wanting to believe

a critical guide to *The X-Files*,
Millennium & *The Lone Gunmen*

robert shearman

with additional material by
lars pearson

mad norwegian press | des moines

Also available from Mad Norwegian Press...

Dusted: The Unauthorized Guide to Buffy the Vampire Slayer
by Lawrence Miles, Lars Pearson and Christa Dickson

More Digressions: A New Collection of "But I Digress" Columns
by Peter David

AHistory: An Unauthorized History of the Doctor Who Universe
by Lance Parkin

THE ABOUT TIME SERIES
by Lawrence Miles and Tat Wood

About Time 1: The Unauthorized Guide to Doctor Who (Seasons 1 to 3)
About Time 2: The Unauthorized Guide to Doctor Who (Seasons 4 to 6)
About Time 3: The Unauthorized Guide to Doctor Who
(Seasons 7 to 11) [2nd Edition now available]
About Time 4: The Unauthorized Guide to Doctor Who (Seasons 12 to 17)
About Time 5: The Unauthorized Guide to Doctor Who (Seasons 18 to 21)
About Time 6: The Unauthorized Guide to Doctor Who
(Seasons 22 to 26, the TV Movie)

Coming soon from Mad Norwegian Press...

Chicks Dig Time Lords

AngeLINK NOVEL SERIES
by Lyda Morehouse, winner of Shamus Award,
Barnes and Noble "Maiden Voyage" Award.

Resurrection Code (all-new prequel)

Copyright © 2009 Mad Norwegian Press (www.madnorwegian.com)
Jacket & interior design by Christa Dickson.
Photograph of cover silhouettes by Kelli Griffis.

ISBN: 9780975944691
Printed in Illinois. First Edition: August 2009.

Table of Contents

The X-Files: Season 4

Millennium: Season 1

The X-Files: Season 5

Millennium: Season 2

The X-Files: Fight the Future

The X-Files: Season 6

Millennium: Season 3

The X-Files: Season 7

Table of Contents

X Introduction

I'm sitting in the foyer of a cinema in Leicester Square, London. In my shirt pocket are two tickets for the new X-Files movie. (They don't quite fit in, but I like that - I can hardly believe the movie was even made, and so whenever I glance down and see tickets for it sticking up onto my lapel, it's somehow reassuring.) My wife Janie will be watching it with me. I've sent her away for half an hour, though, to go to the toilet or look at the popcorn stand or something; I told her I wanted to sit down here and record this moment for my book. She rolled her eyes a bit at that - she's been rolling her eyes a lot at me lately as I've worked on this thing, but it's all right, I've got used to it - and off she went. Bless her. She's put up with a lot recently. Not least sitting through First Person Shooter and the entirety of The Lone Gunmen.

But I do need to record it. This *is* momentous. I never dreamed that The X-Files would be back. I'd heard talk about it on the Internet for years, of course, this fabled second film. I didn't trust a word of it. The X-Files' time had been and gone, I thought. It wasn't until I actually saw a trailer for I Want to Believe on YouTube, complete with Billy Connolly looking vaguely feral and Duchovny and Anderson looking vaguely middle-aged, that I conceded it just might be happening after all.

And I hit upon the idea that before the movie opened, I'd like to watch The X-Files again, just to whet my appetite for it. Janie readily agreed to watch it with me; she said that might be fun. She stopped smiling when I told her I thought we should watch every single episode, in order, and that I'd write up what I made of them all as we went along. And that, just to keep it exciting, I'd throw in Millennium and The Lone Gunmen too. The Lone Gunmen, after all, was a bona fide spin-off - you could hardly claim to be watching all The X-Files if you didn't include the adventures of Byers, Frohike and Langly, could you? And Millennium technically wasn't a spin-off - but Frank Black *did* get to meet Mulder and Scully once, and there was that episode where Jose Chung popped up. So we had to do that series too.

Okay, she said... she sighed a bit, but she said okay.

You see, it was The X-Files that had brought us together. I'm a writer, and she's an actress. We were working together on the same theatre production in 1995, and in the dead time of rehearsal breaks we found out that we had a common bond talking about the latest exploits of Mulder and Scully. Pretty soon we were watching the episodes together on her sofa one evening. Within time we were cuddling. It's not something I'll refer to in the main text, but I can well remember that it was during Hell Money that I first dared to put my arm around her, and just what we got up to in the ad breaks of Sanguinarium. There's an affection I have for these stories; for years they were the constant yardstick to my romance with the woman I love. Then in 2002, The X-Files came to an end. Janie and I looked at each other, and decided we'd best get married. It was either that, or split up, or start watching Buffy the Vampire Slayer.

Last night we watched The Truth, the final X-Files story, the last gasp of Ten Thirteen's magnificent stranglehold on telefantasy. We talked about what it was that had made them all so special. And we concluded it was because they never *tried* to be a hit series. Everything about The X-Files seems designed to be uncommercial: its reliance upon an increasingly convoluted storyarc, the bravery it takes in leaving stories unresolved and ambiguous, its refusal to adopt a house style so that it can jump from horror to comedy to character drama at any point. It was a show which caught the mid-nineties zeitgeist, rode it for a few years, and then - rather magnificently - fell off it but kept going regardless. It had never *wanted* to be the biggest sci-fi show in the world, and seemed to shrug it off quite calmly when it stopped being so, still more interested in producing the same extraordinary mix of quirky and imaginative stories it had always done.

And when The X-Files became a global success in spite of itself, Chris Carter followed it up with Millennium. If anything, Millennium is an even more perverse, even more brilliant series. Over its three-year run, it was constantly experimenting, so that it never quite determined what kind of show it actually *was*. There's a certain lunacy to that. But what beautiful bold lunacy.

We were none too fond of The Lone Gunmen, I'll be honest - but we have to admit that here too was something that cheerfully refused to play it safe. None of the series ever felt manufactured. When that kid pops up in the end credits and says so perkily, "I Made This!", you can somehow believe that it really is a family enterprise, that these shows are there mostly to please the makers. And as a result, all of them were free to evolve naturally. The comedy styling of X-Files Season Six has little in common with the horror tales of Season One; the freewheeling madness as Millennium Season Two slides into the apocalypse is cut from a different cloth to the tight claustrophobia of only a year previously when the series purported to be a procedural detective show.

That's what's been so fascinating about watching it all in order. Seeing how Chris Carter and his production team never felt limited by audience expectations, that they were constantly pulling at the seams and seeing what would happen. You see actors grow: not just Duchovny and Anderson and Henriksen, but William B Davis, and Mitch Pileggi, and Brittany Tiplady. You see writers find their own styles, and run with them: Vince Gilligan, Darin Morgan, David Amann, and - most wonderfully, maybe - Carter himself, who can in one story bog his story down in overwrought pretension and in the next produce something so dizzyingly fresh and free. If the producers are ever complacent, it's rare; the series constantly reinvent themselves, never stand still for long. At their very best, and right into The X-Files' final year, Ten Thirteen were trying to redefine exactly what can be achieved on network television.

This isn't just a guide book, it's a personal journey of sorts. All I've wanted to do is react to each and every episode as sincerely as possible. It's a nature of criticism that at times I will be too dogmatic in my views, but it's only a measure of how I got caught up in my quest to watch everything. I'm aware at times that I come across like an excitable child - loving a story so much one week that I want to shout it from the rooftops, then recoiling from another with angry frustration when it doesn't do what I want. You won't agree with some of what I've written. You may be incensed that your favourite episode is slighted, or another that you can't abide is being held up as the epitome of what TV drama can produce... in a few years' time, when I watch the episodes again, I'm quite sure I'll disagree with myself too. I hope so. This isn't intended to be a dry plod through two hundred and eighty-four (phew) separate stories. Just as I hope your own revisits to The X-Files and Millennium won't be. If this book does anything, I'd like it to prompt a few people to do as I did - blow the dust off the DVD boxsets in the corner of the sitting room, watch them all over again - and argue with me as they go along.

A few words of warning. I couldn't assume that everyone reading this book had an encyclopedic knowledge of these series, especially as we're dealing with a core property that, on original broadcast, lasted nine years. A large number of X-Files fans saw the majority but not the entirety of the show (and it's even more of a toss-up as to how much of Millennium or The Lone Gunmen they experienced), and have understandably forgotten a fair amount of what they did see in the intervening years since. As a roadmap for anyone who needs it, then, my editor - Lars Pearson - has written story summaries to every episode examined herein.

Another warning: Those who use this book as a reference guide only, using it to cherry pick which episode they should watch, will find spoilers here aplenty. To that end, though, I do offer a star rating guide, so you can quickly see whether I'm offering a thumbs up or not without necessarily having to read the text. One star means I thought it was execrable. There are a few of those. Five stars means it's not just a good X-File, or Millennium, but a triumph of television drama. I think the five stars reviews outweigh the one star reviews. My opinions are necessarily skewed. Once in a while I write sci-fi for television myself, so my interest in the series is inevitably from the bias of a writer. Janie saw the series from an acting viewpoint, and couldn't help but judge them on a performance level - and I found her interpretation of how those performances developed invaluable.

The audience from the last showing of The X-Files: I Want to Believe is now coming out of the auditorium. It's hard to gauge what they thought from the expressions on their faces. Some look satisfied, but some look rather stern. I refuse to be put off by the stern ones - who knows, maybe they're all suffering from toothache, and their grimaces are nothing to do with the quality of the movie whatsoever. It's time to go in. To get my first fresh fix of Mulder and Scully for six years. Janie should be lurking around somewhere - oh yes, there she is. And if I'm lucky, she may have bought me an ice-cream. She has. She's wonderful.

We join the queue. I get out our tickets. In we go.

I hope it's good.

Rob Shearman

1.1, Pilot

Air Date: Sept. 10, 1993
Writer: Chris Carter
Director: Robert Mandel

Summary   At FBI Headquarters, Dana Scully - a doctor who's been with the Bureau for two years - is assigned to work with Agent Fox Mulder, an Oxford-educated psychologist and violent crimes investigator. Mulder has developed an obsession with "The X-Files" - cases pertaining to unexplained phenomena - and Scully is to evaluate the validity of his work.

The agents travel to Bellefleur, Oregon, to investigate the latest in a string of mysterious killings, where the victims featured two strange marks on their bodies. By exhuming one of the victims, Mulder and Scully find the corpse resembles an orangutan and has a strange piece of metal lodged up its nose. Mulder suspects that extraterrestrials are involved in the deaths, and confides to Scully his belief that alien beings kidnapped his sister at age eight.

They soon come to suspect the catatonic son of the local sheriff, Billy Miles. Mulder postulates that aliens have planted a device in Billy's head that revives him to take victims into the woods as part of a genetic mutation experiment. Billy awakens and takes a young girl, Teresa Nemman, into the woods. Mulder and Billy's father follow and witness a bright light from the sky intensifying over Billy and Teresa - once it fades, Billy makes a full recovery and Teresa is found alive.

Mulder and Scully discover that their evidence from the case has been destroyed, save for the metal chip from the corpse - which is possibly an alien communications device. Scully tells her superiors that she can't debunk Mulder's findings and turns over the chip - whereupon an FBI official with a fondness for cigarettes (henceforth called "the Cigarette Smoking Man") places it in a Pentagon storage room, alongside similar devices.

Critique   On its own terms, as a TV pilot, this isn't half bad. The direction is terrific, already reaching for that feel of a feature movie truncat-ed into forty-five minutes. The opening set piece, in particular, with a girl dying in a whirl-wind of leaves and bright lights, is marvellous. And there's a pace and an energy to the whole thing which rattles through its rather complicat-ed plot with so much abandon, you find your-self working hard to keep up - but you do so quite willingly, because the enthusiasm shown is infectious. For all its darker themes of abuse and dread, and its ghoulish set pieces of coffins being knocked open, there's an eager puppy dog feel to this: it's just revelling in the joy that such an unlikely TV pilot is being *made*.

Unsurprisingly, the core elements of the show hardly seem to be in place yet. David Duchovny forces his way through a part which is largely maverick bluster; you can tell Mulder's eccen-tricity is supposed to be endearing by the way Scully keeps on smiling at it in spite of herself, but it's mostly just irritating. It's not Duchovny's fault necessarily - scenes which require him to be lounging about on an aeroplane hitting tur-bulence, indifferent to the panic around him, just scream Wacky Character Moment and don't exactly allow for much subtlety. Duchovny is required to play Mulder here not as the tortured hero on a quest, but as Remington Steele, or as David Addison from Moonlighting - he looks a bit bemused when the script asks him to stop clowning around and talk sincerely about his missing sister. Gillian Anderson, though, is ter-rific - the great strength of the episode is the way it makes the sceptical outsider not just the audi-ence's point of view, but an *intellectual* point of view. And it's the clash between the two intel-lects of Mulder and Scully that, ironically, allows the characters to bond: the joy of Mulder danc-ing when, following an encounter with a bright light in a rainstorm, he realises that he and Scully have lost nine minutes; the way in which Scully can only laugh with genuine delight at the absurdity of Mulder's conclusions.

But actors aside, what's surprising is how many of the series' staple ingredients are intro-duced here, and introduced so well: a govern-ment cover-up and colleagues turning out to be spies, let alone alien abductions and strange implants. Considering it's quite clear in retro-spect that no-one could have any idea of the significance of, say, the Cigarette Smoking Man - let alone whether the pilot would defy the conservative climate of TV scheduling and get optioned for a series - it's remarkable how much of this ties into what will follow. Chris Carter presents us with a whole barrage of UFO folklore tales, from missing time to alien autopsies, and keeps all the balls juggling in the air.

The story itself doesn't really work; Mulder realises the truth about Billy Miles on sudden guesswork. And the conclusion is all a little pat, as if confronting Billy's father with what he already knows is going to affect a change in the aliens' plans. But even if the plot is a bit rusty, its component parts are fresh and exciting. And what you're left with is the promise of a series brave enough to conclude its stories messily, in which the bad guys can go unpunished and the good guys go unrewarded. It's in that final sequence where the government is seen burying the evidence, which is tantamount to telling the viewers that the entire hour they've just watched has counted for nothing, that shows The X-Files at its bravest, and in which the show finds its feet. (***)

1.2, Deep Throat

Air Date: Sept. 17, 1993
Writer: Chris Carter
Director: Daniel Sackheim

Summary   Test pilot Lieutenant Colonel Robert Budahas goes missing - the sixth such disappearance from Ellens Air Force Base in Idaho since 1963. An enigmatic man (henceforth called "Deep Throat") with governmental connections approaches Mulder, claiming to have an interest in his work, but advises him to drop this case. Mulder persists, eventually concluding that the military has been conducting test flights of planes equipped with technology from a UFO.

Budahas reappears with no memory of his work. Mulder sneaks into a restricted area at Ellens and sees what appears to be a UFO in flight - but is then captured and subjected to medical procedures. Scully captures a base official and trades the man for Mulder, who is left with no memory of the UFO sighting. Deep

Throat later offers to continue giving Mulder certain information so he can get at "the truth" - and also tells him that aliens have been at work on Earth for a "very, very" long time.

Critique   This feels like a second pilot, much more confident in its pacing and its tone, with both Anderson and Duchovny giving the leads a depth that is surprising this early into the run. A skilfully scripted story of cover-up and paranoia, it sets up the overall themes of the show so well, it almost seems like a primer. That's all the odder when you consider it's actually a very atypical episode: it's concerned not with moments of horror, but of wonder - the sequence where Mulder is caught in the light of an overhead UFO is one of the series' defining moments - and no-one dies.

What's so great about Deep Throat is the way it balances its political themes with something much smaller and more intimate. Mulder and Scully get to argue over the nub of what The X-Files is about: surely the government is allowed to have secrets from the public it represents, but where do you draw the line? The moment when a US soldier, returning Mulder from captivity, tells Scully that their actions have done nothing but endangered the nation, echoes Jack Nicholson's final words after his arrest in A Few Good Men - and for all the excitement of seeing the little guys go after the system, you can't but help feel there's some truth to what they say.

But the most haunting parts of the episode are the domestic, the way that Mrs Budahaus wants her husband back only to be horrified by the sort of man that is returned to her. She's abandoned at story's end to a fate of fear and intimidation from not only the military, but the man she married. Most telling of all is Mrs McClennon - the smiling wife of another "returned" test pilot, who's adapted all too easily to her lobotomised husband and enthuses about his fly-fishing hobby as he sits by her, picking hairs out of his head. We get beautiful displays of UFO lights in the sky - the sort that stoners can chill out to - but are reminded of the very human cost.

Jerry Hardin is really very good at the eponymous Deep Throat - as the series goes on, and the actor himself clearly gets confused over whether he's friend or foe, he can look somewhat uncomfortable - but here he captures both the threat posed and the lifeline offered well. There's a real pathos in the final scene, where he acknowledges that the information that Mulder acquired has been stolen from his mind; Deep Throat knows far more than his young acolyte, but still dare not reveal the truth. Rather brilliantly, the second episode of The X-Files has offered us all the proof we need that the government is colluding with aliens in some form - but Scully hasn't seen this proof, and Mulder has forgotten it. It's like a mission statement. The audience now knows what our heroes need to rediscover. (*****)

1.3, Squeeze

Air Date: Sept. 24, 1993
Writer: Glen Morgan and James Wong
Director: Harry Longstreet

Summary   Three victims are found in locked rooms with their livers torn out - a modus operandi that Mulder says has occurred at thirty-year intervals all the way back to 1903. A fingerprint at the crime scene points suspicion at Eugene Tooms, an animal control officer. Mulder hypothesises that Tooms, who can elongate his body to slither through ventilation shafts and such, is a genetic mutant. His biology dictates that he sleeps for a thirty-year stretch, then awakens and must consume five livers before re-entering a hibernation cycle. Tooms targets Scully as his final victim, but is captured and thrown in a cell with only a tiny slot so that guards can feed him.

Critique   This is the first in a long line of human mutant stories, and one of the eeriest. It works like a surreal painting, tricking the brain into accepting the preposterous. The teaser is a perfect example of this, as you keep finding ways to take the images it presents so matter-of-factly at face value, and persuade yourself that a man is capable of spying from a drain, or creeping through a ventilator. Since this is the first X-Files episode not to rely upon accepted urban legends but to invent its own slice of the paranormal, it's clever that the absurd never seems *too* absurd, that we can by degrees find the impossibility of the premise credible. It does

this by allowing the horror to work by suggestion, and not hitting the audience with special effects: by the time we finally *see* Tooms climb up a building and squeeze his body through a chimney pot, we've already adjusted to the absurdity and can be suitably repelled.

Because it is, of course, absurd - and what's so smart about the episode is that by pursuing the investigation of Eugene Tooms with such realism, it makes its flights of fancy seem logical. You have to admire the chutzpah of a story which keeps on showing the FBI react to Mulder's theories with such contempt - quite acceptably - rather than hiding the mockery from sight. It's pre-empting the audience's own response. That said, after the conspiracy of Deep Throat, the small-time machinations of Agent Tom Colton climbing the ladder to promotion and standing in Mulder's way seem *extremely* unsubtle. After an episode in which the government is revealed to be a foe, a story in which our heroes' colleagues sneer at them feels decidedly forced. Full marks, though, to a story which shows Mulder and Scully working as an effective team; Mulder may come up with the explanations, but it's Scully's profile which first captures Tooms. There's no better example in Season One of what each lead character brings to a case - Mulder's there for the maverick flights of imagination, but Scully's professionalism and constant questioning save the day.

Squeeze sells itself as a quirky piece of horror, and it's as memorable and as scary as it tries to be. It boasts a creepily subtle performance from Doug Hutchison, playing Tooms more as amoral monster than as evil villain, which makes him seem all the more inhuman and terrifying. It makes the scene in which the retired cop soliloquises about death camps all the more uncomfortable - it feels not only unnecessary but tasteless to boot, and the episode is so much better than that.

Oh, and it's odd to hear Colton to talk of a colleague rising the ranks by striking lucky with the World Trade Centre bombings. It's not the first time that the series will anticipate the events of 9/11... (****)

1.4, Conduit

Air Date: Oct. 1, 1993
Writer: Howard Gordon, Alex Gansa
Director: Daniel Sackheim

Summary   When a teenage girl named Ruby Morris goes missing near Sioux City, Iowa, the case bears hallmarks of an alien abduction. Ruby's brother Kevin begins producing scribbles containing all manner of information, and Mulder speculates that Kevin has become a conduit of sorts for alien transmissions. Ruby is eventually found in the woods alive, and her mother insists that Mulder end his investigation. Mulder is left haunted by similarities between this case and his sister's disappearance.

Critique   There's a lovely scene here. A young boy has been filling pages upon pages with binary notations since the abduction of his sister - and it's only as we look at them from high that we see how they form a mosaic portrait of her. It's both shocking and moving, and it's a great metaphor for the series too, that sometimes the truth can only be observed from an unusual perspective.

That said, it's pretty much the only notable thing about this disappointingly formulaic outing. We've seen it all before - weird lights in the forest which turn out to be headlamps rather than spaceships, alien abductees, and Mulder and Scully being threatened by the government. I wouldn't mind, but this is only episode *four.*

Director Daniel Sackheim does his best to energise the material, but in the main he tries too hard. A dull conversation about a school romance in a library doesn't look more dramatic because it's shot like the climax of a conspiracy thriller, it just looks silly. But that's nothing to an interrogation scene in which the clichés of the good cop / bad cop are played so lazily, the whole thing smacks of parody.

It's a storyline so linear, and so without twists or surprises, that the episode can only find depth by tapping into Mulder's quest for his missing sister. But there's little of the sense of obsession which so concerns Scully in Duchovny's performance. And although there's an interesting irony at the end, where it's a mother's concern for her daughter's privacy rather than government interference which buries the truth, it's a fatal anticlimax to such a tedious episode. (*1/2)

1.5, The Jersey Devil

Air Date: Oct. 8, 1993
Writer: Chris Carter
Director: Joe Napolitano

Summary   After a homeless man is found dead - and partially eaten - near Atlantic City, Mulder connects the event to a similar fatality in 1947. Some of the locals believe that a "Jersey Devil" - a feral humanoid - is operating in the area. Mulder suspects that Detective Thompson has been covering up the Devil's existence to protect the tourist trade. After finding the body of a male Devil, Mulder is attacked by its mate. The police kill the female despite Mulder's protests, but forensic evidence suggests that the female recently gave birth. Elsewhere, the Devils' offspring roams the countryside.

Critique   To be charitable, just for a moment - it's only to be expected that a new series will put out feelers to find out exactly what it is *about.* And from this episode, we can conclude that The X-Files definitively isn't about Mulder bonding with neanderthal women and calling them beautiful. The show hit gold early on, with an excellent UFO episode and an excellent monster episode. It's followed them up with a bad UFO episode and a monster episode which can only be described as risible.

Once you settle into the right mindset, watching The Jersey Devil can actually be very amusing. It's hard to work out what's funniest - maybe it's the heavy handed dialogue between Scully and Mulder in the warehouse as they reflect upon evolution and the innate beast in Man. (The way in which Scully draws parallels between a killer of folklore and kids running riot at a birthday party is especially worth a chuckle, if only as you wonder how Gillian Anderson isn't chuckling along with us.) Or is it the sequence where a tramp gives Mulder his lead - a hasty sketch of a woman with long hair - to which they both react with hilarious gravitas? No, it must surely be the sorrowed anger in which Mulder reacts to the death of the cannibal cavegirl, shot dead in the woods with no dramatic build-up but just because the episode had reached its running time.

The sub-plot of Scully going out on a date feels wrong, but it's at least entertaining. I'd have enjoyed the story much more if we'd focused upon her dinner conversation, perhaps even found out what she ordered for dessert. And the scenes with Scully at a party for her godson, doubting whether she could ever manage to be a mother, could be an ironic foreshadowing of the later seasons. But we're talking, what? Three minutes' screen time? For the rest of the episode we're left with a conservation story so clumsily obvious, even the mute neanderthal looks embarrassed. Moreover, after a series of episodes of cover-ups for national security, we're given a tale of police obstruction motivated by wanting to preserve the casino tourist trade. It's hard to care about, even harder to keep a straight face. (*)

1.6, Shadows

Air Date: Oct. 22, 1993
Writer: Glen Morgan, James Wong
Director: Michael Katleman

Summary   Two men are found dead in Philadelphia, their throats crushed from within as if by psychokinetic force. Their investigation leads to Howard Graves, who worked for HTG Industrial Technologies. Graves was murdered, it transpires, to cover up the fact that his company sold parts to Middle Eastern terrorists. Mulder suspects that Graves' ghost is now protecting his secretary, Lauren Kyte, because someone similarly wants to silence her. The agents discover that another HTG official, Robert Dorland, arranged Graves' murder. Graves' shade draws their attention to an incriminating computer disk, facilitating Dorland's arrest. Afterward, Lauren tries to strike up a new life for herself as an office worker in Omaha.

Critique   Shadows is hit by the same uncertainty of tone that affected The Jersey Devil - here is an episode made by people who can't be sure what the series is capable of yet. The big difference is that, in its simplistic way, Shadows succeeds in being a perfectly competent piece of TV. There are some great special effects and a couple of memorable set pieces (the crushed throat sequences are especially good, and the scene where a man is beaten up by an invisible presence could easily have been laughable but is genuinely effective).

Duchovny and Anderson are on fine form too, giving their relationship a light, bantering quality that is easy on the ear. But you could argue they've caught the mood perfectly - this episode really is so lightweight it's almost throwaway, The X-Files conceived as Almost Any Other Generic Programme. This could so easily have been a template for the series, where two amiable FBI agents help out ordinary uncomplicated people who've had brushes with the paranormal. It trots along affably enough. But it's telling that it almost chooses to be less interesting than it should be - starting off as a tale about a poltergeist with surrogate father issues, in the last act it becomes more concerned with the mundane urge to expose a corrupt businessman. This somehow turns the whole poltergeist into nothing more than a deus ex machina, as if the whole phenomenon only existed to help the police out with their enquiries. And by resolving the wrong plotline, the story feels odd and unsatisfying as it dribbles to its end, as if you've been watching an episode back to front - quite a few X-Files start off by examining what appears to be a routine case only to uncover something abnormal behind it, but this may be the only one that does it in reverse.

It's fine. It's not terrible. It's fine. But the lack of focus makes one point emphatic: it's just not *about* anything. Even The Jersey Devil had something to say, however crass the message, but this has no ambition except to trot along and tell a simple story in forty-five minutes. There are worse ambitions to have, and those forty-five minutes pass painlessly enough. But you'd be hard pushed to remember them.

There are lots of unanswered questions here, and they're mostly an attempt, I think, to overcome this sense of emptiness, to give a mystery and a significance to things where there's none to be had. What is the importance of the Thomas Jefferson plaque that Lauren has been carrying about all episode? And why exactly does Mulder want to see the Liberty Bell? (It's an

X-Files cliché that the agents will try to point out the meaning of the story with a pretentious coda, but this one is really grasping at straws.) The final scene, at least, is a joke on the audience. The ripple in the coffee is nothing more than a train passing, not a poltergeist leaping to Laura's defence. But this anticlimax can only work if we'd *had* a climax beforehand, and only reminds us that Howard The Ghost is still out there. What's he going to do now, solve more cases for the CIA? Forget Millennium - Poltergeist Crime Buster, that should have been the spin-off. (**)

1.7. Ghost in the Machine

Air Date: Oct. 29, 1993
Writer: Alex Gansa, Howard Gordon
Director: Jerrold Freedman

Summary Benjamin Drake, the CEO of a high-tech firm named Eurisko, is mysteriously electrocuted after deciding to pull the plug on the company's Central Operating System (COS) project. Mulder's former partner, Jerry Lamana, asks for help with the case, and the agents soon identify Brad Wilczek - the designer of COS, who left Eurisko after a dispute with Drake - as a person of interest. After another technical mishap causes Lamana to fall to his death, Wilczek - falsely, to Mulder's mind - confesses to Drake's murder.

Deep Throat tells Mulder that COS is an artificial intelligence that killed Drake (and Lamana) in an act of self-defence. Mulder convinces Wilczek to craft a COS-neutralizing computer virus, then loads it into COS' network and apparently kills it. Government agents take Wilczek away for questioning - hoping to coerce him into working for them - even as a remnant of the COS system shows signs of life.

Critique Here's an episode that has been given a good kicking by fans over the years, and you can see why. It's rather silly and contrived, it shamelessly steals from 2001: A Space Odyssey to no great effect... and it's yet another episode which feels like it's groping around blindly to find out what the show's tone might be. It's easy to see in retrospect what's going on. The three

main teams of X-Files writers each offered their first inspired script for production, then had to follow it with something speedy and workmanlike as fill-in. Chris Carter goes from Deep Throat to The Jersey Devil, Morgan and Wong from Squeeze to Shadows. The same thing is true here with Gordon and Gansa - but although Ghost in the Machine may be throwaway tosh, it's terribly *likeable* throwaway tosh. And I'd take it over the dull and earnest Conduit any day of the week.

The killer computer may be a cliché, but at least it's a cliché that is addressed - I love the moment when even its creator is amazed that it has the required voice synthesiser programme necessary to make its threats. Watching it now in 2008, the episode feels rather charming, as all the talk of artificial intelligence and advanced technology is conducted to the background whirr of DOS programs and floppy discs. If it's an unintentional charm then it's no less engaging for it; this may be the most dated of X-Files, but the story still works. Sequences which involve our watching victims from the computer's point of view are surprisingly tense - the murder by elevator couldn't have been achieved more simply, but is lovely. And when Mulder and Scully get access to the building, with all electrical systems turned against them, there's a palpable sense of danger the series hasn't offered in weeks.

It's not clever and it's not subtle. Wayne Duvall plays Agent Jerry Lamana, the FBI partner from Hell, with a restlessness so nervy he makes Mulder look positively stable. And Rob LaBelle is the sort of eccentric untidy genius that is only an inch this side of pure caricature. But they're both fun to watch, in a cartoon like way, and their performances fit an episode which may never flatter the audience's intelligence, but never insults them by being dull either. (**1/2)

1.8, Ice

Air Date: Nov. 5, 1993
Writer: Glen Morgan, James Wong
Director: David Nutter

Summary In Alaska, a scientific expedition to drill into the Arctic ice and find samples dating

back to the dawn of humankind goes hideously awry when the expedition members killing one another or committing suicide. Mulder and Scully take a team to investigate, and conclude that the scientists came into contact with a type of parasitic worm - one that causes a murderous aggression - that came to Earth on a meteor and has lain dormant for about 250,000 years.

A member of Mulder and Scully's team is found murdered, and Mulder is wrongly suspected of being the worm-infested killer. The team members discover that two worms in the same host will slay each other, and nearly "cure" Mulder with the one worm left at their disposal. Fortunately, Dr Nancy Dasilva is identified as the real culprit and receives the curative worm, whereupon the survivors evacuate the base - and the military burns it to the ground, destroying all evidence of the case.

Critique   If Ghost in the Machine steals from 2001, then Ice lures The Thing into a dark alleyway and mugs it. Why is it that the one is so disdained, and the other is a fan favourite? It must be because however derivative Ice may be, it finds a way of taking its borrowed material and finding within it something which defines The X-Files. This must surely be the most influential episode ever made - as the seasons go by, we'll see many brazen attempts to copy it wholesale. And what Morgan and Wong so skilfully extract from The Thing is its desperate paranoia and its fear of identity loss. "We are not who we are" is the chilling statement that runs through this episode, and there is surely no better mantra that sums up the entire series. It's the more cynical flipside of "The truth is out there."

What makes Ice so extraordinary is the way that, for the first time in the series, it makes Mulder and Scully not mere observers of the unexplained. The X-Files will always work best once it realises the most satisfying stories are the ones where our leads *are* the story, not just commentators upon it. The sequence in which our heroes train guns on each other is brilliant for the conviction both Duchovny and Anderson show - this is *real* paranoia. And it's the way in which Mulder and Scully are made afraid of each other, yet come through the experience with even deeper loyalty, that makes Ice such a pivotal story. On the surface it's a yarn about arctic worms, but it's really about how much

Mulder and Scully can trust each other.

This story is such a claustrophobic slice of horror that it's easy to forget how witty Morgan and Wong's dialogue is, and how well-rounded the supporting characters are. (I love the professor who can still get enthused listening to ages-old recordings of football games, and the way he retreats more and more unhappily into this world as the situation worsens.) There's a terrific guest cast - Xander Berkeley, as Dr Hodge, takes what could have been played as an obstructive stereotype and makes him diligent and credible. And isn't that Felicity Huffman, future Oscar winner, rolling about on the floor trying to resist something slimy being inserted into her ear?

And just a word about the teaser. How good is *that*? Two men with guns pointing at each other, decide without word to commit suicide instead. It's the look in their eyes which sells it - the first reaching a moment of bold resolution, the other looking on with confusion and then terrified acceptance. It's shocking and macabre and very very X-Files. (*********)

1.9, Space

Air Date: Nov. 12, 1993
Writer: Chris Carter
Director: William A Graham

Summary   Michelle Generoo, a communications commander at NASA, finds evidence that someone is sabotaging shuttle launches and asks Mulder and Scully to investigate. The agents direct their attention to Lieutenant Colonel Marcus Belt - a NASA supervisor who flew a space mission in 1977 that came into contact with a mysterious face seen in the landscape of Mars. Ever since then, the face entity - evidently wanting to stop mankind from venturing into space - has resided in Belt and used him to hamper NASA's efforts. Belt re-asserts enough control to help save the current shuttle flight from disaster, then hurls himself to his death.

Critique   The oddest thing about Space is watching the science fiction of The X Files come into collision with the science fact of NASA. Suddenly we're presented with a world in which scientists aren't long haired eccentrics but men in suits being engineers and listing countdowns. It seems on the surface only natural that a series so interested in alien life and government dealings would put the two together and look at the space programme - but this flavour of realism is strangely disconcerting.

No, wait. Let me start again. The oddest thing about Space is how much it's hated. If you look at any online poll - and there are many - Space always rests at rock bottom. It's the true turkey of The X-Files, the Worst Episode Ever. And sometimes a reputation can be so notorious that it colours all impressions of the episode itself. Certainly, watching Space again, I found myself at times less wondering what was happening to Colonel Belt and more what, exactly, was supposed to be so bad about it in the first place. I wonder whether it really is that collision, of The X-Files taking a step towards science reality and making the series' concerns with monsters and UFOs look a little exposed. There's no question that one of the episode's biggest flaws is that Mulder and Scully have literally nothing to do but stand in mission control and emote in the background - pensive expression for when the astronauts are in danger, thumbs up for when they pull through. But it's hardly the worst crime that The X-Files can commit, particularly within a first season which is still only beginning to realise how to put them at the heart of a story at all.

I wonder too whether it could be the way that, having looked at the familiar myths like poltergeists and bigfoots, the series turns its attention towards a far more controversial myth - that of American heroism. For the villain of the piece to be a space veteran, a man that Mulder all but begs an autograph from, is hard enough - that he's a villain because he's cracking up is even worse. American heroes are supposed to be solid, not flaky. The whole episode is an analysis of how the public have turned against this heroism - how space exploration, once so highly honoured, is now a footnote buried deep in the newspapers. For once we see a man prepared to conceal the truth not as a cowardly diversion, but to protect NASA from more ammunition that might shut it down. I don't really buy Mulder's puppy dog shock that Belt would lie to the press - but I loved the way that by the end of the episode, Michelle Generoo is

prepared to take part in exactly the same cover-up her principles oppose.

Fair enough, NASA seems a bit understaffed, and the episode relies a lot upon stock footage. It looks cheap. But even here this only serves to demonstrate how NASA has been undermined since the glory days of Mulder's youth. And the fact we haven't the budget to cut to the crew of the space shuttle brings a claustrophobic verisimilitude to those scenes in which the scientists battle to save the lives of the astronauts - it's all done by crackling microphone, and somehow those men in space seem ever more isolated.

At the end of the day the plot strains a bit with its tale of alien possession and ghostly faces. It loses focus by having Generoo run off the road after she sees such a face in the rain - the episode is so much more effective when you can believe nothing supernatural is happening beyond Belt's paranoid fantasies. Ultimately the story doesn't give itself time to resolve anything, so that the final act feels very confused. Belt's suicide, whilst rather touching in conceit, feels something like an afterthought because we can't really see what his death is saving the world *from*. And why emphasise the unlikelihood of Mulder and Scully finding one file in ten thousand, only to then have them do just that? It's when the episode tries to give the sort of climax we've come to expect from The X-Files that it trips over itself. I wish it had the courage of its convictions more, that it had gone even further with its realism, with its strangely languorous pace. But then, it'd probably be even more unpopular than it already is - if such a thing were possible. (***)

1.10, Fallen Angel

Air Date: Nov. 19, 1993
Writer: Alex Gansa, Howard Gordon
Director: Larry Shaw

Summary Deep Throat advises Mulder that US satellites registered a mysterious object - possibly an alien spaceship - falling to Earth in Wisconsin, and that he has twenty-four hours to investigate before a retrieval team sterilises the area. Mulder gets arrested while trying to photograph the object, causing an FBI oversight committee to contemplate firing him and closing down the X-Files.

Mulder comes into contact with Max Fenig, a member of a group that tracks UFO sightings, and who has a scar that's consistent with alien abduction. Military radar detects a much larger craft moving into the vicinity, and Fenig is compelled - perhaps by an alien communications device lodged in his cerebellum - to go to a warehouse. Mulder witnesses Fenig floating in a strange blue light before he disappears entirely. Afterward, Mulder's superiors move to close down the X-Files, but Deep Throat overrules them - advising that Mulder's occasional insubordination is preferable to his going rogue and meeting the "wrong people".

Critique   Fallen Angel teases us with offers of something significant right from the get-go. It opens in a forest where someone is attacked by strange lights. We've seen this played out twice already. Except this time there's no false reveal, it's not headlights from a truck... there's an alien, it's real and it's fast, and it's just done something nasty to the local law enforcement!

But after the opening credits, you quickly realise this is all smoke and mirrors. To be fair, smoke and mirrors is an essential house style on The X-Files, but for all the earnest shouting from Mulder, nothing really seems at stake here. There's a killer alien in the woods, brilliantly realised by eerie point of view camera shots - which just runs away without further comment. Instead we focus upon the tale of alien abductee Max Fenig. Max is a nerd, has many amusing lines, and is charmingly played by Scott Bellis - and as an actual fan of the X-Files, he anticipates a group following that hadn't yet been born. But all he offers is the most pedestrian of storylines; even Max is unaware of his abductions, so the story is energised only by Mulder's theorising, and all the climax can do is show that theory happening. There's no twist, no surprise, and no resolution.

It's telling that the real threat of the story isn't invisible aliens or UFO abductions, but that Mulder and Scully might lose their jobs. It's a little hard to believe that the X-Files is in such danger of being shut down, because Mulder spends most of the episode accepting it with resignation or ignoring the prospect altogether.

The last few minutes, though, are terrific - Mulder's attack upon the FBI officials who are judging him, "How can I disprove lies that have been stamped with an official seal?", is played by Duchovny with an angry dignity. The final scene, in which Deep Throat reveals he may not be on the side of truth after all, and has saved the X-Files for his own ends, is great. But pivotal moments like this, stuck after the action of the episode proper has played out, suggest Fallen Angel has more purpose than it actually has. Really, this story is another Conduit, offering little we haven't seen before. But it's done with style and wit - nothing much may happen, but it at least happens entertainingly. (***)

1.11, Eve

Air Date: Dec. 10, 1993
Writer: Kenneth Biller, Chris Brancato
Director: Fred Gerber

Summary   When two men die in identical circumstances in Connecticut and San Francisco, Mulder and Scully find that the victims' daughters - Teena Simmons and Cindy Reardon - are identical twins. Deep Throat tells Mulder about the "Litchfield experiment", a 1950s eugenics program designed to create a supersoldier; girls born to this program were called "Eve". Deep Throat arranges for Mulder and Scully to meet with the institutionalised Eve 6, who reveals that the Eves were gifted with enhanced strength and intelligence, but eventually developed homicidal tendencies.

The agents further discover that Dr Sally Kendrick, designated Eve 7, cloned herself into Teena and Cindy's ova when their mothers received in-vitro fertilisation. Kendrick hoped to eliminate the flaws inherent in the Litchfield experiment, but Cindy and Teena - who have a psychic awareness of one another - developed lethal inclinations even sooner in life and murdered their fathers. Kendrick kidnaps the girls in the hopes of rehabilitating them, but the twins poison her. The girls similarly try to kill Mulder and Scully, but are captured and thrown into the asylum that houses Eve 7. Soon afterward, the last of the Eves at liberty - Eve 8 - arrives to collect the girls.

Critique Even this early on in its run, The X-Files had developed a clear formula. Something odd happens, Mulder gets a theory, everyone else is sceptical, Mulder turns out to be right. Part of Eve's cleverness is that it turns our expectations right on their heads. Mulder's confidence that this is a story about alien abduction is wrong; he finds another theory, that the murderers are adult psychotic clones wanting to kidnap their younger counterparts, and that's wrong too. It's rare for an X-File to come along in which the suspense is more than eeriness from composer Mark Snow and murky lighting, but to do with the twists of plot and genuine story misdirection. The result is that we get a mystery which actually intrigues and surprises the viewer.

I'm naturally scared of children anyway - who knows what's going on in those little heads? - so Eve had me chilled from the start. The way in which Teena manipulates Mulder into believing that his alien story is true, feeding him lines about red lightning and men from the clouds, is brilliant - and the calm with which she tells him that the aliens wanted her father for "exsanguinations" is one of the most subtly unnerving things the series has offered. Some have criticised the acting ability of the little twin girls, but there's something about their vacant performances, deliberate or not, which makes them all the more inhuman. Harriet Harris, in a whole range of multiple roles as the Eves, is quite extraordinary, biting at Mulder and Scully in the asylum with frenzied madness. But she's somehow even more disturbing as the "good" Eve 7, who offers the girls the chance to be just like her, through the questionable sanity of anti-psychotic drugs.

The only fly in the ointment is the characterisation of the regulars, possibly because this is the first episode written by freelancers. Mulder has shown his selfish obsessive nature many times, but the glee with which he finds out a little girl has been abducted just because it bolsters one of his theories feels very off-key. And Scully is rather colourless here - besides needing to have in vitro fertilisation explained to her, the good doctor is told by Mulder, of all people, the function of the heart! Jerry Hardin, too, looks a bit all at sea; back to a role of genial provider of exposition for no obvious reason, his performance becomes awkward and unusually mannered.

It's a clever story, though, and one which in its themes of eugenics and supersoldiers predicts the main plot for the show's later seasons. If only they had explored it with the same elegance and guile that is shown here. (****)

1.12, Fire

Air Date: Dec. 17, 1993
Writer: Chris Carter
Director: Larry Shaw

Summary After various members of the British aristocracy are set ablaze, Phoebe Greene - Mulder's former lover, now a detective for Scotland Yard - asks for his help in protecting Sir Malcolm Marsden at his home in Cape Cod. Mulder deduces that a pyrokinetic - someone capable of mentally enhancing and directing fire - is at work. Scully's research finds that two of the victims had an Englishman named Cecil L'ively in their employ.

L'ively ingratiates himself to the Marsden family, but the agents confront him at the Cape Cod home. Greene splashes L'ively with a fire accelerant, causing him to burn out of control while the family is rescued. Scully estimates that L'ively's injuries will heal in a month, leaving it unclear how authorities will effectively incarcerate him.

Critique Some of the fire effects are quite good.

But the rest of this - what on earth is going on here? It seems as if Chris Carter is on a mission to undermine Mulder's character as badly as possible. What happened, did David Duchovny forget to send him a birthday card or something? Carter saddles Mulder with a phobia of fire - never to be heard of again in the series. And you can only feel that it's for a Vertigo-like payoff, that Mulder will face his demons to save the day. But as he huddles on the floor whimpering, leading to the unintentionally funny moment of an entire flotilla of strapping firemen jogging past him as if he's a corpse - you feel embarrassed for him, and really hope that his act of heroism will be big enough to overcome this shame. In the event, though, what we get is a sequence where Mulder flaps ineffectually at a burning curtain with a towel.

This, though, is nothing to putting him under the spell of a femme fatale so uncharismatic that it beggars belief. Phoebe Green has the cards stacked against her right from her introduction, where she finds it amusing to say hello to her old friend by pretending that his car has been wired with explosives - for no greater reason, it would seem, than a jolly jape. But as played by Amanda Pays, whose atonal British accent has the nasal quality of someone drowning in snot, the character is irredeemable. For all Mulder's claims of her brilliance, there can surely be no-one more stupid working at Scotland Yard. Scully is able to solve the entire mystery sitting at her computer desk, whilst this glamorous vixen is out snogging her partner. Did she really also have to be so unprofessional that she's caught in a clinch with the English lord she's supposed to be protecting - isn't that labouring the point just a tad? Of course, we don't care about Phoebe Green - her only importance is how much it weakens Mulder's character to see him so helpless in her company. Laid low by fire and an old flame, this isn't a good week for Mulder.

Or for anybody else. The plot is so thin it's ridiculous. When the end of an act shows Scully a picture of the man we know has been guilty since the precredit teaser, you know this is not a story that has many surprises up its sleeve. It doesn't have much point either. Cecil L'Ively is a man who wanders all over both sides of the Atlantic setting fire to things. He'll do it to the aristocracy, but if he's bored he doesn't mind popping down to the local pub and doing it there instead. He is that dreadful thing, a motiveless baddie, who uses his unexplained paranormal powers for evil just because he *can*. There is some attempt to suggest he's stalking Lord Marsden because he's attracted to his wife, but since there's even less a spark between them than there is between Phoebe and Mulder, this doesn't convince - and it doesn't help that the teaser has already shown him killing another English aristo already. Did he fancy *his* wife as well? It's telling that the most unnerving scene is the one where L'Ively tries to persuade two young children to smoke; it's utterly pointless, mind you, but at least it's sinister.

And I haven't mentioned the quality of the *English* accents.

But, you know, the fire effects were good. Well. Some of them. (*)

1.13, Beyond the Sea

Air Date: Jan. 7, 1994
Writer: Glen Morgan, James Wong
Director: David Nutter

Summary After Scully spies a ghostly image of her father, she learns that he's just died of a heart attack. Meanwhile, two college students go missing, and the agents' only recourse is Luther Lee Boggs - a death row inmate who's felt a connection to the spirit world ever since his first execution attempt was halted.

Boggs offers to provide information on the missing students in exchange for a stay of execution; Mulder doubts Boggs' alleged psychic abilities, but Scully pays more heed when Boggs recites personal details about her father. Mulder and Scully save one of the students with Boggs' help, but the kidnaper - Lucas Henry - escapes with the second. Scully falsely tells Boggs that he's been granted a reprieve; Boggs knows she's being duplicitous but helps anyway. The authorities kill Henry and recover the second student; Scully declines Boggs' offer to hear a last message from her father - afraid to let herself believe in psychic phenomena - and Boggs is executed.

Critique Beyond the Sea's greatest fault is that it is so much more ambitious and thoughtful and affecting than anything we have seen in the series previously. As a result, it hardly seems to be the same show. The culture shock is extraordinary. It's as if a well-meaning and occasionally scary programme about aliens has been given a shot in the arm - and a shot in the brain too. It's such an advance in quality that it jars. How can this be the same X-Files that offered us Fire only one week previously?

It feels like an act of bravado. The series hadn't taken off yet; drowning amid bad ratings and general indifference, it seems to be a programme ripe for cancellation. Several years later Glen Morgan and James Wong went all guns blazing into Millennium when they were certain it was to be axed, and gave it an intended finale that was shocking and bold and unforgettable. Beyond the Sea is a much subtler affair, but it's no less an act of creative fervour, a cry that if the show is going to go down, then it'll go down with something exceptional.

What Morgan and Wong have done here is taken the ambiguity of the series and put it centre stage. There is a serial killer on death row who appears to have a psychic connection with the other world, and offers Scully a chance to talk to her dead father. We can be sure that Boggs is lying - but now how much. And Scully, the arch sceptic, is transformed into a woman on the edge - at once an FBI agent putting herself in danger to open herself up to extreme possibilities, and yet also a daughter who's still seeking parental approval. The choice that Scully is given at the end - between closure or further ambiguity - is the making of her as a rounded character; she refuses to give in to the manipulations of a murderer, just as she backs away from the fear that he might be for real and throw her scientific certainties into question. She opts for doubt and uncertainty over hard fact rights and wrongs, favouring the love she feels her father had for her over any bald statement on the matter. It's also a moment which is the making of the series itself - the acceptance that the beauty of the unexplained is that sometimes it just remains unexplained.

Gillian Anderson is quite outstanding, especially with her reaction to Mulder's clumsy use of Scully's first name when showing sympathy for her loss, and her childlike need to question her mother about her father's pride even as his ashes are being scattered. There's also the blazing anger with which she confronts Boggs to tell him that she will execute him herself if his mind games have killed her partner. Brad Dourif as Boggs, the murderer turned visionary, gives her everything to play off. It's a part which so easily could have been grandiose and barnstorming, but it's played with great generosity. Dourif never seeks sympathy from the audience, and you warm to him in spite of yourself - by never justifying his actions, nor hiding his fear of impending death, you see that the serial killer is just a terrified little man wanting nothing more from his last moments of life than a bit of attention. The accepting despair on his face when he

is denied that, when he realises he will die without his turn in the spotlight, is surprising and moving.

This is brilliantly plotted - awash with all sorts of moral dilemmas about state execution and the nature of faith - and subtly disturbing. (The story Boggs tells of his victims watching him as he eats his last meal, lined up in the corridors as he's walked to execution, is quite wonderful. It's only topped when he's led to his death a second time, and we see on Boggs' face the sickened realisation that he'll have to suffer that haunting guilt all over again.) Beyond the Sea is one of those times where The X-Files touches genius. As the series lurches onward in its quest for an identity, it is the fact that this story exists, that it can be capable of a drama so profound, that gives you reason to believe it will find one. (*****)

1.14, Gender Bender

Air Date: Jan. 21, 1994
Writers: Larry Barber, Paul Barber
Director: Rob Bowman

Summary A number of people die in the midst of sex, always with a person of one gender entering the crime scene but another leaving it. Mulder and Scully follow leads to a reclusive, religious (and evidently genderbending) sect known as the Kindred. They find that one of their number - Brother Martin - has been literally seducing people to death, with the victims experiencing pleasure that mankind was never meant to survive. Mulder and Scully confront Martin, but the Kindred take him away. Later, Mulder and Scully find the Kindred compound vacated - with Mulder believing, based upon a crop circle of sorts, that they've departed Earth.

Critique It *looks* great enough; Rob Bowman's directorial debut is visually striking, contrasting the bright autumnal colours of the Amish-like community with the synthetic pulse of the night clubs. And it's interesting, too, to see an episode in which the decadent lifestyle of easy sex and loud music collides with a society which is all about restraint and denial. I love the way that the Kindred, with their religious orthodoxy, regard the errant Brother Martin as an alien - it's a clever twist on an ongoing theme, and on what we've come to expect from the series' most potent buzzword.

Or almost, anyway. Because the episode then decides to reveal that the Kindred really *are* aliens. Who can shapeshift and change gender. Oh, and are responsible for crop circles, apparently. A story which begins as something different and subtle - if, to be honest, a little out of left field - finishes up instead entirely clichéd. No explanations, no answers, and no purpose behind the ambiguity, the episode just stops: the aliens disappear as the police track them down, leaving behind no clues, no resolution, no point.

For an episode too which seems to prod at post-AIDS promiscuity, this is all very tame. If you're going to call your story something as lurid as Gender Bender, with all the deviance and fetishism that implies, then, for God's sake, *be* lurid. The sequences in which Martin picks up his victims are about as sexy as an omelette. For this episode to have worked it'd really have had to go for the jugular, emphasising explicitly the reason Martin wanted to escape the austerity of the Kindred in exchange for fun and shagging. Instead we just get wall to wall austerity. When Scully gets seduced she doesn't get turned on, she just gets sleepy. It's a fair indictment of a story which should have been too controversial to be boring - but which faithfully bores all the same. (*1/2)

1.15, Lazarus

Air Date: Feb. 4, 1994
Writers: Alex Gansa, Howard Gordon
Director: David Nutter

Summary Scully and Agent Jack Willis - her former mentor and lover - respond to a tip-off and keep watch for an impending heist by Warren Dupre and Lula Phillips, two married bank robbers. The following skirmish results in Willis and Dupre both taking fatal gunshot wounds. They die on the operating table, but Dupre's consciousness somehow transfers into Willis' body and re-animates it.

As "Willis", Dupre captures Scully and tracks down Lula. Dupre weakens because Willis' body is diabetic and requires insulin - where- upon the treacherous Lula stops him from getting any, admitting that *she* tipped off the authorities to the heist in the first place. Dupre snatches Lula's gun and kills her, then dies from his illness as the authorities determine Scully's location and rescue her.

Critique Considering this is an episode about a man who has two separate souls battling inside him, it seems almost appropriate that this is so tonally schizophrenic. At times the story plays like a sly black comedy - the sequence where the attempts to revive one man on his death bed causes another body to jump about in the background is both eerie and funny at the same time. And I love some of the more dispassionate dialogue about rats eating faces of dead criminals: we're dealing here with an FBI which is *so* cynical that they barely regard their fugitives as human. Seeing that we're in a story in which Scully's ex-lover gets saddled with the psychotic behaviour of the convict he's spent a year bringing to justice, that comic tone seems appropriate for the irony. This is, let's face it, one of the sillier premises offered by the series - so silly, in fact, that Mulder's bizarre theory of psychic transference, based on nothing more than a blip on an EEG machine, looks almost self-parodic.

Christopher Allport, though, hasn't been let in on the joke. He plays the muddled agent in question with a gravitas that borders upon the histrionic - he's doing his level best to take this role seriously and mine every ounce of passion from it, damn it. The music follows suit, Mark Snow giving the action an urgency it hardly deserves. And suddenly even Mulder is calling Scully "Dana" once again, and telling FBI agents that the search for his partner is deeply personal to him. It's all curiously overwrought.

And what that leads to is a conclusion which is one half a glimpse of FBI procedure (down to discovering a phone location by isolating a single sound of an overhead aeroplane, and including rather impressive sequences where the authorities set up a siege) and one half a story in which tattoos keep appearing and disappearing, dependent on which soul is supreme in Willis' body. With everyone's emotions played at full volume, The X-Files has never yet been such a gulf in tone. It's all somewhere between a drama which is po-faced and earnest, and cheesy sci-fi hokum that barely passes the slightest analysis.

It's a pity, because there are some good ideas in here. It's the sort of story which even a year later the series would have made competently well, and known how to balance the tone correctly. As it is, you've got something which feels all over the shop. And the story's just got too many twists up its sleeve - when Scully first tells Dupre that he's inhabiting a body that is diabetic and requires insulin, you might think she's making a particularly clever bluff. But she isn't - it's a measure of the on-the-nose dialogue and plotting that people say *exactly* what they mean - and so for the sake of coincidence we sacrifice what could quite easily have been a piece of character building instead. Similarly, the only sincere thing the episode has going for it is the love between Dupre and Lula - one of the best bits of the story is to hear Willis' taped report on the pair, exposing him in envious obsession. To find that Lula has double-crossed Dupre right from the start betrays the characters, and betrays the whole point of the X-File: that this is the story of a man who so couldn't bear to lose his wife that he came back from the dead to find her. There's an attempt to imitate Tarantino here, but what Tarantino understood is that his hip criminal lovers are honest to each other: what makes them terrifying is that their amorality is consistent, that they can butcher and love at the same time. This story portrays Lula as shallow and treacherous, because she's a criminal, and that's what criminals *are*. The FBI agents who regard their fugitives as barely human were right, it seems. (*1/2)

1.16, Young at Heart

Air Date: Feb. 11, 1994
Writers: Scott Kaufer, Chris Carter
Director: Michael Lange

Summary   Agent Reggie Purdue alerts Mulder when a note at a crime scene bears the same modus operandi as John Barrett - a criminal who died four years ago, after Mulder helped to capture him. Mulder and Scully find that Barnett was a test subject of Dr Ridley, a disgraced physician who experimented to find a cure for progeria, an aging disease. Having been grafted with salamander cells, Barrett has de-aged twenty years and is now equipped with a super-healing factor.

Barrett kills Purdue and tries to murder Scully at a cello recital - but is shot dead by Mulder. Government operatives try and fail to recover Ridley's work, unaware that Barnett stashed the man's findings in an airport locker.

Critique   The first half of the episode is really very good, enlivened by an exciting and comprehensible revenge plot, and a terrific performance by David Duchovny at his most paranoid and guilt-ridden. For a while it's really not an X-File at all, beyond the mystery concerning why an apparent dead man is making threats upon Mulder and his friends. It's well directed and tense, and even though it plays like a fairly standard cop movie, complete with courtroom flashbacks and hapless FBI agents getting offed because of a rookie's hesitation, it's convincing and engaging.

Then, suddenly, things get very odd. It becomes a government conspiracy episode, complete with Deep Throat popping up to talk of shady deals and corruption. It mutates into a story of peculiar and unexplained science, in which people grow younger and amputees get hands grafted from salamanders. And it all gets unnecessarily operatic - quite literally, in its showdown in a concert hall - as Mulder is required to face a Moral Dilemma in gunning down a murderer who just happens to hold the secret that could change the lives of all mankind. And more, he can also Find Redemption, as he's challenged to re-enact or correct the mistake he made all those years ago on his first case.

All of this makes the story strangely top heavy, and more than a little pretentious. Mark Snow doesn't help with a score that wants to echo The Omen, with lots of choirs going nuts singing in Latin around every corner. And what gave the episode its hook, a chance to see a more personal side of Mulder as he is forced to face his youthful demons, gets sacrificed as it strains to be about global concerns. It's another in a string of stories which don't really know what they want to do - and so, by trying to do everything at once, bog down the plot.

I like the flirty handwriting expert, though. She seems to know Mulder very well - just how often off screen does he slope around her microscope, asking her advice on graphology? I wish she would become a regular. You'd have an FBI agent who deals with the paranormal, his sceptical partner who prides herself upon her scientific rationale, and, in the middle, a woman offering coquettery and handwriting analysis in equal measure. I'd watch that. (**)

1.17, E.B.E.

Air Date: Feb. 18, 1994
Writers: Glen Morgan, James Wong
Director: William A Graham

Summary When Mulder and Scully attempt to track down a UFO that fell to Earth near the Iraq / Turkey border, they discover that Deep Throat has been feeding them misinformation to keep them away from the grounded alien spaceship and the extraterrestrial biological entity (E.B.E.) inside. Deep Throat insists that the public isn't ready to know certain secrets, but Mulder trails the UFO to Washington state and - in collusion with the Lone Gunmen (three conspiracy theorists named Byers, Frohike and Langly) - infiltrates a military installation there.

Once inside, Mulder learns that the E.B.E. has been killed. Deep Throat arrives and tells Mulder that after the notorious Roswell incident in 1947, the major world governments agreed to kill any E.B.E. that fell to Earth in their territory. As one of three men to have personally exterminated such a creature, a repentant Deep Throat hopes to use Mulder's work to one day expose the truth. Meanwhile, Mulder is less certain than ever as to what to believe.

Critique It's hard to know where to begin assessing E.B.E. After a flurry of mediocre episodes which signpost their plot twists clearly for all the world to see, this one comes out of left field. It revels in obfuscation, and is deliberately frustrating. It's a story about disinformation, in which Mulder and Scully are fed lie after lie and denied even a hint of true resolution. Is there a better scene to sum up the series than Mulder risking his life as he races towards a box containing his fabled alien - only to discover it's missing, presumed dead? Is there any episode in which the theme of the programme, its conspiracy and paranoia and deceit, are better summed up or handled so deftly? E.B.E. sees the future of The X-Files, and sums it up in microcosm.

And that, of course, leads to the frustration I mentioned earlier. Throughout its run audiences would complain about the lack of proper answers, realising that with every mythos episode all we would be given would be fresh questions. By summing that up, E.B.E. also risks coming off as very cold and very schematic. It's like an Escher print - there's no beginning, and no end, because for all the characters' search for a truth, there's no simple truth we can seize upon to expose the lies surrounding it. Jerry Hardin has been used rather poorly as Deep Throat of late, only there to prop up weak storylines and give them the sense of a greater conspiracy. And his performance has suffered as a result, clearly feeling uncomfortable as a man whose only function is to offer exposition, then vanish mysteriously into the shadows once more. That's not a character - that's a macguffin. Here, though, he is blindingly good, playing a man who might be hero or might be villain - and who might even be both. He tells the truth, but he decorates it with lies, and by doing so re-establishes the emotional core of the show: Mulder and Scully can trust no-one but each other, and nor can the viewer.

For what is such a marvellous slice of paranoia, there's a scene of great comedy to enjoy with the introduction of the Lone Gunmen. Truth be told, I've never been that convinced by the acting ability of this trio, but here - in what appears to be no more than a one-off appearance - they don't try to play for laughs or cuteness, and are much funnier as a result. Unlikeable and creepy, they are the epitome of the paranoia this episode is all about - a paranoia which, as Scully suggests, gives them ironically a sense of importance and esteem they don't deserve. It's why, perhaps, for all its obvious cleverness, E.B.E. still strikes me as vaguely dissatisfying - as if, underneath, it knows that all the intrigue and subterfuge The X-Files are playing with here are masks for a rather hollow centre. If so, it's an interesting critique of the show, and one that I'd argue gets addressed in the second season when Scully's fate is put at the heart of the conspiracy episodes and they acquire a greater emotional pull. But for the moment E.B.E., as good as it is, leaves an odd taste in the mouth. It's only in Deep Throat's speech about his personal encounter with alien life, and how he has been atoning ever since for his role as its executioner, that suggests something truly heartfelt. And it's a peculiar irony that we *still* cannot be sure that even that flicker of emotion isn't yet another lie. (****)

1.18, Miracle Man

Air Date: March 18, 1994
Writers: Howard Gordon, Chris Carter
Director: Michael Lange

Summary Scully brings to Mulder's attention the case of Samuel Hartley, an eighteen-year-old working at the Miracle Ministry - an evangelical church in Tennessee. Samuel's touch formerly cured the sick, but it's now turned deadly, and before long he's arrested on suspicion of murder.

The agents find that the parishioners "killed" by Samuel were actually poisoned by Leonard Vance - a burn victim whom Samuel once brought back from the dead. The event left Vance physically scarred, and he now seeks to discredit the man who resurrected him. Locals who believe that Samuel has turned evil beat him to death, but Samuel mysteriously appears before Vance - who promptly commits suicide. Mulder and Scully leave town after learning that Samuel's body has gone missing from the morgue.

Critique The religious debate on offer here is something of a camouflage, I think. At its heart, this is a tragic tale of a man who has a great talent; it defines him, it gives him purpose - and then he loses it. And he is left torturing himself about what he did to deserve that, how something so valuable was squandered. It's a classic idea - the Salieri of Amadeus is driven to despair when he believes he's been destined for mediocrity, Ernest Hemingway shooting himself when he believes his genius for writing has deserted him. And it humanises this tale which, with all its religious themes, could easily have been distancing - fundamentally, each of us fears that we will never achieve anything great, or even

worse, that the greatest of our achievements are behind us. Scott Bairstow plays the faith healer with miracle block with tremendous dignity, always with the conviction that he has once been an instrument of God, and has now been forsaken for his pride and turned into a murderer. After all the monsters we have even by now seen on display in the series, to put at the centre of a story an *examination* of what special powers can do to a man is hugely refreshing.

For the most part, too, it's a good story well told, and it's great to see Mulder and Scully acting in concert during an investigation. Scully's Catholic faith makes her less sceptical than usual, but more damning of the mercantile way that Samuel's gifts have been exploited than Mulder; he is happier making quips about Elvis. And Mulder too has a journey in this episode, as his own faith is held up to the light and examined - not in God, but in the way he has defined himself by the abduction of his sister.

It's here, though, that the story gets a bit stuck, with Mulder having visions of little girls all over the place. Subtlety would have been so much more effective - the passion with which Duchovny questions Bairstow about his "pain" is so much more successful than the sequences in which he starts chasing minors in red dresses. But unsubtlety is the direction the episode takes. Before too long Samuel is being murdered, his shadow clearly mirroring Christ upon the cross - then he's coming back as a ghostly vision to challenge and forgive the traitor in his flock - and then, most speciously of all, he even gets to stage a witnessed resurrection from the dead. Whereas all these phenomena can be explained away, either as prickings of conscience, body snatching, or simple directorial bluntness, the fact that the story presents them as fact on screen robs the episode of any ambiguity. And, it must be said, of much of its power too - Samuel was so much more effective when his fall from Grace was something we could all find resonance with.

There's still lots to enjoy here. Somewhat surprisingly, the Evangelists are not held up to the ridicule one might expect, and though their faith is never endorsed it is still treated without cynicism. And I love the idea of an unwilling Lazarus, taking revenge on his saviour because he'd rather be dead than ugly. It's a fault of the plot that he waits ten years of such ugliness before bothering to vent his displeasure - but it's a good twist all the same. (***1/2)

1.19, Shapes

Air Date: April 1, 1994
Writer: Marilyn Osborne
Director: David Netter

Summary In Browning, Montana, a savage creature attacks Jim Parker and mauls his son Lyle - but when Jim shoots the beast dead, it reverts to the form of Joseph Goodensnake, a Native American. Mulder informs Scully that the case might be related to the very first X-File, in which a series of murders in 1946 were attributed to a vicious animal that became human when the police shot it. A Native American mystic tells Mulder about the Manitou, a malevolent spirit who turns men into beasts. Lyle's injuries infect him with the Manitou taint and he becomes a were-man - who kills his father and in turn is slain by Mulder and the local sheriff. The matter seems settled, but the mystic suggests that the Manitou will return, as is its pattern, in about eight years.

Critique Mulder and Scully investigate the case that opened the X-Files, way back in 1946! Dear God, protect us from episodes which try to prop up their lame storylines by tying them to the series' background. It doesn't give them greater moment, it just makes them look as if the writers are desperately trying to find another hook. We've seen Mulder's first case explored, and seen both Scully and Mulder work with ex-partners and ex-lovers... so it just doesn't work. Whatever sense of importance you try to attach to Shapes, it's a bog standard werewolf idea, without twists or insight or the least freshness to offer. Early on, Scully tells Mulder it's clear he's been expecting every clue he's so far uncovered - and so have we. Of course we have. We know the hackneyed genre. The difference is that Mulder continues to act puzzled for the next half-hour by what the investigation turns up, whilst the audience can happily chant out every thudding predictable turn of events.

It doesn't do The X-Files any good when we get episodes like this, which take on monster stories so familiar that we know every trick and trope before the characters. It makes Scully look stupid at the end when she *still* believes she may have been attacked by a mountain lion. We can see she's in a laboriously slow werewolf story, so why can't she? Hasn't she ever seen An American Werewolf in London? Hasn't she even seen Teen Wolf? Well, we have, and they were better. Yes. Even Teen Wolf.

There are some nice directorial flourishes from David Nutter. I like the way the funeral pyre dissolves to the lit cigar of the man who killed the person being cremated. The werewolf transformation scene is quite convincing too. But the script is witless and overwritten, the acting (especially from Renae Morriseau, as Lyle's aunt) one-dimensional and pompous, and the overall pace is turgid. At the very end, Wise Native American Guy - I don't know his name, let's call him Talks-in-Long-Monologues - says to Mulder he'll expect to see him in another eight years for the next werewolf cycle. "I hope not," Mulder replies. It's the first thing said in the entire episode which has a note of sincerity to it. (*)

1.20, Darkness Falls

Air Date: April 15, 1994
Writer: Chris Carter
Director: Joe Napolitano

Summary When thirty loggers go missing in Olympia National Forest, Mulder and Scully join an excursion to discover what happened to them. Mulder concludes that the logging operation released dormant green mites that were altered by radiation from a local volcano. The mites swarm in darkness and consume human flesh after cocooning their prey.

Stranded when a trap set by eco-terrorists ruins their car tires, Mulder, Scully and a forest ranger spend a harrowing night with the light of just one bulb - powered by a generator that's rapidly running out of fuel - to keep the mites at bay. Doug Spinney, the only surviving member of the eco-terrorists, retrieves a jeep and attempts to drive Mulder's party to safety, but the jeep's tires are again punctured by an eco-terrorist snare. Spinney runs off as the insects swarm and cocoon Mulder, Scully and the ranger. Government agents rescue them and provide life-saving treatment. Mulder learns that the government will use a series of controlled forest burns and pesticides to eliminate the mites.

Critique If you go down to the woods tonight...

I like this a lot. It borrows much of Ice's basic premise - that of a base under siege from creatures reawakened after hundreds of years by human interference - but it has a paranoia and a tension all of its own. At heart it's another monster episode, but this time Mulder and Scully aren't on the outside looking in, and are genuinely ensnared as the prey in a tight little horror movie. Chris Carter keeps the story simple - rarely for him - and puts our heroes in a situation where the darkness will kill them, more than a daylight's distance from rescue. We quickly find the nature of the threat, and from that point on the agents' only goal is to survive. It's not subtle, but it's not supposed to be. Instead this is a masterful exercise in tension, and it's fascinating to watch how Mulder and Scully begin to panic and come apart at the seams.

There's a vague conservation theme here too, pitting ecowarriors against loggers, and showing how the extremists on both sides may have condemned each other to death. But wisely not too much is made of this - Carter would rather focus upon our fear of insects in their millions, and upon our fear of the dark. Even though these two fears are frankly incompatible (insects are drawn, of course, to the light), Carter merrily just tells the audience that these are different *kinds* of insects, sits back, and lets the terror games start. There are many great sequences here, but the best must be Scully's horrified fascination as she watches the unstoppable predators pour down the walls into their hut - right before she freaks at realising that she too is covered with them.

There's such a grim inevitability about our heroes' demise, that the ending can't help but disappoint a little. But even if they are rescued in the nick of time, it's still shocking to see Mulder and Scully lose the fight against the monsters for once, and have to be cut out from cocoons and taken into quarantine. As effectively as it can, Darkness Falls has shown Mulder

and Scully die, lost and screaming beneath a swarm of killer bugs. It's easy, too, to criticise the special effects - the insects aren't *that* convincing - but there's still something very creepy about seeing people attacked by green dots, buzzing away at them like angry static. (****1/2)

1.21, Tooms

Air Date: April 22, 1994
Writers: Glen Morgan, James Wong
Director: David Nutter

Summary When Eugene Tooms (1.03, Squeeze) comes up for parole, Mulder's assertion that Tooms is a century-old mutant who kills people in order to eat their livers sounds so outlandish that Tooms wins his release. Mulder keeps surveillance on Tooms, but Tooms uses his super-stretching ability to steal one of Mulder's shoes and beat himself with it. Walter Skinner, an assistant director at the FBI, warns Mulder that he's not above the law.

As is his custom, Tooms kills five people and eats their livers, then prepares to go into hibernation for thirty years. Mulder and Scully deduce that Tooms will "nest" in his former apartment building, which has been replaced by a shopping mall. Mulder finds Tooms underneath an escalator at the mall and barely escapes with his life. He then triggers the escalator's machinery, ripping Tooms to death.

Critique The plot goes a bit awry, but the moments are excellent. Because it's an episode with a lot of continuity baggage (It's the first sequel! Skinner makes his debut! The Cigarette Smoking Man actually speaks!), it's hard to spot that maybe its true legacy is that here is the first time that The X-Files tries its hand at comedy. It's a jet black comedy, to be sure, but no less funny for all that. From a teaser which leads you to believe that Tooms will use his stretching powers to make a prison break, but in which the only stretching he can satisfactorily accomplish is the crossing of his fingers for luck, you can tell this going to be about the reversal of expectation. And the parole hearing, in which Mulder in all po-faced solemnity berates Tooms for being a hundred-year-old hibernating cannibal mutant, is genuinely laugh out loud stuff. It's a neat subversion of the series' premise for us to see just how *ridiculous* The X-Files' plots are if you try to describe them out loud.

Morgan and Wong are savvy enough to realise we've already seen Tooms kill people in grisly ways in Squeeze - and so all that's left in the sequel is to see him being foiled instead. The sequence in which Tooms tries to invade a suburban house through the toilet is great - the tug of war he gets involved in, with a housewife unblocking the drain, is very funny. But what's brilliant about the comedy is how unsettling it still is: even more than in Squeeze, watching Tooms contort through bars makes the brain struggle to match what's being presented so plausibly with what we know is impossible. There's that moment where Tooms breaks into Mulder's flat, not to kill him, but to injure himself and frame our hero - it's a joke, it's a twist on what we were expecting, but it's also disturbing. The end of the act, which shows Tooms using his own fingers to make his cheeks bleed, is utterly grotesque.

But best of all, perhaps, is a single scene between Mulder and Scully on a stakeout, sitting in a car, talking about sandwiches and loyalty and love. It's funny, it's touching, it's true - and it's the best we've yet seen Duchovny and Anderson perform together.

This story doesn't offer the same shocks as Squeeze, but it does provide instead greater and subtler surprises. Less obviously a horror story than its predecessor, it feels somehow more sophisticated, an examination of what the series' clichés are, and where the series will go from here. And it's brimming with confidence. The story itself may not be up to much - it's more a series of set pieces, and very little investigation - but for its breezy macabre wit alone, this is that rare thing: a sequel which is better than the original. (****1/2)

1.22, Born Again

Air Date: April 29, 1994
Writers: Alex Gansa, Howard Gordon
Director: Jerrold Freedman

Summary A police detective summons Mulder and Scully when a fellow police officer dies while speaking to Michelle Bishop, an eight-year-old girl. Michelle claims to have visions of Charlie Morris, a detective who was killed nine years ago. Mulder notes that Morris' death coincided with Michelle's conception. Morris' soul has been reincarnated in Michelle's body, and he's been using psychokinetic power to kill those involved in his death. Michelle attacks Morris' former partner - Tony Fiore, who betrayed him as part of an insurance scam - with telekinesis, but Mulder and Scully intercede and convince Michelle to relent. Fiore confesses to his role in Morris' death, and Michelle loses all memory of these events.

Critique The X-Files has already given us a great creepy little girl story - but I *like* creepy girls, how can you ever have enough? In this instance the acting from the girl in question is terrific, but the story is much more humdrum. Part of the difficulty is that this wants to be both a telekinesis episode - with a lovely teaser of a two-hundred-pound man being blasted out of a window by the will of a child - and also a reincarnation episode. Either one of the starting points would have been interesting; to link the two so spuriously makes them both feel a bit woolly, and *still* doesn't really provide enough meat for forty-five minutes of television.

It all starts intriguingly enough, but within a quarter of an hour, we're in a revenge drama in which all the members of a corrupt cop ring are being bumped off one by one. What's surprising is how enjoyable this is, never mind how predictable. The set pieces are nicely done, especially the death by hanging whilst caught in the doors of a bus. And there's a strange quirkiness to the imagery of the episode - the repeat of the abused doll, the origami animals, the deep sea diver in the fish tank - which make a very ordinary story seem just a little bit extraordinary after all.

The characterisation of Mulder and Scully is a little off, perhaps, but it's interesting to see

Mulder genuinely rail against Scully for her scepticism. Beyond showing a frustration that may well by now have been shared by a sizeable chunk of the audience, it also suggests the growing tension now that the future of the X-Files feels under threat. Scully gives as good as she gets, though, rightfully hitting back at Mulder in a scene where he tries to push a girl into hypnotic regression against the wishes of her mother or doctor. I'm amazed that the mother lets Mulder watch young Michelle's first swimming lesson at the story's end - if I'd been her, I'd have pushed him into the pool. (**1/2)

1.23, Roland

Air Date: May 6, 1994
Writer: Chris Ruppenthal
Director: David Nutter

Summary   Mulder and Scully visit a research facility where scientists tasked with developing a new jet engine are being systematically killed. The head of the first victim, Arthur Gamble, was frozen after he died in a car accident - and Mulder soon concludes that this event enabled Gamble's consciousness to attain a higher level of being. Since then, Gamble has been mentally influencing his twin brother - Roland Fuller, a janitor at the facility - to continue Gamble's work and vengefully murder his associates.

The last surviving team member, Dr Nollette, overhears Mulder's theories and starts to thaw Gamble's head. Nollette confronts Roland - who has hit upon the magical computation needed for the jet engine to obtain Mach 15 - and confesses to thieving Gamble's work. The agents convince Roland to relent from murdering Nollette, and Gamble's consciousness dissipates as his head assumes room temperature. Afterward, Mulder argues that Roland is innocent and wins his release.

Critique   Hang on, haven't we just watched this one? In Born Again, a child is controlled by a dead man wanting to take revenge on his colleagues. In Roland, it's a child-like man being controlled by a dead man who - well, just guess what he's after. Born Again might seem the more generic of the two episodes, and lacks both the

mental disability thread and the shiny hardware of the story, but it's still *better*: you can understand Charlie Morris' motivation in a way you never quite can for Arthur Grable. So, to sum up, this is the story of a man who directs his twin brother to kill people because... they're carrying on his work after his death. Not subverting it, or exploiting it, just using it. I thought that was the point of science. Isn't that just a tad self-obsessed, even for a psychotic head in liquid nitrogen?

The deaths are good. I love the dispassionate way the camera only just glimpses Dr Surnow being sucked to his death, concentrating instead on Roland absorbed in his janitor duties. And the white chalk corpse outline of Dr Keats, with the head smashed into little frozen pieces, is priceless. The acting is good too: Zeljko Ivanek gives a standout performance as the autistic Roland, treading the thin line between eerie and sympathetic very skilfully.

But at the end of the day, the biggest mystery to be solved here is why the producers chose to schedule two identical plotlines back to back in the running order. It almost feels like the series is running out of steam, which is why it's a relief that the finale and a new direction are just around the corner. (**)

1.24, The Erlenmeyer Flask

Air Date: May 13, 1994
Writer: Chris Carter
Director: RW Goodwin

Summary   Deep Throat tells Mulder to find Dr Secare, a fugitive who has demonstrated superhuman strength, toxic green blood and the ability to survive underwater. An unidentified killer (henceforth known as "Crew-Cut Man") murders Dr Berube, one of Secare's associates. Scully finds Berube had in his possession bacteria with nucleotides that don't exist on Earth, and thus must be extraterrestrial in origin.

Deep Throat informs Mulder and Scully that Berube was engaged in research to determine the effects of alien viruses on human subjects, and that Secare was one of Berube's patients. With black ops agents - acting without sanction or knowledge of the highest levels of government - destroying all evidence pertaining to the case, Deep Throat stresses that Mulder must find Secare. Mulder does so, but the Crew-Cut Man kills Secare and takes Mulder prisoner.

With Deep Throat's help, Scully infiltrates a containment facility at Fort Marlene, Maryland, and steals an alien foetus. Deep Throat arranges to exchange the foetus for Mulder's life and insists on making the exchange himself. Mulder is released as promised, but the Crew-Cut Man kills Deep Throat. Two weeks later, FBI higher-ups hand down word that the X-Files are to be closed.

Critique "Trust No One." Changing the motto in the opening title sequence is a trick that becomes hackneyed through overuse in future seasons, but the first time it happens is a real shock: it signifies that however familiar the trappings of the episode, something off-kilter has taken place. And so it turns out to be. On the face of it, there's so much here that feels like an echo of what we've already seen. There's Deep Throat sending our heroes on yet another mission with cryptic clues - but this time Scully at last vents her frustration, telling Mulder that he gets off on the conspiracy of it all. There's a repeat of the ending of this season's second episode, with Mulder bought back from government authorities - but this time there's a real price to pay, and Deep Throat gets executed. There's even a replay of the same closing shot from the pilot episode - and now there *are* no X-Files; the agency has been shut down, Mulder and Scully have been reassigned. There are no new cases to look forward to.

The Erlenmeyer Flask promises new information, but delivers only scraps. But what's clever about it is that it makes us feel we're watching the same series through a sudden harsher light, with all the tricks and clichés of the show coming back and biting. It makes it a disquieting experience, one in which we get our first sense of the power of Mulder's opponents - "I'll protect you" are the last words Dr Secare hears Mulder say before being gunned down in his arms. You get the impression that Mulder

and Scully are in no position to promise *any-thing*, that they've only been allowed to carry on with their work this long because they hadn't quite upset the status quo enough to be worth bothering with - but that now they've drawn attention to themselves, they can be easily squashed. Conceived as a possible finale to the series, this would have been a brave, even nihilistic conclusion. What's remarkable is that this isn't as depressing as it ought to be. There's a real sense of wonder to the episode, as Chris Carter pours on the moments of revelation - Scully's amazement at finding the alien foetus, Mulder investigating the laboratory full of hybrids. Just as the X-Files are closed, and their informant is killed before our eyes, we have a sense at last of a bigger story opening up before us.

Did I say revelation? Well, maybe not. This is The X-Files. It'll become a staple ingredient of the conspiracy episodes that more is suggested than is ever explained. And the same thing is true here: Chris Carter's script almost falls over itself with its excitement to talk about genome projects and DNA experiments, and barely finds the space to provide a connecting narrative. The reason why this episode works almost *because* of this, rather than just in spite of it, is because it has a dynamism behind it which feels so fresh. The plotting unravels by the end - it's undoubtedly very clumsy the ease with which Scully blags a password and is able to steal just about the most important alien lifeform the government owns - but you buy it because the payoff is so very good. Deep Throat's death is shocking because it's done in such a matter-of-fact way, but also because it feels like a real *consequence*. We've heard him talking endlessly about how his connections to Mulder have endangered his life, and we at last see, when he puts his head over the parapet for long enough, the reality of those fears. The rush of non-explanations that the episode seems to offer the audience are thrilling stuff, because you can honestly feel that to get these table leavings of truth, the series' format has been wrecked. (****)

2.1, Little Green Men

Air Date: Sept. 16, 1994
Writers: Glen Morgan, James Wong
Director: David Nutter

Summary With Mulder and Scully stuck doing routine FBI work, one of Mulder's allies in Congress - Senator Richard Matheson - tells him that some sort of UFO incident has occurred at an abandoned radio telescope in Arecibo, Puerto Rico. Mulder goes there but finds only a terrified native - who renders a drawing of an alien before dashing into the jungle and mysteriously dying, as if of fright. Mulder sees a bright light, complete with an alien silhouette, then falls unconscious. The two agents escape as a Blue Beret UFO retrieval team shows up, but Mulder finds all evidence pertaining to the incident has vanished, leaving him at square one.

Critique   The teaser is beautiful. Not just because is it a wonderful display of computer animation, but because it's also the first time a series about the possibility of alien existence has stopped to look up at the stars above with awe. The effect is that when Mulder speaks of the closure of the X-Files it affects us too - we have been denied the knowledge that the Voyager project could have given us. (It hearkens back to Space, where it's acknowledged we live in an all-too real world which finds space exploration irrelevant.) But what makes Little Green Men so brilliant is that it emphasises just what the absence of the X-Files has done, not only on that intellectual level, but to Mulder and Scully. It's telling that we see a redefinition of Mulder's quest, via a flashback sequence of his sister being abducted. And Duchovny's Mulder is fantastic - here is a man who has become so disillusioned by pen-pushing banality that he's begun to doubt not only his mission but his own experiences. This is Duchovny's best performance yet; too often in the first season he seemed underpowered beside Gillian Anderson, but here he approaches the role with a fresh confidence and a real verve. It's as if in the sea-son break Duchovny has realised what the series is about, and how he can take centre stage in it.

It's a new confidence shared across the board. It's a Morgan and Wong script, so you expect the dialogue to be good - but this is a *fantastic* script, unsensational and subtle as it may be, which reinvigorates the series and its themes with great aplomb. The X-Files are no longer a symbol of the spooky and the bizarre, but of sincerity and truth. The sequence between Scully and Mulder in the car park is superb; it's almost painful to see how the paranoid Mulder has had to reject Scully, and how it's her concern for him which overrides her sense of personal danger. When she later tracks him down in Puerto Rico, and he says that his faith in himself has been so badly shaken that he now has to believe in *her*, it's a simple but moving reaffirmation of what the heart of the programme is.

Because this *does* play like a pilot, and a very good one. It asks the questions that the first season never had the time to answer, but which need to be addressed so the series can move forward. Mulder is so obsessed with finding aliens, but what will he do once he finds them? The answer, which is as much of a shock to him as it is to us, is to freak out, pull a gun and start shooting. It's almost as if the whole alien encounter quest is a lie, that deep down Mulder is just another terrified little man we see as a patsy getting killed in many an episode teaser; the FBI may have taken away his ability to get to the truth, but he wouldn't know how to handle the truth if it were given to him on a plate. The closure of the X-Files, then, is less about the denial of Mulder's mission, but more the enforced separation from Scully. It's a theme which will play to the first third of the season to great effect.

Mitch Pileggi has also undergone a transformation; somewhat overacted in Tooms, he now feels like a core player. That's quite an achievement in only his second episode. The scene in which he rejects the Cigarette Smoking Man in favour of Mulder is terrific - like Mulder and Scully themselves, Skinner is having to adjust his values. It offers a character who could so easily have been the obstructive face of bureau-cracy a door to redemption, and it's a mark of this new sophisticated X-Files season that the moment counts for so much.

It's not an episode that The X-Files fans were expecting, and its reputation isn't great. But I think this clever and claustrophobic little tale, which does so much not only to refresh the show but to analyse what it's actually about, is one of the very best. (*****)

2.2, The Host

Air Date: Sept. 23, 1994
Writer: Chris Carter
Director: Daniel Sackheim

Summary Mulder is bored when he's assigned to the seemingly routine murder of a sanitation worker in Newark, but an unidentified inform-ant advises him to take more interest in the case. In due course, Mulder encounters the Fluke-man: a quasi-vertibrate creature that reproduces by incubating its larva in humans. The Flukeman escapes into a sewage treatment plan-et, but Mulder drops a sewage gate and slices the monster in half. Scully speculates that the Flukeman was the result of a Russian freighter disposing nuclear waste from Chernobyl. Meanwhile, the severed Flukeman, unbe-knownst to the agents, is still alive in the sewer system.

Critique This is a decent old-fashioned monster story, given a new spin by being set in the new X-Files-less FBI. What gives it an extra buzz is that it's Mulder, still in the throes of depression, who all but rejects the case - witness his disgust as he ventures down into the sewers on what he assumes is one more round of routine humilia-tion - and that it's Scully, still trying to find a way to give her former partner some purpose, who takes the steps to determine the unusual nature of his assignment. In addition, the mysterious phone calls telling Mulder that the successful outcome of the case is imperative for the reopening of the X-Files, and Skinner's own reluctant admission that lives would have been saved had the X-Files been active, give this deliberately familiar story of monster maraud-ings a greater sense of depth.

There are some lovely ideas, too, about the

way the FBI is ill-equipped to deal with prose-cuting legal proceedings against a human fluke. It's comical to imagine a sea monster being brought to book in a courtroom, but it also helps illustrate that gulf between the show that was (in which Mulder and Scully get to pursue cases only limited by imagination) and the show that *is* (in which Mulder is still stuck on wiretap duty).

It all peters out after half an hour's worth of action, and more's the pity; the sequence where Skinner admits that he's at the behest of his own superiors in repressing Mulder's work feels like a satisfying climax, and it's disappointing that it's followed by another ten minutes of running around sewers once again. But this is largely a skilful horror story with some great (and grisly) set pieces - the revelation of the fluke by autop-sy, the sanitation worker coughing up a parasite in the shower. If by the end of the story you might feel this is just an ordinary X-File, then bring them on: as a baseline episode, this has enough flair and pace to satisfy. (***1/2)

2.3, Blood

Air Date: Sept. 30, 1994
Story: Darin Morgan
Teleplay: Glen Morgan, James Wong
Director: David Nutter

Summary In Franklin, Pennsylvania, seemingly random members of the public go mad and kill twenty-two people. Mulder concludes that the perpetrators - as part of a covert experiment - were exposed to a type of insecticide that chem-ically induces fear and makes them see murder-ous messages (such as "Kill 'Em All") in digital displays. Edward Funsch, a laid-off postal worker, succumbs to the condition and takes to a campus tower with a rifle. Mulder apprehends Funsch, but sees a last message - perhaps real, perhaps imagined - in his cell phone: "All done. Bye bye."

Critique I don't think this really works. Which is a pity, because it's a clever idea, and a witty script. The problem may just be that it's too complex a premise to be explored within a sin-gle episode - the notion of a town being sub-jected to controlled paranoic bouts of violence is brilliant, and you could easily imagine it as a movie. But without the space to analyse it, the revelations (even for The X-Files) are illogical and forced, and any sense of plot progression is abandoned in favour of set pieces.

And the set pieces are great. There's something not only disturbing but very funny about seeing people being dispassionately urged to commit murder by the electronic panels of microwave ovens and cash dispensers. The problem is that they're all the *same* set piece. There's something wrong with the structure of a story when you begin to realise that any of one these scenes - the great depiction of lift claustrophobia, the woman being told to kill a mechanic before he can rape her - could be the precredit teaser. They all have the same purpose, and much the same effect. And the only reason we focus upon Edward Funsch is because he's the guy we're going to watch go to pieces in the final act; however, since it takes forty minutes of screen time before Mulder even meets him, you get the nagging sense that we could be following any one of these storylines. There's no special significance to Funsch - and it feels odd at the end of the episode, after his homicidal breakdown has been thwarted, that the people behind the paranoia seem to call off the experiment. Since the strength of William Sanderson's performance is that his killer is such an ordinary man, it's strangely anticlimactic that the story relies upon him to wrap up the conspiracy.

Minute by minute there is tons to enjoy. I love the scene where Mulder thinks he might be the latest victim of subliminal control, only to realise he's watching a TV commercial for a gym - that's knowing and witty on all the right levels! But what we've got here is a whole string of first acts, and then a garbled final act which for some reason takes its signature from Vertigo. It's disjointed and not a little frustrating.

It's odd, too, that Mulder and Scully seem to be openly working together, without restrictions or the need for secrecy. In the atmosphere of sustained paranoia this episode generates so well, it might have given the story a bit more focus had it tied in with our heroes also being forced to look behind their backs every moment.

You can't write off an episode which so clearly wants to criticise the blandness of American small town values, the insidious way in which advertising controls our lives, and gun culture. It has heart and intelligence. I could only have wished for a bit more narrative and coherence. (***)

2.4, Sleepless

Air Date: Oct. 7, 1994
Writer: Howard Gordon
Director: Rob Bowman

Summary Mulder is assigned a new partner, Alex Krycek, and told to look into a pair of anomalous deaths in New York. An enigmatic figure named only "X" tells Mulder that the military once conducted experiments to determine if removing the need for sleep would create a more aggressive type of soldier. The only survivor of this project, Augustus Cole, hasn't slept since and has consequently developed the ability to endow people with dreams so powerful that they kill. The agents intercept Cole, who's been eliminating those connected to the project, hoping to atone for his squad - in their capacity as military lab rats - massacring a village in Vietnam. Mulder asks Cole to give testimony on the military's actions, but a despairing Cole tricks Krycek into killing him. Afterward, Krycek reports to his secret boss: the Cigarette Smoking Man.

Critique The biggest shame of the episode, I think, is that it reveals Krycek as an enemy too early. Nicholas Lea is so convincing as a junior agent keen to impress Mulder, and to run around in his mentor's shadow, that you just can't help but wish there was more of a chance to see the pair in action. And to wonder what greater impact Krycek's treachery would have had after he'd built up a greater trust in the audience. It's rare for The X-Files to *rush* a conspiracy, after all; that said, if we're considering the game the series plays in setting up characters who might be friend or might be foe, it's good to see Mr X at last, in a fine introduction well played by Steven Williams.

All in all, there's such a strong sense of a new chapter opening here, with the conspiracy against Mulder and Scully gathering apace, that it almost threatens to overwhelm the plot proper. Howard Gordon is offering another of his patented revenge stories, in which a man with powers knocks off his old associates - we've seen a lot of these already, and there are more to come. What dignifies this above, say, Gordon's last contribution (1.22, Born Again) is the sincerity of the revenge on display. This isn't something small like cops stealing money, this is Vietnam - and what's skilful about Gordon's script is that he makes the cliché of Vietnam war guilt feel very personal and even sorrowful. The idea of making soldiers more aggressive by removing the solace of sleep is a fascinating one, and it means that the victims almost seem to be *waiting* for death as a release, haunted by the evil that they have done and could not prevent. Tony Todd as the executioner plays a man only offering mercy killings to his brothers in arms, and manages to be both very powerful and strangely sympathetic - the scene in which he murders Henry Willing is in particular a tour de force. If in the last act the revenge story runs out of steam, it's still provided an X-File so nebulous and amoral it almost feels like sleeplessness. Wonderful imagery distinguishes the story too - the sequence in which the doctor is confronted by all the soldiers on which he operated, one of whom we've already seen killed, is especially striking.

Add to this a beautiful scene between Duchovny and Anderson over the phone, in which they're on the brink of being actually *nostalgic* about their partnership together. On the face of it it's so odd, this early on in The X-Files' history, but it does much to mythologise a team we had no reason not to take for granted in the first season. As the Cigarette Smoking Man indicates, the spine of the series now seems to concentrate on the importance of Mulder and Scully being separated. Arguably as The X-Files develops its second season, and it's only now finding what key elements it will need to rely on to ensure its longevity, it's already yearning for simpler times and more innocent adventures. It's very clever, too - it gives the whole series a different scale already, the sense that it's been running for longer and more successfully than it has, and suggests a halcyonic state to which the show *must* return. After so cunningly in recent episodes showing us what the absence of the X-

Files means to the series intellectually, it now hits us with an emotional charge too. (****)

2.5, Duane Barry

Air Date: Oct. 14, 1994
Writer / Director: Chris Carter

Summary In Marion, Virginia, an institutionalized FBI agent named Duane Barry takes hostages, demanding to be taken to the site where aliens purportedly abducted him. Mulder and Krycek negotiate with Barry until an FBI sharpshooter winds up wounding the man. Barry is taken to the hospital, where an examination finds bits of metal in his gums, abdomen and sinus cavity, plus extraordinarily small holes drilled into his teeth - all signs of an alien abduction. Scully, speculating that one of the metal pieces in Barry was placed there as if to catalogue him, leaves Mulder a message telling him as much - just before as Barry escapes and bursts in on her. [To be continued.]

Critique It's the teeth which always get me. Not simply on a gut level - because, let's be honest, the sequence showing lasers cutting into Barry's mouth makes Marathon Man seem tame - but because it's such a *minute* detail. From the word "go" the series has been concerned with UFOs and alien abductions, but this is the first time that the trivial, even mundane, details are examined in ever more disturbing detail. It's what at last makes the premise of the series seem real - death and abduction are big staple concepts, but aliens that wire your mouth open so they can drill holes in your teeth? That seems personal, somehow.

What makes Duane Barry such a standout episode is its apparent simplicity - the majority of it is concerned with a hostage situation, and the conversation between two characters. It's dialogue heavy, and feels at times like a filmed stage play. And that makes the moments of violence that much more shocking, and the tension that much more palpable. For the most part it works perfectly well as an episode devoid of any genre trappings, and it's the playing of the story as a claustrophobic police drama rather than as science fiction which gives it the veracity it needs. Just as Beyond the Sea played obviously on Silence of the Lambs, and seemed to reinvent what The X-Files could do, so Duane Barry, more subtly, does here. Barry himself is not an evil Hannibal Lecter, and it's Mulder's willingness - even eagerness - to be persuaded by him and get inside his head which makes him truly dangerous. Ambiguity makes the story work - not only the ambiguity of Barry, who may be an alien abductee or psychopath (or both), but of Mulder, whose apparent intent is to save the lives of hostages, but who may just jeopardise their lives to even a scrap of truth about his sister's fate. David Duchovny and Steve Railsback (playing Barry) are both excellent here, portraying two men linked by obsession and delusion.

What's clever, though, is how at the end of the day it's that obsession which keeps Mulder safe - it's only when he listens to Scully, and begins to doubt Duane Barry's story, that he endangers his life. It's not too much of a stretch to view the episode as being a parable about faith: we shall often see Mulder risk his life to pursue an ideal, but never quite as bluntly as we do here. He gives himself over to a maniac, and has himself vulnerable at gunpoint, just because he wants to believe. One of the most unexpected moments in the episode takes place when one of the hostages, at last released, turns to Barry and tells him his story has convinced her - it's a surprisingly nervy moment, coming as it does at a point in the story where the audience is being discouraged to believe it any longer. But this is the kind of trick that Chris Carter so skilfully plays for the entire episode, batting around our sympathies and expectations. It's exhilarating.

This is a career best for Chris Carter, who never wrote or directed as powerfully as this again - or as simply, or as passionately. And it remains one of the real standout episodes of The X-Files: a story which, by being so atypical in tone, somehow seems to sum up what the series is about. (*****)

2.6, Ascension

Air Date: Oct. 21, 1994
Writer: Paul Brown
Director: Michael Lange

Summary Barry kidnaps Scully and takes her to Skyland Mountain in Virginia, the site of his alleged abduction. Mulder and Krycek pursue, but find Barry alone, raving that "they" will leave him alone now that he's given them Scully as a guinea pig. An unidentified helicopter departs the area; Barry later has a heart attack and dies while in Krycek's custody. Mulder concludes that Krycek - who disappears - killed Barry and is working for the Cigarette Smoking Man. With Scully missing, Skinner does what he thinks the shadowy figures dogging Mulder will fear most: reopening the X-Files.

Critique This has a job to do, and it does it well enough. That job is to follow Duane Barry, to move the counters into position so that Gillian Anderson can leave the show temporarily to have her baby, and to reopen the X-Files for her to slot back into on her return. It doesn't have the depth of the episode from which it takes its momentum - but that is rather the point. After the claustrophobic dialoguefest of Duane Barry, this is designed to open out its implications onto the series at large. And to have scenes on top of a cable car in the mountains to boot.

But what's telling is that the episode still works best when it's echoing the intimacy of the previous week. Mulder's interrogation of Barry is a terrific reversal of the power games we saw there, and both Duchovny and Steve Railsback seize the scene with the same gusto as before. And although by necessity, as fugitive and scapegoat, Barry doesn't have any of the same danger now that he's an abductor rather than a *latent* threat, he still commands the same ambiguous sympathy. The sequence in which he plaintively begs the trooper to leave him alone so he won't be forced to kill him is especially memorable.

For the most part, Ascension excites when it wants to. The first half of the episode is taken up with a chase, and whilst it's unusual to see The X-Files get its thrills quite that simply, it does it very well. And in the scenes of intrigue, whether it be X talking of the government's policy to deny everything, or the Cigarette Smoking Man making Krycek realise his status is only of a pawn, it crackles with energy. The dialogue may be arch and portentous, but at least it's *about* something. It drops the ball only in the final few minutes. Ascension is crying out for a sense of climax, after all the failures of the chase, after all the misdirection and subterfuge. Instead Mulder exposes Krycek... by finding a cigarette butt in his car. That's it. If William B Davis smoked a pipe, or a bong, or something *identifiable*, then the discovery might have more impact. And amazingly, Skinner not only doesn't laugh Mulder out of his office, but reopens the X-Files as a response. To deny the viewer a confrontation here is bad enough; to give the X-Files back so easily, after so many episodes in which their removal had such consequence, feels a criminal waste. It's ironic that an episode which so obviously tries to follow the talk-led Duane Barry with action adventure and pursuit, finishes up being so resolutely anticlimactic. (***1/2)

2.7, 3

Air Date: Nov. 4, 1994
Writers: Chris Ruppenthal, Glen Morgan, James Wong
Director: David Nutter

Summary In Los Angeles, the corpse of a businessman displays signs of a vampire attack. Mulder captures a suspect - a blood bank employee who calls himself "The Son" (a.k.a. John) - and places him in a cell that's filling with sunlight, in the hopes of frightening information out of him. However, the sunlight appears to make John combust and die.

Mulder follows a lead to "Club Tepes", where he meets an enigmatic woman named Kristen. She admits that she and John engaged in "blood sports" until he met two other vampires and the group's propensity for violence increased. The three vampires have been pursuing Kristen ever since. Mulder finds himself drawn to the woman and sleeps with her. The vampire trio - including John, who claims to be immortal - shows up to confront Kristen. After initiating the ritual to turn herself into a vampire - as a

vampire can only die for good at the hands of one of their own - Kristen starts a fire that engulfs her and the vamps. Mulder escapes, and later watches as four bodies - burnt to ashes and bone - are found in the rubble.

Critique It's not just the absence of Gillian Anderson - in tone, in pace, and in theme, this episode feels different to everything we've seen on the series before. For that reason I want to cherish it, for its courage in refusing to play safe when one of the two leads is absent for the first time. But there's bravery, and there's sheer self-indulgence.

Modern vampire novels, as popularised by Anne Rice, focus on blood fetishism, turning their amoral antiheroes into something seductive and compelling. But it's a fine line to tread, and if it's not left as subtext - if the vampires themselves start giving turgid speeches about their lifestyle choices - they become narcissistic bores. They can too easily come across as the sort of people who, in an attempt to be "other" and stand out from the crowd, only lose their identity in subculture trappings. That's when they're being happily boastful and bragging of their superiority. Then they start to angst, cursing their immortality and their isolation, as if wallowing in sadness lends them a greater depth.

To be fair, at first you get the sense that the episode is going to laugh at the wannabes and their self-obsessed pretensions. The interrogation scene of John is actually very funny, as Mulder refuses to take the purple prose dialogue of his undead captive seriously. But this is The X-Files: the monsters have to be real. And as soon as the man shrivels up and dies in sunlight, Mulder determines to look into vampirism more carefully. And he drags the audience with him, making us listen to speech after wearying speech of self-justification so precious you want to give the bloodsuckers a slap. We don't expect Mulder to listen to the woes of the werewolf culture, or to sit in awed fascination as the fluke monster eulogises about his intestine fetish. As a result, there is little that is erotic or shocking about the sex scenes, in which Mulder yields to the attentions of Kristen - we feel instead we've been witnessing an especially tedious bout of foreplay, and that's never as much fun to watch as to take part in yourself.

To depict Mulder mourning for Scully is one thing, but the psychology behind his eagerness to abandon all FBI caution and run to the arms of a murder suspect is just muddled. To be as tonally jarring as this is, as I say, bold - but to get Mulder's character so backwards is a crucial mistake, and the one thing that could have anchored the experimental style on display here has been removed. It feels odd at the beginning to have Mulder as sceptic (although I suppose he can't believe in *every* gothic legend), and it almost feels as if he's having to compensate for Scully's absence. But he throws away all his training and procedure, looking for most of the story less like an FBI agent and more like that Anne Rice stereotype, the fascinated initiate. So rather than bending a vampire tale to the demands of The X-Files, the reverse happens: the scenes become increasingly formulaic, the most clichéd of all being the bathroom scene where Mulder cuts himself and produces blood for Kristen to kiss away. With Shapes last season, I argued that there's no point in taking a werewolf story and doing nothing *with* it: 3 is a lot more stylish, and has some fine moments (the loaf filled with blood, for example), but it suffers from exactly the same problem. It's a bore, because we've seen it all before - and so Mulder looks stupid for showing surprise at what the audience has taken for granted.

Duchovny and Perrey Reeves (playing Kristen) undoubtedly have chemistry - but then, since they were dating at the time, that isn't so unexpected. (Indeed, it suggests a reason why the long, long, *long* scenes between them feel so self-indulgent. A lot of fans dislike this episode because they see Mulder having a fling with a woman who isn't Scully - I've no problem with that in itself, but with Mulder so badly defined, I just got the awkward sense that all I was watching was Duchovny copping off with his girlfriend.)

The early scene in which Mulder returns to the X-Files basement is truly effective. What should have been a moment of triumph instead becomes a sequence in which he is forced to consign his former partner to her own case file. It's a spark of real emotion in an episode which otherwise plays fast and loose with passion and woe, and yet feels nothing. And when it takes

itself too seriously, as in the dreadful accounts of domestic abuse, it's aspiring to something more worthy than it ever has the wit or the imagination to pull off. At the end of the story, we see Mulder on a hillside looking depressed. And no wonder - last week his best friend was abducted by aliens, and now his new squeeze has blown herself up so comprehensively that she hasn't even left behind any body parts. That's rejection. Poor Mulder. He was miserable at the beginning of 3, and he's miserable at the end. It's been a waste of time for him, and for us. (*1/2)

2.8, One Breath

Air Date: Nov. 11, 1994
Writers: Glen Morgan, James Wong
Director: RW Goodwin

Summary A comatose Scully reappears without explanation at a local hospital. The Lone Gunmen discover that Scully's DNA has been tinkered with and her immune system has been gravely compromised. X informs Mulder that government operatives complicit in Scully's kidnapping will soon search Mulder's apartment - and advises Mulder to kill the men in "self-defence". Scully's sister Melissa tells Mulder that Scully is slipping away and that he's needed by her bedside. Mulder abandons his chance at revenge to visit Scully - who recovers, in large part, because of the strength of Mulder's beliefs.

Critique Glen Morgan and James Wong play a similar game to the one they presented in Beyond the Sea last year - they dangle a moral dilemma in front of our heroes, tempting them with closure, only instead to have them turn their back upon it to visit their partner's side in hospital. But in this instance the drama is all the more powerful - Mulder is offered the chance to execute Scully's abductors, or to say goodbye to his dying friend - and chooses redemption over retribution. Scully recovers unfeasibly swiftly after this, but you can conclude that's the point of this little fable - that Scully's survival depended upon Mulder's own strength. Throughout the episode he courts retaliation and resignation. He holds a gun to the Cigarette Smoking Man's head, he tells Skinner he's quitting the

FBI. And in a funny way, both enemy and ally give Mulder the same speech in response; their refusal to accept that Mulder give himself up to revenge or despair is what saves his soul. It's rare for an action series to show in conclusion that all of Mulder's frenzied activity, his refusal to sit back and do nothing, is useless - and it's in the still moments that he can help Scully instead.

In that way it's very much a story about life and death, and the choices we make between the two. Melissa says early on that we hide the dying away in hospitals because we're embarrassed by them, but that there is nothing unnatural about death. Mulder's exasperation with her, and what he calls her political correctness, is wholly understandable - but what she says is the core of this episode. Every major character here is either staring death in the face (Skinner's out of body experience as a dying soldier parallels Scully's own, the Cigarette Smoking Man looks up at Mulder's gun with calm confidence), or are called upon to inflict it (X executes the man who stole Scully's blood because Mulder cannot do so, but makes clear that he represents what Mulder must become; Skinner is appalled that Mulder wants revenge upon the Cigarette Smoking Man, but becomes implicit in an attempted murder by giving him the Man's address). It's the decision between being active or passive. And, in the middle of all this is Scully and the decision *she* must make. We see her as the little girl who shot a snake and tried to revive it as it died in her hands. Then she's the woman who sits just out of reach of all the people talking to her, on a rowing boat in her own imagination, listening to the living and the dead and not being one nor the other.

One Breath certainly flirts with pretension. Scully's scenes in the boat could so easily have been risible, the long sequences of revelatory monologue overwritten tosh. It's certainly a trap The X-Files will fall into in the future. But there is such a sincerity to the emotion on display, and such a careful handling of the episode's profoundest themes, that One Breath is a triumph. If it has a fault, it's that it's doing too much too soon; the story feels too important to be tucked away at the start of the second season, not when there are over seven more years - my God - left to run. The confrontations on display are so major, and the dilemmas faced seemingly so pivotal, that it seems unfair that the show must

now put the toys back into the box and resume its duties as an anthology series. That's just circumstance, however - no-one could have foretold quite how long this story had left to play out - and it doesn't affect the impact of this gorgeous piece of work. (*****)

2.9, Firewalker

Air Date: Nov. 18, 1994
Writer: Howard Gordon
Director: David Nutter

Summary Mulder and Scully respond to a distress call from a team of vulcanologists at Mount Avalon in Washington state, suspecting that the expedition leader - Dr Daniel Trepkos - has been killing his colleagues. However, Mulder learns that apart from Trepkos, the team members have been infected by a silicon-based, parasitic lifeform that a robot probe (the Firewalker) released from the base of the volcano. The remaining researchers, including Trepkos' lover Jessie, die as the lifeform causes spore-filled shoots to burst out of their chests; Scully is nearly infected, but survives because the spores must be inhaled almost immediately upon release. Afterward, the agents allow Trepkos to take Jessie's body and disappear into the caverns of the mountain.

Critique The moments of body horror are well directed and nicely gruesome, especially the scene where Scully is still attached to Jessie at the time of her grisly death. This episode is following in the footsteps of Ice and Darkness Falls - rather too obviously, really, with parasite infections and forced quarantines and the ilk - and after the rush of conspiracy episodes, you can see the wisdom in getting back to the claustrophobic terrors that make a staple X-Files diet. The problem is that this really isn't all that claustrophobic: its sister episodes worked principally by propounding a simple premise and following it with rigorous conviction. Firewalker, on the other hand, has no real sense of place or purpose - we kept on being *told* to feel the isolation and the menace, but the story doesn't build and the plot barely gains momentum.

The error is compounded with the character of Trepkos. It's peculiar as a West Wing fan to see Bradley Whitford so cast against type, here playing a crazed Brando a la Apocalypse Now. He's a confused and underwritten character, and he's clearly supposed to carry the weight of the episode on his shoulders - but for all Whitford's efforts, he's clearly miscast. He can't make much of his frequently pretentious dialogue, or give him a coherent motivation. When, at the story's conclusion, Mulder and Scully pretend he is dead so he can go into hiding with his dead girlfriend, it only emphasises the gulf between the grandeur the episode believes it's lending him, and the low impact he's actually made. There's clearly meant to be something ambiguous in this, even tragic, but instead it comes out of nowhere, and looks as if this ho-hum monster yarn is aiming for something momentous. It doesn't even get close. At best, it's a less than average episode, with some ugly neck worms. When the second season has been deliberately making its audience yearn for The X-Files to find some stability, it's extremely disappointing that we now realise this is the sort of thing we've been looking forward to. (**)

2.10, Red Museum

Air Date: Dec. 9, 1994
Writer: Chris Carter
Director: Win Phelps

Summary In Delta Glen, Wisconsin, a number of teens are found wandering, dazed but alive, with the words "He / She is the One" written on their backs. Mulder and Scully cast suspicion upon the Church of the Red Museum - a local cult who believes in soul transference. They eventually find evidence of a wider conspiracy: local cows are being treated with an unidentified substance, and Dr Gerry Larson - who is found dead in a plane crash - has been injecting the town's teenagers with the same material.

Mulder hypothesises that Delta Glen is part of an experiment to study the effect of alien DNA on humans who consume the altered beef, using the vegetarian Red Museum members as a control group. The Crew-Cut Man who killed Deep Throat arrives to eliminate persons and evidence, but is shot dead by the local sheriff. The agents fail to identify the substance injected into the teens, leaving the case unsolved.

Critique This is the one about the religious cult who wear red turbans. And the drugged children with the words "He is One" inked across their skin. It's also the one about a voyeur hiding behind a family's mirror making videotapes. And about growth injections in cows causing aggressive behaviour in meat eaters. Just as you think you might have got a handle on this episode and what storyline it's following, it suddenly cuts to two characters we've never seen before dying in a plane crash, around the halfway mark. And then it gets very confusing. The story changes direction altogether to be a conspiracy tale involving alien DNA and the man who murdered Deep Throat offing farmers.

It's a mess, frankly, with more red herrings than any plot can comfortably bear, and a focus that's so constantly shifting that if you look for a theme long enough your eyes go wonky. But for all that there's something rather beguiling about an X-File that revels in doing too much, and an arc storyline that comes at you out of left field and wrongfoots you entirely. It's not a pretty story - as the various plots get ditched untidily, so the stack of coincidences grow ever higher - but there's a real chutzpah to this. After so many episodes conceived in the absence of the X-Files, here comes one which tries to make up for lost time by telling at least three stories at once. And after all the to-ing and fro-ing, there's something very satisfying about the story ending on a note in which a mysterious conspiracy player is killed not by Mulder or Scully or a man smoking cigarettes, but by a bit-part sheriff raving over the death of his jock son. To see The X-Files mythology story collide so devastatingly with an episode that feels so much more disposable has a wonderful irony to it. (***)

2.11, Excelsis Dei

Air Date: Dec. 16, 1994
Writer: Paul Brown
Director: Stephen Surjik

Summary At the Excelsis Dei nursing home in Worcester, Massachusetts, invisible forces rape nurse Micelle Charters and push an orderly to his death. Mulder and Scully find that another orderly, Gung Bituen, has been supplying the normally vegetative patients with hallucinogenic mushrooms and herbs grown in the basement. The herbs restore the patients to health, but also put them in connection with the spirit world - and enable the angry spirits of people who died in the building to wreck havoc. Stan Phillips, one of the patients, overdoses on the drugs, whereupon the spirits flood a bathroom and nearly drown Mulder and Charters. Bituen drugs Stan unconscious, halting the attack. Afterward, the spirits dissipate, Bituen is deported and the patients lose their newfound stamina.

Critique One Breath dealt very effectively with the themes of how we respond to the dying, how we're embarrassed by the sight of them and want to shut them away. Excelsis Dei is the idiot's version. We're presented with the old folks' home from hell, in which every single worker is cruel, uninterested, or abusive. (Except for the lowly Chinaman porter, who instead gives the inmates magic mushrooms which are probably poisoning them.) It's an episode in which everything bad is presented so unsubtly that you find yourself recoiling from the slap of it all. A nasty nurse in the teaser isn't just attacked, she's actually *raped* by her invisible assailant. And there's a sour atmosphere to the whole proceedings, in which only Scully shows the slightest concern that a woman's been sexually assaulted. The story implicitly suggests that because Nurse Charters is unsympathetic, she had it coming to her. It's tasteless.

The story plays with themes that are laudably weighty. A rape victim whose attack cannot be substantiated, so is treated as a fantasist and a troublemaker. The use of illegal drugs to alleviate the suffering of the elderly. The way in which we regard the old as second-class citizens. But if the themes are treated as glibly as they are here, paying them no more than lip service as the story limps ploddingly on towards another issue, then surely it would have been better not to have raised them in the first place. Pointing a finger at a topic is not the same as exploring it - indeed, when you're telling a story as confused as this one, in which a bunch of spirits come back from the dead because patients are overdoing their homeopathic treatment, it looks as if the subjects are being used for cheap sensationalism.

There's a decent atmosphere to the episode, and some of the ghost effects are eerie. But this is a very stupid script, with set pieces that are either by the numbers (the orderly being pushed out of the window) or utterly ludicrous (Mulder being left to drown in a bathroom filling with water). There's little structure to any of this, no climax, no resolution. There's no characterisation, beside the kneejerk and the vile. There's no point, because it has nothing to say it hadn't already hammered home in the teaser - nothing is developed, nothing is countered. And ultimately, there's no heart. What a thoroughly depressing instalment. (*)

2.12, Aubrey

Air Date: Jan. 6, 1995
Writer: Sara B Charno
Director: Rob Bowman

Summary Detective BJ Morrow, a police officer in Aubrey, Missouri, who is pregnant through an affair with her boss, mysteriously finds herself digging up a body in a field. Mulder and Scully identify the corpse as Sam Chaney, an FBI agent who disappeared in 1942 while pursuing a serial killer who carved the word "sister" onto his victims' chests. The agents also question Harry Cokely, age seventy-two, who was convicted in 1945 of raping a woman and similarly carving "sister" on her.

Mulder determines that Cokely's rape victim gave up her child for adoption, that BJ is Cokely's granddaughter, and that it's possible for a murderer's memories to pass on to his descendents. Cokely's memories - made dominant in BJ by her pregnancy - goad her into nearly murdering her grandmother Linda Thibedeaux, but BJ slays Cokely instead. After an unsuccessful attempt to abort her son - who might one day inherit the family curse - BJ is placed on suicide watch in a sanatorium, with the child's father petitioning for custody.

Critique There's a theme running through the episode of nature versus nurture - and whilst the conclusion it reaches, in typical X-Files style, might be a little muddled, it makes for a fascinating hour of television. It's one of those stories where the plot itself ends up feeling somewhat contrived and pat: a police officer is revealed to be the granddaughter of a murderer, and starts re-enacting his killings in her dreams. But what makes this sing is the quality of the script around it. It's a very *female* script; first-time writer Sara B Charno explores mother-hood, pregnancy, and rape, and does all of them from a wholly realistic perspective. The dilemmas that the women in this story face are simple ones - an unmarried woman deciding whether to abort the baby that's the product of a secret affair, a married rape victim unable to live with the child that's the result of her attack. The real climax of the episode occurs when the one attacks the other: Mrs Thibedeaux pleading with BJ, making her realise that they have both been made what they are by the actions of one man fifty years ago, is quite sensational, and frightening, and strangely moving.

What especially makes this episode stand out is the way it becomes a character study of one woman, BJ Morrow, putting her centre stage in a way that is quite rare for the series. A police detective with human fears and real world problems, she gives the story an emotional truth we haven't seen on The X-Files in a standalone episode for quite a while. Deborah Strong seizes the part and gives it dignity. It all begins to go awry only when the plot-mechanics require her to become a possessed monster - both writer Sara Charno and Strong have done their jobs *too* well in making BJ seem fully fleshed out, and so making her finally the tool of genetic inheritance feels off key. It's a perfectly decent idea, but it turns a real person into a puppet of the paranormal - and, for once, I found myself resisting the necessity of the story over the pull of the character.

For the most part, though, this is gripping stuff. The precredit teaser is superb, hitting us with domestic awkwardness and fifty-year-old murder - the sharp contrast of both so startling, it made me reel. There are some great scare moments: the sequence where BJ finds the word "sister" carved into her chest as she wakes from a nightmare is fantastic. And I love the juxtaposition of Mulder and Scully in this one. It takes Mulder to come up with the theories of evil genes and to make the leap of faith into science fiction. But it's Scully who can make intuitive leaps of her own, who can recognise there's a

very *human* reason why BJ would lie to Mulder, needing to hide both her affair and her pregnancy. Mulder's surprise at Scully here speaks volumes - but also gives Scully a far more interesting function than being sceptic to the believer. (***1/2)

2.13, Irresistible

Air Date: Jan. 13, 1995
Writer: Chris Carter
Director: David Nutter

Summary When mutilated corpses start appearing in Minneapolis, Mulder suspects that the perpetrator is a "death fetishist" who has been acquiring existing bodies but will soon resort to murder. The fetishist, Donnie Pfaster, ritualistically murders a prostitute and, having briefly encountered Scully at a police station, decides to make her his next victim. Pfaster kidnaps Scully, who grapples with him and sees the face of a demon. Mulder tracks Scully and rescues her; Pfaster is arrested, and Mulder deems the case - involving no paranormal influence that he can discern - is as disturbing as any X-File.

Critique Chris Carter's last episode featured a peeping tom with a leaning towards paedophilia. This week he offers us a necrophiliac in all but name. Give this man a commission for Millennium this instant! After a first-season fascination with UFOs, it's interesting to see Carter drawn more and more to real-world evil - and this episode is the first we've seen with virtually no supernatural elements in it whatsoever. Indeed, that's the point of this outing, made explicit by Mulder's coda: it's somehow *safer* to believe in alien flying saucers and monsters that go bump in the night than it is to engage with true-life psychosis. It's a brave inversion of the series' themes, and one which provides not a few jokes into the bargain - it's wonderful to have a law authority, for once, calling in Mulder and Scully because they believe in outlandish UFO theories, only to be told by the FBI agents that it's something much less fantastical and much more disturbing.

There are two common criticisms levelled at

this episode. One is that Carter wimps out from his real-life horror story by having Scully see Pfaster morph into a demon. But this is not simply the story of a death fetishist - it's *Scully's* story, at last coming to terms with her experiences during her abduction, and it seems psychologically telling to me that she finds it safer to imagine Pfaster as something inhuman. It's the contrast between these two images - a creature with horns, and a too-ordinary man obsessing over the right shampoo for his victims' hair - that provides the meat of the drama. There's no textual evidence that Pfaster really *does* become a demon; instead it's a metaphor for the way both Scully and your typical X-Files viewer is best able to make palatable Pfaster's madness. The second complaint is that it's another episode in which Scully is kidnapped and tied up - but this too, surely, misses the point. In Ascension she was given over (we still imagine) to aliens; here she is taken by an all-too human psychopath, and this time she's no longer protected by the science fiction of the show and is obliged to fight back. In a very real way, this is a story in which Scully needs to face her demons to survive.

Gillian Anderson gives another astonishing performance. The confessional honesty of Scully's therapy session is one of the highlights of the season; I love the way she approaches the autopsy, something for which she'd usually show utter detachment, with the revulsion of a person who's never seen a corpse before. (The voiceover at this point, in which Scully has to re-establish to herself what an autopsy actually *is*, speaks volumes.) But best still is Scully's insistence to Mulder, even after Pfaster has been apprehended, that she's "fine" - said so forcefully even as she's already unravelling.

There's an anger and a conviction to this episode that makes it stand out from the majority. Nick Chinlund is wonderful as Pfaster - we too see him as a monster, but somehow his obsession becomes eerily identifiable too. It's clever that we never see him kill, or indeed hurt, anybody; he always seems to us like a curious child, and that makes him so much more insidious. And it's the insidiousness of that evil, the way a fascination can grow into an obsession, that makes this story so genuinely chilling. (*****)

2.14, Die Hand Die Verletzt

Air Date: Jan. 27, 1995
Writers: Glen Morgan, James Wong
Director: Kim Manners

Summary Mulder and Scully travel to Milford Haven, New Hampshire, after a quartet of teens conduct a silly, contrived dark ritual - and one of them winds up dead, his eyes and heart torn out. Meanwhile, the members of the local Parent Teacher council, who are actually Satanists, grow concerned about the degree to which they've let their faith lapse. Unbeknownst to them, a substitute teacher named Mrs Paddock - who killed the teen - has arrived to pass judgment over them. When Paddock kills one of the council members with a giant snake, the surviving three Satanists decide to murder Mulder and Scully to appease their dark master. However, Paddock decides that it's too late, and ritualistically compels the Satanists to kill themselves. She flees town, leaving the agents empty-handed.

Critique The teaser is laugh out loud funny. We realise that the PTA of a school, so concerned about the students' production of Jesus Christ Superstar, aren't banning it because it's blasphemous but because they're a secret satanic cult. This sets the tone for an episode as atypical as Irresistible, but coming at the banality of evil from an entirely different angle. The principle joke here - and it's a very good one - is to look at the way religious faith has been so watered down and paid nothing but lip service, its rituals and doctrines reinterpreted so that only what's comfortable is adhered to. But rather than this being Christianity, it's devil worship on display, treated here with the same Sunday School vapidity.

For all that it's a parody of organised religion, it asks one pertinent question: if all the things we say in church have *any* meaning at all, how can we dare treat them in such a cavalier fashion? If you believe Christ really died for your sins, how can he be something you regard as an optional extra for use only at Easter and Christmas? And if you believe that Satan really does exist, and is all that is evil, and has ownership of your soul, how can this not be the central focus of your life? So this is the story of the devil, delightfully played by Susan Blommaert as the genuine substitute teacher from Hell, bumping off all her acolytes which show such little faith. And as she does so, you can't but help picture, say, St Paul coming back and taking a pop at all the fair weather Christians who only affirm their faith at their own convenience.

But it's a joke against The X-Files too. This was intended to be Glen Morgan and James Wong's last contribution to the show, and they exit with an affectionate pisstake of the format. This time the monster Mulder and Scully are pursuing is nothing less than Satan itself - who proceeds to misdirect them at every turn, run rings around them, and make them look like the stuffed shirts they are. It's the sort of joke we'll come to expect from Darin Morgan, Glen's brother, but this is the first time it's been used, and it catches us by surprise. There may be no stranger - or funnier - scene in the show's history than the one where our heroes listen to fifteen-year-old Shannon detail her child abuse. It begins earnestly enough, but as the litany of dark deeds tips over into self-parody it becomes impossible to take seriously - she begins to recount the tale of how her sister was murdered, and how she's given birth to three children, sired by her own father, who were ritually sacrificed as babies. What's hilarious is that Mulder and Scully listen with poker faces, and never get the gag. It's probably the blackest joke The X-Files ever attempted, and what's being sent up is the very house style of the show itself. The last message on the blackboard from the satanic Miss Paddick - "Goodbye, it's been fun working with you" - is clearly a fond wave from Morgan and Wong themselves, who've just spent an hour deconstructing the show they've worked so hard to build up over the last year and a half.

For all the comedy, it has some great set pieces - the raining toads, the death by python - and Morgan and Wong have their cake and eat it; these sequences are not only very funny but genuinely macabre too. If you wanted to criticise, you could point out that Mulder and Scully achieve nothing whatsoever - but since that's the crux of the joke, that'd seem rather churlish. This is meant to be the last hurrah of the two writers who've done more than anyone to establish what The X-Files is capable of, and aren't

above a final creepy laugh at its expense. If you take the show as seriously as the characters themselves, then the episode is probably lacking. But on its own terms, this is just about perfect. From the dispassionate way Miss Paddick dishes out the embryos for dissection, to the Young Frankenstein gag of lightning striking every time her name is mentioned, the jokes are thick, fast, and deliciously witty. (*****)

2.15, Fresh Bones

Air Date: Feb. 3, 1995
Writer: Howard Gordon
Director: Rob Bowman

Summary   After two Marines stationed at an immigrant processing centre in North Carolina die in a voodoo-related manner, Mulder and Scully find a group of Haitian refugees living in squalor. The Marines were killed as part of a standoff between Pierre Bauvais, an imprisoned revolutionary who wants his people to go home to Haiti, and the domineering Colonel Jacob Wharton, a voodoo practitioner. Wharton ritualistically compelled the Marines to kill themselves because they filed complaints about his abuses. The Colonel has Bauvais beaten to death, then instigates a ritual to take Bauvais' soul. Bauvais briefly rises from the dead and seems to kill Wharton - who is actually trapped alive in a buried casket, screaming for dear life.

Critique   There are scares and twists galore here - but they're pretty much confined to the last ten minutes. Before that we get an efficient tale about stress within the military, the oppression of illegal immigrants, and voodoo curses. It's well-told, and well-acted (especially by Daniel Benzali, as a colonel who can command dread respect without ever raising his voice). Howard Gordon follows a familiar storyline of revenge executed by supernatural means - he really is *very* fond of this - but it's done with intelligence and a respect for Haitian customs. It's all just a bit ponderous, that's all; the voodoo curse against the FBI agents is very much a slow burn affair, and you can't help but feel that the storyline may have benefited from one more set piece murder somewhere in the middle to prop up the flagging action.

I'm being harsh. The direction and lighting, as usual, give the whole episode the atmosphere it needs - there's a real collision between the familiar image of a US military base and the exotic unfamiliarity of Caribbean lore, and it genuinely gives the story an air of being something quite different. For once you feel some fear that Mulder and Scully, who are often just witnesses to the unexplained, are here being sucked ever deeper into rites they don't understand. And the slow pace does pay certain dividends: the surreal attack on Scully in the car, as a man climbs out from a wound in her hand to throttle her, is all the more effective for being the result of a long set up and not being The X-Files' trademark shock stunt. The final moments too are superb, and very scary - it's a satisfying twist, one you can in retrospect see has been long seeded into the story, but is so cleverly staged that it still catches you by surprise. (***1/2)

2.16, Colony

Air Date: Feb. 10, 1995
Story: Chris Carter, David Duchovny
Teleplay: Chris Carter
Director: Nick Marck

Summary   A shape-changing alien bounty hunter arrives on Earth and sets about murdering abortion clinic doctors. Mulder takes an interest in the killings because the victims are absolutely identical. Unbeknownst to him, they also possessed green blood that turns toxic upon exposure to air.

Mulder's missing sister Samantha suddenly appears at the Mulder family home. Samantha claims to "been returned" from her abduction, at age nine or ten, and placed with a foster family. She now thinks that she and her adoptive parents - whom she identifies as aliens - are in danger from the bounty hunter. Scully places the four remaining doctors, all code-named "Gregor", under federal protection, but the bounty hunter finds and murders them. Soon after, Mulder shows up at Scully's hotel room - mere moments before the *real* Mulder calls her. [To be continued.]

Critique   This all feels very odd. In part this could be because Colony is the beginning of the

first "proper" two-part story - Duane Barry felt self-contained, and Ascension worked in tandem because it was trying to be so tonally distinct. But this story is very clearly just half of a bumper length episode to be concluded next week. It's why the opening sequence, where Mulder has a heart attack in the Arctic, counts for nothing. Yes, it's all very well to flashback to a moment of jeopardy shown in the teaser, but when that moment turns out to have not even the slightest *relevance* to anything that follows afterwards, it can only be forgotten. And that's not the only structural oddity on display: there's a lot of running around and some well-directed action scenes, but the pacing of the episode is much slower than usual, and the action we're offered feels faintly repetitive. Shock moments don't work as well as they should, because we've already seen too much of the set up: Scully finds an alien foetus, some minutes after she'd already seen a CIA agent stamp on it; Scully is amazed to find four cloned doctors, in spite of the fact we've already encountered another four already; Scully discovers in the cliffhanger that Mulder is a shapeshifter, mere *seconds* after we've seen yet another example of the creature's morphing ability. It's not that any of these moments are bad as such, and it'd be unfair to say that they're boring, because they're not; Colony is always an entertaining enough romp. It's merely that we're not used to our set pieces being spelled out quite this laboriously.

And the characters are a little off too. Mulder is almost gleefully gullible throughout the episode - it even prompts Scully to ask whether he's changed his entire "trust no one" stance. Whereas Scully, on the other hand, gets criticised for being paranoid. In Mulder's case his gullibility hits him at a particularly inopportune time, since this is an episode where he goes to his family and finds that his abducted sister has just turned up. He is so accepting of this - even reassuring his mother that he can't see who else the woman could be, a whole scene *before* "Samantha" explains her history to him - that it makes what should be momentous feel somewhat trite. If you compare this realisation of his entire adult mission with, say, his crazed terror when he meets aliens in Little Green Men, it doesn't ring true at all. This is a character who will question and doubt everything, especially when the basis for his entire adult quest is handed to him simply on a plate.

But for all of its problems, the episode should surely be commended for wanting to take the already fraying seams of The X-Files mythology, and to tie them to *something*. That's the biggest shock about this episode - that after forty episodes of hiding in the shadows and being so ambiguous that even the actor playing Deep Throat clearly can't work out what side he's on, there is some honest attempt to develop the ongoing storyline. If Samantha's return (in some form) feels from the perspective of the entire series' run a bit too much too soon, if an alien bounty hunter wandering around like the Terminator feels uncharacteristically unsubtle - well, it's still exciting. And it's still gives you the promise that there's a major shift taking place within the series. (Oh, and that Mulder's going to have a heart attack in the Arctic at some point. Mustn't forget that.) (***)

2.17, End Game

Air Date: Feb. 17, 1995
Writer: Frank Spotnitz
Director: Rob Bowman

Summary   The ersatz Mulder takes Scully hostage. Samantha tells Mulder that aliens have been attempting to found a colony on Earth since the 1940s. The Gregors were trying to develop alien-human hybrids using foetal tissue from abortion clinics, but the aliens didn't sanction the endeavour - so the bounty hunter was dispatched to slaughter the participants. The hunter offers to trade Scully for Samantha; Mulder's plan to save both women fails and the hunter plunges, along with Samantha, into a river.

Mulder follows a clue to a clinic that's staffed by many Samantha duplicates, but the hunter follows and kills the women. X helps Mulder backtrack the hunter's arrival to the Arctic - but when Mulder goes there, the bounty hunter leaves him to perish from exposure and escapes in a captured submarine. On Scully's behalf, Skinner dutifully roughs up X and makes him reveal Mulder's location, facilitating a rescue. Mulder's only consolation is the bounty hunter's claim that the original Samantha is still alive.

Critique   Sometimes you just get tired of being told something is of significance, that something dramatic is happening, when at heart there's nothing but emptiness. There's lots of audience pleasing scenes here: Skinner and X have a fight in a lift! Mulder is required to sacrifice his sister's life for Scully! Mulder goes to certain death in the Arctic to get answers from the Alien Bounty Hunter! But, as Mulder admits in the closing scene, he doesn't find what he was looking for. And really, for all the revelations that seem to have come thick and fast, the series is in no different a place than it was before.

It's perfectly all right to engineer moments of high drama, even when they're essentially artificial. It all depends on their being done well. Some of them here are. The second half of the episode concerns Scully's attempts to find Mulder, as he's off on a personal mission and refuses to risk his life by letting her know where he's gone. The scene where X is surprised to find that it's Scully who has summoned him, and his refusal to have anything to do with her, gives a real frisson as two major characters finally meet. (The succeeding one between X and Skinner feels comparatively forced and unnecessary - a chance for some fisticuffs, but it's an encounter so easily resolved that Skinner gets the information he wants by saying the right thing to convince X off screen.) Similarly, the scene in which Mulder tracks down the bounty hunter on board the sub is brilliantly directed and suitably tense - but can only reveal the same information that was offered to us by the clones twenty minutes previously. You can't help but feel that after such a long build-up - and polar navigation no less! - that the confrontation scene would give us at least a crumb of something new. And it's a little hard to understand therefore why Mulder's useless quest has given him any new faith whatsoever. (It's a lovely final speech, but as with so much else in this episode, for all that it *sounds* good, what does it actually mean?)

It's a shame, because you can see the opportunities here for some powerful stuff. But they're largely squandered because the big dilemmas are dealt with so peremptorily. This is an episode - let me say again - in which *Mulder is persuaded to trade his sister's life for Scully's*. That's throwing away the object of his lifelong quest, to save the partner who has accompanied him along the way, and may now be more important to him than the quest itself. That should be huge, that should be a climax. Instead Scully is only told the scene's importance after it's over, and Mulder's only allowed to agonise over his decision once it's already been made. The wonderful irony of Mulder at last finding not only his sister but a roomful of them is great in concept, but within a minute of this discovery, the handy assassin has stepped in and closed off that avenue of storytelling. The scene where Mulder tells his father that he's lost Samantha once more is *awful*: you can see the emotional pitch it wants to reach, but Peter Donat is so stiff and disapproving as Mulder's father, and Mulder himself is so cowed, it looks like nothing more than a ten year old being told off for getting a bad school report.

To be charitable, it's a symptom of how confident the series is that it can waste big scenes like this, by packing them into a single story with the overexcitement of a kid opening all his Christmas presents at the same time. And it's a sign of how rich The X-Files has become in its second season that it has so many elements to juggle in the first place: most of the key players and themes in this story didn't even feature in Season One. The X-Files will learn better how to play its mythology episodes, with a steadier pace and more focus. (They won't necessarily be any more revealing, but at least most will excite on a moment to moment basis.) And at its worst, End Game may be an empty thrill - but it's still, for the most part, a thrill. Even if, as you watch it, it's hard to work out exactly what you're being thrilled at. (**)

2.18, Fearful Symmetry

Air Date: Feb. 24, 1995
Writer: Steven De Jarnatt
Director: James Whitmore, Jr

Summary   An invisible force wreaks havoc in Fairfield, Idaho, killing a workman - just as an elephant appears out of nowhere and dies forty-three miles away from its zoo. Scully and Mulder interview zoo workers Ed Meecham and Willa Ambrose, as well as Kyle Lang, an animal rights activist. They also meet Sophie, a zoo gorilla who knows sign language.

Mulder speculates aliens are stealing the zoo animals, impregnating them through artificial insemination and taking their offspring - then returning them miles away from home, temporarily invisible. Sophie vanishes in a burst of light, after signing "man save man", then re-appears miles away and is killed by a car. Mulder is left to theorise that Earth's rate of animal extinction is such that the aliens were attempting to conserve various species before they die off.

Critique   Cards on the table here. I'm a big animal lover, and themes of conservation are very dear to my heart. There's a rare anger to this episode, and it's refreshing to see an X-File with such genuine passion behind it. It's actually about something of concern, and after stories about shapeshifting aliens, voodoo and devil worship, that's to be commended.

But... this isn't a very good story. The teaser is wonderful: an invisible elephant knocks a small town about for six, and later dies of exhaustion before the sympathetic gaze of a little girl. It's brilliant and bizarre and moving. But the plot which follows is so confusing that all that impact soon dissipates. I know The X-Files is about ambiguity, and I regularly applaud it for not feeling it has to provide answers at every turn. But there's a world of difference between ambiguity and vague fuzziness. If we accept that aliens are abducting zoo animals - and in some uncharacteristic way that seems to be criticising man for not being ecological - why are they being brought back invisible? Why do they keep ending up a couple of miles from where they're abducted, so they're just left to die on the roads? And, on a human level, exactly what is going on between Willa, Kyle and Ed? Half the time they're all pitted against each other as enemies, then they become allies, and the story never quite seems to want to chart how the one becomes the other. It's sloppy - you can sort of see what the story is trying to do, but it can't quite be bothered to make anyone's motivations clear, so ultimately the script's efforts to distinguish their various points of view counts for nothing in the chaos of shifting sympathies.

The discussion of animal rights is even-handed, and as in Darkness Falls last year, it's dramatically more interesting that the script doesn't come down in favour of either the zookeepers nor the conservationists. But the writer's own emphasis on the tragedy of the animals is overegged; there's a strange dignity to the elephant's death, a shock when the tiger is killed - but by the time Sophie the gorilla is knocked down by a car, the sheer catalogue of disaster feels almost comical. No episode which features an elephant autopsy can be judged a complete failure, though. And while playing Willa, Jayne Atkinson is sincere enough in her concern for her gorilla's welfare that you almost forget she spends her time emoting to an actor in a hairy costume. But that word "almost" is the final judgment, I'm afraid. This tries hard, and it cares, but for all its good intentions they're not highlighted in a story told well enough to pull them off. (**)

2.19, Dod Kalm

Air Date: March 10, 1995
Story: Howard Gordon
Teleplay: Howard Gordon, Alex Gansa
Directed By: Rob Bowman

Summary After the U.S.S. *Ardent*, a Navy destroyer escort, goes missing in the Norwegian Sea, a Canadian ship rescues survivors - who later die from a sort of hyper-aging. A trawler captain named Henry Trondheim transports Mulder and Scully to the *Ardent*, but someone steals Trondheim's ship, stranding them. The trio also experience accelerated aging; Scully theorises that the *Ardent* is drifting near a meteor that's augmenting their free radicals - chemicals that harm DNA and cause the body to age. Mulder realises that the ship's desalinised water is the source of their contamination, but that the recycled sewage water aboard is safe. Trondheim locks himself in with the "safe" water, but drowns when the ship's hull weakens and the sea gushes in. A greatly aged Mulder and Scully lapse into unconsciousness, but Navy SEALs rescue them as the *Ardent* sinks. Based on Scully's journal entries, doctors rehydrate the agents back to youth and health.

Critique The ending, of course, is a major disappointment - inasmuch as there really *isn't* one. Dod Kalm borrows from last season's Darkness

Falls, by trapping the regulars in a claustrophobic setting from which there is no escape, and then providing an escape anyway. But Darkness Falls gets away with it by delivering a chilling coda that the government have to contain a new predator for the sake of mankind's survival. Dod Kalm has nothing like that to distract us. So instead it brings our heroes to the point where death is the only satisfying conclusion the story can offer, and then cheats entirely.

One could argue that if the writers can only devise a plot which paints them into a corner so awkward there's no realistic way they can get out, then they shouldn't write the story at all. But that would be a shame, because Dod Kalm offers a meditation on death so touching that I think the series as a whole would be poorer without it. Darkness Falls derives a lot of its drama from putting Mulder and Scully in a pressure cooker situation, and watching as they lose patience with each other. Dod Kalm, on the other hand, treats the characters with greater dignity: this is a demonstration of how far the faith our heroes have for each other has developed. The story offers a series of betrayals - the teaser shows a crew mutinying to escape death, a treachery which is fruitless as both those who run from the ship and those who stay aboard age to death in the same way. A criminal named Olaffson is left aboard ship by his fellow pirates; Trondheim seals himself in the room with the only safe water, and condemns himself to drown alone. Mulder and Scully survive by looking out for each other. And there's a tender melancholy to the scenes in which they wait for death together, in which Mulder confides in Scully how tired he is, how Scully assures Mulder there's nothing to fear as he loses consciousness. They both refuse to drink the last of the uncontaminated water, as neither can bear to sacrifice the other.

I'd have been happier still had Trondheim merely given into his fear and greed, emphasising the difference between him and the FBI agents more forcefully. That the story also makes him a deliberate murderer robs the story of some of its subtlety. (And that he's killed Olaffson at all is very muddled - it's not clearly directed, and once Trondheim lies about Olaffson's "escape", Mulder and Scully never

seem to question why the man never again shows up.) In truth, the story doesn't need Olaffson at all - our heroes deduce that the water storage tank is safe to drink because the pipes haven't corroded, so we hardly require the exposition offered by a redundant character. But (ending aside) this is a lone weak spot in a story which positively brims over with atmosphere. There's little explanation to what's going on - several contradictory alternatives are offered - but what should be a weakness only highlights how desperate Mulder and Scully are, searching for answers that cannot save them.

The ageing make-up is a bit of a mix - Scully looks like a credible old lady, Mulder rather more like a man wearing several layers of latex. It's an undeniable barrier to our accepting a story which already has so much against it, lacking both detail and conclusion. But as a showcase for Duchovny and Anderson this is first rate, and better yet, as a character study of Mulder and Scully it achieves moments of real beauty. It's not the strongest of tales - but from scene to scene, as a piece of writing, Howard Gordon delivers a little gem. (***1/2)

2.20, Humbug

Air Date: March 31, 1995
Writer: Darin Morgan
Director: Kim Manners

Summary Mulder and Scully look into the murder of a circus performer, the latest in a string of forty-eight similar cases going back twenty-eight years. The agents encounter all manner of circus folk at the man's funeral in Florida, and more performers soon die horribly. Lanny, a man whose congenital twin (Leonard) is growing out of his side, eventually confesses that Leonard has been somehow separating himself from Lanny's body - and killing people in the act of trying to "join" with them. Mulder and Scully try and fail to capture Leonard - not realizing that he's been eaten by the Conundrum, a circus performer who specializes in consuming virtually anything.

Critique I love what Humbug stands for. It's a celebration of human diversity, of eccentricity and freakishness that looks more normal the longer you stay in its company. The final rant against genetic engineering, which makes it clear that if science had its way Duchovny would be the human norm, is both persuasive and very funny. And the episode is hugely influential upon The X-Files - it's from this point that the show realises it can sustain itself not only upon po-faced conspiracy episodes and monster runarounds, but by tweaking its own format. It's from Humbug that most of the truly *clever* X-Files episodes will be born, freed from linear plotting and able to be much more experimental.

But - and it's a disappointed "but" - I don't think on its own terms that Humbug is very good. If you look at almost any scene in isolation, its wit and intelligence is clear. Taken as a whole, though, it's something of a bore - and that's because it has no structure, no pacing, and little story. The concept is very simple: a series of murders are being enacted upon carnival folk. But the investigation always feels so secondary to writer Darin Morgan's comic turns of grotesquerie, and the killings themselves are devoid of tension and, even worse, *momentum*; each time someone dies the plot doesn't progress at all, it's simply another curious set piece.

This is extremely frustrating. There are so many great scenes - Mulder's arguments with his vertically challenged landlord, the sequence in which the FBI exhume a potato - but increasingly these sequences feel draining, because there's no developing story to give them context. Every time a clue appears to be uncovered, it's revealed to be another con, another gag. The dwarf who's brought out from under Scully's trailer really *is* just fixing the plumbing, the potato exhumation is just an opportunity for the sheriff to shake his head sadly and comment on how badly Mulder and Scully's investigation is going. And it *is* - they don't solve anything, and only we the audience appreciate the joke of how the geek who'll eat anything turns from victim to predator. It's a good joke too, and a nice reversal of the opening teaser in which we see an apparent monster being attacked in a swimming pool. It's just that by this point, I was tired of jokes and wanted some crumb that was a little more substantial. There's a scene in which Scully visits the freak museum only to be sold a cheap trick; as I watched it, and realised that yet again we were being offered another piece of sleight of hand, I despaired.

There's a brilliant writer at work here, and Humbug stands out as something of true talent compared to the formulaic episodes around it. It's also massively undisciplined, and the points it raises are muddled by too much cleverness. I'm glad Humbug was made, because it helped to stretch the series and show, ironically, how eccentric and freakish its premise is. But it lacks the simple emotion that make the best episodes work and the best of Darin Morgan's later episodes sing. There's one moment, in which Lanny reveals his heartache on discovering his own conjoined twin hates him enough to leave his body - it's inspired, because it makes the extraordinary horror suddenly very human and very personal. But its effect is lost somewhat amidst the freewheeling chaos on display. (***)

2.21, The Calusari

Air Date: April 14, 1995
Writer: Sara B Charno
Director: Michael Vejar

Summary When two-year-old Teddy Holvey is mysteriously lured to his death in Arlington, Virginia, Mulder comes to wonder if poltergeist activity is responsible. Teddy's father also dies in a freak accident - his tie caught in a garage door opener - and suspicion soon falls upon Teddy's eight-year-old brother Charlie.

The agents encounter Romanian holy men, the Calusari, who insist that evil resides in Charlie. The root of the problem is soon revealed as Charlie's stillborn twin Michael - the brothers' souls weren't properly "divided" at their birth, meaning that Michael's wrathful shade can manfiest. Michael's ghost attacks Scully, but Mulder and the Calusari perform a ritual over Charlie that banishes Michael's spirit. The leader of the Calusari warns, however, that while the "evil" is temporarily banished, it knows who Mulder and Scully are.

Critique The season's coming to an end, and everyone's getting a bit tired. That's the best reason I can find for this pale retread of The Exorcist, with more than a smattering of Omen II thrown in for good measure. The annoying thing is that the reason why those movies are scary is because they put evil into a modern domestic setting, and yet it's that jarring collision here which makes the episode so ineffective. The teaser is the most disturbing sequence in the story, as a two year old follows an errant balloon in front of a funfair train - it's horribly credible, and it's genuinely startling that a piece of network television is going to lead us into its opening credits with the death of a toddler. But within minutes, we're in a story in which Romanian mothers-in-law shout curses whilst trying to sacrifice chickens - it immediately puts you at one remove from the real-world horror, and feels like the premise for a sitcom to boot.

So what starts as a meditation on child abuse, and the way in which parents can inflict illnesses upon their offspring deliberately by Munchausen by proxy, becomes all too quickly a tale about long-bearded men in frock coats and hats intoning about the evil eye and drawing comparisons between a small child and Hitler. It's so tremendously crass, and leaves Mulder and Scully precisely... nowhere. They seem to spend entire long sequences of the episode standing in corridors, or watching from the windows of hospitals. In the end, they achieve nothing; Scully gets to be menaced by a phantom, whilst Mulder has the task of holding a child by his feet as strange old men pin him down by force and daub him with blood. I found this last sequence the most disquieting of all, with Mulder tellingly not *even given any lines* for several minutes. I know that as FBI agents go, Mulder is on the unorthodox side, but his standing by mutely as a terrified child is exorcised feels grossly wrong. It's a measure of a bad episode when our heroes can only watch the conclusion takes place, but it goes off the rails altogether when they abandon police procedure by doing so.

The dialogue is pretty good - when it's not in Romanian or being incanted. There's a terrific scene in which Evil Child cruelly mocks his grieving mother by asking to be taken to the park and ride on the train which flattened his brother. It's a rare moment of real horror, and so much more effective, say, than a sequence in which he sticks his mother high up on the wall. Less is more. The Calusari *looks* good, but there's something stale and pointless at its heart. (*1/2)

2.22, F. Emasculata

Air Date: April 28, 1995
Writers: Chris Carter, Howard Gordon
Directed By: Rob Bowman

Summary Mulder and Scully are assigned to find two convicts - Paul and Steve - who've escaped from Cumberland Prison in Virginia. They learn that a deadly disease started making the rounds at the prison after a severed pig's leg showed up in the mail. The agents backtrack the problem to Pinck Pharmaceuticals - a company that explores rain forests for potential drug application. Pinck found a type of insect in Costa Rica, Faciphaga Emasculata, which contains a parasite that attacks the human immune system and generates pustules as part of its reproductive cycle.

When Steve dies from the infection, Paul tries to escape to Toronto. Mulder intercepts Paul, wanting living proof of Pinck's wrongdoing, but an unidentified sniper shoots Paul dead. Mulder and Scully realise that the prisoner who received the pig's leg and the Pinck scientist it was intended for have the same last name - meaning those responsible can pass off this field-test of F. Emasculata's effectiveness as a simple postal error.

Critique For its first half, this episode jogs along quite merrily as a simple contagion story: there are prison refugees out there, and they're infected - somebody stop them before they end the world! Then it all suddenly takes a left turn and becomes a thoughtful analysis on disinformation, on cover-up, and the public right to truth. It makes for a pretty full hour, but in all honesty neither plotline is quite given the attention it deserves.

What we've got instead feels like two really interesting first drafts. The disease part of the episode is suitably unpleasant, with pus being squirted out of festering boils left, right and centre. And I love the grisliness that the only way to determine whether Scully is infected is to strap a beetle onto her skin and get it to bite her. But it's all compromised hugely by having Scully behave *exactly* in the opposite manner to how

one should conduct oneself in a tense quarantine situation. Taking no precautions for herself or for the others trying to contain the threat, she walks around without protective clothing, cuts open sacks of diseased bodies, and directly kills one scientist as a result. Frankly, it's remarkable that she *wasn't* infected - her survival could be an X-File in itself.

Mulder's own manhunt story is efficient enough, although it seems to lose interest in the convict's girlfriend as soon as she reveals where her lover is headed. (Presumably she dies horribly. Well, them's the breaks.) Where it gets interesting - if a little muddled - is in the way his assignment to the case is shown to be a set-up by the Cigarette Smoking Man. Using Mulder as a stooge, he's engineered his involvement in order to *suppress* the truth - almost, it feels, to rub Mulder's nose in his own ideals. Mulder and Scully argue over whether or not the truth should be made public, and these scenes present a genuine moral dilemma that's at the heart of what the series is about. It's easy to suggest that the episode barely qualifies as an X-File at all - there's nothing alien or paranormal about what's going on - but that's entirely the point, I think. Even our heroes can't work out why they should be involved, until they're forced to look at the nature of conspiracy and cover-up from a whole new angle.

There's something very confused about F. Emasculata. In its rush to implicate the government, it doesn't bother to make clear quite how this entire threat has been arranged. It's quite clever, this idea of using a guinea pig in a jail to analyse a contagion, and picking someone who has the same name as one of the pharmacists so that any leak can be passed off as an administrative error. But... even writing that out, the scheme seems headache-inducingly convoluted. It's indicative of the problems of the episode - some bits (like Scully's story) are too sloppy, others are too contrived. But for all that, it's a strangely satisfying episode. It's tense and exciting - and pretty disgusting - and for all the muddle, it feels as if it's *about* something, that it has some meat on its bones. There's a welcome intelligence at its core, even if it hasn't been revealed as cleverly as it might. (***1/2)

2.23, Soft Light

Air Date: May 5, 1995
Writer: Vince Gilligan
Director: James Contner

Summary   Detective Kelly Ryan, a former student of Scully's, asks for help in solving missing persons cases that all feature mysterious burn marks being left at the scene of each disappearance. Mulder and Scully turn their attention to Dr Chester Banton, a fugitive and former researcher at Polarity Magnetics. Owing to a mishap with a particle accelerator, Banton's shadow has taken on black-hole-like qualities - and is now capable of consuming people. Banton tells Mulder that the government wants to drain his brain of knowledge, and that his death would result in the "shadow force" within him getting free. X and his associates try to capture Banton, who accidentally kills Ryan and then attempts to destroy himself in the particle accelerator. The effort fails, and X takes Banton to a facility where government researchers can study him indefinitely.

Critique   I'm reliably informed that the science in this episode is even more absurd than normal. And I can quite see that if you care about physics, seeing supposed geniuses walk about getting elemental definitions of quantum particles wrong must be frustrating. My interest in such things is minimal, though. Vince Gilligan's debut script is witty, exciting, and has an engaging idea as its premise. A killer shadow is such fun - it takes the cliché of the evil twin we've seen recently and gives it a fresh twist. Tony Shalhoub gives a wonderfully manic performance as a man who murders in spite of himself, who can't help but kill the police if they get too close to arresting him. And it's clever too that Gilligan takes the standard lighting style of the series, all darkness and shadows, and turns it into a character itself. Director of photography John Bartley rises to the challenge, and plays up the atmosphere to the point of parody; the scene in which Mulder's shadow is merged by X's is especially effective.

It's one of those stories where Mulder and Scully get to investigate properly, coming up with theories that they later build on or retract. The contrast that they make to the new detective on the block, the short-lived Ryan, is telling. The first series regularly presented doomed characters in the police force who stole the credit for our heroes' discoveries, but here the stereotype is given greater dignity; Ryan is just a woman struggling to make her way through the boys' club of the FBI. What she lacks is Mulder and Scully's banter, their sense of humour - and what makes her sympathetic is that she reminds us of the less-certain Scully from the beginning of Season One. Ryan is what Scully was like before she had her eyes opened to extreme possibility, a woman with a chip on her shoulder who's trying too hard. Both Mulder and Scully come off well in Soft Light, surprisingly so considering it's yet another in a series of episodes in which they're seen to fail objectively. It works, though, because it builds upon the sense that the X-Files are being used as a patsy, to do the dirty work of the government unawares. It's great to see Steven Williams as X get more screen time, and to be exposed in all his amoral glory. The fact that Mulder at last confronts X on his loyalties makes you feel that all the setbacks he suffers this week have nevertheless advanced him somehow - and, in doing so, the series itself.

And if we're left in any doubt where The X-Files is going, with its greater distrust of the powers that be, there's no better illustration than the brilliant closing scene. Shalhoub is fixed to a chair, bombarded with flashes of light, as one single tear rolls down his terrified face. There'll be no escape for him - he's another one of the guinea pigs we met last week. And the grinding of the machine that tortures him continues long after the episode has properly ended, and the theme music over the credits comes as a blessed relief. (****)

2.24, Our Town

Air Date: May 12, 1995
Writer: Frank Spotnitz
Director: Rob Bowman

Summary In Dudley, Arkansas, when a federal poultry inspector considers shutting down the Chaco Chicken processing plant, he's killed in what looks like a tribal ceremony. Investigating the man's death, Mulder and Scully find a multitude of bones in a nearly lake - evidently the remains of eighty-seven people who've gone missing in the area in the past fifty-nine years. It transpires that the founder of Chaco Chicken, Walter Chaco, spent some time with the Jale tribe in New Guinea, thereby discovering a means by which the people of Dudley could extend their lifespans by eating human flesh. Chaco captures Scully, but protests when the townsfolk kill and eat one of their own: the late inspector's wife. Mulder saves Scully and Chaco Chicken is closed - but not, it seems, before the townsfolk take Chaco away, grind him up and feed him to a bunch of chickens.

Critique Sometimes you can just try too hard. The title already points to satire - it's a nod towards the play by Thornton Wilder, which promotes family values in folksy Americana. And the theme which runs through the episode, that of a society poisoning themselves only when they let in outsiders, is a clever one - it can apply just as easily to religion or to race. That it here refers to cannibalism is rather witty, and sets up the story as being in the same vein as Die Hand die Verletzt, where otherwise ordinary people are shown espousing one corrupted value amongst all the usual homesy ones. The rebellion against Chaco at the end, where he talks about how the community has lost its faith and will destroy themselves if they attack their own kind, makes its point explicitly. But Frank Spotnitz just pushes at the metaphor too hard for credibility's sake. Whereas it's possible to accept a small group leading an entire town into unwitting cannibalism, it looks comical at the end when virtually everyone in the area lines up for their spot of human chow. It makes the theme too pat, it dilutes the effect of the collective guilt. The Scooby Doo conclusion, where Mulder pulls the mask off the executioner,

counts for nothing when everybody else is running about being just as culpable.

The episode works best when it's drawing parallels between animal and human behaviour. Mulder is disgusted to learn that chickens get fattened on remains of other chickens. Scully cannot tuck into her own bucket o' wings when she's made to contemplate the idea that people have been snacking on each other. It takes a wrong turn when it starts suggesting that all the cannibals have found some gift of eternal youth; it's as if Spotnitz doubted the power of his own story, and was eager to find another spin to put upon it. By reaching out for the paranormal, he robs the story of a subtler horror. As I say, sometimes you can try too hard.

And sometimes you can simply not try hard enough. Rob Bowman's direction has its moments - I love the way that a corpse sinks face down into the chicken feed with a slurp. But by emphasising the usual tropes of The X-Files - the gruesome and the eerie - he misses the lightness of touch necessary to make Spotnitz's strange black comedy work. "Good people, good food" is the slogan of Chaco Chicken, and we needed to see that - that these were good people, good husbands and wives, good neighbours out of Thornton Wilder - to give the story any point. Mark Snow is on autopilot too, giving Chaco the same horn anthem he gives any character who's taken a little too much from a tribal culture. It played all the way through Fresh Bones as well - but Fresh Bones worked as a story built on voodoo shocks, and the comparison doesn't help the slyer, more mocking Our Town at all.

Oh, and enough with Scully getting captured and bound this season. The first time was essential for the long term mythology of The X-Files, the second was a deliberate echo of that. By now, though, it's getting repetitive. It's disrespectful towards Scully, only undermining her status as a competent FBI agent. And it's disrespectful towards us, because it's lazy storytelling. Once you've built an entire arc around Scully's abduction by aliens which resonates throughout an entire season, you're not going to sell easily a ten-minute abduction by an old man who runs a chicken company. (**)

2.25, Anasazi

Air Date: May 19, 1995
Story: David Duchovny, Chris Carter
Teleplay: Chris Carter
Director: RW Goodwin

Summary A hacker named "the Thinker" breaches the Defense Department's computer systems, stealing every drop of information the Department has compiled about UFOs since the 1940s. The Lone Gunmen pass the data along to Mulder, and find that it's written in Navajo - a language used for encryption purposes in World War II. Meanwhile, Mulder's behaviour becomes increasingly erratic, and Scully finds that someone has been lacing his apartment water with hallucinogens.

The Cigarette Smoking Man visits Mulder's father Bill - an old associate of his - to discuss the theft of the files, which contain Bill's name. Bill starts to come clean to his son about his work for the State Department - but Alex Krycek appears and shoots Bill dead. Mulder pursues Krycek, takes his gun and moves to kill him - but Scully shoots Mulder first, to preserve the forensic proof that Krycek murdered Mulder's father.

Scully takes a recovering Mulder to New Mexico and introduces him to Albert Hosteen, a Navajo code-talker. Hosteen sets about decrypting the Thinker's files, which make mention of Scully and her former kidnapper, Duane Barry. He also mentions the Anasazi, a tribe that vanished six centuries ago and was apparently kidnapped by aliens. Albert's nephew shows Mulder a train car filled with alien bodies, each with what looks like smallpox vaccination marks on their arms. Mulder hides in the train car as the Cigarette Smoking Man moves to suppress an array of evidence, ordering his men to incinerate the contents of the train car. [To be continued.]

Critique It's perhaps wrong to look to the mythology episodes to reinvent The X-Files: as the series continues, we'll see the standalone stories evolve and become more playful, whilst the conspiracy arc gets ever further enmeshed in a house style years old. Anasazi is one of the reasons, though, why there's always such a sense of anticipation for these event episodes. It's fresh, and it's exciting, and it reinvigorates the series just as it seemed in danger of becoming predictable.

Its brilliance mostly lies not in its new revelations, but in looking at old relationships from a jaundiced eye. It's a touch of genius to make Mulder psychotic for most of the episode; his frustration with the FBI, which has been simmering for the last few weeks in particular, leads him to punch Skinner - his verbal attack on Scully, as someone who was only assigned to his side in the first place to discredit him, brings to a head the last feelings of distrust between the pair and lances them. Everything is being re-examined from a sideways perspective - even Mulder's boredom with the comic relief of the Lone Gunmen feels refreshing - and at the heart of this, of course, is Mulder's own obsessive nature. His delight upon discovering "the Holy Grail" of secrets, only to be so furious when he thinks he's been sold just another hoax, is schizophrenic - his confused response to his father's hug, which he only returns when the man is dying in his arms, is another high point. The second series has been a year in which Duchovny has nailed Mulder, and his performance here is superb. And all the better for being so understated: rather than playing against the character, the psychotic Mulder is disturbingly believable. It's with some relief we learn he's being poisoned by drugs, but all the more powerful for the possibility he might not have been.

But all of this would count for little were it simply a character study of Mulder. It's through Scully that we make sense of it all. Gillian Anderson is extraordinary here, baffled and frightened by her best friend's behaviour, until she finally is obliged to save him from himself by shooting him. The chemistry between Anderson and Duchovny now makes all the emotional twists and turns not only fully believable - and that's a tall order with so many crammed into one episode - but also gut wrenching. It's an illustration of how far the series has developed that the biggest drama it now offers is not one of alien encounters but the destruction of their relationship.

Mind you, there *are* aliens. After the tortured

confrontations earlier in the episode, it almost feels like a relief when Mulder steps into the boxcar to see what's inside. But this isn't business as usual. The realisation that the alien corpses piled up there have smallpox vaccination marks, coupled with Scully's information about experiments upon humans, takes the series into new and darker areas. The implications are honestly chilling. And The X-Files sud-denly seems less a bit of escapism about the FBI chasing monsters, and something nastier and much angrier. The cliffhanger is a good one. The image of that boxcar on fire is powerful - although the dialogue before has already made clear that Mulder must have escaped. What sells it is the real sense that The X-Files is starting another chapter. (*****)

3.1, The Blessing Way

Air Date: Sept. 22, 1995
Writer: Chris Carter
Director: RW Goodwin

Summary Scully returns to Washington, D.C. to find that her copy of the stolen Defense Department files has been taken. Meanwhile, the Cigarette Smoking Man reports to a shadowy consortium of men (henceforth called "the Syndicate") with an interest in global affairs.

Albert Hosteen and his family find Mulder lying near death close to the train car. Mulder straddles the divide between life and death, and speaks with the spirits of his father and Deep Throat. Upon recovering, Mulder visits his mother and asks about one of his father's photographs from the early 1970s - which shows Bill Mulder with a number of the Syndicate members.

A metal detector at FBI headquarters registers a computer chip embedded in the base of Scully's neck, and a doctor removes it for her. At Bill Mulder's funeral, a Syndicate member (henceforth called "the Well-Manicured Man") warns Scully that his colleagues have rashly targeted her for assassination, but that he believes her death would unduly draw attention to them. Krycek and an associate search Scully's apartment for the stolen files, and the associate mistakenly shoots Scully's sister Melissa.

Skinner takes Scully to Mulder's apartment and tells her that *he* took the stolen files for safekeeping, but Scully - unsure of who to trust - covers him with her pistol. As footsteps sound outside, Skinner and Scully level their guns at one another... [To be continued.]

Critique You have to admire the gall of this. Here we have a sci-fi show with guns and aliens and monsters, and it's the opening of a new season after a really good jeopardy cliffhanger, and against the odds the series is a hit! And what do you do? You present an episode full of Navajo rituals and dreams and poetic language from imaginary people. Is it brave? Absolutely. Does

it work? Not really, no. But the bravery wins through for me.

After Anasazi focused upon past events through the tint of psychosis, The Blessing Way looks to interpret the future through something spiritual. It's a clever contrast. Mulder's dream encounters with his father and Deep Throat are oddly moving, even though the lines are frankly dripping with pretension. Jerry Hardin is not the most naturalistic of actors, and many times has looked stilted as he's tried to navigate his way through overwritten dialogue - it could almost feel like an act of cruelty that he's been inflicted with the teenage verse he recites here. What's remarkable is that these sequences work as well as they do. They give a sense of importance to Mulder's recovery and to his renewed purpose afterwards. And the poetry is offset with moments of brutality which slap you across the face - we cut from Hardin's monologue to a scene where the boxcar aliens panic as they're gassed by cyanide.

But the main reason why these long scenes of Mulder touching his inner self do not offend is that they contrast with Scully's own more prosaic methods of self-analysis. She even tries hypnotic regression therapy, but pulls away, scared of what she might learn. There's a terrific (and possibly unintentional) irony on display in this episode: as Mulder looks inside himself, so Scully finds a microchip inside her body. And as we see Mulder heal from that discovery, so we see Scully remove the chip - the very act which will give her cancer in Season Four. The Blessing Way, for all that the title directs you to Mulder's adventures with the Navajo, is really about Scully, about how she copes with the death of her partner and the loss of her vocation. And just as Anasazi sees Mulder deal with growing paranoia as he's under threat for his life - only to lose a family member in the process - so the same thing happens to Scully. The scene where she meets John Neville's Well-Manicured Man at the funeral, where he oh so smoothly tells her that his consortium wants her dead, is very well-written: it's taut and subtle, as opposed to the florid opaque sequences with

Mulder floating about listening to the dead. That paranoia builds up to a fantastic cliffhanger as well, as Scully and Skinner turn their guns upon each other.

The Blessing Way is flabby and unfocused. The one thing that the audience wanted it to do - to show how Mulder survived a blazing boxcar - it resolutely fails to make clear. It takes the audience on a strange journey which contrasts disciplinary hearings at the FBI with floating ghosts in the heavens. It's an irritating episode. It's a fascinating episode. And it's done with such conviction that even if you don't believe a word of it, to quote The X-Files - you *want* to believe. (***1/2)

3.2, Paper Clip

Air Date: Sept. 29, 1995
Writer: Chris Carter
Director: Rob Bowman

Summary   Mulder enters his apartment and convinces Skinner and Scully to back down. The Lone Gunmen study Bill Mulder's photograph and identify Victor Klemper, a former Nazi scientist living in America. Mulder and Scully visit Klemper, who divulges that the photograph was taken at the disused Strughold Mining Company in West Virginia. The agents travel there and find an astonishing number of medical records from the 1950s and beyond. Suddenly, the lights go out and alien figures scuttle past. Mulder witnesses an alien spacecraft fleeing the scene, then escapes with Scully as hit men secure the site.

Krycek and his thugs ambush Skinner and take the stolen data. The Cigarette Smoking Man orders the goons to kill Krycek because he botched Scully's murder - but Krycek flees, still in possession of the data. Mulder and Scully find that Kemper has been murdered (or very coincidentally had a heart attack). The Well-Manicured Man tells them that after an alien spaceship crashed in Roswell in 1947, Nazi scientists were granted admission to America as part of "Operation: Paper Clip". Genetic material was harvested from millions of Americans via their smallpox vaccinations, with the goal of creating an alien-human hybrid. When Mulder's father threatened to expose the project, his daughter was taken to ensure his silence.

Mulder visits his mother, who confesses that Mulder's father decided which of their children he would surrender.

Skinner tells the Cigarette Smoking Man that Albert Hosteen has memorized the stolen data's contents and recited it, per the narrative tradition of his tribe, to twenty other men. The threat of the information getting out forces Syndicate to lift the death threat on Mulder and Scully, whereupon Scully goes to visit her injured sister - and finds that Melissa has died.

Critique   I get the sense that Chris Carter is rather an excitable chap. When he's set loose on the mythology shaping episodes he goes a little mad, and gets so carried away with new ideas and concepts and directions that you're left somewhat reeling. Paper Clip is a very enjoyable hour of television, but almost in spite of its frenetic pace, not because of it. Almost every scene seems determined to offer a new revelation, or a new confrontation so fraught in its emotional implications you feel it could be used to carry an entire episode. So, on the one hand, you have scenes in which a German war criminal - who Carter takes pains to tell us is the most determinedly evil man to have escaped the Nuremberg trials - pops up to give Mulder and Scully a clue. They then find an entire mountain stuffed full of filing cabinets that contain nothing *but* clues. And then, to make sure they interpret these clues correctly, the Well-Manicured Man arrives to help them out. And amid this veritable onslaught of new information are scenes in which Scully has to react to Mulder's survival and the fatal wounding of her sister; in which Mulder must demand of his mother whether she chose to put his sister up for abduction rather than him, and sees an entire spacecraft overhead to confirm all he has believed is true. The result, inevitably, is that the explanations feel a bit hysterical, and the emotional payoffs a bit cheap.

Not that there's anything wrong with the ideas or the set pieces on display. On the contrary, there's a pleasing sense that in its third season, The X-Files is fulfilling the promise made in the second: find a way of tying these sci fi escapades into something more human and relevant. The growing impression there's been human experimentation - with, at last, a totally blunt allusion to Mengele's work on the Jews in

World War II - gives the whole conspiracy a new, darker focus miles away from the bright lights of UFOs. And just as the UFO back story was tied into something personal, here Carter ups the stakes too, and gives the Mulder story a background that smacks of Sophie's Choice. It's very clever. And, potentially, very powerful. It's only undermined by the way in which the episode is reluctant to let the ideas breathe - almost as if it's too frightened by what they imply, happier to run on to the next set piece.

Perhaps it's not surprising, then, that it's the subtler moments which have the greater impact. This is an episode of power reversals. The Cigarette Smoking Man finished the second season in the position of archetypal villain, the one at last who gave the order to kill Mulder. By the end of Paper Clip he's been outed as a man desperately trying to cling to the failing respect of the consortium who employ him: he's a stooge, a henchman, and even his own assassins phone him up to promise revenge. Skinner emerges as a hero, having been set up only last week as a potential traitor; it's telling that the most triumphant moment of the episode is his, as he at last is able to challenge the Cigarette Smoking Man directly after a season of prevarication. And, best of all, is the way Mulder leaves the choice of continuing the quest or not to Scully - he offers no arguments, he just accepts that her interests in exposing the truth are as earnest as his. It's a scene of quiet dignity for both of them, and helps to redefine their entire relationship.

For those reasons, the barrage of new information is humanised. The conspiracy players no longer feel like faceless automatons but like frustrated individuals. And Mulder and Scully too feel more exposed, more real. That's Paper Clip's success, that for all its plot complications, it's let something more simple out. That's even wittily reflected in the way that Skinner foils the Cigarette Smoking Man, relying not upon the technology of computer tape but the oral traditions of the Navajo. It may not strictly make sense - when exactly did Albert Hosteen have time to memorise those detailed files, let alone teach them to twenty other men? - but the metaphor is perfect. (Less so is the one about the white buffalo, but let's pass over that - after all, the episode itself quickly does too.) (****)

3.3, D.P.O.

Air Date: Oct. 6, 1995
Writer: Howard Gordon
Director: Kim Manners

Summary In Connerville, Oklahoma, lightning strikes kill an improbable number of people. Mulder and Scully identify the culprit as Darin Peter Oswald: a nineteen-year-old whose electrolyte balance enables him to control electricity and fire lightning bolts. Oswald harbors a crush for Sharon Kiveat, a former high school teacher, and nearly murders her husband. The agents confront Oswald, who generates a lightning bolt that kills the local sheriff, but is left so drained that he falls unconscious. Afterward, Oswald is institutionalized and forced to undergo treatment.

Critique It's that Howard Gordon staple again - a man with paranormal powers bumps off people who get in his way. What gives D.P.O. part of its kick, though, is that this time the villain in question isn't acting out some sort of masterplan, there's nothing operatic about the reason for his revenge. It's a study instead of a small town failure, of a boy whose only inspiration from remedial class was to get a crush on his teacher, whose own mother ignores him because he's not important enough to interrupt her diet of trash TV, whose own best friend is called Zero. Given his extraordinary ability to conduct electricity, he has no ambition at all - he plays video games, he fries cattle, he makes the traffic lights change so he can sit and watch car crashes. This isn't a monster in any sense of the word. There's a telling scene where Mulder asks Darin if he'd consider himself a lucky person as the only survivor of a lightning strike - and Darin's dull slackjawed response is one of bemusement. His teacher later reveals she only ever took pity on his attentions because there was something unlucky about him. This is the story of a person whose life changes quite suddenly, and who hasn't the imagination to realise it. He lives the same dazed life he always did, wasting time and drinking beer, and once in a while killing the bullies who made his pathetic existence that smidgen more uncomfortable.

As a story it doesn't have many surprises, and the last act in particular is very predictable. But there's a peculiar anger to this tale, both in its writing and its direction, which give it its energy. Howard Gordon never tries to sentimentalise Darin - but never holds back either from making it clear that the focus of all this horror is a boy who's only looking for some affection or some purpose. He wants to use his powers to impress a schoolteacher, and can't decide whether that's best done by killing her husband or by saving his life as a human defibrillator. So he does both. It's that lack of foresight which makes him so very believable. He wants to be *special*. The harsh irony is that he hasn't the wit either to be a very good monster or a very good hero - his own understanding of his potential is as random as the cars which knock into each other as they run the traffic lights.

Jack Black, as the loser friend, is terrific, giving a hint of the comic timing for which he will become renowned. Giovanni Ribisi is even better as Darin, neither seeking the audience's approval or fear. The last scene of him in a cell, watching TV as passive a drone as his mother, is as arresting an ending as the show has given us. To the strains of "Live Fast, Diarrhoea", as he flips the channels with dead eyes, he finally achieves his goal: we see him on TV in a hit television series called The X-Files. It's a sudden shocking image, with Chris Carter's name on screen, that The X-Files too has become a commercial phenomenon, that it's a part of the network TV scheduling being pumped out and giving the slacker generation something to engage with an hour each week. I don't want to labour the point too much, but it's the beginning of a postmodern approach to the series, with the understanding that it's famous enough now to shape the culture it's commenting on. (***)

3.4, Clive Bruckman's Final Repose

Air Date: Oct. 13, 1995
Writer: Darin Morgan
Director: David Nutter

Summary The murder of several fortune tellers cause Mulder and Scully to encounter Clyde Bruckman, an insurance salesman who seems to possess psychic abilities. Bruckman says the killer is also psychic, and predicts that Mulder will die at the man's hand after stepping into a pie. The agents put Bruckman into protective custody at a hotel, but the killer - working there as a bellhop - moves to eliminate his psychic rival. In the ensuing scuffle, Mulder steps in a pie in the hotel kitchen, which gives him enough warning to dodge the killer's knife. Scully shoots the killer dead, but she and Mulder learn afterward that Bruckman has committed suicide.

Critique This is a little slice of genius. Once in a while, you hope that with any good TV show an episode will be made that redefines the series' whole potential. Clyde Bruckman is that episode for The X-Files. From this point on, every year, you can see the writers trying hard to match it, every now and then producing something as clever and as moving and frankly as profound as this. This is an inspiration for The X-Files, this is its finest hour.

And it's about little men with little lives. I find it fascinating that the response of the staff writers to the epic scale of Chris Carter's opening scripts is to write about ordinary people with ordinary ambitions muddling through with their extraordinary powers. We are presented here with two men who have a psychic ability that lets them see the future. Both of them are plagued by what this ability suggests - if the future is predetermined, then what possibly can be the meaning of life? One is a bellhop who becomes a serial killer, as eager to ask of his fortune-telling victims some small insight into why he commits such appalling acts as he is to remove their eyeballs and entrails. The other is a life-insurance salesman who loses at the lottery and dreams every night of the disintegration of his own body, forever knowing the manner of death of each person he meets.

If, suggests Darin Morgan, you have no control over what you do, how can there be any achievement, or any guilt? Mulder cannot understand why Bruckman is so disdainful of his gift, but for Bruckman it's a gift he has done nothing to earn. Our serial killer is clearly disgusted by the things he does, but cannot see how he can prevent them. When he finally meets Bruckman, and realises at last he can discuss matters with a fellow psychic who might understand, his eager delight to find a rationale for his evil is almost childishly touching. And so is his relief when Bruckman gives him the answer he's been seeking - there's no psychological explanation, he's not as deep as that, he kills people because he is a homicidal maniac. A stereotype, a caricature. A character that Darin Morgan hasn't even bothered to give the dignity of a name. The bliss on the killer's face is palpable - he's just an ordinary man after all, albeit one who likes to remove people's organs.

But Bruckman can't let himself off the hook so easily. Although he believes in predestination, in the worthlessness of choice, he is obsessed about the millions of tiny coincidences that shape events. What must have happened to a woman to make her want to collect dolls, what chance was there that the Big Bopper was fated to be sitting on the very plane that killed him? As Bruckman admits, quite literally, he cannot see the wood for the trees. When warning Mulder he'll get his throat slit, he gives equal weight in his description to the flavour of the pie that he'll step in. As the serial killer searches for meaning in his acts, so Bruckman wearily cannot help but find meaning in all the trivial details of life he sees.

What this cannot make clear is just how *funny* this is. Darin Morgan has a brilliant ear for comic dialogue - but more, for comic subversion. The police aren't talking about Mulder as their spooky expert, but a TV psychic calling himself The Stupendous Yappi. It's Mulder who's thrown out as the sceptic. And Morgan ensures that whenever his script is being profound, he undercuts it with anticlimax. The effect is honestly dazzling. You can tell this is intellectual stuff, but there's such a wealth of gags on display you never feel it's being pretentious.

And nor is it heartless either. Darin Morgan's script is brilliantly clever, but its themes of futility run the risk of being cold and unfeeling. And as an episode which examines death from every angle - even Laurel and Hardy get turned to skeletons - it could so easily have been depressing. Peter Boyle, who like Morgan deservedly won an Emmy for his work here, gives Bruckman a lightness of touch, and even his defeatism has an air of amiable pathos. His affection for Scully dignifies him. When he talks

of his own suicide, and her response to it, he describes it as being very sweet and very tender. And that's exactly what Boyle's performance shows us. Because at the heart of the story there is the positive belief in free will, that the future *can* be shaped. Bruckman kills himself because he *knows* he kills himself - he never learns that Mulder's life *can* be saved. There always has to be a matter of choice in our actions, or the universe is too grim to contemplate. The dog cannot help eating its dead owner when it has no food, but that's because it's just a dog. We have to do better. If we don't, we end up just as puppets, taking no pleasure in our good or our evil because fundamentally neither have much to do with us.

Fundamentally, the troubled questions Morgan poses here are best answered by the writing of the episode itself. Life might seem random, a cruel joke. FBI agents may feel relieved to learn they won't die of lung cancer, but only because they don't know they'll be knifed to death on the toilet moments later. Buying a boat rather than life insurance becomes a bad move if you're going to die in a car crash soon, leaving a widow and a young child. But if you can create something special, if you can add to life a little piece of art like Clyde Bruckman's Final Repose, then you're doing something right. Because an episode like this isn't random - it's finely wrought, and thoughtful, and compassionate, and is a triumph of individualism. A little slice of genius indeed. (*****)

3.5, The List

Air Date: Oct. 20, 1995
Writer / Director: Chris Carter

Summary After Napoleon "Neech" Manley gets the electric chair, persons related to his incarceration start dying horribly. Mulder concludes that Manley's spirit is honoring a pledge to eliminate the five men he believes wronged him. One of Manley's fellow inmates, Roque, owns a list of the men fated to die - but the prison warden, whose name is on the list, questions Roque and beats him to death. Mulder and Scully discover that Manley's spirit now resides in a

prison guard named Parmelly, who's become the lover of Manley's wife Danielle. She shoots Parmelly dead upon learning that he's really her late husband, but Manley's spirit retains enough potency to kill the warden in a car accident.

Critique   Chris Carter's writing and directing debut last year caused quite a stir, so there was a lot of anticipation for this follow-up - and, it would appear, from Carter himself, who almost superstitiously gave himself the same fifth episode slot in which to repeat his success. This time he's halfway there. The direction is very good; the long precredit sequence is excellently handled, and the episode that follows it is suitably grim and claustrophobic. It's a good looking, if decidedly grisly, hour of television.

But direction is only as good as the script it serves, and The List's feels barely cooked. Another revenge drama, another story in which a man comes from beyond the grave to wreak vengeance. The twist this time is the list itself, a catalogue of the five people who are to be the victims. Carter tries to inject some suspense into our finding out who these victims are to be, in what should have been a neat reversal of the format; the tension in the prison grows not so much from the killings, not in such a brutal community, but from the expectations of those killings. Death itself almost feels to the inmates like an anticlimax.

There's irony for you. But it's only an irony of sorts; this isn't an episode that's big on subtlety. Its real problem is that each victim is given so little character that you hardly care whether they're being bumped off or not; Carter makes a crucial mistake in giving the first four of the five so little screen time that they only seem to have been introduced to be offed moments later. Only JT Walsh as the prison warden is given any dimensions whatsoever. But he's such a stereotype that every time he appears he only looks less believable; in the first few scenes Walsh's performance alone suggests a depth, but the more he's required to battle with a script that has him jump through the same repetitive hoops, the more shallow he becomes.

Mulder and Scully do nothing of any use in the episode. The bit at the end where Mulder complains that he feels they've both missed the point of the story is quite bold. But since what they've misunderstood is such a familiar story-line, it makes them both seem unusually stupid. That the agents stand there as a car drives past that will claim the fifth victim only emphasises how much this story just passed our heroes by. They weren't the only ones. (*1/2)

3.6, 2Shy

Air Date: Nov. 3, 1995
Writer: Jeffrey Vlaming
Director: David Nutter

Summary   In Cleveland, a number of women with an interest in Internet dating are found dead, their bodies rapidly decomposing and covered in an unidentified slime. Skin samples from a crime scene are found to contain no oils or fatty acids, suggesting to Mulder that the killer has a biological deficiency that compels him to eat people's fat. When the murderer, Virgil Incanto, targets a new victim - Ellen Kaminski - he is forced through circumstance to kill his landlord and a snoopy detective. Kaminski shoots and wounds Incanto when he attacks her, leading to his arrest.

Critique   You can get an idea of what might have happened here: first-time writer for the show looks back over episodes he has liked. And so he invents a new Eugene Tooms, this time with a predilection not for livers but for adipose tissue. So far, so obvious - there's a very first season vibe to this, which pleases when it's making Mulder and Scully go back to rigorous, investigative procedure to solve the case, and frustrates when it expects the audience to be impressed by what are becoming X-Files clichés. But a retread of Squeeze can only go so far, and it's when writer Jeffrey Vlaming puts in more personal touches that make the story different. It's full of little details which feel somewhat tacked on, even irrelevant, but give this episode a rather unusual flavour. For example, the sexism displayed by the police detective in one scene is odd, but contrasts well with the way throughout the episode that women are objectified and seen as prey. The landlady with the crush on the killer is given an awful lot of screen time for the minimal role she has to offer, but provides good dramatic irony - here's a woman who is drawn to Virgil's charisma, but because she doesn't have the shyness (or the fatty excess!) of the victims he stalks on the Internet, Virgil is repulsed. I'm reminded of the cartoon character in the adult comic Viz - he's so obsessed with the fantasy sex he can get from porn, he's blind to the fact that his attractive wife is in her lingerie only too eager to please him. There's a clever comparison made here - if the women looking for love on the web prefer to stay behind their computer keyboards rather than take a risk at real relationships, so Incanto the predator is just the same. Offered real affection by a woman down the corridor, he'll beat a hasty retreat to the safety of the modem. Real love is scary.

At the time this episode was filmed, the concept of Internet stalking was rather a new one - access to the World Wide Web was certainly not the standard that it is today. This gives the story a rather dated feel, especially in the way that it seems to characterise all people who use email and chat rooms as fat and desperate. But there's a real sympathy shown for these people too, those of us who are more scared of rejection than they are of meeting serial killers. Ellen Kaminski may have no self-confidence and be a few pounds overweight, but there's a resolve to her as well, and a capacity for happiness - there's something very truthful about the way that as soon as the man she wants is in her apartment, she can't resist logging on to tell a friend all about it. There's something very celebratory in the sequence where Ellen saves Scully's life by shooting Incanto - it'd be a stretch to say it was a feminist statement as some have claimed, but it's great to see a victim so coldly furious about the way she's been treated and empowering herself.

2Shy is, at heart, a story about love, and the hunger that we feel for it. The fumbling joy that one of the victims, Lauren Mackalvey, feels when some man at last is prepared to like her for herself, is very sweet - and it's heartbreaking that she realises in her moment of death that she's just been used. If the episode makes the point a bit bluntly at the end, implying that Incanto's worst crime is not that he's a murderer but a love rat, it's still that betrayal of those vulnerable women's feelings that leaves the greatest impression.

It's a little too formulaic to be truly satisfying.

It doesn't help that Mark Snow's score echoes the one he composed for Squeeze a little too closely for comfort. And some of the subplots Vlaming puts in just feel a bit forced - quite what was the point of the landlady's blind daughter? But it jogs away at a fair pace, it's nicely grisly (the scene where Lauren turns to slush prior to the autopsy makes you squirm and laugh at the same time), and it has a heart to it. I wouldn't say I loved it, but I'd go on a date with it. (***)

3.7, The Walk

Air Date: Nov. 10, 1995
Writer: John Shiban
Director: Rob Bowman

Summary An invisible force at an Army hospital murders the family members of various servicemen, then makes the servicemen suffer by preventing them from committing suicide. Suspicion falls upon the vengeful Leonard "Rappo" Trimble, a fellow veteran and quadruple amputee who seems capable of astral projection and wants to goad the servicemen into killing him. Trimble murders the wife of General Thomas Callahan, then traps Callahan in a room with scalding steam. However, another of Trimble's targets, Lieutenant Colonel Victor Stans, dissipates Trimble's mental force by entering his room and smothering him with a pillow.

Critique It's another supernatural revenge story! That makes, what, the third this season alone? Just like Jeffrey Vlaming did with 2Shy last week, John Shiban has used a staple X-File plot as his debut script, and has put real blood and passion into it which raises it high above the trappings of its clichés. Right from the start there's a conviction to this, whether it be in the suicidal despair of Stans (making a truly memorable teaser), or in the way Scully fights her corner against military bureaucracy. The story of soldiers suffering from post-traumatic stress has already been explored in Sleepless - but The Walk brings it up to date by making this explicitly about the Gulf War; the scene in which Trimble accuses Mulder (and the audience) of watching the action play out on TV like a video game, all to enjoy cheaper oil, has a righteous anger to it which is gripping.

As a story it's a bunch of set piece deaths and chills. Some of them are scary - the child dying in the sandpit is unusually disturbing. Some of them, like the murder of Roach in his cell, feel like the plot is going through the motions. But it's not within the plotting that The Walk sings, but in the emotion. It's a revenge drama which has less interest in killing its victims than in making their lives a living hell. Death becomes something of a release, a mercy which Callahan refuses to give Trimble, insisting he should suffer to stay alive like everybody else. When Mrs Callahan tells her husband she doesn't *want* to come to terms with her loss, her death by astral projection feels strangely anticlimactic compared to the much more affecting display of despair shown minutes earlier. In plot terms, Trimble's murder seems predictable, even perfunctory - but within this theme of characters forced to live on beyond their inclination, there's almost something redemptive in it. And that makes the conclusion neat and satisfying.

Like 2Shy before it, it's not a great X-File; it's all a bit too obvious, and it doesn't really give Mulder and Scully enough to do. But it's very well written, and very well directed, and stands out as a superior piece of television on its own terms. (***1/2)

3.8, Oubliette

Air Date: Nov. 17, 1995
Writer: Charles Grant Craig
Director: Kim Manners

Summary When fifteen-year-old Amy Jacobs is abducted, Mulder and Scully meet Lucy Householder - a woman who was similarly kidnapped when she was eight and held captive for five years. Lucy displays a psychic connection to Amy's mind and physical experiences, and Amy's captor is soon identified as photographer's assistant Carl Wade - the same man who kidnapped Lucy seventeen years ago. Wade drowns Amy as the authorities close in, but Mulder shoots him dead. Amy seems beyond hope - until Lucy dies in her place, with five litres of water manifesting in her lungs.

Critique There is one key moment in Oubliette which demonstrates how far The X-Files has grown. It's a story in which Mulder develops a sympathy for a woman who as a girl was a kidnap victim, and it's a sympathy that the police and Scully feel is clouding his judgment. For half the episode the inevitable connection isn't spelled out, until Scully finally suggests that his empathy has something to do with Samantha's abduction. The quiet anger of Mulder's response, and the look of absolute betrayal on his face, is terrific. "Not everything I do or say or think or feel is about my sister," he tells her. The complexities of a man cannot be traced back to one key moment, and his pity for Lucy Householder is based upon a genuine horror of what she went through as a child and a wonder that she has survived in society since. It's a call for recognition that Mulder is a real character, not just a series of impulses which relate to some series bible backstory - it's the antithesis of episodes like Conduit, where the fate of a young girl is given extra depth only by making it a clumsy metaphor for Mulder's own mission.

And stripped of that, Oubliette has a sincerity that makes it emotionally raw and hard to watch. The kidnapper is played as an ordinary, even boring man without fanfare, without showman quirks. He's all the more unsettling because he's so terribly mundane. There's no glamour to our unwitting psychic either - Lucy is plain, dull, and shockingly unsympathetic. She has clearly no intention of helping Mulder solve the case, no interest in the young girl whose abduction so mirrors her own. She's selfish and unreasonable - a credible portrait, in fact, of an abused woman who has struggled back into the community. Even at the story's end she doesn't know why she's involved herself; her sacrifice, drowning on dry land as Amy is pulled from the lake, is all the more powerful because it doesn't feel like a conscious act of heroism.

Just as the episode refuses to trade on X-Files lore, it also denies the audience the usual bag of tricks and set pieces. This makes it a very atypical outing, and a very sober one. There is a strong supernatural element to the story, as Lucy begins to experience Amy's suffering, but it's so downplayed you could almost believe it's working as a metaphor for the woman coming to terms with her childhood ordeal. It's an episode which gets its scares not from goo or gore, but from an obsessed man taking flash photographs of a terrified captive in the dark, where you feel tension from whether he'll give into her pleas for a glass of water. The harsh tone is also unrelieved by any rapport between Mulder and Scully - this is the first in a number of stories where they're clearly adversarial. It's interesting that Scully doesn't disbelieve Mulder's theories because she can't intellectually accept them, as is the norm, but because she distrusts his emotional state. Duchovny responds by giving one of his best performances, appalled by the life Lucy has suffered and the coldness she receives in response.

This is deceptively very ordinary, but that is its power. It's perhaps unsurprising that Charles Grant Craig never wrote for the series again; this is too uncomfortable and too real to fit into the usual mould. Craig only uses the paranormal trappings of the show to reflect back on us all our normality, and the results aren't pretty. Difficult to watch, difficult to like, it's nevertheless one of the series' boldest and greatest achievements. (*****)

3.9, Nisei

Air Date: Nov. 24, 1995
Writers: Chris Carter, Howard Gordon, Frank Spotnitz
Director: David Nutter

Summary Suspecting that a mail-order video of an alien autopsy is genuine, Mulder and Scully backtrack the tape to a video piracy operation in Allentown, Pennsylvania. There the agents obtain files that identify members of the Mutual UFO Network, and also satellite photos of the *Talapus* - a salvage ship tasked with finding a Japanese submarine that sank during World War II.

Scully meets with the Network members - who are all women with alien abduction stories similar to her own - and learns that they too have removed pieces of metal implanted in their necks. Worryingly, Scully also learns that the abductees are progressively contracting an unidentified form of cancer.

Mulder finds the *Talapus* berthed in Newport News, Virginia, and also discovers a hidden alien spaceship that the *Talapus* evidently recovered from beneath the sea. Senator Matheson gives Mulder information suggesting that after World War II, Japanese scientists - much like their Nazi counterparts (3.2, Paper Clip) - relocated to America and worked to create a human-alien hybrid. It now seems that the government is moving to silence these men.

Mulder discovers traincars in Quinnimont, West Virginia, that are part of the government's secret railroad / alien autopsy operation. X phones Scully to warn that Mulder is in danger, just as Mulder jumps atop a moving train car. [To be continued.]

Critique Splitting the plot between Mulder and Scully only emphasises how thin the one part of the story is compared to the other. Mulder gets to run around an awful lot, and when he isn't running he's jumping over things or off things or on top of things. It's all quite breathless stuff, but if you take too close a look, it seems rather funny: an entire team of black ops are sent to a small boat, shouting and waving their guns about, but Mulder is still able to evade them and soundlessly dive into the sea without their noticing. And Mulder's attempts to catch a train, for all his running and panting, are to be foiled - he misses it twice! - but that's okay, because he can just jump on top of it from a bridge. It begins to feel all a little like Planes, Trains and Automobiles reinvented as an action movie. It's unfair to carp - it's exciting and directed with great energy (perhaps, at times, a little too much), and it's hard not to feel for the customs guard, who having got Mulder the file he wanted only has to look out of the window to see Mulder can't wait around because he's in Running Mode again. The opening teaser is brilliant, full of tension and real shocks, and the last image before the credits, of an alien being zipped up in a body bag, is great. And however much I might make fun, the cliffhanger looks great too, as Mulder rides off against X's warnings to find answers...

But for all the frantic to-ing and fro-ing, it's in the Scully sections of the story where we get revelations. The growing realisation that she has not been abducted by aliens but by human eugenicists is very powerful, and cleverly

underlines how this series of The X-Files is more concerned with human horror than the supernatural. As ever, Gillian Anderson is fantastic; having avoided confronting her memories earlier in the season, she is now face to face with women who recognise her and share her experiences. After all the big set pieces surrounding her abduction, and all the melodrama, there's something so down to earth about seeing ordinary housewives rattle their implants at her, looking for all the world as if they belong to a suburban book club. It makes the implications of what has been done to Scully so much more mundane and yet so much more shocking - as is emphasised by the realisation that these abductees are all dying of that most terrible and banal of all illnesses: cancer. The sequence where Scully watches and rewinds the video autopsy to look at the face of the man who experimented on her is one of the most subtly disturbing things the series has shown. Paper Clip introduced the idea of Axis powers involved in barbaric acts against prisoners of war; Nisei shows pictures of it, explicitly, and has the guts to suggest that it's still going on. The fantasy of a UFO-spotting show has turned into a drama in which one of its lead characters discovers they're the victims of a modern holocaust. It may not be tasteful, but it's not bland. (***1/2)

3.10, 731

Air Date: Dec. 1, 1995
Writer: Frank Spotnitz
Director: Rob Bowman

Summary Mulder finds himself aboard a train on which Dr Shiro Zama - one of the masterminds behind the government's alien experiments - is transporting a creature of some sort in a quarantine car. An assassin kills Zama, whereupon both Mulder and the assassin - who claims to work for the National Security Agency - find themselves trapped in the explosive-laden quarantine car, unable to open the door without Zama's pass code.

Aided by Agent Pendrell, Scully finds that her neck implant was designed to harvest neurological data, artificially replicating the brain's mental process to know the subject's every thought. They also discover that a Japanese firm made the chip, and that Dr Zama had it delivered to Hansen's Disease Research Facility in Perkey, West Virginia. Scully goes there and finds some former test-subjects, who claim the location was once a leper colony. She also encounters a senior member of the Syndicate (henceforth called "the Elder"), who explains that Dr Zama conducted his experiments on lepers and destitute members of society. Scully concludes that the government's clandestine experiments on the effects of radiation on human subjects - which supposedly ended in 1974 - were never discontinued, and that the quarantined creature isn't an alien. Mulder maintains that the creature is a alien-human hybrid, and the assassin says the creature is an attempt to create an army impervious to atomic and biological weapons. Scully phones Mulder with Zama's pass code, having gleaned it from the autopsy video, but the assassin attacks Mulder. X shows up and slays the assassin, then flees with Mulder as the train car explodes and kills the creature.

Critique   731 is one of the most satisfying mythology episodes. As ever, of course, it piles revelation upon revelation with almost dizzying gusto. Even by this stage of the series, not even a third into its run, the back story can barely be made sense of. But what makes these revelations stand out are that they're not based upon the introduction of new gimmicks - we're only a few weeks from black oil, folks, and the bees are just around the corner - but about altering our perception of what we've already got. For all the complications of the mytharc, the episode depends upon the most simple of narrative techniques - a countdown to a ticking bomb - and Mulder risks his life upon *his* understanding of the mythology over Scully's. He believes the conspiracy to be fundamentally about aliens. Scully has new information, and insists to Mulder that the creature in the train compartment is not an extraterrestrial, but a human victim of horrific experiments. If Scully's right, the bomb will dispose of the evidence. If Mulder's right, the powers that be will need to rescue the alien, and save his life in the process.

All the boundless energy of Mulder is contained for the majority of the episode within a single boxcar on a train. The X-Files does long scenes of claustrophobia well, as Duane Barry proved, and Duchovny and guest star Stephen

McHattie (playing the assassin) have a rapport which makes the increased desperation of the countdown gripping. But these scenes come as a relief to the sequences in which Scully explores the death camps. When she looks down into an open grave, where the genetically wounded have been left to rot, it's impossible not to conjure up images of concentration camp horrors. As I suggested before, the metaphor clearly runs the risk of being sick and frivolous. What makes it work - I think - is the very sincerity of the performances, and the way that the script too refuses to shy away from the allegory. In a strange way, it's because it's such an unsubtle statement of disgust, that man is capable of such atrocities, that gives it its purpose; if the teaser flinched from showing the American soldiers gunning down the unnamed in death squads, if it tried to put a sci-fi gloss on it, it'd be unthinkable. As it is, this feels like an angry indictment of twentieth-century politics: not only for the gunfire, but the dispassion with which the soldiers peer over the pit to check for survivors, and then so casually *turn back and walk to camera.*

The frustrating thing about The X-Files, of course, is that the people who wrote it had no idea how long the story would last. This new development would be a fitting turning point for the series, making the government conspiracy in which it's dabbled so much tougher and more potent. As it is, we've six and a half seasons still to run, and it's the nature of a programme built upon intrigue and suspense that these revelations will *have* to be overturned. Of course there will be aliens. The show would have no life without them. 731 therefore cannot help but offer a false perspective on what The X-Files means. But it doesn't matter for now; on its own terms, this is brave and furious work. Even if the plot will later have to be put into reverse gear, the images it evoked cannot be.

All this, and a lovely scene where Agent Pendrell shows he has a crush on Scully. What could be better? (*****)

3.11, Revelations

Air Date: Dec. 15, 1995
Writer: Kim Newton
Director: David Nutter

Summary   After a number of murders involving people who faked manifestations of stigmata, Mulder and Scully venture to Loveland, Ohio, and interview Kevin Kryder, a fifth grader whose palms started bleeding in class. Mulder suspects that Kevin is faking his wounds - a means of appeasing his father, who thinks Kevin is the son of God - but worries that the stigmata-killer will target him. Scully's religious background, however, makes her wonder if Kevin has a connection to the divine.

The killer - a recycling-plant owner named Simon Gates - kidnaps Kevin. Mulder rushes to intercept Gates at the airport, but Scully follows a hunch that she's meant to protect Kevin and finds them at Gates' recycling center. Gates pulls Kevin and himself into a giant paper shredder; Gates dies, but Scully finds Kevin clinging to a platform, even as wounds on his palms instantly heal.

Critique   This is a showcase for Gillian Anderson, and she runs with a script which gives her ample opportunity to reflect upon Scully's beliefs and doubts. The final scene in particular, where she sits in the confessional and tries to pick up the remnants of her Catholic faith, gives her a chance to shine.

But for all the stigmata and bleeding wounds, this is a peculiarly bloodless episode. It asks an important question: why can a series like this feel comfortable depicting scenes of the secular paranormal, but shy away from the unexplained nature of miracles? And I'm not really sure it has to wit to provide a satisfactory answer. It's all very well making Scully do a volte face, and become the one who believes, the one who's prepared to open her mind to extreme possibility. But by making Mulder *so* sceptical in response, and so hostile to Scully's journey, it feels less like an analysis of faith and its power, and more like a strange "body twist" storyline. Revelations wants to be an earnest discussion of religion, and the way in which a twentieth-century society based on science can interpret it - but in all the scenes where that can be examined, it looks like nothing more than Freaky Friday. That final scene in the confessional is very good - but it's a cheat, because by having Scully say out loud that she can no longer discuss the themes of the episode with Mulder, she denies him his own journey within the story. And it should have been as much Mulder's tale as Scully's - if the question is raised of how a sceptical scientist can rationalise matters of faith, then surely it's as valuable to ask why a freethinking believer like Mulder should be so aggressive to it?

This may not have mattered had there been emotion elsewhere in the episode. But Kevin (yes, there's a story about a Second Coming, and he's called Kevin, but it isn't a comedy) shows precious little passion for anything. In the scene following his mother's death, you have to forcibly remind yourself that she hasn't just grazed her knee, he seems so fundamentally disinterested. There are people out there who want to save Kevin, and there are those who want to harm him - but it's only Scully, believing she may have been chosen by God as his protector, who seems to take what's going on personally. The story then denies her a climax; she finds Kevin in a paper mill, but is barely involved in the final struggle to save him. Kenneth Welsh throws himself and the kid into a paper feeder, and the child survives by hanging onto the sides. When Scully can't even look after the kid when he's washing in the bathroom, when two minutes after turning her back on her charge he's abducted, it's hard to see quite what message God might have for her.

And if you're going to do an episode about the religious paranormal, I'd argue you have to be slightly more careful than in your average X-File. In humdrum episodes you might buy a villain who can burn with his hands - even though no line of explanation is ever offered. But you'd be hard pushed to justify dramatically a boy who can be in two places at the same time - for one helpful scene only! - because Scully points out one barely remembered saint could do it. Take a serious subject by all means, but then take the subject seriously. Give it more rigour than you'd normally need to. Or else you risk offending the audience - or, even worse, as here, just boring them. (**)

3.12, War of the Coprophages

Air Date: Jan. 5, 1996
Writer: Darin Morgan
Director: Kim Manners

Summary In the sedate town of Miller's Grove, Massachusetts, swarming cockroaches kill an exterminator. Mulder learns from Bambi Berenbaum, an employee for the USDA Research Service, that the government established a research facility in Grover's Mill to study cockroaches. Scully and Berenbaum both suspect that a type of cockroach that's aggressive towards humans has been imported into the area.

Mulder discovers a metallic cockroach and takes it to Dr Alexander Ivanov, a robotics expert who thinks it could be a reconnaissance device sent by aliens. Scully, meanwhile, focuses her suspicion on Dr Jeff Eckerle, an alternative fuel scientist she believes transported a species of vicious dung-eaters into the area. Mulder confronts Eckerle, who tries to shoot him and thereby ignites a source of methane gas. The resultant explosion kills Eckerle and obliterates the research facility.

Critique Darin Morgan's previous two X-Files comedies worked by having Mulder and Scully as the straight guys to the larger than life characters around them. War of the Coprophages looks inwards, and finds hilarity within the FBI agents themselves. We have a Scully who - whilst washing the dog or cleaning her gun or doing sundry things to while away her weekend - finds a rational explanation each time a Mulder makes her a frantic phone call about killer cockroaches. We see Mulder beg for Scully's assistance - until such time as he meets *another* scientist, called Bambi of all things, and can give Scully's attentions the brush off with "not now"s and "whatever"s. It's the methodical and self-obsessed characters writ large. And both Anderson and Duchovny reveal a comic timing which is absolutely faultless.

Like Humbug before it, there may not be much point to hang these jokes on. But unlike Humbug, that pointlessness is part of the point - Mulder is chasing at first a monster story which gets shot down in flames, and then an alien story which keeps contradicting his own experiences. (The way he listens to Bambi's theory that all UFO sightings are nothing more than insects - or that alien visitors will be robot bugs and not the greys of science fiction - is with a sort of resigned patience that is very funny.) Anticipating Jose Chung's From Outer Space, this is a story all about perspective changing - and does with comic effect what 731 did two weeks ago much more grimly. Morgan allows us some moments of gross-out horror, some of which are truly unnerving - and all of which echo classic moments from the series. (My favourite must be the cockroach crawling under the skin, which goes back as far as Ice.) But he has his cake and eats it too: what we think of as supernatural can be explained by allergy, or drug psychosis, or even straining too hard on the toilet. Morgan names the town Miller's Grove, a conscious reference to Grover's Mill, the location of the Martian landing in Orson Welles' radio version of War of the Worlds - and thereby evokes the hysterical reaction which greeted the broadcast where listeners thought the fiction was real. Watching the town panic is very funny, but there's a serious point to be made here too - shows like The X-Files, which pride themselves on their paranoia, are deliberately creating a state where viewers will see conspiracies and intrigues that don't exist. Maybe accidentally, Morgan puts his finger on the direction of Season Three - that there's something much more human and mundane behind the scenes. And that Mulder's quest, even his FBI presence in Miller's Grove, might aggravate the tension, and create the very smokescreen that the authorities want.

It's not *too* serious a point, though. This is an episode, after all, in which Mulder and Scully get covered in exploding shit. Yes, it's *that* good. (*****)

3.13, Syzygy

Air Date: Jan. 26, 1996
Writer: Chris Carter
Director: Rob Bowman

Summary Mulder and Scully link a number of strange deaths in the town of Comity to Terri Roberts and Margi Kleinjan - two girls who appear to have telekinetic powers. For a fee, an astrologer named Madame Zirinka tells Mulder that an impending planetary alignment set for January 12th means a) that everyone in town is acting a bit goofy, and b) that cosmic energy will focus on people born in 1979.

Margi and Terri vie for a boy - Scott Simmons, who's impaled to death on a garage door - and unleash their telekinetic powers at one another. A maelstrom wreaks havoc on the town police station until Scully shoves the girls into an interrogation room. After the planetary alignment ends at midnight, the girls lose their powers and become two perfectly ordinary teenagers.

Critique It's a comedy X-File! It features a town which is driven to panicked hysteria. Mulder and Scully snap at each other and parody their characters. Scully gets very jealous about Mulder and a blonde woman... but this episode has no cockroaches in, and little of Darin Morgan's wit.

Syzygy certainly isn't helped by being the episode after War of the Coprophages, to which it bears more than a passing resemblance. But I'm not sure that even scheduled more sensitively this would have been a success. It may replay some of the jokes seen in last week's story, but it lacks the tone that gave them a context. War of the Coprophages had a spot-on confidence, it knew *precisely* what it was doing. Syzygy is skittish and inconsistent, it jars, it misses beats. To be fair, that's exactly the point - this is a tale about misalignment, about people not connecting. But - and it's a big "but" - comedy is such a fragile thing, and it really needs precision control. You really only laugh when the comedian makes you feel comfortable with his talent, and Syzygy deliberately flouts that; it'd much rather you squirmed.

And, as a result, it's simply not very funny. A typical X-File can work on many levels - it can be thoughtful, or scary, or exciting. If it's going to plump for comedy, however clever the intent, it still pretty much needs to be able to make you laugh. The Mulder / Scully interplay is rather witty, but the style is too cruel and hectoring to raise a smile. Some of the characters have comic potential - the astrologer who doesn't trust the federal government enough to talk to Mulder until his credit card clears, or the paediatrician who is hiding not Satanism but transvestitism. But they're robbed of a proper context in which they can amuse, because the story is so intent on heightening everything that it forgets to give them someone normal to play against. Cosmic forces or not, Detective White should not be the most gullible woman in the US police force; by playing her as stupid, the episode becomes a cartoon, and Scully's jealousy of a woman that dense demeans her.

We keep on getting clips of the Keystone Kops on television - on every channel in fact, which is a joke that's never set up or explained. The finale in the police station is clearly intended to be a throwback to this. But slapstick and farce demand pace and energy, and Syzygy's problem is that it's all rather laboured. This is because the story offers no surprises. We know the villains are a couple of cheerleaders from the teaser, and when the plotline is thuddingly predictable the comedy gets sucked out.

That said, no episode which has the central conceit that spiteful teenage girls are evil can be entirely bad - it's what I always suspected during sixth form. Margi and Terri are thoroughly irritating, right down to their superficial Valley-girl speak, but that is clearly intentional. And as hard as it is to watch, it's interesting to see the subtle schisms between Mulder and Scully that have played out over the last few episodes made large and obvious. Nisei and 731 showed how the two agents are now fundamentally at odds with their understanding of the mythology storyline, and the episodes surrounding anticipated it (Oubliette) or developed it (Revelations, War of the Coprophages). It's disconcerting to see something which has been so subtly handled now dressed up in neon lights with an arrowed sign pointing towards it - but it's fascinating too. Chris Carter has established the house style of The X-Files as something which plays softly softly and buries itself within ambiguity - for one week only, as the stars are in sync, he takes the lid off. Anderson and Duchovny clearly enjoyed the comic exploration of their relationship last week; it's to their credit that they make the more callous treatment of it here so hard to stomach. That's the best joke about Syzygy - that its biggest running gag could only have worked had the show

around it been worse and not made us care so much about its characters. (**)

3.14, Grotesque

Air Date: Feb. 2, 1996
Writer: Howard Gordon
Director: Kim Manners

Summary   Agents Bill Patterson and Greg Nemhauser arrest John Mostow, an art student they believe has been a serial killer for three years. But when the deaths continue, Mulder tells Scully that when he and Patterson were students together, Patterson believed that an investigator could best catch monsters by becoming one himself.

Mostow claims that a dark spirit possessed him and made him commit the murders. Mulder and Scully subsequently find Mostow's apartment filled with sculptures and paintings of gargoyles. When Nemhauser's body is found smothered in clay, Mulder spies clay on Patterson's hands and accuses him of so intently studying Mostow that he too has become a killer. Mulder grapples with Patterson, briefly glimpsing him as a gargoyle, but ultimately arrests him.

Critique   The idea that one can best catch a killer by getting inside his head is a fairly familiar one. It's a form of psychological profiling that predicts the advent of Millennium later in the year. And, once that concept is introduced, it's not a premise that is going to offer the plot many twists or turns. But that is not its point. Because Grotesque certainly surprises, and shocks, and even appals - this is the closest The X-Files ever gets to staring into the face of insanity.

There's an attempt at a red herring, suggesting Nemhauser may have been infected by a bite and become possessed. But where this episode is so clever is that it uses the clichés of a standard X-Files plot, with its easy acceptance of the supernatural, to produce a story which is ever more frightening for being so psychological and *real*. Like Irresistible last year, this is The X-Files grown up, using its predilection for the paranormal to wrongfoot us into thinking this is something safe and fantastic, when it's really a study of the potential for evil within us all.

Howard Gordon's script is a masterpiece of brooding terror - a terror not often felt in The X-Files, because it has less to do with jolts of violence than the subversion of character. After two episodes which have flipped Mulder and Scully's personas to comic effect, it's fascinating to see one where Mulder, to find a murderer, is prepared to lose his identity completely within that killer's obsession. Mostow claims that there is a demon living inside him, but for once that plays out entirely as metaphor. Agent Patterson has spent three years trying to catch Mostow, and now he's succeeded, he has so much of Mostow's anger and madness inside him that he's compelled to reenact the same crimes. To catch Mostow, he himself had to drop into the abyss; he calls Mulder to the case to punish his favourite pupil, to invite him to drop into the abyss himself. You get a sense of what Mulder must have been like as the genius of his youth, an agent so driven that he was prepared to sacrifice his own sanity in order to understand a crime. This is why he now pushes Scully away - why she's forced to question his mental state - and how she is able, at last, to rescue him from drowning in the same evil that Patterson has. It's the fact that Mulder *has* a Scully that saves his soul - and that Patterson never had one that damns him.

David Duchovny is extraordinary here, giving his best performance yet seen in the series. The sequence in which he demands information of Mostow, *needs* to find the demon so much he punches him in frustration, is acted with a controlled frenzy that is startling - it's a shock when Mostow, through a mouthful of blood, tells Mulder that the monster may already be inside him. Duchovny doesn't go for histrionics; he understands entirely the tone of this story, that it isn't plot-driven but a mood piece. In this, he's superbly supported by Mark Snow's mournful score and John Bartley's cinematography of reds and blues.

If this were simply the study of a serial killer, it'd be a cut price Silence of the Lambs. But, typical of this season, Mostow is no Hannibal Lecter but a terrified little man lost in a delusion. And the story callously has no time to waste on him - it's a study instead of Mulder, surrounding himself with the gargoyles, living

and breathing and becoming the evil he wants to touch. As such its wider concerns are less about crime profiling than about obsession itself. The extraordinary teaser emphasises that, as Mostow the artist labours over his still-life drawing, all charcoal and blood and passion, the scratching across the canvas sounding manic and desperate. In story terms, it takes a similar idea to Season One's Lazarus - and it's a measure of how far the series has grown that that feels childish and silly in comparison. (*****)

3.15, Piper Maru

Air Date: Feb. 9, 1996
Writers: Frank Spotnitz, Chris Carter
Director: Rob Bowman

Summary Working from the salvage ship *Piper Maru*, a diver named Bernard Gauthier examines a submerged World War II fighter plane and finds the pilot still alive, his eyes swilling with a strange black oil. Every crewmember save Gauthier soon contracts radiation sickness, and Mulder notes that the *Piper Maru* was operating in the same area as the *Talapus* (3.9, Nisei).

Now infected with the "black oil" from the pilot, Gauthier returns home to San Francisco. Mulder and Scully question him, but not before the oily substance transfers into Gauthier's wife Joan, and Gauthier loses all memory of the incident.

Mulder shadows Geraldine Kallenchuk - the manager of the salvage brokerage - to Hong Kong, but Krycek murders her. In Washington, D.C., the assassin who killed Melissa Scully shoots Skinner, hospitalising him. Mulder intercepts Krycek at the airport and demands the stolen data in Krycek's possession (3.2, Paper Clip). Krycek agrees to lead Mulder to its location in Washington, D.C. - but Joan approaches Krycek in private, and the black oil transfers into him. [To be continued.]

Critique I'll admit it, I'm not an expert on kids. I've not had one of my own. But I think if I did, I'd want to give it a name that would ensure it'd not get beaten up in the school playground; life can be hard enough as it is without having a silly monicker to carry about for the rest of your natural. But when Gillian Anderson named her little baby Piper Maru, and Chris Carter promised he'd name an episode after her, he at least lucked out. After all, Anderson might have gone down a more conventional route, and Carter would have been stuck calling this episode "Trish".

Overall, this is pretty heavy going. Piper Maru feels such an awkward mix of plotlines that stutter and stall and never quite come to life. Scully spends the episode on exposition detail - she meets a friend of her father's, who just happens to be the one survivor of a misadventure in the Pacific Ocean fifty years ago. The black and white flashbacks are quite stylish - and there's something exciting about a mutiny - but too much of the tale is told in guilt-ridden monologue. Scully fills up the rest of the hour getting angry about her sister's murder - as if she just *knows* it's a mytharc episode, so it's time to let that particular trauma bubble to the surface once more - and getting tearful with nostalgia about playing hopscotch at a naval base. Gillian Anderson makes it all work, but there's very little heart to much of this.

And, as these mythology stories tend to play out, Mulder pursues his side of the investigation by running around a lot. This time he runs so far he ends up in Hong Kong; it's nice that The X-Files is aiming for a more international flavour, but since the scenes which determine the location consist of little more than people eating noodles, it all feels somewhat arbitrary. The best guest appearance is Jo Bates as the coolly amoral Geraldine Kallenchuk - she's gunned down, though, just as soon as we meet Krycek, and that's rather a pity. (It does make for a great sequence, however, leaving Mulder handcuffed to a dead body on the other side of a locked door, with her killer moving ever closer towards him.) It's good to see Krycek again, but as soon as we do it's all talk about the digital tape we last heard mentioned in Paper Clip; the viewer is just expected to remember the macguffins of episodes broadcast four months previously with no context given. And it's another element thrown into the confusing mix.

Oh, and Skinner gets shot. I like the Skinner scenes, actually. They're to the point. There's little more pointed than a bullet to the stomach.

Piper Maru is the first of a two-parter, of course, and relies upon an audience's willingness to tune in the week following to see whether something more edifying can be pieced together. There are a few good set pieces, mostly involving eyes clouding over during alien possession, and that might persuade them. But if I were Gillian Anderson's daughter, I'd probably be a bit miffed to share a name with such a lacklustre episode. I think she'd have been better off if she'd been called Grotesque - now that was a good one. (**)

3.16, Apocrypha

Air Date: Feb. 16, 1996
Writers: Frank Spotnitz, Chris Carter
Director: Kim Manners

Summary Upon returning to Washington D.C., Krycek escapes after his body emits a blinding light. Mulder conjectures that the "black oil" is a medium by which an extraterrestrial entity can move from host to host. Meanwhile, Scully finds forensic evidence proving that Skinner's assailant was Louis Cardinal, the same man who killed her sister.

Krycek gives the Cigarette Smoking Man the stolen data in exchange for the location of the salvaged UFO. Mulder arranges a meeting with the Well-Manicured Man, who says that American pilots downed the alien spaceship in World War II, but the radiation hazard made retrieval impossible.

Scully arrests Cardinal when he tries to finish off Skinner, and makes him reveal that Krycek is heading for an abandoned missile site near Bismarck, North Dakota. She and Mulder rush there, but the Cigarette Smoking Man's soldiers prevent them from investigating further. The black oil exits Krycek's body and returns to its spaceship, leaving Krycek trapped inside a missile silo. Later, Mulder informs Scully that Cardinal has been killed in his cell, the death made to look like suicide.

Critique I'm not convinced that this episode is much of an improvement.

Good things: most of the scenes with the Cigarette Smoking Man. There's a marvellous bit of black comedy where he stands over a man suffering from radiation sickness, and instructs the doctor to burn the body - only to be reminded that the patient hasn't died yet. And we catch a further glimpse of this little man, sitting at home on his own drinking and smoking and watching black and white movies, waiting for the conspiracy to order him to commit further acts of evil. I also enjoyed the sequences where it makes clear that the cliché of alien possession is not necessarily a pleasant thing to be freed from - the scene where the black oil slowly pours out from all the orifices on Krycek's face is sickening. And the episode is bookended by two terrific moments - the shock of seeing a young Bill Mulder and Smoking Man back in the 1950s already concealing the truth, and the horror of Krycek buried alive inside a silo, screaming for help with no-one to hear.

But after the way that 731 found a moral depth to the mythology stories, this all feels very much like an empty runaround. Attention is given to the trivial; we're sold the capture of Luis Cardinal as some sort of climax, but he's utterly unimportant, a henchman who has been given barely a handful of lives over his short time on the series. (He's also not much of a threat, as he surely must be the worst assassin ever employed. He kills the wrong Scully sister, he fails to kill Krycek. He only wounds Skinner at point-blank range, and gets captured when he returns to finish the job. Mulder supposes that Cardinal's death in the cell is the work of the conspiracy group, but he's so incompetent that it's just possible he fell over shaving.) Scully puts her finger on it later in the graveyard, when she feels empty after Cardinal's capture, reflecting that there's no sense of justice. Why should there be? The X-Files has this habit of turning walk-on parts into characters of greater significance than they deserve; it worked last year in Red Museum when the killer of Deep Throat reappeared, because it was a shock which detoured the story. But here, for all that Anderson excels at the moment of coming face to face with Melissa's murderer, it's nothing but smoke and mirrors.

There's something just a little bit complacent about this episode. There are fan-pleasing appearances from the Lone Gunmen, skating around an ice rink for a bit of comic relief. There's a moment in which Mulder thanks Skinner for his support, which somehow feels wrong - Skinner may have given the X-Files the tacit help that endangered his life, but his character depends upon the authority that Mulder reacts against. And the Syndicate members really do seem to do nothing but sit around in the same darkened room all day looking concerned - what seemed shady and mysterious at the beginning of the season now looks just a little comical. Don't they have homes to go to? (**)

3.17, Pusher

Air Date: Feb. 23, 1996
Writer: Vince Gilligan
Director: Rob Bowman

Summary   Agent Frank Burst asks for Mulder and Scully's help in capturing "the Pusher", a serial killer who can directly control the minds of others. The Pusher is identified as Robert Modell, a for-hire assassin who places ads in magazines. Scully finds Modell's medication, and theorises that his powers stem from a brain tumour that will eventually kill him. His murder spree, it seems, is just a final kick of excitement.

Modell mentally commands Burst to have a heart attack, killing him. Mulder and Scully corner Modell in a hospital, but Modell compels Mulder to play Russian roulette with himself and Scully. By setting off the fire alarm, Scully breaks Modell's concentration and facilitates his capture, leaving him a dying shell of a man.

Critique   Like Robert Modell himself, the pusher of the title, this is an episode that seems ordinary and forgettable enough to begin with, but slowly insinuates itself into your head. It takes a typical X-Files premise - this time the supernatural gift our villain has is that he can control other people's wills - but acts against type by making Modell not a superman after all but something of a loser. This is a person who has amounted to nothing his entire life, and only through a brain tumour is given a psychic ability as he dies. Rather than be cured, he chooses instead to be special, to have a purpose. Robert Wisden's performance as Modell is spot on: he appears to have charisma in spades, but it's a *borrowed* charisma, a charm that isn't really his.

All his talk of samurai codes is just a fantasy - here is a man who even when turned into something unique is still so shallow, he needs to pretend to be a martial arts hero. As such, this is one of the best examples of the Season Three theme, that of evil being a mundane and human and somewhat pathetic thing. The last scene is just beautiful, as Scully turns away from Modell dismissively, unwilling to waste any more time upon the little man who wanted to be big. He could be the older brother of D.P.O., or the cousin of the murderer in Clyde Bruckman's Final Repose seeking an identity - and it's through people like him, the weak ones who pretend to be strong but have so little imagination, that the atrocities seen in 731 are allowed to happen.

The plot is a little ungainly at first, as it tries to play a Dirty Harry on us and send Mulder scurrying after a serial killer's obscure clues. But the moments of hypnotised suicide are wonderful, Modell being cruel to the point of allowing his victims enough consciousness so that they can experience the horror of setting themselves on fire. It's the perfect slice of the macabre that we watch portly Agent Burst being talked into a heart attack over the phone, and what provides the twist of the knife is that he dies for nothing, staying on the phone long enough that Modell's call can be traced, a number Modell gives up perfectly cheerfully when asked. The runaround chasing of the villain is a tad formulaic, maybe, but it's easy to argue this is just an example of Modell's own childish lack of imagination. But once he's caught in a hospital the story takes on a tremendous electricity, the tension ratcheted up to the extreme. What's surprising is that after so many episodes in which a schism has been placed between Mulder and Scully, Pusher becomes a story about how one can save the other. Scully's concern for Mulder going in to confront Modell on his own is palpable - and the sequence where she sees on camera that her partner has been ambushed at gunpoint is a delicious shock moment. The Russian roulette scene is one of the great set pieces in the entirety of The X-Files, as a grimly silent Mulder is pulled as a puppet between Modell's evil influence and Scully's supportive pleas. That he would rather shoot himself than pull the trigger on Scully is telling, and it's only as he allows her to cause a distraction that Mulder can shoot at

Modell instead. A story about a mediocrity who perversely can control the lives of those greater than himself, this becomes a tale of how Mulder and Scully as a *team* are able to defeat him.

Vince Gilligan's dialogue is witty and clever and captures the comic rapport between Mulder and Scully that has only been handled as well by Darin Morgan. And he has the invention to take a somewhat hackneyed idea and get all the depth from it that he can. His debut script, Soft Light, showed real promise; this sophomore effort is a triumph. (*****)

3.18, Teso Dos Bichos

Air Date: March 8, 1996
Writer: John Shiban
Director: Kim Manners

Summary   At the Teso Dos Bichos site in Ecuador, a team of excavators unearth an urn containing the remains of a female shaman. The urn is taken to the Museum of Natural History in Boston, where Dr Alonso Bilac - failing to convince his fellows that the item is sacred to the Secona Indian tribe - ritualistically invokes a jaguar-like spirit that starts murdering the team members. Mulder and Scully investigate the strange deaths, and Bilac disappears into the tunnels beneath the museum. The agents soon find him dead in an air vent as dozens of house cats mass in the tunnels. Mulder and Scully escape, and no sign is found of the evil cats afterward. Reassuringly, Mulder learns that the State Department has decided to return the urn to its native land.

Critique   Actually, the much derided sequence of the killer kitty cats isn't *that* badly handled. The editing is quick, the lighting suitably dark, and even though they might have picked cats that looked a tad more feral, there have been worse monsters on show. So it's a cautious thumbs up for the cats. Well done, all. Now - what about this disaster of an episode that surrounds them?

Earlier in the season, John Shiban took an X-Files staple story and found something fresh to bring out from within it. That's not true here. This is a retread of a cursed mummy movie without a mummy in it, in which museum staff are being picked off one by one by a jaguar spirit until an artefact is returned to its home country. It needed *something* to give it a little flavour of its own. A sense of irony, maybe. Instead we've got a plotline which is turgid and predictable, characters so wafer-thin they're merely defined by their jobs, and dialogue that is at best functional, at worst banal.

It's not Shiban's fault that the main guest star, Vic Trevino, recites every deathly line with the same languorous pace. He's playing a man who uses hallucinogenics to commune with an Ecuadorian god - as you do - and interprets the stoned part of the performance a little too well. It probably *is* Shiban's fault that Anderson and Duchovny barely make an effort here, looking bored and unconvinced by the proceedings. Only Janne Mortil puts in a little effort as graduate student Mona Wustner, and gets ripped apart by pussy cats for her pains.

These days The X-Files makes bad stories from time to time; it's what you'd expect from a series which is so obviously experimenting, not every idea can pay off. This is the first time since Season One, though, that a script has been produced that is this achingly unambitious. There's really no excuse for this sort of thing by now. (*)

3.19, Hell Money

Air Date: March 29, 1996
Writer: Jeff Vlaming
Director: Tucker Gates

Summary   When a man is burned alive in an oven in San Francisco's Chinatown district, Mulder and Scully coordinate their investigation with Detective Glen Chao. They discover a secret gambling operation in which players draw tiles from jade vases in the hopes of winning prize money, but must surrender some or all of their organs if they lose. One such player, Shuyang Hsin, tries to win money for his daughter's leukemia treatments, but ends up losing an eye.

The agents come to realise that Chao - torn between his duty and his Chinese heritage - is either covering for the operation or directly aiding it. They discover several freezers filled with human organs, unaware that another game is in progress. Hsin loses, but Chao suddenly smash-es one of the jade vases and reveals that the game is rigged, triggering a brawl. Chao kills one of the men intent on taking more organs from Hsin; Mulder and Scully arrest Chao and the operation's ring-leader. Those involved keep quiet about the affair, prompting the ring-leader's release. Chao is later captured and burned alive.

Critique   This is a very unpopular episode, and it isn't hard to see why: for starters, it's not really an X-File at all. Whereas there have been episodes (like Irresistible and Grotesque) which turn out eventually to have no supernatural elements, the trick in the storytelling is always that edge that they *might* be there. Hell Money doesn't provide us with an easy target, there's no serial killing spree to stop. Instead there's a process of routine exploitation going on, as unglamorous as it is ugly, and that's a less interesting thing to pit our heroes up against. And it's arguable too whether Mulder and Scully make that much of a difference. They show up, they judge, they leave again - and the banal evil of a lottery of body parts carries on, protected by a culture which hides it behind a wall of silence.

But it'd be unfair, I think, to regard any of these factors as mistakes. There are several stories in which Mulder and Scully spend too much time on the sidelines observing - the most recent offender, for example, is The List. That was an example of narrative laziness, and that's really not what's happening here. The script hasn't forgotten the FBI agents, it's instead making a point about their irrelevance. Detective Chao points out that they're coming at the Chinese culture altogether too bluntly, that they think all the words and symbols they see can be translated, that the real meaning behind what a society does can be discovered so easily. They will always be nothing but observers; Chao, however, has to straddle both his police work and his heritage. We've seen examples of this before - most notably in Shapes, of all things - but it's fascinating here because it turns the tables back on our heroes. We're used to seeing them walk merrily through many a plotline interpreting the folklore and myths of other nations as if they've a God-given right to do so; only last week, Teso dos Bichos provided a ver-

---

sion of it to stultifying effect. Seen from Chao's point of view, Mulder and Scully seem clumsy and arrogant. And by implication, the audience are made to feel just as arrogant - a bold decision is taken to isolate us still further by having so much of the dialogue subtitled from Cantonese, keeping us at one more remove from the characters. It's fascinating to see, in a series about aliens, how Mulder and Scully tackle an alien culture - and fare so badly. The sequence where they turn upon Chao in his office and interrogate him is profoundly unfair, and one week away from an episode which again turns upon our perceptions of our heroes, makes them seem badgering and unsympathetic. Chao may be corrupt, he might take payment from a gambling ring, but one senses he is caught miserably between being born American and being of Chinese descent - he's trying to fit into both cultures at the same time. When he turns upon the gamblers, it isn't that he finds the idea of a game trafficking in body organs necessarily *wrong*; it's that the game is rigged that makes him disgusted. Its existence isn't the issue, just its unfairness.

It's a hard episode to love. The tone is as black and as cynical as we've ever seen in the series. The premise may be macabre, but the style is resigned and defeated. It's interesting too, in a season in which the idea of human experimentation has been broached, and innocents are reduced to "merchandise", to have a story where that quite literally becomes true. The story does drag a little; although BD Wong is excellent as Chao, some of his supporting players labour the Cantonese very badly, and difficult scenes of subtitles become all the more strained. Lucy Liu, long before she became famous as a Charlie's Angel, is guilty of this - an even worse offender is Michael Yama as her father. There are also few of the trademark set pieces we expect in an X-Files story. An autopsy in which a live frog pushes out from a stomach makes a notable exception. Again, you feel the lack of shocks is rather the point of this deliberately dreary story, but it does mean that a plot which so atypically sidelines our heroes as much as this one does is doing itself no favours by further testing the audience's patience.

It's not a story you'd want to see too often, and it's not an experiment you'd want repeated. But however cold its heart is, Hell Money is sin-cere and purposeful. Any lottery can be regarded as a way to make the poor poorer and a minority very rich indeed. When the lottery ticket you're buying costs you not just an arm and a leg, but maybe your eyeball and a slice of your liver, its evils are all the more obvious. This episode is a flawed gem. (****)

3.20, Jose Chung's From Outer Space

Air Date: April 12, 1996
Writer: Darin Morgan
Director: Rob Bowman

Summary   Scully agrees to meet with Jose Chung - one of her favorite authors, who's writing a gimmicky book about alien abduction - to tell him about a recent case involving teenagers: Chrissy Girogio and her boyfriend Harold Lamb. The pair vanished for a time, then reappeared and claimed aliens had abducted them. Their accounts of the incident kept changing, to the point that Mulder believed aliens were responsible, but Scully suspected Chrissy was traumatized from being sexually assaulted.

A dead man, Major Robert Vallee, was soon found in an alien costume. Mulder wondered if the military was faking UFO flights to fool invading forces, but another officer, Lieutenant Jack Sheaffer, claimed that aliens had indeed taken him and the teens. Whatever the truth, unidentified men in black made off with evidence pertaining to the case. Mulder tells Chung that publishing an account of this incident will only serve to humiliate those involved, but Chung opts to finish the book anyway.

Critique   Widely touted as The X-Files' greatest episode, this is writer Darin Morgan's masterwork, his final script for a series to which he introduced irony, self-awareness and a willingness to explore beyond the constraints of traditional storytelling. He regards it as his best story for the programme, the one that best sums up his approach, and it's certainly true that it's stuffed full of more ideas and cleverer tricks than you might have thought possible within forty-five minutes' screen time. It's Morgan's take on The X-Files writ large - a series in which the truth palpably *isn't* out there, because it's the series' very intention to celebrate ambiguity.

It is, as I say, very clever. It's also pretentious, overwritten, and desperately self-indulgent. Jose Chung is the sort of thing you get when you find an extremely talented writer and tell him he's a genius once too often. Clyde Bruckman's Final Repose and War of the Coprophages, as is Morgan's style, are about the ways stories work, about how there's a veneer of artifice to everything within them that we see or remember. If memory is subjective, then so must be the tales we tell. The X-Files is the perfect stamping ground for Morgan to explore these themes, because subjectivity is so much part of its bread and butter, even in the most familiar and hackneyed monster of the week plot. The difference between Clyde Bruckman and Coprophages is that in exploring these post-modern attitudes to narrative reality, they never forget that there's an audience out there watching who need to be entertained. The sleight of hand tricks in both stories are delightful, because however pessimistic Morgan's messages about fate and the way people behave, there's a fundamental sweetness to the comedy. You care for Bruckman, even if he himself sees his life as an abject failure. You care for Mulder and Scully in Coprophages, even if their stereotypical natures are being held up for ridicule.

This episode is heartless in comparison. It's not that its outlook on life is harsher, or its treatment of characters more jaded. (In fact, there's an innocence to Blaine Faulkner, who *wants* to be abducted so he need never find a job, that is very touching.) It's simply that with all the pyrotechnics of Morgan's structure there really isn't much *room* for heart. Some of the gags are great. The opening teaser is note perfect, as apparent aliens echo the incredulity of the humans they're abducting when they too have a UFO encounter. And there's a whole raft of one-liners so skilful and well judged; Morgan has a tremendous gift for comedy. But comedy is largely about timing, and there's such a greedy attempt to cram as much into this episode as possible, to make it his final masterstroke, that his jokes have no space to breathe. And it was always the jokes which humanised Morgan's characters - if they're not working, they just look like puppets of the writer. Detective Manners becomes a running gag of censored

expletives, the Man in Black drowns within his verbose speech patterns. Morgan wants to write a story which reveals its secrets like a series of Russian dolls, and that's great - but there *aren't* any secrets to reveal, except for the nature of that structure itself. And once that's been established, that Morgan wants to emphasise an ever more fractured set of perspectives, you look for something more tangible to grab hold of. A plot, a character, a moment of emotion, anything. And there's little there.

I think the heart of the problem is that Charles Nelson Reilly simply isn't as good as Peter Boyle. Chung has much of the same show-stopping brio as Boyle's Clyde Bruckman - but Reilly's performance is arch and knowing, he plays the joke, he doesn't let himself *be* the joke. With Scullys and Mulders being deliberately misremembered and misrepresented according to different observers, you need someone to anchor the story, and Chung just isn't credible enough. The most real characters in this episode are the two teenagers on a date. And it's within them that I find the humanity that I'm looking for. Bookending this tale is a very sweet love story, of a fledgeling relationship utterly destroyed by big government and alien conspiracies and memory implants. At the end, Chrissy has come to realise she's not a victim of date rape at the hands of hapless Harold - but he's irrelevant to her now, her experiences have inspired her to greater causes than romance. He may still profess his love, but it looks trivial beside the ever-complicated subterfuge of the story. It's a great ending. It also, I think, sums up my problem with Jose Chung's From Outer Space, which finds simple love far less interesting than displays of literary flair. This manifestly *isn't* a case of the Emperor's New Clothes; the fanbase is right - this is dazzling and brilliant, the episode *is* as clever as it thinks it is. I just don't care very much. (**)

3.21, Avatar

Air Date: April 26, 1996
Story: David Duchovny, Howard Gordon
Teleplay: Howard Gordon
Director: James Charleston

Summary With his divorce pending, Skinner meets a woman - Carina Sayles - in a hotel lounge and winds up spending the night with her. Skinner experiences the image of a crone as he and Sayles have sex, then awakens to find Sayles dead. He's suspected of having killed Sayles, and Mulder wonders if forces within the government are trying to discredit Skinner and remove him from the FBI. Mulder also considers the possibility that the crone - which has appeared in Skinner's dreams since he served in Vietnam - is a malevolent spirit (a "succubus") that's preying upon him.

Skinner's wife Sharon is injured in a car accident. Mulder and Scully track down a government man who arranged for Sayles to "randomly" meet Skinner and then murdered her. Skinner goes to visit Sharon and briefly spies the crone in her place, then listens as Sharon tells him something. The information allows Skinner to dash to the rescue and shoot the killer as he corners Scully, saving her. Skinner is cleared of Sayles' murder, and he decides to postpone his divorce.

Critique "The truth is, we don't know very much about him." This is fascinating, a character study in a series which up 'til now has chosen only to focus upon Mulder and Scully, keeping all others nicely ambiguous in the background where they can be potential friend or foe. At the end of Apocrypha Mulder went as far as to thank Skinner for his support, something which would have been unthinkable at the beginning of the season where the Assistant Director was still being played as a potential assassin to Scully. With Avatar, there is an acceptance now that Skinner must be regarded as a stable element in the series. It closes some storytelling doors, but it opens up others.

Many have complained that for a Skinner-focused story, this didn't reveal very much that was new about him. I disagree. What we have here is an analysis of a control freak who has lost control. This is what a tacit support of the X-Files has done to him. On the one hand, after the attempt on his life was botched earlier in the season, there is now a conspiracy to discredit him. On the other, it's implicit that his marriage has broken down as a consequence of his support for the X-Files cases too. It's clear that he is a man who likes simple facts and answers - the

contradictions in his life that have been created by his disillusionment with the authority he once looked to, and was a part of, have caused him to shut himself away emotionally. There is a human cost to seeking the truth, even if in Skinner's case the only way he can seek it is passively, to sit back and allow those of greater imagination to seek it for him.

In that case, it's highly credible that while doubting himself and his cause as his marriage crumbles around him and he's subjected to bad dreams, Skinner can't be sure whether or not he is the killer the conspiracy has framed himself to seem. He rejects Mulder and Scully's offers for help - and, at the end of the episode, seated back behind his desk, cannot yield to their demands for the truth. He's not going to reward their efforts with his trust, or his thanks - he'll shut them out, do his best to put things back the way they were. The Skinner we see in Avatar is a man who had to be passionless to stay alive, just as he had to escape from who he was with drugs to keep himself together in Vietnam. Scully might suggest at the beginning of the story that they don't really know who Skinner is - and that's as true at the end; Skinner can't allow himself to *be* known, perhaps for fear he'll find out he doesn't know either. From his introduction in Season One he has been a cipher, and perhaps deliberately so. It's only his growing connection to the X-Files, one feels, that has given him an identity at all.

For the most part this plays out as a strange but winning balance between conspiracy thriller and something more supernatural. The succubus idea is played with an ambiguity that allows us to believe that the old woman that Skinner sees in times of crisis may really just be in his head. And there's an emotional power to the image, that a man who refuses help as steadfastly as Skinner now sees the protection he was offered when he was wounded in Vietnam. It suggests too that he has married a guardian figure who is prepared to look after him, no matter how much his silence drives her away. There's a realism to the bruised dialogue between Skinner and his wife which is unusual in a show which rarely bothers with awkward domestics. And that is reflected in the reality of the police case drawn against Skinner, and the way his enemies at the FBI move to dismiss him from his job.

In the final act the story stutters. Crucially, the episode needed to decide whether the death of the prostitute was due to paranormal influence or conspiracy plotting. Each reading of the event works - but there are clues for both which don't make sense once either one is proved. If Skinner has been framed, then why does the prostitute have phosphorescence around her mouth, and how could Skinner know to save Scully at the hotel? And if the succubus story is true, then much of the FBI storyline just doesn't fit at all. Rather than provide a way through two conflicting interpretations, we cut unhelpfully back to Skinner in his office, the charges against him dropped. With so much of the episode setting Skinner up so damningly as a murder suspect, you're left with a nagging doubt that what's been uncovered is enough to clear his name. And with so much at stake, the resolution feels rushed and confusing.

Perhaps the story doesn't really work as either a Don't Look Now ghost story or as a conspiracy piece - neither plotline develops into anything as substantial as initially promised. But Mitch Pileggi is great, and Howard Gordon's dialogue throughout is so terse and so real that this still carries quite a punch. And for opening up its characters a little further, even by acknowledging there *are* characters to open up, The X-Files' landscape has shifted subtly. (***)

3.22, Quagmire

Air Date: May 3, 1996
Writer: Kim Newton
Director: Kim Manners

Summary When a number of people are savagely eaten by something at Heuvelmans Lake in Georgia - a tourist spot known as the home of "Big Blue", a Loch Ness monster-type of creature - Mulder becomes convinced that Big Blue is real. However, certain evidence (such as a boot shaped like a dinosaur foot) suggests that someone is faking Big Blue's "appearances". As more deaths occur (including that of Scully's dog Queequeg), Mulder concludes that the monster's sudden interest in eating people owes to a drop in the local frog population. Mulder makes a final bid to shoot Big Blue, but merely injures a large alligator. The goal of finding Big Blue seems hopeless - even as a giant serpent, away from spying eyes, swims freely in the lake.

Critique This is such a lovely little comic episode which feels so wonderfully familiar - it's a no-nonsense Season One monster story played as a tongue-in-cheek romp. But what is striking about that familiarity is that we've never really seen an episode like this before, and pretty much never will again. The comic episodes of The X-Files have either revelled in black humour, or been deliberately quirky and postmodern. Whereas Quagmire's joy is that it's just *fun*; this is The X-Files as non-fans imagine it, a disposable little adventure story which plays like a live action Scooby-Doo. There's something very winning about its innocence, about seeing Mulder and Scully acting like an old married couple with cute dog in tow, hunting down a Loch Ness wannabe. The jokes aren't subtle, but they're very likeable - you've got to love the stereotyped Sheriff straight from Jaws who is adamant that the lake will stay open until he has a close encounter of his own. And the characters are broad caricatures who were fun to watch as they get ever closer to becoming monster food.

It's all hugely enjoyable and light as a feather - and after a season dealing with such weighty themes, and with an even grimmer season ahead of us, it's a joy to sit back and chuckle at an X-Files episode so lacking in pretension or cynicism. There's a cracking pace, spooky moments in darkened woods, and a huge body count - what could want anything more? And just as you ask yourself that question, we get a seven-minute conversation between Mulder and Scully, sitting on a rock surrounded by water, waiting for rescue. Mulder makes small talk asking Scully about cannibalism; Mulder tells stories of his childhood desire for a peg leg; Mulder nearly shoots a duck. And amidst the gentle comedy, Scully is able to ask Mulder what drives him, what keeps him so obsessed. It's one of the most perfect illustrations of the differences between the two agents' personalities ever portrayed in the series, and whereas entire stories will be given over to this comic disparity in future seasons, it's probably never achieved as subtly as it is here. It's beautifully played by Duchovny and Anderson, and even if you suspect it might be the most obvious bit of padding ever conceived, it makes this already delightful little gem something rather magical. (****)

3.23, Wetwired

Air Date: May 10, 1996
Writer: Mat Beck
Director: Rob Bowman

Summary Looking into a string of sudden murders, Mulder and Scully find evidence that the perpetrators became demented after watching television. While watching video tapes taken from the killers' homes, Scully becomes paranoid to the point of thinking that Mulder is in collusion the Cigarette Smoking Man. Mulder observes a cable technician affixing a strange device to a utility pole, and the Lone Gunmen confirm that the gadget uses different colors to make people violent. Being red / green colorblind, Mulder proved immune to the effect. A panicking Scully returns to her mother's house, but is eventually made to see reason. Mulder later discovers that X has ended the covert TV experiment by shooting the cable tech.

Critique We've seen the majority of this before. For starters, it's a retread of the episode Blood, where people were reduced to paranoid psychosis by images they saw on electrical displays. Wetwired uses the same premise, but more bluntly - television is a more obvious medium than, say, a microwave oven, and seeing the images directly through the victims' eye is less interesting than the black comedy of neon words urging people to murder each other. Then there's thrown in a touch of Anasazi, except this time it's Scully who is driven to see Mulder as the traitor. Again, it's less subtly done here - Mulder's paranoia in Anasazi has a slow building effect, and when he finally turns on his ex-partner the grounds for his attack on the more hurtful because they are credible: Scully really *was* sent to spy on him. This retread here feels like an attempt to give Anderson the same opportunities for barnstorming that Duchovny had a year ago, and the scene where she pulls a gun on him at his mother's house is brilliantly performed - but it means less because her accu-

sations are clearly without real substance. If you add to this the dramatic moment where Mulder shouts at X that he's a manipulative coward and threatens to shoot him if he won't give answers - a mirror image of the scene Anderson played with X in 731 - you can be left with the impression that Wetwired is a greatest hits compilation rather than an episode in its own right.

And yet... this really works rather well. It may be simpler than Blood, but it's also a lot more engaging. There we had a clever premise which didn't quite translate into an actual *plot*; here writer Mat Beck remedies that, very wisely, by making the premise contingent upon our heroes. Blood missed the trick of having either Mulder or Scully affected by the subliminal messaging. Wetwired may not have found much more to say about the idea than Blood had, but by making it about the way Mulder and Scully trust each other, this is considerably more exciting. And because the episode unashamedly focuses upon the relationships of the two leads, it can produce rather stunning scenes out of left field: the sequence where Mulder is called upon to identify a body he thinks might be Scully's is ultimately just a red herring, but the way Duchovny shuts down when he gets the news and refuses to show an emotional response to the Lone Gunmen is very affecting. And it highlights what is so moving about this episode - just how much our heroes need each other. Scully's greatest fear is that Mulder is not the pillar she needs him to be; his simple assertion that she is the only person he trusts is therefore very powerful. And yes, whilst Scully's bout of paranoia cannot compete with the same depth as the one Mulder had in Anasazi, it benefits here too from a simpler approach away from the mytharc and its complications. When Mulder turns on Scully at the end of Season Two, it's self-consciously part of an Important Episode. When Scully does it to Mulder here, it can be allowed to feel more intimate and personal.

And, surprisingly, at the end of the episode, after all the usual assurances that the evidence has been destroyed and the villains killed before Mulder can take them into custody - there's a revelation after all. We discover at last that X is in the employ of the Cigarette Smoking Man - and that he may have aroused his boss's suspicions. His days are surely numbered. (***1/2)

3.24, Talitha Cumi

Air Date: May 17, 1996
Story: David Duchovny, Chris Carter
Teleplay: Chris Carter
Director: RW Goodwin

Summary In Arlington, Virginia, a man who can change his identity via shapeshifting lays hands on some shootout victims and miraculously heals them. The Cigarette Smoking Man captures the healer - Jeremiah Smith - from his job in the Social Security Office and interrogates him, but Smith later escapes.

Meanwhile, Mulder's mother has an argument with the Cigarette Smoking Man, then suffers a hemorrhage and is hospitalised. Mrs Mulder scribbles the word "palm", thereby directing Mulder's attention to a lamp in her home - which contains a stiletto akin to the Alien Bounty Hunter's weapon of choice. Smith surfaces at Scully's apartment and they rendezvous with Mulder - whereupon the bounty hunter appears and marches toward them. [To be continued.]

Critique You see, the thing about The Brothers Karamazov is that it was written by a genius. What Dostoevsky was doing in his Grand Inquisitor scene was setting out a debate about Man's relationship to God and to the servitude that implies. It's not an easy read, but it is extraordinary. It's rather sweet, really, that Chris Carter was so influenced by one of the great Russian novelists for this episode - there is a long conversation between the Cigarette Smoking Man and Jeremiah Smith which riffs off it wholesale - but it's worthy and pretentious and utterly undramatic. And just as you think, thank God that's all over... the Cigarette Smoking Man pops back into Smith's cell to do the whole thing all over again!

It's astonishing that a season can end this way. This last year of The X-Files has seen it grow in sophistication, and in depth, and its writing even in the humblest monster of the week stories has been sparkling. But the script for Talitha Cumi is *awful*. If these Karamazov patches alone were the problem, you could perhaps forgive the episode for biting off more than it could

chew in a couple of misjudged set pieces. But this is an episode in which no-one speaks as if they're human. The dialogue is verbose, dripping with tautologies and metaphors - and the scenes that ought to have some power, like Mulder confronting the Cigarette Smoking Man in the hospital, or fighting X in the car park, are prefaced by lines that feel as if they've been translated badly from Serbo-Croat. The upshot of all this is that all the emotion of the story has been crushed. Last year's Anasazi had a kick not just for the rush of plot twists, but the passion which those twists provoked. Here we get nothing new. End Game has already done a lot of these scenes of import (and done them badly, albeit better than the ones shown here). Another family member of Mulder or Scully is in critical condition, so we can get another hospital scene. There's lots of shapeshifting. Mulder demands to know where the Cigarette Smoking Man lives - just as he did in One Breath. There are vague promises of Samantha, and vaguer news about the colonisation. And there's an unbelievably poor sequence where Mulder finds an alien weapon by rearranging the letters in a message his mother so cryptically left for him. I understand that victims of strokes can jumble up the letters in words, and that's why she lets him know an alien weapon is hidden in a lamp by writing the word "palm". But it's confusion for the sake of it, and there's a meanness to it - it smacks of the idea that Chris Carter gave Mulder's mother this trauma *precisely* to make a simple clue just that bit harder to understand. We know that all these characters are subject to the mechanics of the plot, but if the series wants us to care about these relationships it doesn't help that it's so heavy handed with them - this just steps over the line into cruelty.

But then, this episode isn't meant to be helpful. On the contrary. It's about obfuscation, and about drawing out a narrative beyond its natural conclusion - you can really feel the gears grind in this instalment, as Chris Carter and company find a way of streeeetching out the plotlines for years to come. Talitha Cumi is about nothing, and advances nothing. You could forgive it even that, if it didn't do it with such a grandiose swagger. (*)

The X-Files: Season 4

4.1, Herrenvolk

Air Date: Oct. 4, 1996
Writer: Chris Carter
Director: RW Goodwin

Summary   The agents and Smith elude the bounty hunter. Smith takes Mulder to a Canadian farm community where identical boys and young duplicates of Mulder's sister Samantha are tending fields of plants. The goal is to produce a lethal kind of pollen that bees will spread as part of an alien colonization effort. Scully determines that six identical Jeremiah Smiths were using their government positions to create an inventory of humanity, and that each person who's received a smallpox vaccination has been "tagged" with a genetic marker. Before Mulder can learn more, the bounty hunter slays Smith.

The Cigarette Smoking Man and the Elder (3.10, 731) identify X as a security leak and send an assassin to kill him. X is shot outside Mulder's apartment, but uses his blood to scrawl the letters "SRSG" before dying. Mulder accordingly visits the Special Representative to the Secretary General office at the United Nations, and speaks with Marita Covarrubias, a worker there. She claims to know little about the Canadian farm that Mulder mentions, but tellingly hands him photographs of the duplicate boys and Samanthas. Afterward, the Cigarette Smoking Man instructs the bounty hunter to lay hands on Mulder's mother and heal her, purportedly because Mulder will be less dangerous if he has something to lose.

Critique   The sundrenched landscape of hills and countryside is a jolt, and the wonderfully creepy teaser - in which identical children watch as a repair man falls to his death from a beesting - gives us a promise that this opening episode will be a refreshing change to the pretentious tosh of the last. And it mostly is - there are still purple passages to wade through, but they're fewer and further between. (Though the conversation between Mulder and Scully in the hospital is turgid in the extreme - if you look into Duchovny and Anderson's eyes, you can see the effort required even to reach the end of their sentences.)

But it's a terribly disappointing episode nonetheless. Jeremiah Smith promises Mulder significant explanations of the conspiracy. Although they drive together through the night into Canada, and then go on a ten-mile hike across country, they never quite get around to having the necessary conversation. Just as Mulder anticipates the audience's impatience and demands that *something* is put into easy words of one syllable, that is the moment when the shapeshifter assassin turns up and everybody has to start running again. There is a lot of running in this episode. I don't mind running per se, and any form of action is a welcome relief after Talitha Cumi. But when it's used in such an unsubtle way just to eke out a series' precious secrets still further, it's ridiculous.

So what do we learn from all of this? Nothing coherent, but there's an awful lot about bees. Cue lots of scenes where the characters flap their hands about, warding off stinging insects. Bees were first introduced as a conspiracy element in the War of Coprophages last year, but that was clearly intended to be a Darin Morgan joke about the tortuous convolutions of the mytharc - whether by accident or design, Chris Carter has taken that parody plot line seriously. Although bees provide a metaphor for workers and drones, with all the lack of individuality that implies, they are also a fundamentally undramatic menace - inasmuch as it's very hard to get a good scene of tension if your hero is required to wave his arms around as if he's a windmill.

More tellingly, it's frustrating that Mulder is required to make a choice between saving his mother's life or going to the Canadian hills to talk about bees. We've seen this dilemma before - in Beyond the Sea and in One Breath, where either Scully or Mulder are given the option of going to a loved one in hospital, or pursuing some nebulous truth. Up to this point the series has always demonstrated the greater wisdom in choosing love over answers. Herrenvolk reverses that conclusion - and that's surely a retrograde step, to suggest that the weight of Chris Carter's mythology is worth more than the characters who prop it up. It feels emotionally wrong, and all the more frustrating that Mulder effectively sacrifices his mother for answers so unhelpful and expressed so lackadaisically. Elsewhere, Scully uncovers facts of her own about smallpox tagging - which are potentially fascinating, but revealed in as painfully and undramatic way as possible. So we end the episode with the sense that Carter is not prepared to develop the mythology he's got, but just throw instead more random elements into the mix as he goes along. (Bees? I just want to say that again. Bees? I ask you.)

In spite of everything, there's some powerful stuff here too. X's death is gloriously melodramatic, as he writes the contact details for Mulder's next informant in his own blood - but it's very tensely directed, and the moments where you see his blood actually pump out from his wound, and his eyes harden as he expires, are exceptional. And I love the final scene, as the Cigarette Smoking Man clearly blusters for reasons to have the shapeshifter save the life of Mrs Mulder, his one-time lover. It's a welcome moment of heart in a dismayingly cold instalment. There's a nice irony here too, one that wrongfoots the viewer used to X-Files structure and expecting yet another casualty in the series premiere - that the very obstacle that prevents Mulder having his mother healed by Smith is the means to her recovery. (*1/2)

4.2, Home

Air Date: Oct. 11, 1996
Writers: Glen Morgan, James Wong
Director: Kim Manners

Summary The discovery of a dead, malformed infant in Home, Pennsylvania, draws Mulder and Scully's attention to the Peacock clan - a family who's spent a century doing their best to avoid civilization. Generations of inbreeding have made the three Peacock brothers intensely savage, and the agents come to suspect that they're holding a woman prisoner and are forcibly impregnating her.

At the Peacock farm, Mulder and Scully discover that the captive - and the object of the brothers' desire - is actually their mother, a mul-tiple amputee. Mulder and Scully shoot two of the brothers after they go berserk and murder the local sheriff and his wife, but the third brother escapes with his mother. They quickly set about trying to restore the family line.

Critique Glen Morgan and James Wong are back on The X-Files - dragged back kicking and screaming, too, from the look of things, after the cancellation of their series Space: Above and Beyond. Of all the series writers, they're the ones who have tested and expanded the format of the show the most, and all their Season Four episodes will do the same thing. If anything, they're more unforgiving of The X-Files now it's a big hit, there seems to be an anger to the way they take its conventional limitations and smash them. Home kicks off their reign of terror in as controversial away as possible. It's the first episode which had its US broadcast prefaced by advisory warnings, and Fox promptly took it out of syndication. Its teaser kicks off with a child being born with the help of rusty kitchen instruments - a fork to prod it out of the womb, scissors to cut the umbilical cord - and the screaming baby is then taken out and buried alive in the mud. The senses are revolted.

The episode is of course, much criticised - but it is actually very *hard* to be more revolting than this. There's a brutality to the story which is sickening - there is probably no murder as tense in the entire series as that of the sheriff and his wife. But it's hardly just a collection of disturbing set pieces and gore. Instead it's an attack on US values and the family system, and more raw and more blunt than you could ever have expected on network television. Morgan and Wong have been down this path before with episodes such as Blood and Die Hand Die Verletzt, but they look like gentle pokes with a stick compared to this searing indictment of the American way. The sheriff, with his folksy trusting ways and his cherished view of his home as a place of innocence where everyone can leave their doors unlocked, dreads the effect of the FBI coming to town because it will destroy the values he holds dear. The Peacock brothers, latest in a line of centuries' inbreeding, who are making babies with their mother kept strapped under the bed, fear the exact same thing. It's a none too subtle contrast between cheery American values and its darker underbelly - and the fact that the sheriff is called Andy Taylor is one gag too far - but it's curiously effective. Andy Taylor and the Peacocks coexist peacefully because they've never threatened each other; it's only as the barriers of heritage are eroded away, as represented by Mulder and Scully, that the two destroy each other.

The most sickening thing of all, of course, is not the violence or the blood but the way that the mother is not a victim of her sons, but an eager compliant to it. This is the American family boiled down to its very basics - the urge to breed, to perpetuate the loins. The mother's diatribe against Scully - that it's clear *she's* not a mother - is a wonderful foretaste of themes to be explored, but also a twist upon the conversations between Mulder and Scully earlier where he talks of her settling down and populating the world with über-Scullies. It's the fact that man is reduced to his most bestial here which is so telling, and so disturbing. It's not mindless depravity on display here, but something much more searching and pessimistic about the human condition, a statement that for all our veneer of civilisation we follow animal needs to procreate and protect our offspring and homes.

An episode like this will always divide its audience, but that is part of the point. It's not meant to be easy viewing. And you feel that it is making a critique on The X-Files, which for three years has been offering a steady diet of murder and mutants, without ever really engaging with the implications honestly. Mulder and Scully wisecrack through the story; at times it feels it's an attempt to keep their humanity, and at times it seems more awkward, as if Morgan and Wong are objecting to the format of a show which has our FBI agents witness atrocities on a weekly basis only to bounce back ready for the next case. You could be tempted to say to Morgan and Wong that, to be fair, it's not such a crime for a show to be escapist fun - but as an invective against complacency, their point still stands. You wouldn't want The X-Files to be like this every week, but for the once it's fascinating.

And it is, as well, absolutely terrifying. It does its job - no X-Files has generated tension as thick as this one. If Home were about nothing more than providing unease and dread, it'd still be a great achievement. (*****)

4.3, Teliko

Air Date: Oct. 18, 1996
Writer: Howard Gordon
Director: Jim Charleston

Summary   A disease centre in Philadelphia asks for Scully's help when four African-American men go missing. One of them turns up dead, his lack of pigment suggesting a contagion is at work. Scully finds the man's pituitary gland missing. Clues lead Mulder and Scully to arrest Samuel Aboah, an immigrant from West Africa. Marita Covarrubias directs Mulder to Minister Diabria, a diplomat who tells him a folk story about the Teliko: evil spirits who drain their victims of life and color. Mulder theorises that the Teliko are actually members of an albino clan who compensate for their lack of a pituitary gland by ingesting other people's hormones. Aboah escapes, but Scully kills him when he attacks Mulder.

Critique   Once in a while you can feel this episode struggling towards saying something interesting. There's obviously such a great conceit here - a man that can drain the melanin from a body, and leave black man as white - that it's somehow startling that the theme of skin colour and what it would be like for a man to escape his racial stereotype is largely ignored. The way that the immigration worker turns on Mulder, because he can't realise why a man who has been a victim of police brutality might instinctively run from authority figures, is great. But otherwise you feel this needn't be about melanin at all. It could be about... well, let's say livers.

Because this is a straight retooling of Squeeze and Tooms. The story could at least have had the wit to disguise it - but alongside Aboah's skill in turning black men albino, and his curious ability to keep long sticks down his throat, he also can hide himself in impossibly confined spaces. Even this conscious retread of an X-Files favourite might have worked had it had any new images to offer us, but whereas Eugene Tooms in a tight corner looked credibly eerie, Aboah peeking out from a trolley drawer just looks comical. If you're going to create a mutant with a special power, then focus on that: giving him several unconnected powers just dilutes the character and what he stands for. And there might have been some more time to spare exploring the themes already raised instead.

It's not just a rehash of the mutant monster story, mind you. It also goes down the path of the old tribal folk myth - in this case recited to Mulder by a character never seen before and never seen again. And just to score at hat trick, it even drags in a nod to the conspiracy, by having Mulder pursue Marita Covarrubias for information. She looks as befuddled by his talking to her as we are - you almost sense she's dying to tell him that they're not doing one of the "important" episodes this week, but a disposable one no-one'll remember. "Don't bother me again until it's a two-parter," her expression says, "with at least a hint of a cliffhanger." The phrase "Deceive inveigle obfuscate", scattered liberally throughout the episode - including a motto on the credits (for some reason), and in a painfully bad bit of Scully monologue at the end - all seems to suggest a greater weight to this story than it even begins to attempt to justify.

The final act is quite fun, with lots of tense action in a ventilation shaft, and Mulder getting paralysed by a dart. And there's nothing necessarily *wrong* with most of this. It's just achingly formulaic. God knows there are worse episodes out there - but not many this forgettable. (**)

4.4, Unruhe

Air Date: Oct. 27, 1996
Writer: Vince Gilligan
Director: Rob Bowman

Summary After a young woman goes missing in Traverse City, Michigan, Mulder and Scully find that the victim's passport photos, taken minutes before her abduction, render terrifying images of her. Mulder attributes the phenomenon to "psychic photography", suspecting that the girl's abductor isn't even aware that he has the ability to generate images of his fantasies on film. The missing woman is finally found, lobotomized and repeatedly saying the word "unruhe" - German for "trouble" or "unrest".

Scully identifies the perpetrator as a foreman named Gerry Schnauz, but winds up as his prisoner. Schnauz becomes intent on removing the

"unruhe" that he thinks is afflicting Scully, and moves to lobotomize her with an icepick. Mulder identifies Schnauz's location by studying more altered photos, and arrives in time to shoot Schnauz dead.

Critique It's interesting that in the week that Millennium launches, and steals The X-Files' time slot in the process, that the parent series produces its own take on serial killing. With Home and now Unruhe, the fourth season of The X-Files feels much grimmer than before. This plays with many familiar elements of a standard episode, but with an added realism. We've seen many dead bodies in the show, but Scully's disgust at finding the body of one of Schnauz's victims - Alice Brandt - has a conviction to it that has rarely been portrayed. The clichéd ending, in which Scully types up her report via voice-over, is played unlike any we've seen before; she looks sick and expressionless. For once the supernatural element isn't the X-File at all, it's something tangential that even the killer isn't aware of. When Mulder is keen to find out the truth behind it, and in doing so appears to trivialise the murders that they reveal, Scully is palpably so revolted by the case that she rejects him: the thought photography is of no interest to her, it's a superficial detail measured against the brutality on display. It almost feels like an episode which is casting off the trappings of The X-Files formula, seeing them as childish concerns weighed against the brutality of real-life crime. It's honestly as if the people in charge of Chris Carter's production company, Ten Thirteen, are acknowledging that The X-Files is really something of a silly bauble compared to their bright shiny new series premiering that very week.

Yet it's these thought photographs too which give us the best metaphor of Schnauz's evil - a man so warped, he has the power to warp pictures as well. Schnauz is one of the most terrifying of X-Files villains, because he sincerely believes he's only helping his victims. Clearly a product of parental abuse, he has turned the fantasies of the howlers, creatures which take the blame off his father, into an obsession. The sequence where Scully is his prisoner, and does her best to convince him of this insanity, is quite extraordinary - all the more chilling because you can't help pity Schnauz, even as he prepares to lobotomise Scully with an ice pick through her eye. Of course this is a man who can misshape photographs - against all our instincts, he does a similar thing to the viewer's sympathies. And so begins a running theme that we can see through Vince Gilligan's episodes, as he examines the monstrous and the inhuman with an apparent geniality that only makes them *more* horrifying as he brings them closer to our understanding.

Some of the plotting, perhaps, is a little tenuous - the significance of the six fingers in Scully's abduction photo lost me somewhat - but Vince Gilligan's dialogue is superb. Crisp and cold and very scary, this is one of the series' underpraised masterpieces. (*****)

4.5, The Field Where I Died

Air Date: Nov. 3, 1996
Writers: Glen Morgan, James Wong
Director: Rob Bowman

Summary Mulder and Scully assist in locating the leader of a doomsday cult - Vernon Ephesian - and his six wives. Mulder feels oddly drawn to one of the wives, Melissa, who seems to channel different personalities. He eventually comes to believe that Melissa has been reincarnated several times, that she was a Civil War nurse named Sarah Kavanaugh and that *he* was her fiancée: Sullivan Biddle, who died in the war.

Mulder immerses himself in the concept that he and Melissa were lovers, to the point that he emulates several of his former personalities and insists that he, Scully, Samantha and the Cigarette Smoking Man have previous histories together. However, Melissa refuses to accept Mulder's beliefs and returns to her husband. Officials are obliged to release the cult members, who make good on a suicide pact. Mulder finds Melissa's body, clutching a photograph of Kavanaugh.

Critique What I admire most about the returning team of Morgan and Wong is that they aren't afraid to fail. If that sounds like a backhanded compliment, then I suppose it is. But it's sincerely meant, all the same. It feels like they have

nothing to prove any longer, and the value their work brings to The X-Files is to stretch the format and see whether it snaps. Otherwise you'll be in a position where you're watching Teliko every week - cribbed, it must be remembered, from episodes Morgan and Wong wrote in the first place. The Field Where I Died doesn't even feel as if it's part of the same *series* as Teliko. It's very indulgent, and unwieldy, and at times a little embarrassing to watch, but the one thing it isn't is a safe retread of old glories.

This feels like a showcase for actress Kristen Cloke, who was a regular on Space: Above and Beyond, will come to play Lara Means on Millennium and still later will become Morgan's wife. It also gives Duchovny a chance to stretch his acting muscles too. Both of them are required to play long emotional monologues, flitting between past lives. (And, especially in Cloke's case, past accents.) Neither holds back from giving bold performances, in every sense of the word - they're brave, and they're not necessarily subtle. To be fair, both Cloke and Duchovny are very good. To be fairer still, neither of them are quite good enough. All their sequences of past life regression are unflinchingly captured on camera, every tic and vocal inflection on show - it's such a self-conscious thing to put the actors through, and for all the tears and the gnashing of teeth, it's a bit too contrived to be moving.

What was that about gnashing of teeth? A lot of fans took against this episode because it was revealed that Mulder's soul partner in many a past life wasn't one Dana Scully, but instead the guest star of the week. On the contrary, I thought this was one of the best things about the story, something which took it from the obvious and pat. The idea of Scully and Mulder being connected as friends through the centuries shows a far greater and more touching understanding of their character dynamic. It is, as Melissa says, a beautiful idea that gives life some meaning, the notion that throughout our lives we are dancing around the same people we care for. The problem is that in its forty-five minute slot, Morgan and Wong come undone by putting a few too many ingredients into the mix. The contrast between the present day crisis, featuring a Koresh-like suicide cult, and the slaughter of an American civil war battle, has a certain elegance to it. But when Mulder becomes a Jewish woman escaping from the Nazis, with Samantha as her son, and the Cigarette Smoking Man as a Gestapo officer, the premise is stretched so thin it breaks. (Besides the fact that the Cigarette Smoking Man was clearly alive in the war from what is revealed in Apocrypha, the level of coincidence at work here can only undermine the simplicity of the central love story.)

After the events of Unruhe, it's interesting to see Scully call Mulder once more on his selfish quest for the truth over and above a concern for the innocents they are trying to protect. It's a welcome burst of reality in a story which too rarely acknowledges the world outside Mulder's fascination with his former selves. The Field Where I Died features one of the series' most downbeat endings, as Mulder picks his way through the bodies of fifty people the FBI couldn't save from religious suicide - but the impact of this tragedy has been kept at arm's length for so much of the episode that it's hard to be affected by it. And, it must be said, we're now so used to poetic talk in The X-Files which is overwritten and pretentious, that when the episode opens with Duchovny reading something as good as Robert Browning, we still switch off with the expectation it's just Chris Carter being wanky again. In some ways, though, that's a fair summing up of the problems here, where the established tone of The X-Files series makes the episode look precious and weird. It is also its strength too. The Field Where I Died stumbles around a lot, and isn't clear about what it wants to say, but you get the impression there's nothing else on TV quite like it. (***1/2)

4.6, Sanguinarium

Air Date: Nov. 10, 1996
Writers: Valerie Mayhew, Vivian Mayhew
Director: Kim Manners

Summary   A surgeon in Chicago liposuctions a man to death, then claims that he was possessed by demons. Mulder and Scully soon find evidence that nurse Rebecca Waite, who's also a witch, has been strategically planting pentagrams at the hospital to to influence the physicians there to commit murder. However, Waite dies in a manner that suggests she was hexed, and the agents come to believe that she was actually protecting the patients from Dr Jack Franklin. Mulder pegs Franklin as a practitioner of the dark arts who uses ritual sacrifice every ten years to extend his lifespan. Franklin completes his master ritual and strips off his own face, then escapes. Soon afterward, a Los Angeles cosmetic clinic hires "Dr Hartman", a young and dashing surgeon.

Critique   You've got to chuckle when a nurse warns a patient in the trailer that there won't be any blood - and opens an episode which is literally *awash* with the stuff. When I first saw the episode in the UK, it was so butchered by the censors that it made little sense. Seeing it in its full unexpurgated glory, I can better appreciate this wickedly subversive little tale. Yes, you need a strong stomach to watch it, but that's surely the point. This is a dissection of cosmetic surgery, of the urge we have to go under the knife and have all sorts of incisions made just so we better conform to an idea of beauty. We hide ourselves from the real procedure of this, like the patient in the teaser we don't want to see the blood, would rather believe our body didn't have blood inside it at all. So to see a liposuction become a sequence where a man's insides are literally pumped out, to see the laser used to make nasal adjustments burn a hole right through a man's cheek and out the other side, to see the acid burn away an entire face - we're being shown the true implications of what those little nips and tucks mean.

It's not a subtle script; it's a gimmicky mix of hospital reality and witchcraft, the clinical nature of the one set against the mythic trappings of the other. It feels like a first season idea, where Mulder and Scully are incidental witnesses to a tale which has little interest in them. Had it been made at the beginning of the series, indeed, this would be of little interest - but this Season One concept is given a Season Four brutality, and the results are genuinely disturbing. The amount of blood on display is gratuitous, but what's effective about it is how quickly you adjust to it, how soon you stop squirming. It's the matter-of-fact tone on display which is the most disturbing thing of all. By the time Dr

Franklin is cutting off his own skin as a do-it-yourself facelift, we're almost desensitised to it. At the top of the story I was of the opinion that nothing now would get me near a hospital again - by the end I was, worryingly enough, taking it in my stride. Had it been a double length episode, who knows? Like Mulder, maybe I'd be checking out my nose in the mirror too.

It's a nicely structured story, carefully directing us to believe that the witch in the hospital is the villain, not the doctor she's attacking. And it is well paced too, so that Franklin's scheme and the importance of the victims' birthdays - which correspond to witches' sabbaths - comes to light logically and coherently. The ending is pants, though; this is a schlock shocker, and I don't think it has earned the right to let its satanic surgeon win the day. It feels like one ending too many, when the saving of Dr Shannon's life in the final act provided a natural reason for Franklin's rejuvenation to fail. But this is nevertheless a solid adventure, even if it's decidedly amoral tone and its body horror will always make it an X-File too strong for some to stomach. (***1/2)

4.7, Musings of a Cigarette Smoking Man

Air Date: Nov. 17, 1996
Writer: Glen Morgan
Director: James Wong

Summary   Mulder and Scully visit *The Lone Gunmen* office, where Frohike says he's pieced together the history of the Cigarette Smoking Man. Simultaneously, across the street, the Smoking Man sets up a rifle and eavesdrops on their conversation...

Frohike claims that the Smoking Man became a ward of the state after his father was executed as a Communist spy and his mother (a smoker) died of lung cancer. As an Army captain, he was recruited by the shadow conspiracy that runs the government to assassinate JFK. After doing so, he enjoyed his first cigarette.

By 1968, the Smoking Man was operating with complete anonymity within the government. He arranged Martin Luther King's assassination. But for all his power, the Smoking Man had a personal setback - he wrote political thrillers, but failed to get any of them published.

By 1991, the Smoking Man did everything from starting wars to influencing the Oscars and the Super Bowl. The fall of the Soviet Union briefly left the Smoking Man without an enemy to fight, but he found a new purpose when an alien was pulled from a wrecked spacecraft, and an associate of his - Deep Throat - killed the creature. In time, the Smoking Man pulled Mulder and Scully into his machinations, trying to conceal the truth about the existence of aliens.

Recently, a magazine accepted one of the Smoking Man's stories. He was excited to the point that he quit smoking and wrote his resignation letter - then discovered that magazine editors changed his ending. Inconsolable, the Smoking Man bought a packet of cigarettes.

Frohike finishes his account and leaves the Lone Gunmen's office. Luckily for him, the Smoking Man refrains from pulling the trigger, snug in the knowledge that he can kill Frohike any time he pleases.

Critique   The tease that Glen Morgan and James Wong play upon their X-Files audience escalates here. In fact, from the very beginning, with almost breathless excitement, the episode promises to tell us the whole truth about the Cigarette Smoking Man! And then - by showing him responsible for the assassination of Kennedy, and Martin Luther King, and for rigging the results of Oscars and sports events, and for not even returning Saddam Hussein's phone calls - it really does everything but. The answers that the viewers are craving are handed out here on such a large plate, you can only take them as a delicious parody. And it's a joke so cleverly told that it creeps up on you by degrees. The Kennedy section seems to be played straight - there are indications of the fiction behind it all that Mulder's first spoken word ever was "JFK", but in its establishment of the Cigarette Smoking Man as the most infamous assassin in modern American history, it just about takes itself seriously. Then the second section repeats the story - this time it's King, and our gullibility is being tested. We begin to see the man's life as a metaphor, a cycle of gun shootings and a half-smoked butts.

And then, most delightfully, we come closer to the present day. We see the Cigarette Smoking Man as the sad boss from hell, giving all his colleagues identical ties as Christmas presents, bashful when asked where he will be spending the holidays. He's a man who's tortured by his urge to write pulp fiction, only to receive insulting rejection letters. A man who can reflect to Deep Throat how in creating history he'll always be anonymous, and yet secretly would rather create fiction. The irony is that he's only too good at controlling real life whilst the make-believe is embarrassing drivel. The joyous glee with which William B Davis plays the scene where he finds he's been at last accepted by a publisher, and dashes off his resignation letter so he can fulfil his dreams, is genuinely touching and beautifully silly. And the piss-take of Forest Gump, as he sits upon a park bench reflecting on how life is like a box of chocolates, is one of the funniest jokes The X-Files has ever made.

What is so clever about Musings of a Cigarette Smoking Man is not that it's a pure comedy (because it isn't) or a mythology episode (because it isn't that either). It shifts between the two, just as we suspect the story shifts between a truth of sorts and an impossible fiction. It sends up The X-Files' ability to find answers, suggesting that the entire spine of the back story is never to be coherently explained. That, in spite of the show's by-line, there is no truth out there. The whole point of The X-Files is ambiguity. This extends even to the making of the episode itself; Chris Carter and Glen Morgan reputedly couldn't agree on which parts of the story were true, and William B Davis was frustrated and confused. The original conclusion to this story had Frohike shot dead by the Cigarette Smoking Man - in spite of all the jokes surrounding him, all the new softness he'd been written with, at the last moment he'd have taken out one of the regular characters. The tonal shift would have been jarring, maybe *too* jarring - but that would have been the point. But there's a clever elegance to the broadcast story, with the Smoking Man giving Frohike the "second chance" that is the title of his novel. And there's an added frisson to the section where Davis is appalled to see his story at last in print ("This isn't the ending I wrote!") when you remember that Morgan and Wong may have been moved to say the same thing.

By no means an easy episode, it deliberately sets out to alienate the viewer, and to be ultimately anticlimactic. But it's a real grower. There's a depth to this, and the power of those contradictory impressions of The X-Files' boogeyman haunt you long after the story is over. It promises to be a character study, and it's everything but - because there is no real character to study. It's the daring realisation of this that makes Musings one of The X-Files' true masterpieces. (*****)

4.8, Tunguska

Air Date: Nov. 24, 1996
Writers: Frank Spotnitz, Chris Carter
Director: Kim Manners

Summary   A military salvage team liberates Krycek from his imprisonment in a missile silo (3.16, Apocrypha). Mulder begrudgingly forms an alliance with Krycek, accepting that the man wants revenge against the Cigarette Smoking Man and the Syndicate. At Krycek's direction, Mulder and Scully intercept a Russian courier transporting an item of great importance: a four-billion-year-old space rock. But when an exobiologist drills into the rock, black worms emerge and render him comatose.

Marita Covarrubias tells Mulder that the courier was outbound from Tunguska, Siberia - the site of an infamous explosion possibly caused by a meteor strike in 1908. Mulder and Krycek find a gulag where the workers are mining extraterrestrial rocks, whereupon Krycek reveals that he's in league with the people running the camp. Mulder is captured and - alongside several other prisoners - is restrained on a table. Pipes above them spew the black oil into their faces, allowing oil-worms to wriggle inside their bodies. [To be continued.]

Critique   "There is no truth. These guys, they make it up as they go along." I'm beginning to dread the mythology episodes. The long unspeakable bursts of dialogue, the overcomplicated plots, the huge exposition with no revelation. When Tunguska opens with Krycek summing up what I've come to fear from these stories, my heart lifted. It was as if Chris Carter had heard my cries of bored anguish from the sofa.

And, yes, this feels in tone very much like one of those runaround episodes of random elements. There are lots of sequences at airports - Dulles, JFK and one in Honolulu - before the episode finally comes to rest in Siberia. Mulder travels the globe, while Scully is stuck at home fending off internal matters at the FBI. But there's a *focus* to this story, there's the sense that a comprehensible plot is being followed. And rather skilfully, Carter and Spotnitz marry the fantastical trappings of their grand plan to the human rights concerns, the black oil plot colliding with a tale showing human experimentation in gulags. The final sequence of Mulder - held under chicken wire, being tortured as little alien worms burrow up through his nose into his eyes - not only makes one of the finest X-Files cliffhangers, but rather graphically revisits the themes of concentration camp atrocity introduced in 731. This time round, though, it's not the Holocaust that is being invoked, so much as Dostoevsky via House of the Dead.

It's remarkably well directed by Kim Manners; for once, a conspiracy episode has the same movie-like scope of the more satisfying standalone stories. There is action / adventure which finds within its thrills and tension the point of the story - it doesn't have to pause every few minutes for pretension's sake and a bit of a catch-up. If anything, there's a bit too much action: I'm quite sure there must be a great drinking game to be played watching this, downing a point every time Krycek gets beaten up. One can understand emotionally why Mulder and Skinner would punch Krycek on first impulse, but it turns our heroes into something thuggish and stupid - and repeated as often as it is here it actually begins to seem comical.

But overall this is great stuff. It pulls the same trick as Colony did, opening with a teaser that won't be broadcast until the end of the following episode. In this case, though, it actually works - you can already see by Tunguska's end how Scully's defence of her partner will lead her to risk contempt of Congress... and can only wonder about what has become of Mulder, who clearly hasn't made it out of his black oil operation easily. It leaves you with greater anticipation for what will happen next than has been felt in the series since Anasazi. (****)

4.9, Terma

Air Date: Dec. 1, 1996
Writers: Frank Spotnitz, Chris Carter
Director: Rob Bowman

Summary Mulder recovers from the black-oil infestation and flees from the gulag. Krycek happens upon a group of locals who are all missing their left arms. The men believe that amputation is required to save those infected by the black oil, and dutifully cut off Krycek's arm without his permission.

Meanwhile, Vassily Peskow - a former KGB assassin - accepts an assignment from "Comrade Arntzen" to eliminate persons connected to the extraterrestrial rocks. Peskow kills the comatose exobiologist, then beats Mulder and Scully to Boca Raton, Florida, and murders Dr Chung-Sayer - a nursing home doctor who was the intended recipient of the courier's space rock. The agents realise that they were manipulated from the start by someone who wanted to keep the space rocks out of American hands. Meanwhile, Peskow reports to "Arntzen", the now-one-armed Krycek.

Critique By God, this follow-up episode is awful. This takes all that made Tunguska work - all its coherence and suspense - and flushes them away. There is virtually no structure to it at all, and its answer to how to resolve the lingering plot developments of Tunguska is... to add new ones. Lots and *lots* of new ones. Euthanasia patients being treated as test subjects, KGB agents assassinating members of the conspiracy, lots of snide power jockeying between the Cigarette Smoking Man and the Well-Manicured Man in a sequence which looks as if they're competing to see which one can come up with the most arch comeback. In fact, a lot of this feels like the writers have set themselves a game: the scene between Skinner and Scully outside her apartment has the two rabbiting exposition at the other with as many subordinate clauses squeezed in as possible. (Mitch Pileggi wins by coming up with one sentence which boasts no fewer than *eleven*.)

There's such a lack of attention in this episode to anything which makes decent dramatic sense, it almost makes your head spin. Mulder's escape from the Gulag, to the bizarrely comatose reaction of all the armed guards about him, is so mechanical that David Duchovny's face barely twitches. The last we see of him in Siberia, he's being advanced on by a pissed-off truck driver intending to cut off his arm - the next, he's at a congressional hearing in DC impossibly speedily, promising Scully he'll explain how he escaped later. (He doesn't.) Gillian Anderson is required to speak ever more complex and ever less interesting speeches, until at last you can see her give up and switch on the autopilot. It's dreadful, boring, and facile. Just as you think the dialogue has got as bad as can be, Mulder stands in front of Congress and tells them they should all be in contempt for not believing in aliens. In response everyone looks bemused. I know I was.

It's not entirely bad. I enjoyed the conversation between Mulder and his neighbouring prisoner, discussing the persistence of life. A man who spent two weeks making a knife with which to kill himself loses the desire to die in the fashioning of it - and finds strength in the stubbornness with which the black oil that is killing him has clung to its own existence. It's a fine scene, and it's *about* something. Peskow, the KGB assassin with the affable demeanour, is rather charismatic - it's a shame that this episode marks his one appearance, because what The X-Files is lacking in its villains is charm. And I liked the moment where Krycek's false hand is revealed; it ought to have been the final image of the episode, frankly. Instead we get the Cigarette Smoking Man binning the report summing up this episode with a bored nonchalance that's just a little *too* apt. (*)

4.10, Paper Hearts

Air Date: Dec. 15, 1996
Writer: Vince Gilligan
Director: Rob Bowman

Summary Dreams lead Mulder to conclude that the incarcerated John Lee Roche - one of the first serial killers he profiled for the FBI - killed more victims than was believed. Worse, fresh evidence suggests that Roche abducted and killed Mulder's sister Samantha. Roche recites details pertaining to Samantha's disappearance, but refuses to divulge more unless he's taken to the crime scene. Disobeying orders, Mulder takes Roche to Martha's Vineyard and thereby proves that he's lying about his involvement with Samantha. Mulder speculates that his extensive profiling of Roche created a mental link between them - one that enabled Roche to riffle through Mulder's memories. Roche escapes and kidnaps a little girl named Caitlin, but Mulder tracks Roche and kills him in the course of saving her.

Critique Vince Gilligan has a disturbing ability to take serial killers and make them pointedly ordinary; there is nothing Silence of the Lambs-like in his approach to his human monsters, nothing which can glamourise them. But nor does he demonise them either. John Lee Roche is the successor of Robert Modell from Pusher and Gerry Schnauz from Unruhe, a man who is as interested in the details of his vacuum cleaner sales as he is in the trophies of this child murders. Gilligan is able always to show us the human being behind the sociopath, and Roche is eerily sympathetic as a man who does nothing threatening until the final reel. There is something truly macabre in his opening scenes with Mulder, the way they greet each other calmly as familiar acquaintances. And what this achieves is the unthinkable - you spend the episode almost hoping that Roche really *is* the man who molested and killed Samantha, because it would somehow give closure, it'd bring peace. When Mulder and Scully visit Frank Sparks, some twenty years after the abduction of his little daughter, it's clear from the way he greets the FBI at the door that he's been keenly waiting for news all this time, that the mystery has never for a single day stopped haunting him. He talks of how it's better to know than always to wonder - and yet, conversely, how relieved he is that the child's mother is dead so she's spared the news.

And it's that contradiction which is at the core of Paper Hearts' success. You want to find out the truth. You dread finding out the truth. David Duchovny's performance - one of his very best - captures that dichotomy brilliantly, digging at the dirt with his bare hands eager to discover the body of his sister, relieved and yet anguished when he realises that the corpse on the autopsy table is not Samantha, meaning that she still has not had the resolution he needs.

It's the most moving episode since Beyond the Sea in Season One, and it reflects many of its themes. There's that familiar ending in which Mulder is given the choice between learning the truth, or doing the right thing - but this is a sick twist on it, where the most humane thing he can do is shoot Roche in the head. And it's a clever reversal of Grotesque, too, which sees Mulder profile a killer so well that he gets into his head; here, he's profiled Roche so well that the man can return the favour, get inside *Mulder's* head, and feed him clues in his dreams.

It's fascinating to see how The X-Files continues to evolve towards realism, now putting credible spins upon the UFO mythology that formed the very fabric of the opening season and a half. To see the abduction scene from Little Green Men played once more, but this time with a terrifyingly human explanation, is brilliant. What is even cleverer, though, is the insidious way that Gilligan shows how destructive Mulder's obsession really is. In Grotesque it was hinted that he was allowing his profiling to awaken a monster within; here the beating of Roche is only the start, and Mulder's performance in this episode is starkly unheroic, losing his gun and his prisoner and endangering another child. Roche allows Mulder his fantasy to rescue Samantha from a car, and the look of joy and accomplishment on Duchovny's face is truly heartbreaking - but it's an illusion Roche has sent to affect his own escape. It's that genuine contrast between the satisfaction offered by the easy answers of X-Files "the hit sci-fi show", and the consequences of what happens when reality gets in the way, which makes Paper Hearts such a standout. (*****)

4.11, El Mundo Gira

Air Date: Jan. 12, 1997
Writer: John Shiban
Director: Tucker Gates

Summary At a shantytown in the San Joaquin Valley, California, two brothers - Eladio and Soledad Buente - compete for the love of Maria Dorantes. Maria and her goat are soon found dead, the mutilated state of their remains suggesting that the fabled Goatsucker (a.k.a. "El Chupacabra") - a hairless monster with an enormous head - killed them.

Scully suspects that Eladio is carrying a fungal infection that's catalyzed by a specific enzyme that Mulder believes is alien in origin. More deaths occur, and Eladio's head swells as he transforms into El Chupacabra. He and Soledad have a fateful encounter, and accounts differ as to what happened next. Perhaps aliens took one or both of the brothers - or perhaps they're roaming the countryside as Los Chupacabras.

Critique This is trying very hard to be clever. But if cleverness were only about intent, then we could all be geniuses. John Shiban's last script, Teso dos Bichos, was an achingly unambitious take on Latin American culture. El Mundo Gira returns to that culture but, by contrast, wants to be a story within a story, commenting upon false perspectives and shifting narratives; it describes itself as a Mexican soap opera, and consciously contrasts scenes of great emotion with fictional equivalents on a television set. It takes metaphors of illegal aliens, and in what is becoming a Season Four theme, draws parallels between the sci-fi tropes and their real-world symbols.

And it's rubbish, really. Because a metaphor only works if it isn't underlined each time it's made. The nudge and wink that Scully gives the audience that "this time the aliens are the victims" is a mark of subtlety compared to a conclusion which allows the immigrants to see the FBI as alien greys. Whilst there is an earnest message here about the way we turn our backs upon the poor and itinerant, the story emphasises it to the point of absurdity by the end where two men - deadly to the touch, with heads like the elephant man's - are invisible to the affluent West. And the recurring theme of storytelling, that these people resort to the myth of the chupacabra to give some meaning to their simple lives, is patronising in the extreme. There is a sympathy at work, I'm sure, but it's suffocated by the very mawkishness of the story's conceit, and the sledgehammer tactics with which these themes are played. And Mark Snow's incessant guitar music helps matters not a jot. Yes, these people are Mexicans! We do get the idea.

It's an episode at its best when Ruben Blades plays a policeman so laconic, his uncaring racism seems not an issue being explored but a world-weary honesty. But he is performing *against* the script, and by the end his character is lost in a spree of unengaging melodrama. Skinner comments in the final scenes that the story is very hard to make much sense of, and the script treats this like a metatextual observation on the ambiguity of narrative. In fact it's a slap in the face of an audience who have been struggling hard to find a way through an episode somehow both very convoluted and yet wholly obvious, and struggling even harder to care. Acknowledging an incoherent script within the script itself doesn't magically solve the problem, it just adds a veneer of smugness to it. Teso dos Bichos was rubbish without pretension. With that added ingredient, El Mundo Gira manages to be even worse. (*)

4.12, Leonard Betts

Air Date: Jan 26, 1997
Writers: Vince Gilligan, John Shiban,
Frank Spotnitz
Director: Kim Manners

Summary An auto accident decapitates an EMT named Leonard Betts - but his headless corpse, undeterred by this, later walks out of the morgue. Scully examines Betts' head and finds that he was riddled with cancerous tumours. Mulder hypothesises that Betts, gifted with an extraordinary healing factor, could be the next stage in human evolution.

Needing tumours to survive, Betts - after regrowing his head - sets about targeting people with cancerous growths. The agents pursue Betts, leading to a confrontation in which he tries to remove the cancer he senses within Scully. She kills Betts with defibrillator pads, but can't escape his haunting words when, later that night, she awakens coughing and stems a nosebleed.

Critique   As soon as the word "cancer" was mentioned, alarm bells should have gone off. We were told, quite bluntly, that Scully would get cancer as far back as Nisei, but the series has been so clever about making mention of it recently - Jeremiah Smith healing the Cigarette Smoking Man in Talitha Cumi, the black cancer of Tunguska - that the inevitability of it has been hidden in plain view. So this story manages to pull off an astonishing coup - playing like a standard monster episode, it gives a powerful punch in the closing few minutes when it reveals that the cancer-eating mutant wants to feed from Scully. It's so skilfully done, too; using the same apologetic words with which he killed a smoker earlier in the episode, Betts provokes a horror of recognition as he turns to Scully and says, "Sorry, you have something I need."

This is what Teliko should have been. The story is another in a series of Eugene Tooms rip-offs - the mutant with the need for a particular part of the human body, be it livers / melanin / cancer cells - but its familiarity here is its strength, burying its twist ending beneath the standard X-Files tropes. But it's more than that, taking Vince Gilligan's penchant for the ordinary villain - a man who kills only out of desperate necessity and with genuine regret - and making Betts into a sympathetic figure. The tone of the episode plays not as horror, but as grisly black comedy. For the first half of the story, at least, no crime has been committed and Mulder and Scully can indulge in some genuinely funny banter about blinking craniums and body parts bins without appearing callous. It's very gory, but all in a clinical way - this isn't the gore of violence, but of the medical macabre. As a result, Leonard Betts for the most part plays like a likeable shaggy dog story. The X-Files is more ludicrous than usual, with men regrowing heads, but that's part of the fun. There's a real sense that Mulder and Scully are in this investigation for the pursuit of the absurd, with the wild theories about evolution spikes and photographic auras entertaining even them. There's an amiable quality to the story which makes its final moments all the more of a kick in the teeth. In the stark and harsh Season Four, this is the first episode to come along which feels light and frothy - and it deliberately makes the unkindest cut of all. (****)

4.13, Never Again

Air Date: Feb. 2, 1997
Writers: Glen Morgan, James Wong
Director: Rob Bowman

Summary In Philadelphia, Ed Jeres, a recent divorcee, visits a Russian tattoo artist and gets a Bettie Page-like tattoo with the words, "Never Again". Soon after, the tattoo begins speaking to Ed and incites him to kill his downstairs neighbour, then dump her body in an incinerator.

Back in Washington, D.C., Mulder is compelled to take some vacation time. Scully reluctantly follows a lead to Philadelphia, where she happens across Ed. An attraction forms between them, but a potential night of passion is thwarted when the tattoo tells Ed "Kiss her and she's dead" - and he opts to sleep on the couch.

Scully learns of the neighbour's death, and forensic evidence suggests that the Russian's ink contains an ergot alkaloid that causes powerful hallucinations. Ed goes mad upon learning Scully's occupation and nearly shoves her into the incinerator, but gains enough resolve to burn the tattoo off his arm. Afterward, the Russian's business is shut down, pending an investigation.

Critique This episode was originally intended to air before Leonard Betts, and Gillian Anderson has said that had she known that Scully's frustration expressed here - something that drives her to walk on the wild side - was to be seen as a result of her cancer shock, she'd have played it differently. In a way, of course, it belittles what Morgan and Wong are setting out to do here, to give Scully's behaviour an *excuse*. And it hearkens back to their last episode, in which they tried to give the Cigarette Smoking Man a character study, and were allowed free rein only because outside forces decreed that it was an unreliable narrative. What the cancer does to Scully here has much the same effect - what was intended to be a blistering depiction of her bitterness can be read more simply as illness trauma.

And, I must admit, I think that's the episode's great saving grace. The difficulty with series television is the way that the characters necessarily have to behave in stereotypical ways to keep the stories moving. Mulder and Scully routinely behave in recognisable patterns, because if they didn't, if Scully spent too long complaining that she finds Mulder selfish, it stalls the plot. And you reach a position, some eighty-six episodes in, when it all but becomes too late to give Scully's complaints such an airing. It demeans the characters to hear them bitch about things they ought to have bitched about long ago - if it bothered Scully that she didn't have a desk, it makes her look silly that she only gets around to raising the point three and a half seasons into the programme. Essentially Mulder and Scully *are* functional hero characters, who are obliged to be two-dimensional - what gives them a reality is the work of the actors who flesh them out so well and give them the illusion of greater depth. When the writers step in once in a while and give Scully a bit of extra background for a week, it can only run contrary to what Anderson has been doing. And by lending Scully the irritation and self-analysis she has here, it only emphasises how thinly drawn she is in other episodes. You *need* an excuse for her behaviour. The cancer has to do.

There's a West Wing episode in which CJ goes to visit her father, and ends up sleeping with Matthew Modine. I'm quite sure that it was seen as being an exploration of the character, putting it into a different context. But it doesn't; what we have on display doesn't feel like CJ at all. Seeing Scully as angry and bored and believing her life is pointless isn't really Scully either. Instead it's the writers picking up on the complaints on the fan message boards. Why hasn't Scully got a desk, why isn't her name on the door? There are even references to Moose and Squirrel, the nicknames the fans have given Mulder and Scully because of the similarities seen to the Rocky and Bullwinkle cartoon. Rather than being an accurate depiction of Scully, it's only a justification of fan hobbyhorses. What's supposed to be an intimate study of Scully becomes instead outward looking, a view of the character as seen by outspoken fanfic writers. It gives Scully no extra dimensional, making her dialogue one note, one tone. Scully becomes the victim of Mulder's selfish boor. It's about as reductive a representation of The X-Files leads as you can have.

Gillian Anderson makes it work. She finds a way to ally the Scully that has been through so much to this Scully on the edge. And Rodney

Rowland gives her wonderful support as her almost-lover. Morgan and Wong are very good at their dialogue, and they give their fanwank-nod moments of real conviction. It's well directed, it's well scored. The final scene, the story ending on an unfinished sentence and an awkward silence, is beautifully well done. It's by no means a bad episode. It's just a self-indulgent one, that has an earnestness it doesn't really deserve. At the end of the day, rather than be being a groundbreaking examination of Scully, it's a story about a man who kills women being egged on by a talking tattoo that sounds like Jodie Foster. It's telling that the scenes in which his life is shown as one of repetition and failure are more affecting than Scully's - you can believe in this man, whose life goes in circles, drowning in his own mediocrity because he comes to the episode with no other baggage. When Scully is shown as being the same thing, you feel the urge to remind her that she hunts fluke monsters, catches serial killers, and gets abducted by aliens. She's not got such a boring life, really. (**1/2)

4.14, Memento Mori

Air Date: Feb. 9, 1997
Writers: Chris Carter, Vince Gilligan, John Shiban, Frank Spotnitz
Director: Rob Bowman

Summary When Sully is formally diagnosed as having a tumour between her sinus and cerebrum, she decides to visit the similarly afflicted abductees in Allentown (3.9, Nisei). All of the women have perished save for Penny Northern, who's near death. Finding that one of Northern's physicians, Dr Scanlon, has seen progress on combating the cancer, Scully submits herself for treatment.

Mulder catches a UFO network member, Kurt Crawford, taking files from the one of the dead women's computers - and thereby learns that the abductees underwent treatment at the same fertility clinic. The man who murdered X (henceforth called "the Gray-Haired Man") murders Crawford, whose body dissolves into a green goo. Mulder breaks into a federal research facility to access the fertility clinic's mainframe, and finds several Crawford duplicates there, grown from ova harvested from the women (including Scully) during their abduction. Discovering that Scanlon is involved, Mulder calls a halt to Scully's treatment. Scanlon disappears, and Northern dies.

Critique There's a hilarious moment in this, when Mulder tells Scully he's been reading the letter she wrote to him in her diary. "I decided to throw it out," she tells him, looking suitably embarrassed. Unfortunately, there's not a laugh intended in this rather mawkish tale of cancer treatment and stolen ova. Scully may be a great doctor, but a writer she isn't: though it's a nice structural conceit that the episode is chaptered by extracts of Scully's prose, they are by and large impenetrably dense and tortuous. The opening teaser, composed of nothing more than Scully narration, is especially poor - and full credit should go to Gillian Anderson for making it to the end without taking a breath.

There are four writers on this episode, so it comes as no surprise that the script feels as self-conscious as Scully's letters. With the formal acknowledgement of Scully's cancer it all feels deliberately important, but, truth to tell, there's not a lot that's new on display. There's a shock reveal of a roomful of cloned doctors, as there was in Colony. There's a sequence where Mulder demands of Skinner the whereabouts of the Cigarette Smoking Man... what's that, the third time now, surely? There are big revelations from finding Scully's name on file, as in Paper Clip. And there are lots of hospital scenes, of course, which might have had considerably more impact if they weren't by now a staple of so many mytharc X-Files episodes. Poor Sheila Larken, playing Scully's mother - it's rare she appears in an X-File without being required to stand tearful over a hospital bed. I could almost believe she got the job because she brings her own prop with her.

But there is still a power to much of this episode, and that's down to the sincerity of the performances. Larken brings an anger to the scene where she attacks Scully for not telling her of the cancer sooner, and it feels utterly right from a woman who's had to grieve so much in the last couple of years. David Duchovny is ter-

rific when he's in denial that Scully's cancer is inoperable, reduced to a slightly stammering boy with no wisecrack behind which he can retreat. As Penny Northern, Gillian Barber brings an honest dignity to her role of cancer victim, acting as the still point of calm for Scully as she prepares herself and her friend for death. And Gillian Anderson is, as ever, wonderful: responding to her cancer first with the clinical detachment of a medical doctor, then angry embarrassment when the nosebleeds start. There's no more moving moment than when she gives in to treatment, and telephones Mulder to tell him the truth is in *her*. In spite of the complexity of so much of her monologues, it's the clear simplicity of Anderson's perform-ance here which is so haunting. She finds strength in the end in Penny's death, in wanting to battle on as best she can. The final scene of bravery and acceptance is a tour de force for both her and Duchovny.

It's well directed too - from the opening shot of white light and corridors which so symbolis-es near death experiences, to the way that all the hospital equipment looks as frightening and cruel as the experimental devices we see in Scully's abduction. It's all made very well, and is performed with great heart - and it makes a very mannered script feel genuinely affecting and real. (**1/2)

4.15, Kaddish

Air Date: Feb 16, 1997
Writer: Howard Gordon
Director: Kim Manners

Summary Three hate-filled teenagers murder a Hasidic man named Isaac Luria, who was engaged to a woman named Ariel Weiss. Soon, one of the teens is also found dead with Luria's fingerprint on his body. Mulder and Scully find that Luria's body is still in his coffin, but they wonder if he's risen from the grave to exact vengeance.

Kenneth Ungar, a Judaic scholar, tells Mulder about the golem: a creature formed from mud, given life by an inscription of the Hebrew word "emet". Mulder suspects that Ariel's father Jacob has created a golem with Luria's features. Meanwhile, Luria's other two murderers - plus Curt Brunjes, a disseminator of anti-Jewish

propaganda - are slaughtered. Events converge at a synagogue, where Ariel and the golem con-duct a wedding ceremony. After a dangerous scuffle with Mulder and Scully, Ariel proclaims her love for the golem and alters the inscription giving it life, terminating its existence.

Critique It's appropriate that Howard Gordon's last solo script for the series is a supernatural revenge drama, because he's done more than any writer to make it a staple story of The X-Files. But this is one of his very best. The plot mechanics offer nothing unexpected, as a golem kills off one by one all the men involved in the murder of a Jewish fiancé - but there's a real anger to this tale of anti-Semitism and hate between differing cultures which marks this episode out as something special. Gordon makes the very convincing point that the likes of Carl Brunjes, who peddles Jew-hating litera-ture from his presses but would never dare raise a finger against a Jew himself, is just as guilty as the three Nazi thugs who beat and shoot a defenceless man. And Gordon could so easily have turned the Jewish community into anoth-er portrait of the Native Americans seen in Shapes, or the cults of Gender Bender or Red Museum - strange outcasts with their funny lit-tle religions and ghastly folk tales. But the way he shows a society who so routinely suffer prej-udice, that Mulder and Scully too - quite cor-rectly - can be seen as part of an establishment disrespecting their customs, gives the story the dignity it requires. There's always something very dangerous about episodes which take their lead from minority groups - the series risks fum-bling and patronising them, whilst using their mythology as cheap fodder for monster tales. But Kaddish refuses to sentimentalise Ariel's father (excellently played by David Groh), showing that however justified his anger, he too has been a terrorist.

Best of all, though, is the way that in the last act the revenge drama shifts focus and becomes instead a love story. That Isaac was brought back to life so that Ariel could say goodbye to him on their wedding day gives the episode a real heart - and the final sequence, in which she weds the macabre remnants of her love, and then destroys him and reduces him to mud, is extremely moving. It's a story about truth: the words that bring the golem to life mean "truth", and truth is the mantra used by Brunjes to justify his persecution of the Jews. For a series which routinely uses "the truth is out there" in its opening credits, to have the word so abused and twisted here is truly effective. And it's about the power of words too; not for nothing does Brunjes own a printing press, the lies and propaganda from which fuel the anti-Semitism in the neighbourhood. It's words which can create life, but by changing a letter in Yiddish "truth" becomes "dead", so words can destroy as easily.

Its biggest problem is its position in the scheduling. Intended to air before Leonard Betts, the story was never meant to tie into the cancer arc. Coming straight after Memento Mori, this deceptively traditional tale looks as if it's cheating on the consequences of Scully's illness. Its love story, too, is buried beneath the showier and more unsubtle histrionics of the week before. Had this been broadcast after El Mundo Gira, a story which got its Mexican love story wrong as much as Kaddish got its Jewish love story right, it would be better appreciated. As it is, this is a fine if unremarkable story, distinguished in the cynicism of Season Four by showing rare soul. (***1/2)

4.16, Unrequited

Air Date: Feb 23, 1997
Story: Howard Gordon
Teleplay: Howard Gordon, Chris Carter
Director: Michael Lange

Summary   The unexplained death a military officer causes Mulder to investigate Nathaniel Teager, a Green Beret who was held prisoner in Vietnam for twenty-four years. Mulder speculates that Teager learned from Viet Cong guerrillas how to conceal himself from a person's field of vision, thereby manifesting a form of invisibility. Moreover, Mulder suspects that the government is using Teager to eliminate the three generals who signed his death certificate - preventing them from testifying about the military's treatment of South Vietnamese soldiers.

Teager kills the second officer involved, then goes gunning for the third - General Benjamin Bloch - at a re-dedication ceremony for the Vietnam Veterans' Memorial. Skinner thwarts the murder attempt, and an FBI agent kills Teager as he flees the scene.

Critique   Kaddish was a victim of poor scheduling, and so Scully's cancer story was unceremoniously dropped at a time when the series really needed to demonstrate it was taking more care of its characters than that. But there's no excuse for Unrequited, filmed after Memento Mori. To avoid bringing up the matter altogether, the story is set earlier in the season, before Paper Hearts, which you can only learn if you're the sort to pay especially close attention to the on-screen dating given at the bottom of the screen, and be prepared to compare it to the dating on episodes broadcast a couple of months previously. Even if you *are* watching the screen that intently - in which case, you're probably taking the mytharc even more solemnly than Chris Carter - it makes it no less an act of cowardice on the half of the production team. We're used by now to the fact that the events of mythology stories rarely impinge upon the standalone ones, and we accept it (grudgingly) because its format is one of an anthology show. But there's a world of difference between Mulder not discussing the spaceship he saw last week, and Scully not coming to terms with the illness she is *dying* from. To misquote the show: don't open doors you're not prepared to go through, guys.

It's not as if the episode couldn't have done with a little more substance than a few cancer references might have given it. This is very thin stuff. Never has a story been so blatantly padded: the (long) teaser scene is replayed later in the episode to no new dramatic effect. Marita from the UN is pursued by Mulder to give information we've already worked out for ourselves - it's likely that the third general under threat will be the only one still alive with a speaking role, and - heaven's alive! - that turns out to be the case. There's an interesting metaphor here about the way Vietnam veterans were treated after the war, and here's a soldier so ignored that he is actually invisible. It's not subtle, but the analogy works - or *would* work, perhaps, unless the first words of the episode raise the theme directly, and the last scene has Mulder explaining it in detail for those of us who have missed it.

And somewhere within the padding there's a good story. Mitch Pileggi is given a large chunk of the dialogue, but is never allowed to make the case *personal* - as a Vietnam vet himself, what freshness might the episode have contained if it had given him something interesting to say from that perspective? The three set pieces (one repeated) of assassinations, successful and foiled, are well set up - if the same care had gone into the scenes linking them, this night have been rather exciting. As it is, the episode becomes a barrage of conspiracy theories which don't get the attention required to make sense, and war guilt platitudes which keep changing our allegiances towards the characters. Teager is a cold assassin, but also a hard-done-by victim who wants to return medals to widows. Sleepless and The Walk both had a take on the military which was insightful; in Unrequited, the generals are cynical liars, and the soldiers cheer in crowds as if they're at a Status Quo concert. It's not good enough.

In spite of all this, it's watchable. It's well directed by Michael Lange, and the action - what there is of it - trots along nicely. It's never boring. But it's so unambitious, and feels very much like a first draft script rushed into production. That would be annoying enough anyway. But at a point in the series where one of the lead characters is, for the first time, undergoing a genuine life change, it feels doubly wasteful. (**)

4.17, Tempus Fugit

Air Date: March 16, 1997
Writers: Chris Carter, Frank Spotnitz
Director: Rob Bowman

Summary Sharon Graffia, the sister of abductee Max Fenig (1.9, Fallen Angel) tells Mulder and Scully that Max has died in an airplane crash. At the crash site, the agents note a nine-minute discrepancy between the time on the victims' wristwatches and the time of the disaster. Meanwhile, an "airplane investigator" named Garrett disposes of evidence pertaining to the incident.

Armed men try to kill the airport controllers who last spoke with the downed plane, but one of them - Louis Frish - tells Mulder and Scully that a second airship approached Flight 549 just prior to an explosion. Scully returns to Washington to secure protection for Frish, but Garret tries to kill her in a bar - and shoots Agent Pendrell instead.

Mulder theorises that an alien vessel drew close to Flight 549 in mid-air, but was shot down by a third airplane. He calculates that the second airship crashed into Great Sacandaga Lake and goes diving there. Mulder locates the wreckage of an alien spaceship - just before a bright light overtakes him. [To be continued.]

Critique This is the best conspiracy episode we've seen in nearly two years, precisely because it is *about* a conspiracy and the mysteries which surround it, and not men in darkened rooms talking in purple prose. It's told very clearly, with remarkably little baggage, and the plotting is good and intriguing and blissfully well managed. As it is a story about UFOs and abductions, with the cover-ups being something shadowy rather than steeped in mytharc continuity, it has the breeziness and energy of a Season One adventure, but done here with a Season Four budget and a Season Four efficiency. It's a breath of fresh air.

And it's so beautifully directed too. This is the first indication we get of Rob Bowman gearing up to take the mantle of the feature film. Its scale is wonderful, from the stunning teaser of an in-flight tragedy, to the car chase on the runway avoiding an incoming aeroplane. Crash investigator Mike Millar's encounter with a UFO above the lake is a really beautiful.

It's an episode of great performances - Tom O'Brien and Joe Spano bring a realistic conviction to the respective roles of Louis Frish and Mike Millar, making the disaster of an aeroplane crash seem very real. Both of them, either in the anger with which Spano refutes Mulder's alien claims, or in the scene in which Sergeant Gonzales demonstrates a terrible guilt of responsibility upon realising that a blip on the air traffic control screen equates to rows of body bags, make this alien encounter story feel properly grounded. (****)

4.18, Max

Air Date: March 23, 1997
Writers: Chris Carter, Frank Spotnitz
Director: Kim Manners

Summary Military frogmen - the source of the bright light - place Mulder under arrest but later release him. Frish is incarcerated on suspicion of murder and lying to federal investigators. Agent Pendrell dies. The agents learn that Sharon Graffia isn't related to Fenig after all, but is an associate of his with a history of mental illness.

Evidence from Fenig's trailer suggests that he boarded Flight 549 with something he believed was incontrovertible proof of the existence of aliens. Mulder theorises that an alien spaceship froze Flight 549 with a tractor beam so it could retrieve Fenig and his item, but the military shot the spaceship down. Fenig's item was divided into three parts - two pieces were confiscated, but the third was in Fenig's luggage. Mulder retrieves it from Syracuse and leaves for Washington on a plane, but Garrett follows and grabs the piece. As before, a UFO freezes the plane and spirits Garrett and the item away; Mulder lands in Washington empty-handed.

Critique And, amazingly, they don't drop the ball.

Concluding instalments of two-parters in The X-Files are notoriously unsatisfying. After the play box has been opened in part one, and promises are made that will affect the future of mankind / all life on Earth / ratings at sweeps (if nothing else), the toys are all shut away again. It's true to a certain extent here too; Mulder's alien evidence is stolen, the conspiracy agents cannot be brought to justice, and Scully is left to pontificate in the traditional pompous summing up. But there's still something very solid about all this, because it feels that the episode in question is all *about* closure, and the inevitability of loose ends dangling. And Scully's speech is nicely punctured by a gag from Mulder, and we enter the story rarely on a note of optimism and wonder which seems to dignify characters who have died and the quest they were on.

Although Max is dead, this is very much his story. We are given a moving impression of a frightened man who only ever wished to be alone - but was chosen by bad chance to be something important, an abductee. And so against his better judgment he becomes a rebel, and dies in the process of trying to expose a greater truth. Scully likens Max to Mulder, and it's only right that Mulder takes his mission so personally, seeking a way to make sure that Max cannot be just forgotten as another nut. The flashback sequence where Mulder hypothesises how Max died is breathtakingly good, and is probably the most subtly frightening thing in the whole of Season Four; we know that we are watching a disaster in the making, and that none of these terrified people on the aircraft will survive. Agent Pendrell too gets killed; it's a sad, unheroic way to go, dying not to save the woman he's had a crush on but drunkenly getting in the way of her bullet, and I love it for that. Just as I love too the way Scully can mourn him without ever having learned his first name - to kill a comic relief character so matter-of-factly is wonderful, and in Scully's insistence that Pendrell must not die we see her nose bleed, a reminder that she can't hold back death even from herself.

The plotting perhaps isn't as to height as it could be. Joe Spano and Tom O'Brien, who were both so essential to the success of Tempus Fugit, get dropped from the story rather perfunctorily. And the sequence where Max is abducted midair is so good that the climax to the episode, where the same thing happens to Garrett, can't help but feel a little repetitive. But there is an emotional power to this story which makes these flaws forgivable - what the episode does is take a look at Mulder's quest from a new, more innocent perspective, and give it a heart in the process which has arguably been lost somewhat through the plot convolutions of the last few years. If this isn't the equal of Tempus Fugit, it isn't far off - and together they make the most satisfying "event" multiparter that The X-Files has done. This could have been The X-Files movie itself - tight, satisfying, witty and touching, and re-examining the series goals with a new vigour. (****)

4.19, Synchrony

Air Date: April 13, 1997
Writers: Howard Gordon, David Greenwalt
Director: James Charleston

Summary An elderly man warns two cryogenics researchers at the Massachusetts Institute of Technology - Jason Nichols and Lucas Menand - that a bus will run over Menand. They ignore him, and the bus kills Menand as predicted. Soon after, the elderly man somehow freezes another scientist named Dr Yonechi to death.

Lisa Ianelli, Nichols' girlfriend and fellow researcher, tells Mulder and Scully that Nichols has tried - and failed - to develop a cryogenics compound akin to the one that froze Yonechi. She also suggests a means of reviving Yonechi, but the attempt incinerates him instead.

Mulder pegs the elderly man as being Jason Nichols from the future, who's come back to alter history. Nichols, Yonechi and Ianelli perfected the freezing solution five years hence, and Nichols - having failed to save Menand - opted to kill Yonechi instead. The older Nichols grabs his younger self, and they both burst into flames. Undeterred, Ianelli continues work on the cryogenics compound.

Critique I'm a real sucker for time travel stories, so I'm more forgiving of this than most fans. But Synchrony is an odd beast - it's so tentative about the very science fiction nature of its concept, it holds off even acknowledging it until over halfway through the running time. The biggest weakness here is Mulder's leap into theorising that the old man assassin must be a visitor from the future - typically he'll ask Scully if she can come up with a likelier explanation, and for once you want to shout at the screen that hundreds automatically spring to mind! It's such a defined genre, the fantasy of going into the past, that Chris Carter once said it'd be a subject too awkward and hackneyed for The X-Files ever to touch. That it feels so odd here is partly because it tries too hard to justify its inclusion in the series at last, and you feel that Carter's earlier assertion weighs heavily on the production team and makes them self-conscious: had the old Jason Nichols at the start of the story more openly admitted that he was from forty years hence, the episode could have

relaxed a bit more and had some fun playing with the concept of the paradox.

As it is, then, although there are some great scenes here - the freezing is a suitably creepy, and the sequence where the luckless Dr Yonechi is brought back from the dead only to burst into flame is smashing - the story never gives itself the time (ironically) to do much more than chase after a mysterious old man carrying a chemical compound. The potency of the climax, where Jason is hugged to fiery death by his older self, is underplayed. It's all a bit too cold, as if the writers were so intent on concealing the impossibility of the premise that they never really explored the consequence of it. Whilst I applaud the view of time travel that is so very X-Files, and so very far from the utopian excitement it usually inspires - offering instead a nightmare world without history or hope - Howard Gordon and David Greenwalt never find the passion to make this nightmare really credible. It's a concept, nothing more. It's as schematic as the papers being busied over by all these super-intelligent research scientists.

But, for all that, it feels fresh. It's a very simple X-Files episode; there's a spate of killings to be solved, and a mystery to be explained. It doesn't add up to much, and the characters aren't very engaging, but it's solid and watchable. It's a rarity in Season Four, a high concept tale that is told without pretension - or, it must be said, without much ambition. It does its job. It's only shame is that it's a concept with such potential that it's galling to see it explored with such little joie de vivre. (**1/2)

4.20, Small Potatoes

Air Date: April 20, 1997
Writer: Vince Gilligan
Director: Cliff Bole

Summary The tabloids run wild when five children in Martinsburg, West Virginia, are born with vestigial tails. All of the women attended the same fertility clinic, but Mulder notices a telltale scar on the lower back of a janitor, Eddie Van Blundht. Paternity tests reveal that Van Blundht fathered the five children, but he escapes by changing shape to resemble a deputy. Mulder posits that Van Blundht similarly disguised himself as the women's husbands (and in one case, Luke Skywalker) to have sex with them.

The agents visit Van Blundht's home and find his father's mummified remains. Scully concludes that Van Blundht Sr's skin acted like a muscle, and that Van Blundht has the same trait. Van Blundht locks Mulder up and takes his place, then returns to Washington with Scully. They share a relaxed evening and nearly kiss - until the real Mulder bursts in, having escaped, and places Van Blundht under arrest.

Critique   This is what Vince Gilligan has been working toward all season, with his tales of monsters who are desperately ordinary, even mundane. Eddie Van Blundht, who has a tail and shape shifting abilities, is a loser - his high school sweetheart, crazy enough to watch Star Wars nearly three hundred times and allow herself to be impregnated by Luke Skywalker, defines him as such and sees herself as superior. What we have here is a gentle and witty exploration of what makes someone feel they're an underachiever, a man who stubbornly takes more pride in the silent "h" in his surname than in his magical ability to change his form, a nebbish who is given great powers but lacks the imagination to do anything constructive with them. Gilligan has spent the year working away at his depictions of men who need to make themselves feel special by bizarre means - and he finishes up with poor Eddie, who is so insecure he literally changes into a new shape to get the respect he craves. In retrospect, the sequence where he poses as his father, just to pour scorn on his loser son who will always be "small potatoes", is terribly sad. You feel that the hurtful contempt his father showed him is something so endemic to Eddie's understanding of who he was, it would be impossible for Eddie to impersonate him as someone supportive. And the scene where, disguised as Mulder, he hears a list of his every failing from the mother of his new child, his face falling at each new criticism, is wonderfully cruel comedy.

But it's in the final act, when Eddie becomes Mulder, and goes to work at the FBI, that the story has its real twist. The episode could very merrily have had its fun from watching Mulder reinterpreted as an idiot who can't spell "inves-tigation" and has no idea what Scully is ever talking about. What gives it a kick is that, for all this, Mulder is revealed to be the bigger loser still - a man with geeks for friends, with no bed to sleep on, and so emotionally stunted he hasn't had the wit to make a pass at Scully in four seasons. The scene where our new Mulder seduces Scully is superb, because he succeeds not by being a bumbling Eddie we've come to expect, but a man who bothers to listen to what a woman is saying and to be empathetic. Duchovny is extraordinary in these sequences - he captures to great comic effect the way that Eddie's face slumps, but also gives his false Mulder a winning and sympathetic gentleness that is extraordinarily charismatic. And Gilligan's dissection of ordinary losers punching above their weight at last includes Mulder himself. The hypothesis of the episode, that we are defined by others' responses to what we look like, is only partly true: the "Mulder" that Eddie creates could never have solved an X-File, but he'd have had a lot more fun, and been a more caring man into the bargain.

It's apt that Darin Morgan is cast as Eddie, as the story already owes a debt to his comic writing in Season Three. But there's a charm and intelligence here which is Gilligan's own, and a finer display of storytelling all round. Morgan's work feels like an attempt to reinvent The X-Files radically; Gilligan is a more cunning writer, he wants to analyse it from within. And it's why the little digs at the characters and the series clichés feel truer here, because they're not breaking the rules to make their observations. This is essentially a story which takes an entire strand of X-Files mythology - the shapeshifter - and uses it to comic effect; it's the cliffhanger of Colony made into a perfect joke.

The episode has its faults. The comedy may be a little too infectious, so that Mulder as himself breaks the tail of a corpse and tries to hide the evidence, when it would have been surely more effective had he been characterised as someone much more mechanical and efficient. It's a joke for the sake of a joke, and it spoils the contrast needed between the clumsiness of Eddie's Mulder and the real Mulder. A greater concern is in the way that we're invited to see as comic hero a man who is using his mutant abilities to commit rape. As you watch, you put the implications of what Eddie is doing to one side, partly because Darin Morgan plays the part so winningly, and partly (let's face it) because the word "rape" is never actually mentioned. But it's there all the same; this is a man who uses his shapeshifting abilities to deceive women into sex, and for all the comic pratfalls and the merry tone of the episode, you have to deliberately *ignore* what Eddie's up to if you don't want a bad taste left in your mouth. I suspect it may only a flaw in retrospect - that Gilligan had a blacker comedy in mind, in which he made that balance between Eddie's charm and a more nefarious deceit part of the point. But if that's the case, it gets lost in the execution. Maybe it's better that way; the final act sequence between Duchovny and Anderson on the sofa plays brilliantly as domestic comedy, and too much would be lost if it had overtones of the usual "Scully in Jeopardy" tension we've seen so often before. Part of the joke is surely that when Mulder arrives to save his partner in the nick of time, it isn't from human sacrifice or lobotomy, but from a snog. The actors and the director find a tone which is joyous and bubbly, and it works a treat - it's only when you remind yourself of the grubbier implications of Gilligan's script that you wonder whether the plot could have been adjusted to have matched that tone.

Those qualms apart, Small Potatoes is a little gem. Vince Gilligan has brilliantly taken the crueller, colder freedoms of Season Four, of little men and disillusionment, and found a fresh and funny way of exploring them. It's this balance of laughter and despair which will prove the true template for the next few seasons of The X-Files, not Scully's cancer or Mulder being driven towards suicide. (*****)

4.21, Zero Sum

Air Date: April 27, 1997
Writers: Howard Gordon, Frank Spotnitz
Director: Kim Manners

Summary   Skinner brokers a deal with the Cigarette Smoking Man to get Scully treatment for her cancer, and in exchange becomes the Cigarette Smoking Man's minion. In this role, Skinner destroys evidence when a bee swarm kills Jane Brody, a delivery worker. Mulder learns about the incident when an informant, Detective Ray Thomas, sends him photographs of the crime - but Thomas is later killed execution-style.

Skinner delivers a piece of honeycomb to Peter Valdespino, an entomologist, and learns that the bees have been engineered to carry smallpox. More killer bees attack an elementary school in South Carolina, but Skinner tells medical workers to treat the victims for smallpox, not bee stings. Mulder accuses Skinner of killing Thomas, but Skinner claims that his gun was stolen - a frame-job that Mulder helps Skinner dodge. Soon after, the Cigarette Smoking Man instructs Marita Covarrubias to give Mulder false information.

Critique   Most conspiracy episodes trip over themselves with overwritten dialogue and a rush of non-explanations. Zero Sum is very different; the sequence after the opening credits is six minutes of dialogue-free action, and it's quite brilliant: we see Skinner stare into the face of his Faustian deal with the Cigarette Smoking Man, cleaning toilets to remove evidence, hiding in ventilation ducts, and burning bodies. It is usually considered a weakness that these episodes offer no revelations, but for once that's the story's real strength. This is the world of The X-Files as viewed by a supporting character who for the best intentions has got caught on the wrong side of the conspiracy.

Mitch Pileggi looks much more comfortable here than he did in last year's showcase Avatar; rather than being about some experiment using bees, as the plotline would suggest, it's instead about a criminal who wants to be caught. Skinner is torn between seeing Mulder here as threat and as salvation - you can see how desperately he *wants* his best agent to expose his part in the cover-ups, and the relief that would bring. Skinner has come a long way since he made that fateful decision to back The X-Files explicitly at the beginning of Season Three; the Cigarette Smoking Man now wants to toy with him, give him a glimpse of how far he's fallen by making that bargain to save Scully's life. In Avatar, Skinner was framed for the murder of a prostitute; Zero Sum is much more confrontational, and therefore much more interesting, as Skinner realises how he is *genuinely* complicit in the shooting of a police officer and the infection with smallpox of a playground full of children. It's not a story with a climax - which does make the final act a little unsatisfactory - but that's part of the point, there's no easy ending here. Skinner comes to realise that by trading with the devil, he's ransomed his soul.

The episode only really stumbles when it offers the viewer what they've had before: Mulder threatening Skinner at gunpoint, Skinner threatening the Cigarette Smoking Man at gunpoint... they're big scenes, but they carried far more weight the first time we saw them. And the story does get somewhat top-heavy. It ends upon the realisation that Mulder's new contact, Marita Covarrubias, is in league with the conspiracy - but the lisping blonde has been used so perfunctorily ever since her introduction, denying information and then retreating back into the shadows like a bad parody of Deep Throat and X, that the moment counts for nothing. At this stage it would have seemed a bigger twist had she *not* been corrupt. These nods towards the greater arc feel a mistake - it's not an episode which has much to say, so in conversations between Skinner and the Cigarette Smoking Man, it can only retread familiar ground. But where it succeeds is in its style - those excellent sequences of death by bee - and in the shock value of seeing a deliberately familiar story through the fractured view of another character. (****)

4.22, Elegy

Air Date: May 4, 1997
Writer: John Shiban
Director: James Charleston

Summary Angie Pintero, a bowling alley owner, spies a young woman caught in the alley's machinery - then also finds her lying dead in the street. Mulder investigates a number of similar incidents, and comes to question Harold Spuller, a mental patient, who met each of the slain women prior to their demise. Spuller also gets a vision of Pintero - who moments later is found dead from a heart attack.

Mulder concludes that anyone who's seen such "ghosts" is near death themselves. Scully becomes alarmed, as *she* saw one of the slain women while staunching a nosebleed. The agents find that one of Spuller's caretakers - Nurse Innes - has been taking his medication, which leads her to commit the murders. Innes attacks Scully, who shoots her in the shoulder. Spuller dies from respiratory failure - and soon afterward, Scully sees a vision of him.

Critique The murder investigation itself is a bit ho-hum, with all the requisites clichés in place - a hugely unsympathetic police chief who badgers the innocent suspect, the killer coming out of left field in the last act with dubious motives and little characterisation. (The nurse did it. It's signposted from the very first appearance, though, because she's the only woman working with the mentally ill who looks grumpy.)

If writer John Shiban doesn't seem much interested in the X-File itself, though, it allows him to give greater attention to the relationship between Mulder and Scully, with particular emphasis on Scully's cancer. The result is terrific. After so many scenes in this series where the two lead characters have been required to come out with awkward bouts of revelatory dialogue which are utterly unsayable, there's something hugely moving in the final sequence where Mulder rounds upon Scully's own dishonesty in facing up to her illness. It has a complexity and sincerity which is unforgivably rare in the series' use of the cancer storyline, where it's either been ignored altogether or cheaply sentimentalised. This is an episode about death, with a premise that the dying are able to see visions of ghosts - and it's therefore a story in which the characters are being forced to confront death, their relationship to it, and their very *proximity* to it too. The scene where Scully sees her first vision, as she is washing away her telltale nosebleed, is one of the most chilling things the series has offered this year - as in Leonard Betts, it's what the concept of the week reveals about Scully herself that is so affecting. The conversation she has with her counsellor, an echo of the similarly brilliant one in Irresistible, is a highlight of the season, with Gillian Anderson on top form. That she is asked to consider not only her fear of mortality, but her fear of letting down Mulder, is wonderful - it turns the whole cancer arc on its head, and makes her illness a much more personal failing.

This is not an easy episode to watch, and there's a funereal atmosphere to it that makes it one of the series' most depressing outings. But for once I don't feel it's glorying in the cancer storyline for the sake of melodrama, or to give Anderson a good acting role. It's a strangely quiet and contemplative little episode; it's every bit the elegy that the title suggests. (****)

4.23, Demons

Air Date: May 11, 1997
Writer: RW Goodwin
Director: Kim Manners

Summary Mulder awakens in a hotel with blood on his shirt, two rounds missing from his pistol and no memory of what happened to him. He and Scully soon find the bodies of abductee Amy Cassandra and her husband David - and worry that Mulder killed them.

Meanwhile, Mulder has flashbacks of the Cigarette Smoking Man visiting the Mulder household and acting curiously intimate around Mrs Mulder. A toxicology report indicates that Mulder's memory loss stems from an injection of a drug called ketamine; further evidence establishes that David and Amy Cassandra died in a murder-suicide. When Mulder learns that Amy's therapist, Dr Charles Goldstein, specializes in memory retrieval, he orders Goldstein to recover his missing memories. Goldstein agrees and drugs Mulder, then menacingly approaches him with a needle. The police arrest Goldstein, but a deluded Mulder flees to his childhood home and flails a gun at Scully until she talks him into relenting.

Critique This feels like the wrong episode at the wrong time. We're building up to a crescendo on a storyline in which Scully is confronting her brain cancer - so it's strange that here we see Mulder falling over and clutching his head whilst Scully worries over *his* possible aneurysm. I'm sure it wasn't the case, but it looks like David Duchovny wanted his chance to do a little bit of terminal disease acting too. We've seen Skinner deal with the devil to save Scully's life, we've seen Mulder fight for the truth behind Scully's condition - it all feels like

a strange Season One throwback that Mulder would let some quack bore holes into his brain now, when Scully needs him most, to uncover the secrets behind his sister's abduction.

It's a particularly pointless detour, because it doesn't reveal anything whatsoever. The flashback sequences are masterpieces of editing - but there's only so many times they can intrigue when on each successive appearance they only repeat the same lack of information. The episode gets off to a great start, with an interesting mystery to solve: is Mulder a murderer? The first half of this story works because you're waiting to find out what really happened in the long weekend that Mulder cannot remember. We get flashes of an explanation, but no real payoff, and we are largely left as much in the dark as we were when we started. Mulder must have been in the room when Cassandra killed herself and her husband, and was presumably too tripped out to care. How he got himself back to his motel room, though, is left unclear. I can forgive an episode which hints it might answer big back stories to the mythology, and then deny us. But to lose interest even in the answers set up in your own plotline is just bad storytelling.

For all the angst on offer, we're given very little that is new. And it means that when the story aims for big dramatic climaxes - the scene where Mulder points a gun at Scully, or confronts his mother over his paternity - we're left unengaged. The sequence in Paper Hearts, for example, in which Mulder prods his mother's memories about the abduction of Samantha - and is so forgiving when after her stroke she can't remember details - is so much subtler and truer than here, where he's so childishly rude that she's obliged to slap him round the face.

But that is what Demons is - a slap around the face. It's relentlessly unsubtle. Scully tells Mulder that if he wants to learn the truth, he should probably find a better approach than to resort to trepanning. I'd really rather respect a hero who had worked that out for himself. But then, this is a character who lets somebody drill into his skull to find out what relationship his mother had with a man, and only *afterwards* thinks he could just go to her house and ask her. He should be relieved she slapped him. Imagine what a silly chump he'd have felt had she just come out and told him - all that head trauma for nothing! (*1/2)

4.24, Gethsemane

Air Date: May 18, 1997
Writer: Chris Carter
Director: RW Goodwin

Summary   Anthropologists in Canada discover what appears to be an alien body entombed in two-hundred-year-old ice, but an assassin named Scott Ostelhoff kills most of the team members. Ostelhoff fails to locate the alien corpse - which Mulder finds and transports to a warehouse for further examination.

Scully studies ice core samples taken from the base camp, then arrests Michael Kritschgau, a member of the Pentagon's research division, when he tries to kill her. Kritschgau is taken to Mulder for questioning, where he details an elaborate scheme to deceive Mulder by planting a fake alien corpse for him to "find" in Canada. Ostelhoff makes off with the corpse, and Mulder is taken aback when Scully tells him the men behind this hoax must have also given her cancer. Soon afterward, Scully is asked to identify a body in Mulder's apartment, and tells FBI officials that Mulder has died from a self-inflicted gunshot wound. [To be continued.]

Critique   Like most mythology episodes, this attempts to do too much. But rather than do so on a purely narrative level, with lots of exposition as usual, it asks us to accept rather too much of an *emotional* shift. That, at the least, is more interesting - and if Gethsemane doesn't quite work, it has a passion behind it which makes it gripping. Scully and Mulder are both shown here on different personal quests, both as obsessed as the other with finding their own truths. Anderson is excellent in the scene where Scully's brother Bill challenges her continued assurance that she's fine, and asks what on earth so selfishly drives her to work through her cancer and deny herself to her family. Duchovny has the harder job to do, needing in the space of a single episode not only to be jubilant that evidence for alien existence has at last been found, but then be so disillusioned by the hoax of it that the idea he'd take his own life is a credible one. It's here that the story falters - as far back as Deep Throat, Mulder was asked why he stubbornly clung to his beliefs in the wake of so much proof to the contrary, and he answered it was because such proof was never convincing enough. Nor is it here. We know of course that Mulder hasn't killed himself, that it's merely another way of doing a season cliffhanger. It's the most contrived part of the story, and for all its genuine shock value, it feels as fake as the alien in the ice.

Chris Carter's script, though, is mostly clean and thorough. The discussions between Mulder and Scully about their individual faiths, and the way that the proof of God or the proof of extra-terrestrial life might change who they are, is particularly effective. There's a subtle skill to the way that Mulder and Scully are contrasted here, which makes shocking sense of the framing device in which Scully appears to denounce Mulder to the FBI. It's an episode of betrayals - Scully to Mulder and to her family, and Mulder to Scully. (Bill's observation that Mulder has abandoned Scully in her hour of need to pursue an alien carcass in the mountains is very pertinent.) Gethsemane works because it strips The X-Files down to its basics - Mulder's eagerness to believe over Scully's need to hesitate - and has never more convincingly expressed that dynamic. For a story which more or less takes the series' core elements and reboots them, asking us once again whether anything we have seen over the last four seasons can be substantiated, the ending (however bogus) is still thrilling. It feels that the series may be moving into a new direction, the emphasis more upon justifying the belief in the paranormal rather than just complacently accepting it each week. We know, of course, that by this stage a movie has been commissioned, and so Season Five effectively has to be put into a holding pattern, setting up its storylines only as far as the cinema will allow. But rather than just treading water, instead of spreading its mythology ever outwards, there are hints here that it might look inwards and become more analytical. That may be a fascinating thing. (****)

Millennium: Season 1

1.1, Pilot

Air Date: Oct. 25, 1996
Writer: Chris Carter
Director: David Nutter

Summary Frank Black, a former FBI agent, relocates to Seattle with his wife Catherine and young daughter Jordan to begin a new life. However, the murder of a peep show dancer prompts Frank to offer his expertise as a criminal profiler to his former boss, police Lieutenant Bob Bletcher.

The authorities prove sceptical regarding Frank's deductions, including his belief that the murderer thinks he is purging Seattle of sin. Frank tells Bletcher that he possesses the ability to see what the killer sees - that he can mentally put himself in the killer's head, and become part of his or her darkness. He quit the FBI after jailing a killer who photographed his victims - and a second, unknown party sent him Polaroids of Catherine. Later, the Millennium Group - an organization of former law enforcement officials, gathered to battle dark forces related to the oncoming millennium - offered to help Frank understand the nature of his "gift". Peter Watts, a senior Group member, has become one of Frank's key allies.

Frank realises that the killer works in a police forensics lab. The murderer attacks Frank, raving about the final judgment and how "the thousand years is over!", but Bletcher shoots and kills him. Afterward, someone (henceforth called "the Polaroid Man") sends Frank Polaroids of Catherine and Jordan.

Critique The first image is like a frozen snapshot - and then, almost at the flick of a switch, the action starts and heavy rain comes pouring down. It sums up the tone of the new series very well, of something dark and threatening ever encroaching. Right from the start, with the sequences of blood running down walls to the syncopated dance beat of a peepshow, this is a programme which is marking itself out as being cruder and nastier than its more obviously populist sister show - but what's remarkable is that however brutal the episode is, there's a com-

pelling beauty to it too. David Nutter's direction is *so* good that it lends an elegance to the imaginings of a crazed killer. And I wonder whether that is a distraction, whether Nutter can't help but give an artistry to what is meant to be so bleak and confrontational, to the point that it somehow prevents the audience from getting too shocked.

It's a pretentious point to make, I admit, but I hope a valid one. If there's a theme to the pilot, it's of that same pretension. Chris Carter sets up the notion that the world is an amoral cesspool of violence and fear, where even the cops are so desensitised to what they see that they can make jokes about it. And in opposition to this, there's Frank's yellow house - the symbol (too boldly stated) of sanctuary, where his idyllic family can be unaffected. As his wife Catherine says, in one of the most effective scenes, that's an impossible dream; Frank may buy his perfect daughter a little puppy (!), but he'll still receive in the mail an envelope of Polaroids to show him his family is being stalked. It's not a subtle point, and at times it's made far too obviously - most wincingly, in a scene where Bletcher comments that he's never seen anything more terrifying than an abductee in a coffin with her eyes and mouth sewn up, and Frank tops it by comparing it to his daughter suffering with a fever. But for all that it's sincerely meant; Carter's view of Millennium is very different, say, from the one Morgan and Wong have when they run the second season. If the world is such a bleak place, there has to be some contrast, there has to be something pure for Frank to protect - or else he'll get sucked into the maelstrom like everybody else.

And the strongest element to the pilot is Frank himself, Lance Henriksen seizing the part with a confidence that makes him immediately a more credible character than either Mulder or Scully could be for an entire season. There's a compassion and a genius to him - but also, most interestingly, a backstory of breakdown and failure which makes Mulder's own crisis of sister abduction look tacked on in comparison. I'm concerned that there's not enough emphasis given to Frank's profiling ability; it's all very well to have characters repeatedly ask him how he's able to see inside the crimes, but Carter's insistence that it's not a supernatural gift is somewhat thwarted by a story told at such great pace that it gives little time to make this clear. On the one hand you get scenes where we see Frank study CCTV footage, and pick out the words of Yeats from the killer - that is, conducting an investigation through brilliant but entirely naturalistic means. On the other, there's a suggestion that the killer knows instinctively that Frank has the same psychic gifts he has, and that tips the story into being something more fantastical. At this stage the series quite rightly wants to emphasise the differences between its more gritty approach and the sci-fi hokum of The X-Files. But it's because of The X-Files that this pilot was the most highly rated on national television, and Chris Carter had a tough balancing act keeping that audience happy whilst establishing Millennium as a completely different beast. In seasons to come, as we shall see, it reluctantly becomes another series about the paranormal, before finally accepting that it's a spin-off to be concluded within The X-Files storyline. But at this stage it has higher ambitions than that, and although I find the ambiguity of Frank's gift interesting, I wonder whether it was the right way to play it.

At once this is a stronger pilot than The X-Files had four years ago. It's more stylish, better acted, better written. But it fails perhaps to make it clear what it's about, or who it's for. The first X-Files episode was, for all its frills, very simple. This feels like it needed a feature-length running time to explore its millennial themes properly, to collide the worlds of procedural police work and Nostradamus prophecies. It's brave and clever and startling. But it will need to establish what sort of programme it actually *is* very quickly. (****)

1.2, Gehenna

Air Date: Nov. 1, 1996
Writer: Chris Carter
Director: David Nutter

Summary In San Francisco, a savage beast dispatches a young man, and a large amount of human ashes are found in a park. Frank links one of the victims to an apocalypse cult that funds itself through telemarketing ventures and punishes, possibly even kills, its disobedient members. Clues implicate Gehenna Industries; one of Frank's colleagues, Mike Atkins, finds a stockpile of weapons at a Gehenna warehouse. The beast causes Atkins to become injured inside an industrial-sized microwave, but Frank directs the authorities to dismantle the operation.

Critique This benefits from a slower pace than the pilot, allowing us to get to know Frank and Catherine, and to get a better feeling for the Millennium Group and what it stands for. The scene between Catherine and Bletcher over coffee is a stand out, in which Catherine shares her views on the Polaroid Man and Frank's subsequent paralysis when he couldn't protect her. Chris Carter makes it clear at the end of the episode - after Frank has tried to take care of his family at a distance of several hundred miles, and Catherine comes to San Francisco so she can take care of *him* - that the union of this couple is the moral heart of the series. They'll both do their best to shield the other from "the bad man". The scene, too, where both of them discuss the origin of evil is impressive, because it ought to be unsubtle and clumsy, but instead at once feels both a natural conversation and honestly profound.

Around it, though, is a somewhat humdrum story. I love this idea of a telemarketing company being a front for a terrorist cult - the notion that selling rubbish nobody wants is allied to apocalyptic forces is very neat. But there's too little made of this clash of the mundane and the biblical (although the scenes within the centre are striking, in which mantra about hair products are flashed upon the wall as if at Belshazzar's feast). It's a little hard to understand why a case such as this should so upset Frank and cause him to question the nature of what he believes in. It's a thoughtful piece, and the core elements are fascinating - but they seem adrift within a plot that feels curiously without direction. It's typified by the use of "Gehenna" itself, an old Hebrew word for Hell, which suggests something epic but here is merely the name of a holding company Frank finds on the Internet.

Giving this episode a millennial flavour does little to make it seem grander; it just ends up being a little confused. (**1/2)

1.3, Dead Letters

Air Date: Nov. 8, 1996
Writers: Glen Morgan, James Wong
Director: Thomas J Wright

Summary   While tracking a serial killer in Portland, Frank is asked to partner with Detective Jim Horn - a potential recruit for the Millennium Group. Frank theorises that the murderer is making an impression on a world he fears has reduced him to a mere number, but Horn proves increasingly unable to handle the inhumanity and gruesomeness inherent in the case.

Frank deduces that an optician named Janice Sterling is the killer's next target. The killer walks into a trap, but Horn nearly blows the case by ruthlessly beating the killer up. Enough admissible evidence remains to file charges, and it becomes evident that Frank - unlike Horn - copes with his job by drawing strength from his family.

Critique   The difficulty I've had getting to grips with this series so far is that Frank's insights into the criminal mind, via flash imagery rather than investigative prowess, are not in themselves very dramatic. They ask the question *how* he's able to do that, but never answer. Morgan and Wong's first script for Millennium is more interested in the *why*. If it doesn't have any answers either, you feel that's part of the point. Frank Black is shown here reflected through the work of another profiler, a man who has spent so long inside murderers' heads that he's become sickened by them and lost perspective. What's so effective about this is that Jim Horn, played with nervous intensity by James Morrison, is not some idiot rookie but a man whose psychological studies of the killer are erudite and convincing. He's a presentation of what Frank could be - a man who can no longer deal emotionlessly with the brutality he faces, who sees the world as a dark and cruel place from which he cannot protect his son. And it's fascinating to see, writing about a man whose profiling has driven a wedge between himself and his family, who is separated from his wife and has metered custody of his child, how Morgan and Wong are setting the stage exactly for where they'll put Frank Black in Season Two once they're in charge.

The only problem here is that it makes Morrison's profiling rather more interesting than Henriksen's. Lance Henriksen is as solid as ever, and in his quiet brooding way here is a man in whom you can place your trust very willingly. But Morrison plays the more *human* of the two - and it's hard not to feel that it's that very humanity that the show is crying out for. Objectively Frank Black is the better detective - but Jim Horn is the most *interesting* one here, someone who is constantly questioning the clues he discovers, and finding within each frustrating setback a personal slight. This is all framed within a well-told story of a serial killer, a (deliberately) ordinary man with no ties whatsoever to millennial angst or prophecy, and it's the very routine nature of the case, and the almost mechanical way in which the plot unfolds, that the juxtaposition between Black and Horn works so well. What Morgan and Wong have presented us with is a gripping and sincere portrait of human ugliness at its most banal, and what that can do to a man whose job requires him to be steeped in it. As the fourth season of The X-Files shows how the monsters can be ordinary humans, Horn finds to his dismay that the humans for whom he once had so much sympathy are now just monsters.

It tries a bit too hard at times. The scene in which Horn is drowning within the case, seeing each vehicle as the same orange van, each passer-by a suspect, makes a subtle character arc very obvious. And the teaser sequence, in which we're subject to Jordan's nightmares of clown faces and loss, are frankly irrelevant. But at its best this episode works because it's very *clean*; it's the first episode which tells a simple story without clutter, and with real passion. This is the world of the profiler, endlessly hunting down killers. And the effect that can have. A weaker episode would have tried to sensationalise this, as in The X-Files' wonderful Grotesque, turning Jim Horn into some sort of monster himself. It's so much more effective, at the end of the story, to see that his career ends upon a despairing anticlimax. (****)

1.4, The Judge

Air Date: Nov. 15, 1996
Writer: Ted Mann
Director: Randy Zisk

Summary When someone sends a human tongue to a woman named Annie Tisman - the latest in a series of severed body part incidents - Frank realises that a criminal mastermind is at work. The genius in question, "the Judge", has been recruiting violent offenders to right perceived injustices. The tongue was taken from a retired cop whose false testimony sent Tisman's late husband to jail.

Frank and Bletcher capture the Judge, but he's released on lack of evidence. However, the Judge's latest henchman - an ex-con named Bardale - decides the Judge is guilty of hypocrisy because he avoided arrest. Frank apprehends Bardle, but not before the man kills the Judge and feeds him to some pigs.

Critique It's high time that the series tackled the issue of vigilantism - it's been bubbling under the surface ever since the concept of the Millennium Group, with their secret agenda, was first mentioned. But this episode doesn't make a very interesting study. The plot is very contrived, as the eponymous judge hires ex-convicts to sever body parts from the people he wants to punish, then offs his lackeys whenever he feels they're not up to scratch. It's barely a subtle premise, and the script unfortunately elevates the lead villain to high camp - the fact that he has to put on a black mask every time he wants to pronounce judgment makes him look comic-book silly rather than threatening. There's an issue to be explored here, but not like this - and with Marshall Bell playing the Judge as lunatic of the week, there's very little to engage the brain.

There are some interesting concepts - the scene in which the Judge offers Frank Black a job has an arrogance to it that is entertaining, and in some ways predicts the storyline that'll run through the whole of the next season. But even the plotline doesn't find the Judge a particularly credible foil for Frank, and has him fed to his own pigs in a manner so matter-of-fact it's almost funny. It's as violent and grisly as you would hope for from the series: the teaser which shows a woman getting a bloody tongue in the mail is especially nasty. But after a while all the body parts on display, divorced from any credible narrative, just begin to seem comical. By the time we're watching a leg passing through an X-ray, we're past caring. (*)

1.5, 522666

Air Date: Nov. 22, 1996
Writers: Glen Morgan, James Wong
Director: David Nutter

Summary In Washington, D.C., a man named Raymond Dees blows up a pub, then calls 911 and keys the numbers 522666 - the phone pad equivalent of "Kaboom". Frank deduces that Dees hopes to become infamous though his actions, but proves unable to thwart his explosive endeavours. Dees tells Frank that he's planted a bomb in his car, whereupon the authorities - who are eavesdropping on the conversation - shoot Dees dead. No explosive is found, and the media reports of Dees' death give him the fame he so desperately desired.

Critique This is the first Millennium episode to play it entirely straight - no flashes of paranormal inspiration from Frank, and instead we get the first proper examination of a killer and why he's driven to do what he does. It plays like a routine police thriller, and I mean that as a compliment - free at last from the self-conscious trappings of pre-millennial angst, the series is allowed to find both subtlety and real depth. Glen Morgan and James Wong develop the idea of direct profiling that they demonstrated in Dead Letters, and in doing so, Frank Black is rewritten not as some peculiar maverick but as the brilliant lynchpin of an FBI investigation. They make him more interesting, more credible, and more dramatic.

And being the first real analysis of what makes a man get his thrills from murder, the episode is suitably clever at drawing out the clues to Raynond Dees' psychosis. Here is a man who develops a joy from not just being a killer but a victim too, eventually putting himself in the throes of a bomb explosion just so he can survive it and triumph over it. This is the little man wanting to be big, to be a hero who rescues Frank Black from the rubble, to be America's favourite on morning talk shows. And it builds to a tense climax, impeccably paced, as Dees engineers his own suicide by FBI sniper - ensuring, to Frank's disgust, that right until the end he maintained the power that he wanted. 522666 is significantly less flashy than most of the episodes in the season, but is something of a neglected gem. It manages not only to be a chilling study of one man's madness, but an indictment upon the modern obsession with celebrity. (****1/2)

1.6, Kingdom Come

Air Date: Nov. 29, 1996
Writer: Jorge Zamacona
Director: Winrich Kolbe

Summary   When two ministers die in a manner consistent with the Christian persecution of heretics in the Middle Ages, Frank theorises that the killer wants to destroy faith itself. More specifically, the perpetrator - Galen Calloway, a high school teacher - wants vengeance for the death of his wife and daughter in a fire, and is committing the murders to exterminate his personal faith. An explosive-laden Calloway takes a congregation hostage, but Frank points out that Calloway, despite his heinous actions, hasn't abandoned faith in God. Calloway agrees, then shoots himself in the head.

Critique   There's a certain macabre fun to be had here, watching the clergy bumped off in murders that recall the medieval execution of heretics. Although it must be said that the best death is the first - in a very impressive teaser showing a vicar burned at the stake - and that the killer's imagination becomes progressively more ho-hum from that point on. But for all its pretence to the contrary, this episode really isn't about religion at all, so the deaths are just gimmicks, in the same way that Theatre of Blood offering murders in the manner of Shakespearean deaths isn't a serious treatise on Renaissance drama.

The metaphor being offered here - that the murderer, grieving the death of his family, is

angry against God and is therefore trying to kill his faith - is so obvious that it leaves you expecting some new twist. The climactic scene in the church, through well played by Lance Henriksen and Michael Zelnicker, really gives us nothing that hasn't been spelled out already, and the resolution of the crisis is so predictable that it hurts.

There's something to be said, in all fairness, for a Millennium episode that is as blunt as this one, and doesn't get bogged down in trying to be too cryptic. But there has to be a limit; Jordan is given a long (far too long, actually) introduction to death, via the fate of a poor wounded bird that has crashed into her window one Sunday morning. The fate of the bird leads her to question her own mortality, and whether she'll one day lose her parents. Fair enough questions for a four year old, but you have to wonder - in a series where she knows all too clearly that Daddy is "stopping the bad men" - whether this being her brush with life's greatest pratfall is the best way it could have been presented. And within the context of the episode, with a man driven to commit terrible (and overelaborate) murders because he's in mourning, it can only look cheesy in contrast.

Lindsay Crouse looks very awkward indeed as Millennium Group member Ardis Cohen, Frank Black's partner of the week, but Lance Henriksen gives the episode a dignity it doesn't really deserve. With Frank centre stage, and once more relying upon his wits more than his special powers, the episode is rarely less than entertaining. But it's a particularly superficial addition to the series. (**)

1.7, Blood Relatives

Air Date: Dec. 6, 1996
Writer: Chip Johannessen
Director: James Charleston

Summary   A young man named James Dickerson attends funerals in the Seattle area, receiving some affection by pretending to be a friend of the deceased. Soon after, relatives of the deceased - specifically, those hugged by James - are found dead. Frank at first suspects James of the murders, then realises that James' caretaker Connor has an unhealthy interest in the boy, and has been killing anyone who gets too close to him. Frank incapacitates Connor when he tries to kill James' mother, facilitating his arrest.

Critique   This clearly takes its cue from The X-Files' Irresistible, and you can see why, a few years later, writer Chip Johannessen was asked to write its sequel. But whilst Donnie Pfaster's character was designed as an outrage against depravity, in the most extreme way The X-Files could devise, this instead becomes a thoughtful analysis of loneliness and what passes as civilised behaviour. James Dickerson is a young man whose only pleasure is to ingratiate himself within strangers' families at funerals, to pretend to feel their pain as they mourn, to offer solace - and to steal little mementoes of a life he's only able to glimpse. These funeral sequences are brilliant; the teaser, in particular, showing how James so subtly moves his fingers from the dress to the skin of a dead jock's crying mother. As Bletcher says, the distinction between a tame cat and a feral cat is determined by the right human contact at the crucial time of its infancy - and, abandoned into foster care as a baby, Dickerson has been trying to connect back to the concept of family ever since.

Blood Relatives is a study of a sociopath, and it invites the audience to treat Dickerson as the most repulsive of serial killers, one who not only violates the bodies of his victims but also their trust, who gets under the skin of their grief and tries to share in it. And then the episode does a remarkable thing - it humanises him. It finds reasons for his behaviour, it allows Catherine Black to profile the criminal in an astute but more forgiving way than her husband (and how great to see Megan Gallagher in a role that gives her more than just looking concerned on the sidelines). By the time the story establishes that Dickerson isn't the murderer, the job's already done; it almost doesn't matter that the need for a (very good) plot twist exonerates James, even if he *had* been the killer, Johannessen's subtle writing would have already done much to make him sympathetic. And no easy answers are offered, crucially. In the last scene, James is still buying newspapers, still checking the obituary columns, still looking for a chance to fit in.

Favourite scenes include the one where Frank and Catherine discuss the case as they carry the sleeping Jordan to bed, for the little girl to open her eyes and dozily ask what "depravity" means; however much they try, they cannot protect her innocence. And the sequence in which Connor feeds James like a pet clearly indicates the way that Connor sees other people, as things to be indulged or destroyed. It's another of those well-crafted episodes in which Frank's profile feels like an intellectual study of deduction, and the way he does it in concert with his wife's counselling gives it extra depth. And Catherine's concern for Frank's safety is given an extra dimension - they need each other against the crippling loneliness that has caused James Dickerson such despair. Beautifully done all round, what starts as a story about extreme alienation becomes, to paraphrase the motto of a later title sequence, a portrait of ourselves: "This is who we are." (*****)

1.8, The Well-Worn Lock

Air Date: Dec. 20, 1996
Writer: Chris Carter
Director: Ralph Hemecker

Summary   Connie Bangs, age thirty-two, tells her sister Sara, age nine, to lock herself in her room, then is found dazed and wandering the streets of Madison Park, Washington. In her role as a victim's counsellor, Catherine realises that Connie's father Joe has sexually abused her for years, and that Sara is the product of their union. A dogged Joe runs away with Sara to a cabin where the family spent vacations, but Frank tracks them and enables Joe's arrest. Connie gains enough courage to testify against her father.

Critique   It's very well acted, especially by Megan Gallagher as Catherine and Michelle Joyner as Connie. And it's clearly well intentioned - it's good to see an episode which tackles issues of child abuse so earnestly, rather than just churning out a serial killer story of the week. But it does feel that Chris Carter has tried so hard to tackle the subject with the right gravitas, he's shied away from making it a full-blood-ed drama. The embarrassment with which the case is treated by the authorities is very clear, and the points made about the way that families collude in secrets against themselves is powerful and real and shocking.

But - and it's a big "but" - Carter's sense of outrage against the insidious crime means that he robs the episode of any ambiguity whatsoever. After twenty years of regular abuse, it would have been only natural had the family acclimatised to it so fully that not only the father and the daughter, but the rest of the household, would have treated it as the norm. The mother's reaction shows what the story might have been, as she's appalled by the way that her routine life has been shattered by the abuse coming out into the open. But all the siblings around Connie show not only support, but full corroboration. And when within the first ten minutes of the story facts come to light that reveal eight-year-old Sarah is the product of an incestuous relationship between father and daughter, it's really an open and shut case. Joe Bangs is a monster. Once he goes on the run with Sarah, and knocks Frank Black down in his car, every shred of humanity has been removed from him.

And this is a great shame, because it makes an abuse that survived so long because it was subtle become so blatant that it not only kills any dramatic suspense, but also takes a very real issue and trivialises it. It's typical of the episode that Sarah doesn't get any voice whatsoever - had she reacted to the beginnings of the abuse, or even appeared to accept it in her naivety, then there would be some depth to this. As it is she's treated as an object by the episode, just as she is by her father. There's some attempt to give a real credibility to the trial sequences, by ensuring that five months elapse between Bangs' capture and his sentencing, and in a better episode that structural jolt might even have been shocking. But there's nothing to be jolted by, because the examination of the legal system which delays the judgment is still too superficial. The courtroom proceedings are incredibly brought to a crisis because an incest victim undergoing counselling cannot answer a question on the stand *once* - and Catherine has to hold her hand so she can say the words that will condemn her father. The final scene is *terrible*; having established only minutes before that the locked door is a metaphor for the family's secrets and lies,

Catherine brings that very lock to Connie so she can throw it over a bridge into a handy dam. It sums up all that is wrong about this story - it turns the complex into something easy and obvious.

For all that, it's a measure of how sincere are the performances that the episode still has a certain power to it. And although Carter's plotting is awful, the dialogue is simple and heartfelt. Its failure is that it errs on the side of caution, in wanting to discuss a taboo subject that needs to be brought out into the open. It's right that the show wanted to do this. It should have just done it a bit more fearlessly. (**)

1.9, Wide Open

Air Date: Jan. 3, 1997
Writer: Charles D Holland
Director: James Charleston

Summary   When a married couple is found bludgeoned to death, Frank finds their young daughter Patricia hiding inside a vent. It becomes evident that the killer thwarted the family's alarm system by hiding himself during their open house, and has attended several open house events. Frank realises that the murderer - a school crossing guard named Cutter - is trying to prove that people aren't nearly as safe in their day-to-day lives as they'd like to believe. The authorities and Frank set a trap for Cutter at an open house, leading to a scuffle in which a family dog pushes Cutter over a banister to his death.

Critique   There are interesting ideas in this tale of a killer who attends open house viewings then hides in the cupboard, all the better to slaughter those living in the household later. But the M.O. is spotted by Frank whilst the credits are still playing over the screen, and that remains the most distinctive thing about the whole case. There's a little of the flavour of Blood Relatives here, with a stranger insinuating himself into a home for nefarious means - and it's telling perhaps that the little girl who's left alive as a witness is called Patricia Highsmith. (Ripley, the most famous creation of Patricia's crime-writer namesake, had a similar talent.) But there's little of the creepiness or the danger that the premise should suggest, and the killer remains largely anonymous. That he's felled by a dog knocking him over some banisters is as half-hearted a climax as he deserves.

For a while there's the hint the episode might take its cue from the dilemma posed to Frank and Bletcher, whether to interview the little girl only to risk her reliving her trauma. But the episode is too half-hearted about it; it's so careful that Frank and Catherine are supportive of each other that it never has either one of them raise a voice in the debate, and Bletcher's constant reminders that the girl is a material witness don't so much resemble a police detective under pressure as a whining dog being asked to be let out. It's all too mechanical, too passionless, and the plotline dribbles out in as anticlimactic a way as possible, complete with repetitive scenes of Catherine helping the orphaned girl draw pictures with crayons.

It's solid enough, I suppose, but routine and utterly uninspiring. It's the series on autopilot, and it's worrying that this early into its run, one of the boldest shows on television seems to have settled into a lazy rut. (*1/2)

1.10, The Wild and the Innocent

Air Date: Jan. 10, 1997
Writer: Jorge Zamacona
Director: Thomas J Wright

Summary   A thug named Jim Gilroy tries to rape a young woman named Maddie Haskel - but her boyfriend, Bobby Webber, interrupts the proceedings and knocks Gilroy unconscious. The pair hits the road with Gilroy as their prisoner, but Webber becomes increasingly unstable and murders anyone who gets in their way.

Webber continues his rampage in the interest of getting Gilroy to reveal the location of Haskel's son Angel - whom Gilroy stole years ago and sold for $7,000. Gilroy reveals that the Travis family adopted Angel. Haskel finds that her son is well cared for by the family, and decides to leave him with them. Webber protests to the point that Haskel shoots him dead; the police arrest her and Gilroy.

Critique   This is a curious mix of the cloyingly sentimental and the unremittingly bleak. It doesn't quite work, but it deserves great credit for trying to be so tonally different from the episodes around it; it's also the first story which works as a genuine mystery, with suspense generated not from the killers' identity but the meaning behind their quest. In some ways it's reminiscent of Hardy's The Mayor of Casterbridge, not only for its tale of a man selling a family for cash, but also for an ending in which the tragic character can look upon a child and, for his own sake, wish that it need never hear any word about who its parent was.

The real difficulty of this episode - which plays out like a Southern melodrama - is that it doesn't allow much room for Frank Black or his profiling: he's reduced to chasing the two young killers on a mission to find a baby. The final scene in the prison is touching, in which Maddie tells Frank he's the only man who's ever treated her right - but it only emphasises how little Frank had to do with the drama itself. This is a story that would actually have worked better removed from the Millennium series, done as a fable about the evils of man and the death of innocence - a plot more suited to Cormac McCarthy than Chris Carter. The tragic climax is great, where Maddie finds her baby Angel, and then gives him straight back to the adoptive parents who will prevent him from becoming the violent murderer her boyfriend has turned into just to help her. And, of course, the resolution offers no function to Frank Black or to the FBI, who all turn up after the drama's played out.

The story is structured well, giving light to the ever-darkening ugliness by the way Maddie narrates letters to her missing child. And the performance that Heather McComb gives is lovely. For all its bleakness there's a sincerity here, and an honest attempt to do something different with the Millennium format. The Millennium scenes frankly feel shoehorned into a drama that doesn't need them - but a quirky failure like this is still to be applauded. (***)

1.11, Weeds

Air Date: Jan. 24, 1997
Writer: Frank Spotnitz
Director: Michael Pattinson

Summary A teenager named Josh Comstock is kidnapped. The next morning, Josh's parents discover the body of another teen - Kirk Orlando - in Josh's bed. Josh's father sees "331" - the number of a hotel room where he had an affair - painted in Josh's room, and Frank theorises that the killer sees himself as a holy figure who's exposing dirty secrets. Josh is safely returned after his father admits to his adultery, but Orlando was murdered after his father failed to recant a sin of his involving money.

The son of Robert Birckenbuehl - a man who killed another boy in a hit-and-run accident - is taken, and Frank advises Birckenbuehl to publicly confess his wrongdoing. Birckenbuehl does so, but his son remains missing. Frank locates the boy and captures the killer - a community leader named Edward Petey. Birckenbuehl's guilt is such that he hangs himself.

Critique As a portrait of a community in fear, this works very well indeed. A killer is preying upon the teenage boys of a middle-class neighbourhood, all of them belonging to families who moved to an expensive area to be safe from violence. The way that the town simmers with recrimination and vigilantism is credibly done; it becomes clear that Frank Spotnitz is exploring the very hypocrisy of complacent American values. The imagery of the episode is highly effective - the murderer sees the people around him as corrupt and decaying - and the reason that he is taking the children, to punish the fathers for their own crimes and misdemeanours of infidelity and financial impropriety, is apt and turns him into some warped modern-day Pied Piper.

Where the episode suffers is in individual characterisation. Because Spotnitz (rarely for Millennium) chooses to frame the story as a whodunit, it spends a lot of time introducing figures as potential suspects rather than giving a great deal of depth to any of them. When the killer is finally revealed there's no dramatic impact at all - he's just another nondescript middle class man, indistinguishable from the oth-

ers. It's probable that this was Spotnitz's very point, that the identity of the murderer is almost irrelevant, that the corrupt town did this to itself - but if so, it still produces a somewhat anticlimactic conclusion. And much of Spotnitz's actual plotting feels overdone - there's no real *reason* for the kidnapped boys to be made to drink human blood, there's no especial *need* for the cattle prod, other than the fact that they're suitably grisly Millennium gimmicks. This is an example of an episode where the basic concept is sound, and the theme a powerful one - but the actual plot details seem underdeveloped or random. There are worse crimes for an hour of television, of course. And if a lot of what's on offer here seems like staple fare - serial killers leaving bloodied messages - then at least it's done with a sense of angry purpose. (***)

1.12, Loin Like a Hunting Flame

Air Date: Jan. 31, 1997
Writer: Ted Mann
Director: David Nutter

Summary Frank and a Millennium Group member named Maureen Murphy travel to Boulder, Colorado, where a killer targets young lovers and leaves their naked bodies in artistic poses. Frank realises that the killer, a pharmacist named Art Nesbitt, is making the slain couples emulate the happy sexual encounters he thinks he should've had prior to marriage. After rescuing two of Nesbitt's intended victims, Frank stops Nesbitt from poisoning his wife - whereupon Nesbitt poisons himself instead.

Critique The psychology on display here feels a little glib. A married man hasn't had sex with his wife for eighteen years, and so embarks on a series of killings showing his victims in various forms of carnal congress. The sequence in which the poor wife is questioned by Frank and his associates feels uneasily less like a police investigation and more like a guest spot on Dr Ruth. But for all that this is a decent little episode, its problem is that really it offers nothing new. It's so routine a serial killer adventure that it almost forgets to put any jeopardy into the story - Frank pursues his investigation with perfect ease, and at the climax when the murderer is apprehended he helpfully kills himself rather than offer any threat. Even the pharmacist's victims seem happily consenting as he records them having sex and gives them lethal injections.

It means that there's something of a hole in the story where the tension should be, and so writer Ted Mann artificially creates some by making the police detective unusually brusque and surly. When later on Kent admits that he too has sexual problems as a result of his work, you feel that this may have had a certain relevance after all, but it's really nothing much more than thematic colouring. It's helped enormously by Doug Abrahams' performance being so strong, and playing against the stereotype by making Detective Kent credibly sympathetic in spite of himself. Harriet Harris is largely wasted in the part of Maureen, Frank's new Millennium partner, reduced to most part to standing in the background and being patronised.

It also falls into the familiar Millennium trap of opening with a visually arresting first death in the teaser, and then failing to deliver on subsequent ones in the main narrative. The teenage couple discovered positioned like Adam and Eve acting out the fall of Man is eerie and strangely beautiful, but there's no follow-up: the next death is just a couple of swingers found sitting on a park bench. It's as if Ted Mann's imagination ran out as surely as the killer's. And it typifies an episode which has good moments, and is at least efficient and watchable - but doesn't really deliver anything special, doesn't try to be anything other than average. (**1/2)

1.13, Force Majeure

Air Date: Feb. 7, 1997
Writer: Chip Johannessen
Director: Winrich Kolbe

Summary   When two twin girls - Lauren and Carlin - die under mysterious circumstances, an enigmatic Millennium Group outsider named Dennis Hoffman finds an astrological conjunction symbol carved on each of them. Hoffman believes that the deaths are related to a planetary conjunction that will occur on May 5, 2000, when the solar system's seven innermost planets will align and a cataclysm will ravage Earth.

Frank and Hoffman discover that Lauren and Carlin were two of twenty copies of the same girl, created by a man in an iron lung so that the best of humanity could survive the 2000 disaster. The remaining eighteen girls are taken but later found at The Atrium in Pocatello, Idaho, and are relocated to protective custody in a bus. The man in the iron lung dies during a power failure, but the girls - along with Hoffman - go missing. Frank finds that The Atrium was engineered to serve as a sort of ark, surmising that the missing parties will return there on May 5, 2000.

Critique   "Welcome to the world of the truly bizarre." Arguably there's not much of a story here, just a collection of ideas - but the ideas are fascinating, and so well examined. After a spate of episodes which have trod the same unambitious path and turned Millennium into something like a formulaic cop show, this one comes out of left field, reminds us what the title of the show is, and offers the series an entire new direction. It's about what the impending apocalypse might actually *mean*, free from the quasi-religious influences and seen from a scientific perspective of cosmic alignment and cloning; it's especially apt that our new Noah explains his philosophy while kept alive inside an iron lung - he's surviving not through faith at all, but through a medicine delivered by electrical cable and plug. Rarely for an episode of Millennium, too, it's without villains, without murders - however grotesque he is in appearance, the dying man wanting to give humanity some twisted chance of recovery is sad and lonely and sympathetic.

A lot of the imagery here is borrowed from The X-Files, most obviously in every scene featuring identical clones - but because it's all been placed within a different framework, that of a very human urge for survival rather than something concerning little green men, it still feels very fresh. And all the more macabre: the sequences involving the suicides of these girls is eerie enough, but somehow not as strange as the idea of these perfect but characterless drones being representative of mankind. It's telling that the story keeps them mute, when it's clear that they can talk fluently in their real lives - what Iron Lung has done is reduce these daughters of his into nothing more than symbols, not real people at all but flag-bearers of a new generation. The suicides feel increasingly like acts of independence.

Brad Dourif (formerly Luther Lee Boggs in X-Files 1.13, Beyond the Sea) is making a habit of turning up halfway through first seasons of series, only to give a barnstorming performance in an episode which bravely redefines what a show is capable of. His portrait of Dennis Hoffman makes the man's paranoid theories of armageddon frighteningly plausible, and finds within this Millennium Group wannabe the right level of social awkwardness and frustration to make him entirely real. He's helped by great dialogue from Chip Johannessen; indeed, all the dialogue in Force Majeure is crisp and thoughtful, and of a standard higher than we've been recently used to. And Johannessen too reinvents Frank Black; always before the stoic purveyor of psychic revelations, here he's a man in denial of forces stronger than himself, telling Hoffman in frustration that he doesn't *want* to understand. The last scene is a particularly haunting one, as Frank realises that however much he might protect his family from the brutal banality of serial killers, he still has no power over time and the countdown to armageddon. Millennium has found a new theme to play with, one that will come to characterise the mood of the second season, and it's something rich and dark. (*****)

1.14, The Thin White Line

Air Date: Feb. 14, 1997
Writers: Glen Morgan, James Wong
Director: Thomas J Wright

Summary In a hospital, Frank happens across a mortally wounded woman who bears a knife mark on her hand that's similar to a scar on his own palm. Twenty years ago, Frank and his fellow FBI agents tracked down Richard Alan Hance, a Vietnam veteran turned serial killer. Frank and a quartet of agents searched for Hance in an abandoned building; Hance slaughtered Frank's comrades, but Frank arrested him after incurring the hand slash.

Frank deduces that Hance's former cellmate, Jacob Tyler, thinks he's a reincarnation, of sorts, of Hance. Adopting Hance's methods, Tyler places an anonymous tip so officials will search an abandoned building and give Tyler a chance to massacre them. A gunfight ensues - Frank tries to convince Tyler of his true identity, but Bletch, seeing Tyler with a gun, shoots and kills him.

Critique It's a return to the serial killer format, but it's never been done before with as much verve as it has here. On the face of it this is very derivative: the way that we're shown the victims' acquiescence to murder from the killer's point of view is pure Tarantino, and the profiler interviewing a serial killer to catch another is a Silence of the Lambs cliché. And yet Morgan and Wong turn the familiarity upon its head. The Tarantino device is given a great twist by the way that it allows Frank to *refuse* to be killed, by dint of being one of the murderer's victims already. It also helps show that Tyler is a man whose entire personality has been entirely subsumed by his cellmate's, that he's a passive character in his own sick fantasy. And that eight-minute sequence where Frank interrogates Hance as a TV version of Hannibal Lecter is maybe the single best scene in the whole season. Against type, Hance is charmless, his desire to be represented in cable TV movies (and not by Anthony Hopkins, but Gary Busey) splendidly trite, the only anguish he feels is at the constant hum of the fluorescent lighting he has to suffer day and night. Both Quentin Tarantino and Thomas Harris have done much - brilliantly - to give the serial killer format some wit and glamour; Morgan and Wong use the same tropes only to show the lives of mediocrities.

It was a trait of the first season of The X-Files to pump up a weak storyline by making the case refer to our heroes' past - that hoary old cliché is used again here. But it's used to great effect. There's a real culture shock to be had seeing Frank Black as an FBI man with a gun, and the episode becomes an analysis of what defines his attitude towards violence. The same character defining sequence where Frank is wounded, and has the opportunity to kill a defenceless man, is given to us from three different angles - most grippingly, in a dream where Frank plays himself *and* his doomed partner. By refusing to take the life of a murderer, Frank is haunted by the other lives who have been sacrificed by his mercy - it's a replay of the dilemma which faced Mulder in Young at Heart, but it has far greater impact here because we're dealing with a character we've never even seen holding a weapon before. For Mulder it was just angst of the week, for Black it's truly a life changing moment, and one which tells us precisely who he is and how he approaches his gift. And deliberately or not, it sets up the character breakdown of Frank at the top of Season Two, when by resorting to such means he loses his family. Catherine's bold statement that he could no more have killed Hance than her or Jordan seems eerily prophetic; as in their earlier episodes, Morgan and Wong are poking at the safe yellow house of domesticity established by Carter, ready to snatch it away when they take charge. (*****)

1.15, Sacrament

Air Date: Feb. 21, 1997
Writer: Frank Spotnitz
Director: Michael Watkins

Summary   Frank's brother Tom celebrates the baptism of his newborn son with his wife Helen, but a kidnapper makes off with her. A sex offender named Richard Green becomes the prime suspect. Meanwhile, Jordan demonstrates a psychic sensitivity to Helen's plight - which suggests that she's inherited her father's abilities. Frank finds Helen embedded in a basement wall of the Green family home, but still alive. He deduces that Green's father is a lunatic who was using his son to procure victims, and ends their murder spree.

Critique   ... and the other trick that The X-Files performed to bolster a mundane storyline was to have it concern a hitherto unmentioned ex-lover or family member. So welcome Tom Black and his unfortunate wife Helen, never to make a reappearance in the series, to be this week's victims of a kidnapping. There's some great moments here - the scene where Tom turns upon Frank and accuses him of bringing bad luck upon the family, that he's so steeped in violence and crime that he infects all those who touch him, is especially striking. And it gives

some extra weight to those otherwise peculiar scenes where it's hinted that Jordan is inheriting her father's psychic abilities. (In doing so, surely, Ten Thirteen is abandoning any pretence that Frank's profiling isn't supernatural - it's an understandable but somewhat disappointing conclusion to reach, as the ambiguity was so much more powerful, and it was more interesting to believe that the flashbacks we saw were merely visual representations of his deductive prowess.) But it's clever nonetheless that here in Sacrament, there's a suggestion that Jordan too has been tainted by her father - that, like her aunt, she'll be adversely affected by her relationship with Frank.

That said, Frank Spotnitz shies away from the implications of his emotional story. When in his desperation Tom breaks into Frank's files, and takes a gun to the suspect's house, it should have been a turning point in the drama. Spotnitz has already examined the implications of vigilantism within the series; having one of Frank's own adopt the same measures would have been a fascinating development of this. But the opportunity is thrown away, and a sequence where Tom attempts to kill a man on his own doorstep is passed off as nothing more than padding. When later on Peter Watts gives Frank evidence of the killer's torture techniques, Tom insists he can handle the information - and Frank shrugs acceptance, even though it's quite clear from the way he boiled over into attempted murder that he can't! It's as if the Black family are being given special dispensation, and it makes a mockery of Bletcher's requested orders for Frank to stay away from the case - we know at the end of the day he'll turn a blind eye, accept Frank's analysis, and thank him.

What makes this work is a terrific portrayal of despair and grief from Philip Anglim as Tom, and a sensitive script by Spotnitz. The plotting may be a bit humdrum (and not very persuasive - I'm at a loss why a ten-second conversation with someone at an airport would lead a woman to accept without comment a stranger at her child's christening). But the incidentals are well done, and the ending - in which the sister-in-law tacitly blames Frank for her own abduction, and Frank leads Jordan away - is very powerful. (***)

1.16, Covenant

Air Date: March 21, 1997
Writer: Robert Moresco
Director: Roderick J Pridy

Summary　Frank is asked to draft a psychological profile of Sheriff William Garry - a Utah man accused of murdering his wife and children - to aid a jury in convicting him. Garry has confessed to the crime, but Frank suspects he's so consumed with guilt over another event that he thinks he did the deed. Frank learns that Garry's pregnant wife discovered her husband was having an affair, and couldn't bear the thought of bringing another child into a world of adulterers. *She* murdered their children - deeming them angels, and wanting to keep them that way - then killed herself after telling Garry it was all his fault. Frank encourages Deputy Kevin Reilly, who has been lying on Garry's behalf, to come forward and spare his friend the death penalty.

Critique　This is Millennium's version of Twelve Angry Men. Frank Black is brought in to provide a profile examination for a confessed murderer so that the state can recommend the death penalty, and scratches away at the truth until he exonerates him for the crime. Tightly plotted and boasting extremely good dialogue, the script by Robert Moresco showcases exactly why the series works best when it plays upon deductive reasoning rather than psychic revelation - it's because Frank solves the case with such analytical precision that makes this story so gripping.

And it's why it's so subtle, too; it'd be so easy for this to be a simple statement against capital punishment, with Frank depicted merely as a man with a liberal agenda. Moresco takes pains to have a scene in which Garry's lawyer asks Frank for his opinion about the subject, exactly so that he can refuse to answer. This is not an episode of simple statements: we have a credible presentation of a police sheriff who believes himself guilty of multiple homicide, all because he knows that the deaths are a reaction against his adultery. The story ends upon a note of suspense which is to be congratulated: Frank has provided the judge with his new evidence, but it will take further testimony to convince the

jury to overturn the guilty verdict. The final dilemma is placed upon the shoulders of a deputy police chief who has lied for Garry for six months to preserve the reputation of the man's wife - and there is genuinely no dramatic indication whether he will come forward or not. That the innocent man pleads with Frank to let him be executed, and that Frank refuses him is wonderful. That it refuses to supply a happy ending is great, but that it can't even decide whether or not the truth would *make* that happy ending is greater still.

If the episode has a fault, it's that Frank's support is a little on the weak side. It's commendable that Frank's influence enables pathologist Didi Higgens to stand up for herself and become more than a yes woman, but Sarah Koskoff plays the part with a little girl naivety that isn't as subtle as the script demands. The story demonstrates, without prejudice, how easy it would be for intelligent well-meaning people to accept Garry's confession, and it'd have been surely more effective had Higgens been characterised as someone of greater intelligence - Frank's victory would have been all the more rewarding. Jay Underwood, too, plays the part of the lawyer with a youthful gusto that makes him seem at times like he's auditioning for the Scooby Doo team. But they're weak links in what emerges nonetheless as one of the great "simple" Millennium episodes, in the days when the series could still be written as a straightforward crime series. Had the show stayed as fresh and clever as typified by Covenant, it could happily have stayed in that groove a lot longer. (****1/2)

1.17, Walkabout

Air Date: March 28, 1997
Writers: Chip Johannessen, Tim Tankosic
Director: Cliff Bole

Summary　Frank is found at a bus station with no memory of recent events, save for a lingering sense that someone died. It's gradually revealed that he took part in a clinical trial of an antidepressant drug called ProLoft - possibly because it affects the temporal lobe, and thus might cure his empathic talents. The test subjects in the drug trial became increasingly savage until one of them perished. Dr Daniel Miller, a man who experiences visions similar to Frank, is run over by a car after a meeting with Hans Ingram, the man who oversaw the clinical trial. Frank deduces that a drug called Smooth Time was administered during the ProLoft trial, which had an enraging rather than calming effect. Ingram is arrested for distributing the drug, as part of his goal to counteract the nation of "zombies" his drug company helped to create. Frank tells Catherine that he entered the trial because Jordan might have his empathic talents, but that he'll guide her if that's the case.

Critique This must have entered production a little before The X-Files episode Demons. In both stories, our heroes have amnesia of events which are violent and shocking, and discover to their horror that they've been seeking treatment from unethical doctors using controversial methods to tap into their brain powers. Demons is a rather muddled and unrevelatory affair at best, and Walkabout is the superior story. For a start, it's a greater contrast to see Frank Black losing his reserves of emotional sang froid: within the first ten minutes we witness him not only try to smash down a glass door with his bleeding fists but also - and in some ways more shockingly - collapse dumbly into Catherine's arms when she finds him in hospital.

But those ten minutes still make the most interesting part of the episode. After that, and despite a bravura performance from Henriksen which really tries to find new areas of Frank Black to explore, this is a curiously passionless affair. To its credit it lacks the pretensions of Demons. But the mystery surrounding the trials of experimental antidepressants isn't nearly as exciting as the mystery of why Frank Black was involved in such trials in the first place. The episode sets the idea that these two puzzles are somehow connected, and that Frank will find that connection when he investigates - but, as it turns out, the solution is offered only as an epilogue, Frank admitting to Catherine that he was worried about Jordan's burgeoning psychic ability. The remedy - that they'll keep an eye on her and make sure she's all right - is especially pat and unsatisfying after the extreme ways Frank tried to confront the issue at the beginning of the story.

There's an interesting idea at the heart of this, about the way America is anaesthetising its population into zombies. But Gregory Itzin plays the doctor who wants to wake everybody up from their medicated cheer as a two dimensional madman; similarly, Zeljko Ivanek's performance as the discredited doctor who suffers from visions lacks the subtlety that would make the comparisons between him and Frank Black especially meaningful. What begins as intriguing becomes rather plodding and formulaic, before descending into silliness. The opening sequence of trial patients freaking out to their drugs is disturbing and bizarre - the later ones, with whole armies of extras flapping about like geese, are laugh out loud funny.

It's nice to see an attempt to do something different with Frank's character - even if it doesn't generate the domestic drama that it might have done: poor Megan Gallagher, on learning that her husband is keeping secrets from her under an alias, remains stubbornly supportive of him. (Just wait until next season, love - oh, how the sparks will fly!) It does at least give Terry O'Quinn, who's been doing a fine job as Peter Watts in a largely expository role up to now, a chance to ruffle his feathers a bit. (**)

1.18, Lamentation

Air Date: April 18, 1997
Writer: Chris Carter
Director: Winrich Kolbe

Summary Dr Ephriam Fabricant, a serial killer whom Frank helped to convict, disappears from the hospital where he was donating a kidney to his dying sister. Frank and Peter Watts question Fabricant's wife, Lucy Butler, but Frank is startled when Butler receives an e-mail that references his own street address.

Fabricant's abductor removes his *other* kidney, then allows him to stagger dazed into an emergency room, and Catherine finds the missing organ in her refrigerator. A man who bears features similar to Butler appears at the top of the Black household stairs. Bletcher helps Catherine and Jordan to flee, then searches the house. He sees Lucy at the top of the stairwell, but she quickly transforms into a demon creature (henceforth called the "Gehenna Devil"). The abomination cuts Bletcher's throat, then leaves his body dangling from a wall stud.

Fabricant warns Frank that "the base sum of all evil" took his second kidney - and that the same evil has its eye on Frank. Rattled, Frank withdraws with his family to a remote cabin. [To be continued.]

Critique This is a classic piece of misdirection. Chris Carter introduces us to yet another serial killer, credibly builds him up as the most fearsome that the show has yet presented - and then trumps him. It's a sick joke that we never see this most amoral of murderers outside a hospital bed, and that our sympathies are called into question in the scene where he has a second kidney removed without anaesthetic. Carter is far too clever to suggest that Fabricant is a victim, and by preserving his evil makes Lucy Butler stand out as something very strange and new and terrifying. The moment where a dying Fabricant tries to warn Frank that he has greater evils than him to face is effective because of the very frightened earnestness with which it's conveyed - there's something demonic out there, and it knows where Frank lives. Sarah-Jane Redmond is outstanding as Lucy, inviting both the audience and Frank to patronise her as just another gullible woman romancing a prisoner on the Internet, and the cat and mouse game she plays with both the police and with the audience is frankly unnerving.

The whole story is an intentional jolt to the show. It's not just that the episode kills a series regular, but that it does so with so little remorse or closure; the murderer can walk free and mock Frank as she does so. It's also that Bletcher sees, in his last living moments, that Lucy Butler is something outside the series' established genre - she is unapologetically portrayed as an incarnation of evil, and suddenly a lone man standing before her with a gun, and the type of drama programme he represents, looks inadequate before it. The third act of the episode is genuinely horrifying, because the sanctity of all that Millennium has established as safe is taken away from us. Frank's yellow house has been invaded, and from the moment Catherine finds a human kidney in her fridge, there's a sense that the series is moving into uncharted waters. This is a triumph. Millennium is an extraor-

dinary programme, never comfortable standing still, always trying to work out what sort of drama it should be, and radically redefining itself. Lamentation represents a time when it makes one of its biggest shifts, and never does it make a shift with greater confidence or subtlety. The final sequence of Frank and Jordan looking out over the mountains, the one thing that will never change, is a tacit reminder to the audience that this is a pivotal point for the programme. That something as ugly and as brutal as Millennium ever got complacent at all is a major failing - we've grown used to the death on offer each week, we've become desensitised to it. Lamentation is a shock to the format. There'll be formulaic episodes again, to be sure, but to a different formula - and never more without the possibility that they're only there to lull the viewer into a false sense of security. (*****)

1.19, Powers, Principalities, Thrones and Dominions

Air Date: April 25, 1997
Writers: Ted Mann, Harold Rosenthal
Director: Thomas J Wright

Summary While Peter investigates the death of Eddy Pressman - a man who died surrounded by occult symbols - Catherine tells Frank that he should return to work. The police arrest a man named Martin for killing a nanny, and Frank senses that he's somehow connected to Bletcher's murder. The case against Martin collapses, but he confesses to killing Bletcher and later commits suicide.

Frank deduces that Pressman was murdered to get the Millennium Group's attention. He speculates that Martin's attorney, Al Pepper, was involved in Martin's demise. Peter and Frank find Frank's mentor, Mike Atkins, dead in a hotel room, a sacrificial knife in his chest. Frank spies the killer escaping, and follows him into a grocery store. Frank variously spies Pepper, then Martin, then Lucy Butler, pushing the same shopping cart. Finally, Pepper exits with a bag of groceries - and is killed by a bolt of energy projected by a young man named Sammael.

Peter tells Frank that after Pepper became clinically dead from a heart attack six months ago, he changed the focus of his legal work. Sammael confesses to killing Pepper because he wanted to prevent the man's future actions. He also indicates that Frank won't see him again, because it's "painful for him to remain".

Critique   By turns surprising, intriguing, moody and pretentious, Powers is the oddest episode of the first season. It's a slippery thing, which unhelpfully refuses to be what you expect, or what it promises to be. It takes the new lease of life that Lamentation gave the show, its acceptance of an overt supernatural agenda, and not so much runs with it as sets off at such a pace that you're left out of breath struggling to keep up. It's so tonally different from any Millennium we've seen before, as the episode riffs off a new storyline of angels battling demons, with mortal man the uncomprehending spectator. In a late scene, Sammael tells Frank that in such a struggle Frank's own survival is completely incidental, and that change of scale is at once thrilling and bold, and also rather deflating. It's almost as if we've been witness to a new programme which only serves to demonstrate how irrelevant all the concerns of the previous instalments are, that we've little reason to care about the fates of Frank and Catherine Black and their cute as a button kid.

But I suspect that this jarring tone is precisely the intention. If Lamentation shook up the format, Powers breaks its down. It's not an especially satisfying episode in its own right, because for all the different ideas put into the mix, there is nothing which is offered as a new template we can hang on to. The impact, however, of scene after scene is extraordinary: Al Pepper's repeated invitations to Frank to take a job for him (echoing Mann's early attempt of a similar theme in The Judge) recalls Satan tempting Jesus - Richard Cox's performance of patronising suavity isn't necessarily subtle, but becomes increasingly chilling the darker the story becomes. And amid all these somewhat metaphysical scenes of power struggle, there are moments of horrific brutality; the killing of the babysitter in the park is very graphic, as is the scene where Martin is goaded to slit his own throat in his cell. The overall effect is that the episode is like a gadfly, flitting from moment to moment. And whilst that doesn't make for an especially comprehensible yarn, it does produce

an episode that is genuinely uneasy viewing.

What glues this all together is Lance Henriksen, turning in one of his very best performances as Frank Black. Here Frank is a man shaken to the core, unwilling to return to work, no longer having faith in his own abilities, grimly aware that the sanctuary of his home has been invaded. The dread with which he confronts the ghost of Bob Bletcher in his sitting room - and the way in which he can no longer be sure of the difference between the world of reality and the world of dream - is especially powerful. It's a portrait of a man who, like his audience, can no longer be sure what series they are investing in. (****)

1.20, Broken World

Air Date: May 2, 1997
Writers: Robert Moresco, Patrick Harbinson
Director: Winrich Kolbe

Summary   When a woman goes missing in North Dakota, Frank senses a connection to a series of horse killings going back two-and-a-half years. The perpetrator, Willi Borgsen, derives almost sexual pleasure from murdering horses and has escalated matters to kill humans as well. Frank deduces that Borgsen was raised on a farm where mares' urine is harvested for pharmaceutical treatments, and their foals are sold to slaughter. He tracks Borgsen to a slaughterhouse, interceding when Borgsen tries to kill Claudia Vaughan, a veterinarian. A scuffle follows, and a group of horses trample Borgsen to death.

Critique   This account of a serial killer in the making, and Frank's attempts to tutor a man away from his baser impulses, would have been a useful addition to the season a couple of months previously. As it is, it feels as if the series has outgrown it somewhat - Frank is back to offering profiles with a detachment so clinical it offends the husband of an assault victim, and has a scene where he talks about the very human life he has with his family away from the job. It's unhelpfully scheduled within the season, then, and feels like a throwback - which is a pity, because it has a far stronger script than many of the mid-season serial killer tales, and has a new perspective to offer the format.

After a handful of episodes in which Millennium has upped the ante and wanted to confront evil on as grand a scale as could be, there is still something very refreshing in the depiction of a man who is scared of his own desires and who is trying to decide whether he's a killer at all. Claudia Vaughn is surprised that Frank feels pity towards him, but it's in his struggle, that resistance to his carnal instincts, that makes Willi so credible. Once he gives himself over to killing women, sadly, the character becomes much more generic, developing the clichéd trait of leaving cryptic messages and talking in platitudes about his amoral stance to the world. That may well, of course, be the scriptwriters' very message, that Willi dehumanises himself entirely once he becomes a murderer, but it does squash a lot of the emotion out of the story. And the ending is a real botch-up: there's some poetic justice in having the killer stampeded by angry horses, but after the point has been made earlier that horses are so naturally trusting that they'll calmly accept even the worst cruelty, it feels glib and trite when it's suggested they're taking revenge. And it's a double pity, because that very image, of the victims waiting patiently for their killer and accepting their fate without complaint, resonates all the way back through the season. The horses that are destroyed, dumb and compliant, seem to represent the very helplessness of the innocents we've seen slaughtered in this series, whether it be the clones who no longer speak in Force Majeure, or the acquiescent dead from The Thin White Line.

The script is mostly very sharp. I love the way that Claudia takes Frank to task for seeing the butchery of horses as only a stepping stone to more serious crimes. And, continuing a theme, Frank seems culpable of turning Willi into a murderer, giving him the attention that Peter Watts wants to deny him: the relationship between the two, with Willi asking Frank as serial killer expert what he should do next is very nicely macabre. It's a decent story, well-intentioned and crisp enough in its own right - but at the far end of Season One, it's both too familiar and too tentative to make much impact. (***)

1.21, Marantha

Air Date: May 9, 1997
Writer: Chip Johannessen
Director: Peter Markle

Summary Frank allies himself with Yura Surova of the Moscow Police Department when a man named Yaponchik leaves a trail of mutilated bodies. Surova tells Frank that the name "Yaponchik" denotes a Russian bogeyman who's sometimes blamed for the Chernobyl disaster. Frank deduces that Yaponchik has been patterning the murders to boost his reputation, and that Surova believes Yaponchik is the Antichrist.

Surova mortally wounds Yaponchik with a shot to the head, and Yaponchik is hospitalised. Frank recalls that the book of Revelation mentioned that the Antichrist will heal a fatal head wound, even as Surova goes to the hospital and finds himself unable to finish Yaponchik off after the man tells him "you are not the one". Surova helps Yaponchik reach the hospital's helicopter pad, where unidentified men airlift Yaponchik to safety. Afterward, Surova attends a religious service where it's said that when the "evil one" walks the Earth, the Lord is soon to come.

Critique There's so much effort put into Maranatha that it seems almost churlish not to be more impressed by it. Its use of the Russian setting is very persuasive, and the notion that after the collapse of Communism the Soviet people have taken solace in the superstitions of the past is fascinating. But there's such a barrage of detail in here - from the collection of old Russian icons, through to the apocalyptic meaning behind Chernobyl, from the appearance of a mystical bogeyman, to the real-world dealing of assassins and mob politics - that the plot rather gets lost in the mix.

And that's a pity, because the atmosphere is great. I loved the way that, at the start of the story, it's stated that the Russian approach to death is to make a cross and accept fate - it gives a remorselessness to the demon Yaponchik that makes him genuinely disturbing. Three weeks after Lucy Butler came to symbolise the American idea of evil, with the sanctity of the home being invaded and family life being torn apart, the Russian concept of the devil is shown to be steeped much more within folklore and tradition. As a result the final act has an almost epic intensity to it, in which Yura tries to kill a being he fears may be immortal, and is won over to his side.

But I'm not sure that what this suggests for the future of Millennium is so promising. The X-Files quickly fell into the trap of alternating simple monster tales and conspiracy episodes that were wilfully obscure. Millennium is caught between a rock and a hard place as well - the first season offers us serial killer investigations which have become through repetition increasingly predictable, and as a relief is now presenting tales of Biblical armageddon and battles between good and evil so symbolic that it can only leave human concerns dwarfed in comparison. Powers, Principalities, Thrones and Dominions was a brave attempt at constructing a story which was mythic and ambiguous, against the very nature of a cop drama series necessitating stories with a beginning, middle and *solution*. It worked once, but left Frank nowhere to go, and had to make a dramatic virtue out of his impotence. Maranatha tries the same thing, but here Frank is largely forgotten altogether, no longer the prime mover in the series but an ordinary man buffeted about by forces of chaos. It's a neat moment at the end of the episode when, leaving the church, he echoes a Russian greeting and unwittingly states that the end of the world is nigh. It's ironic and chilling - but it's further evidence that Frank Black is a stooge.

The advantage that The X-Files has is that, whenever it gets too convoluted or pretentious, it can kick back the week later and give the audience something lighter. At the moment the relief offered from these episodes of confusion and apocalypse are brutal stories about sadists - the only colours on the Millennium pallet are black and black. Maranatha is an interesting experiment for the production team, and credibly feels very different - but it's a dangerous template for the future. (**)

1.22, Paper Dove

Air Date: May 16, 1997
Writers: Walon Green, Ted Mann
Director: Thomas J Wright

Summary   While the Black family visits Catherine's parents, her father Tom asks Frank to visit an associate of his, CR Hunziger, who's dying of cancer. Hunziger is refusing to see his son Malcolm - who was convicted four years ago of murdering his wife - and Tom hopes that Frank's insight into the criminal mentality will convince CR to visit Malcolm before he dies. Frank examines the evidence and becomes convinced that Malcolm is innocent, and that the real killer slew four other women.

Meanwhile, a man named Henry Dion reports to the Polaroid Man after killing a Maryland housewife - a crime that the Polaroid Man wanted done while Frank was in the vicinity. Frank apprehends Dion after he kills his own mother; Malcolm is thereby proven innocent and visits his father. The Black family returns to Seattle - but the Polaroid Man abducts Catherine at the airport.

Critique   And yet, unexpectedly, for the season finale, Millennium does find a tonal nuance that makes it feel both epic and domestic comedy. It's an unlikely style, it's true, and examples of it in Paper Dove are as black as anything Ten Thirteen have yet produced. But it's there all the same - a standard serial killer storyline with the murderer reimagined as the sort of henpecked man you'd expect to find in a sitcom. This is a killer who cheerfully goes on camping holidays with his dead victims just so he can share quality time with them under the stars. As Frank Black realises, he lives with a woman who never shuts up, and so only murders women to make them good listeners, to allow him to be amiable and chatty. The drama neatly subverts our expectations; there's a wonderful scene where Henry Dion comes across a single mother in the woods, and you can only believe he'll slit her throat. But Dion is in his domestic element, he has a woman to talk to and feel comfortable with already (albeit one buried amidst leaves and wrapped in plastic) and so he can relax, be charming, and help bandage her son's hand. The brilliantly funny but amoral conclusion we reach is that Dion is a better man so long as he has a dead body by his side. When we finally meet his mother, we can only understand why he needs the company of women who are peacefully dead - she's loud, patronising and nagging. Never before has the series invited us to urge the murderer on - and when he finally snaps and shuts his mother up for good, the effect is cathartic. When Frank finds him, Dion can only do a comic "oops", as if he were in a farce, and deliver the story's funniest line: "At last we found a way to communicate."

It's insidious, of course; after so many episodes where we've been looking at a serial killer from a profiler's point of view, we finally see one from his own perspective as a fall guy. The plotline is formulaic, but it needs to be for the joke to have its effect: the killer isn't a mastermind, he's a bumbling everyman. And therefore it's all the more surprising, with the case wrapped up and everybody happy, that the season ends abruptly on Catherine's abduction by the mysterious Polaroid Man. The bubble has been burst. The X-Files ends its seasons on big cliffhangers that threaten to change the entire course of the series (but never actually do). Millennium ends on an afterthought that is low key and so undramatic it dares you to think of it as all an accident, that Frank's worrying for no reason, that everything's going to be okay - and from this point on, the series will never get back to what it was.

The first season of Millennium is an oddity.

It's clearly more ambitious and more accomplished than The X-Files' first season - actually, even compared to the *fourth* season of the parent series, running alongside it, Millennium's first year mostly holds its own on an episode by episode basis. Where it falters is in its characters. There are half a dozen actors who could be termed regulars alongside Lance Henriksen, but without exception they remain functional ciphers. Bill Smitrovich's finest hour as Bletcher was his last; Terry O'Quinn appears in most stories as sidekick but is, as yet, denied a personality to go with his professional mien. It's ironic that the best chemistry shown between Henriksen and Megan Gallagher is in this final episode, away from the yellow house, just before their marriage is undermined forever. The only relationship which really works is between Frank and his daughter Jordan - she's required to do little more than beam toothily and show excitement or love whenever her daddy is in the room, and it says much for the very real spark between Henriksen and Brittany Tiplady that these scenes always feel natural and charming. Duchovny took a season to find his feet as Mulder, but the connection between him and Anderson is what sold The X-Files. At this stage, a year into Millennium, Lance Henriksen's performance as Frank Black pretty much stands alone. It's credible and engaging, but it hasn't had the support around it to becomes especially *likeable*. That may be the biggest problem Millennium faces as it prepares for its second year. (****)

The X-Files: Season 5

5.1, Redux

Air Date: Nov. 2, 1997
Writer: Chris Carter
Director: RW Goodwin

Summary In flashback, it's revealed that Mulder found Ostelhoff keeping watch on his apartment. A scuffle led to Ostelhoff's face being shot off, whereupon Mulder and Scully - convinced that the FBI was spying on them - decided to fake Mulder's death so he could act with impunity.

Ostelhoff's ID card grants Mulder access to the Defence Advanced Research Projects Agency (DARPA), where Kritschgau finds him. Kritschgau claims that Mulder is investigating a hoax stretching back to the 1940s, when the military used the Roswell incident as a smokescreen as part of a secret program to boost the economy through military build-up, and to harvest DNA from virtually every American born after 1945. Meanwhile, Scully finds that the ice samples from Canada contain unique cells capable of creating life, and she deduces that her cancer stems from exposure to such material.

Soldiers take Kritschgau away for questioning, but Mulder uses DARPA's subterranean tunnels to enter the Pentagon. He finds dozens of alien bodies on gurneys, an index system of human DNA and a metal vial tagged for Scully - which he hopes contains a cure for her cancer. Mulder takes the vial and leaves, but the Lone Gunmen later find that it only contains deionised water. [To be continued.]

Critique The satellite channel Sky One bought the first broadcast rights to The X-Files in the UK. As the series grew in popularity, however, and Fox released special compilation tapes of the mythology stories ahead of transmission, Sky were obliged to skip these episodes altogether. (It had the curious effect of making The X-Files seem like two separate shows altogether - both featuring the same characters, but in completely different genres. The one running weekly on television being an anthology of monster stories, the other a series of self-important TV movies. It's odd, in retrospect, how true that really was.)

I first saw Redux as the middle third of a rented video from Blockbuster. I'd already seen Gethsemane, and duly watched it again in compilation form to get myself in the mood for the concluding hour and a half. It's hard to describe the shocking change in tone - from the sweeping majesty of the Yukon Mountains and a story aiming at epic drama, to a forty-five minute stretch of people walking down corridors. It looks as if the budget has run out for Season Five already, and we're only on episode one! And these people haven't even got the decency to walk down corridors *quietly* - no, they are accompanied by a long monologues in voiceover, as both Mulder and Scully interminably drone on in Chris Carter's tortured poesy. It's always jarring to hear either one of the characters in inner voice, because it sounds so peculiarly stilted, and so unlike the heroes we've grown to care for as real people over the past few seasons. But when they're both doing it - a scene from Mulder followed by a scene from Scully - and they're both in exactly the same mannered style, the effect is almost hilarious. Director RW Goodwin tries to divert the audience's attention from the effusion of chat chat chat by bringing on all manner of flashbacks and stock footage. Kritschgau's long, *long* explanation of US history since the end of World War II is made only the more confusing by fast edited news images ranging from the Gulf War to nuclear bombs to Vietnam.

It's hard to exaggerate how shoddy and lazy this all feels. It's The X-Files rewritten as self-indulgent exposition, with all the drama sucked out. The few scenes of exciting dialogue - Scully telling the FBI committee about Mulder's death! - are shown in full twice, and are still repeats from Gethsemane, from pity's sake. At the end of the episode, after half an hour of Mulder doing little more dramatic than trying to open doors with a key card just so he can find a cure for Scully's cancer, he finds out all he's managed to get his hands on is water. So he's wasted his time and then. And ours. Hey ho.

And I can't believe we're going down the Skinner-as-traitor route again. The only way this will be justified is if it turns out to be true - but the production team aren't going to do that, and the shock "villain in the room" reveal will be Section Chief Blevens - a character so important to the framework of the series that, barring his appearance in the Season Four finale, we haven't seen in *ninety-four episodes*. As it is, there's not even the slightest drama to be had from this blind alley, just Skinner and Scully shouting the same lines at each other like petulant children. In a corridor. Naturally. (*)

5.2, Redux II

Air Date: Nov. 9, 1997
Writer: Chris Carter
Director: Kim Manners

Summary Scully's cancer takes a turn for the worse. The Cigarette Smoking Man decides to deal with Mulder by offering to tell Mulder the truth about extraterrestrials - if Mulder quits the FBI and comes to work for him. However, the Elder disagrees with this strategy and authorizes the Cigarette Smoking Man's death. Soon after, the Cigarette Smoking Man tells Mulder that the vial he stole contains a tiny microchip that, when inserted into the base of Scully's neck, will cure her cancer. In fact, the removal of Scully's chip triggered her illness.

As part of his offer, the Cigarette Smoking Man arranges for Mulder to meet with his sister Samantha. She claims that since Mulder saw her last, she was cared for by a foster family, then told that the Cigarette Smoking Man was her father. Samantha's discomfort with the reunion causes her to leave without telling Mulder her whereabouts. Mulder refuses the Cigarette Smoking Man's deal.

At a FBI inquiry about his "death", Mulder intuitively fingers Section Chief Scott Blevins as the mole who has been unduly keeping tabs on him and Scully. An assassin slays Blevins, and another shoots the Cigarette Smoking Man. Skinner tells Mulder that although the Cigarette Smoking Man's body wasn't found, the blood loss was such that nobody could have survived. The chip works as intended, and Scully's cancer goes into remission.

Critique At least this story has the semblance of drama. The best pieces of the episode are, inevitably, those which have and have an honest a motion to them - the fantastic conversation between Mulder and Bill Scully about the sacrifices that have been made simply so Mulder can fail in his quest, the fear Scully shows as she apologises to her mother for abandoning her faith. And, best of all, the scenes which Mulder and Scully share together, the affection and bravery of both of them played excellently by Duchovny and Anderson.

But however well the episode succeeds in dealing with the intimate, it's in the bigger picture that it typically flounders. The scene between Mulder and Samantha is well played, and it's interesting to posit the idea of a Samantha who, now found, wants to keep away from her obsessive brother. But it's a necessary ingredient in a story which is already filled to the brim with angst and dilemma - Mulder is up on a murder charge, and Scully is fading fast, so do we really need Samantha to enter the frame now? If we could believe this as a real resolution, it would be worth it. But we can't. What we have here is an episode which makes a lot of fuss bringing events to what only *pretend* to be climaxes.

It's a measure at this stage of how little we can trust the series that when it tells us something it may even itself believe to be the truth, we know it will only reverse it later if it needs to spin out the story still further. If this episode really did show the Cigarette Smoking Man's demise, all well and good - there's something very apt about his being gunned down as he clutches a portrait of Mulder and Samantha as children. But we're now so conditioned to disbelieve any statement on the show, the moment is rid of all power - and, true to form, no body is found, so we know that he'll show up again soon or later. In which case, why bother with a subplot in the first place? By the end of Season Five, the Cigarette Smoking Man will be back working for the Syndicate as if nothing has taken place, so Redux II looks like a substantial waste of time in retrospect. As in Gethsemane, the characters are required to have a change of heart suddenly to justify the urgency of the plotting - it's a great idea to have the Syndicate decide to assassinate the Cigarette Smoking Man, but we get no real reason for it, and so it's hard to believe it counts for anything. And, of course, it later transpires it doesn't.

It'll be good to get back to some decent stories now, preferably with beginnings, middles and ends. Too many of the mythology stories are lacking in any one of these three props. Redux and Redux II brazenly decided to forego the whole lot of them at once. (**1/2)

5.3, Unusual Suspects

Air Date: Nov. 16, 1997
Writer: Vince Gilligan
Director: Kim Manners

Summary   In a flashback story from 1989, a woman named "Holly" recruits Byers - a future member of the Lone Gunmen - at a computer show to help locate her kidnapped daughter, Susanne Modeski. Byers' hacking skills enable him to obtain a decrypted file on Modeski, and a fellow computer expert named Frohike agrees to help decipher it. When Holly identifies the kidnapper as her psychotic ex-boyfriend - one Fox Mulder, an FBI agent - another hacker named Langly is asked to crack the FBI mainframe to learn more about him.

The trio discovers that "Holly" actually *is* Susanne Modeski, that she lied about Mulder, that she worked on experiments involving paranoia-inducing gas, and that she's manipulated them to get the file decrypted. The group tracks down a warehouse where the gas is stored, but Mulder tries to arrest them. Government officials try to seize Modeski, and the resulting shootout ends with Mulder getting sprayed with paranoia gas. X appears and briefly intimidates Byers' group, then departs. Byers and his associates are released when Mulder confirms their story. Soon afterward, government agents capture Modeski.

Critique   As the Redux episodes indicate, with Season Five filmed *after* the movie it leads into, The X-Files this year automatically becomes self-reflexive. No great steps can be taken in the back story, or in the relationships, which have not already been anticipated during the writing of Season Four. Nothing can be introduced that cannot be undone. And instead effort can be used to plug gaps that don't necessarily *need* to be plugged. Beyond the necessity of making a story which could fit in around Gillian Anderson and David Duchovny's shooting schedule and use them at a minimum, there's no great use to an episode which shows the Lone Gunmen coming together or their first meeting with Mulder.

What Vince Gilligan produces is this year's equivalent of Musings of a Cigarette Smoking Man. Both purport to be establishing stories for supporting characters. But whilst Musings is bold and unsettling, Unusual Suspects is throwaway and charming. I'm not sure that's necessarily a fault - there's something very winning about a story told in a clear straightforward fashion after the murk of the Redux instalments. However, it very much relies on just how amusing the audience finds the Lone Gunmen to begin with. As characters who shamelessly hand out useful exposition, they function pretty well as comic relief bit parts, but I don't honestly think that any of the performances here have the weight to carry a whole story. Perhaps that is why Gilligan plays them so cautiously - *too* cautiously - because for all the extra attention foisted upon them, there's nothing in their origin story which offers any surprises. Frohike and Langly are the same social misfits we already know, with no dimensions added - there's nothing to suggest that they're any different to the characters we know from the present timeline. John Harwood is something of a revelation as Byers, playing innocent rather better than the knowing we're used to - but there's very little to be learned here, and he's not strong enough an actor to pull off the moral outrage needed in the warehouse scene with X. Duchovny, tellingly, makes a greater impression with his few minutes' screen time as a more confident and straight-laced Mulder. But I think Gilligan may have been trying to be a bit too smart with his suggestion that the reason that Mulder is so obsessed with aliens is because he was subjected to a dose of paranoia gas. Redux offered us a Mulder who was a gullible dupe, and this feels like the comic flipside of that. But the gag's just a bit too pat, and it threatens to turn a whole character's motivation into a simple punchline to a joke.

If this feels like a harsh judgment on an episode intended as a fun stopgap, then it is. There's lots to enjoy here. Signy Coleman makes a terrific femme fatale; Richard Belzer is funny enough as the sceptical detective John Munch that it doesn't matter if, like me, you can't spot the in-jokes from his appearances in Homicide. And there's something very sweet about seeing Byers, a man named after JFK but who remains naive enough never to have questioned the circumstance of his namesake's death, opening his mind to a new and more exciting world.

But this is, nevertheless, an episode largely concerned in suggesting to the audience that the government is being conspiratorial... five seasons into a hit series which has turned that argument into a cliché. It's a likeable enough little romp, but it's too leisurely to be exciting, too predictable to be revealing, and - most crucially - not really funny enough to be a comedy. I still think the most delightful joke about it is that, for its hundredth episode, The X-Files broadcasts a story boasting no aliens or monsters, which has no mention of Scully, and features Mulder only as an unlikeable bit part. In a series as hyped as this one was, with a feature film on its way, to celebrate a milestone like that is genuinely funny. (***)

5.4, Detour

Air Date: Nov. 23, 1997
Writer: Frank Spotnitz
Director: Brett Dowler

Summary   Forced to attend a team-building seminar in North Florida, Mulder is excited when some locals go missing and there's talk of an invisible monster. Mulder and Scully take some associates and look for the creature, but members of the group keep getting pulled into the ground. Scully is also pulled downward, and finds herself in a small cave with some of the missing team members. She wards off a savage, predatory man with her gun, gaining enough time for other agents to rescue her. Mulder suspects that the "predators" are linked to Ponce De Leon's quest to find the Fountain of Youth in the same area, and might just be defending their territory. The agents depart, leaving the creatures to themselves.

Critique   You can see why this would have seemed like a good idea. A back to basics monster story, featuring our heroes largely on their own and bantering off each other: after the angst and confusion of the cancer episodes, this was clearly designed to be a light-hearted adventure in the style of Season Three's Quagmire. Indeed, it replicates so much of that story's structure that it cannot be a coincidence - there's even a five-minute bit of dialogue between the two leads in which they just sit and chat. But the principle difference between the Detour equivalent of the "conversation on the rocks" is that Quagmire's wasn't just funny, but also touched upon matters of character. There were laughs to be had at watching Mulder and Scully being forced out of their comfort zone as action heroes and forced to stay still and *talk* for once, but they weren't laughs at their expense, and they made them feel richer as a result. The scene here doesn't really move much beyond discussions of which Flintstones wife the agents most identify with, and Scully singing about bullfrogs. It all earns a smile, of course it does. But if Tarantino realised that comic potential was to be had from stock genre characters discussing popular culture and fast food, he also used it as sharp relief to the clichés of what those characters stood for, and made their world seem all the more cold and brutal as a result. There's nothing to be gained from making Mulder and Scully concern themselves with Hanna-Barbera cartoons, because it in no way challenges our perception of how they ought to behave - it just makes them seem a bit more cartoonlike themselves, and the scene seem rather self-conscious. We aren't watching Mulder and Scully relax, we're watching Duchovny and Anderson relax their portrayals, and that isn't even nearly the same thing.

Comedy and charm are great things to aim for, but Detour seems to be satisfied with the *intention* alone; it's so busy telling us how cute the interplay between our heroes is it forgets to make it any good. You can see an episode like this working were it in the hands of Vince Gilligan - bizarrely, though, it's been written by Frank Spotnitz, someone you'd want on your side in a tussle with a conspiracy arc, but not the first man you'd call upon to tell a joke. There's a lethargy to the humour here, which is unfortunately echoed by the lethargy of the monster story itself. The result is a very ponderous episode in which Mulder and Scully wander about through some woods without either tension or effective comic relief.

Even this might have worked; getting Mulder and Scully out of the corridors and on an investigation in the great outdoors seems fresh, a throwback to Season One. But there's no investigation on offer. They stumble into the mystery by chance when they bail out of a team building seminar (which is, admittedly, a funny idea). Scully literally falls into a hole and finds the lair of the invisible monsters. And the rescue team just happen to discover them, even though the episode tries to derive most of its chills from the unlikelihood of this. Coincidence is fine, and a show like The X-Files depends upon it - but there's so much of it here that it doesn't leave room for anything else. And to cap it all, at the end of the episode, Mulder declares with no evidence that these strange (and rather crap looking) monsters might be sixteenth-century Spanish conquistadors who have found the Fountain of Youth. It's so utterly left field it feels self-parodic. And it's a further failing of this episode, even though it's setting itself up as a comedy, that it hasn't earned the right to be that preposterous. (**)

5.5, The Post-Modern Prometheus

Air Date: Nov. 30, 1997
Writer / Director: Chris Carter

Summary   Mulder and Scully answer a letter from Shianeh Berkowitz, an Indiana resident who mysteriously found herself with child eighteen years ago, and is now pregnant again after being gassed uncounscious by a Frankenstein-like creature. Her son Izzy has named the monster - which lives in the nearby woods - "The Great Mutato".

It transpires that twenty-five years ago, Dr Francis Pollidori accidentally created the Mutato as part of his genetic experiments. Pollidori's father - thinking his son's actions hateful - hid the Mutato from him in the intervening years. Dr Pollidori becomes outraged upon learning this and murders his father, then tries to pin the crime on Mutato. The locals form a mob, but everyone involved hears Mutato's story and learns that Pollidori Sr was trying to help Mutato find a mate - meaning that a number of the townsfolk are Mutato's children. The mob dissipates upon realizing that Mutato is one of their own, and the agents take Mutato to see his favourite performer, Cher.

Critique   This is something of a fan favourite, and it's not hard to see why. It's undoubtedly brave, a work of confidence borne out by the success of a show which is now prepared to experiment so completely with its style and format. It's got a witty and - sometimes - rather clever script, with jokes that repay careful viewing. (I love the idea of this modern-day Frankenstein, talking in prose as thick as Chris Carter at his most purple, of how he learned of culture through "home media centres".) And it has Mulder and Scully dance at the end. As Izzy's mother says, what's not to love?

Well, it's the direction, frankly. Chris Carter the writer has come up with something playful and light and charming. And Chris Carter the director has stamped all over it and made it so arch and obvious and dull that it kills it stone dead. Filming in black and white isn't simply a matter of turning the colour off - it has a grammar of its own, a different understanding of shade. Post-Modern Prometheus has none of the beauty of the Universal pictures it emulates, and instead looks cheap and nasty. The performances are all over the place. John O'Hurley decides to play Dr Pollidori as a mannered parody, and the result isn't witty or referential, it's just badly acted. Dana Grahame is terribly annoying as a journalist who has the facial tic of a chicken. And Pattie Tierce plays a Jerry Springer-watching, blue-collar mother so broadly that it could strip wallpaper. Mark Snow's music channels Danny Elfman, just so we know what we're watching is comic and cartoonlike - as if it weren't already obvious from the constant lightning bursts, and the lingering camera shots which transform each member of the town into a grinning caricature. "We need to speak to the writer!", Mulder says at one point. Leave the writer alone. Set the dogs on Chris Carter's alter ego.

And the comic-book setting is a dreadful mistake, because this play on post-modernism just doesn't make any sense. A comic has action, a way of jumping from frame to frame fast, cutting to the chase. By contrast this is languorous and self-indulgent. Halfway through it decides to mimic more obviously the horror films of the thirties rather than comics, and the mob all pick up flaming torches for no other reason than parody. But no horror film of the type would dare be as slow and as talky as this. There is a lot of fun to be had, I'm sure, in an X-Files episode mimicking a whole new genre - but it requires a consistency and an understanding of the form. Post-Modern Prometheus is so pleased that it's breaking the format that it doesn't ever choose a new one to adopt. It ends up as a mess.

It's a shame, because there are great ideas here. I love a town which feels like an X-Files audience, cheering Mulder on when he's believing in the monsters, and spitting in his food when he so unsportingly thinks it's a hoax. And there's something fun about a "monster" who comes to adore Cher because of the way she treats a misfit in the movie Mask. But these jokes work because of a real-world understanding of the characters and their links to contemporary culture - something which, as far as it can, the tone of the episode does its level best to stifle. (**)

5.6, Christmas Carol

Air Date: Dec. 7, 1997
Writers: Vince Gilligan, John Shiban, Frank Spotnitz
Director: Peter Markle

Summary Scully gets a cryptic phone call that's traced to the Marshall Sim residence, and upon going there discovers that Marshall's wife Roberta has been murdered. Marshall confesses to the crime - even though he has a credible alibi - and is later found hung in his cell. Scully comes to wonder if Marshall and Roberta's three-year-old daughter Emily - who looks strikingly like Scully's dead sister Melissa - is actually Melissa's offspring, given up for adoption in 1994. However, a paternity test determines that Scully herself is Emily's mother. [To be continued.]

Critique Dana Scully isn't the sort of person you'd much want to share Christmas with. She's a malcontent, she's a sulker. And she'll never relax long enough to open a present without someone knocking at the door giving her DNA results, she'll never have time to unpack before dead people leave messages for her on the ansaphone. With David Duchovny absent filming elsewhere, this becomes another episode which is forced to fracture the regular format, and here it's the Scully family who get the attention rather than the Lone Gunmen. Sheila Larken gives her best performance yet as Scully Mum, at last able to show some emotion beyond hospital bedside grief, showing understandable impatience at her daughter's refusal to enjoy a holiday. And Pat Skipper is great as Bill; insensitive he may be, but he's also very real, and every time he appears in the series it's to deliver uncomfortable home truths to his sister. His attack on her for being selfish, for investing too much emotion in a murder victim's daughter, is intellectually spot on. And it takes an adoption worker to reject Scully's application to become Emily's guardian, pointing out how unsuitable and emotionally detached a mother she'd be, for Scully to unravel at last and reveal the trauma she's been concealing ever since her cancer was cured.

The reason, then, why this episode works is all sleight of hand. We are conditioned to see Scully as the hero, and to enjoy the stories from her point of view. Even when Mulder is running around being brilliant and eccentric and solving things, it's nevertheless Scully who provides the audience perspective. And it's now only with Mulder absent that she's somewhat skew-wiff, and we can see her as the weird and melancholy woman she is. Though, like the Dickens allusion in the title suggests, this is an episode composed of visitations from the past - the memory sequences are all done without the usual pretension, and have a tremendous amount of verve. And because the dead Melissa Scully has a presence, in the phone calls but also in the way the family discuss her with such social awkwardness, you can buy the idea that this child born in 1994 could be her daughter. The cliffhanger at the end, revealing that it's Dana's instead, is dramatically perfect - we realise the inevitability of it as it happens, but the revelation has been so cleverly hidden in plain sight that it still carries quite a punch.

Gillian Anderson gives a terrific performance, refusing to sentimentalise a Scully who feels so uncomfortable around the people who love her, and is much more at ease demanding autopsies and opening murder investigations. This is a measure of what the X-Files has done to her. And you can look back to those deleted scenes from the pilot now, in which she's been given a boyfriend and a life outside the FBI which is relaxed and supportive and normal, and just see how impossible it is now to imagine her being characterised that affably. Even as you realise that her methodical approach is right, you still wish she could let go of it all and just be *happier*. And John Pyper-Ferguson is excellent as the sceptical Detective Kresge, a Scully to her Mulder, hinting years before it happens of the relationship Anderson will enjoy with Robert Patrick.

And the group-written script is really sharp too. This isn't exactly subtle as a character study, but the natural dialogue goes a long way to disguise that. The one moment where it all feels a bit too blunt, when Melissa tells Scully of the impact one can make on strangers' lives, is immediately undercut by having the speech compared to the motto in a greeting card. In its own quiet and unshowy way, this episode is just as atypical as Post-Modern Prometheus, but it's so much more rewarding. (****1/2)

5.7, Emily

Air Date: Dec. 14, 1997
Writers: Vince Gilligan, John Shiban, Frank Spotnitz
Director: Kim Manners

Summary   Putting his hacking skills to use, Frohike finds a social services record citing one Anna Fugazzi as Emily's mother. Mulder and Scully wonder if Emily was somehow born of Scully when she was abducted three years ago, and suspect that the conspirators behind this have a special interest in the girl. Emily's health deteriorates, and a cyst is found on the back of her neck that contains a toxic green substance - possibly the same fluid the Alien Bounty Hunter had in his system.

Mulder follows a clue to the Dimsdale Retirement Home, where evidence suggests that the elderly female patients - Anna Fugazzi included - gave birth a few years ago. He locates ampoules containing human embryos, and escapes after encountering a pair of alien shapeshifters akin to the bounty hunter. Emily dies, but the secret parties involved in her birth move to secure evidence pertaining to the case and steal her body.

Critique   Mulder catches up with the story, and immediately this all becomes a little more formulaic. What Bill Scully said of his sister is true - it genuinely feels as if Mulder can hijack Scully's life, and before long last week's emotional little mystery is a conspiracy episode full of chases and green blood and shapeshifting aliens. It's very telling that the Scully family all but disappear from the story, popping up again only in the final scene - when, with a jolt, we realise that Scully's sister-in-law has had the baby she's been carrying. Real life has continued regardless as Scully gets herself sucked ever deeper into an X-File, and she's become an aunt without even noticing. When Mulder is on the scene, and The X-Files format kicks back into touch, there's little time to focus upon the domestic - and that's exactly *why* Scully is now the way she is.

Only the teaser has the mark of deathless prose stamped all over it, but it's so well filmed, as Scully turns to sand in a desert, that it has a beauty all the same - and the only bit of the voiceover accompanying it which makes much sense, as Scully concludes she is "alone, as ever", is ominous and affecting. However, it's not as moving as it would like to be. Emily is doomed from the get-go, and the episode can do nothing to dress that up. After the cancer storyline it feels too soon to see yet more sequences of people standing around emoting as they watch the dying in hospital. And beyond drawing on the kneejerk emotional impact of seeing a small child die, there's very little about Emily with which we can sympathise. She barely talks, and her only human moment is laughing at Mulder when he pulls his Mr Potato Head face at her. That it works at all is testament to the sincere performance - as ever - of Gillian

Anderson; the scene where Emily undergoes a CAT scan, so soon after Scully herself has been through the same procedure, has a real power to it. And the episode's final moments, in which Scully finds her cross necklace within Emily's coffin, are wonderful; they echo the teaser brilliantly, and give a rare symmetry to a mythology story. (***)

5.8, Kitsunegari

Air Date: Jan 4, 1998
Writers: Vince Gilligan, Tim Minear
Director: Daniel Sackheim

Summary Mulder and Scully organize a manhunt when Robert Modell - a murderer with the power to influence people's minds (3.17, Pusher) - escapes from prison. The prosecutor who put Modell away is soon found dead - and a Japanese ideogram at the crime scene displays the word "kitsunegari", i.e. "fox hunt".

The agents ascertain that Modell has an interest in Linda Bowman, the prosecutor's wife - but Mulder realises that Linda, not Modell, killed her husband. He suspects that Modell has been covering for Linda's crimes - a theory confirmed when Linda approaches uses her own power of mental suggestion to make Modell's heart stop. Linda confuses the agents with her mental talents until Scully shoots her. As she's taken away for medical treatment, Mulder and Scully discover that Linda and Modell were twins.

Critique Once you get past the unlikely twist - that Modell has a sister with a brain tumour which gives her the same power as her brother - this is a great deal of fun. It doesn't have the power of Pusher, but Kitsunegari is a very different sort of beast; Pusher worked as a character study of a little man trying to be big, whereas the sequel is more about plot and action. Even if you suspect that the episode is an excuse to trot out all the set pieces they forgot to use the first time round, they're still very *good* set pieces. A man wielding a bat comes to believe he's holding a snake. A woman amiably electrocutes herself whilst holding a relaxed conversation with Mulder. A man covers himself with blue paint and then drinks himself full of the stuff, in what must be one of the most bizarre images we've seen on the show for quite a while.

And Mulder is convinced that Scully has shot herself in the head right in front of him. It's exciting stuff, and this time much more emphasis is given to the way that Modell and his sister are playing mindgames with their victims. The scene in which Linda openly mocks the FBI agents by alluding to the murder she's committed with painting puns is very clever indeed, creeping up on you subtly as you begin to spot the references.

It lacks Vince Gilligan's trademark wit, but it showcases his very clean storytelling style. If the climax scene where Mulder and Scully point guns at each other doesn't have the same intensity of the one in Pusher, it's still a very neat echo of it, and this variation on the theme takes the mind control idea suggested two seasons ago to its logical conclusion. And the scene in which Linda talks Modell into a mercy killing is gorgeous; it's excellently played by both Robert Wisden and Diana Scarwid, and for its sincerity it's surprisingly moving. It's a rare moment of heart amid all the twists and tricks, and it helps raise Kitsunegari above the average. (***1/2)

5.9, Schizogeny

Air Date: Jan. 11, 1998
Writers: Jessica Scott, Mike Wollaeger
Director: Ralph Hemecker

Summary In Coats Grove, Michigan, a disagreement between sixteen-year-old Bobby Rich and his stepfather Phil ends with Phil dying after being buried. When Bobby becomes the prime suspect, his therapist, Karin Matthews, claims that Phil physically abused the boy. Soon after, another of Matthews' patients - student Lisa Baiocchi - stands up to her father, whereupon an unseen force kills him.

Mulder discovers that Matthews' own father Charles died after being pulled into the mud some twenty years earlier, but he finds only roots in the man's casket. Further investigation reveals that Matthews herself was the victim of childhood abuse, and that her rage has become entwined in the life force of the trees in the area. By pushing her patients to imagine that they were abused, Matthews has been enabling the local roots to come to life and kill the teens' fathers. As Mulder and Scully find Charles Matthews' corpse in his daughter's basement, a deranged Matthews commands the roots to start pulling Bobby into the mud. Matthews relents - and the trees go quiet - when Ramirez, an axe-wielding local, kills her.

Critique As Mulder says of Bobby Rich, this is a hard kid to love. Looking at it coolly, the premise makes little sense, spotlighting a woman who is channelling the presence of her dead father and protects teens on whom she projects her own childhood abuse by controlling murderous trees. It's hard not to make that sound a mite contrived. And the plot, such as it is, lurches around somewhat, before coming to an awkward end when a mysterious axeman shows up to chop off the villain's head at the right moment.

And yet, in spite of all that - maybe in part even because of it - there's a weirdness to Schizogeny that makes it very chilling. There's a creeping sense of dread to this horror tale; the idea behind it may be preposterous, but it's treated with such realistic dialogue and true emotion that it just convinces. We've seen teenage angst in The X-Files before, most memorably in D.P.O. For a while Schizogeny seems to be a replay of that, as a bullied kid appears to become a supernatural murderer. It's so Howard Gordon it hurts. But that's the twist - Bobby seeks popularity by courting a notoriety he hasn't earned. The theme of the episode may well be that of child abuse, but it's treated far more subtly than the horror story around it would suggest, as we learn that the children are being made to *believe* they are victims as opposed to being teenagers undergoing usual acts of rebellion. David Mamet's play Oleanna caused a furore by making its target a political correctness which demonises and codifies all forms of male behaviour as sexual abuse - and Schizogeny does the same thing, portraying a child counsellor who is able to turn ordinary and innocent relationships into something obscene. It's a very brave idea - and a very *dangerous* idea - and it works wonderfully well thanks to a script which treats its characters and the distances between them with honesty. The aching gap between parent and child, both hurting from the mistrust of the other, is excellently drawn - there are no simple aggressors in these wars between the generations, just people who are confused and blindly hurting the other.

The first half-hour is terrific, with director Ralph Hemecker bringing the eeriness to the fore, and making this a more honest-to-God scary slice of X-File than has been offered in ages. And if Chad Lindberg at times tries too hard to affect a Nicolas Cage drawl while playing Bobby, he impressively avoids making his misunderstood teen either too sympathetic or too unlikeable. If by the end the nods towards Psycho and the lack of explanation tip the episode over the edge into nonsense, it remains for the most part a genuinely intriguing mystery with lots to say about the modern day witch hunt culture of cod psychology. (***1/2)

5.10, Chinga

Air Date: Feb 8, 1998
Writers: Stephen King, Chris Carter
Director: Kim Manners

Summary Scully lends medical assistance in Amma Beach, Maine, when a number of the locals inexplicably start harming or killing themselves. Attention soon focuses on Melissa Turner, a widow who sees a reflection of each victim - and the manner of their injuries / deaths - before each incident occurs. Melissa is rumoured to be a witch, and it's suspected that her daughter Polly inherited her spell-casting talent. However, the real cause of the trouble is Polly's doll Chinga - which Polly's late father, a fisherman, found in one of his lobster traps.

More people die, and Melissa spies a reflection of herself with a hammer buried in her head. She nearly carries out the deed, but Scully - deducing that Chinga is responsible - melts the doll in a microwave. Melissa is saved, but a lobster fisherman later finds the scorched Chinga doll in one of his traps.

Critique With its celebrity guest writer in place, Chinga was hyped as an event episode. So it seems a bit disappointing that so much that is being offered here we've already seen recently, and done with more verve: people being forced to kill themselves by a stronger will was on display only two episodes ago in Kitsunegari, whilst Elegy's depiction of a character seeing ghosts of the nearly deceased was only at the end of the previous season. For once what the viewers would have wanted was something entirely new, outside the show's comfort zone, a different slant on the series altogether - The X-Files as re-imagined by the greatest horror writer of the twentieth century. It's unfortunate that this "fresh" perspective seems to be a collection of the familiar.

At his best, Stephen King's genius is for taking the mundane and making something bizarre out of it - his great innovation with horror was to put it in a world of Coca Cola and rock music. And as his writing matured, so did the way that however outlandish his plots, they were characterised by real people with recognisable feelings and emotional journeys that felt true and moving. You can see why King would seem like a great match for The X-Files - in many ways, he created the template. But it's in his prose that King excels, not in his screenplays; he has a blind spot about what works well on screen. Anyone who has sat through Rose Red or Maximum Overdrive will know that; King still believes that his own laboured mini-series of The Shining is better than Kubrick's film masterpiece. It comes out of the very different way the media work - what is subtle and beguiling in book form looks obvious and clunky when translated directly to TV. King's tale of a killer doll would probably have been a likeable potboiler on the page - on the screen it feels so on the nose, it makes you wince. The X-Files can do generic, but rarely so bluntly.

This may have been why Chris Carter stepped in with his rewrites. What Carter did was to make the story more of an obvious pastiche, so that the lack of subtlety would be part of the point. This is a Carter who's just stepped off Post-Modern Prometheus, and is clearly relishing playing about with parody. To this end we have a repeat of the running gag from War of the Coprophages, where Scully and Mulder are separated and conduct the investigation by telephone. There are some good jokes here - I especially enjoyed the one where we're led to believe Mulder is watching porn, only to discover he's genuinely watching "World's Deadliest Swarms" as he claimed. But the gag of showing how boring our heroes' lives are away from each other

was better handled by Darin Morgan, and feels increasingly off the mark here. Far cleverer is the reluctance with which Scully eventually has to solve the mystery by bringing up "extreme possibilities" - the little sigh says it all. It's as if she understands too that this is *always* the way these stories play out, and in his absence she has to play Mulder too. It's a nice development of a theme played more seriously in Christmas Carol, and nicely anticipates Bad Blood, where the two approaches made by Mulder and Scully are held up for caricatured study.

The irony of all this is that King is rather a better comedy writer than Carter is. Had he been commissioned to do a spoof, we'd have ended up with something jet black and very funny. As it was, we've been offered a Stephen King Horror - a knowing nod to the audience right from the start when we see a Maine license plate. This curious half breed is unlikely to satisfy Stephen King fans or X-Files fans over much, both of whom would be looking for the depth that the other's involvement would seem to have removed.

But in spite of the clumsy feel of Chinga, there is something still very watchable about it. It's atonal, it's dissonant. The comedy is forced, the horror unsubtle. And that's what makes it something of a guilty pleasure. There's nothing quite so atypically awkward in all of The X-Files as the fisherman's story about a father bringing up a doll from the sea floor and deciding to give it to his daughter as a present - spend some *money* on a gift, Dad, why don't you - and then skewering himself on his own grappling hook. But it strangely works - it's utterly unbelievable, it doesn't fit into this series of government conspiracy and cancer angst whatsoever, it feels more like an urban legend told around a camp fire - and that's its joy. If Chinga could have been just that bit crazier still. If it had just said, "we've got Stephen King for a week, let's revel in it, let's go mad," then however bad the results, it would at least have been *distinctive*. At the end of the day, Chinga entertains as a bit of silly nonsense, but it doesn't have the courage of its convictions to become something *memorable* too. (**1/2)

5.11, Kill Switch

Air Date: Feb 15, 1998
Writers: William Gibson, Tom Maddox
Director: Rob Bowman

Summary Donald Gelman - a co-inventor of the Internet - dies in a police shootout facilitated by an anonymous tip-off. Mulder and Scully look into Gelman's death, coming to suspect that Gelman created a sentient computer program. Gelman evidently released the program onto the Internet so it could evolve, but the program is now capable of self-defence, and can blast ground locations by hijacking laser-equipped Department of Defense satellites.

The agents encounter Esther Nairn, one of Gelman's associates. Nairn and her boyfriend, David Markham, hope to upload their minds into the illicit AI, thereby achieving a melded consciousness that can live forever. Mulder identifies an equipment-laden trailer that serves as the AI's home node, and finds Markham's body inside. The AI traps Mulder with animated machinery, but Scully pulls him free as Nairn uploads her consciousness. Moments later, at Nairn's direction, the DOD satellite destroys the trailer and her physical body.

Critique I'm not sure this episode makes a lot more sense than Season One's Ghost in the Machine. For all its greater style and shinier hardware, it pretty much tells exactly the same simple story - that of a sentient computer that kills in order to defend itself. But what style, and what hardware! William Gibson and Tom Maddox achieve exactly what Stephen King's episode failed to do, to produce an instalment of The X-Files which feels as if it's written outside the house style and is more relative to the work of the celebrity guest responsible. I'm not a reader of Gibson's cyberpunk, so perhaps Kill Switch is no more than a stereotyped view of his writings - but its dealings with artificial intelligences and virtual realities feels very fresh and new. And even if I don't understand a lot of the jargon, it has the ring of truth to it - I had the thrill of watching an episode of technobabble which felt rather more persuasive than normal. As with any episode this year, Kill Switch's greatest pleasures come from the internal portraits of Mulder and Scully. Just a week before Bad Blood defines the limits of this, we're treated to a vision of Mulder's nightmare - a scenario in which he's threatened by busty breathy nurses who cut off his limbs, and is rescued by a kickboxing Scully, blowing the hair out of her face in a way that can only be described as supercool. What's great about it is not only that it's very funny, but it's also slanted enough from reality to be quite disturbing too - we laugh as we're taken far from our comfort zone. There is no more comic moment in the story than Mulder's pathetic attempts to get a snarling, martial-arts expert Scully to take pity on the fact that his arms have been severed, offering up the stumps to her like a poodle wanting to be petted.

It's not an episode with a lot of depth, but it has a real heart to it. The Lone Gunmen scene, in which they all but kow-tow to Esther, is quite charming. And as preposterous as the notion might be, there's something truly celebratory about Esther's victory over body death, her escape into the Internet, sending out the message "Bite Me" to her geeky fans. It's the sense of humour which humanises Kill Switch for all its technology, and sets it apart from the earnest Ghost in the Machine; Esther talks admiringly about the AI's comic murder of Gelman in a beautifully overelaborate teaser. The plotting is, I think, a bit confusing; there's a lot of running around, but you're never quite sure where they're running to. And the final sequence in the trailer park is utterly superfluous, and feels like an attempt to wrench this quirky little episode back to the standard X-Files clichés. But the incidentals have a wonderful confidence to them, the special effects are great, and there's a macabre wit to it all which makes this story a winner. (****)

5.12, Bad Blood

Air Date: Feb 22, 1998
Writer: Vince Gilligan
Director: Cliff Bole

Summary Mulder and Scully compare their version of events when a case in Chaney, Texas, ends with Mulder staking a "vampire" who's actually a teenager wearing false fangs. In Scully's account, she and Mulder went to investigate several dead cattle - and one dead tourist - that had two telltale puncture wounds and were completely drained of blood. Scully autopsied a second victim while Mulder accepted a pizza delivery at her hotel room. Scully found that the victims' last meal was pizza - and dashed back to the hotel as Mulder become groggy from chloral hydrate-doped pizza, and the delivery boy, Ronnie bared his fangs. After a quick chase, Mulder staked Ronnie. Mulder agrees overall with Scully's account, but his retelling greatly differs in tone.

The agents return to Texas when a coroner pulls the stake from Ronnie's body and he returns to life. Scully accepts some drugged coffee from the dashing Sheriff Lucius Hartwell, who's really a vampire, and slumps unconscious. Mulder traps Ronnie inside his coffin, but a crowd of vampires - who live at the Rolling Acres RV Camp - overpower him. The agents awaken to find the entire RV Camp empty - the vampires would prefer to keep a low profile, and Ronnie, who's a bit of a moron, was spoiling things for them.

Critique   Now that's how you tell a vampire story! Early X-Files too often relied upon taking a core horror tale, milking it for all it was worth, and adding nothing to the mix. One of the best examples is 3, in which Mulder walked the wild side with vampires who took their blood fetish so seriously, they smacked of angsty teenagers. For a story which wants to take examine Mulder and Scully's very stereotypes, it's terribly clever that Vince Gilligan has pinned his concept of telling the same adventure from two different skewed perspectives upon such a clichéd folk myth, using its very familiarity for comic effect. In most episodes, it's Mulder and Scully who are the reassuring constants, and we react with surprise or horror to the case they're investigating - here it's wonderfully reversed, so it's our heroes who are shown to be peculiar, whilst the vampire story seems normal in comparison. I love the idea of these very amiable twentieth-century vampires, trying to be good neighbours, despairing with a sigh and raised eyebrow when one of their kind goes about killing people and letting the side down. In 3, one of the vampires

was a cool rock chick - here it's a tubby pizza delivery boy, wearing false fangs because he's watched one too many Bela Lugosi movies.

And this is very much the backdrop to a wonderful comedy which takes the idea of analysing Mulder and Scully as far as it can go. Darin Morgan has done fine work deconstructing Mulder and Scully as icons, right back as far as Humbug, and Gilligan has further explored that. His is a more affectionate comedy style, realising that what makes them endearing is all the stuff you'd normally cut from the dialogue so the story has more time for action or chills, allowing our heroes to have their neuroses and quirks hang out for all to see. What he does here is a step beyond that. In Small Potatoes, Mulder could be reassessed from the perspective of a shapeshifter wearing his body, and the conceit was a *plot* one, the monster of the week allowed the opportunity for Gilligan to expose just how trivial Mulder's life was. Bad Blood doesn't feel the need to come up with a premise to justify its take on the characters - as far as Mulder and Scully are concerned, as far as the vampires they interact with are concerned, the adventure follows the usual protocol. It's only we the audience who can see the difference, just as only we saw that Post-Modern Prometheus was taking place in black and white (no-one needed to suddenly notice all the colour had been drained, and the Great Mutato didn't have a strange power to turn everyone monochrome).

It's a new trend in the series, and a sophisticated one - the gimmick here isn't supernatural, but structural: in a series as crazy as The X-Files, where anything can happen, we're now being invited to step back from the inner "reality" of the programme and see it as a television show which can be told backwards or forwards, and with obvious inconsistencies. I think the comparison with Post-Modern Prometheus is telling - there, though, Chris Carter made the fictional nature of the story very obvious, framing it all within a comic book, making it look like it was a 1930s movie. The brilliance of Bad Blood is that it's just as fictional, but far more subtly done - and if a viewer turned on the episode halfway through they wouldn't easily spot that what was being shown on the screen isn't to be taken literally. The same adventure is told in exaggerated form twice, but the exaggeration is not so over the top that you'd be alerted to it -

we've already seen on the show, sometimes just through sloppy writing, Scully coming across as someone either taken for granted or whinily shrewish, or Mulder as an insensitive monomaniac or cheeky chirpy genius.

And, of course, as with most attempts to discuss the craft of comedy, this makes it all sound very cerebral and stodgy. When, naturally enough, it's actually blissfully funny. There's lots of great laughs to be had from the contradictory accounts of both the vampire story, and the way that Mulder and Scully see each other. What makes it clever is the way that the agents aren't just portrayed as each other's polar opposite - because however amusing that might be, it'd be dishonest to the characters we know. There are telling moments when both have the chance to show affection for the other - Scully's very real concern for Mulder's little "overreaction" with his wooden stake, the tactful way Mulder leaves Scully alone on stakeout with the police chief she knows she fancies. Season Three's Syzygy showed a Mulder and Scully at loggerheads for comic effect, and the result was something almost too strident to watch. Whatever disputes they may have in Bad Blood, here they work well professionally as a team. Scully either slopes off sadly to do another autopsy because she wants the good opinion of the selfish man muddying up her bed - *or* she blasts her partner with anger and the insistence that everything she does is for him. It almost doesn't matter; because whether she goes to carve up another body placidly or kicking and screaming, carve up another body she does. In the same way, either as braggart or someone walking on eggshells, it's charmingly clear that all Mulder wants to do is to impress his partner - even holding off telling her the reason why shoelaces are an important clue for greater dramatic effect. For all the arguing and the sneers on display, it makes Bad Blood something warm and optimistic - the final scene in Skinner's office, where the agents grudgingly support each other, becomes something almost triumphant. They feel for each other the way that the sheriff feels for vampire misfit Ronny Strickland - they make the other look bad, but in the end they have to accept they're both "one of their own". (*****)

5.13, Patient X

Air Date: March 1, 1998
Writer: Chris Carter, Frank Spotnitz
Director: Kim Manners

Summary   The Syndicate becomes alarmed when mass groups of alien abductees are mysteriously compelled to gather at certain locations, where they are burned alive. The perpetrators are faceless aliens who hope to stop the colonization efforts of the Syndicate and their alien allies. Krycek captures a young boy, Dmitri, who witnessed one such mass slaughter and is now riddled with the black oil. He offers to trade Dmitri to the Syndicate for all data pertaining to a vaccine against the oil, and then meets up with his lover, Marita Covarrubias. Dmitri escapes, after infecting Marita with the black oil.

Meanwhile, Mulder takes an interest in "Patient X" - an abductee named Cassandra. Scully discovers that Cassandra has a neck implant and claims to have been taken at Skyland Mountain, the site of Scully's own abduction (2.6, Ascension). However, Cassandra's son, Agent Spencer, warns that his mother is just mentally disturbed.

A large number of abductees - including Scully, Cassandra, the assassin who shot the Cigarette Smoking Man and Dmitri - are compelled to gather at Ruskin Dam in Pennsylvania. Scully looks about the crowd just as a spaceship of some description appears - and faceless aliens bearing flame weapons start incinerating those assembled. [To be continued.]

Critique   There's a fascinating experiment going on here - and I don't necessarily mean the one that drips black oil onto Russian boys' faces. The last couple of episodes have worked principally on suggesting that there is a Mulder and Scully stereotype, one that can be subverted to comic effect: the dream sequences of Kill Switch and the entirety of Bad Blood depend upon an audience's expectation of how predictably our heroes will behave in any given situation. Patient X tries to shift the goalposts. Mulder no longer believes in aliens, and is adamant that they are the smokescreen of darker government agendas. Scully, her chip back in her neck, and talking to fellow abductees, has become the open-minded one. She gently prods her partner towards extraterrestrial explanations - and visibly recoils at his contempt. Full marks to the production team for showing how deeply unsympathetic Mulder is without his quest to ennoble him - this feels a very real depiction of someone grieving the purpose of his life. Opening with Mulder rejecting alien experience publicly certainly isn't subtle - and since when did Mulder get to give talks about this sort of thing at the UFO fans' equivalent of a Doctor Who convention anyway? - but it gives the refocusing of Mulder a clarity rare in these mythology episodes. We've seen little hints of Mulder's new world view over the season - most jarringly, I think, in Post-Modern Prometheus, where he tells Izzy's mum that he's no longer sure he believes in "that stuff", which feels like an attempt to crowbar continuity development into an episode that wants to be as standalone as it's possible to be. But it's only in these mytharc stories that we can really get a measure on how our heroes are progressing - and Mulder's stance here is dramatic and shocking.

The question is, I suppose, whether there's much point to this sudden twist in the characterisation. The audience is all too keenly aware that the feature film is set to be released in the summer, and that it's going to be a big showstopper with tons of aliens and spaceships and things. (Probably.) Any shift that can happen here is only temporary, and all this to-ing and fro-ing can be seen as merely a means of avoiding any *real* plot development or character growth, nothing more than running on the spot until the cinemas open. But it works because Duchovny and Anderson, typically, both play the truth of characters whose core beliefs are crumbling. After seasons of scepticism, there's something touching about Scully *finally* witnessing an alien spaceship of her very own. (And true to X-Files form, Mulder doesn't get to see it. It almost seems you have to *believe* in the first place before you're shown any evidence!)

These aren't the only shocks on offer. It's a truly visceral episode, the second (after Home) to be prefaced by a warning about its content. The sequence of faceless men emotionlessly incinerating living people is terrifying, and makes for a truly effective cliffhanger. And the image of Dmitri, the kid who was in the wrong place at the wrong time, filled with black oil, his eyes and mouth sewn up to prevent its release, is maybe the grisliest yet in a series which thrives upon acts of cruelty and torture. It's a conspiracy episode, so you expect the inevitable scenes of men looking worried in darkened rooms muttering about timetables - but just as you get complacent once more, you react to scenes of genuine horror, such as Marita's interruption in the phone box by an oil-dripping Dmitri. (****)

5.14, The Red and the Black

Air Date: March 8, 1998
Writers: Chris Carter, Frank Spotnitz
Director: Chris Carter

Summary Scully is found alive after the Ruskin Dam incident, but the assassin and Dmitri are dead and Cassandra has vanished. The Well-Manicured Man captures Krycek, offering his freedom in exchange for a Russian-developed black-oil vaccine in Krycek's possession. Krycek agrees, and the Well-Manicured Man tells the Syndicate that resistance against the alien colonists is now possible, especially once the vaccine is successfully tested on Marita.

Under hypnosis, Scully recalls that the slaughter in Pennsylvania was interrupted when a second ship assaulted the faceless beings - who've self-mutilated their faces to prevent infection by the black oil. Cassandra was levitated upward into the second vessel.

The Syndicate captures one of the faceless aliens, and deliberates on whether to turn him over to their allies or instead ally themselves with the rebels. The Well-Manicured Man favours the rebels, and Krycek - now in the Well-Manicured Man's employ - tells Mulder that the resistance movement against the colonists will fail unless the captured alien is saved. Mulder and Scully try to rescue the captive from Wiekamp Air Force Base, but they run into an alien bounty hunter. A UFO appears and a second faceless alien approaches the bounty hunter with a flame-thrower. What happens next isn't clear - Mulder awakens after a flash of light to find all the aliens gone.

Afterward, Agent Spender refuses to read a letter from his father - the Cigarette Smoking

Man, who's holed up in a cabin in Canada.

Critique The hypnosis scene is gorgeous. The combination of Gillian Anderson's awed acting, and the gorgeous slow-mo special effects, give a real feeling of wonder and majesty that has (deliberately) been lacking in The X-Files for some time. And it's partly because it's a regression sequence that it works so well - the series has become so established now that mere appearances of spaceships can look too blunt and can be taken too complacently. But because this is channelled through the experiences of Scully, it moves us; there's a marvellous stylisation to this, the eerie beauty of ambiguity. This simple scene is one of the best in Season Five.

Nothing else can really match that. It settles down into being a typical mythology runaround, with Krycek and Mulder having a tussle, members of the Syndicate growling at each other, and our heroes getting in trouble with the military. It's very complicated, but the simpler scenes of confrontation are very well handled. Mulder and Scully discussing Mulder's lack of faith, and how even Scully as a non-believer who followed him anyway is no longer prepared to do so, has a real power to it. And Chris Owens is terrific as an angry and frustrated Agent Spender, drawn forever into a world of UFO abductions whilst he only wants from his job respect and stability - the scene where he shows Scully his own childhood regression tape is outstanding. Nicholas Lea is required to do silly things like kiss Mulder, and give all manner of earnest exposition, but Krycek earns something of a series best in the scene in which he convinces himself that Mulder is an ally in his battle against alien colonisation.

It doesn't really build to anything concrete, mind you. There's lots of interesting sabre rattling about vaccines and rebel alliances, but it all trickles out very inconclusively. The sequence where Mulder encounters the two warring aliens is clearly intended to be a life-changing moment, but it's rather anticlimactic, perhaps because you feel all it's really doing is putting his character back on the road he should never have come off in the first place. Ultimately you can't help but feel that for all the ideas on display, this episode hasn't so much set things up for the movie as just shuffled them around into

a slightly different position. The fact that Fight the Future depends so little upon the activities here leads you only to suspect that the approach here was needlessly cautious: if this two-parter wasn't all that relevant anyway, Chris Carter could have afforded to have given us some closure to it here after all. (***)

5.15, Travelers

Air Date: March 29, 1998
Writers: John Shiban, Frank Spotnitz
Director: William A Graham

Summary In 1990, a sheriff and a landlord catch a tenant, Edward Skur, in the act of draining the insides out of a human. The sheriff shoots Skur, who mutters "Mulder" before dying. The incident prompts Mulder - still a year away from working on the X-Files - to visit former FBI agent Arthur Dales.

Back in 1952, Skur was suspected of being a Communist, but escaped when Dales and Agent Hayes Michel were assigned to arrest him. A young Bill Mulder approached Dales and told him that Skur - along with two associates, now deceased - once worked for the State Department. Dales learned that the authorities performed xeno-transplantation surgery on the three men against their will, and grafted a spider-like lifeform to their bodies. Mulder wanted the truth about this known, but Michel became Skur's next victim when a spider-creature exited Skur's mouth and crawled into his.

Dales offered to help Skur and met him at an empty bar, where a fight ended with Dale overpowering and handcuffing Skur. Mulder and a Bureau aide purportedly took Skur into custody, but Mulder later released Skur - in the hopes that by letting him live, the crimes done against him might one day be exposed.

Critique Though clearly a stopgap episode imposed upon the production team when cast availability became an issue, Travelers cannot be better placed. After an episode in which the phrase "resist or serve" replaced the motto in the title sequence, this story takes on extra resonance. It uses the Communist witch hunt of the fifties as its backdrop, and regularly juxtaposes the idea of "serving" as being a patriot, with "resisting" as being branded a traitor. It's wonderful to see The X-Files finally gets its claws into the House Un-American Activities Committee, and it's a chilling reminder that the FBI, as the central home for the X-Files, was once party to such horrific attacks on civil liberties. As the conspiracy story picks up momentum for the movie, it seems fitting to show us what the conspiracy is a metaphor *for*: the use of hysteria to control the populace, the government actively making scapegoats of innocents to strengthen that control, the creeping fear of anything or anyone that could be deemed "alien".

Although largely rejected by fans at the time for being an irrelevance in a truncated season, this now feels fresh and urgent. With the absence of Scully, and the reduced role of Mulder, this was never going to be a popular favourite - but from the perspective of a show which de-emphasised these characters in its final seasons, this stands out as being a story *about* the X-Files themselves, and what it is they represent. Arthur Dales is no Mulder, he's no hero, he's no expert profiler. He's an ordinary man who is changed because of his brush with the unsolved cases stacked in the FBI basement (you've got to love the explanation why they're not filed under "U"). He becomes a rebel by accident, a "Communist" in the making, all because he has a human desire to find the truth, and the truth stands for a freedom that the government fear. The depiction of Mulder's father, too frightened to expose the lies he knows, or even to save Dales' life, is very sympathetic: we've seen Duchovny's Mulder battle against a comparatively liberal nineties FBI, but poor father Bill was up against a paranoia of far greater power. It's a perfect fit in this fifth season, in which the government are *using* the popular myths of UFOs to conceal their darker agendas, to see that they were doing the same thing with Marxism forty years before.

It's earnest and it's well-meaning, and the dialogue is angry and tight. The only pity is that the monster grafted into Skur's body, the eugenics experiment that Dales seeks to expose, isn't very effective. It's not that it isn't grisly enough, and there's nothing actually wrong with the way that it *looks*. But in a story which has been so well shot to reflect the murkiness of both the sets and the politics, the spider scuttling from mouth to mouth breaks the credibility. In truth, it makes the episode look a bit too much like it's from The X-Files, when its overall power comes from being so determinedly atypical. It's a collision of styles which doesn't pay off, which gives the metaphor of conformity gone wild a silliness it could well do without.

After years of saying how The X-Files took its inspiration from Kolchak: The Night Stalker, it's apt that Darren McGavin plays the older Agent Dales. And that, just as the Lone Gunmen took on the role of substitute leads earlier in the season, he fulfils the same function here - he's not a character we trust from The X-Files, but McGavin is so much the series' spiritual father he might as well be. (****)

5.16, Mind's Eye

Air Date: April 19, 1998
Writer: Tim Minear
Director: Kim Manners

Summary Marty Glenn, a young blind woman, is mysteriously made to watch through a killer's eyes as he murders someone - and is later implicated when she's found at the crime scene. Mulder believes that Glenn is innocent, and finds evidence that her sightless eyes are dilating in response to mental images. Mulder learns that the killer's modus operandi matches that of the death of Glenn's mother - and conjectures that Glenn gained her "sight" because a mental connection was forged between Glenn and her mother's killer. Fingerprints prove that the murderer, Charles Gotts, is Glenn's father. Glenn misdirects the agents as to Gotts' location, then kills him and is arrested for the crime.

Critique This is solid, if unspectacular. The writing's greatest strength is a return to a simpler style of storytelling that hasn't been seen on the series much these last couple of seasons - but it's somehow its greatest failing too, as once the premise is established there's really not much depth to be mined from it. It's odd that we've reached this position in The X-Files, where an episode featuring Mulder pursuing a hunch and trying to protect an innocent suspect can feel so naïve and old-fashioned. Tim Minear's dialogue is crisp, but the actual story is rather ponderous, and the murderer so lacking in dimension that the revelation that he's Marty's father comes across as pure contrivance.

But the episode works nonetheless, thanks to a superb central performance from Lili Taylor as Marty. She gives the best guest star turn of the year, lending a strength, an anger, and a redeeming humour to a blind woman who has adapted the world to her disability. In the opening scenes, Duchovny plays Mulder with the same wisecracking cynicism that has made him seem so much colder in the wake of his faith being shattered - but he clearly admires Marty hugely, and his growing concern for her has a winning sincerity. The rapport between them is excellently judged, Mulder's affection for her never patronizing, her response to him puzzled and abrasive but tinged with respect. Only in the final scene does the relationship trip into sentimentality - up until that point there was a dignity and truth to the characters that gives much impact.

The plot is rather predictable, and the pacing is on the slow side. For a story which has a device of a woman seeing through a killer's eyes, it's surprising how little advantage is taken of this dramatically or visually - some of that bravura camerawork that was used, say, in Demons, might have gone a long way to give this a bit of a jolt. But although you know it just *had* to happen, the sequence in which Lili Taylor first sees herself is terrific. (***)

5.17, All Souls

Air Date: April 26, 1998
Story: Billy Brown, Dan Angel
Teleplay: Frank Spotnitz, John Shiban
Director: Allen Coulter

Summary Dara Kernof, a mentally handicapped sixteen-year-old who's confined to a wheelchair, inexplicably starts walking and ventures out into the street. Her father sees her kneeling before a shadowy figure - just before the figure disappears in a flash of light and Kernof is found dead, her eyes burnt out.

Mulder and Scully learn that Kernof was adopted and that the shadowy figure is stalking her three identical sisters. Two of the remaining girls die, and the agents suspect one Father

Gregory of the crime. However, Aaron Starkey, a social services worker who's a demon in disguise, kills Gregory.

Scully's family priest, Father McCue, deduces that they're dealing with a seraphim - a four-faced angel who, according to an apocryphal story, sired four mortal children who themselves have the souls of angels. The story says that God sent the seraphim to collect the girls' souls, thereby protecting them from the devil. Scully finds the last girl, Roberta Dyer, but Dyer changes into her daughter Emily - who then asks Scully to release her. Scully does so, thwarting Starkey from taking Dyer as the shadowy, angelic figure generates a bright light. Starkey disappears, and Dyer's eyeless body is found afterward.

Critique And sometimes, when the episode is over, you just stare at the closing credits and say, "what"?

So, this is the one about a killer who's hunting down four girls. And burning their eyes out. But it's okay, because the killer is God. Yes, God. That's right. And it's doubly okay, because the girls are disabled, and not "meant to be"... I'll let that one sink in a moment. And when Scully gets the chance to save the last victim's life, she's persuaded - get this - by a vision of her dead daughter to let her die as was intended. The daughter who was, unless we forget, *also* killed earlier in the season because she too wasn't meant to be. (To be fair, at least in Emily, the girl was an alien hybrid with green acid blood. And she wasn't disabled. Did I mention that these other girls have no right to live because they're *disabled*? Okay. Good. I thought I had.)

Now, let's ponder. What sort of message is being sent out here?

As with Miracle Man and Revelations, there's an interesting point being raised here. Why are we happy to watch Mulder accept all manner of things paranormal, from alien intervention to urban legend, and yet baulk at a supernatural which forms the basis for a living religion which, accepted or rejected, is still a cornerstone of Western society? One flippant answer would be that Mulder enthusing about UFOs is *fun*, whilst Scully getting weepy over Christ really truly isn't. I think Gillian Anderson's great,

---

but All Souls, with its repeated shots of Scully sobbing in confession boxes, is raiding the cookie jar of angst just one too many times. And a more serious answer, which All Souls throws into sharper relief than its sister episodes, is that it denies our heroes a central role. Mulder and Scully can hunt down a man who eats people's livers, or chase alien vaccines, and they're being active participants in the drama, they're making a difference. The concept of religious faith in The X-Files, though, is a passive one - and that's a shame, because worship in itself is not passive at all. In the scheme of a show about criminal investigation it negates the FBI's role if all that happens is either predestined, as Scully suggests here, or is operating on a morality outside our ken. In any usual X-File we would be horrified by the death of innocents. In a Christian context, however, why should death be seen as a bad thing? At the start of the episode, Mrs Kernoff talks about how she knows the murder of her adopted daughter was for the best and we react against it - but this is precisely what the episode itself concludes.

Looking at death from a different angle is fascinating, and it's something that will be revisited with greater impact in Closure. But this needs to be given more time and intelligence than All Souls can offer. To pull this off the plotting must be clear and purposeful. Instead we get awkward sequences in which the girls are being fought over by God and the Devil, and because both sides appear to want the same morbid thing, it's impossible to work out what the conflict is about. In either case, the girl is toast - with one, though, there'll be a nice special effect of smoke issuing out of her eye sockets. The drama lurches around all over the place: one moment Scully is at her feet, encountering the (ridiculous) image of an angel with shifting faces, the next she's up and about and asking her reverend to look it up in the Big Book of Obscure Winged Creatures. The framing device of Scully narrating the story to a priest is interesting, but puts the events at one further remove, and fatally gives them the standard X-Files pretension of poetic monologue. If the story had any chance of working, it needed its shocks of God and the Devil contrasted with the real and mundane; as it is, the tone of the whole episode is so overwrought that it looks heightened and artificial. By the time of sacri-

fice, it almost looks parodic.

And that's why All Souls is such a terrible episode. If you're going to open this can of worms, if you're going to be that bold - then follow through with it. When Scully lets a girl die for God's glory, we don't need a priest's reaction, we need Mulder's, if only to ask her what the hell she thought she was doing. We get the odd mumble of disbelief from Duchovny earlier in the episode, but nothing discussive, nothing to justify his involvement. Indeed, he's shunted into the background simply so he *can't* question what's going on here. There is a place for the difficulties that All Souls raises about faith and attitudes towards death, but only if the debate is engaged honestly. This is cheap. It sells itself upon knowing that Gillian Anderson is very good at playing emotional trauma, and upon the contrived continuity of having her see Emily. There's no heart to this, and no point. It's abysmal. (*)

5.18, The Pine Bluff Variant

Air Date: May 3, 1998
Writer: John Shiban
Director: Rob Bowman

Summary Mulder's heretical views on the government lead Skinner and US Attorney Leamus to assign him to infiltrate a militia group that possesses a biotoxin. Scully deduces that the toxin stems from a secret governmental weapons program, and that shadowy figures in the government have manipulated the militia group into pulling a bank heist - a means of contaminating cash with the toxin, and thereby testing its use against a general populace.

Mulder participates in the theft, but Scully figures out which bank is being robbed and alerts authorities to seal off the building, preventing the toxin from spreading. One of the militia group's leaders - August Bremer, actually a government agent - kills his rival for command, Jacob Haily, and escapes. The government covers up the operation, even as Mulder realises - though he can't prove it - that Leamus was part of the toxin scheme from the start.

Critique Since Mulder had his psychotic episode in Anasazi, every season of The X-Files has featured an episode towards the end of its run where one of our heroes thinks the other is a traitor. This one is cleverer than most, offering neither drugs nor trepanning nor subliminal messaging to make the premise work. Instead what we're given is a reasonably straightforward thriller, as Mulder goes deep undercover to infiltrate a terrorist group. It feels strangely less like an X-Files episode, and more like a precursor to 24, with which it shares a similarly tense atmosphere, a sense that every other character is a traitor or a double agent (sometimes to the point of ridiculousness), and scenes of torture against the hero. Oh, and some terrific set pieces along the way - especially welcome in a season which has put such things somewhat behind them recently - the bank heist and the horror in the cinema are both particularly memorable.

Sensibly, the episode reveals Mulder's innocence a third of the way through; the mystery is sacrificed, of course, but there's only so often we can play scenes where Scully and / or Mulder suspect the other without them looking foolish. What is revealed behind this apparent betrayal, though, is rather subtle: it's Mulder's speech against the government in Patient X which has brought him to the attention of these terrorists in the first place. It's clever that the broader paranoia shown in the mythology episodes can be shown to have grimmer real life consequences here, and poses in the final act the very cogent question of where a series like this really stands. After all, half the time it's an FBI show where Mulder and Scully bring felons to legal justice, however monstrous or paranormal their nature. And the other half they are battling against the very government who establish what is legal in the first place. It reminds me of Travelers, where we're reminded that the FBI has a rather uglier past than the series often acknowledges; here we see that Mulder's new rationalism has darker connotations. So we get sequences where we're asked to consider whether Mulder will kill a civilian to keep his cover safe or not - and the get out, that another gang member kills him instead, hardly provides an answer. The man dies anyway, and Mulder couldn't save him.

All of this makes the story much richer. The Syndicate of the mythology episodes might

infect victims with black oil, but they never do anything quite as blunt or as *real* as breaking Mulder's fingers to test his loyalty. If in the final act there's a sense of too many bluffs and too many twists, the message is still clear - that The X-Files' quest for the truth, and the desire to expose it whatever the cost, leads to the paranoid fundamentalism we see in Jacob Hailey. And the single-minded obsession that the end justifies the means we'll later see given life in characters like Jack Bauer. (****)

5.19, Folie a Deux

Air Date: May 10, 1998
Writer: Vince Gilligan
Director: Kim Manners

Summary Gary Lambert, a telemarketer in Oak Brook, Illinois, believes that his boss, Greg Pincus, is a monster who's turning Lambert's coworkers into the undead. Lambert becomes unhinged and takes his officemates hostage with an AK-47, causing a stand-off in which Mulder briefly sees a monstrous form where Pincus is standing. A SWAT team member kills Lambert, and Scully attributes Mulder's perception of Pincus to "folie a deux" - a delusion shared by many people in a tense situation.

Mulder's recalls Lambert's claims that the monster was "hiding in the light", and finds five X-Files with similar descriptions. Mulder's obsession with Pincus becomes so outlandish that Skinner has him institutionalized. Pincus transforms into a large insect creature and approaches Mulder with the intent of injecting a toxin into him, but Scully arrives and chases Pincus off. Scully vouches that Mulder is of sound mind, and tells Skinner that her own sighting of Pincus as a monster must owe to "folie a deux". Pincus and his undead minions disappear and set up a new telemarketing centre in Missouri.

Critique Vince Gilligan's latest comedy is a more generic affair than Bad Blood, but it's also the logical extension of it. There we saw a Mulder and Scully portrayed in extremis, the one a man so inclined to his own hunches that he will "overreact" with a wooden stake, the other a woman whose comparative caution pushes her into the role of grumpy sceptic. Here their worldviews are seen through the perspective of a man who sees monsters everywhere, who thinks that his boss at work is someone who sucks the souls out of his employees, his fellow workers in telemarketing sales reduced to zombies. It's a pretty good, if rather obvious, joke; what gives it a punch is the way that gun-toting Gary Lambert is really just another Mulder, the sort of man who'll execute a zombie he's certain is already dead, just as Mulder will drive a stake into a pizza delivery boy he's certain is a vampire. And the rest of the world represents Scully - the sort who are rather embarrassed by these insane ravings, who'd much rather the man shouting "monster" at the top of his voice would really just sit down and shut up now, please - even if, by that attitude, you risk being turned into zombies. Even if, by that attitude, you're little more than a zombie already.

So what we've got here is something which Bad Blood, for all its cleverness, could not really do - provide a comedy and an effective monster story at the same time. The vampires in Bad Blood may be killers, but never pose a serious threat - whereas Mr Pincus, who prides himself on being such a *nice* boss, is likeably ordinary in his human state and eerily creepy without it. Kim Manners shoots the man-size insect brilliantly: a thing of shudders and twitches, it looks unreal enough that you think it *may* be a delusion, and its appearances are so fleeting it doesn't give you the luxury of a definitive judgment. The sequence in the hospital ward, where Mulder like a child rails out against the so-called imaginary monsters outside his bedroom window, are especially effective. That's a metaphor for Mulder's character right there, and it's rarely been so wittily or tensely made.

And whereas Bad Blood ultimately concluded that Mulder and Scully may be at loggerheads about their methodology, but ultimately are closer than they might wish to admit, so Folie a Deux succeeds by making this the point of the story. Scully thinks Mulder is crazy, but as he tells her, she's his one in five billion, she's the only one who'll ever stop long enough even to *consider* believing him. Mulder tells her she'll only see the monsters if she's willing to do so, and the scene where she is able to view the nurse as a zombie feels like a breakthrough

moment: her science has given her no proof, but it's her *faith* that lets her believe and enables her to save Mulder's life. The penultimate scene between them is a beauty: she's in denial and still can't express what she saw, but admits that she and Mulder have a shared madness. A folie a deux. Is there any more touching description of their relationship? (****)

5.20, The End

Air Date: May 17, 1998
Writer: Chris Carter
Director: RW Goodwin

Summary   A chess match between two masters - a Russian and twelve-year-old Gibson Praise - ends with Gibson moving, as if warned by precognition, and avoiding an assassin's bullet. Tests establish that an area of Gibson's brain (the "God Module") is exhibiting a startling amount of activity, and Mulder wonders if Gibson is a "missing link" - proof that man has some relationship to alien beings. Moreover, Gibson's psychic powers are so formidable, he stands a chance of explaining each and every X-File.

Scully feels conflicted when Mulder becomes overly friendly with his former girlfriend, Agent Diana Fowley. Meanwhile, the Syndicate recalls the Cigarette Smoking Man from Canada, asking him to deal with Gibson before he exposes all of their secrets. Fowley is wounded while guarding Gibson, and the Cigarette Smoking Man delivers the boy to the Well-Manicured Man. Later, the Cigarette Smoking Man reveals to Agent Spender that he's his father.

In the fallout from these events, the Justice Department opts to close the X-Files entirely. The Cigarette Smoking Man steals into Mulder's office, takes Samantha's file - and covers his deed by torching a good portion of the X-Files.

Critique   For the first time in the series, Vancouver is referenced - the teaser sequence was shot in the stadium there with seventeen thousand fan extras. It's a farewell gesture to the city in which the show has filmed over the past five seasons. And it provides the key to this episode, one which has the stated purpose of leading into the feature film but which is actually far more concerned with behind the scenes conclusions. (And it's the first time in The X-

Files that the factual reality of making the series has weighed against the fictional, even down to the title; for it to make sense we're meant to know that Duchovny and Anderson are moving to Los Angeles, but yet Mulder and Scully are staying exactly where they've always been.) It's for that reason too that so many old characters line up to take their curtain call. The Cigarette Smoking Man is brought back by the Syndicate, which is very welcome - but it lacks the dramatic force it might have had, because the reduction of standard mytharc episodes during Season Five has meant his absence hasn't been particularly noteworthy. Krycek is back too, but against narrative sense - last time he was seen already working against the Syndicate, and now he's both their special ops soldier and chauffeur, jobs you'd have thought he wasn't best equipped for with only one arm.

And look, we've lots of familiar elements to play with as well. Gibson Praise is yet another "key to the whole X-Files", the one who can provide all the answers. He's just a cuter version of Jeremiah Smith, or a walking talking chess-playing MJ file. The X-Files are under threat again as well, and are shut down just as they were at the end of Season One - only this time they've only been under noticeable threat for less than fifteen minutes' screen time before the plug is pulled. The sheer speed with which they're junked is a shock, and it's quite a surprise to close down the very department as introduction to a feature film trying to reach a new audience. But it's hard to believe in either of these big end of season gestures of the epic, because we've seen them before.

And yet... The End works in spite of itself. Tonally, it's very odd. All the elements that seem so familiar are being considered from a slightly skewed perspective. The Cigarette Smoking Man is not the man we last saw, a pawn, a stooge, a government bureaucrat. He's lost all the respect he once had for his superiors and no longer is fawning to impress them; he deliberately goads the Well-Manicured Man, refusing any longer to trade in euphemisms about the murders he commits. There's a swagger to his attitude that suggests he's gone a tiny bit mad, and he's much more interested in pursuing his son Jeffrey than even paying lip service to polit-ical agendas. All this gives the character a freshness which entirely justifies his return from the wilderness, and William B Davis clearly has a ball playing this more expressive version of the man. And the Mulder / Scully relationship is under new examination thanks to the arrival of Diana Fowley, played very skilfully by Mimi Rogers as an X-Files supporter you still can't help but dislike. This is far cleverer than, say, the way Phoebe was handled in Fire as Mulder's old love interest - the jealousy that Scully shows seems not only sexual but professional. Fowley appeals to Mulder that he needs a partner who is more supportive of his beliefs - and the irony is that she does this just at the time when Scully is, as Frohike puts it, taking a walk on the wild side and genuinely entertaining the concept of extreme possibilities. It almost feels like it's a desire to prove herself anew to Mulder that she waves Gibson's existence under the nose of the Attorney General - and, in showing off, puts the X-Files under dangerous scrutiny.

With its portentous title, The End suggests it's about big themes and climaxes. The surprise of it is that it's really composed of lots of intimate scenes of real emotion. In the end Gibson Praise is used dramatically *not* as the key to alien existence, but as a conduit to explain a love triangle between Scully, Mulder and Fowley. The Cigarette Smoking Man's finest moment is not setting alight the X-Files office, but telling Spender at last that he is his father. The very first thing that Scully needs to have from the Lone Gunmen is not an exam of Gibson's brain, but gossip about Mulder's ex-squeeze. This is what makes The End so very off centre, the deliberate placing of relationship drama over the action. We're about to dive headlong into a big budget feature film, and we're getting there via something a bit like soap opera. And it's where The End excels, because the dialogue is crisper and more honest than we're used to from Chris Carter, and the scenes are played more delicately. This is the true direction for Season Six, where the relationship between the heroes is given foreground attention at last. The End paves the way for a new beginning - and it has little to do with the black oil and the bees and the conspiracies of a government. We'll leave all that for the movie. (***1/2)

Millennium: Season 2

2.1, The Beginning and the End

Air Date: Sept. 19, 1997
Writers: Glen Morgan, James Wong
Director: Thomas J Wright

Summary   Members of the Millennium Group upgrade the security system on Frank's computer as the Polaroid Man ties up Catherine in a cellar. Peter tells Frank that the time has come for him to learn more of the Group's secrets - and that the Polaroid Man's fixation with Frank is related to the Group's interest in him. Frank deduces the Polaroid Man's location, leading to a fight that ends with Frank brutally stabbing the Polaroid Man to death. Catherine, horrified at having witnessed her husband's brutality, asks for a separation period. Frank accommodates her by moving out.

Critique   In their eagerness to reformat the series, Glen Morgan and James Wong rather clumsily stumble over themselves. There's much to be impressed by: the first act is suitably tense, as Frank frantically works against time to catch Catherine's abductor before he makes it onto the freeway. And the depiction of Frank Black as a man who finds himself suddenly powerless and out of control is brilliant, Lance Henriksen bringing such pain and self-doubt to the part that the key moments where he picks up a gun to turn vigilante, or in his rage stabs the Polaroid Man to death, have tremendous force. The point that his profiling is turned against himself is well made too, as the abductor chillingly narrates the sequence of events that lead Frank to his moral breakdown.

There's an interesting sequence in which Frank and Peter Watts talk about sacrifices made upon the way - and much is sacrificed here too. I've been crying out for consequence in this series, but now that Catherine reacts so strongly against Frank and packs his bag so he can move out, it's hard not to feel that this is all too much too suddenly. In spite of her statement to the contrary, Catherine comes off as ungrateful rather than confused. Morgan and Wong could have reached the same dramatic position, with Frank obliged to leave the safety of his family unit, much more sensitively - the moral turmoil that both the Blacks find themselves in is credible, but so abrupt that it belittles them and their relationship. Catherine is simply not a well enough established character to turn against the star of the show like this and retain the audience's sympathies - we can understand the *logic* of the dramatic beat here, but there's not been enough groundwork within the first season for us to find it emotionally satisfying.

And, in the same way, Morgan and Wong rush at their redefinition of the Millennium Group itself. On the one hand, Peter Watts is given more character development than ever before, and Terry O'Quinn gratefully seizes it. But all the little hints that the Group is something darker and has secret designs for Frank feel forced. That they've chosen this moment to upgrade him to a new level of security, and give him some Lone Gunmen-like techie nerds for comic relief, seems inappropriate. Frank can only look on bemusedly as one of them, Brian Roedecker, waffles on about Soylent Green because it's so wholly irrelevant to the drama at hand or the urgency of the situation. With Frank away from his yellow house, in the episodes to come there would have been credible reasons for the Millennium Group to change their relationship with him.

It's that overwritten quality to the episode which is typified by the Polaroid Man himself. Originally somebody enigmatic and softly spoken, hidden behind his sunglasses, a man whose emotionless connection to Henry Dion in Paper Dove was alien and unnerving, here the Polaroid Man is recast as Doug Hutchinson, who memorably played Tooms in The X-Files. And suddenly you can't shut him up - he waxes lyrical about comets and the apocalypse and theme park rides. Hutchinson gives a typically barnstorming performance, but it's actually *too* barnstorming - he's a caricature of evil with verbal diarrhoea. And he himself states that he's just a cipher to effect a change in Frank Black and the series. He exists only to be the victim of Frank's rage. Crucially, it makes that moment of rage seem contrived, too schematic. And seeing that it's the pivot for the new series, that's a big mistake. (**1/2)

2.2, Beware of Dog

Air Date: Sept. 26, 1997
Writers: Glen Morgan, James Wong
Director: Allen Coulter

Summary Peter encourages Frank to investigate when a pack of dogs butchers two retirees in the puny town of Bucksnort. Frank finds that the residents are terrified to go out at night, and discovers an obelisk depicting the ouroboros, the mark of the Millennium Group.

An old man talks with Frank about the importance of the Group, and stresses that the balance of good and evil is becoming destabilised as the millennium approaches. He also claims that one of the residents, Michael Beebe, has upset the area's balance by building his home in the wrong location. Frank asks Beebe to move out, but a dog pack surrounds them. The old man burns Beebe's house down, restoring some of the area's equilibrium.

Critique For the first half this trots along well enough as an X-Files episode, with Frank Black looking out of place in the wrong series investigating an isolated town ruled by killer dogs. It's somewhat dismaying that Millennium has so quickly lost its own identity and become a show about paranormal monsters, but it's well directed by Allen Coulter, and the second-act sequence where Frank needs all his wits to survive being locked out in the dark is especially good. But then the plot veers alarmingly away from being a simple little horror story. Frank meets a mysterious old man in the woods, and the story gets derailed into a discussion about the Millennium Group, ouroborouses and the coming apocalypse so vague and elliptical it makes the conspiracy arc of The X-Files look like a shining beacon of coherency. Lance Henriksen looks increasingly bemused by a script which requires him to stray into a completely new genre altogether; RG Armstrong as the old man relies a lot upon enigmatic smiles which only suggest he hasn't a clue what he's talking about either; Randy Stone tries very hard to give some colour to Michael Beebe, the out-of-town stranger under threat, but only manages to make him flambuoyantly camp.

There's a nice running gag about the town's eagerness to welcome Frank as the new sheriff, and there's enough wit in the dialogue to remind us that this is a Morgan and Wong script. But this episode is badly out of tune, and gives further indication that the series is mutating into something rather silly. The radical changes wrought upon Millennium in the previous episode now look like a masterpiece of subtlety: there's an unnerving sense of desperation about the show as it flounders about here, no longer knowing what its house style is any more. (*1/2)

2.3, Sense and Antisense

Air Date: Oct. 3, 1997
Writer: Chip Johannessen
Director: Thomas J Wright

Summary Frank attempts to find "Patient Zero", a ranting African-American who is thought to be carrying a pathogen native to the Congo. In their search, Frank and his allies conclude that Zero isn't infected with a virus, but that an unidentified agency has manipulated them into finding him. An examination of Zero's blood leads Frank and Peter to suspect that the government, under the guise of the Human Genome Project, is developing a means of controlling human behaviour. Frank and Peter locate Patient Zero - actually Dr William R. Kramer, who denies all recollection of being in a delusional state. A photograph suggests that Kramer was behind the massacre of thousands in Rowanda in 1994, leaving Frank to wonder if Kramer's own experiments turned him into Patient Zero.

Critique Lance Henriksen looks much more comfortable in this conspiracy thriller, but it's really just another example of Millennium dipping its toes into The X-Files format. And it has its moments - Clarence Williams III gives a great turn as a taxi driver whose life is turned around by the conspiracy, who opens his eyes to the idea that it's only in the ravings of the insane that any truth can be heard. But it's too thin and too obvious a story to have much impact. The premise is fine; Frank is used to hunt down someone he believes is a plague carrier, but is instead the subject of experiments on the genome to control human behaviour. But right from the teaser the men in black are so deeply unsympathetic, crashing their way through a hospital, that it's hardly a surprise that their professed aims to stay a contagion aren't as altruistic as they claim. There's not much plot here, just a succession of shifting lies - and since it's always clear who the liars are, there's little suspense or excitement to be had.

Right at the end there's a potentially terrific twist, in which we learn that Patient Zero isn't simply a homeless transient after all, but one of the men in charge of the project. But there's no resolution to be had from this, no confrontation - the most the character can do in response to Frank's questions is walk to his office and shut the door behind him. One can only afford an ending of such ambiguity if what's been given beforehand hasn't been as nebulous and drifting as this. (**)

2.4, Monster

Air Date: Oct. 17, 1997
Writers: Glen Morgan, James Wong
Director: Perry Lang

Summary Peter asks Frank to look into the case against Penny Plott, a daycare centre owner accused of child abuse. Frank allies himself with Lara Means - an associate of the Millennium Group - when a boy at the centre dies from an asthma attack. However, Frank is arrested for assaulting a minor when one of the daycare children - Danielle Barbakow - accuses him of attacking her. Worse, a dentist determines that Jordan may have acquired a cut lip through force, raising the spectre that Frank has been physically abusing his daughter. Frank is cleared of wrongdoing when it's revealed that Danielle injured herself, and that he never harmed Jordan.

Critique With the introduction of Lara Means, the second season finally finds its groove. Kirsten Cloke gives a terrific debut, even if she's not always helped by her dialogue. (Giving a character an annoying catchphrase - "Here's my thing..." - lends her no more depth than, say, Frank Black developing a sudden predilection

for the music of Bobby Darin.) But she's intelligent and resourceful and more obviously real than any of the Millennium Group that Frank has shared a case with in the first season - and specifically because she *wasn't* part of Season One, she can discuss with Frank her concerns about armageddon and mystical visions without it seeming contradictory or contrived.

Because this continues to be the problem with Catherine Black. The episode's biggest weakness is the way that she's so quickly become unrecognisable; she's suspicious here that Frank may have committed child abuse, and although pains are taken to state that a dentist is responsible for the investigation into Frank, it's telling that she's seen to offer very little resistance. More bizarre still is the scene where she meets Peter Watts, and refers to him as being like the other woman, complaining that Frank's involvement with the Millennium Group made her feel he'd been having an affair. Megan Gallagher gamely struggles to find the connection between Chris Carter's depiction of Catherine as the essential backbone to Frank's life, and the Morgan / Wong version which sees her as a bitter and selfish harpie. When the new executive producers are stuck with past season baggage, they cheat - when, as with Lara Means, they can start afresh, it's done with confidence.

This is a brave story well told. The theme of vigilantism has been raised in the series before, but never about such an emotive subject as child abuse, and never with Frank the target of the witch hunt. Lauren Diewold gives an unsettling performance as a five year old who'll resort to accusations of abuse to deflect attention away from her own crimes, showing far more range here than she's allowed as the somewhat inexpressive daughter of Scully. Morgan and Wong see the growing evil in the world - the idea that a small child is capable of murder - as the prelude to the apocalypse; it's something only hinted at in the first season, but it gives the standalone stories a refreshing pertinence. The willingness of a community to blame a day care teacher rather than a little girl is fully understandable - it's far safer to believe an adult is capable of evil than a child, and it makes their blinkered hatred somehow sympathetic. It gives Chris Owens, here playing a deputy, a moment of great courage when he chooses to stand out from the mob. It's an important scene too, one which gives this dark episode a chink of optimism.

Ultimately the episode loses interest in the case once Frank is accused of hitting a little girl, and it means that the ending is rather rushed (exactly how is Penny Plott vindicated, or, for that matter, Danielle's guilt proved?). But Lance Henriksen gives a terrific performance, his account of the birth of Jordan and the way she became the centre of his life extraordinary. And in Monster we at last are given some promise of a direction for this new, more fantastical Millennium - one that doesn't try to ape The X-Files, but find stories that only Millennium could tell. (****)

2.5, A Single Blade of Grass

Air Date: Oct. 24, 1997
Writers: Erin Maher, Kay Reindl
Director: Rodman Flender

Summary   Daniel Olivaw, a Native American, is found dead after a group of masked men force him to ingest rattlesnake venom. Frank finds evidence of rituals intended to commune with the spirit world, deducing that a lost Indian tribe blended into other tribes hundreds of years ago - but is now attempting to reunite as part of a prophesy. The tribe members take Frank prisoner, convinced that his visionary talent identifies him as "the one" who will relate a prophecy given by their ancestors. Frank is forcibly given rattlesnake venom, and experiences visions suggesting that the tribe will reunite and the buffalo shall return. The authorities rescue Frank and arrest the tribe members, while a quartet of buffalo escape from a rodeo and take to the streets.

Critique   This is a misstep, but at least it's Millennium's own misstep. It doesn't feel as if it's trying to be The X-Files, it doesn't lurch about trying to redefine the format of the show. Indeed, if anything, it's a sincere attempt to look at the apocalypse from the perspective of another culture, and to explore the implications of Frank's visions.

It must be said, it makes that attempt very badly. Ten Thirteen routinely come unstuck when they try to explore Native American rituals - and this one is so inaccurate a foray that even the archaeological expert Frank befriends says that it's all just cobbled together nonsense. And the suggestion that what was once presented as intuition and skill is now something so mystical it can be interpreted by the Iroquois would be more irritating if it reached its conclusions less vaguely: as it is, the meaning behind Frank's visions of coyotes and spirit roads is so obscure that it can be easily ignored. A Single Blade of Grass's worst fault is that it's just very tedious: there's virtually no action, there's tons of academic talk that, by dint of being a made-up synthesis of different tribes, doesn't actually mean anything, and it ends upon a prophecy of buffalo that is just banal. One reference in the first act to a circus coming to town is *not* effective foreshadowing.

But the episode does, at least, show a willingness to tackle the new themes of Millennium that Glen Morgan and James Wong have brought to the fore. It's not tiptoeing around the countdown to armageddon, it isn't just putting numbers on a screensaver and muttering about conspiracies. It's an ugly mess of a story, to be sure - a dull, lumpen thing without urgency or climax. But however badly it plods, at least it's plodding to the beat of its own drum. (*)

2.6, The Curse of Frank Black

Air Date: Oct. 31, 1997
Writers: Glen Morgan, James Wong
Director: Ralph Hemecker

Summary   On Halloween, Frank briefly spies the Gehenna Devil who killed Bletcher (1.18, Lamentation) watching him. He recalls a previous Halloween in which, at age five, he encountered a local resident named Mr Crocell. Having witnessed the carnage of World War II, Crocell was curious to know if the spirits of the dead might return to Earth. Frank replied that ghosts don't exist, and a depressed Crocell later killed himself.

In the present day, Frank visits his old house and becomes resentful enough to throw eggs at it. A series of recurring numbers draw his attention to Crocell's address, and a verse from the

Bible that reads: "Why should it be thought incredible by you that God raises the dead?"

Frank goes up to his attic and encounters Crocell's ghost - who advises him to abandon the Millennium Group, protect his wife and daughter and live out a normal life, giving up the fight to avert the apocalypse. In response, Frank returns to his old house and cleans the egg yolk away - in open defiance of the Gehenna Devil.

Critique A Single Blade of Grass makes reference to the contradictory symbol of the coyote, that it can be both trickster and creator. Glen Morgan and James Wong are the coyotes of Ten Thirteen. Their return to The X-Files on Season Four was by way of a series of experiments which seemed designed to pick holes within the format - and their inheritance of Millennium for its second season has been all about removing the show's foundations. When Frank Black throws eggs at his yellow house, that's the creative team turning Chris Carter's beacon of hope and light into an abandoned ghost house. But what this episode makes clear is that it's not merely been an act of sabotage. The Curse of Frank Black is the show taking breath, pausing to look at itself and where it is heading. It turns Frank Black into a myth, a boogeyman for the local children, the murder of Bob Bletcher and the visions Frank suffers reinterpreted as fodder for teenage horror stories. The destruction of the family itself is seen as the twist in a grisly tale of blood and curses, shorn of the real emotion of marital breakdown.

This is all very clever, and not a little amusing. But what's most impressive is how, coyote-like, Morgan and Wong use their tricksy reinterpretation of the past to create something striking and new. The slow pace of the tale sets up a ghostly encounter from Frank's childhood. And it's within that encounter that Frank is given a clear mission brief, and as a result, so is the series. Crocell speaks from Hell, telling Frank that the apocalypse is inevitable - and all Frank needs to protect the souls of those he loves is to sit back, like everybody else, and not lift a finger to resist it. And boogeyman Frank is transformed into a hero again - and not a hero with special powers of psychic visions, but a hero simply because he has the gall to make a stand. The final sequence sees Frank return to

the yellow house, and set to work sponging off the stains and the dirt. There's a future after all. And Frank is determined to be a *part* of that future. He won't give in to temptation, he won't stop.

It's simple, and it's brave, and it's curiously moving. With very little dialogue the episode instead relies upon catching the expressiveness of Lance Henriksen's face, showing all his despair and frustration and confusion. And the comparative lack of music from Mark Snow gives this a brooding atmosphere. The constant references to Acts 26:8 may be a little overdone, but the payoff is so well realised that it's forgivable - it's as if letting the possibility of the supernatural into the world gives Frank the chance to hear the message he needs, and for the show to evolve. And there's great support from Dean Winters as Crocell; the black and white flashback scene in which this suicidal veteran begs a little boy to tell him that the afterlife might exist, and offers him a cigarette as his "trick or treat", is weird and profound. (*****)

2.7, 19:19

Air Date: Nov. 7, 1997
Writers: Glen Morgan, James Wong
Director: Thomas J Wright

Summary A man named Matthew Prine experiences a vision of nuclear devastation, and kidnaps a group of schoolchildren. Frank realises that Prine meant to kidnap nineteen individuals - in accordance with Revelation 19:19 - but only nabbed seventeen children and the bus driver. Prine is caught while attempting to secure the last child, claiming that World War III is inevitable.

Frank deduces that Prine took the children in the belief that one of them will bring peace to the world. With Lara Means' help, Frank finds the children trapped in an aluminium quarry. A tornado kills Prine but also frees the children, leaving them miraculously unharmed. Frank is left to wonder if Jessica Cayce, the local sheriff's daughter, is the foretold peacemaker.

Critique This is a mostly successful blend of clear first season storytelling with second season themes. It's the first time this year that such a straightforward plot has been attempted, with

Frank working with local authorities to find a group of abducted children. There are some great stand-out moments in the first half - the terrific teaser, as a man finds within a barrage of overlapping news reports a prophecy of the coming armageddon, the chilling way that upon hearing the prayers of the frightened children he joins in with zealous fervour.

Strangely, it runs out of steam somewhat by the third act. Once Matthew Prine is in custody, the dramatic potential of having Frank profile a captive kidnapper is somewhat squandered, and it's up to Lara Means to save the day. That the finale relies upon driving Prine around and seeing when he scratches the back of his hand - something Lara identifies as a "tell" he makes whenever he feels anxious - is anticlimactic to say the least. Psychologically interesting it may be, but it makes for rather contrived drama. But the literal deus ex machina of the hurricane, felling the abductors and freeing the children, works rather well; the suggestion that there are higher forces at work is a logical consequence of the story's themes, and provides a suitable twist when it suggests that the kidnap actually saved the children's lives from natural tragedy. (***1/2)

2.8, The Hand of Saint Sebastian

Air Date: Nov. 14, 1997
Writers: Glen Morgan, James Wong
Director: Thomas J Wright

Summary Peter asks Frank to help solve the murder of a scientist named Dr Schlossburg even though the Millennium Group hasn't sanctioned the case. The pair of them travel to Germany and dodge both assassination attempts and another Group member - Cheryl Andrews - who's arrived to bring Peter to heel. Peter tells Frank that the Group's origins stretch back a thousand years, when the Knights Chroniclers were warned about the upcoming millennium. They believed that a holy relic - the hand of Saint Sebastian - could grant them the knowledge to overcome a great evil at that time. Peter believes that Schlossburg discovered the Chroniclers' burial ground and was examining a mummified corpse found there.

Frank deduces that Andrews set Peter up with the intent of humiliating the Group, but German authorities arrest Andrews and her gunmen. Peter speculates that tattoos on the corpse are secrets ready to be discovered, but Frank says that whatever knowledge the man had died with him.

Critique You can't but help feel this isn't any longer the show that Lance Henriksen signed up for. The overriding image I have of this is Frank Black slowly sinking into a peat bog, and the look of weary bemusement on Henriksen's face as he finds himself up to his neck. It sums the episode up entirely. This is the story in which it's finally revealed that the Millennium Group, in the first season inspired by real life concerns and based upon research with FBI profilers, is actually a religious cult dating back to the birth of Christianity. It has its own passwords and oaths, it's something of factions and initiates. And it's running about in Germany this week trying to find the severed hand of Saint Sebastian, which will grant the possessor knowledge of how to survive the millennium. Apparently.

So far, so very Indiana Jones. It's silly, but potentially quite exciting too. What it damages is the character of Frank Black. Season Three will show how Chris Carter drives as firm a wedge as possible between the character he created and a man who'll aimlessly accept this mumbo jumbo. This is Frank's first opportunity to walk away from the pretentious gobbledegook, and you can see the despair on Lance Henriksen's face that the character he has worked so hard to give real credibility doesn't do so; it cheapens the man that he not only listens to this nonsense patiently, but that he doesn't even think to question it. Later on, after he's denounced Cheryl Andrews, he tells us that she's failed a test. And the sad fact is that it's rather Frank who has failed, and it's the integrity of his character that's been sacrificed.

In itself there's nothing necessarily wrong with wanting to reformat the series, even to change its very genre in the way Morgan and Wong are doing. But they do so with such little depth. The characters are dreadful. Roedecker, at heart a Lone Gunman without the charm, makes his third caricatured appearance, a gangling overacted mass of catchphrases and film quotes. The German detective Heim has learned all about policing from American cop shows, so talks continually in phrases borrowed from Kojak. And the plotting is just as cartoon-like, composed of inelegant conspiracy twists, and multiple crosses and double-crosses. There's no moral centre to the programme any longer, no real meaning. It's sold out. What was intended to be a depiction of the darker days of the late twentieth century has become something wholly atonal, a joyless comic book. There's an atmosphere of such desperation to this series now, as cast and crew struggle to find out what its internal reality might possibly be worth. (*)

2.9, Jose Chung's Doomsday Defense

Air Date: Nov. 21, 1997
Writer / Director: Darin Morgan

Summary Frank looks into the mysterious electrocution of Joseph P Ratfinkovitch, a man who was excommunicated from the Selfosophy self-help movement for reading a heretical story by Jose Chung (X-Files 3.20, Jose Chung's From Outer Space). Chung, who is conducting research on arising belief systems about the millennium, comes under threat when Mr Smooth - another Selfosophist - mails him a doll stuck with knives. The deed emulates Chung's newest story, which ends when a psychopath kills the author.

A Nostradamus scholar is murdered, and Frank deduces that someone is targeting persons believed to be Nostradamus' three Anti-Christs. Chung correctly predicts that a movie theatre worker will die, and Frank concludes that Chung will be the next target.

Mr Smooth angrily confronts Chung at gunpoint, then flees with Frank in hot pursuit. Smooth falls to his death, even as the *real* Nostradamus killer slays Chung and is quickly apprehended. Afterward, Frank reads one of Chung's books, Doomsday Defense, in which he predicts that the new millennium will usher in "one thousand years of the same crap".

Critique On the face of it, this could look like the most blatant X-Files crossover of all, as a guest character from its third season takes a starring role here. But it's nothing of the sort; this is no more like an X-File than - well, it has to be said - than it's like an episode of Millennium. For one week the series has been shanghaied by the comic imagination of Darin Morgan. Whether it's the right moment for the programme to be so further destabilised is questionable; what was fascinating about Morgan's foray into The X-Files was that it gave a twist to a massively popular hit and forced it to look at itself differently. His critiques of Millennium feel a little more like he's kicking a puppy with a broken leg. On its own terms this is a brilliant episode; it's a dazzling script packed full of jokes, with ideas to spare, and directed with real zest by the author. Charles Nelson Reilly, whom I found somewhat mannered and cold in Jose Chung's From Outer Space, is extraordinarily good here, and if he wholly dominates the proceedings, at least Lance Henriksen offers amiable support.

At its heart, though, let's make no mistake about it - this is a gloves-off attack upon the solemn pretensions of the show. The sequence where Chung angrily defends his right to wallow in sarcastic humour, pricking at the so-called profundities of the world, is very telling. Doomsday will come, Darin Morgan tells us, not in a dramatic way, not with floods but with indifference. Everybody throughout history has always believed that they were living at a significant time of great change - but all we can be sure of is that the next millennium will bring us another thousand years of crap. Morgan derides the series' entire foundation as being self-worshipping tosh. And he saves his most damning indictment for the cults that grow up around such inward looking pretension; Selfosophy is clearly a Hollywood religion, a parody of Scientology - and one of the best jokes is seeing a washed-up actor played by David Duchovny go on to be a box office sensation on the back of his self-help mantras. It's clearly a parody too of the Millennium Group, and the new direction Morgan's brother has steered the programme towards with its obsessions about Masonic-like rites. Jose Chung sees the Millennium Group as being part of the same noxious package - and Peter Watts says they won't touch Selfsosophy with a bargepole. (They'll stare down evil incarnate, he argues, but evil incarnate doesn't sue.)

With its message of "don't be dark", the episode allows us to see fictional versions of Frank Black, a variant who waltzes cheerfully into crime scenes delivering snappy one-liners, chatting up the women and refusing to look at corpses because blood depresses him. It's wonderful to see Lance Henriksen having some fun with his alter ego, and showing off his gift for comedy. But this is a show which relentlessly is dark - that's its raison d'etre. And it's apt that although Jose Chung is able to talk away the threat posed by a Darin Morgan psycho, he's utterly unprepared for the appearance of a *real* Millennium serial killer. There's something rather profound (in spite of the reaction Morgan would have to that word!) about the author's larger than life comic creation being destroyed by the uncompromising and humourless world of Millennium. The episode leaves us no direction for the show to follow, no hope that it may yet find its feet. But for forty-five minutes it's a whirlwind of ingenuity and imagination and *fun*. (*****)

2.10, Midnight of the Century

Air Date: Dec. 19, 1997
Writers: Erin Maher, Kay Reindl

Summary At Jordan's Christmas pageant, Frank encounters a young man named Simon - who explains how the "fetches" of people who will die soon walk the churchyards on Christmas Eve. Meanwhile, Jordan draws the figure of an angel, claiming that her late grandmother helped her do it. Frank realises that Jordan's drawing is identical to one he drew in 1946 on the day his mother died.

Lara tells Frank that she too experiences visions related to various crimes, but that hers entail an angelic figure warning her of danger. Frank visits his estranged father Henry, who explains how Frank's mother correctly predicted the date of D-Day - and that Henry's brother Joe would die at Normandy. Linda Black finally predicted her own death, and claimed her ghost would move an angel figurine to show she was waiting for Henry. Frank's father gives the fig-urine as a gift to Jordan, who claims that her grandmother "wants her to have it". Afterward, Frank and Jordan see several fetches of people who will soon die - including Henry, who's at peace with the world.

Critique For all of this season's apocalyptic obsessions, the most interesting episodes have been those which have looked inward and given studies of its lead character. This is the perfect companion piece to The Curse of Frank Black; the first looking at the way that Frank has been mythologised, and by doing so being the most intimate portrait of Frank yet seen - and this story doing the reverse, starting as something introspective and then billowing out, and ending as an examination of the fractures that rare talents can cause to relationships. The series is so comfortable with what Frank stands for that it can use his dealing with the banal - putting up Christmas decorations, buying Danny Dinosaurs in a toy shop - as comic effect sequences. But there's a real pathos underling these scenes of normality - these moments of ordinary happiness are things he gets wrong, and he struggles through Christmas as a ritual he just can't properly get a grip on.

We see different members of the Millennium Group, all of whom are as bad at the festivities of the mundane as Frank is. Peter Watts holds joyless parties, and at them speculates gloomily upon death and destiny. Lara Means, forever tormented by visions of angels, sees them everywhere she goes hung from trees or embossed on greetings cards. Concern yourself with the bigger questions of life and meaning, and you cut yourself off from love and from family. That is the source of Catherine's anger here, as she sees Jordan show signs that she's got a special gift, and risks dooming herself to the same compromised life that her father has. Is it better to be mediocre and fit in happily with everybody else, rather than be unique and labour under the burden of a talent you never asked for? What would you wish on your child - that they stand out from the crowd, or get lost within it?

And, at the centre of this episode, is the stunted relationship between Frank and his father. Darren McGavin gives a heartbreaking performance as a man who became distanced from his wife because of her special gifts, and in the process was estranged from his son too. The long scene between McGavin and Henriksen is beautifully well done - it's hard, and it's awkward, and very honestly written and performed - and out of it comes something truly redemptive. Beneath all the social embarrassments of this story, where characters find it difficult to reach out for the people they care for and somehow can't stop hurting, there's a real passion which makes this episode truly special. And the sequence at the end, where at the midnight of the century Jordan and Frank can see as ghosts on the street all those who are due to die, all those who have been lost - and see the newly forgiven Henry Black amongst them, is exceptionally moving.

It's less obviously stylish than The Curse of Frank Black, but it's more emotive and fragile. And the direction by Dwight Little is terrific; the elisions between past and present are made with increasing subtlety, the moment where a lamplighter gives flame to a lantern in slow mo on what appears otherwise to be a modern day street of electric bulbs is beguiling and beautiful. (*****)

2.11, Goodbye Charlie

Air Date: Jan. 9, 1998
Writer: Richard Whitley
Director: Ken Fink

Summary Frank and Lara look into a series of apparent suicides which Frank believes are actually murders. A man named Steven Kiley has been befriending terminally ill patients, tying them up and forcing them to activate a "suicide machine". Frank and Lara determine that "Kiley" is actually Ellsworth Beedle, a nurse who believes that he's sending his victims to a plane of existence subscribed to by people in Tibet, West Africa and Mexico. Beedle is arrested but released on lack of evidence, and later meets with several of his coworkers at the home of Mabel Shiva, his assessor. Frank and Lara track Beedle down - but arrive to find his colleagues have committed suicide, and that Beedle has disappeared.

Critique Right from the start, even with the quotation on the black screen before the teaser,

there's the suggestion here that this will be a regular serial killer thriller story as typified by the first season, a refreshing return to basics. In fact what we get is rather better than that. Many of the stories have shown murders from the killer's perspective, as if the evils they were committing were acts of mercy or justice. Goodbye Charlie goes one further, teasing us from the opening with what appears to be a murder dressed up as assisted suicide - and then muddying our moral certainties about the sanctity of life as the drama goes on. Tucker Smallwood is quite magnificent as Dr Steven Kiley, the man who'll despatch his victims (?) / patients (??) with kind homilies and karaoke - it's a careful performance which plays the very ambiguity itself, smiling and sincere, but perhaps smiling just a little *too* widely, being just that little bit *too* sincere. Richard Whitley's script shows both the compassion of the man, and his anger at the unfairness of suffering - and, in the clever climax, you're utterly floored as you realise that all the suicide notes and mouth gags are entirely voluntary. The plot refuses to be predictable - Lara is certain that Kiley's body will be found amongst the happy dead, but the parting message, "I didn't make the choice", is very funny and very real.

If there's a problem here, it's that age-old problem when a writer puts in so much work to building up the complexity of their killer, it doesn't leave much room in the story for Frank. Here he is partnered with Lara Means, and both of them exchange their doubts about euthanasia. But Lara has all the best lines, Kristen Cloke at last balancing the tone of the drama with a keen sense of humour. Frank's best moment occurs when, visiting the Samaritans to snake out the killer, he confides to an assistant there about his visions of evil. It's gently absurd and rather telling that Frank can't hide behind a lie, and lets out his angst to a disinterested stranger so easily. (****)

2.12, Luminary

Air Date: Jan. 23, 1998
Writer: Chip Johannessen
Director: Thomas J Wright

Summary Catherine introduces Frank to Mr and Mrs Glaser, whose son Alex disappeared in the Alaskan wilderness. In violation of the

Millennium Group's wishes, Frank tries to find Alex and learns that he adopted the name "Alex Ventoux". Eventually, Frank finds Alex in the wilderness with a broken leg, and carries him to safety. Alex disappears after being hospitalised; Frank explains to Alex's parents that "Ventoux" is the name of the mountain that Petrarch scaled five hundred years ago - an act that ushered in the Renaissance, and which suggests that Alex's actions are similiarly heralding the coming of a new age.

Critique   It's a relief to see a story in which Frank Black is allowed to be a hero, plain and simple. Not the pawn of some Masonic cult. Not a man who is bruising from a broken marriage. Indeed, much of the pleasure derived from Chip Johannessen's script is the way it restores so much of the integrity of Season One's Frank, confronting head on the machinations of the Millennium Group and doing the right thing in spite of its insistence to the contrary: the scene in which he refuses to define himself as a "candidate", but rather as a father and as a husband, is terrific. And that he acts in concord with Catherine is refreshing too - for the first time this season, she's portrayed sympathetically; she may be estranged from Frank, but she only wants to help him, and is the only one who'll stand by him when he needs it.

The plot is simple - perhaps rather *too* simple - as Frank takes off to Alaska to look for a missing boy in the woods. As this is a story about helping a family, rather than battling against armageddon, the cold and dispassionate Millennium Group can't be bothered to intervene. The astrological symbolism is laid on a bit thick, but the point that there's a new covenant to be made is welcome. Just as Alex is finding a new identity, so Frank and Catherine are forging a new relationship too. There's a suggestion here of the second season finally stabilising somewhat, away from the hysterical grief and bitterness that so beleaguered its first half. There's a real beauty to the landscape of Alaska, something cleansing and pure, and it ties in well to this lovely little fable of determination and renewal. (****)

2.13, The Mikado

Air Date: Feb. 6, 1998
Writer: Michael R Perry
Director: Roderick J Pridy

Summary   A young woman is executed live on a website after the number of hits on the site equals a number that's scrawled on the wall behind her. The second time this occurs, the given number corresponds to an FBI case file pertaining to a serial killer named "Avatar", who's been quiet for twelve years. Avatar starts sending out coded messages, one of them containing the words "The Mikado".

Frank tracks Avatar to a disused theatre in San Francisco, one with a Mikado poster out front. Avatar shoots at Frank, leading to a harrowing chase in which Frank corners a hooded figure with a gun. Frank whips off the figure's hood, revealing that it's another of Avatar's kidnap victims, and realises he was nearly tricked into shooting her. Avatar escapes, and Frank suspects that he'll surface in another forum.

Critique   The fascination the episode has with the wonders of new technology makes this look rather dated. But that's hardly its fault - and the fascination is really very persuasive, so before long the twenty-first century viewer is as gripped by the possibilities of remote servers and video conferencing as Frank Black and Peter Watts. This is just as well, because it's a serial killer story played out in front of a computer screen, and even Frank finds his profiling stunted when bounced off nothing more mystical than plugs and wires. The story works too because the devices it plays with are old and true: the sick voyeurism with which people turn to a website to see a woman being murdered is matched only by the prurient curiosity we the viewers feel as we too watch the screens refresh to display another horrifying image. You don't want to look, but it's hard to resist - and that's the clever appeal of an episode like The Mikado, which turns us all into spectators, and turns death into performance art.

As in recent episodes, there's evidence that the second season is trying hard now to rid itself of its chaff - this is the last appearance of techie geek Brian Roedecker. Ironically, of course, this is also the first instance in which his character really works: placing the nerd at the heart of the story, and watching his complacent face become ever more appalled by what the technology he so worships can host, is one of the most satisfying parts of the drama. Michael R Perry's script goes to the trouble of taking the character and humanising him by degrees - so it feels rather a waste that he's put out to pasture as soon as he finds a level to play on.

The use of the Gilbert and Sullivan song is really nothing more than to give the episode a title and the killer a quirk - as if his obsession with murdering people on webcam wasn't quirky enough. And although the final act is exciting, it's not really very satisfying - this is the second murder story in three weeks, and once again the killer gets away with it. But the sequence in which Frank trails Avatar to his lair, only to appear on the killer's Internet site himself, is great - and the way in which it forces Peter Watts and Roedecker to become audience members like the rest of us as they watch the danger he's unwittingly put himself into is gives a real frisson. (***1/2)

2.14, The Pest House

Air Date: Feb. 27, 1998
Writers: Glen Morgan, James Wong
Director: Allen Coulter

Summary The murder of a young man displays the modus operandi of Woodcock, an inmate at a psychiatric ward nicknamed "The Pest House", but Frank and Peter find that Woodcock is too infirm to have done the deed. Other killings are patterned upon urban legends, as based upon the criminal preferences of inmates Bear and Purdue.

Frank learns that Edward, a nurse at the Pest House, has been "stealing the inmates' dreams" in an attempt to drain away their violent tendencies and cure them. Edward goes berserk, and a psychiatrist - Dr Stoller - observes him morphing into some of the inmates. Purdue stabs Edward to death, leaving Frank to theorise that Edward absorbed the inmates' sins to the point that it changed his shape.

Critique This is great fun, Millennium reinvented as a slice of good gory horror. On the face of it this is just a set of clichés from lots of different movies all flung together - and whilst that's true, that is also rather the point. Wes Craven's Scream franchise had done this, relying upon an audience's familiarity with the stereotypes to give a fresh perspective on a series of shock moments. The Pest House takes much the same attitude, as Frank meets the inmates of a psychopathic mental home, and watches as the very different types of murder they represent are acted out. But because it's less knowing with the comedy than Scream, this parody of every urban legend you can think of becomes scary in its own right. And there's a great idea at the heart of it: a man who's capable of draining the evil right out of people, but can't help being tainted by it himself. There's a strange pathos to the murderers - living forever in seclusion, only sustained and differentiated by their insane dreams of violence, then suddenly sucked dry and left with nothing that makes them who they are any longer. So as we watch the cliché in action we're also aware that these clichés are the only things that give these mental patients any validity.

The only problem, really, is that being a parody of any number of scare fests, the story requires Frank to play along as a stereotype too. Cue scenes in which he leaves the killer hiding in the back seat of a car to murder the nameless gas attendant, or any number of instances of walking down darkened corridors like a sacrificial victim. Morgan and Wong do Frank no favours by revealing their culprit far too early - by spoiling the mystery, it only makes Frank look a bit slow in not understanding the same twist that we already do. And Melinda McGraw is stuck giving a performance as Dr Stoller, who earnestly wants to give dignity to her patients, and yet within the confines of the clichés looks an idiot for obstructing Frank in his pursuit of a crazed killer. To act out the urban myth of the car chased by a man who's only trying to warn her of the maniac sitting behind her, Stoller has to think Frank is more dangerous than any of the criminally insane she's treating. However, Michael Massee is great as Purdue, giving real ambiguity to a man who's not only a repulsive serial killer but also someone tragically scared of losing his identity - his stabbing of Edward, as he says, seems like an act of sane courage. It's a credit to a story which on the surface seems like little more than an ironic joke, that in the last act it's able to question our attitude towards murder as well as it does here. (***1/2)

2.15, Owls

Air Date: March 6, 1998
Writers: Glen Morgan, James Wong
Director: Thomas J Wright

Summary   After a piece of petrified wood - thought to be part of the cross on which Christ was crucified - is unearthed in Syria, a man named Helmut Gunsche steals it from an airport in Jordan. This exacerbates a rift in the Millennium Group - one faction, "the Owls", believes that if a major theological event fails to occur before the millennium arrives, a thousand years of secularism will follow. However, Peter and his religiously motivated associates, "the Roosters", fear that the Owls took the crucifix shard to weaken them.

Peter recommends that Frank and Lara investigate the theft in the hopes of healing the Group's divisions. Lara suspects that the Owls didn't steal the artefact, as it would tear the Group apart. However, Frank vents his disgust with the secret society aspects of the Group - which he aided in the belief that it was a criminal investigative firm - and threatens to wash his hands of the organization.

Peter ostracizes Lara from the Group when he discovers that she's had contact with Mr Johnston, an Owl who infiltrated the Roosters and was murdered by Gunsche. Meanwhile, two men claiming to be Group members approach Frank, armed to kill him. [To be continued.]

Critique   The first two-part mythology episode of Millennium is rather like a two-part X-Files story: cluttered and confused and clumsy, but at moments providing some real thrills into the bargain. This is very much what The Hand of Saint Sebastian *should* have been like - obsessions about religious artefacts aside, this episode has the slower pace to explore the Millennium history properly and with the necessary gravitas

to make it credible, and to give characters the opportunity to react emotionally to it rather than just get buffeted along by the whims of plot. It helps hugely too that Owls comes on the heels of a good run of solid, straightforward stories, which have done much to put a bit of structure back into the series' framework. This time Frank Black, confronted with the demands of the Millennium Group, is able to express with due anger his frustration: how what appeared to be a criminal profiling unit is actually a secret cult with a god complex.

Though I'm not convinced that this is the right direction for Millennium, it at least feels like it *is* a direction, and not just a ragbag of random elements. The old man in the forest, the passwords, the dark halls of initiation, concern with mystical objects - they're all back, but this time they're contrasted with the reality of a recognisable family unit. Frank and Catherine Black are mutually supportive, and it's interesting how just that relationship gives a spine to the more fantastical elements around it. There are some good set pieces here - the opening teaser in Damascus is exciting, as is the murder of Johnston in his car - but the best bits of the episode are still the sequences involving *characters*. Frank's rejection of Peter Watts, Peter's rejection of Lara Means: this is where the real drama lies, and these betrayals are contrasted effectively by the growing reconciliation between the members of the Black family.

For this reason this all feels very satisfying and tight, even as you suspect it's really not about anything very much. The warring factions of the Millennium Group, bizarrely named the Owls and the Roosters (maybe that old man in the woods is something of an ornithologist?), feels as immediately contrived as the power struggles within the Syndicate in The X-Files: without any clear idea what the agenda of either faction can be, it all seems somewhat too abstract. The sequence where Peter Watts looks with awe upon a charred piece of wood ought to be terribly silly, but the story is told with such confidence that it has a certain grandeur to it. (***1/2)

2.16, Roosters

Air Date: March 13, 1998
Writers: Glen Morgan, James Wong
Director: Thomas J Wright

Summary   Frank's assailants escape after a shootout. Lara visits Frank along with the Old Man (2.2, Beware of Dog), who's actually the Millennium Group's leader / mentor. The Old Man explains that after World War II, Nazis were relocated to countries south of the equator as part of "Project: Odessa". One of them, Rudolph Axmann - the oldest surviving member of Hitler's inner circle - aided with the downfall of Communism but is now trying to destroy the Group.

Gunsche kills the Old Man, which causes the Group to set aside its differences. Peter apologies to Frank and Lara for how he treated them, and the Group undertakes a concerted effort to eliminate the Odessa members. Gunsche and Axmann are killed, and a senior member of the Group - identified only as "the Elder" - takes up the Old Man's post. Searching his predecessor's shack, the Elder finds the piece of the cross that Gunsche stole.

Critique   Dull and flabby, this takes the ideas of Owls and utterly fails to make anything dramatic out of them. When the biggest source of conflict in the episode is an argument between Frank and Catherine over how much exposition to give, you know you're in trouble - and there's a *mass* of exposition here, as all the characters perform a clumsy dance around each other telling stories about secularism and Nazis and icons but still never answering a straight question with a straight answer. Owls set up the tease that at last Morgan and Wong might knit something solid from all this makeshift mythology they're creating - and Roosters lets us down.

When Thomas J Wright is allowed a few moments of atmosphere, he seizes upon them. The gun battle in the teaser, the murder of the Old Man - whenever the script bursts into life with a spot of action, the director makes the most of it. (*1/2)

2.17, Siren

Air Date: March 20, 1998
Writers: Glen Morgan, James Wong
Director: Allen Coulter

Summary   Immigration officials discover a young woman locked in a freighter hold - put there after four of the crew died of exposure - but accounts differ on how she arrived aboard ship. Jordan tells Catherine to help the woman, claiming she will somehow save Frank's life. Frank identifies the stowaway as Tamara Shui Fa Lee, a Chinese national from Hong Kong, who was lost to sea in 1988. Lee is initially uncommunicative, then starts speaking in English.

Frank loses consciousness after seeing a vision of Lee, then finds himself in an alternate reality where he never joined the Millennium Group and the Gehenna Devil killed Jordan. Back in the real world, Frank recovers as three of the freighter crew, thinking Lee is evil, try to kill her. Frank saves Lee, who loses her ability to speak English and therefore cannot provide further insight about his life.

Critique   I'm a sucker for alternate reality stories, and the sequence where Frank is seduced into a life in which he's still living with Catherine and Jordan and never joined the Millennium Group is very touching - it's an indication of how much trauma Frank has been going through that his fondest wish is a beautifully effective scene of sharing a Chinese meal and teaching his daughter how to use chopsticks. But as fun as the fantasy is, it's not especially revelatory - and I think that sums up the episode as a whole. It all feels curiously undeveloped, as if the idea of a Chinese ghost tempting the unwitting into illusions of happiness in itself is a twist. It's a great *premise*, but a premise needs to be explored, not just bluntly served to us uncooked on a plate.

As it is, I can't help but feel a trick was missed with Siren. If there had been more time to examine Frank's alternate life - if there had been some ambiguity whether it had been true or not, had Frank himself started to believe it were true and his history with the Millennium Group the delusion - then this may have been a fascinating character study. But the very title of the story gives away the nature of the threat here, and by the time Frank encounters the mysterious siren who'll propel him into his own desires we've already passed the halfway mark of the running time. This *ought* to have been about Frank, and what it is he's seeking from life, and whether the sacrifices he's made for the Millennium Group are justified - and, indeed, the dying fall of the epilogue focuses entirely upon that. But it takes the story so long to reach that point, after two acts of meandering with a ho-hum story about illegal immigration, that the potential for something really interesting is squandered. What we're given instead is something light and obvious, a potboiler of a yarn. With a bit more care this could have been the bookend to a loose trilogy exploring Frank's attitudes towards his gift, the thematic sequel to The Curse of Frank Black and Midnight of the Century. This is a slight bit of hokum about an unexplainable phantom more really suited to The X-Files - it passes the time, but it's not really *about* anything. (***)

2.18, In Arcadia Ego

Air Date: April 3, 1998
Writer: Chip Johannessen
Director: Thomas J Wright

Summary   Two lovers, Juliet "Sonny" Palmer and Janette Viti, escape from a women's prison. Frank deduces that the women escaped because Janette is pregnant, having been raped by an African-American prison guard named Ernie Shiffer. However, Peter's investigation reveals that Janette has a placenta previa, and could bleed to death if she gives birth without proper medical care.

Frank locates the fugitives, who believe that Janette's baby is a "miracle child". During a stand-off with the authorities, Frank helps to deliver Janette's child - who has white skin, and thus can't be Shiffer's offspring. Janette bleeds to death, and a distraught Sonny goads the police into killing her. Afterward, a middle-aged couple adopts Janette's child.

Critique   It means well, and it's good to see a story attempted which tries to pull at the heart

strings a little. But an uncharacteristically crass script from Chip Johannessen kills this one dead in the water. It's so relentlessly unsubtle - every prison guard we meet is lecherous and corrupt, there's not a shred of human decency to any of them, and not a shred of reality as a result. And the two lesbian prisoners on the run, believing they're having to protect a virgin birth, are too naïve and cloyingly sweet for words. It only makes the police's response at the siege to shoot them on the spot look like hysterical overkill.

But hysterical overkill is what In Arcadia Ego is all about. It boasts the most ridiculous prison break ever - these guards must be the stupidest in the world, and it's a wonder that all the other inmates haven't escaped before now. The drama feels so heightened and artificial you suspect that this must be the point somehow. But it's not: every character point, every plot development, every dramatic beat, they're all played with the same melodramatic excess. Frank's revulsion at the use of guns on the chase for the convicts, the inhuman lack of conscience from the rapist guard who believes that impregnating a lesbian is a joke, the disgust shown by the mother in the waiting room when her child is smiled at by someone *gay*. There's a limit to how much cynicism a story can take before it buckles - even the man taken hostage by Sonny and Janette is revealed to have ulterior motives.

And by the end of the story the plotting becomes so predictable, and yet reaches for such tragic catharsis, that it's actually funny. Sonny's death in slow mo in a hail of bullets, letting herself die because she can't go on living without Janette, is especially overwrought - her last words being a declaration of love which has been repeated so often they've become nothing more than a trite catchphrase, her last act being to drop to the ground the flattened bullet which has represented her belief in their cause. "It should have ended better," Frank tells Peter - and he hasn't even *seen* the end yet, where he passes the baby into the foster care of the two most terrifyingly fundamentalist Christians he could find, whilst glimpsing the face of the Virgin Mary in the indentations of a bullet. Ouch. (*)

2.19, Anamnesis

Air Date: April 17, 1998
Writers: Erin Maher, Kay Reindl
Director: John Peter Kousakis

Summary Catherine provides counselling services in Rowan, Washington, when five high school girls claim to have seen a vision of the Virgin Mary. Lara takes an interest in the case, suspecting that one of the girls - Clare McKenna - is a genuine visionary. Moreover, the high school drama teacher, Ben Fisher, claims to be part of "The Family" - a breakaway faction of the Millennium Group dedicated to mentoring people with such talents.

Alex, the deluded son of a reverend, tries to shoot Clare after thinking that Jesus favours her over him. Catherine overpowers Alex, but not before Fisher dies shielding Clare. Afterward, Lara gives Catherine DNA evidence suggesting that Clare is a descendent of Christ and Mary Magdalene.

Critique This suffers in part from being broadcast a week after In Arcadia Ego. They both deal with a similar premise - about the incongruity of God choosing such unlikely apostles for his message. In the place of the lesbian convicts we're now given a high school brat called Clare whose life is magically transformed when she starts seeing visions of Mary Magdalene and talking in Gnostic texts. The most effective parts of the story are those where she bitterly states how in being marked out as "special", her life has been ruined forever - the sceptics may think she's just a wild child wanting attention, but who would want her every action to be under scrutiny from believers?

This is a little better than In Arcadia Ego, but, in truth, not by much. Whereas In Arcadia was simplistic to a fault, Anamnesis to the contrary is wilfully obscure. There are little moments of humanity, but the script is more concerned with the series' ever-increasing obsession with religious iconography. Here it's the shroud of Turin, and the suggestion that Clare is the direct descendent of Christ and Mary Magdalene. It's an indictment of where the series is that it would have made more of a dramatic twist had it transpired Clare's visions *weren't* for real. But the script makes Catherine Black's doubts seem ever more ridiculous and close minded until, by the end, even she is knocked into dumb acceptance by a set of miracles.

And it's such a pity, because effectively what Millennium is doing with these stories is cutting off the dramatic potential of debate. Even The X-Files, in which Scully the sceptic loses out almost every week to Mulder's outlandish theories, understands that within the to and fro of that debate lies the show's appeal. It's the suspense of characters finding out the truth, not the frustration of a character withholding the truth, and then revealing a truth which is ever more dependent on an academic understanding of early Christianity, that makes a story work. On The X-Files, then, a tale involving a girl who has come to believe she is some sort of messiah is *about* faith and its limits - on Millennium, it's just another example of biblical prophecy as we head ever further downwards towards the apocalypse.

The double shame of this approach here is that, with Lance Henriksen away, Megan Gallagher and Kristen Cloke are foregrounded for once. There's some hint of these two very different characters bonding together on the same case, but most of the potential for seeing how Catherine and Lara bounce off each other is wasted by a script that would rather revel in exposition. And by the end of the story it's all become so confused that we're invited to find significance within almost anything: the shifting weight of a black angel statue, or a passer-by carrying the same edition of the Bible as Catherine. There's no focus at all. The teaser is brilliant, an energetic sequence showing how an assassination is attempted in a school, all performed in dumb show to the music of Patti Smith. And naturally enough from that we're led to believe that the episode will be about this very emotive subject, about a gun culture society that will produce the killings at Columbine High (which took place almost exactly a year after this episode was transmitted). Instead it's lost in the now all-too-familiar mix of miracles and proselytising. (*1/2)

2.20, A Room With No View

Air Date: April 24, 1998
Writer: Ken Horton
Director: Thomas J Wright

Summary After an intruder kills a high school student and kidnaps one of his classmates, Landon Bryce, Frank's visions suggest that the Gehenna Devil / Lucy Butler is behind the incident. A long-haired man torments Bryce, but Butler comforts him - all part of an effort to break down Bryce's self-esteem and make him accept that he's mediocre.

Frank and Peter find that Teresa Roe, the school councillor, long ago succumbed to Butler's teachings and has since aided in her crimes. Roe identifies the farm where Butler is holding Bryce, enabling the authorities to rescue the teen and other captives. Butler and the long-haired man - clearly two aspects of the same being - disappear.

Critique Recent episodes have focused upon the ordinary singled out to be special. This is the flipside to that, as talented children are taken away, locked in rooms, and taught how to be mediocre to an unceasing background of elevator music. They're shown that the greatest ambition to have is to have no ambition at all, that love isn't a passionate colour but a dull blue. It's an extraordinary episode of claustrophobia and tension, and the violence enacted against these captives in the name of love is all the more terrifying because it's rarely physical - they're instead robbed of their very identities. When new prisoner Landon Bryce rejects his breakfast, and as a punishment is told he will never hear his name again, Ken Horton's script taps into a fear far subtler and more powerful than ones we are used to on this show. And as Landon's will to express himself fades away, as he gives in to the tender caresses of the woman enforcing on him his anonymity, so we're presented with as startling a depiction of evil as we've yet witnessed.

Lucy Butler is the perfect Season One villain to return to Millennium. Her very ambiguous nature, the way that she distorts reality around her so she can seem to represent evil itself, means that she's in the very small crossover space where the serial killer stories of Season One bounce off the fantasy stories of Season Two. Sarah-Jane Redmond is even better here than she was in Lamentation, her performance all the more unnerving because it's so *sincere*: as she seduces these poor teenagers, and sucks their very personalities out of them, she is at once persuasive and threatening. Many fans were bemused by Lucy Butler's presence in this episode, wanting something more tonally consistent with her back story as the murderer of Bob Bletcher - but what's brilliant about it is that it ties in perfectly with the many-headed elusive figure Bletcher saw as he died. Lucy is unknowable, unpredictable, and something so much more powerful than merely being a revenge killer looking for a sequel. Frank never finds Lucy in this story - she's the *concept* of evil itself, something sly and insidious that cannot be confronted or beaten.

It's the most frightening story of the second season, precisely because it doesn't attempt to tie into some mythology, and it never tries to present a rationale wider than itself. But it's also one of the most optimistic. The schoolteacher who has watched so many children of soul and intelligence fail to make the grades, gives an angry diatribe against the way the world codifies and belittles all those people it cannot put into neat categories. This is a story all about the strength of human resistance, about personality and spirit, and how Landon finally triumphs over all attempts to make him a lesser person than he knows he can be. For many, love will be blue - but what Frank's battles against Lucy Butler and her ilk stand for is something richer and unique and more colourful. If the ending feels abrupt, then that may well be deliberate - the ordeal is over, just suddenly, and the captives will have to find their own individual ways to deal with the consequences. Evil flits away into the dark, and the real test of character will be to pick up the pieces left behind. In a season that's been heavy on exposition and easy on sense, this compelling chamber drama of little struggles and little victories is frightening, beautiful, and profound. (*****)

2.21, Somehow, Satan Got Behind Me

Air Date: May 1, 1998
Writer / Director: Darin Morgan

Summary Four devils disguised as elderly men - Abum, Blurk, Greb and Toby - stop at a late-night coffee shop to swap stories. The quartet realise that each of them had run-ins with Frank, who could see their true forms. Blurk happened across Frank while tutoring a serial killer, Perry, whom he eventually betrayed to the authorities. Abum was using a meter maid to torment a mundane man named Brock, who committed suicide. Greb pushed a network censor to commit murder. And Toby saw Frank after becoming engaged to a stripper named Sally - who killed herself when Toby broke up with her. Frank observed that Toby must be terribly lonely, and the demons - concurring that they're all in that state - shuffle out of the coffee shop to their various lives.

Critique Darin Morgan's final script for Ten Thirteen is typically atypical. If it's also his weakest, then it's still bold and trying to find new ways to tease the format of the show.

This plays like one of those old British Amicus movies, a portmanteau of four different short stories. That they're told in a doughnut café one night by a collection of horned demons gives it an extra twist - that they've all in some form had encounters with a mysterious sombre looking man who can see them all for what they are binds the tales together. It all starts promisingly enough; the first story is a lovely parody of the serial killer plot, with our narrator urging a young man to beat the record slayings of a murderer he admires. There's much to enjoy here: the demons all groaning at the lack of imagination the killer shows as he gravitates towards prostitutes, the way both tempter and temptee chat about true crime books and murder memorabilia as if swapping top trump cards. Morgan is here attacking America's own fascination with the serial killer phenomenon, and by implication the Millennium series too - and it's done with much economy, not a little wit, and a clever ending.

The problem is that, of the four stories, it's the only one that feels especially relevant to the series it's spoofing. The second tale is a peculiarly anodyne affair about the banality of everyday life, and how mindless repetition of irritants can drive a man to suicide. (Even the fellow narrators find this one and its philosophy a little disappointing.) The third tale offers not so much a parody of The X-Files - although there's one sequence where we see the filming of an alien autopsy to Mark Snow's theme music - but a parody of a specific incident which happened to Darin Morgan whilst writing War of the Coprophages. It's a tale of a network censor who goes mad, after taking a script apart for its liberal use of the word "crap": Morgan's cockroach comedy for the third season was censored heavily because it had the audacity to refer liberally to the dung the monsters fed off. It's either an in-joke that's impossibly obscure, or a writer's petty revenge - either way, it's not especially revealing. And in both stories Frank Black makes only the most token of appearances; indeed, in tale two Frank's only involvement is to get a parking ticket. It's almost as if in Morgan's joie de vivre, he's forgotten what television show he's satirising. And it's a telling comment on the show itself, perhaps, that it's now so nebulous and vague, that its house style is so indistinct, that Morgan can't find much to get his teeth into.

The fourth tale is sweet and engaging, being the love story between a demon and an ageing stripper. It's Darin Morgan at his best - he returns to the pole dancing clubs and laundromats of earlier tales and shows how love can transform the seedy into something bright and dazzling. Frank has little to do in this story either, but his judgement upon the grieving demon whose nature has pushed his lover into suicide is sympathetic and wise: "You must be so lonely." It's rather fitting as a final statement from the writer who at his best tried to show us the sad comic face behind the cruelty, who created Clyde Bruckman and Jose Chung. As the penultimate story for Millennium, however (as it was certainly believed to be at the time), Somehow, Satan Got Behind Me feels a waste: self-indulgent and irrelevant at worst, and at best only sporadically funny (**)

2.22, The Fourth Horseman

Air Date: May 8, 1998
Writers: Glen Morgan, James Wong
Director: Dwight Little

Summary Frank and Peter are held in quarantine after examining the body of a man who died from a virus. Men in hazmat suits inject Frank and Peter with a vaccine, then release them. Meanwhile, the contagion slays a family while they're having dinner. Lara fails to return Frank's phone calls, and Frank later finds her formally being inducted, in secret, into the Millennium Group.

Frank tells Peter of his belief that the Group wants to control the world, urging him to probe its operations. In response, Peter predicts an earthquake and says that if it arrives when he claims, Frank must accept full membership in the Group without complaint. An odd-sounding Lara phones Frank to say that he should trust the Group - just as the foreseen earthquake strikes. [To be continued.]

Critique With Morgan and Wong now certain that the series would not be recommissioned for a third season, they decided in their final two-parter story to confront the Millennium Group directly. All the familiar arguments between Frank and Peter about the Group's purpose, or between the Blacks about Frank's loyalties, are rehearsed here once more - but this time with a new clarity, and with the added bonus that they actually have a *purpose*. For once a discussion will result in a changed opinion, or a doubt, or a new direction for the characters - rather than just lose itself in circles, the scenes feel properly like drama. There's a new conviction to the writing, and it's one that's seized upon by the actors. Megan Gallagher's rage against the Group that has destroyed her marriage looks at last not like self-absorbed whining but something earnest and true, and Terry O'Quinn has never been better than here, playing Peter Watts as a man desperately shutting his ears against Frank's pleas for reason, even as his own beliefs start to crumble. Lance Henriksen is clearly relieved: the relish with which he agrees with Megan Gallagher that they're dealing with an insidious cult is the relish of an actor who has regained a faith in his own character. It feels too that Morgan and Wong are clearing away the detritus of their failed vision for the series - all the secret cults, all the hunting for Christ's cross, frankly all the *pretension*, all are revealed to be the window dressing for a power conspiracy much more banal and much more believable. It's interesting how Millennium's mythology comes at this late stage to resemble The X-Files' own: an ever-complicated and obscure set of baggage hiding something that's much more human and sordid. If The X-Files were facing cancellation at this stage, rather than the prospect of a movie franchise, maybe it too could have reined itself in as effectively as Millennium does here. "There is no millennium!" insists Frank, at one electrifying moment. The apocalypse isn't six hundred days away, it's now, it's already here.

And the nature of that apocalypse is terrifying. The scene in which the perfect American family celebrate Mother's Day and bleed to death over their roast chickens is the single most shocking thing Millennium has ever attempted. Gruesome and sick and even slightly funny - the strains of the muzak still playing as the family drown in their own blood - it's one of the most disturbing things I've ever seen on network television. Broadcast straight after an ad break, and playing with the same sunny blandness of a commercial, it's all the more disconcerting. Serial killers now feel like the stuff of nostalgia compared to this; Frank is fighting a plague. The scale is massive. For once all the talk about the end of the world seems real. For a series which has traded upon the notion of armageddon so much that it has inevitably come to feel a little trite, that's a great achievement. (*****)

2.23, The Time is Now

Air Date: May 15, 1998
Writers: Glen Morgan, James Wong
Director: Thomas J Wright

Summary Frank receives news that his late father bequeathed him a cabin in the woods, even as Peter breaks into the Millennium

Group's computer systems. Peter learns that the Soviets genetically enhanced the virus after finding it in Africa, but that the contagion was released into the wild when the Soviet Union fell. He also believes that the Group developed a vaccine in 1986 to protect its own members.

Lara becomes increasingly unstable, stricken by potent visions of a day of reckoning. Peter intervenes when two members of the Group attempt to capture her, leading to a shootout. Frank arrives after the altercation, is unable to determine the outcome and gets Lara medical attention. Paramedics wheel a catatonic Lara away, but not before she gives Frank her portion of the Group's vaccine.

Frank takes Catherine and Jordan to his cabin as the virus spreads, and Catherine insists that Jordan be given the vaccine. Later that night, Catherine develops symptoms of the contagion and - while Frank sleeps - dies after wandering off into the woods.

Critique This contrasts well with The Fourth Horseman, as it's a far more intimate episode about the characters we know and their individual destinies. The power of it comes not, strangely, from the way that we're given a credible portrait of the world ending, but that it brings out so much personal bravery. Peter Watts, at last questioning his faith, gives his life (we suppose) as he tries to save Lara Means. Lara gives away her vaccination against the plague to Frank, sacrificing her own chance of survival; Catherine insists without hesitation that Jordan be saved, and walks out into the forest to die alone. The cumulative impact is tremendous. The Millennium Group state that they are not interested in the fate of the individual, only concerned with the bigger picture - and this episode demonstrates, by focusing upon the sufferings of those individuals, just how monstrous that makes them. It's horrifying and tragic, and actually uplifting - all these people we've seen behaving all season with so much selfishness, putting their own interests aside when the chips are down.

And, right at the centre of the episode, amidst all these quiet scenes of Frank and his family preparing for the end, is a nine-minute piece de resistance. To a Patti Smith song we see the world through Lara Means' madness. It's obviously self-indulgent, but it also succeeds in somehow personalising all the global catastrophe and chaos, and cleverly making the horror of armageddon the province of one woman being driven out of her mind. It's beautiful and disorientating and very, very brave. And it manages to justify the intimacy of the episode, and by lending it the scale that it would otherwise lack. It somehow sums up the boldness of the Morgan and Wong vision of Millennium. It's been a frustrating year, often lost within pretension and obscurity - but, at its best, it has tried to be the most radical thing on television. Was the second season a mistake? Quite probably. Was it any good? Only sometimes. But when it *was* good, it's because it had the courage to take the risks it takes here. The first season of Millennium is the most consistent, but it lacks the chutzpah shown here, to take the chance of either falling flat on its face or being a slice of genius. It's fitting that in the final episode Morgan and Wong are as questing as ever, wanting to put onto the screen a descent into insanity that is surely one of the most alienating things ever broadcast in series TV.

The final scene is perfect too. Broken up by static, hearing snatches of panicked news reports, Frank Black stares dumbly at us. Jordan asks about her missing mother, but is distracted to laughter by the sight of her father's hair, which has inexplicably blanched overnight. And she cuddles into his arms happily. It's the best conclusion to the show imaginable. Morgan and Wong have met the series' cancellation head on, and used it to turn out a thrilling and unforgettable piece of television.

... hang on, what do you mean, Millennium has just been renewed for a third season after all? Bugger. (*****)

X The X-Files: Fight the Future

Release Date (US): June 19, 1988
Release Date (UK): August 21, 1998
Story: Chris Carter, Frank Spotnitz
Screenplay: Chris Carter
Director: Rob Bowman

Summary   In 35,000 BC, two Neanderthals investigate a cave in what will become North Texas. A savage alien kills one of the Neanderthals, but the other one stabs the alien to death. Black oil pours from the alien's wounds, and oil-worms infect the surviving Neanderthal. In the modern day, oil-worms infect a boy and four rescue workers at the same locale. Agents of the Cigarette Smoking Man round up the quintet and take them away for study.

Meanwhile, Mulder and Scully look into a bomb threat directed at the Federal Building in Dallas. An explosive destroys a building across the street, and although the agents manage to evacuate the structure beforehand, an FBI review board faults their actions and moves to have them reassigned.

Mulder is approached by an associate of his father, Dr Alvin Kurtzweil, who wishes to aid his work. Kurtzweil tells Mulder that the building in Dallas contained a quarantine lab operated by the Federal Emergency Management Agency (FEMA), and that the lab that was destroyed as part of a cover-up. The explosion was arranged so that the oil-infected boy and three of the rescue workers from Texas would be found in the rubble and officially listed as killed in the blast, even though they were dead beforehand. Scully examines the corpses, and finds them undergoing cellular breakdown.

The Syndicate gathers in London, alarmed because the remaining rescue worker's body - which they kept for further observation - is being "digested" as an alien gestates inside him. Whereas the Syndicate believed that their alien allies sought to control mankind with the virus as part of a colonization scheme, in reality the virus will transform humanity into aliens. The Well-Manicured Man quarrels with his colleagues, who advocate further contrition towards the aliens to buy more time.

On Kurtzweil's advice, Mulder and Scully investigate FEMA operations in North Texas and discover a remote corn crop along with two large domes containing bees. Kurtzweil insists that the corn pollen has been genetically engineered to carry the alien virus. When the time is right, the bees will spread the virus and cause a widespread epidemic, allowing the White House to suspend Constitutional government as per FEMA's authority in time of a catastrophe.

Scully falls comatose when a bee from the Texas domes, having hidden itself in her clothing, stings her and infects her with the virus. Posing as ambulance workers, the Cigarette Smoking Man's agents spirit Scully away. The Well-Manicured Man carries out the Syndicate's instructions and has Kurtzweil killed, but disobeys further instructions to eliminate Mulder. Instead, the Well-Manicured Man tells Mulder of the alarming discovery that the alien virus - which arrived on Earth millions of years ago and has been lying dormant underground since the last Ice Age - will transform mankind into aliens. The Well-Manicured Man provides Mulder with the coordinates of Scully's location and a weak vaccine of the alien virus, hoping that the introduction of the vaccine into the aliens' lair will disrupt their plans. Mulder departs as the Well-Manicured Man gets back into his car... which explodes, killing him.

Mulder arrives at the stated coordinates in Wilkes Land, Antarctica, and finds a remote outpost manned by agents of the Cigarette Smoking Man. Mulder enters an alien spaceship via an underground passage, finding numerous people in liquid-filled cells. He finds Scully in one such cell and gives her the vaccine, which via Scully's cell contaminates the spaceship's entire system. The Cigarette Smoking Man and his men withdraw as the vaccine makes their equipment go haywire; Mulder and Scully escape just as the spaceship emerges from the ice and departs.

Afterward, the Syndicate destroys most of the evidence pertaining to this case. Scully gives the FBI review board the only tangible piece of evidence remaining - the virus-carrying bee that stung her - and regains some credibility with her superiors, allowing her to recommend that such matters must be investigated. The Syndicate starts up its corn and bee-growing operation anew in Tunisia, even as the FBI reopens the X-Files.

Critique The original intention seems to have been that the TV series would have ended at Season Five, leading into a movie franchise. You can imagine how much this would have changed both projects. Season Five would have had the job of providing a clear and satisfying conclusion to all the complications of the mytharc, allowing a feature film to offer perhaps a story focusing upon an actual alien invasion. There's a sequence where Mulder pisses on a poster for Independence Day - it's quite funny and not a little arrogant, but it's utterly irrelevant too, because it's within a movie which doesn't even try to compete with the spectacle offered by that blockbuster. In a way a movie on that scale would have been unrepresentative of the show, would have turned the series of ambiguity and conspiracy into a popcorn event. But what we're given instead feels so achingly unambitious, so utterly familiar, that any change would surely have been a good thing.

Effectively, Fox's desire to keep The X-Files running on television derails what the movie might have been. And that, in its turn, derails the fifth season. The first four years of the show may well be wildly inconsistent, but they at least feel *purposefully* inconsistent: if you feel that Chris Carter and his team are making it up as they go along, they are still making it up with confident strides. Season Five has many charms, but it essentially has to run on the spot for twenty weeks, it can't afford the creativity to spiral off into areas unknown for fear of contradicting a movie filmed beforehand but released afterwards. For the first time, The X-Files stutters. It's lost forward momentum. And once it's done so, it never really gets that momentum back - the series will run for a good few years yet, but without that sense of mission. It's not necessarily a terrible thing either; playing with a mixture of styles, allowing comedy and experimentation to come to the fore, frees The X-Files from much of its pretension and produces many episodes of great imagination. But it inevitably

changes the idea that the show is actually *about* anything cogent or, indeed, coherent. The X-Files movie represents the series at its peak, when it was part of the zeitgeist. It's a big mountain in the middle of all the TV episodes, but at the summit of this mountain there's actually very little to find.

To have derailed an entire season, the movie had to do something special to justify it. And it doesn't. It plays for the first hour in particular like an old-style mythology episode - something which could have been set in Season Two, say, when the characters were a bit more idealistic, and the mytharc a lot simpler. But for all its movie aspirations, the pace is much slower than the majority of what we've seen on TV. It takes Mulder and Scully the length of an entire episode even to get to Texas, where the action of the movie has started. It all looks beautiful, but the direction is ponderous, self-indulgent. There's precious little to show a movie audience why Mulder and Scully have become so iconic; they run around a lot, but show no investigative prowess at all. The whole adventure is only solved in *one scene*, where Mulder is *given* a cure and coordinates by a nameless man in a car. It's terribly lazy, and does nothing to dignify our hero at all - the only great skill he shows in the climax of the movie is his ability to rent a snow plough.

Watching the movie straight after Season Five, it's evident too that the characterisation is all over the place. This is the consequence of trying to be too clever, of thinking a writer can slot future *events* into a shooting schedule, but not people. The Cigarette Smoking Man is right back to how he was played two years before the movie was released, with none of the new direction the attempt on his life gave him. Mulder is the alien believer, almost scared to use the word "extraterrestrial" in front of old stick-in-the-mud Scully, who has nonetheless spent Season Five believing in such things more readily than her partner. Other characters (Skinner, the Lone Gunmen) appear only as a nod to the fanbase, adding nothing. For the Well-Manicured Man, his end has come. A bizarre and clumsy scene in which he reacts to his grandson breaking a bone seems to, at least in part, motivate him to betray the consortium he's been leading since Season Three. And look, that's Martin Landau and there's Blythe Danner, utterly wasted in thin guest parts. Armin Mueller-Stahl, a wonderful actor and a great casting coup, is given so little to do in his big baddie cameo as Strughold - one of the Syndicate members - that he barely bothers to articulate properly.

It's a curious, misshapen beast, this movie. A confusing mesh of black oil and bees, it never bothers to explain what's at stake, or what can be done to resolve it. The Antarctic section is visually stunning, but it's as if Mulder has wandered into the headquarters of a James Bond villain, and yet without encountering *any* opposition - and with only one injection of vaccine - foils his enemies' nebulous plans. For a story which spans the globe and thirty-five thousand years, there's no scale to the plot whatsoever. And when, in the final moments, Strughold drops to the ground the letter informing him that the X-Files have been reopened, I defy any floating viewer to work out why that should be such a big deal.

It's not without its moments. The way that our heroes mistake the sound of bees for engines. The wit of the first Mulder and Scully kiss being interrupted by a bee sting, and that Scully is so much the doctor that she can diagnose herself as she keels over. The sequence where Mulder sums up his entire character to Glenne Headley's disbelieving barmaid is very funny. But they're few and far between in a movie which is only too aware of its importance, but forgets to do very much to earn it. It's a bad film. Both as a continuation of a TV series, and as a movie in its own right, it fails to deliver.

And don't even get me started on Scully's amazing bee, which travels in her collar all the way from Dallas to Washington, through a frantic chase in a cornfield and an FBI enquiry, before bothering to pop out its stinger and say hello. It demonstrates a lot more tenacity during the movie than I was able to summon. (*1/2)

The X-Files: Season 6

6.1, The Beginning

Air Date: Nov. 8, 1998
Writer: Chris Carter
Director: Kim Manners

Summary A review board threatens to reassign Mulder and Scully unless they can produce solid evidence that extraterrestrials exist. Skinner informs Mulder of a strange death in Arizona in which the corpse has a hollow chest cavity. Mulder conjectures that an alien virus gestated a creature within the man, which then tore its way to freedom.

The Cigarette Smoking Man tries to contain the situation, hoping that the uber-psychic Gibson Praise can track the alien-creature. Gibson escapes and finds Mulder and Scully, but an agent of the Syndicate ("the Black-Haired Man") re-captures the boy. Events converge at a power plant, where the alien kills the Black-Haired Man, but both it and Gibson are locked in the reactor room. FBI agents cordon off the area; Gibson watches as the creature seems to bathe in the reactor's power.

The Cigarette Smoking Man meets with Agent Spender, his newfound ally. Agent Fowley recovers from her wound, and files an edited report to protect Mulder's investigation. The review board terminates Mulder and Scully's assignment to the X-Files, and makes Assistant Director Kersh their new boss. Scully keeps one of Gibson's medical exams, which suggests that all humans contain a "genetic remnant" that's active in Gibson. But if so, then all of humanity has some genetic alien inheritance.

Critique The movie has made the mythology stories feel redundant. Even if you liked the thing, what it did was bring the whole confusing arc to a big-budget crescendo - it was playing on being the *ultimate* explanation of that storyline. To follow that straight away with *another* mythology story would be wholly anticlimactic, but that's the format for the series now. Every season has to open with something about aliens and government conspiracies, even though this time around there's not even the pretence of an urgent need for one. There's not even a big cliffhanger to solve, but the traditional X-File season opener rolls around anyway. So what we get in The Beginning is really anything but a beginning. Instead it feels like a lukewarm serving of leftovers - a small and low-budget sequel to an event movie that makes the cardinal error not only of summarising that movie in such a way that it feels like an embarrassing load of old tosh, but leaves Mulder and Scully in their age-old roles of believer and sceptic again. Both characters are *supremely* irritating here - Mulder is all arrogant bluster, jeopardizing all he believes in with his incessant recklessness, and Scully seems to have cast aside seasons of development.

And there's a reason for that. This is Chris Carter's reformat of the series, in anticipation of the new audience he's expecting to switch on the television having enjoyed the movie. It's a mistake, of course, that he's assuming there'll be an influx of new viewers at this point, rather than the gradual exodus you'd expect at a sixth year. But it explains the simplification of what we see here, Mulder and Scully reduced to easy-to-understand stereotypes. It's one of the reasons the audience will lose faith with the series from this point on - however spectacular it may have been on its own terms, the follow-up to the movie reveals it as the Emperor's New Clothes. Nothing has been resolved, nothing deepened. In fact, if anything, with Mulder and Scully reduced to their Season One characters, the reverse has happened. Whereas the show before used the idea of our heroes chasing aliens as a theoretical concept, with lashings of ambiguity to give it some suspense, here it's become bald reality. And now that an alien has been revealed, we see it's just a collection of clichés - it bursts out of its victims' chests, it hides in the dark, it rips people apart. In trying to consolidate and streamline the show for these potential new viewers, Chris Carter has made it look like everything else.

The Gibson Praise sequences are more interesting, and it's striking that Praise clearly sees Scully's concern for him as being no less selfish than that of the Syndicate, who have (rather shockingly) opened up his head to poke at his brain. The suggestion that he, and by extension the whole human race, may be extraterrestrial is fascinating, and gives the laboured mythology something new to tinker with. But the plotting here is ungainly - Scully's one function this episode is to keep an eye on a sick kid, and he's abducted right under her nose.

The best parts of the episode are those that suggest long-term changes for the show's future. It's clever, having reopened The X-Files at the end of the movie, that the series doesn't just plonk Mulder and Scully back into their original jobs as if nothing has happened. They're given little to work with here, but agents Spender and Fowley are potentially very interesting obstacles for our heroes, and the idea that the agents *running* the X-Files could be working against the very characters who symbolise it is fresh. Spender has a legitimate reason for so disliking Mulder, since he feels his mother has been lost because of Mulder's quest - it's a mistake, though, never to mention this during the episode itself, because a potentially sympathetic character comes across as something of an arse. Fowley is the more complex of the two (and the more subtly performed), and suggests she can play the ambiguity of a new Deep Throat - the twist this time being that she's feeding Mulder information from *within* the X-Files.

But taken as a week of series television, and the first of an exciting new season, this episode scuppers its potential. It opens wittily enough on bright sunshine, as if to symbolise a change caused by the move to Los Angeles, and then offers the viewer no substance. It's a better season opener than Redux, and has none of its pretension. But it's still very poor. And I've no idea what that Homer Simpson joke was trying to achieve. (*)

6.2, Drive

Air Date: Nov. 15, 1998
Writer: Vince Gilligan
Director: Rob Bowman

Summary   In Nevada, the police apprehend Patrick Crump and his wife Vicky for driving at an extreme speed, whereupon Vicky thrashes her head until it explodes. Mulder and Scully disobey orders to look into the case, but Crump escapes, captures Mulder and forces him to drive due west - the only means of alleviating the tremendous pain in Crump's head.

Scully finds that the Department of Defense has an antenna array that runs through the edge of Crump's property, and speculates that this particular type of military communications might have matched the resonant frequency of the human skull. Crump has rising pressure in the labyrinth of his inner ear, but driving west along lines of electromagnetic force alleviates the condition. Mulder arranges for Scully to meet him in California, intending for her to insert a large-bore needle into Crump's inner ear and thereby save his life. Crump fails to last that long, and is dead on arrival.

Critique   It'd be tempting to suggest that Vince Gilligan has taken to heart a lesson from the staid season opener - if you don't keep moving, you're dead. Right from the start, with a trailer that teases the audience they're watching a live news report, you get the feeling that the show is experimenting with style and structure once more. In a series which will get increasingly playful this year, Drive seems a comparatively restrained affair, but that's partly because Gilligan skilfully hides the risks he's taking with the format. For all of its emphasis upon car chases, Drive plays out largely as a dialogue, a hostage drama that riffs off Duane Barry and Gilligan's own Folie a Deux, by pairing Mulder with a victim driven to desperate measures. But the twist here is that the victim is not simply an expository tool, to convince a readily open-minded Mulder about aliens or giant insects, but a man as confused about what is happening as the audience is. He's the mystery itself, not just someone to explain it.

And the effect this has is twofold. On the one side it turns the episode into a genuine character piece, as Mulder and Crump develop from their antipathy a growing bond. The drama is not only in *why* Crump is suffering, but how through his paranoia and pain he will come to rely on a man he distrusts as an authoritarian Jew. Bryan Cranston cleverly portrays a character who at first invites our disgust, but wins our sympathy precisely because he never appears to seek it; the way in which he calls for the respect of being called "Mr Crump" gives him a peculiar dignity, and the way in which he learns to extend that same respect to Mulder is oddly touching. (It's easy to see why Gilligan later cast Cranston as a similar sort of anti-hero in Breaking Bad.) And the final scene, in which Crump bravely accepts the prospect of being turned deaf by Scully's operation if it will save his life, is beautiful and life-affirming. It's a testament to how well these characters play off each other that a man we initially write off as a violent racist comes to represent by the story's end the indomitability of the human spirit.

And the second effect is that it ensures that Scully isn't relegated to playing the bystander. Instead she's the one who has to puzzle out the mystery, come up with the wild theories, and do a bit of honest to God *investigation*. It's been such a long time since Scully has been treated as a brilliant FBI agent rather than as a victim, a second string, or an emotional whirlwind. It gives Gillian Anderson a chance to elicit one of her strongest performances in ages, the scene at the end where she stands her ground against Kersh and refuses to apologise for breaking protocol an especial delight.

In essence this is Speed, given a terrific X-Files spin - the bomb isn't on the bus, it's in the ear. The audacity of that is almost witty enough in itself to carry the episode along. It only falters at the final explanation, which just about makes sense but is really too rushed to satisfy. And having driven Crump as far west as he can go, Gilligan can only kill the man in the final reel. Duchovny plays the failure brilliantly, but the story hasn't honestly earned this gravitas - if you're going to set up a plot where the hero needs to win through against overwhelming odds, it feels a lazy cheat if you don't show him doing so. Speed would not be a more meaningful film if Keanu Reeves had died in a bus explosion, and Drive isn't any cleverer because Vince Gilligan couldn't think of a better ending. It's the quality of the dialogue that allows us to be affected by Crump as much as we are, so that this lack of resolution isn't the damp squib it ought to be. (****)

6.3, Triangle

Air Date: Nov. 22, 1998
Writer / Director: Chris Carter

Summary   Mulder ventures out to sea when satellite photos show the *Queen Anne*, a British luxury liner that disappeared sixty years ago in the Bermuda Triangle, sailing along peacefully. A storm wrecks Mulder's motorboat, and he boards the *Queen Anne* just as Nazis arrive looking for "Thor's Hammer" - something they believe is an atomic bomb but is actually an atomic scientist. Some of the persons on the ship look like Mulder's associates: an OSS agent travelling with "Thor's Hammer" resembles Scully, while Skinner, the Cigarette Smoking Man and Agent Spender are present as German officers.

Back on the mainland, the Lone Gunmen inform Scully of Mulder's disappearance. Scully tries to obtain clearance to find Mulder using Navy swath imaging, and sees Assistant Director Kersh and Agent Spender reporting to the Cigarette Smoking Man. Skinner slips Scully the imaging information, enabling her and the Lone Gunmen to find a cobweb-filled *Queen Anne*, exploring it in tandem to events with the 1939 passengers.

On Mulder's version of the *Queen Anne*, a fight breaks out between the Germans and British servicemen. Mulder tells the OSS-Scully that she must save history by preventing the ship from reaching Germany, and gives her one last kiss before diving overboard, in the hopes of returning to his own time. Scully and the Gunmen leave their *Queen Anne* and find Mulder, convinced that he dreamed his experiences there.

Critique   It's a triumph of style over substance, yes, but you can't argue with a triumph, and the style is *so* good it puts a big grin on your face for an hour. A week after it's taken on Speed, The X-Files turns to The Wizard of Oz for inspiration - and in doing so throws off any pretension of being anything other than delightfully silly. There's something very satisfying about seeing Mulder, now an icon in his own right, after years of battling aliens and monsters, finally square up to the Nazis. And even better that these aren't real Nazis, the ones that inspired the concentration camp metaphors of the third season, but the ones from Indiana Jones, comic-book nasties played here by all our favourite guest stars. Mulder's wisecracks about the German army needing to dress up warm for Russia are great fun, but only because these are never seen to be anything but cartoon characters, the dream-Nazis of popular culture. There's a Cigarette Smoking Man with pronunciation that's so bad that it ends up being part of the fun, Spender allowed to cut loose and rant like a proper villain rather than a sulky boy hiding in the basement, and Skinner charmingly parodying the ambiguity he's been playing all these years and turning out to be an American-loving ally who tells our heroes to get their "asses out of here". If there's a fault to all this cross-casting it's only that perhaps it's too soon into the life of some of these characters to have the impact it deserves - James Pickens Jr sporting a Jamaican accent isn't as funny as it should be, because we haven't seen enough of Kersh in context yet.

And at last Chris Carter is allowed to showcase his directorial skills properly. Post-Modern Prometheus was an undisciplined mess in which he threw in everything but the kitchen sink. Triangle, in contrast, only works because it requires strategic control of the action to a level we've never seen in the series before: each act filmed in one take, steadicam operator following the actors up and down corridors. There's a precision to all of this which is literally jaw-dropping. The moment in which the two Scullys cross each other's paths on split screen is punch-the-air wonderful, but it's only a stand-out sequence from a truly magnificent piece of clockwork. And yet, for all the atmosphere aboard the *Queen Anne* in 1939, the best scene of all is the twelve-minute one, performed in real time, of Scully dashing around the FBI trying to find a way of reaching Mulder. It plays like farce, and it plays as action adventure - it's that perfect synthesis of comedy and thrills that only The X-Files at its best can aspire to... and it's yet *still* only about Scully going up and down in a lift and barging into offices.

Ultimately, of course, Triangle isn't *about* anything more profound than a demonstration of great skill, but that's one of its principal pleasures. It would only have taken a moment of

earnestness to pop the balloon. At the very end, as Mulder lies in his hospital bed, he tells Scully that he loves her. Scully rolls her eyes, says "oh brother", and leaves. It's great because it's heartfelt and true, and at the same time exquisitely silly. And it sums up this shining gem of an episode very well. (*******)

6.4, Dreamland

Air Date: Nov. 29, 1998
Writers: Vince Gilligan, John Shiban, Frank Spotnitz
Director: Kim Manners

Summary Mulder and Scully follow up on a tip-off and visit Area 51 in Nevada - the Holy Grail of UFO mythology. During a stand-off with Area 51 officials, an Air Force plane flies overhead - which somehow causes Mulder and Morris Fletcher, an Area 51 official, to switch bodies. Mulder capitalizes on the chance to infiltrate Area 51, while Fletcher - freed from the confines of his appalling suburban life and family - returns to Washington with Scully.

The Air Force plane crashes; one of the pilots is found fused into a rock, while the other - Captain Robert McDonough - swaps bodies with Mrs Lana Chee, a seventy-five-year-old Hopi woman. Area 51 officials theorise that the plane, equipped with an antigravity system, created a tear in the space-time continuum. Mulder attempts to steal the plane's flight recorder, but Morris - sensing that Mulder is causing trouble - phones Area 51 and rats "himself" out as a mole. Area 51 soldiers drag "Morris" away, while Scully wonders if the man's wild claims about being Mulder have some merit. [To be continued.]

Critique The most memorable ten minutes of Small Potatoes show Mulder from a new perspective, as the hapless Eddie Van Blundht steals his identity and lives out his life at the FBI. Dreamland takes the same comic premise, and stretches it out over an hour and a half. This is an amusing episode, certainly - there's a lot of pleasure to be had from seeing Mulder adapt to the domestic family from hell, failing to cope with a shrewish wife who wants sex and bad-tempered children who want piercings. Duchovny is brilliant at playing the fish out of water as he does here, a man who finds social interaction more alien than little green men. And as Fletcher, Michael McKean is a comic actor skilled enough to walk into the show and make *his* Mulder more than just a series of role reversal gags.

But role reversal gags are really all we get. The brilliance of Small Potatoes was what it showed us about Mulder; Eddie may not have been able to spell his job, but he was amiable and engaging enough to fit into Mulder's shoes and be a better person than the original. Morris Fletcher, on the other hand, sees his borrowed body as an excuse to flirt, smoke, and weasel. It's not subtle, nor is it meant to be - but it's not especially funny either in itself, because the responses are too predictable. Eddie desperately wants to fit in; Morris doesn't even try, and for all the raised eyebrows Gillian Anderson can muster, it's hardly credible that her Scully wouldn't be more suspicious of him. Especially considering there's a scene in which Mulder-as-Morris explains to her exactly what is going on, within the context of a series which uses shapeshifters once or twice every year, her rejection of the facts makes her look unreasonably stupid. It's the worst scene in the episode. Farce depends upon the idea that none of characters have the space or the time to explain all the misunderstandings that are going on.

But there's plenty of time here, because the pace is so very slow. It's an episode too convinced of its own hilarity, so repeats the same jokes too often. Morris behaves like an arse at work, and Mulder is tyrannised by his new wife. There's only so many times the same shtick can be shown without offering the viewer a new slant on it. The longer the gag is spun out, the less amusing it becomes. There's something very witty (and typically Vince Gilligan-like) about showing the amoral goons behind Area 51 as ordinary men with ordinary lives, and it's shocking to see such nobodies gun down a civilian and set fire to the evidence. But it's those subtler character moments which work best, like Mulder's search for the car keys that will get him out of his home, rather than the contrived set pieces, such as the dance to the mirror sequence riffed off the Marx Brothers.

It has enough funny moments not to be dismissed out of hand, and Duchovny and McKean are enjoying themselves so much, it seems churlish not to join in. But there's not enough meat to sustain a full episode, let alone a two-parter. The ten minutes of Small Potatoes had more to say, and said it better. (***)

6.5, Dreamland II

Air Date: Dec. 6, 1998
Writers: Vince Gilligan, John Shiban, Frank Spotnitz
Director: Michael Watkins

Summary Mulder avoids incarceration when Area 51 officials discover he took the wrong flight recorder, and conclude that "Morris" was running a scam on the FBI. Meanwhile, Scully forces "Mulder" at gunpoint to admit that he's really Morris. The effects of the space-time tear begin reversing themselves, and an Area 51 official - having deduced the Mulder / Morris body swap - enables Mulder and Morris to stand in the same spot where the initial transfer occurred. They return to their original bodies as time reverses itself and none of those involved can remember what happened.

Critique The best joke is the one that doesn't relate to the body swap conceit at all - it's very funny (and strangely touching) to see the reason the mole at Area 51 contacted the X-Files in the first place was not to give information, but to ask for it - "Agent Mulder, do aliens exist?" That the bureaucracy that holds the Men in Black in place is so strict that even *they* don't know what they're up to ties in nicely to a tale which shows the banality of government conspiracy. Even an amoral man like this one just wants to know what we all do deep down - does his life actually have any meaning?

But beyond that, frankly, we get very little we haven't seen in part one. Michael McKean gets the best moments: his mocking of the Lone Gunmen, telling them that all the truth they publish is just stuff he makes up on the toilet, is joyous. For the ending to work, however, Morris Fletcher is required to become a caring husband and a nice guy on the slimmest of pretexts, which undermines the whole caricature he portrayed in the first place. And as a story which literally "unhappens", with barely any build-up, it feels determinedly inconsequential. There's so little at stake in the episode proper that it frequently seems characters are just drifting from scene to scene - the reset button at the end only emphasises that.

It's a fun premise, and with greater consideration could probably have given the stars their chance to be comedians for a while. But at an hour and a half, it's in no way justified. If you see individual scenes out of context, Dreamland is fun and sprightly, but at a long yawning stretch it lacks structure and point. (**)

6.6, How the Ghosts Stole Christmas

Air Date: Dec. 13, 1998
Writer / Director: Chris Carter

Summary Mulder and Scully charmingly spend Christmas Eve looking into a condemned house in Maryland that's purportedly haunted. Mulder relates a tale from Christmas 1917, in which a heroic young man named Maurice and a beauty named Lyda - a pair of star-crossed lovers - killed themselves. Since then, three double murders have occurred in the house in the last eighty years, all on Christmas Eve.

The agents are separately approached by an older couple who claim to live in the house. The couple use a combination of psychology and illusions to trick each agent into believing that their partner will try to kill them - leading to Mulder and Scully, both injured by gunshots, stalking each other through the house. Each of them refuses to kill the other, whereupon their wounds miraculously vanish. Maurice and Lyda chuckle how they "almost" got Mulder and Scully to off themselves, and disappear in front of an open fireplace. Mulder and Scully leave the house, steady in the knowledge that they're not alone this Christmas season.

Critique Chris Carter is the hardest writer on the series to categorise. Watching the episodes back to back, it's relatively easy to discern the styles of Vince Gilligan or Darin Morgan, to pick out the recurring themes of Howard Gordon or John Shiban. But Carter is a true chameleon - it's difficult to believe the showrunner responsible

for the pretentious monologues of the mythology episodes could in Season Six not only write but direct episodes as playful and as clever as Triangle and Ghosts. It's remarkable that as The X-Files changes its tone, so too does its erstwhile head writer. I'm not entirely convinced that being such a chameleon gives Carter's writing much depth - I rather distrust someone who can change hats this easily. But whereas before I've found Carter's forays into experimental humour rather self-conscious and cynical, How the Ghosts Stole Christmas is a real delight, bursting with heart and life.

And this is a story, I hasten to add, that has as its climax Mulder and Scully crawling across the floor, leaving thick blood trails behind them, believing themselves dying from gunshot wounds, to the cheery strains of "Have Yourself a Merry Little Christmas". Essentially this is a macabre tale of ghosts psychoanalysing Mulder and Scully and their relationships towards each other - much as thousands of fans were doing on the Internet, all phantom-like and insubstantial. Mulder is dismissed as a narcissist, a man whose self-obsessions are "paramasturbatory". Scully is lonely and frustrated and only follows Mulder because she needs to prove him wrong. The central joke is that they're caught in a snare by two spirits who prey upon lovers and urge them to re-enact their suicidal passion - and Mulder and Scully really aren't up to the job, neither of them having the emotional maturity to even *speculate* about love.

It's something which could seem very shallow and self-reflexive, but it's an absolute charmer, because (for once) Carter's writing and direction are perfectly in sync, understanding the parody but never giving too much emphasis to it. And the four-hander drama is perfectly acted, not only by Duchovny and Anderson who gauge the laughs and the scares to a tee, but by star turns from Lily Tomlin and Ed Asner. They play the comedy as well as you'd hope and expect - I love Asner's yearning for old-fashioned hauntings without all the "psychology crap", and the flirtatious way that Tomlin shows Duchovny the gunshot wound her ghostly character endured in life. But it's the pathos which makes these characters sing - following on from the very ordinary men in black in Dreamland, we have here ghosts with pressing concerns about whether they'll get taken off the tourist literature, spooks who age and get disillusioned with the loves they've died for.

The story could have done with a few more scares. The riffs on Tell-Tale Heart are very smart, and the revelation that Mulder and Scully are identifying their own corpses under the floorboards should have been shocking. It's only Mark Snow who spoils the proceedings by pointing out the comedy - had he just shut up for the first act, the atmosphere would have been genuinely creepy. And the episode suffers a little from its placing in the season: after a whole slew of comic stories which derive their humour mostly from challenging our perspectives on Mulder and Scully, some of the impact is lost when it's being done yet again. It feels like we've opened our Christmas presents a mite too early to enjoy the main event. But these are minor niggles - this is a little bit of magic, utterly unrepresentative of the series and yet somehow summing it up entirely. There may be no lovelier scene in the entire run than our heroes retreating to the sofa on Christmas morning together to open the gifts they've promised not to buy the other. (*****)

6.7, Terms of Endearment

Air Date: Jan. 3, 1999
Writer: David Amann
Director: Rob Bowman

Summary   In Hollins, Virginia, Wayne and Laura Weinsider learn that their soon-to-be-born child is deformed - a situation worsened when Laura dreams about a demon taking the baby, then awakens to find it missing from her body. Mulder senses a classic case of demon foetal harvest, i.e. when a demon hosts his seed in a woman and later collects the offspring. Suspicion falls upon Wayne, who - unbeknownst to Laura - is also married to a woman named Betsy. Mulder finds evidence indicating that Wayne is a demon who has adopted many guises - and killed a number of wives - over several decades.

Betsy also claims that her unborn child has vanished. The agents catch Wayne in the act of seemingly burying Betsy's child - when actually, he's unearthing it - and the local sheriff shoots

him dead. Mulder deduces that Wayne, although a demon, wanted a human baby and was aborting the demonic ones that his wives produced. Meanwhile, Betsy - herself a demon, but far more evil than Wayne - was doing the reverse and burying her human children. Betsy escapes with her latest child, a truly demonic offspring.

Critique   The emerging theme of the sixth season seems to be that of the extraordinary revealing itself to be deeply mundane. The schmoes at Area 51, the ghosts that haunt lovers to death, all of them are trapped in the same routine domestic disappointment as the rest of us - and meanwhile Mulder and Scully find it impossible to adapt to that *real* world at all. It's very funny. And it's a logical extension of the way that alien mythology was suggested as being human in Season Three, and the very banal villains of Gilligan's work in Season Four. But I do wonder whether taking the bizarre and *normalising* it sucks some of the fun out of it all; one of the joys of early X-Files was the way it treated the bizarre with awe. The bizarre these days just wants to settle down in an ordinary family and have kids.

Bruce Campbell's demon skilfully manages to be both an everyman who hankers after a normal healthy child, and a prince of lies who can convince his own wife she's murdered their baby. It's in his performance that the episode captures a style of jet black comedy the best, the eagerness with which he looks at each of his wives' pregnant bumps, the sulky disappointment as he realises he's going to have to do all that devil shtick again and rip his demonic brood from the womb in a ring of fire. But for the second time this year a guest star is allowed to steal all the laughs; the biggest problem with Terms of Endearment is that it gives Mulder little to do - beyond making wild leaps of deduction remarkable even for him - and Scully practically nothing. It's a typical fault from a first-time X-Files writer to use the heroes just as expositional tools to knock his plot into touch - and it only ever works if the plot is very solid. This one isn't: it's a lovely conceit, and has a smashing twist at the end, but it really provides nothing more than a single character study. And for all Campbell's hard work, Wayne isn't a particularly interesting little devil. The scene where he's horrified to discover that his wife Laura is still alive is very funny, and his obvious jealousy of the three strapping children he meets at a client's house rather touching. But David Amann's script requires that Wayne has a certain ambiguity about him, for Betsy's *real* villainy in the last act to be a shock - and so the story falls between two stools, not having enough comedy to explore the premise properly, and not enough suspense to provide much drama.

But there's still much to admire here - it's a very brave story, mixing scenes of dead babies being incinerated with themes of a warped sit-com. It may not fuse together as well as it should, but it's an entertaining episode, and the tone of the piece is so markedly discomforting that it arrests the attention. The scene where Betsy reaches out and interrupts her devil nightmare is brilliantly done, it's grotesque and very funny. And Lisa Jane Persky's performance as wife Laura is terrific, giving her scenes a sincerity and strength. (***)

6.8, The Rain King

Air Date: Jan. 10, 1999
Writer: Jeffrey Bell
Director: Kim Manners

Summary   Mulder and Scully travel to Kroner, Kansas, which has been ground zero for freak weather conditions for the past thirty years. In particular, they investigate a local man - Darryl Mootz, the self-proclaimed "Rain King" - who claims to have used his influence over the weather to end a prolonged drought.

Mulder hypothesises that just as the weather can influence people's moods, the reverse is also true. In this case, the subconscious emotions of Holman Hardt, the local meteorologist, are causing the varying weather conditions. After Mootz lost his leg in a car crash during a hailstorm, Hart subconsciously felt guilty and facilitated Mootz's career as the "Rain King". However, Hardt's unexpressed feelings for Shelia Fontaine, Mootz's ex-girlfriend, trigger a destructive rain. The agents bring Hardt and Fontaine together as a couple, bringing the storm to an end.

Critique   The cow in the tornado is very funny. It's not simply that it suddenly gets sucked up into the air like magic, it's the querulous moo of surprise it makes as it does so. When my wife saw this episode on first broadcast, she laughed out loud at the moment. Ten years later, watching it once more, she laughed again. Getting my wife to laugh at anything is hard enough, but at the same thing twice? Comic genius.

But a romantic comedy cannot work by flying cows alone. This is the first time The X-Files has tried its hand at the genre, and it has a lot of fun with the tropes, even ending with the heroes trying to reconcile two sweethearts at a high school reunion dance. Some of the best jokes are provided by the very awkwardness the show has with the format - Scully's reaction to the idea that Mulder is going to save the day by giving dating advice is priceless. And the premise itself is a real charmer: that a man has been so besotted since school by someone that the weather itself is affected by his hope and despair. Jeffrey Bell's script makes a lot of the concept, and manages to be both wryly amusing and rather touching, whilst passing comment too upon the state of play between Mulder and Scully. It's telling that no-one, even the apparent loser Holman, can believe that the two of them have never got it together. For all the mismatched loves in this story, from romantic gestures that are as varied as hail which falls in the shape of hearts, to a secretary who proffers her lover his false leg as an olive branch, still no-one has failed to understand affairs of the heart quite as profoundly as our heroes.

The problem is in the casting. The story hinges upon the idea that Holman has never told Sheila how he's felt in all these years - it'd be like a frog declaring love to a swan, he says. But actor David Manis is no frog; he wears *glasses*, it's true, but he's slim, well-spoken and intelligent. And Victoria Jackson, most critically, is no swan either. There's not an ounce of subtlety to her performance, never suggesting that there's anything more to discover than the shrill bubblehead exterior. Not only does she kill most of the comedy scenes she appears in, lacking the delicacy to make them charming, she also kills the plot - there's virtually no chemistry between her and Manis... or *anyone*, come to

that. Her acting is so broad it's playing in a separate bubble to everyone else. The one real contrivance of the plot is that, for reasons of farce, she needs to fall in love with Mulder; it's not really fed by the dialogue, so it needs the actress in question to sell it instead. The story falters on this point, as it does on so many others, because Jackson has no interest in making Sheila Fontaine a real person. She's the comic caricature she plays on Saturday Night Live. And with the guest star performing on one note, and riding roughshod over the jokes in the script, it's hard to care about the romance. In an ordinary X-File you can often get away on plot mechanics alone, but romance depends upon character. You can sit back and admire Rain King in concept, but the execution fails to convince.

But the cow in the tornado? Really, very funny. (***)

6.9, S.R. 819

Air Date: Jan 17, 1999
Writer: John Shiban
Director: Daniel Sackheim

Summary After Skinner falls ill, a discoloration starts making its way across his body. A shadowy figure phones to say that the assistant director has twenty-four hours to live. Scully finds that fast-replicating nanobots are building dams in Skinner's cardiovascular system, working their way toward causing a heart attack.

Mulder believes that Skinner's malady is related to a security check being run on Senate Resolution 819, which would entail exporting the same nano-technology that's killing Skinner to third world countries. Additionally, Mulder finds that his ally, Senator Matheson, is somehow involved in the intrigue and ends their friendship. Skinner becomes clinically dead until the shadowy figure uses a remote control to make the nanobots go dormant. Skinner recovers, then tells Mulder and Scully to drop any investigation into the matter and reports to the shadowy figure: Krycek, who can reactivate the nanobots at any time, and now commands Skinner's loyalty.

Critique After a whole series of comedy episodes, it's refreshing to get a story which feels more like a traditional X-File: cue chases in alleys, sinister scenes in underground car parks, Skinner growling at everyone, and lots and lots of hospital action. The problem is that it's also a return to the sort of murky storylining which promises so much but delivers little. The premise is terrific - Skinner is poisoned somehow, and has twenty-four hours to live. Already a walking dead man, he and our heroes have to find out who murdered him. So far, so DOA - and with on-screen reminders of how many hours Skinner has remaining, the stage is set for a taut thriller.

But that isn't what we get. Considering the urgency of the situation, the plot seems to amble along; it might be the fault of director Daniel Sackheim, or John Shiban's script, but the episode as a whole lacks any real tension. The story relies upon our finding shock in a) the idea that a minor character last seen in Season Two, Senator Richard Matheson, might be a villain after all, and b) in the return of Krycek, a character who lost comprehensible motivation some time around the middle of Season Four, and here sports a long beard just to conceal his identity until the final scene. There's no resolution, either to the conspiracy (we never find out how Skinner was poisoned) or to the crisis (Skinner is pronounced dead, and then is revived by Krycek's magic box). And so the entire adventure seems only to exist to demonstrate that Krycek has a hold over Skinner. We've been here before. When the Cigarette Smoking Man had control over Skinner in Season Four, it was at least tied into a Faustian pact to save Scully's life; this is the rather less dramatic reason that Krycek has something like a TV remote control that can make poor Walter's skin go blotchy.

There's one lovely scene, in which Skinner confesses to Scully that he's never been the support to her and Mulder that he should have been, that his entire life has been squandered by caution. But deliberately or not, the impact is cheapened by the ending, in which Skinner goes back to being his usual surly self, refusing to acknowledge their concerns, and putting himself ever deeper into the thrall of the conspiracy. (And considering what's about to happen to that, was it really worthwhile?) One step forward, two steps back. We've got the return of edgy X-Files here, but I don't think we're better off for it. (**)

6.10, Tithonus

Air Date: Jan. 24, 1999
Writer: Vince Gilligan
Director: Michael Watkins

Summary   Scully is assigned to help Agent Peyton Ritter, who's found a series of crime-scene photos that don't correspond to the times they were purportedly taken. They wonder if the photographer, Alfred Fellig, is killing people and taking snapshots of the event, then returning to take photos for the wire services.

Scully confronts Fellig, who claims that Death once passed him by in a contagion ward and took a nurse by mistake. Fellig has been immortal ever since, able to innately sense when people are about to die. By photographing death-acts, Fellig hopes to capture Death's image on film so that he can look into Death's face and die.

Fellig senses that Scully will soon die, just as Ritter bursts into Fellig's apartment and fires recklessly. A bullet strikes Scully, but Fellig implores Scully not to look into Death's face. Fellig does so himself, trading his life for hers.

Critique   For a while this episode looks as if it's simply going to be a retread of Clyde Bruckman's Final Repose; Alfred Fellig is a man who can sense when people are going to die, and grimly parades the streets with his camera looking for a chance to photograph the event. But this turns out to have a flavour all of its own, and finally emerges as one of the most thoughtful and profound X-Files episodes in ages. The genius of Clyde Bruckman was that it was so spoiling with ideas that it was like a dizzying burst of comic energy. Tithonus, on the other hand, is a more methodical affair, building up to a long discussion about the meaning of death, the release it can offer, and the anguish it can cause if denied. The cleverness of the episode is that it showcases Gillian Anderson, playing a Scully who has stared death from cancer in the face and been pulled back from the brink, who has examined and prodded at and cut up countless examples of it on the autopsy slab. This is a hardened Scully, who is teamed up here with a young and enthusiastic agent,

sceptical to her outlandish theories. It's become increasingly hard to watch Scully's fresh-faced counterpart in the title sequence each week; Gillian Anderson waving around her torchlight seems so young and naïve there in comparison. When she berates Fellig for showing no compassion towards those he can see are about to die, she is in a way berating herself, a woman who can so calmly study the photographs of the dead, who can oversee the bodies of a crime scene without breaking a sweat. It's a measure of how much humanity Scully has left that she can argue with Fellig that a person can never want too much life, that there is a whole world of experiences to explore that should never be taken for granted. Coming on the heels of episodes like How the Ghosts Stole Christmas, Rain King, and the Dreamland two-parter, which typify just how far our heroes have strayed from having ordinary lives, this is very touching and very telling. And it also saves her life. The immortal Fellig feels no sympathy for the dying, but envies them for being able to take part in an adventure he's denied - he chooses to take Scully's death from her, because of all the doomed people he has photographed, she's the only one with whom he has had a conversation, and the only one who deep down is in danger of being as emotionless as him.

Although Clyde Bruckman is a comedy, it ultimately offers a very pessimistic view of life. Tithonus is an altogether grimmer affair, its presentation of a man who expressionlessly collects images of the dying macabre, the very whine of his camera shrill like a mosquito. But in the way that it presents death as a release, as something which once resisted you'll spend an eternity searching for anew, it clearly shows how rich a thing life should be. Geoffrey Lewis plays Fellig like a man faded, like a sepia photo, a man of such little feeling that he makes the dying look more alive in contrast. It's a terrific performance; it utterly rejects any sympathy, and for that very reason it achieves a calm dignity which is so much more powerful.

Bizarre, chilling, and yet strangely life-affirming, this is one of the best X-Files episodes. Season Six has been experimenting widely with tone, and it's gratifying to see, as it returns to the style of creeping unease that made it so famous, that it still has the power to be original and meaningful as it does so. It's hard to imagine any other television series being able to pull off a story like this. (*****)

6.11, Two Fathers

Air Date: Feb. 7, 1999
Writers: Chris Carter, Frank Spotnitz
Director: Kim Manners

Summary   The faceless alien rebels (5.13, Patient X) move against the Syndicate and their alien allies, murdering a medical team working in a train car in Arlington, Virginia. Their patient - the formerly abducted Cassandra Spender - is deliberately left alive, which threatens to bring down the Syndicate's core conspiracy...

For fifty years, the Syndicate has sided with the alien colonists and laboured to create an alien-human hybrid for them - purely a means of buying time to develop a vaccine against the black oil and formulate a proper resistance. But now, they've succeeded in spite of themselves. Cassandra is the first true alien-human hybrid, and if her existence becomes known, the colonists will initiate the invasion of Earth.

One of the rebels kills the Second Elder and takes his guise. The Cigarette Smoking Man deduces this and sends Agent Spender and Krycek to kill the infiltrator. Krycek does so, then tells Spender that the Cigarette Smoking Man has been orchestrating Cassandra's abductions.

Scully's research determines that Cassandra was first abducted on the same night that Samantha Mulder vanished. Meanwhile, Cassandra realises her importance to the colonists' plans - and implores Mulder to stop them by shooting her. [To be continued.]

Critique   "Full Disclosure!" screamed the trailers for this two-parter. They might as well have said, "We Know We Promised You Answers in the Movie, But We Forgot To Put Them In - Sorry, Here They Are!" The mythology episodes have become such a mass of exposition masquerading as drama that it's only to be expected that this one, the first in what sounds like an exercise in ticking the boxes, should be a monster of Redux proportions. It's much, much bet-

ter than that. And that's partly because there really *isn't* that much of disclosure on offer, so we get the chance for some suspense to seep through - and partly because what disclosure exists is being offered in a refreshingly different way.

And what's different is that the episode is largely narrated by the Cigarette Smoking Man (although, I suppose, from this point on he should be referred to by the slightly disappointing name of Mr Spender). Much has been done to make the character lose his impact over the years, either deliberately by undermining his iconic status in Musings of a Cigarette Smoking Man, or accidentally by killing him off then effortlessly bringing him back from the dead. It's a testament to how powerful an enigma he really is, though, that Two Fathers makes the impression that it does, our first *real* look into the soul of the enemy. William B Davis seizes on the script he's clearly been waiting for all these years, reflecting upon his failures and his last hopes with a wounded pride and a world weariness that gives him great dignity. The conspiracy tale is looked at laterally, from the point of view of a man who isn't afraid to kill one of his associates - Dr Openshaw - for the greater good, but does so with solemnity, finding within his pawn of a son none of the qualities he admires in his adversaries. Chris Owens gives his best performance yet too, at last given an opportunity not to play Spender merely as some tittle-tattling weasel, but a man who for his own different reasons is seeking the truth as deeply as Mulder. His mother has been returned to him, and the relief he shows is moving - as is his growing realisation that the man he has allied himself to is responsible for the experiments upon her. The sequence where Spender is sent to kill an alien spy to prove his worth recalls The Godfather, and has much of that movie classic's edge.

With all the drama going on between Spender and Son, there's not much attention given to Mulder or Scully. But for once that feels like a positive thing; with the agents genuinely sidelined and unable to make an impression upon events, Chris Carter and Frank Spotnitz finally get dramatic mileage out of the leads' removal from the X-Files. It's their very absence from the heart of the episode that emphasises that events are reaching crisis point, and gives the sense that things are out of balance. It helps to justify a curiously abrupt cliffhanger, in which Mulder is told by Cassandra that to stop an alien invasion he must shoot her dead. It's almost too hasty to be credible, but this sudden shift of Mulder into the limelight after forty-five minutes of his treading water is an effective jolt. (****)

6.12, One Son

Air Date: Feb. 14, 1999
Writers: Chris Carter, Frank Spotnitz
Director: Rob Bowman

Summary   Operatives for the Centers for Disease Control (CDC) stop Mulder from shooting Cassandra. Diana Fowley tells the agents that Cassandra has contracted an extremely dangerous virus, but Scully finds records suggesting that Fowley spent years working as an operative of the Syndicate.

Mulder encounters the Cigarette Smoking Man, who is unusually candid with him about the Syndicate's history. The Cigarette Smoking Man confirms that the conspiracy originated with the Roswell incident in 1947 - those involved first came together at the State Department, but later privatized the effort. They forged an alliance with the alien colonists as a means of staying the enemy's hand... but in 1973, the Syndicate members were required to give some of their family members, Cassandra Spender included, to the aliens in exchange for an alien foetus. They were tasked with creating an alien-human hybrid that could survive the "viral apocalypse" the aliens wanted to unleash on humanity, but they never planned to succeed. Bill Mulder objected to the pact, but later capitulated and gave the aliens his daughter Samantha. He also suggested that DNA from the alien foetus could be used to develop a black-oil vaccine.

The Cigarette Smoking Man says that thanks to the alien rebels, the Syndicate's plan lies in tatters. The aliens will mobilize, and a state of emergency will be declared owing to a massive outbreak of the alien virus carried by bees. With little option, the Syndicate members intend to save themselves and their families by facilitating the invasion.

The Syndicate members and their relatives - including Cassandra - are taken to El Rico Air Force Base in West Virginia, with the expectation that they will receive the alien-hybrid genes. However, the faceless aliens arrive and incinerate everyone present - save for the Cigarette Smoking Man and Agent Fowley, who flee the scene.

Disgusted with his father's actions, Agent Spender implores Kersh to reinstate Mulder and Scully to the X-Files. Afterward, the Cigarette Smoking Man, deeming his son a grave disappointment, shoots him.

Critique   Typically for a mytharc episode there's a lot of exposition to wade through - but, for once, it manages to feel both urgent and dramatic. Indeed, the long conversation between David Duchovny and William B Davis, which so threatens to be a replay of scenes we've witnessed too often before, as Mulder waves a gun in the Smoking Man's face and shouts a lot, is the real highlight of the story - very well acted, and truly interesting. The simplified version of The X-Files backstory makes sense and builds nicely towards an ironic climax, in which the Syndicate are finally wiped out after consorting with the enemy just that little bit too long. And there's a genuine sense that the show, at last, is closing a chapter and moving onto something new.

What could so easily have been an instalment which ticked lots of continuity boxes is given a real power, once again, by William B Davis. Two Fathers showed he was capable of a really complex performance, and he develops it further here, so that it's the emotional centre of the episode. The guilt and the awkwardness with which he approaches his betrayed wife is quite wonderful, the scene where he so regretfully shoots his disappointment of a son strangely affecting. Chris Owens, too, continues to play a Spender who is fully real; his redemption is honestly touching, and the way in which he insists that the X-Files be reassigned to Mulder and Scully has a touch of triumph to it. It's a shame that just as the series gives him some dimension that it takes the easy step of writing him out. As an ally there was much that could have been done with him, and Owens shows signs here that he might easily have been a replacement lead in the event of Duchovny's departure - as had been rumoured when he was first brought into the series.

That said, too much attention is given to whether or not Diana Fowley can be trusted or not. This is only her third full appearance in the series, and there simply isn't enough reason for the audience to care about her loyalties one way or the other - had the sixth season given her as much screen time as it had Jeffrey Spender, the to-ing and fro-ing here might have made some impact. As it is the normally excellent Mimi Rogers flounders; she doesn't seem to know which way to play the character either, and she ends up not being so much ambiguous as just bland.

For what's intended to be a pivotal episode, its greatest moments are little moments. Cassandra's smile of acceptance as she's at last to die with her torturers, the look of cool horror on Krycek's face as he realises that the conspiracy is doomed and that all bets are off. It's a confusing story, to be sure - but what can you expect after five and a half seasons of the writers' attention on the show's mytharc, extending some aspects and truncating others beyond all sense? But this reaches for both significance and closure, and mostly works. (***1/2)

6.13, Agua Mala

Air Date: Feb. 21, 1999
Writer: David Amann
Director: Rob Bowman

Summary Arthur Dales (5.15, Travelers) directs Mulder and Scully's attention to Goodland, Florida, where some sort of tentacled sea creature has slaughtered a family. A tremendous hurricane rolls into town, stranding the agents and a few locals in an apartment building.

The tentacled-thing attacks a deputy, causing his body to melt. Mulder speculates that the "creature" is the water itself, taking whatever shape it needs to attack and reproducing itself inside the human body's water content. The survivors shoot out the building's sprinkler heads, spraying the area with fresh water and disrupting the creature's reproductive cycle - making it helpless until the storm passes.

Critique The second season set up expectations for the reopening of the X-Files, and the return of a traditional monster episode, then botched it with the dull and derivative Firewalker. And, sad to say, much of the same thing happens here - except this time the story can't even take itself seriously enough to instil even the slightest bit of tension. To be fair, as a comedy the first half plays rather well; the banter between Mulder and Scully in the car is very amusing, and the scene they share with Darren McGavin's Arthur Dales is a real highlight. But David Amann's script is so intent on being witty and wry that it never finds the time to settle down and deliver an effective plot. He populates the story (and only at the halfway mark) with a whole array of characters so broad that they detract from the claustrophobic setting - the comic stereotypes on display here are too big for such an enclosed space. And by the end of the story, with Scully delivering a baby, it's almost as if she too has forgotten she's in a tale about sea monsters who can turn their victims into salt water. She barely even registers that Mulder's fighting for his life, or that a tentacle is lifting another man off his feet - it's as if she's given up on the horror side of the episode altogether.

There are some chuckles to be had - I love the sequence where Mulder and Scully both try to talk to the deputy with torches in their mouths. But it's hardly Oscar Wilde. Halfway through a season which has continually toyed with the balance between comedy and horror, this is the one where it comes crashing down: the laughs aren't clever, and the scares are silly. (*1/2)

6.14, Monday

Air Date: Feb. 28, 1999
Writers: Vince Gilligan, John Shiban
Director: Kim Manners

Summary Mulder tries to deposit his pay check on a seemingly typical Monday, but visits his bank just as Bernard Oates, a janitor, tries to rob it. Scully arrives to find Mulder, and the standoff ends with Oates detonating the dynamite strapped around his waist - killing everyone in the building, the agents included.

Time resets itself to Monday morning, and Mulder and Scully - unable to remember the previous "day" - go through various permutations that always lead to the fatal bank heist, followed by Monday morning again. Only Bernard's girlfriend Pam recalls the previous loops, and she tells Mulder that time is stuck in a groove until they find the "right" sequence of events. Mulder remembers a few details in the next loop, and has Pam brought into the bank so she can help talk Oates into aborting the robbery. Oates tries to shoot Mulder, but winds up killing Pam - the fated act that allows time to roll forward to Tuesday.

Critique   Though cut from the same cloth as Groundhog Day, this episode comes to very different conclusions about fate and predeterminism, and acquires an original taste of its own. In the one, Bill Murray lives the same day over and over again, with everyone about him behaving in exactly the same predictable way. Once he's learned the score, he's able to conduct the world as if it's his own symphony. In Monday, however, it's as Mulder says - that there are so many variables in the events that unfold, different words used on Bernard's note to the teller, Mulder falling over his shoes in different ways, that no matter how many times the same day will play out there'll always be hope for something unique that will break the cycle. Groundhog Day, for all that it's a comedy, reduces characters somewhat cynically to mechanical toys; Monday, for all that it's a tragedy, is much more optimistic about the chaos of free will. Man's impulses *cannot* be predicted, nor controlled so simply.

It's interesting that for Gilligan and Shiban's conceit to work they have to take Mulder and Scully out of the traditional X-Files setting: for the repeated hell of the story to work, the ordinary events have to be as mundane as possible. Mulder's here not concerned with alien abductions, but with paying in a cheque at the bank; he'll be foiled not by the machinations of a conspiracy, but by an ATM being out of order. This might normally be considered something of a cheat. It's only because this season has gone so far as to show Mulder and Scully's domestic lives already for comic effect that it doesn't feel forced - and it has the double purpose of suggesting from the start that this too is a comedy. The mirrored ceiling, the waterbed - all recall

Dreamland, a story in which the reset button was also used, and with no dramatic consequence. As we watch Mulder wince as his bed springs a leak - again and yet again - we're reassured that this will turn out well; no matter how often he dies, it's established that this must be a joke. And by wrongfooting the audience's expectations, the writers brilliantly allow Pam's very real despair to be all the more shocking. It conceals from us the obvious way out of the loop, that she must die, that there is no happy ending after all: that this isn't a conceit in which the universe wants to keep Mulder alive, but instead wants Pam to be dead. And as she lies on the ground, suffering from a fatal gunshot wound, the wonder in her face as she realises this order of events hasn't happened before is powerful and moving. It's telling that in a series which has sometimes used the device of pretending to be solemn only to reveal it's a comedy, that we at last have a story where we see the reverse. It plays upon the idea that this is another example of Season Six's foray into "X-Files Lite", to deliver something which is intriguing and tough and quietly profound. (*****)

6.15, Arcadia

Air Date: March 7, 1999
Writer: Daniel Arkin
Director: Michael Watkins

Summary   Mulder and Scully pose as a married couple, hoping to explain a number of disappearances at "The Falls at Arcadia" gated community in San Diego County. In time, Mulder discovers that the homeowner president, Gene Gogolak, made a number of trips to the Far East and learned about the tulpa - a Tibetan thought creature. With the Falls having been built on an old landfill, Gogolak has been mentally manifesting the tulpa as a garbage creature to punish / kill the residents if they break the neighbourhood rules.

The tulpa tries to slaughter Scully because Mulder has broken many rules, prompting him to dash to her rescue. In his absence, Gogolak - who's able to summon the tulpa but not control it - becomes the creature's next victim. With his death, the tulpa goes to pieces.

Critique Of course, the principle pleasure of the episode is seeing Mulder and Scully go undercover as a yuppie married couple. Anderson and Duchovny clearly have great fun turning their characters on their heads, Mulder gushing and just a little bit stupid, Scully perky and polished. It's Mulder's chance to send Scully up, by claiming his wife is a gullible New Ager, by indulging in winsome lovey talk and talking about how he and his wife spoon like cats - the best Scully can come up with in retaliation is calling her husband "poopyhead" through gritted teeth. So many stories this season have played upon the joke of putting our heroes into a domestic setting, and it clearly reaches its apotheosis here, in an episode which requires them to expose the very artificiality behind suburban happiness. Where having a pink flamingo on your lawn, or your mailbox propped askew, may just be non-conformist enough to summon up a monster.

But what makes this setting so delicious is the way the anarchy of The X-Files destroys what appears to be the American Dream. Daniel Arkin's script may not be exactly subtle, but there's a lot of anger here amongst the fish out of water jokes. Cami Shroeder, playing one of the residents, may claim that there's no dark underbelly to this community, but these perfect homes are constructed on layers of landfill. It's a neat play upon the traditional horror cliché of a house being built upon an Indian burial ground - only in Arcadia could the evil underneath be the garbage of corporate America. And if Gogolak's visits to the East, where he's learned how to make an avenging tulpa from the earth, seem a little silly, then that's surely the joke - it's the collision between Tibetan folklore and the WASP population of Californian prosperity which makes this seem so fresh. If the monster itself looks a bit rubbish - well, that's apt, because rubbish is what it literally is.

In the final act the story runs out of steam; when the episode can no longer trade off domestic comedy or social satire and becomes instead a slice of horror the plotting ends up somewhat rushed. Abraham Benrubi's Big Mike reveals that he wasn't killed by the tulpa as we all thought - only to be killed by the tulpa a moment later, in a twist that's as unnecessary as it is puzzling. It's not really clear why Gogolak is murdered by his own creation, and Arkin

throws away the moment when the cowed neighbours refuse to save him. But for all the confusion of the last few minutes, the coda is excellent, as Mulder and Scully drive away leaving behind a community of neighbours who *still* respond to the pressures to conform and won't acknowledge what evils they have been facing. (****)

6.16, Alpha

Air Date: March 28, 1999
Writer: Jeffrey Bell
Director: Peter Markle

Summary Karen Berquist, an expert on canine behaviourisms, tips off Mulder when two crewmen are savaged to death aboard the freighter *T'ien Kou*. The bodies were found inside an otherwise empty crate belonging to Dr Ian Detweiler, who claims that a near-extinct type of dog - the Wanshang Dhole - was inside.

Mulder deduces that a Dhole attacked Detweiler while he was in China, and thereby turned him into a shapeshifting trickster who becomes a murderous animal at night. Detweiler realises that Berquist knows too much and transforms into a savage dog to murder her - but Berquist deliberately positions herself in front of an upper window, causing them both to plunge to their deaths.

Critique No matter how good the effects, there's a limit to the number of times a dog with glowing red eyes pouncing on a human can be interesting. I make it twice, three at a pinch. By the time we reach the climax, and the dog in question launches itself at its sixth victim, you'll be wondering what on earth makes this tale of a shapeshifter man who turns feral at night any better than the risible first season story Shapes. Well, Jeffrey Bell's dialogue is better, admittedly, and Duchovny and Anderson as ever play their initial banter well. But this is the *sixth* season now, chaps, and if the show is going to do a werewolf yarn it really needs to do so with more invention than is seen here.

Instead what we get is a muddled subplot about a canine expert who can't relate to people but who has nevertheless fixed her attention upon Mulder. Melinda Culea plays Karin Berquist as a woman who's borderline autistic very well, but at the expense of any chemistry between her and Duchovny; when Scully first points out that Karin is obsessively in love with Mulder, we've seen such little evidence of it that it feels like one of those strange intuitive leaps we're more used to from Mulder's wild theories. As an attempt to instil a bit of emotion into this repetitive and formulaic tale, it fails utterly. As an attempt to intrigue, to suggest that Karin is the werewolf rather than Detweiler, it's only a little more successful. (*)

6.17, Trevor

Air Date: April 11, 1999
Writers: Jim Guttridge, Ken Hawryliw
Director: Rob Bowman

Summary   After a storm strikes a prison in Stringer, Mississippi, a disciplinary box containing inmate Wilson "Pinker" Rawls is found destroyed. Additionally, the prison warden is found dead - cut in half without any blood splattering his office. Mulder reasons that the storm's electric potential granted Rawls the ability to phase through matter and thereby change its composition. As his power is electrical in nature, an insulating material such as glass can thwart it.

Rawls kidnaps his ex-girlfriend, June Gurwitch, after learning that she bore him a son named Trevor. A scuffle ensues, causing June to drive at Rawls with her car. The passenger-side windshield strikes Rawls, killing him and ending his wish of getting a second chance with his son.

Critique   This is The X-Files at its most generic, given a certain freshness only because we haven't been given a human mutant on a revenge rampage for a while. And I use the word "rampage" loosely; the biggest problem with Trevor is that it has a single good visual gimmick, that of a man who is able to pass through solid objects, and it never exploits it to the full. John Diehl is clearly in something of a quandary working out how to play Pinker; the script makes great mention of his dangerous temper, that this is a man who'll murder a motorist who cuts him up whilst driving, but

also requires him for the climax to be a father dismayed that his own son fears him. Diehl plays the latter but shies away from the former, which means that there's barely any tension in the first half-hour or so at all as he amiably wanders about shirtless through walls, and that there's no surprise or redemption when he finally tracks down Trevor in the final act. This is a workmanlike story which *needs* a couple of good set pieces and a credible villain causing them - and we don't get either.

It's a pity, because although this is hardly an ambitious or original episode, the script by Jim Guttridge and Ken Hawryliw is decent enough. Catherine Dent, in particular, rises to the quality of the dialogue, playing well a woman who's so desperate to escape from her seedy life that she'll throw herself fully into bland suburbia. Though the final act recalls the Millennium episode The Wild and the Innocent a little too closely, there's an awkward realism to Pinker's attempts to reach out to Trevor even as he's terrifying the poor kid which is impressive. But Guttridge and Hawryliw fall into the trap common to first-time writers, giving Mulder and Scully very little to do. Mulder wisecracks just a little too much this episode (although the David Copperfield gag is genuinely very funny); Scully, at least, gets to faze her partner by willingly being open to extreme possibility. Yet as usual with manhunt stories, ultimately all they're able to do is hunt. In a season which could in fact do with some solid traditional storytelling in the mix, Trevor is just a bit too disposable and routine to hold much interest. (**)

6.18, Milagro

Air Date: April 18, 1999
Story: John Shiban, Frank Spotnitz
Teleplay: Chris Carter
Director: Kim Manners

Summary   The agents investigate deaths in which the victims' hearts were removed without cutting marks of any kind, prompting Mulder to wonder if "psychic surgery" was involved. Meanwhile, Scully is intrigued by Mulder's new neighbour, a failed writer named Phillip Padgett.

Mulder arrests Padgett, having found a correlation between personal ads that Padgett placed in the newspaper - a means of finding victims, Mulder thinks - and descriptions of the killings in his book. Padgett is released when another murder happens while he's incarcerated, leading Mulder and Scully to suspect that he's working with an accomplice.

As the agents observe Padgett sitting alone in his apartment, Padgett finds himself conversing with the hooded figure - a character from his novel, whom he envisioned as the perfect killer. The hooded figure tells Padgett that both his novel and his love for Scully must end with her death. Padgett finishes writing his book, then goes to burn it in the basement incinerator. The hooded figure attacks Scully, but Padgett destroys his book - saving Scully's life, at the cost of his own heart being torn out.

Critique   Consider this. Chris Carter comes up with a series about two FBI agents who pursue paranormal cases, with an eye in particular on UFO sightings. He sees it as being a modern day Kolchak: The Night Stalker, something fun and scary that hasn't been seen on network television for a while, something too which is unlikely to be that commercial a show. To that end, against network pressure, he casts an unknown actress as one of the two leads, short and decidedly less glamorous than the suits upstairs have in mind. Why not? After all, The X-Files isn't likely to be a ratings success. Oh, and there'll be no romantic involvement between the two agents - that just isn't what the show's about. And when that show begins to build a following, partly because of the very chemistry between those agents, he'll give interviews insisting that the sexual tension that is clearly on the screen will never be released. The series is a bigger hit than Carter can possibly have imagined - it runs on past its intended ending, it runs on past a feature film. From its cheaper home in Vancouver, it's now being made in Los Angeles. Other writers have come onto the show. And, inevitably, they put to the forefront of their stories the sexual chemistry that was never supposed to be there in the first place. The series is reinvented as something comic, something post-modern, something knowing. And it never stops.

In the teaser, a writer working on a story about Mulder and Scully literally pulls out his own beating heart for inspiration.

The sixth season has been about re-examining what Mulder and Scully are; they've been reimagined in a domestic setting, they've had their lives swapped. They've lived the same day over and over again, giving us the chance to look at every minute aspect of what they do in minute detail. You can see immediately how Milagro fits into this, an episode in which they're explored as fictional characters of a frustrated writer. What's remarkable is that this is in no way, as you might expect, done for comic effect; where Darin Morgan played around with the conventions of writing for The X-Files to point out where it's compromised, Chris Carter does so as a sincere expression of Scully's character: how an FBI agent of such passion hasn't had a proper relationship during the series' run and what a toll her work at the Bureau has placed upon her, how a woman he imagined as a no-nonsense (and plain) doctor has evolved in spite of himself into one of the greatest sex symbols on the planet. It's also a cry of - what? despair? exasperation? - about working on a series which keeps on reinventing itself and won't let its creator go.

Gillian Anderson gives a revelatory performance as a Scully who uncomfortably finds herself opening up to extreme possibility - not only within the X-File she's investigating, but within the stirrings of her own heart. The entire long sequence where she wants to run from the bedroom of her stalker, but is nevertheless so fascinated that she can't leave, walks a knife edge of credibility, but is so deftly written and acted that it works beautifully. John Hawkes too is both sinister and sympathetic as a man so obsessed by Scully that he'll write a novel about her, that he'll become Mulder's neighbour just to get close to her. But in that scene there's a third character, and it's Chris Carter himself, *making* a confused Scully stay where she doesn't want to be, forcing her to examine her own hopes and desires. This is an episode about writing, about how if the writer becomes God and makes his characters do what he tells them against their own inclinations, then the story won't be true or sincere - but if he allows himself to be a vessel for where the characters direct *him,* he may produce better art but end up powerless as a result. When Carter writes Scully out of character, she notices and complains; when, at the end, our fictional writer destroys the logical ending that his own imaginary killer has given him, he's accepting that just because the art is better it's not necessarily the most humane.

It's a piece of self-indulgence, of course. It's vague and it's flabby. And it's by Chris Carter, which means that Padgett's voiceover prose has passages of brilliance and passages of pretension. In some ways, though, all these faults are part of the *point*: this is a study of overwriting with all the mistakes left in, all the frustrations and inadequacies that a writer has to endure. It's deliberately not the most rounded or satisfying episode of The X-Files, but it's nevertheless one of the most personal, and one of the most remarkable. And if after six seasons of being a runaway hit - and still going strong, Carter won't be off the hook for years yet! - the show couldn't afford to make something as inward-looking as this, it shouldn't still be running at all. This is the schizophrenia of The X-Files, and what this story is about: it'll broadcast something as generic as Alpha and Trevor, then follow them with this. The investigation into hearts being taken from victims' bodies is intentionally pointless and illogical - it's what The X-Files *always* does. And it's the work of a writer in a room, all on his own, battling away with all the clichés and the formula into a typewriter. (*******)

6.19, The Unnatural

Air Date: April 25, 1999
Writer / Director: David Duchovny

Summary Mulder consults with the brother of Arthur Dales (6.13, Agua Mala) - who's also named Arthur - concerning an incident in Roswell, 1947, when he was a police officer. Dales was assigned to protect a star African-American baseball player named Josh Exley when a pamphlet surfaced offering a reward for his death. To his surprise, Dales learned that Exley was a shapeshifting extraterrestrial who left his home of Macon, Georgia, to pursue his love of baseball.

Exley flees when an alien bounty hunter from Macon comes calling for him, but Dales figures

out that Exley is going to a late-night "cactus league" baseball game in Roswell. Led by the Alien Bounty Hunter, Klu Klux Klan members interrupt the proceedings. The bounty hunter escapes after stabbing Exley with a stiletto. Dales arrives to find Exley bleeding human blood - a discovery that surprises and pleases Exley as he dies.

Critique And this is the perfect way to follow Milagro. If last week's episode was a cynical tale of writing gone sour, there's a charm to David Duchovny's scripting and directing that is the ideal antidote. Duchovny co-wrote for The X-Files before, but always for stories drowning in mythology twists and providing him, as a performer, the chance to express some angst. It's a measure of how the series has changed that his first solo script is as delightful a comic fable as this one, a little fantasy about an alien who so falls in love with something as frivolous and human as baseball that he abandons his heritage to play in the minor leagues. Exley talks about the game as being useless but perfect, the first unnecessary thing he ever did, and Jesse L Martin plays the part as a man who is utterly enamoured with life and laughter. It's the most optimistic statement about mankind the show has made for quite a long time, and its climax - when Exley dies only to discover to his bemused joy that he's bleeding red blood - has something of Pinocchio about it. The Good Fairy has granted this alien his wish, and he's been transformed into a real boy.

Some of the comedy is a bit heavy handed; recurring sequences in which the young Arthur Dales is accepted into the "Roswell Grays" team are on the saccharine side. But they work because the whole story is structured as a fairy tale; as older Dales says to a disbelieving Mulder, trying hard to tie up everything he's hearing into the established mytharc like a diehard fan, "trust the tale not the teller". And though the way that director Duchovny blurs the action between past and present isn't subtle - a little boy running here, a TV programme there - it still gives this episode a licence to be as sweet and fabulous as it likes. The relationship between Dales and Exley is genuinely touching; Dales will protect him as bodyguard when he thinks that Exley represents a breakthrough in race relations, but once he realises that Exley isn't even black but something far more alien, he'll jeopardise his reputation and his career for his new friend.

It's a pity that Darren McGavin was taken ill during shooting. M Emmet Walsh does a fine job as his replacement, but by giving Arthur Dales a brother (and sister, and goldfish) with exactly the same name, Duchovny breaks that little barrier between the fictional world of 1947 and the real world from where the tale's being spun. I can see that it's the result of a panicked rewrite, but Duchovny jumped the wrong way by trying to squeeze one more joke out of the story, when a far more functional solution would have sufficed - indeed, the story being told by Dales' brother would have put it at one more remove, and made the unreliable narrator that much more explicable. Arthur Dales' strength was always that he was resolutely, stubbornly, *ordinary*; the sort of man who combats McCarthyism not as a hero but as a common man, someone who'll stick by Exley not because he's an eccentric idealist but because he's decent. Now he's become someone you can't quite believe in any longer, and it's perhaps telling that there'll never be an attempt to bring him back.

The highlights of the episode, though, in spite of the fable's charm, are the two scenes between Mulder and Scully, which both have such affection and ease to them. The sequence in which Mulder teaches Scully how to play baseball is especially delightful, and gives this sentimental episode an extra warm glow. (*****)

6.20, Three of a Kind

Air Date: May 2, 1999
Writers: Vince Gilligan, John Shiban
Director: Bryan Spicer

Summary The Lone Gunmen try and fail to infiltrate a defence contractors' convention in Las Vegas, but spot Suzanne Modeski (5.3, Unusual Suspects) while doing so. Byers, who's infatuated with Modeski, learns that she's staying with Grant Ellis - who has ties to a weapons facility in New Mexico. Modeski tells the Gunmen that she and Ellis are in league against shadow men trying to exploit the psychological warfare gas that she developed. However, it turns out that Ellis - on pain of death - has been working for the shadow men, manipulating Modeski to finish her weapons project. With Modeski having outlived her usefulness, a CIA hitman tries to kill her but merely succeeds in slaying Ellis. The Gunmen capture the hitman and give him to the authorities, making it look as if he also murdered Modeski - who goes into hiding to start a new life.

Critique This is a serviceable enough sequel to The Unusual Suspects, inasmuch as it's affable, amusing and has some nice jokes every now and then. But it isn't really funny enough to make much of an impact. There are some lovely gags (I love the way that Langly is prepared to play Dungeons & Dragons in memoriam to a fallen geek)... and some very poor ones too (Langly's sickened reaction to an autopsy must count as the single-most laboured joke the series has ever done). Gillian Anderson is utterly delightful as a drugged Scully, playing the flip side of the hard-nosed FBI agent as a giddy blonde who just likes to flirt and call everyone "cutie" - her autopsy analysis makes the entire episode worthwhile. But, like its prequel, it's a story which takes as its theme government conspiracy and for all of its comic zest can't really find anything new to say about it. It's nicely directed by Bryan Spicer, and the opening teaser of Byers' idyll is beautifully shot, as is the sequence where Langly turns assassin. For all the energy of the performances, for all the inventive camerawork, it's a pretty self-indulgent and slow-paced script which has a few good lines in it. Likeable and good-natured, and utterly redundant, this passes forty-five minutes pleasantly enough, but you'll be hard pushed to remember them afterwards. (**1/2)

6.21, Field Trip

Air Date: May 9, 1999
Story: Frank Spotnitz
Teleplay: Vince Gilligan, John Shiban
Director: Kim Manners

Summary After two hikers are found dead - their bodies reduced to skeletons - in the Brown Mountain region of North Carolina, Mulder wonders if their fate is connected to strange lights that have been spotted on the mountain's peak for seven hundred years. Mulder visits the area and drives over some spore-emitting mushrooms, while Scully learns that the hikers' skeletons were coated in the digestive juice of a plant.

Scully searches for Mulder and is also exposed to the spores, whereupon the agents' perception of events deviates. From Mulder's point of view, he finds the dead hikers alive and returns to Washington, D.C. - where he meets a grey alien and has his theories confirmed. But from Scully's point of view, Mulder turns up alive after his skeleton is allegedly found in the woods and a funeral is held.

The agents realise that a giant plant is digesting them, and that the hallucinogenic spores are keeping them docile while this occurs. Fortunately, Skinner finds and rescues his missing agents, getting them medical treatment.

Critique   Last year Vince Gilligan brilliantly showed in Bad Blood how Mulder and Scully reduce themselves to stereotypes for comic effect. This time, writing with John Shiban, he goes one better. Mulder and Scully are both caught in alternate realities designed to make them complacent whilst a fungus digests them alive, and on the surface it's a retread of those Bad Blood themes. Mulder gets to prove the existence of aliens, Scully's rational explanations are celebrated by characters as diverse as Skinner and the Lone Gunmen and parroted back at her. But as they live out their fantasies, it's the fact that both are trying to find the opposing arguments that will shoot down what they believe in - indeed, to resist being those stereotypes - which allows them to see the truth. Mulder gets everything he wants; Duchovny's wonder and pride as he's able to show off a telepathic alien he's been hiding in his bedroom is very touching and has all the innocence of a child whose dreams have come true. But even as he is being presented with all the proof he's ever looked for, he keeps on trying to behave like Scully, to look for the intellectual opposition for something he aches to take for granted. It's only when Scully too accepts, without the rigour he demands of her, the existence of extraterrestrials

that he knows this must be false. Scully, on the other hand, is made to suffer Mulder's death and burial, and gets increasingly paranoid and angry as everyone praises her for deductive conclusions she no longer accepts. She searches instead for the explanation *Mulder* might have come up with. (And in doing so, neatly foreshadows an entire character arc she'll be obliged to play out in Duchovny's absence during Season Eight.)

What's brilliant about this is that Gilligan and Shiban refuse to make the story that neat or simplistic; as in Monday, they take what could have been a comic confection and make it darker and more questing than that. In Bad Blood the joke was that the audience understood that the narrative was skewed; in Field Trip, both Mulder and Scully's visions are presented as clean and credible and only *slightly* off kilter. The upshot of this is that when they escape, and sit in Skinner's office making a report, it's a genuine shock for both of them and for us to realise that the conventional happy ending is just another part of their complacent fantasy - they're still underground, and they're still being eaten. Typically, the story would end with the realisation that Scully and Mulder need a piece of the other's methods to save themselves, but there's nothing so pat here. The pair survive by chance, by the FBI identifying the bile samples that Scully had sent to them at the start of the story. As the two are driven away in the ambulance, they reach and touch for support - but for all the way they fought back, it wasn't their connection that saved them. Field Trip is a story about the unreliability of stories, and in a season where post-modernism rules the day it's the cleverest and most dynamic example of them all, an episode not just wanting to look inward for comic effect. By analysing the characters' realities it's not merely poking fun at the conventions of a long running sci-fi show, but inviting its audience to question the truths around us we take for granted. (*****)

6.22, Biogenesis

Air Date: May 16, 1999
Writers: Chris Carter, Frank Spotnitz
Director: Rob Bowman

Summary   Dr Solomon Merkmallen is elated when a piece of metal with strange symbols is found on the Ivory Coast, as he already possesses one such piece. Merkmallen tries to consult with a fellow researcher, Dr Sandoz, at the American University in Washington, D.C. However, Dr Barnes - the head of the university's biology department - kills Merkmallen.

Skinner tells Mulder and Scully about Merkmallen's unsolved murder. Notably, Merkmallen and Sandoz both believed that life originated elsewhere in the universe, and that cosmic collisions resulted in microbes entering Earth's atmosphere. Skinner gives the agents a carbon rubbing of Merkmallen's artefact, whereupon Mulder's senses become temporarily muddled.

Meanwhile, Dr Sandoz attends to a patient of his - Albert Hosteen (2.25, Anasazi), who's fallen ill. Analysis of the carbon rubbing confirms that the symbols on Merkmallen's fragment are phonetic Navajo. Further exposure to the carbon rubbing makes Mulder more loopy, and he develops a special "sense" that tells him that Barnes killed Merkmallen.

An autopsy suggests that Merkmallen was exposed - via his fragment - to a type of radiation only found beyond the solar system. Sandoz tells the agents that Merkmallen's fragments are part of a larger puzzle, and that Albert was compiling a complete rubbing from them. Together, the fragments seem to spell out a passage from Genesis. Mulder insists that the fragments prove that life on Earth originated from outer space.

Mulder is hospitalised as his condition weakens. Sandoz tells Scully that the letters Albert translated amount to coordinates for the human genome. He implores her to find more fragments - just before Krycek, who's monitoring these events, kills him. Scully travels to the Ivory Coast and locates where Merkmallen found his fragments... only to realise that she's standing atop a buried alien spaceship. [To be continued.]

Critique   With the Syndicate destroyed, this episode was widely touted as the beginning of a fresh new mythology for the show. So why does watching it give such a strong sense of déjà vu? From the ponderous voiceovers, to the discovery of Some Thing which will prove everything within the X-Files. From Skinner being a traitor (and Scully calling him a liar), from the Cigarette Smoking Man and Krycek showing up like proverbial bad pennies. There are Navajo healing rituals - again - there's even a sequence where a man is murdered to the scream of caged monkeys. And, most familiar of all, this is an episode about big ideas and precious little action. Those ideas are not without interest - that Biblical texts may be extraterrestrial in origin - but in hysterical style the implications of this are made to be so cosmic as to change the existence of mankind forever. The truth is, we've been down this path before - and the story so far really amounts to little more than furtive conversations over phones and chases up stairwells.

What has potential is Mulder's insanity, as the discovered artefact causes his brain to operate on higher levels. Whilst Gillian Anderson is given little more to do than look customarily grim and sceptical, Duchovny at least is able to explore something new. It's curious that as Frank Black drives off into the sunset in Millennium, so Fox Mulder inherits something of his condition here. The cliffhanger too is interesting, if only because the revelation that she's standing on top of a bloody UFO must mean that Scully *has* to start believing in something alien when the series returns for its seventh season. And that just maybe the series too will be propelled away from these disappointing murky hints and towards something a little more dramatic. (**)

Millennium: Season 3

3.1, The Innocents

Air Date: Oct. 2, 1998
Writer: Michael Duggan
Director: Thomas J Wright

Summary Months after Catherine's death, Frank and Jordan relocate to Falls Church, Virginia. Eager to bring justice to those who died in the virus outbreak, Frank starts doing consultancy work for the FBI and reports to Assistant Director Andy McClaren. Meanwhile, a tearful passenger aboard an airplane - who resembles one of the stewardesses - finds a pistol in a bathroom. The stewardess takes the weapon from her and fires several shots through the plane, depressurizing it and making it crash.

Frank gets visions of a downed plane, and meets agents Barry Baldwin and Emma Hollis at the crash site. The agents note that the passenger and the stewardess looked very similar, and that they lived in Salt Lake City. Frank goes there and finds another look-alike of the women named Mary. An explosion destroys Mary's house, hospitalising her and killing her daughter.

Mary tells Frank that her sisters and their children were the true target of the contagion that killed Catherine, and gives Frank the address of the last remaining sister and child. Frank and Emma intercept the sister and her offspring, but a car accident leaves the sister's vehicle dangling off a bridge. The sister deliberately plunges, along with her child, to death rather than let the agents touch her daughter. Afterward, Frank sees three men who were watching them drive away. [To be continued]

Critique Let's get this straight from the start. The best way to have followed The Time is Now... would have been *not* to follow The Time is Now. Obviously broadcasting post-apocalyptic static for a season was hardly an option for new showrunners Michael Duggan and Chip Johannessen, who are obliged to find some way to pull the series back from a virus that's wiping out the world's population, and to curb the fan-

tastical excesses that had alienated viewers during the second season. In a way the season premiere has to feel like a series pilot, a new template (yes, another one) for a programme that has clearly strayed from the path Chris Carter had intended.

It's hard to imagine a way this couldn't have been disappointing. But The Innocents is such a tentative affair that it doesn't feel like it's even trying. It's *competent*. That's the best one can say about it - but also the worst, because however misguided a lot of the second season might have been, however pretentious or frustrating, it'd have baulked at being merely competent. At first it feels like a brave decision to open the episode in a recognisably stable society, in which Frank is able to give piggy backs to Jordan; it intrigues us how we got from those closing images of The Time Is Now to something so normal. Then it dawns on you that it may not be intended to be an enigma, and that the change of tone is more like an embarrassed cough. If Morgan and Wong destabilised the show in their season premiere too quickly, then Duggan forces us back into a safe little box too quickly here as well. There's Andy McClaren - an "old friend" of Frank's at the FBI we've never heard of before, and who automatically takes on the character functions of a Bob Bletcher: a supportive sceptic who'll chew Frank out when he goes too far but clearly has no teeth. There's a new partner played well by Klea Scott - but, crucially, she's given no *reason* to be devoted to Frank and follow his lead so determinedly. We're told that Emma knows of his reputation at the Academy; that's lazy - Old Friend Andy knows his reputation too, and still believes Frank's lost his marbles. What the story needed was a moment of brilliance that Frank could have dazzled her with, persuading her to take his side against all others. And we as an audience needed that moment of brilliance too, we need to be dazzled by Frank once more as well. But this is an episode that doesn't deal in brilliance, only blandness.

A plane crashes, a house explodes, a car is run off a bridge. It really shouldn't *be* bland. The

---

action sequences are well staged, but they lack a context. However big the stunt, it's still going to look like small fry compared to where Millennium has just taken us, and so any follow-up might have done better not to have tried to compete. The best moments of the episode, tellingly, are the quiet ones; Catherine's father accuses Frank of running away from confronting the death of his wife. What's unfortunate is that as he says it, you realise it's what the episode is guilty of too. It's already trying to find a way of containing the emotional power of what happened last year, and make it about something else. We're now asked to entertain the idea that the entire devastation was directed at a series of lookalike women we have never heard of before, and it grates. The final act of the episode relies upon Frank's need to save a mother and child from a plot - but we've been given no background to what this plot could be, and no understanding to whom might be putting it into operation. As a result the sequence feels almost random. It's certainly not a climax to what only reveals itself to be the first episode of a two-parter in the closing credits; never before have Ten Thirteen produced an opening to a feature-length adventure that's so casual you're left surprised there's still more to come. (*1/2)

3.2, Exegesis

Air Date: Oct. 9, 1998
Writer: Chip Johannessen
Director: Ralph Hemecker

Summary   Peter Watts appears at FBI Headquarters, consulting on behalf of the Millennium Group. Mary dies after one of the men who was watching Frank tampers with her IV. Emma examines Mary's ruined house, and finds documents pertaining to "Project: Grillflame", a CIA undertaking. The project, she discovers, was intended to employ "remote viewers" who would psychically commit espionage and foresee the future.

One of the most advanced psychics from Grillflame - tagged as "512" - is identified as an older woman who's likely the mother of the targeted siblings. Frank deduces that the Group targeted 512 and her offspring because they could "see" the Group's operations. The sisters arranged the plane crash - to the point of sacri-

ficing two of their own - to fake the death of one of the little girls, thereby protecting her from the Group. Frank and Emma visit 512 at a missile silo in Virginia, but one of the men dogging them - Mobius - appears there. 512 tells Frank that the Group wants to end the world, then disappears. The sole surviving sister confesses to causing the airplane crash, thereby concealing the truth. Afterward, 512 - accompanied by the little girl from the airplane - travels to parts unknown.

Critique   Whenever Millennium tries to change direction, it goes back to default position of aping The X-Files. In the past that's merely been confined to individual stories themselves. (And it's certainly true of this one, as Mulder and Scully - sorry, Frank and Emma - pursue a conspiracy to breed and eliminate a family of psychics.) But before there's always been the indication that this was a result of crisis, not the game plan itself. However, there's evidence here that suggests that the new Millennium framework is adapting The X-Files structure. Frank is back in the FBI, telling his crazy ideas to a young and brilliant female partner, and the two of them get to run down corridors in underground bases waving guns and flashlights. There are sections of this episode which almost look like The X-Files title sequence.

As a story premise, this one is fine X-Files fodder, but has less impact in the world of Millennium. The psychic here is just another Gibson Praise, really, except she isn't as cute because she's an old woman who spends most of her time with a tube down her throat. And in a show in which the lead character is *also* a psychic visionary, what is the big deal about another? (**)

3.3, Teotwawki

Air Date: Oct. 16, 1998
Writers: Chris Carter, Frank Spotnitz
Director: Thomas J Wright

Summary   When an unidentified shooter kills three teens at a high school rally in Seattle, Emma and Barry suspect student Brant Carmody. Brant himself is found dead soon afterward, his father Chris claiming that he committed suicide. Frank deduces that Brant was indeed the high school shooter, and that Brant's family belongs to a collective effort to create a self-sufficient compound as a means of escaping the projected Y2K disaster. The agents secure the compound, and Chris admits to killing his son because had Brandt been convicted of murder, his mother and sisters would have remained in Seattle and been denied the compound's protection.

Critique The premise of the episode seems a little quaint now, that teenagers will be so disillusioned by fear of the Y2K bug that they'll take to killing sprees. But the details are fine, and subtly drawn: the impact upon a community of a high school massacre is very credible and sensitively handled. This is Chris Carter and Frank Spotnitz's first script since Season One, and they adopt a back-to-basics approach that works very well. The millennium here is seen as a realistic threat, tapping into the growing concern that at the stroke of midnight in the year 2000 all technology will crumble. Hysterical as it may now seem, I remember only too well the people at the end of 1999 who were hoarding food and draining their bank accounts just in case civilisation came to an end overnight. Focusing upon the survivalist group here leads to a thoughtful comment about gun control. (And it's great to see Frank, too, at a shooting range as befits FBI requirements, clearly disdainful of his need to carry a weapon.)

And the back-to-basics approach is used on Frank too. There are no visions here, just the deductive strengths of a good detective. It's a great showcase for Lance Henriksen, bringing out all the intelligence of an expert profiler, and obviously enjoying the way he can now play Frank as a reluctant mentor for the eager Emma. It's not a remarkable story, but it's clearly told, and solid, and refreshingly direct. And Thomas J Wright's direction is terrific - the teaser in particular is stunning, depicting high school celebrations in all their oppressive enthusiasm interrupted by terror and chaos. (***)

3.4, Closure

Air Date: Oct. 23, 1998
Writer: Laurence Andries
Director: Daniel Sackheim

Summary Emma searches for Rick, Peter and Jodi, an armed threesome committing an ever-increasing number of pointless murders. Frank examines Emma's FBI file and determines that twenty years ago, she saw a man named Michael Wynter murder her sister. Wynter later killed himself, but every year since, on the anniversary of her sister's death, Emma has requested a homicide case in the hopes of learning why a person might commit such a foul deed.

The police apprehend Jodi, prompting Rick and Peter to take a bus hostage and demand her release. Peter dies in a shootout, but Rick hijacks Emma's car. Emma drives her vehicle into a bridge at high speed - causing Rick, who isn't wearing a seatbelt, to die after being thrown through the windshield.

Critique There's a creditable attempt to give a bit of depth to Emma Hollis, and Klea Scott works hard to mine some sort of truth out of it. But it's very clumsily done: I'm not sure that giving her a traumatic past where as a child she witnessed the brutal murder of her sister really does her any favours. And having her request a case for motiveless killing sprees on every anniversary, in order to ask herself why death has to happen, is hideously contrived. At best it's a bit unprofessional, isn't it? At worst it's terribly cold, using other people's tragedies just to analyse your own. It's the mistake of passing emotional baggage off as character development. The two things are not the same thing whatsoever, and for all the excessive attention Emma is given, this episode actually reduces her credibility. Taking out a psychopath by driving your car into concrete at great speed, and watching him fly through the windscreen, is not the stuff of good investigative methodology.

And if Emma Hollis is overanalysed, so the murderers themselves are given pretty short shrift. To be fair, that's clearly intentional on writer Laurence Andries' part, but just because you intend your characters to be motiveless doesn't make them more compelling, just more shallow. There's a certain amoral swagger to some of the set pieces which is rather fun - the teaser in which Rick kills a neighbour for snoring, for example, or the sequence where a mountain biker is persuaded into the wrong end of a game of William Tell. But it's all diminishing returns: when Emma asks the killer why he'd want to commit such acts, his inability to answer adamantly does *not* reflect some Dostoyevskian moral abyss, but the innate superficiality of the story. We've seen some fairly dull scenarios on Millennium, but none so two-dimensional that it's fobbed off as being the actual *premise* of the episode.

Lance Henriksen is on the sidelines here, standing back like a guru and passing profiling judgement upon his protégée. It's not a good role for Frank Black; we've seen him cool and detached and emotionally spent, but smug doesn't suit him well at all. (*)

3.5, ...Thirteen Years Later

Air Date: Oct. 30, 1998
Writer: Michael R. Perry
Director: Thomas J Wright

Summary   Frank and Emma travel to Trinity, South Carolina, where a director and an actress have been murdered while filming a movie based upon a case that Frank solved thirteen years ago. In rapid succession, a producer, a publicist, several crewmembers and the local sheriff are all found slaughtered. Frank deduces that the killer is patterning the deaths after horror films such as Halloween and Friday the 13th, and that Emma is the next target. Frank arrests the murderer, actor Mark Bianco - who, ironically, is portraying Frank in the film.

Critique   The teaser is rather fun; there's something rather grisly about watching a couple so dispassionate about fictional murder that as they cavort about they drench each other with stage blood. It's so macabre that it feels like a relief when a *real* killer steps in and offs the pair of them. But those opening three minutes say everything that's useful or witty in this contrast between "real" crime and "movie" crime. As a comedy there are some amusing lines, but the whole concept drowns in overkill. Frank Black

finds out that a movie is being made of a crime he investigated thirteen years previously, and he's to be one of the main characters; had the movie been an attempt at something *good*, and a real dichotomy between truth and fictional plausibility been set up, this could have been very funny and revealing. Hollywood makes many a film based upon true events, and for the sake of dramatic licence distorts events to make them more artificially acceptable - it does not, in itself, mean that all people who work in the movie industry are sleazy morons with the integrity of gnats. Everyone involved in the movie made in this episode is a caricature of self-obsession, from the ingénue who sees the real-life murders only as a means of acquiring a bigger role, to the local sheriff who only cares about the money that the film company is bringing his town and who's prepared to accept a confession so fabricated that even the supposed killer doesn't know what weapon he's supposed to have used. When the characters are as unreal as this, it means that the comedy has nothing to say. And so it isn't very funny.

As with his previous script, The Mikado, Perry shows signs of wanting to comment upon the voyeuristic nature of crime, and even to comment upon Millennium itself. There are hints of something clever here, where Frank is revealed carrying a gun which is against his character, as if he too is being reduced to a movie stereotype. And the way at the end that Emma is identified as being the story's heroine, not the lead actress, blurs the fiction and the fiction within the fiction. But it's crassly done; Emma reading Borges in the bath does not make this metatextual, it just makes it pretension gone awry. That Frank and Emma try to solve the case by watching horror movies is a funny idea, but only demonstrates that the likes of Halloween or Friday the 13th are engaging and suspenseful in a way that this clumsy farrago of in-jokes can never be. By the end of the tale, in which we've seen Frank deliver a talk to FBI personnel always with his back turned, you're hoping that the surprise twist will be anything *but* his turning around to reveal it's only the actor playing his part after all. When the gimmicks are as badly done as they are here, it all becomes predictable.

And the cameo from Kiss is just bizarre. (*)

3.6, Skull and Bones

Air Date: Nov. 6, 1998
Writers: Chip Johannessen, Ken Horton
Director: Paul Shapiro

Summary After a body is recovered in Fingus, Maine, Assistant Director Andy McClaren shares several letters with Frank that mention the town and relate details pertaining to a series of murders. Frank discovers that the letter-writer, a man named Ed, kept journals about the victims - the last being Cheryl Andrews (2.8, The Hand of Saint Sebastian). The journals suggest that Ed isn't the killer, but that he witnessed the first murder and identified forty-two related deaths through newspaper accounts.

Frank concludes that the Millennium Group is behind the killings, prompting Ed to escape before the Group can murder him. Emma identifies the house where the killings took place, but it's bulldozed to the ground as Peter tells her that forty-three "threats" to the stability of the United States have been eliminated.

Critique There's a brooding paranoia to this which suggests that the third season may at last be hitting a groove and start to be *about* something. The tension to key scenes is terrific: Emma uncovering a skull in the mud as an unseen Peter Watts approaches her from behind, or the wonderful sequence where Emma explores the house in which so many Millennium Group executions have taken place, and finds herself unable to cope with her own fears and revulsion.

Reinventing Peter Watts - yet again - as a dangerous foe feels a bit like the producers are squandering the work of Terry O'Quinn in the last few episodes of Season Two, where he credibly played the character as one learning to question his faith in the Group. But O'Quinn is very good here, at his most chilling when he's attempting to sound reasoned and plausible. (Reinventing Cheryl Andrews as victim rather than traitor is much more problematic, but it is at least good to see CCH Pounder again.) All the intrigue and atmosphere go a long way to disguise the fact that nothing really *happens* in the episode, and that nothing major is learned - if

the Millennium Group hadn't been established as a menace after unleashing a plague that made Catherine Black sweat blood, then poking around a mass grave isn't going to make much more impact. But the skill here is the way that Frank is sidelined, so that the story becomes more about Emma and her brush with the Group and its seductive charm. It's telling that this works so much better without Frank, whose character has now become so bogged down with baggage and misdirection, that it requires someone new to give the story a fresh spin. It's to be hoped that this spurs a new direction for Millennium; Johannessen and Horton's tight script does much to excite that possibility. (***1/2)

3.7, Through a Glass Darkly

Air Date: Nov. 13, 1998
Writer: Patrick Harbinson
Director: Thomas J Wright

Summary A man named Max Brunelli, who was convicted of murdering a girl named Mary Flanagan in Oregon, 1979, is granted parole. Soon after, Brunelli becomes the chief suspect when a girl named Shannon McNulty goes missing. Frank deduces that Randie Jarret - Brunelli's attorney - killed Mary and kidnapped Shannon, and has been endowing Brunelli with false memories to cover his crimes. Shannon is saved, Jarret is arrested and Brunelli resumes life in the community.

Critique This borrows a little from Sacrament, and a little from The Well-Worn Lock - a tale of a community's rage against a paroled child killer, and of a family dealing with an abusive parent. And even though it's familiar, it's rather better than either of them. Ironically it's because it doesn't try as hard, not going for extra emotional weight or clumsy earnestness, just telling an interesting story clearly and simply. Thomas J Wright's direction is stylish and effective, and Tom McCleister is smashing as Brunelli - he's hulking and menacing, then sweet and sympathetic, and yet never cheats the audience by trying to lead them to feel one thing or the other.

At first this sets up an interesting debate

about returning convicts to society, and about the dangers of recidivism. It's clearly a moral grey area how we should treat convicted killers, and Ten Thirteen have made rather a habit of suggesting they're irredeemable - right from the first season of The X-Files, we were invited to see that the board who released Eugene Tooms to the world were morons worthy of having their livers eaten. Whilst the story still supposes that Brunelli is a paedophile, the scenes which show the hatred he must endure after twenty years of incarceration are very unsettling, and it's telling that although Frank is keen to avoid a witch hunt, he too speaks out against Brunelli's freedom. I can't help but feel, though, that by revealing that Brunelli was a simple patsy who never committed any crimes in the first place that the story takes itself out of any useful discussion: how much more interesting might it have been had the police been forced to apologise for their persecution towards a genuine child molester? By making him a man so gullible that he was persuaded to believe himself a murderer, he's turned into a holy fool - and it's *easy* to love holy fools, so the audience is let off the hook and permitted to like him without qualms. When he's knocked down by a car, trying to save the life of an innocent, it feels that writer Patrick Harbinson is laying on the sympathy rather too thickly; by the time teenage girls are leaving baskets of fruit on his doorstep and waving at him fondly the story's lost all pretence of objectivity altogether.

To be fair to Through a Glass Darkly, it makes no such pretence. It offers a good, clean detective story, the likes of which you could find on a dozen police series. It's only a shame that, in this season, we should feel grateful for something that has no ambitions beyond competence. (***)

3.8, Human Essence

Air Date: Dec. 11, 1998
Writer: Michael Duggan
Director: Thomas J Wright

Summary Emma travels to Vancouver when her half-sister Tamra sees her heroin-using roommate briefly transform into a reptilian monster. With Frank's help, Emma determines that Wing Ho - a chemist employed by the Hong Kong tri-ads - was left deformed by his work and tainted several heroin batches to expose his employers' operation. The dealers squelch the evidence, burning down a warehouse full of heroin with Ho inside. Afterward, Frank discovers that the metamorphic substance in the heroin was an artificial hormone designed by the US Army six years ago.

Critique This is trying to be different. Gritty and urban and *real*, showing us a view of life on the streets with drug dealers and addicts and pimps. It's a determinedly ugly episode, in which the violence always goes on that bit too long (and leaves scars), and in which everyone seems brutal and harsh. By taking Emma out of the FBI, acting on her own and away from Frank's influence, pursuing an agenda to clear her name from heroin charges and to save her junkie sister, the story gives her a chance to come into her own properly and emerge as a forceful character.

But if you want to do real, then it's probably best done free from a concept too fantastical to be believed: drugs that turn people into monsters. Literally. If it were metaphorical monsters we were talking about, then that would be fine, of course - but when Frank Black asks for toxicology reports that show any chemicals that can alter physical form, you can tell we're out of Millennium country altogether and somewhere back in the heartlands of The X-Files. And that's something which is strangely emphasised when, prowling around a tenement building, Emma faces a broadcast of Kill Switch; it only serves to remind us how much more fun this silliness might be if Mulder and Scully were involved. Since it's Black and Hollis, however, the episode is clearly uncertain of its tone and how monstrous to make the monster, and it settles unhappily on doing nothing with the concept. What we're left with is a story which lurches about with Millennium earnestness pursuing a storyline so ridiculous, it's trying to avoid *looking* at it, and as a result it's extremely dull to watch. The scenes are long and slow and the drama is lost in the murk.

It's far from dreadful. Klea Scott gives her best performance yet, and her Emma shows an anger and resourcefulness which lifts the story. Typically, as in Closure, whenever Emma takes centre stage, the writers are unsure how to write

Frank. Here he's a jobsworth, and is strangely unsympathetic towards Tamra's drug horrors. And then in the final reel he becomes action hero, carrying the aforementioned junkie in his arms out of an inferno. Neither role suits him very well, and Lance Henriksen once again gives a performance which suggests that he too doesn't know what to do with Frank any longer. (**)

3.9, Omerta

Air Date: Dec. 18, 1998
Writer: Michael R Perry
Director: Paul Shapiro

Summary   In Coker Creek, Vermont, a man named Al Ryan is found wandering dazed, claiming an animal mauled him to death. Frank explores the nearby woods and happens upon Eddie Giannini, a mob hitman who was executed by his fellows in 1989. Both Ryan and Giannini, it transpires, were miraculously healed by two women - Rose and Lhasa - who live in a cave.

Giannini's return voids the convictions of his killers, and weakens the government's case against the Santo crime family. The mobsters realize that Rose and Lhasa can testify about the hitmen's attack on Giannini and move to eliminate them - but Giannini and the women elude capture, and take up peaceful living in a cabin.

Critique   This is madder than a box of frogs. For the second time this season, Michael R Perry gets to write a comedy episode - and, like ...Thirteen Years Later, this isn't particularly funny. But it's a heart-warming charmer nonetheless, a Christmas fable about redemption and second chances. The premise is utterly preposterous: a couple of uncivilised girls who live in a forest have the ability to resurrect the dead. They bring back to life a mob hitman, who gamely wants to atone for his sins by confessing to the murders he's committed, and protect these angels of mercy from gangland reprisals when he does so.

And really, that's it. Jon Polito gives a sensational performance as Eddie, the mobster who literally comes to life a new man ("Don't call me

Scarpino"); it's not only gorgeously amiable (his benign and teasing confession to the police is lovely), but touching and moving as he fears that he's endangered the lives of the girls who've saved his. His are the best scenes, and that causes a slight problem. The sequence where he and Frank discuss how they both wish things could be the way they used to be, and Eddie listens to Frank talk about the loss of his family, is beautiful and rightly emphasises the Blacks' grief in this first Christmas without Catherine. (Jordan's own story here is heartbreaking, as without tears or angst she misses her mother, wraps her a present, and hopes that like Eddie she might be resurrected.) But Polito is *so* good that he overshadows the Blacks' story; the long scene where he offers new life to the hitman who executed him is so strong that it dominates the last act.

And, ultimately, it's in that last act that the episode fumbles. It doesn't have an ending. The final scene, in which Eddie has escaped with Rose and Lhasa to a picture card cottage, is just too ambiguous: it's unclear whether they're in heaven after their getaway ambulance exploded, or whether their faked their deaths as a clever ruse. Now, I'm all for ambiguity. But because Omerta so freely changes the rules of the show's reality, it's impossible to work out quite what's at stake by the conclusion. It still manages to charm. But it's a fairly quizzical sort of charm you feel; you want to watch the closing credits with a delighted smile, but it's tempered somewhat by the puzzled frown distorting it. The joy of fables, in the end, is their "once upon a time" simplicity. This fable needed just a bit more clarity at the "happily ever after".

That said (and despite a score by Mark Snow so winsome it leaves your teeth smarting), this is the cheeriest Millennium episode ever made. It's a measure of where the show is at this stage of its run - and perhaps an indictment of it - that it could pull it off. The upside of the third season feeling so nebulous and inconsequential is that bold experiments with the form can be accepted so easily. (****)

3.10, Borrowed Time

Air Date: Jan. 15, 1999
Writer: Chip Johannessen
Director: Dwight Little

Summary Frank deduces that two women who drowned when water spontaneously manifested in their lungs had previously cheated death in some capacity - either by surviving a fatal disease, or miraculously walking away from a car accident. A third victim is found, and it becomes evident that a man named Samiel - an avatar of death - has been causing the murders so that other people can make use of the extra time that the victims were accorded. Frank discovers that Samiel wants to claim Jordan - who survived a bout of meningitis years ago - and implores him to spare her. Samiel is moved to place himself aboard a train that's fated to crash into a river, intentionally drowning so that Jordan can live.

Critique For a while Chip Johannessen's tour de force doesn't even pretend to hide its X-Files influences. People are drowning on dry land, and only Frank can see the connection between them - that they all survived near-death experiences - whilst Emma as his sceptical partner looking for scientific rationale and protecting him denies FBI protocol. It's a terrific premise too, one that Glen Morgan and James Wong later used in their Final Destination movie franchise. But it's all the more eerie here than on the big screen, helped by a great performance from Eric Mabius as Samiel, the thin smiling man who so compassionately robs his victims of life. There are creepy symbolic wristwatches being used at every juncture, and an increasingly weird story structure which flips between Frank's investigations and the fate of four train passengers heading towards disaster. It's the most disconcerting thing we've seen on Millennium all season, and it's fantastic.

This is a wonderful puzzle box of a story, which suddenly steps up a gear when Jordan is taken sick and becomes one of Death's intended. Brittany Tiplady was nominated for an award for her feisty portrayal here of a scared little girl who is dying. But it's Lance Henriksen who impresses, giving a full throttled performance of grief and anger and fear after half a season of barely stretching his acting muscles. It's as if he's been let off his reins at last; the sequences where he turns in frustration on the priest who's reading Jordan her last rites, or confronts Samiel in the street to demand why he's stalking his daughter, are electrifying. The script *demands* that Henriksen be this good - he has to be good enough that when he pleads for Jordan in a prayer so agonised and confused it almost makes you embarrassed for him, that the grim reaper himself sacrifices his life so that Frank's daughter can keep hers.

Beautifully directed by Dwight Little, it's visually one of the most striking episodes in Millennium's run - the little girl watching with ever growing suspicion as she spies Death out of the train window, then staring in bemusement as he drowns in front of her; the fantastic scene in which a woman filming her son on a park roundabout becomes witness to a stranger in the near distance coughing up water. But what really makes this story sing is that it has such enormous heart. And the reason that ultimately it's a Millennium episode rather than an X-File is that it's all about one man who's lost *everything* except his daughter, and as bruised as he is somehow keeps his emotions reined in, at last fighting back with animal pain when even that is to be taken from him. Borrowed Time is a thing of beauty, which restores to Millennium a soul and passion it has been missing for quite a while. (*****)

3.11, Collateral Damage

Air Date: Jan. 22, 1999
Writer: Michael R Perry
Director: Thomas J Wright

Summary Two assailants kidnap Peter's daughter Taylor, prompting Frank to investigate a larger conspiracy. Millennium Group operatives kill one of the abductors, David Couger, who served in the military with Eric Swan, the other kidnapper. Swan reveals that during the Gulf War, he was ordered to deploy a biological weapon against US troops - a test of the weapon's effectiveness against inoculated soldiers - thereby killing his platoon. Swan wants to pressure Peter into admitting that the Group, not the government, sent the order. Peter capitulates, telling Swan details about the weapon's deployment. Taylor, however, ends the standoff by snapping Swan's neck.

Critique   This is magnificent, a story that asks big moral questions of Frank and his relationship with the Millennium Group. What's so clever about it is that it wrongfoots expectations by making us concentrate on Peter Watts' own ethical dilemma. When Peter's daughter is abducted, and the kidnapper only wants information about Millennium, how can he put the organisation before his family? The irony is not lost, of course, that it's the very question that Frank was asked by Catherine throughout the second season. And then, halfway through the episode, in an attempt to locate the kidnapper by keeping him talking on the telephone, Frank clearly changes sides. He suddenly sees that this man, who has infected an innocent girl with a lethal virus and is watching her suffer and die, is wanting the same things he does, that he too is wanting to expose the same truth. And an episode which was so quick to pronounce judgement upon Peter now portrays Frank as a man so desperate to get to the heart of what killed his wife that he's willing to make an ally of someone using the very same thing as a bargaining chip. When Eric Swan asks Frank bluntly why he hasn't tried to bring down the Millennium Group before, it suddenly exposes our hero as a man who's frittered away his anger, who simply isn't as worthy a freedom fighter as he should be. And it pulls us up short.

It's an excellent script by Michael R Perry, one which constantly challenges the viewer to change their perspectives on the characters and with whom they sympathise. And that's helped enormously by a sincere performance by James Marsters as Eric, whose methods to bring to justice a conspiracy are obsessive and appalling, but who still emerges as the character with the greatest integrity in the episode. The conclusion the story reaches is utterly *right*, too, that after all the jostling between Frank and Peter, that neither of them get to confront Eric: instead Taylor Watts fights back against expectation and refuses to play simple victim. Jacinda Barrett is excellent as Peter's daughter, who even when bleeding to death remains an active part of the debates which make up the story. Her growth

from being terrified and helpless, through being reasoning and brave, to finally taking command of her own life and setting herself free, is one of the joys of the episode.

It's a relief at last to see Millennium dealing with the consequences of the second season. And not only the virus that killed Catherine, but at a more fundamental level, with where Morgan and Wong took the Millennium Group and where that left Frank's character as a result. Nothing in the second season approaches that central theme of what the series has now become with as much clarity or intelligence as shown here. (*****)

3.12, The Sound of Snow

Air Date: Feb. 5, 1999
Writer: Patrick Harbinson
Director: Paul Shapiro

Summary   Two Seattle residents perish after receiving audiotapes that seem to contain only white noise - but cause the recipients to hallucinate about the things they fear most, facilitating fatal accidents. Frank receives similar cassettes that induce visions of Catherine. He goes to the cabin where she died, while Emma backtracks the tapes to a duplicating studio managed by Alice Severin. Catherine's spirit tells Frank that she didn't die alone as he believed, but that he was by her side. Emma locates Frank, who concludes that Severin has a great power that the Millennium Group made use of in distributing the tapes. But whatever the Group's motive in sending out the tapes, Frank's memories of Catherine's death have returned.

Critique   Hallucinatory episodes have always had something of a chequered history at Ten Thirteen, frequently pushing the stories into pretension, and big character moments which turn out to be anything but. Millennium, though, has acquired a lot of baggage over the past year with its apocalyptic season finale; last week Collateral Damage gave it a nuts and bolts reappraisal, and this dreamlike instalment acts as a fitting epilogue. It's great to see Catherine Black once more, now purging Frank of the guilt he feels for her death, and providing a real closure to her character - having been the bland wife of the first season, and the bitter harridan of the second, it's affecting here to see her as someone more interesting than either, and who can be loving and forgiving. This new series has rewritten the past several times already, but never so effectively as here, with Catherine correcting Frank's memories of her dying alone to something less bleak and more redemptive. That he held her whilst she died, mirrored here by the way her ghost holds him as he freezes from exposure in the woods, is extremely moving.

To get Frank into this situation, the story grinds its gears horribly. Frank believes that someone is sending subliminal messages of guilt and regret within the white noise on cassette tapes. Knowing this, he nevertheless plays his own tape whilst driving a car, and doesn't seem remotely concerned about the risks he therefore runs to others. Had Frank played the tape as an act of passion, needing to confront his wife once more, then that might not have mattered. But it's typical of a story which is less interested in the mechanics of a story than in its greater themes. The investigation into a woman who sends out these killer tapes is very garbled, so that we're never sure of her motives or even if she's aware of what she's doing - it's not helped by a performance by Jessica Tuck that borders on the criminally arch. And The Sound of Snow is so in love with its imagery that it sometimes drowns story sense within it; Frank seeing Catherine at the yellow house is beautifully filmed, but lacks logic, and lessens the impact of the moment when he opens himself up to encountering her properly in the woods. And a scene in which Alice Severin seems hypnotised by a stranger smoking a cigarette in a bar is so left field, it's baffling.

But it's all so well directed - the entire teaser, in which a girl comes to believe she's driving through a snow storm, is one of the finest Ten Thirteen has ever presented, strange and haunting and beautiful. And Patrick Harbinson's script has an emotional power that packs quite a punch. If at the end of the day this is an episode that skips upon the details, the larger picture it paints is still a treat. (****)

3.13, Antipas

Air Date: Feb. 12, 1999
Writers: Chris Carter, Frank Spotnitz
Director: Thomas J Wright

Summary   Frank and Emma look into the deaths of legal professionals who dealt with murder cases. Frank finds a word clue - "antipas", an allusion to Satan from Revelation - at one of the crime scenes. He also discovers that his nemesis, Lucy Butler, is working as a nanny for the family of John Saxum - Wisconsin attorney general and gubernatorial candidate.

Frank matches a footprint of Saxum's daughter Divina with that of Butler's dead child. Butler's attorney declares that Butler was raped, and insists that Frank take a paternity test. The long-haired man (2.20, A Room With a View) kills Saxum, then pursues Emma as she flees with Divina. Frank drives his car over the long-haired man, who turns into Butler. She's hospitalised, then tells Frank that their baby died, that "all men" come to her in time, and that they could rule the world together. Frank tells Butler that Divina is safe from her, but Butler replies that Frank should be fearful for Jordan's safety.

Critique   The introduction of Lucy Butler was so effective because the very nature of her evil was a surprise; in a series used to presenting killers as something explicable but banal, her almost elemental nature changed the tone of the show. When she returned the year later it was in a story that came at evil from a different perspective, as something which wanted to celebrate in the mediocre and the unfulfilled. It was a sequel so independent, it even refused to have a scene in which Frank encountered his old nemesis. Frank gets to meet Lucy Butler an awful lot in Antipas - they even get to have sex in some weird nightmare sequence - and although Henriksen and Sarah-Jane Redmond share a crackling chemistry on screen, the result is curiously tepid.

The reason for that is that Lucy Butler's evil here is the stuff of any popular horror movie. There's a lot of The Shining, there's a lot of The Omen, there's a sprinkling of Rosemary's Baby - even lesser shockers like The Hand that Rocks the Cradle gets a look in. It's very well directed, and has some great set pieces - but the whole thing feels like a melange rather than a story in its own right. As something amoral and persuasive Lucy is a frightening character; as the harbinger of every horror trope you can shake a stick at, someone who can summon wolves, seduce the unwary and grow horns, she becomes safe and identifiable. Chris Carter and Frank Spotnitz have written an enjoyable confection of scares and thrills, but it's so frenetic a story that it never develops any of its ideas. Lucy inveigles her way into a mansion to possess a couple's daughter and take her as her own. She also comes to Frank in a dream, gets pregnant by him, and accuses him of rape - something too fascinating to be reduced to a throwaway subplot. And then there's the repeated meme of the word "antipas", echoing a similar device in The Curse of Frank Black, and then there's the way that Lucy can transform herself into a man when she's out for murder or into Frank when she wants to deceive. And then there's more... much much more. And, somehow, much less too. Because the whole concoction gets so diluted that any ingredient loses its flavour.

There's a style and a pace to this which make it a fan favourite, and it's great to see a season that's had so little energy now have tons to spare. And it's hard to write off a story, let's face it, which opens with a little girl being devoured by a snake. (**1/2)

3.14, Matryoshka

Air Date: Feb. 19, 1999
Writers: Erin Maher, Kay Reindl
Director: Arthur Forney

Summary Frank, Emma and Baldwin investigate the suicide of Michael Lanyard, a former FBI agent. In 1945, Lanyard tried to solve the murder of Dr Carew, a physicist. Lanyard encountered Dr Alexander and his daughter Natalie, and found that Alexander could somehow transform into a savage criminal named Warren Kroll. A scuffle led to Alexander's death, and Natalie grew up to become a member of the Millennium Group.

Frank concludes that Alexander wondered how men of good conscience could create something as destructive as the atomic bomb,

experimenting on plutonium until it split his personality. Peter tells Frank that Lanyard declined membership in the Group, turning down a personal invite from J Edgar Hoover. Frank realises that Lanyard killed himself upon learning that Natalie was engaged in biological research, horrified that she was repeating her father's mistakes. Peter agrees to Frank's request that Natalie be given her father's journal pages, enabling her to know the full implications of her work.

Critique David Fredericks becomes the second actor to play the same part in both The X-Files and Millennium, reprising his role of J Edgar Hoover here, having portrayed the notorious director of the FBI in Travelers the year before. And Matryoshka has a lot in common with Travelers, both being rather murky exposes of the FBI's early years. Here Hoover's linked to yet another dubious conspiracy; he was one busy feller. There are some interesting things here about the development of the atomic bomb, and the way that in one moment Man had taken from God the means for apocalypse - there's a particularly touching scene where Barbara Bain, playing a mental patient, tells with nostalgia of a time when the concept of armageddon simply wasn't in our heads. At its core this is a reinvention of Stevenson's Jekyll and Hyde, with a nuclear scientist literally becoming a monster; as he acts out the amorality of a society that can develop the means of world extinction, he loses his own humanity.

It's a great idea too tentatively approached. Stevenson had more fun with the concept, and clearly enjoyed the terrors of his Mr Hyde - whereas writers Erin Maher and Kay Reindl seem to find it all rather too distasteful and shy away from it. What they give us instead is a return to the rather tedious agenda of the Millennium Group, and Frank and Peter's animosity towards each other. Haven't we been here already? The 1940s setting is well evoked, but we don't see enough of it, and Millennium squanders its chance to glory in a new setting. Rather a passionless and cold affair, Matryoshka has a lot of intelligence, but not enough clarity. (**)

3.15, Forcing the End

Air Date: March 19, 1999
Writer: Marjorie David
Director: Thomas J Wright

Summary   Jeanie Borenstine, the pregnant wife of a cardiologist, is kidnapped in Brooklyn. A man named Moses Gourevitch and a nurse named Rachel Levinson deliver Jeanie's baby son Max, whereupon Jeanie is returned mysteriously to her home. Frank and Emma realise that Jeanie's abductors belong to a Jewish cult that wants to build a "Third Temple" - a foretold act that will bring about the Messiah's return. Max hails from a long line of priests and is intended to welcome the Messiah to Earth one day. Frank and Emma track the conspirators to a disused Russian bathhouse; Gourevitch tries to escape with Max, but falls to his death. Emma returns Max to his parents, and Frank realises that Peter secretly aided them in thwarting Gourevitch's scheme, preventing the cult from triggering the end times.

Critique   The usually excellent Andreas Katsulas comes adrift in this, playing a Jewish fundamentalist who kidnaps a baby in order to turn it into a priest that can accelerate the end of the world. He'll achieve this mostly, it would seem, by not letting this baby touch the ground. The climax of the story, in which he flaps around waving the infant on a rooftop, only to impale himself on a convenient spike, is so silly it achieves a kitsch brilliance quite accidentally.

And let's not get this wrong - Katsulas is still the best thing about this terrible episode. It's so very solemn and po-faced, all the FBI milling about taking the Revelations prophecy seriously, and not one single person suggesting this is a specious load of old hogwash. Lance Henriksen looks as if he's sleepwalking through the whole thing, his rasping voice brought down to a whisper as if he cannot quite bring himself to say his terrible lines. And the story moves at such a tremendously slow pace you only wish you could speed time up and force the end yourself. This is Millennium at its very worst - pompous and obscure and filled with people muttering one moment about the Millennium Group and the next about Biblical passages, as if either one of them were in themselves any

more important than the fate of a child. Inhuman, a little racist, and very very dull - this season has certainly seen some stinkers but none quite as poor as this. (*)

3.16, Saturn Dreaming of Mercury

Air Date: April 9, 1999
Writers: Jordan Hawley, Chip Johannessen
Director: Paul Shapiro

Summary   When Jordan's empathic abilities draw her attention to a young boy named Lucas Sanderson, she also sees his father Will as evil. Simultaneously, Jordan starts conversing with an invisible friend / protector named Simon, who once lived in Phoenix. Frank notes the similarity to the unsolved murder of Mrs Simon, a pregnant Phoenix resident.

Frank sneaks inside the Sanderson home but is attacked from behind, then awakens to find it on fire. Will perishes while trying to rescue Lucas, who declares, in a demonic voice, "Who's stronger, Frank? Me, or you?" From outside the blaze, Frank and Jordan both see Lucas' face horrifyingly transform into that of Lucy Butler. Afterward, Emma tells Frank that Mrs Simon's dead baby, who was never born, was named Lucas.

Critique   Brittany Tiplady gives an outstanding performance in a story which centres upon Jordan and her growing conviction that a new neighbour is a demon. She shows more range than she's ever been required to prove before, and it's a testament to how sincere is her portrayal that throughout the violent outbursts and the sulky truculence she remains fully likeable and sympathetic. Lance Henriksen and Klea Scott clearly enjoy the change in tone as well, Frank here playing more an anxious father than an FBI investigator, and Emma's awkward attempt to bond with Jordan in her bedroom is the highlight of the episode. Indeed, it's when the story is being so domestic and ordinary that it's at its best, the slow pace making Jordan's distress and Frank's concern all the more credible.

And that's why, when the story becomes a meditation upon evil that it has such an impact; after many episodes which have felt a mite hysterical or clichéd, this one does better by being so low key. Jordan's own childlike arrogance that she can easily distinguish between good and evil is very revealing - she has something of Frank's gift, but nothing of the maturity she needs to question it, or to be affected by its power as she should. That she mistakes the source of the evil, not spotting it comes from a child the same age as her, is at the heart of this: Lucas talks as an adult, and that's shocking, because he has none of the innocence which makes Jordan fallible but also so very human. Writers Jordan Hawley and Chip Johannessen do something very clever with Jordan Black here; it'd be too easy for the series to portray her now as a psychic freak, but they emphasise that for all her supernatural gifts she's also a naïve little girl.

At the end of the day, the revelation of the little boy devil is better in theory than in execution - once a child shows he's evil because his voice reverberates, a lot of the story's subtlety is lost. But the final image of him at the burning window, his face contorting into the face of Lucy Butler, is chilling. And although the point of view shots from the rack of glass eyes are never explained, they're wonderfully macabre. Ultimately a small-scale story about a child's growing pangs gets a bit unstuck when in the final act it takes on bigger themes of inexplicable evil, and its final vagueness is a little disappointing. But up to that point this is one of the most interesting of the Season Three episodes, well written and very well performed. And special mention must be given to Gabrielle Rose, who takes a minor role as the neighbourhood welcome representative, and suggests a real pang of lonely despair in her eagerness to please. (****)

3.17, Darwin's Eye

Air Date: April 16, 1999
Writer: Patrick Harbison
Director: Ken Fink

Summary A young woman named Cassie Doyle - who was convicted for decapitating her father in 1992 - escapes from an asylum where she's believed to have cut the head off an orderly, Roger Cheveley. Doyle happens across Deputy Joe McNulty and convinces him of her innocence. McNulty helps her evade capture, and the two of them have sex in a hotel.

Frank determines that Cassie was raped by both her father and Cheveley - and cut their heads off to "blind" them. Tracking Cassie down, Frank finds that she's decapitated McNulty - while claiming that she would never hurt him - and arrests her. Meanwhile, Emma realises that her father - who is stricken with Alzheimer's disease - is losing more and more of his mental faculties.

Critique Agent Billy Baldwin has been one of the least interesting additions to the Millennium series. Peter Outerbridge is a good actor and deserves rather better than being this show's Jeffrey Spender, only showing up to sneer at Frank and Emma and to approach each case with the bluntness of a mallet. Here, though, he is proved absolutely right, in an episode which cleverly reverses all of our expectations. He complains that the profiling method is passé and simplistic, he asks whether there's any true relevance to all the details of volcanic eruptions and military insignia found written on an escaped mental patient's wall. We are so prepared in this series to find clues within everything, to find conspiracy at each complex turn. And yet, right from the smart opening narration, writer Patrick Harbinson warns us about reading too much into the interconnectedness of events, talking instead about the evolutionary blind alley of Darwin's eye. That is, something which cannot have evolved, and must have occurred through random chance. Random chance is against everything Millennium stands for - it's too thick and obvious and dumb. And it denies the importance of a climax, of the millennium itself having any particular significance whatsoever. As Cass suggests, things may end badly, but not because of any higher purpose.

Harbinson so cleverly sets up the clichés - the government conspiracy which may have found a scapegoat in the cover-up of a spy's murder, the escaped convict who needs to prove her innocence - and the craft of the episode is such that if those clichés were given substance, the story would still be entertaining. The love story between Cass and Joe is very touching and very true: Joe is seduced by Cass' gentleness and her own convictions that she's the victim of a plot - and so are we. That she *is* a killer, as all the evidence suggested, and murders Joe even as she loves him, feels like a violation of our trust as well. Tracy Middendorf plays Cass with such sweet sincerity that even as she's holding her dead lover's head, and still claiming she isn't responsible for his murder, you're still trying to believe her. There's a replay of a shock moment from the early X-Files episode Conduit, when Frank and Emma realise that all the same writing on the wall is a mosaic of a face - but it's so much more effective here. And that's because it reveals Cass' utter self-obsession, it shows us that the details *are* irrelevant and that Billy Baldwin's bigger cruder theories are true after all. It's a measure of how good this story is, and how we treasure the developing intimacy between Cass and Joe - the first hand holding, the first kiss - that we still want the hoary clichés of a weaker script to be maintained.

In the way that Darwin's Eye effectively takes Millennium and its themes and shows them how overelaborate they are - Baldwin's assertion that Frank's methods have had their day is only too telling as we near the series' cancellation - it'd be easy for the story to feel cold or cynical. But the love story, however much it's built upon lies and madness, is touchingly real; and the love between Emma and her father is just as tragic and affecting. The image of a man turning a picture of his dead daughter's face into paper flowers, only too acutely aware that he is losing his mind, becomes a subtle comment upon the despairing sweetness played out in the main plot. (*****)

3.18, Bardo Thodol

Air Date: April 23, 1999
Writers: Virginia Stock, Chip Johannessen
Director: Thomas J Wright

Summary   Dr Steven Takahashi flees to a Buddhist temple and falls ill, his skin blistering. Elsewhere, Takahasi's tip-off enables Emma to find a case with five severed human hands packed in ice - which are growing new cells. Frank locates Takahashi, a Millennium Group member who escaped upon learning the dark extent of the Group's work. Takahashi dies, and

Frank uses a red lacquered bowl in Takahashi's possession as part of a cremation ceremony for him.

Critique   There are some interesting ideas in this. The concept of biochemistry as new alchemy is a good one, and comes complete with the genuinely macabre image of living hands within an icebox. And it ties in well to the sense of technologies passing and becoming redundant - Peter Watts' speculation upon the way red lacquered bowls in Japan, designed specifically to reflect candlelight, have become a dead art with the advent of electricity.

But concepts do not a sound episode make, and Bardo Thodol is so lost within its own obscurity and inconclusiveness that it never sparks. There's the potential here for powerful scenes; Emma is required to betray Frank and enter into confidences against him, Frank confronts a Millennium hitman. But both pass with a lack of consequence that is frustrating. And it says something that in a showdown with Peter Watts, the one thing that Emma can say to get his attention is when she calls him "Bald Man". This isn't moral debating on a particularly intellectual level.

The Tibetan mysticism and preparations for death are no doubt finely observed, but when Frank himself is required to change his character so that he acts as a Buddhist priest, it's a sign this has all got rather pretentious. The chanting from Huun-Huur-Tu is beautiful, mind you. (*1/2)

3.19, Seven and One

Air Date: April 30, 1999
Writers: Chris Carter, Frank Spotnitz
Director: Peter Markle

Summary   When Frank receives Polaroids that have been doctored to make it look as though he's under water, he tells Emma about an incident from his youth in which a young boy drowned. A home intruder snaps photographs of Frank, making him increasingly paranoid.

Frank deduces that someone has been tormenting him using information gleaned from his therapy sessions. The shapeshifting Mabius, having taken the form of an FBI agent, murders Frank's therapist to cover his tracks. Frank saves

Emma when an assailant tries to bury her alive. Emma later goes to Frank's house, arriving as Frank finds himself trapped in the bathroom - which is flooding - and is confronted by her doppelganger, who shoots herself. Frank perceives the bathroom door giving way, then opens his eyes to find the house dry. The corpse of the ersatz Emma disappears.

Critique For the first half-hour this is fascinating, a story that promises to explore Frank Black's paranoias and ask how anyone can cope living inside the heads of madmen for so long. That's an exciting premise - what if Frank could no longer be sure of what's real or what's simply his own imaginings, what if Frank's gift is the delusion of a nervous breakdown? We get tantalising glimpses of nightmares from his past - whether they be the stunningly eerie sequence of watching a boy drown when he was a child, or the return of a man stalking his family with Polaroid photographs. If it has a fault, it's a well-meaning one, that it's an episode that's trying to do too much too quickly: it's hard to buy that the FBI would dismiss Frank twenty minutes into the action simply because they're finding him on edge and neurotic. But it works nonetheless, because it's done using the taped interviews we saw in The Innocents, and because Henriksen himself withdraws Frank into a state of complete mistrust when he refuses to trust anyone. Carter and Spotnitz skilfully play on the audience's doubts too; when Emma sees a man photographing Frank, it gives her and the viewer the proof she needs to believe in him - but it transpires that he's being followed because he's now subject to an FBI investigation of his own. And Dean Norris makes a terrific villain as the man profiling Frank, calmly pointing out to all how irrationally Frank is behaving.

But a story which promises to reveal so much gets washed away in the delight of its own imagery. Once the episode abandons any realism, once evil starts shapeshifting, once Frank is subject to scenes of drowning in a locked room, or Emma confronts her own self committing suicide - the whole becomes merely visually rather than intellectually interesting. And a story which seemed to be doing too much ultimately has done nothing at all; the last ten minutes are bogged down in mutterings about armageddon that marred the worst of the second season. The third season has had many problems, not least at times a certain blandness, but it's also seen a return at its best to well-crafted storytelling. It's dismaying to see it once more go down the slippery path of pretension. Seven and One suggests it's going to be a pivotal episode, a proper analysis of its lead character and what he stands for. But it delivers nothing; he's out of the FBI, he's set up for murder, he's lost his friends and his self-belief. And all that has no doubt been swept away by a delirium he suffered in his bathroom when the toilet overran. It's risible, frankly, and it typifies exactly why it's so hard to relate to Frank or his cases any more. If a plot hinges upon our growing uncertainty between what's real and what's illusory, leaving the audience with no answers whatsoever and no hint of resolution, it undermines not only the journey but the whole fabric of the show the plot has been analysing. (**1/2)

3.20, Nostalgia

Air Date: May 7, 1999
Writer: Michael R Perry
Director: Thomas J Wright

Summary Emma returns to her home town of South Mills, Pennsylvania, where the severed foot of a murdered woman is discovered. Four other women have gone missing, and Frank senses a connection to the death of Liddy Hooper, who is believed to have accidentally drowned. Hooper's day planner mysteriously turns up at the police station, and Frank finds it contains the names of several community men - some of them married - that she had sex with. Frank deduces that park ranger Jerry Neilson killed Hooper in a crime of passion, breaking her foot in the process. Guilt-stricken, Neilson more or less repeated the pattern with the other women as a means of helping the police to catch him. Neilson is arrested after telling Frank where the other bodies are buried, and Hooper gets a proper funeral.

Critique What begins as rather a run of the mill murder story becomes something much deeper and more affecting. Frank and Emma poke beneath the surface of a placid town, and uncover within its uncaring complacency towards the death of a prostitute the beginnings of a serial killer. If it seems somewhat like overkill to make the town a source of happy nostalgia for Emma, the last place she lived where she was happy before the murder of her sister, then the disillusionment she feels when realising that it's just as corrupt as anywhere else makes up for it. Indeed, one of the very best moments is the look of revulsion she shares with the police chief she's known as a kid as they listen to a peeping tom tell how he used to masturbate. The neighbours you think you know and accept may not necessarily be killers, but there's something grim about them nonetheless. And the point is well made when it's shown that the murderer is the only character who, in a flashback, wanted to protect the victim and give her some dignity.

Although the murderer is one Jerry Neilson, the actual culprit is almost an irrelevance. It's clear that he is a product of a community who just didn't give a damn about a girl who was "nuts" enough to sleep around, and that the town itself is to blame. The sequence where Frank takes Neilson down to the scene of the crime, and compassionately allows him to come to terms with what he's done and been re-enacting ever since, is one of the highlights of the entire series. After three seasons we've never yet been shown so directly a man who is crying out to be stopped, a killer who hates what he has become and deliberately leaves evidence of his murders in the hope that he can be captured. In the dying fall of Millennium, a programme which purported to get inside the head of serial killers but which has largely made them distant by making them agents of an apocalypse, it's wonderful to have a story which deals with one so intimately and with such humanity.

One of the most unassuming episodes made for the series, not seeing itself as a showcase for flashy direction or grisly set pieces, Nostalgia is refreshingly solid and unhysterical. It's intelligent without being *clever*. If the series could have produced a few more like it, maybe it wouldn't now be nearing cancellation after all. (****)

3.21, Via Dolorosa

Air Date: May 14, 1999
Writers: Marjorie David, Patrick Harbinson
Director: Paul Shapiro

Summary When a married couple is brutally murdered, the *modus operandi* exactly matches that of convicted serial killer Edward Cuffle - who died three days previously in the electric chair. Meanwhile, Peter tells Emma that the Millennium Group has found a means of reversing Alzheimer's. He offers to give her father the cure if she helps to push Frank out of the FBI so he can do important work for the Group.

The killer is identified as a man named Lucas Francis Barr. Barry Baldwin storms Barr's apartment with a team of agents, but Frank is struck with a premonition and urges everyone to evacuate - just as an explosive device inside the apartment detonates. [To be continued.]

Critique It seems appropriate that the final story of Millennium should be a look back at the serial-killer formula that was the starting point of the series, and is about a murderer who copies the same modus operandi of the man who defined Frank Black's early character. Being the first of a two-parter it takes advantage of the slower pace to make the investigation seem more thorough - the way that Baldwin narrows down a suspect from five-million-to-one is exhilarating, and a welcome return to a scientific procedural approach to the cases. And it allows more time to explore the killings themselves, the murderer here inspecting a home in fine detail before taking his victims from it. There's something very disturbing about a killer who is so calm that he can make the bed after the crime, or leave a glass of water standing in the sink meticulously poured to the very brim.

But the best part of the episode is the added depth that pace affords supporting characters. Peter Outerbridge's Billy Baldwin begins to show a new respect for Frank, privately having a go at this profiling lark all by himself, and looking embarrassed with pride when complimented on a job well done. And the further descent of Emma's father into Alzheimer's is handled excellently, the scene in which he approaches his sleeping daughter with a gun neatly paralleling the obscenities shown in the main plot. That a man can look at his own child and not know who she is, only that he still loves her, is more horrifying than the murders being committed. And even if Peter Watts popping up as spokesman for the Millennium Group every now and then begins to look a little like a pantomime demon, the deal he is offering Emma to save her father's identity looks ever more tempting. (****)

3.22, Goodbye to All That

Air Date: May 21, 1999
Writers: Ken Horton, Chip Johannessen
Director: Thomas J Wright

Summary Baldwin is taken away in an ambulance, wounded but expected to live - until a Millennium Group operative shoves a piece of shrapnel into his chest, killing him. Elsewhere, Andy McClaren tells Emma that he's retiring, and - with Baldwin dead - will recommend her as his replacement as Assistant Director.

Frank accuses Peter of manipulating events to make him rejoin the Group - a confrontation that makes Frank realise that Peter has been cut out of the Group's plans, and will likely be eliminated soon. Emma tells Peter that she can't agree to his Faustian pact, then finds that Group operatives have taken her father from his nursing home.

A repentant Peter rifles through the Group's computer systems, telling Frank how the Group's scientists found a means of turning on the physiological process of learning that normally switches off after childhood. With this knowledge, they were consequently able to graft Ed Cuffle's skills and murderous tendencies into Lucas Barr, effectively making him a pseudo-Cuffle. Peter swears that he's been protecting Frank from the Group, and that he'll send him files of the Group's plans pertaining to Frank if that protection breaks down.

Emma finds her father in her apartment, surgically cured of his Alzheimer's - but disappointed with her because she accepted the Group's offer after all. Frank realises that Emma bargained with the Group and resigns from the FBI, deeming any further affiliation with them a waste of time. He then tracks down Lucas, lead-

ing to a showdown where Lucas' true persona returns long enough for him to commit suicide.

Frank finds the files that Peter promised on the dashboard of his car, becomes alarmed and pulls Jordan out of school. As Peter's study is shown to contain a bloodied corpse, Frank and Jordan leave for parts unknown.

Critique By accident or by design, the direction of this final two-parter echoes the direction of the Millennium series as a whole. What at first appeared to be a relatively straightforward story about a profiler chasing a serial killer becomes instead a far-ranging conspiracy thriller far more about the profiler than the man he is hunting. Lucas Barr is a great character, an otherwise innocent man altered by the Millennium Group. He's honestly horrified by the violence around him; the teaser, in which he phones in to help the FBI whilst watching the news with two corpses as substitute family, is deliciously macabre. It also sums up the whole push and pull of this episode, in which the nuts and bolts horror can only be seen as something softer and more childlike beside the machinations of the Millennium Group. Baldwin's death in the ambulance wrongfoots the audience very cleverly - it gives us a new perspective on the story we've been watching, that an entire scenario of murders and investigations is being masterminded to ensure that Emma Hollis becomes assistant director of the FBI, with Frank pulled along behind her as the tame pet Millennium needs. For all of the second season's attempts at constructing an epic backstory for the Group, they are nowhere more powerful or more insidious than here. Peter Watts (once again) sacrifices his life for Frank when he realises the extent of their culpability; that Emma betrays Frank to save her father feels humane and true, and that is her tragedy. As her computer screen brings up the familiar ourobouros symbol we realise she is now trapped, her former partner rejecting her in disgust, the father whose sanity was the prize only telling her she made a mistake.

It's a tremendously accomplished piece of drama from Horton and Johannessen, and if it doesn't attempt to end the series in as startling a way as Morgan and Wong did the year before, it's none the worse for that. It's intriguing and, as Frank and Jordan escape to valleys new, strangely hopeful. Its impact is only diluted by recent episodes like Seven and One that have predicted this development in the storyline too closely and with less substance. And it is - as all series finales should be - both a celebration of the series' strengths and themes, and a hint that the show had a clearer throughline than it actually did. The brilliance of Goodbye To All That is that it acts as the closure to a TV series which never quite, in three full seasons, ever found out what it wanted to be - and yet somehow is a coherent summation of all its multiple styles and contradictory approaches.

At the end of the day, was Millennium really any good? It's a measure of how successful The X-Files was that this caustic and intimidating series managed to survive for three whole years - and a measure of The X-Files' dwindling popularity that a show like The Lone Gunmen died so quickly. As a result, Millennium feels almost unique in television history, a series which ran for an astonishing sixty-seven episodes and was given the chance time and time again to reinvent what it could be. With most shows it's possible to point to a heyday, a time when it was at

its peak - but Millennium fans will always be divided on whether they prefer the forensic approach of Season One or the mystical style of Season Two. (No-one much seems to champion Season Three. Which is understandable, but rather a pity; for a show that is trying to pick up the pieces of what's been shattered behind it, it ultimately does work towards finding a style of its own, and turns out some terrific episodes.) It's a schizophrenic series, and you can see how Lance Henriksen at times gets confused by the ever-changing tone. But I think that's also what *defines* Millennium. It's a series which is as chaotic and as paranoid in its execution as the times it was meant to reflect. Perhaps nothing is quite as pretentious as a bad Millennium story, but even that pretension is at least of interest after the event: and it's honestly remarkable that a series which began as something so rooted in brutal realism could become so like a dream. Individual stories lack the confidence of The X-Files at its best; but it's a programme where the whole is greater than its parts. It's the most ambitious thing that Ten Thirteen ever attempted, and when it's firing on all cylinders, it's also the most powerful and the most thoughtful. (*****)

The X-Files: Season 7

7.1, The Sixth Extinction

Air Date: Nov. 7, 1999
Writer: Chris Carter
Director: Kim Manners

Summary Scully teams up with Amina Ngebe, a biology professor, to research the symbols carved into the buried spaceship in Africa. They discover that the symbols contain passages from religious texts such as the Koran - and also a complete map of the human genome. Dr Barnes arrives and concludes that the buried spaceship holds the "ultimate" power and represents the origin of life on Earth.

Meanwhile, an increasingly psychic Mulder asks for help from Michael Kritschgau (5.1, Redux), who concludes that the electrical impulses in Mulder's mind are working harder than his body can sustain. Kritschgau prescribes a drug called phenytoin; this slows the electrical impulses of Mulder's brain, but his condition remains grave.

Back in Africa, Barnes captures Scully and Ngebe to prevent them interfering with the ship, but the women escape and Scully returns to Washington. Barnes kills his driver to test his theory that the spaceship can reanimate matter. The man indeed comes back to life - and kills Barnes with a machete. Barnes' body is later found, but the spaceship has vanished. [To be continued.]

Critique In contrast to Season Six's finale, the opening to Season Seven certainly feels more original than anything we've seen played out in the mytharc for quite a while. Although it echoes elements of Season Five's Redux - down to one of our heroes dying in a hospital bed, and the involvement of Michael Kritschgau - it works because it derives its energy principally from putting familiar characters into unfamiliar situations. The sequences on the West African coast, with Scully looking every inch the explorer as she works overnight in a tent decrypting extraterrestrial symbols, gives Gillian Anderson a *mission* that she's been lacking in the show ever since her character was cured of cancer. The new setting is a fresh backdrop too, for an interesting little horror story about supernatural attempts to stop Scully and her colleagues from decoding the mysteries of life. The dead return, locusts descend, and - in a genuinely eerie scene - a mysterious man appears to Scully to tell her that not all truths are for her learning. It's the first time in ages that the macguffin of those ever-elusive world-changing answers are given some dramatic tension, rather than lots of earnest overwritten purple prose.

There is, of course, a fair amount of that purple prose in evidence, mind you. Scully keeps on talking in voiceover to the hospitalised Mulder, suffering from an illness which has "consumed his beautiful mind". Here too there's a new urgency as Skinner breaks protocol to try to slow down Mulder's brain. Mitch Pileggi is great here, disguising the fact that there are long static scenes without much resolution; the sequence where Mulder shows precognitive ability is especially powerful.

As always with the middle parts of these epic three-episode mytharc tales, this one doesn't yield many answers and feels inconclusive - the cliffhanger is especially throwaway. But it's still the most arresting season opener in years, and promises that maybe there's life in the old mythology yet. (***1/2)

7.2, The Sixth Extinction II: Amor Fati

Air Date: Nov. 14, 1999
Writers: David Duchovny, Chris Carter
Director: Michael Watkins

Summary As Mulder falls comatose, Kritschgau tells Scully that exposure to an extraterrestrial source of energy has activated the alien virus that infected Mulder two years ago (4.8, Tunguska). The Cigarette Smoking Man takes Mulder to a private surgical unit, where a medical team transplants Mulder's alien DNA into him - a means of jump-starting the next stage of human evolution. While collaborating together,

Diana Fowley and the Cigarette Smoking Man acknowledge that Mulder is the Smoking Man's son. Meanwhile, Mulder dreams that he's gone into a witness protection program and started up a new life with Fowley. The two of them settle into wedded bliss, have children and stay together unto death in old age.

Albert Hosteen visits Scully and says that Mulder must recover for the sake of humanity. Fowley secretly sends Scully a book on Native American Beliefs and Practices, and Scully finds the letters therein correspond to the symbols on the spacecraft from Africa - and pertain to the as-yet unrealised sixth global extinction. Mulder was taken, she realises, in the belief that his illness is protection against an upcoming plague.

Krycek kills Kritschgau and destroys his work, concealing evidence that Mulder has become part-alien. Fowley tips Scully off to Mulder's location, enabling her to find him alone in the operating theatre. Mulder recovers and learns that Fowley has been murdered - evidently because she questioned the Cigarette Smoking Man's goals and helped Scully. Simultaneously, Scully learns that Albert died after being comatose for two weeks - and thus couldn't have visited her.

Critique Exploring Mulder's character through the use of artificial reality might have had more impact had it not been the overriding theme of the sixth season. But that quibble aside, it's never been applied so directly to the mythology of the series before - the use of it last year was largely for comic effect by seeing how our heroes act like fish out of water in domestic settings. This plays something of the same game, but on a much more epic scale. In Mulder's visions, the Cigarette Smoking Man offers him the chance to tread the path not taken, to live a life free from the responsibility of chasing a nebulous truth of aliens and mysteries. He gives him a house, a wife, children, comfort and security. In one brilliant sequence lasting less than a minute, Mulder becomes husband, father, then widower, as his halcyonic life rushes ever forward. The episode's interest is not so much with the ordinary dreams of extraordinary men, but where these dreams finish up: with all his friends dead, as an old man, Mulder is confronted by a Scully who calls him traitor and coward. By abandoning his mission, by abandoning *her*, the whole world has been sacrificed. The image of the Cigarette Smoking Man standing framed in the window of a suburban house, looking out at the armageddon of alien invasion, is beautifully surreal and grandiose. (And it'll be the only picture of the end of the world the series will ever give us.)

It's not a subtle point - by giving in the fight, everything Mulder stands for goes to hell. But it's a point made with a real passion usually denied these pompous episodes of mytharc; when Scully berates him, the look of agony on the dying Mulder's face, all that embarrassed guilt, is heartbreaking. And neither is it subtle the way he's haunted by dreams of a young boy building a spaceship of sand at the beach - only for the boy to destroy it because Mulder didn't help him the way he was meant to. But the bluntness of the metaphors is welcome in a show where dream sequences are customarily vague and pretentious. It serves as reminder of Mulder's faith as he embarks upon what is due to be his final full year on The X-Files, a rallying cry for the last leg of the race.

It's let down, frankly, by the episode *outside* the dream. What was required as contrast was some good solid storytelling, where Scully rushes to save her partner. Instead Scully is met with a ghost of her own in the shape of Albert Hosteen - and the story buckles badly under the weight of two separate fantasies. It has the effect too of making what's actually *supposed* to be happening seem inconsequential and without substance. It's something about the Cigarette Smoking Man using Mulder as an alien hybrid and operating on him to extract genetic data, etc etc etc. But it seems so convoluted beside the clarity of Mulder's dream that it just sounds silly. And so the three-part storyline is wrapped up in perfunctory style: Kritschgau is murdered without explanation by Krycek, and Fowley isn't even bumped off *on screen*. She evidently redeems herself and gives Scully the information she requires to find Mulder, but her change of heart seems like such an X-Files cliché, it's almost as if writers Carter and Duchovny can't be bothered to show it taking place. "It's a mythology episode," they seem to be saying. In these stories people are *always* changing sides and taking bullets. It's the familiar merry-go-round, we don't always need to watch it happening.

In a way it's hard to disagree - I'd have taken another few minutes of Mulder's life as a happy mediocrity over the traditional mytharc dance. It's as if Chris Carter has finally agreed to concentrate upon the quirkiness the show does so well and pay only lip service to what he always considered the series' backbone. There's so much to enjoy here: William B Davis is quite superb as the benign version of himself, never ageing as Mulder and his loved ones do. And the final scene, in which Mulder and Scully reaffirm their need for each other, is one of the most touching expressions of their love and respect the show ever attempted.

This has been the most peculiar of all The X-Files' mythology stories, where every single episode has deliberately aimed for a radically different tone from the others around them. It may not be the most coherent or satisfying, but it's still the bravest, and it kicks off the seventh season with great style. (****)

7.3, Hungry

Air Date: Nov. 21, 1999
Writer: Vince Gilligan
Director: Kim Manners

Summary   When a customer is slain at a Lucky Boy Burgers in Costa Mesa, California, Mulder suspects that the perpetrator sucked out the victim's brain with some sort of proboscis. Suspicion falls on one of the Lucky Boy employees, Derwood Spinks, but in truth he's just blackmailing the real assailant - his co-worker, Rob Roberts. Stricken with a genetic disorder that makes him feed on brain matter, Roberts winds up killing his neighbour, a private investigator, and Spinks. Eventually, Roberts decides there's no place for him in the world and deliberately charges Mulder and Scully - forcing them to shoot him dead.

Critique   As far back as Pusher, Vince Gilligan has been the master of stories which show the human ordinariness of monsters and serial killers. Hungry takes that rather brilliantly to its logical conclusion, an episode in which the story is told entirely from the monster's point of view, where Mulder and Scully nearing towards the truth are a threat. (It's interesting that Mulder in particular is characterised as a man who is rather cruelly *toying* with his prey; Duchovny in full snide mode would be enough to make any mutant paranoid.) Chad E Donella gives a likeable performance as Rob Roberts, a young man who is so appalled by his biological imperative to snack on human brains that he gorges himself on diet pills to suppress his appetite. It's a very funny satire on a society which mollycoddles the greedy and the lazy, where cod psychiatrists can assure Rob that there's no such thing as monsters, where mantra Rob learns from his self-help videos routinely fail to get him through the day. Best of all is a beautifully funny sequence where Rob is the only thin attendee at an Overeaters Anonymous meeting - getting up on the stage to describe his compulsions of eating brains, he manages to make the entire audience before him salivate. And it's especially apt that the job of such a monster is a server in a fast-food burger restaurant, the most plastic and cosmetic place he could be.

Gilligan's script sees Rob get ever more desperate as he tries to cover his tracks and rid himself of all who threaten his safety - until he has become, without intending it, a bona fide serial killer. It's a particularly perverse script which allows Rob's final declaration that he will stop feeling guilt and be the man his natural urges make him to be so triumphant. This is like Dexter a decade early, there too a series inviting the viewer to be complicit with an engaging character whose own moral code enables him to murder people. The sympathy that Donella gives Rob as he shows his true colours is very touching, as is his realisation that once he has come out of the closet there's no way back in; the only thing he can do now is be gunned down by Mulder and be written off as yet another Monster of the Week. The final moments, seen through Rob's dying eyes as they blur into the credits, are a typically smart touch to this neglected gem of a story. (*****)

7.4, Millennium

Air Date: Nov. 28, 1999
Writers: Vince Gilligan, Frank Spotnitz
Director: Thomas J Wright

Summary In Tallahassee, Florida, Mulder and Scully investigate the grave of Raymond Crouch - a former FBI agent who committed suicide, then somehow liberated himself from his own coffin. Evidence suggests that a necromancer is using dark rituals to raise the dead, and Skinner provides files on three similar cases involving members of the Millennium Group.

Mulder and Scully consult with Frank Black, who has checked himself into an institution for observation. Frank mentions a Millennium Group sub-set who thought they could end the world by killing themselves prior to the millennium. Mulder checks out Frank's list of possible suspects, and winds up trapped in the basement of the necromancer - Mark Johnson - with a quartet of the undead. Frank tracks Mulder and apprehends Johnson; the agents dispatch Johnson's zombies with head shots. Johnson is institutionalized as Frank receives a visit from his daughter Jordan, and Mulder and Scully celebrate the New Year.

Critique If my earlier chapters have said anything about Millennium, it's that it was a curious beast of a television show which over its three seasons was subject to so much change of direction, it never properly settled down to find a house style a viewer could rely upon. By the end its greatest freedom - that almost *anything* could show up on the series, from police procedural drama to visionary fantasy pieces to stories about hunting religious artefacts - became also its greatest limitation. Just what, ultimately, was Millennium about?

And yet, with all its shifts in tone and concerns, Gilligan and Spotnitz still somehow stumble upon a storyline that feels stylistically wrong for Millennium. That's almost something to be proud of. With the series in cancellation denied a chance to have a climax set at New Year 2000, The X-Files kindly stepped in and gave it a conclusion of its own. And after all the storylines about the breakdown in society, about armageddon and paranoia, the climax to Millennium on that fateful day as the twentieth

century shuffles into the twenty-first is revealed to be... four zombies in a basement. No, that's really it. The plan of the nebulous Millennium Group was to resurrect four of its number with a necromancer, and in their undead form take on the role of the Four Horsemen of the Apocalypse.

Now, I have problems with this as a follow-up to Millennium; it simply isn't. But to be fair, we're not watching Millennium any more, this is an X-Files episode, and the themes of a dead TV series should be secondary to the host. Unfortunately, it's also a terrible X-File too. The X-Files at its best works upon a localised threat, something that can be contained within forty-five minutes. It's rarely something simply to be defeated, more to be solved. There's no mystery here *to* solve; there isn't room for Scully's scepticism, so even she is presented with the plain truth of dead men lurching about impervious to bullets. What we get here is an episode, rarely, where Mulder and Scully save the entire world. And the thin shred of credibility upon which hangs the series snaps. Because, joking apart, the concept of armageddon is too vast anyway... and what we get besides is just four zombies. In a basement. The scale is too big. And the story then doesn't bother even to *reach* for it.

There's an undeniable thrill to be had in seeing Frank Black share screen time with Fox Mulder and Dana Scully. But Lance Henriksen is not at his best, clearly resenting the material. The Millennium series constantly presented him with the offer of settling down with his daughter Jordan and giving up the fight against evil - just like Mulder in Amor Fati. Millennium the series shows Black's courage in resisting that temptation; Millennium the episode shows he's caved in. I'd have more respect for the production team had this felt like a deliberate decision, that the Frank we see here has failed - but there's no such understanding. With Chip Johannessen now working on The X-Files, as the only writer who found his way through all three seasons of Millennium and bound those multiple styles into a whole, it's bizarre that he was denied this writing assignment. Vince Gilligan is a terrific writer, but he's not a Millennium writer, and doomsday cults and millennial angst are not within his sensibility. And nor, on this showing, are zombies. No, even within a basement. (*1/2)

7.5, Rush

Air Date: Dec. 5, 1999
Writer: David Amann
Director: Robert Lieberman

Summary Two teenagers in Pittsfield, Virginia - Max Harden and Chastity Raines - take a schoolmate, Tony Reed, into the woods to share their "secret" with him. A cave in the woods has gifted Harden and Raines with super-speed, at the cost of making them addicted to the "rush" this causes.

Mulder and Scully intervene when Harden and Raines cause all manner of super-speed mayhem, including clubbing the local deputy to death with a flashlight. Reed also gains super-speed, and stops the increasingly unstable Harden from murdering his own father. Back in the woods, Harden moves to kill Reed - but Raines shoots Harden dead. Unwilling to live without the rush, Raines positions herself in front of the bullet as it exits Harden's body, killing herself. As Mulder speculates that something inside the cave altered the teenagers' biochemistry but doesn't have any affect on adults, the authorities seal the cave with concrete.

Critique The X-Files has not distinguished itself with its tales of disaffected teens, and I'm afraid Rush is another rather sorry example. Here we have children who need to get a "fix" which will give them a "rush" which in turn makes them antisocial and rebellious, and which ultimately through the high is destroying their bodies. Good students will get corrupted by it, girlfriends will wish they could escape its lure. It's hardly the subtlest of metaphors, and one which feels more than a little lecturing into the bargain; at least the problem kids of Schizogeny or Syzygy weren't the victims of some hysterical reaction against drug abuse. It oddly makes the episode feel rather like a staid middle-aged rant about the evil kids get up to, including discussions from Scully about how teenagers may be psychologically different from the rest of us. It leads to some amusing lines in which it's clear that our heroes are terrified to be thought of as old by the students they interrogate, and a lovely little pout from Scully when it's suggested she's too aged to be affected by the magical forces within the cave. But it also emphasises, in its seventh year, that The X-Files just isn't cool any more, daddio.

There are a couple of terrific set pieces, mind you; the scene where Tony is initiated into the group by having him drive at full speed into a tree is nicely done, and the death by cafeteria furniture is pleasingly grisly. But the basic idea here - that of a cave which makes teens move very fast - is given no more explanation than I just have in this sentence. And it doesn't translate to the screen visually either, relying mostly upon the rushed perpetrators simply... not being visible. (**)

7.6, The Goldberg Variation

Air Date: Dec. 12, 1999
Writer: Jeffrey Bell
Director: Thomas J Wright

Summary A Chicago poker game ends with mob boss Jimmy Cutrona ordering a fatal accident for the big winner - the seemingly harmless Henry Weems, who miraculously survives being thrown off a building. Mulder concludes that Weems has an astonishing "luck factor" that's protected him for years, at the cost of balancing the scales and inflicting hard times on others.

Weems agrees to testify against Cutrona, but Cutrona's men try various means of silencing him. One series of "lucky" events later, Cutrona and his men all lie dead - and it fortuitously turns out that Cutrona's rare blood type is a match for Weems' friend Richie, meaning that Richie can get the liver transplant he badly needs.

Critique The delight of a Rube Goldberg invention is its sheer ingenious pointlessness - that such an intricate machine can be constructed upon a series of cause and effect moments to achieve something utterly trivial. To construct an episode of television which works on the Rube Goldberg structure is a lovely idea, and requires both a playfulness and a sleight of hand to disguise there's such skill *behind* the playfulness. In Jeffrey Bell's script we get the playful-

ness in spades, and much of it is charming: Willie Garson is lovely as Weems, a man cursed with being lucky. But the ingenuity is rather lacking. And that's a shame, because there's a real sparkle to this whimsy, and you really *want* to be seduced by its cleverness. So it leaves you with a sense of disappointment when the cleverness on display just isn't quite clever enough.

Rarely for The X-Files, it's not that there's anything wrong with the story, just the set pieces around it. The script nicely sets up the idea that fate is always going to intervene and save Weems' life from mobsters in as convoluted a manner as possible, that bad luck is going to kick in as a karmic reaction on those around him. For once a story gives itself licence to be as complicated as possible - and it just doesn't go the distance. The gangster deaths should be impossibly elaborate - and a bullet rebounding off several objects before taking out the shooter just isn't witty enough. Nor is the owner of a lottery ticket getting knocked down by a car. Each time Bell shows us a Goldberg machine, we're as awed as Mulder by the multiple variables, and it only serves to remind us at the intricacies the set pieces should have been aiming for. It's as if we're looking at a first draft, placeholder scenes Bell put in before he could come up with something that would *really* knock our socks off.

And as a result the story doesn't work. Without the stunts, we've no choice but to give our attention to the *plot*. And as Weems says to Mulder early on, there's deliberately no *point* to Rube Goldberg's work, that's the charm. So without the dizzying pyrotechnics that are meant to distract us, we focus upon a storyline in which, by necessity, everything that plays out is mechanical, in which the characters are functional cogs. There's an essential heartlessness to that. Almost to counteract this, Bell builds in a story in which Weems is willing to sacrifice his own life to get a new liver for a dying boy - he's trying so hard to put a bit of emotion into the clockwork that he overdoes the mix. And we're left with something which is rather atonal. Just as the story sees a man fluctuate between extremes of good luck and bad luck, so the style can't settle between being something soulless and contrived, and something dripping in sentiment.

For all that, it's a likeable piece of work. As in his Rain King story last year, Jeffrey Bell finds a

whimsy to The X-Files that no other writer seems to mine, and he sets his tales in a universe where the wonders are benign. It's great to see Mulder and Scully smile as much as they do here, free from the angst of drama, or even from the edge of their more caustic comedies. And it's such a well-meaning little bauble that you want to applaud it for its intent if nothing else. (***)

7.7, Orison

Air Date: Jan. 9, 2000
Writer: Chip Johannessen
Director: Rob Bowman

Summary Donnie Pfaster, the death-fetishist who once took Scully prisoner (2.13, Irresistible), escapes after the Reverend Orison visits his penitentiary and time seems to slow down. Scully keeps hearing a familiar tune - the same one she heard the day her Sunday School teacher was murdered - that makes her wonder if Orison acted on divine instructions and freed Pfaster. Conversely, Mulder believes that Orison can "stop" time thanks to a hole in his skull that enables more oxygen to reach his brain.

Orison finds Pfaster and forces him to dig a grave, believing that God wants him to kill the man. However, Pfaster's face briefly takes on a demonic aspect, and he murders Orison instead. Pfaster captures Scully once more and prepares to kill her, but Mulder bursts in and holds Pfaster at gunpoint. After freeing herself, Scully shoots Pfaster dead. Mulder's report exonerates Scully of the deed, but Scully remains uncertain if her need for vengeance came from God or something evil.

Critique A month or so after The X-Files attempted its crossover with Millennium, that series' final showrunner writes an episode which - strangely enough - feels not a little unlike an adventure designed for Frank Black. In a way that's quite appropriate; it's a sequel to Irresistible, the second season tale which by featuring a serial killer with no supernatural overtones and a surprising blunt realism seems to have inspired Chris Carter to create the sister show in the first place. And Orison offers up a lot of Millennium's old standbys. There's a vigilante killer taking out other murderers, there's a heavy religious tone, there's a sequence involving a trusted lead character killing the villain in vengeance. (More on that one a bit later.) And just to remind us that this is an X-File we're watching, here's not only a retread of Irresistible, but echoes of Pusher too, with a man able to hypnotically control others because of a damaged brain. Oh, and endless scenes of Mulder and Scully tediously discussing religion in ways so simplistic they're set at polar opposites; Mulder as the arch sceptic, Scully the devout believer who thinks God may be leaving messages for her in pop songs she hears on the radio.

It's a mess. And a mess at that which cheapens Irresistible badly. The sequence where Reverend Orison is confronted by a Pfaster who is bearing a demon's face makes real and blunt and stupid a moment from the prequel which could clearly be taken as metaphor. By making Donnie Pfaster literally evil, all the hard work that Nick Chinlund put into his disturbed obsessive is undone.

But worse still is the scene where Scully murders Donnie. It's as clear as that, it's murder. Donnie is defeated and restrained by Mulder, and Scully's response is to walk up to him and shoot him dead. It's gloriously directed, don't get me wrong - the slow-mo and the delayed sound of the gunshot make it as shocking as can be - but it's utterly unjustified. It suggests that Scully may be some patsy tool of a God who's been directing her all this time to execute someone, which weakens her terribly, or that she's the type of person who can kill a man and then gets to hide from the consequences (albeit via a little of your old end-of-story-angst), which weakens her further. For all the times that Donnie is called evil in the story, he's actually plotted as little more than a fall guy - knocked out by a prostitute, bested by a reverend, and then shot dead by the FBI. If writer Chip Johannessen intended to set up some moral debate about what Scully had done, he needed not only to make Pfaster a greater threat, but also to give the story the time to explore it. As it is, he's spent half an hour writing a dull retread of old storylines, capped by ten minutes which feel at best dreadfully misguided, and at worst a betrayal of characterisation that has badly damaged the moral fibre of the series. (*)

7.8, The Amazing Maleeni

Air Date: Jan. 16, 2000
Writers: Vince Gilligan, John Shiban, Frank Spotnitz
Director: Thomas J Wright

Summary   A magician named "The Amazing Maleeni" performs an astonishing stage trick that entails his head turning completely around - but he's later found dead, his head parted from his body. Scully determines that Maleeni, a.k.a. Herman Pinchbeck, actually died from a heart attack a month ago and was kept refrigerated. She and Mulder visit Pinchbeck's twin brother, a bank worker named Albert - then discover that "Albert" is Herman, having faked his own death to avoid his gambling debts.

Mulder arrests Maleeni. Also in prison is Billy LaBonge, an amateur magician accused of robbing a courier truck filled with cash. However, the funds are soon found in the possession of a loan shark named Cissy Alvarez. Maleeni and LaBonge are both released, and Mulder concludes that the two of them collaborated from the start. Their plan was to draw the attention of an FBI agent, then get his / her badge number and fingerprint and thus authorize an electronic funds transfer to the tune of millions. By seizing Maleeni's wallet - which contains a playing card with Mulder's fingerprint on it - Mulder thwarts their scheme.

Critique   This feels like it's trying to be the twenty-first century's The Goldberg Variation. Which would be fine, except the twentieth century's counterpart was only screened a few weeks previously. Once again it's a celebration of intricate plot mechanics, where the fascination comes from watching how seemingly trivial events collide to effect a larger outcome. The conceit is much more ambitious this time round, but the plot still feels like a clever Rube Goldberg invention. The only difficulty with that is that it's not quite as brilliant as it thinks it is; the magicians' scheme depends in retrospect upon so many bits of luck (the FBI taking an interest in the case is purely Mulder's whim, LaBonge is very fortunate that the guard with the gun shooting blanks is the one who intercepts him) that it can't but help leaving you reeling not so much at the ingenuity but the implausibility of it all. Had, as in Jeffrey Bell's script, the contrivances been the X-File in themselves - in fate intervening in delightfully overcomplicated ways - then that would have been acceptable. But this time the plot pivots entirely upon human planning - and the story's success depends *entirely* upon our understanding that all that we can see can be achieved therefore by human means.

And this is a cheat. Seeing actual stage magician Ricky Jay in the credits as Maleeni perhaps sets up expectations of a study of magic and conmanship as seen in David Mamet's masterly House of Games. The brilliance of Mamet's movie is that the apparently impossible tricks make perfect sense once they're explained; here, the story resorts to CGI. With a sleight of hand worthy of a conjuror, it tries to answer all the questions it wants to, but deflects us from the one that the teaser is based around - so how *did* Maleeni turn his head three hundred and sixty degrees, then? When LaBonge claims it's easy and manages to contort his arm a bit, Mulder and Scully look duly impressed - rather than come out with the obvious response, "Yes, but it's not your *head*, is it?" Before the opening credits roll, we've already seen that we can't trust the stage magic we see. The story at that point needs to work twice as hard to convince us to trust its storytelling magic as well, and it lets us down just as badly.

It's not without wit. I love the bank manager's hurt reaction when he discovers Pinchback has been concealing his legs and only pretending to be an amputee - "But we bought you a ramp!" And Duchovny and Anderson appear to be having fun. But without the skills of the magician that the story glories in, it's a damp squib of a show: at the end of the day, they did it with mirrors. (**)

7.9, Signs and Wonders

Air Date: Jan. 23, 2000
Writer: Jeffrey Bell
Director: Kim Manners

Summary In McMinn County, Tennessee, a young man named Jared Chirp dies when about fifty snakes manifest inside his car. Mulder and Scully investigate Chirp's pregnant girlfriend Gracie, and their church. Reverend Mackey suggests that the agents check out Chirp and Gracie's former place of worship, the Church of Signs and Wonders, as its members practice snake handling.

Mulder learns that Chirp was sterile and wonders if Gracie's father, the Reverend Enoch O'Connor, sired her child. O'Connor performs an exorcism on Gracie, and she gives birth to a mess of snakes. Mulder comes to realise that O'Connor was protecting his daughter - and that Mackey fathered Gracie's child. Mackey summons snakes to attack Mulder, then escapes when Mulder survives. Later, Mackey joins a church in Hamden, Connecticut, as "the Reverend Wells", and feeds a mouse to the snake that's nestled in his throat.

Critique This one may well be an overripe bit of old nonsense, but it's very well directed, it's got a few shocks up its sleeves, and above all else it has an *atmosphere* which has largely been missing from the series for a while. The snake sequences are very effective - which is a good thing, as there are quite a number of them. And the heart of the episode, the contrast between the rather lukewarm conservative side of Christianity and its firebrand snake-waving evangelist counterpart, is wittily made in an especially good montage of intercut church services.

Ultimately it's rather hard to know what point Jeffrey Bell is trying to make about organised religion here. The fussy quiet little mouse of a vicar turns out to be the killer rather than the hell-and-fury madman whose idea of testing Scully's faith is to assault her over a box of poisonous snakes. It serves as a twist, of course, but surely it can only be that; any comment the story passes upon perception, or upon the way that people should have the right to be true to themselves and question their lives their own way seem to fall by the wayside. In an interesting scene Scully calls Mulder on this, when he tells her about the seductive quality of accepting a religion which hands over all the answers so you don't have to think for yourself any more. She's appalled by the arrogance of this, and so Bell appears to be too - O'Connor may not be the culprit, but he's depicted as being such a violent, self-serving and hypocritical man that Michael Childers' performance can't possibly contain it. Reverend Mackey is the voice of moderation and care, and yet he seems to have living in his throat snakes that he can send out to kill on his bidding. Maybe - and this is the most likely scenario - Jeffrey Bell didn't really *have* a point to make. He just wanted to tell a story that offered up lots of cool images, the sort that just about work on a moment to moment level but don't make much sense afterwards.

And the images *are* cool; we have a woman giving birth to snakes and a man oozing reptile venom. Perhaps that's all we should expect. But it seems a pity to me that in yet another episode which puts religion in the crosshairs, that the story doesn't really seem to stand for anything. It's maybe telling that these stories are usually grounded by Scully and her own battles with faith; here it's Mulder who undergoes the final test of righteousness, and so all the religious spiel ends up as just your everyday slice of supernatural hokum. (**1/2)

7.10, Sein und Zeit

Air Date: Feb. 6, 2000
Writers: Chris Carter, Frank Spotnitz
Director: Michael Watkins

Summary Mulder intervenes when a five-year-old named Amber LaPierre vanishes from her Sacramento home. Amber's parents experienced odd visions before her disappearance, and a handwriting analysis proves that Amber's mother wrote the girl's "abduction note". Tellingly, a similar case from Idaho, 1987, entailed a missing boy's mother - Kathy Lee Tencate - also writing a ransom note with the phrase "Nobody shoots at Santa Claus!"

Mulder's mother leaves a message asking if he's dealing with the case, but he fails to return the call. Later, Scully gives Mulder the news that his mother - who had incurable cancer - has killed herself using sleeping pills and an open gas oven. Tencate informs Mulder that his mother wanted to tell him about the "Walk-Ins" - old souls who live in starlight and protect people's spirits from harm. These Walk-Ins, Tencate says, took Samantha Mulder to spare her suffering.

The "Santa Claus" phrase leads the agents to

a children's play village. Ed Truelove, a tubby man who's been making videotapes of the visitors, is arrested. Afterward, the agents find numerous plots on the grounds - each of them a child's grave. [To be continued.]

Critique There's been a disappointing listlessness to the seventh season, a sharp contrast to the renewed energy that the move to Los Angeles brought to the sixth. With the end of the show in sight (at this stage, that's what the production team were anticipating), there's a sense of everyone marking out time. Certainly you could have expected little better from this, the first of a two-parter resolved to bring to conclusion the mystery of Samantha Mulder; the way we were reminded of the loose ends, in a corridor scene in Biogenesis, had the feeling to it that Chris Carter and company were looking back through their notes to see what story elements still needed to be ticked off the list before they could hang up their overalls and shut up shop for good.

But this is anything but perfunctory. Indeed, it's perhaps the most truly passionate bit of storytelling seen in The X-Files since Scully was dying from cancer. Carter and Spotnitz achieve this by refusing to be melodramatic about Samantha - in fact, if anything, it's about how Mulder's re-emergent obsession with his sister seems rather distasteful as he tries to investigate the abduction of Amber Lynn LaPierre. The mythology episodes are typified by convoluted plotlines and numerous recurring characters - but this is only a mythology episode because Mulder keeps telling us it is. Rather brilliantly, the writers play so much against the usual tone of these Episodes of Great Significance that it makes Mulder's breakdown look all the more unsettling, taking place within what looks like a story about a very real and depressingly routine crime. Mrs Mulder is killed off too, and even here the resulting angst is cleverly misdirected; it says much that she's killed not by a conspiracy (as Mulder believes) but by suicide, that she dies not with the great farewell lines that were granted Bill Mulder and Deep Throat, but on an awkward answering phone message after her son has forgotten to return her call. Teena Mulder has hardly been the most successful

character in The X-Files - mostly because there's been little room for character at all amid the speculation that she may have slept with the Cigarette Smoking Man. But oddly that too works in the episode's favour, giving the death a strange abruptness that feels random, and makes Mulder's insistence it's tied in to bigger revelations and demanding that she be autopsied all the more disturbing.

This is a very emotional episode - and what makes that so successful is that everyone is playing against the expected release of that emotion; it all feels inappropriately channelled somehow. It's a dangerous line to tread, and Duchovny does it quite wonderfully. You can sense him really seize upon drama as powerful as this after so many stories requiring only self-regarding tics and smirks. This is a Mulder who confidently demands that Skinner give him a case that so he can ask all the right questions - and then resolutely fails to ask them, almost stymied into dumbness when Amber's mother asks him if he thinks her daughter will be found. Crisis stories usually bring out the best in our hero - but this is a portrait of Mulder drowning, realising bit by bit that he's too close to this investigation. His breezy assertions at the episode start that Amber is still alive are replaced by a drained defeatism, asking to be taken off the case.

And this is all against an unusually cynical depiction of real life investigation, where the FBI aren't necessarily heroic, or even moved by the gravity of the crime; instead they're taking bets on whether the child will be found alive or not. Where the very sensitivity of the case turns it into a media frenzy, the LaPierres susceptible to any ambulance chaser who wants to be a celebrity. Where, most gallingly, the distraught parents are immediately seen as suspects, and are even prepared to confess to the murder of their own child just to get any amnesty. Santa Claus is a killer in this sort of world.

It's not altogether perfect. Whether intended as self-aggrandising in-jokes, or complaints against a network that cancelled their show, the references to Harsh Realm are very clumsy. And some of the plotting is confused; if Ed selected his victims at a Christmas themed park just days before their abductions, why do neither family ever remark upon the Santa Claus reference in the notes left for them? But this is a welcome

return to an X-File we haven't seen for a while - hard, passionate, and with an urgent story to tell. From where I'm sitting, in the middle of a lacklustre season, it smells strongly of a masterpiece. (*****)

7.11, Closure

Air Date: Feb. 13, 2000
Writers: Chris Carter, Frank Spotnitz
Director: Kim Manners

Summary Truelove confesses to twenty-four murders as the children's bodies are exhumed. Amber LaPierre isn't found, and Harold Piller - a psychic working for the police force - claims to have visited sites where the Walk-Ins turned at-risk children into starlight. Truelove's victims, by contrast, died while suffering. Scully learns that the Cigarette Smoking Man halted a government investigation into Samantha's disappearance back in 1973. The Cigarette Smoking Man believes that Samantha is dead, but asks Scully to leave Mulder ignorant about her fate because it gives him hope.

Mulder, Scully and Piller hold a séance in a house formerly occupied by the Cigarette Smoking Man - and thus find Samantha's diary hidden in a wall. Written by a fourteen-year-old Samantha, the diary mentions medical tests, lost memories and a desire to run away. Scully finds mention of a "Jane Doe" patient - possibly Samantha - in a corresponding police report from 1979. Arbutus Ray, a nurse at the time, claims that she treated "Jane Doe" - who disappeared in circumstances similar to the "Walk-In" interventions when a group of men (the Cigarette Smoking Man included) arrived to collect her.

A little boy - actually the spirit of Piller's missing son - leads Mulder into the woods. He encounters a group of spectral children, Amber included, and has a tearful reunion with Samantha's spirit. Mulder realises that his sister's soul peacefully resides with the Walk-Ins.

Critique It's brave, you've got to give it that. I have a friend who sees this episode as the very nadir of the series, that after seven seasons the resolution to Samantha's story is that she was turned into starlight. But I think it's a reflection of where The X-Files is at this point that the courage pays off so well. It *has* been seven seasons, so by this point, no conventional explanation would have satisfied. Abducted by aliens, murdered by serial killers, or living out in the suburbs somewhere, they've all been served up as truth, then invalidated, then served up once more. And it's a mark of what happens when a series which relies upon big mysteries for its appeal gets extended beyond its natural life, that whatever conclusions it reaches can only be an anticlimax. (It was true with Twin Peaks. It was true with Life on Mars. It may very well be true with Lost - time will tell.) What The X-Files dares is to eschew the meat and potatoes plotting of what happened to Samantha, and gives instead an ending which is pure emotion, something built upon metaphor and the fulfilment of Mulder's character.

For a story like this to work it needs sure control - the ghosts and the sentimentality are going to stretch an audience's credulity more than your average X-File. To this end Carter and Spotnitz give Mulder his own counterpart, a discredited psychic with a mission to find his own son. It's essential that Mulder is as sceptical as the audience must be, and that at its deliberate pace we grow to accept the possibility of the magic ending at the same time that he does. Harold Piller is played with great sensitivity by Anthony Heald, so that mostly works; it only stumbles when the writers try to push the sentimentality too far, as in the contrived moment when Mulder finds in his sister's diary words speaking directly to him, or the sequence where he speculates that all the stars in the sky are lost souls. The relief is that, at the critical moment, Carter and Spotnitz shut up: the last act, in which Mulder is reunited with the loving ghost of his sister, is extraordinarily moving, and it's accomplished by music and lighting and a joyous performance from Duchovny as his character finally reaches the end of his quest.

And this, ultimately, is why Closure, in spite of much clumsiness, has such power to me. That a series which is all about action, and all about spinning out revelations so they can be as epic as possible, can end Mulder's mission so gently in a dying fall. Whether the Walk-Ins rescuing children from certain death is just wish fulfilment or not, it doesn't matter - this is a

story in which Mulder doesn't catch up with his sister, or find her grave, or bring the people who abducted her to justice, it's a story in which he finds peace, and *lets go*. It's about moving on, and acceptance. That Mulder is now free to do that is a series highlight. That Harold, who represents so obviously the Mulder of the past few years, storms away angrily in denial is almost as moving somehow, showing us the journey we've already been on. It's as delicate and touching an end to the Samantha storyline as we could have hoped for. (****)

7.12, X-Cops

Air Date: Feb. 20, 2000
Writer: Vince Gilligan
Director: Michael Watkins

Summary A *Cops* film crew shadows Deputy Keith Wetzel on a raid in Willow Park, California, but some sort of monster flips their car over. Mulder attributes the event to a werewolf, but subsequent killings involve a Freddy Krueger-like slasher and a sort of "wasp man". All told, Mulder concludes that they're facing an entity who appears during the full moon, and manifests as each victim's worst nightmare to feast upon their fear. Wetzel returns to the raided house with the *Cops* crew, then finds himself trapped inside. Mulder arrives and convinces Wetzel to get over his fear; this dissipates the hostile force, which will probably appear elsewhere during the next full moon.

Critique It's ironic that an episode which is a parody of another series altogether is the first in a long time to get the right balance of what makes a good monster of the week story; it's funny, it's clever, and it's actually quite frightening. Certainly for a while it seems to be just a gimmicky joke, writer Vince Gilligan wearing his gag rather than his scare hat. The jokes are very good - the sequences of people acting up to the camera, the way that Mulder so easily falls into the self-important pontificating that is the style of these documentary series, whilst Scully does everything she can to keep out of shot. But there's a smartness to the humour too, as we're forcibly reminded just how *odd* The X-Files really is; by meshing it with a series which prides itself upon hand-held camera realism, it shows scenes of cynical beat cops barely showing patience at Mulder's theories of werewolves and fear monsters. It's great that the series can stand back from itself now and then like this. In the first season Mulder was regularly seen as a laughingstock by his peers, but as the show gained greater audience respect so did the character. Gilligan doesn't merely highlight the absurdity of The X-Files and its heroes for comic effect, as he does in stories like Small Potatoes or Bad Blood - instead, in this new faux verite setting, it makes the clichés seem strange and unnerving.

And that's why what could easily have been a joke episode is able, bit by bit, to erode the viewer's sense of comfort and provide a few chills. In a regular X-File the nature of the threat, that there's some kind of force which makes people see their worst nightmares, would lead to a series of repetitive set pieces. One could argue that the gimmick of the episode is only there to conceal that, but it's also what throws it into sharp relief; we're not watching the story unfold safely via carefully composed camera shots and Mark Snow scored music, we're the eye of the camera, we're in the action and the chaos. If for once the typical viewer can probably work out the twist of this monster long before Mulder does, that's only because he's chasing over the city by night with a paranoid camera crew on his tail. And by the last act this story's style resembles not so much Cops as The Blair Witch Project, as Mulder and Scully explore a darkened crack house by flashlight trying to rein in their own terrors.

If it's not entirely satisfying, that's the style of the horror it's apeing. The Blair Witch Project succeeds precisely because it doesn't allow the audience the reassurance of a conclusion; the only way the story can end is if the protagonist is destroyed by what she fears. Its very abruptness is what's so effective. X-Cops, of course, can't do that - it's a single instalment of an ongoing television series, and so that same inevitable abruptness can only feel inconclusive, and the story only runs out because we reach daylight. In the same way, more disappointingly, Mulder and Scully can never be the victims of their fears. And this means that for all the urgency of the "live" recording, they never quite engage

with the action, they never really stop being observers like us. (****)

7.13, First Person Shooter

Air Date: Feb. 27, 2000
Writers: William Gibson, Tom Maddox
Director: Chris Carter

Summary When a gamer named Retro plays a virtual reality game, he bizarrely winds up dead in real life, apparently slain by a fictional warrior named Maitreya. A second death occurs, and the Lone Gunmen - who are serving as consultants to the game - enter the virtual reality to deploy a patch program. Mulder enters the game and helps the Gunmen escape - but is then trapped, forced to square off against Maitreya. Scully joins the game and battles Maitreya to a standstill, enabling one of the program developers, Phoebe, to implement a kill switch. The game shuts down and the agents emerge unharmed, but later a new avatar appears in one of the game developer's computers: that of Scully as a warrior.

Critique In William Gibson and Tom Maddox's first script for the series, there's an amusing scene in which Mulder gets threatened by a posse of glamorous nurses, who are only defeated by Scully doing ninja. It's funny partly because it's a look at Mulder's own inner fantasies, but also - principally - because it's *short*. First Person Shooter is that little fan-pleasing sequence writ large, a testosterone fuelled, machine gun pumping, breast 'n' bicep bulging ride. And it's almost entirely awful.

There's an attempt early on to make this an argument about the way men channel their macho aggression into video games, but it's really only paying lip service to our intelligence. Mulder has never been as moronic as he is here, getting his rocks off by ogling women, firing guns, and abandoning all higher brain functions as he runs towards a proven killer with all the gung ho enthusiasm of a little boy playing at war. The Lone Gunmen may be comic caricatures, but they've always been characterised by their distrust of corporate America - here, though, they're not only squabbling over their stock options, but also clearly enjoying the adventure in which a virtual reality world they've part created is killing people. Where's the guilt, where's the integrity? In the scene where an exotic danger named Jade Blue Afterglow is interrogated, a whole flotilla of policemen can barely contain themselves in the corridor outside, all but wanking at the thought of the scantily dressed woman. And Ivan, devisor of the game, is an odious little nerd who's only concerned with the money he can make, and barely registers that what he's invented is murderous. If Gibson and Maddox are making a point about male boorishness, it might have been better achieved with even a hint of subtlety. But the women come off no better - Phoebe is the plain girl techie who's really just a Lara Croft wannabe. And in spite of her best endeavours at maintaining some credibility, Scully's sold out too; the programme still manages to end on an image of Gillian Anderson in leather with big breasts holding a large gun.

I'm sure there was an attempt at satire here, but any irony in Chris Carter's direction gets lost within the sexism and the machismo. And as a story it's rubbish - endless sequences of the dullest virtual reality game devised, where there's no problem solving or intrigue, just endless bouts of shooting. (My God, by this time there was a clever enough game of The X-Files available on PlayStation, so it's not as if the creators didn't know there were better examples of the thing out there!) The final act, in which Scully grimly fires on a clan of cowgirls on tanks, whilst the computer programmers struggle interminably about *simply turning the game off* by pressing CTRL-delete, is one of the most unintentionally funny things the series has ever done. Boring, stupid, and actually offensive, this is one of the very worst X-Files ever. (*)

7.14, Theef

Air Date: March 12, 2000
Writers: Vince Gilligan, John Shiban,
Frank Spotnitz
Director: Kim Manners

Summary In San Francisco, the father-in-law of Dr Robert Wieder is found hanging from a skylight, the word "theef" written in blood on a nearby wall. Mulder suspects that witchcraft is responsible, even as the perpetrator - a ritualist named Orel Peattie - microwaves a voodoo doll and thereby chars Wieder's wife to death.

Wieder realises that Peattie wants revenge because he once euthanised his daughter, Lynette Peattie, after she was gravely injured in a bus accident. Scully shoots Peattie to stop him from murdering Wieder, rendering him comatose. However, she wonders if Peattie, as he claimed, could have used his voodoo techniques to save Lynette's life.

Critique This is an unusually solid entry to the flimsy seventh season, with a comprehensible plot, several effective set piece deaths, and a clear resolution. For this relief, much thanks. But "solid" doesn't necessarily mean "inspired" - and one thing that the writing combination of Gilligan, Shiban and Spotnitz left out this time was mystery. As early as the teaser, Peattie is revealed as being the villain behind the piece, and Billy Drago's sneering performance does nothing to disguise the fact. That he's using hexes to curse a family is immediately apparent too. And when we discover why, the last shred of depth that the story might have offered fades away.

Peattie is taking revenge on a respected doctor that he believes to be responsible for the death of his daughter. But the writers go so far to exonerate Dr Wieder from any blame that the story lacks any argument - Wieder alleviated the suffering of a girl with morphine who had thirty minutes to live at best, whose identity he never learned, and with no family members there to intervene. There's a hint of a story here, pitting Dr Wieder's conventional surgery against Peattie's folk medicine, and had the plot seen Dr Wieder deliberately flout the witch's instructions then there might have been something to write about. It'd have been topical too, and this almost becomes a neat reversal of the dilemmas religious believers face when they prevent doctors from operating upon loved ones. It's a theme which features in the En Ami teaser next week, and is disposed of within the first few minutes - it could have been explored more interestingly here. Instead, Dr Wieder is whiter than white, and Peattie, for all the free poultices he gives his landlady, is a bizarre vengeful madman who keeps his daughter's corpse rotting in his bed. When at the episode's conclusion Scully guiltily tells Mulder that as a doctor she'd have done the same as Wieder, it's hardly a revelation - the story has been so firmly biased towards him that it didn't offer him any alternatives.

The sequences where people are hit by Peattie's curses are nicely effective, even if the death by radiation is so signposted in advance that it robs the scene of any real tension. But Scully's temporary blindness is great, and the teaser is delightfully eerie. At the end of the day, Theef pussyfoots around with its assisted suicide theme too gently to say anything profound. It's just too unambitious an X-File to be anything more than a collection of moments, only some of which work. (**1/2)

7.15, En Ami

Air Date: March 19, 2000
Writer: William B Davis
Director: Rob Bowman

Summary The Cigarette Smoking Man asks for Scully's help in securing a cure for cancer - but only if she refrains from saying anything to Mulder, whom he's given up on. The Smoking Man claims that while he possesses miracle-chips such as the one in Scully's neck, he lacks the genetic science behind them. Together, however, they can obtain such data from a federal fugitive named "Cobra" and thus eliminate *all* cancer - indeed, all human illness - in the world. Dying from cerebral inflammation and with only months to live, the Smoking Man hopes that this will secure a better legacy for himself.

Cobra agrees to meet with Scully because, unbeknownst to her, the Smoking Man has hacked into her computer and been trading correspondence with Cobra for months. At the rendezvous, Cobra gives Scully a computer disk with his research - but the Black-Haired Man (X-Files: Fight the Future) shoots him dead, and is then slain by the Smoking Man. The Lone Gunmen examine Scully's disk, but find that the Smoking Man switched it for a blank. Scully is left to wonder if the Smoking Man saved himself at the expense of the human race, even as he tosses Cobra's computer disk into a river.

Critique The title is a clever pun, in French suggesting friendship, in English the exact opposite. It plays on the ambiguity that is the point of the episode - just how far can Scully trust the Cigarette Smoking Man, and is he as irredeemable as we might suppose? William B Davis has been claiming jokingly for years in interviews that he saw his shadowy character as the hero of the show, and he clearly sees a depth to the part that he wants to tap; I'd argue that in spite of his best efforts as actor, there's been really very little of that ambiguity that he now as a writer wishes to explore. And if one wants to write a character study of the Cigarette Smoking Man, why in the dying fall of the seventh season, when he has only one more regular appearance to make? For this to have been dramatically relevant, it would have been better to have attempted a story like this a couple of seasons ago at least, before his plans for the Syndicate turned to ruin.

Or so you might have thought. Instead Davis uses the idea that the character has passed his dramatic peak very wisely; throughout you get the sense of a man who could have affected the lives of billions, now reduced to a failure seeking some last small redemption. And like a dying wasp buzzing on its back, he's to be pitied, but can still sting. It's the reason why Scully is prepared to take off with him and his cure for cancer in the first place - and, as an analysis of the man, it works best as a study of spent and exhausted evil. Davis brings an awkward charm to the scenes in which he tells Scully of his affection for her, or buys her a dress for dinner; he almost scampers with delight at the chance to show off an elderly woman who doesn't think he's a monster. It's unsurprising that Davis as writer captures the portentous Carter-speak of the Smoking Man so well - he's had to say enough of it over the years! - but he gives the dialogue a humanity, an eagerness to please. And the script is wise enough at least to realise when it's delving into pop psychology, and says so, clearly.

The plot itself is all smoke (ahem) and mirrors, but that doesn't really matter. Davis has the generosity to realise that a character study of the Smoking Man is only useful in the way it throws light upon Scully, and seeing the two of them paired together, with Scully genuinely unable to resist the temptations of a man she despises, is thrilling and revealing. After a series of episodes which specialise in sleight of hand, it's great to see a con pulled off which is dramatically tense and keeps you guessing. And at the very end we cannot be sure, in his attempts to seduce Scully and change her opinions of him, just how much the Smoking Man has been affected by her companionship in spite of himself. Certainly the scenes in which he describes himself as a lonely man, or in which he gives up smoking for her sake, are played with a sincerity which seems even to take the character by surprise. The final sequence, in which the Smoking Man throws away the power he has manipulated Scully to acquire, may be a little pat, but thanks to Davis' skills as both actor and writer it's still very moving. (****1/2)

7.16, Chimera

Air Date: April 2, 2000
Writer: David Amann
Director: Cliff Bole

Summary In Vermont, the daughter of a federal judge, Martha Crittendon, sees a raven in her home and then goes missing after a shadowy, long-haired, clawed figure attacks her. Howard Crittendon, her husband, becomes the prime suspect when her body is found buried in their back yard.

Ellen Adderly, the wife of Sheriff Phil Adderly, reports seeing the savage beast that killed Martha in reflective surfaces. Mulder theorises that mirrors are acting as a doorway to a spirit world, enabling a spirit to come to Earth and manifest as a raven. The beast kills a woman named Jenny, and it's revealed that the sheriff was having affairs with her and Crittendon. Mulder identifies Ellen as the killer, speculating that she learned of her husband's adultery and developed a split personality - including the creature-aspect - as a means of coping. Ellen morphs into the creature and attacks Mulder, but her creature-aspect sees its own reflection and goes dormant, leaving her institutionalized.

Critique The plot itself is a little ho-hum, but David Amann's script is very stylish. As a series of horror scenes of suburbanites being attacked

by a monster, it just about passes muster. But as a study of what those suburbanites hope for, and the miseries that lie under the surface of the American Dream, it's acutely observed with fine dialogue and interesting characters. In a way it's a development of the rather more hysterical themes seen in Arcadia last season. But this is much more subtle. Ellen is a domestic goddess who just wants to be a good neighbour, a good mother, the perfect table setter and the perfect hostess. The sequence in which she shyly tells Mulder of the joys of marriage, and exhorts him to go out and find someone who'll protect him from all the darkness he investigates, is a joy; this is a woman so utterly in denial that she's repressed a monster of rage that can't bear to look at itself and attacks whatever challenges her concrete concepts of marital bliss. She's the prissy housewife, her husband the serial adulterer - both could easily have been played as stereotypes, but Michelle Joyner and John Mese bring a realism to the roles that make you feel they are truly trapped in the rituals of a relationship neither can be honest about. And Amann's script brilliantly pinpoints the little awkwardnesses and pitfalls that make up their daily conversation.

Duchovny is very good here, playing a Mulder who begins to enjoy too readily the sense of being in a family home, even as he sees it crumble beneath him. Encouraged by scripts too often to caricature the part these days, here he's sensitive and rational, using profiling skills to narrow in on the nature of the evil. And, as a counterbalance, Anderson provides some great comic relief, stuck in another plot altogether on a pointless surveillance job. The contrast between the Martha Stewart society Mulder is investigating and the seedy nightlife of prostitutes and piss she's spying on is pretty obvious, but in both stories Amann shows us there's something deeper behind the stereotype. It's perhaps a little too ponderously paced to be a classic episode, but it's clever and well crafted, and in a season which feels rather makeshift it's a rewarding stand-out. (****)

7.17, all things

Air Date: April 9, 2000
Writer / Director: Gillian Anderson

Summary By happenstance, Scully encounters Dr Daniel Waterston - her former medical school teacher and ex-lover - when he's hospitalised for a heart condition. The two of them reflect upon how Scully left the medical profession for the FBI because Waterston was married and she feared wrecking his family. His marriage ended shortly after Scully left, and Scully now wonders if she made the right choice.

Waterston's condition worsens, and Colleen Azar - one of Mulder's contacts, with information on crop circles - suggests that Waterston's ailment stems from an inner pain that must be removed. Events cause Scully to venture into a Buddhist temple, where her life flashes before her eyes. She's moved to conduct a healing ritual for Waterston, reviving him. However, she realises that she's not the same person who was once involved with him, and declines to rekindle their relationship.

Critique David Duchovny's first writer / director credit resisted the temptation to study Mulder, instead treating him as audience to a fable that found a new take on the themes of the series. Gillian Anderson, in her one stint as creative head, does the opposite and looks ever inwards. This is a meditation on self-analysis, and the benefit of slowing down. Hence many sequences of slow motion action to a chill-out Moby soundtrack as Scully... Walks down a street! Drives a car! Looks earnest! Looks thoughtful!

The problem is, if you study the minutiae of life too intensely, you may just find that there's little to examine. The characters Scully meets on her quest to self-discovery are, for all the long silences and meaningful hand holdings, dull ciphers. Daniel Waterston, lover from the past, ready with a romantic platitude even with an oxygen drip hanging from his nose; Colleen Azar, who lives in New Age simplicities and patronises Scully's rationale with such wide eyed smugness; Maggie Waterston, so angry and so two-dimensional that after all these years she can so hate a woman her father hasn't seen in over a decade. When such attention is put upon such ciphers as having Special Life Changing Importance to Scully, she's reduced to a cipher too. And Anderson's ever earnest dialogue has the strange effect of leaving you knowing less about a character you've spent seven years developing an affection for than when you started watching.

Anderson's direction is painfully pretentious too; there are some nice stylistic flourishes here and there, such as in the scene where the heart monitor begins to alarm when Scully allows herself to respond to Daniel's affection. But when an episode is composed of so *many* flourishes, regardless of pace or narrative context, they lose all significance. The result is something that at times looks like a dull afternoon TV movie of the week, and at others like a bizarre pop video. The net effect is very tedious indeed. Anderson the director does no favours to Anderson the actress, who comes across as stiff and awkward here, with occasional dips into the overwrought; the scene where she runs back and forth to a Buddha statue is so clumsy, it's honestly hilarious. It's all an attempt at something different, I grant you. But it falls too often into the strained effort of a student filmmaker - and one who's working on a three million dollar budget. (*)

7.18, Brand X

Air Date: April 16, 2000
Writers: Steven Maeda, Greg Walker
Director: Kim Manners

Summary Mulder and Scully venture to Winston-Salem, North Carolina, when a researcher for Morley Tobacco dies, his neck and lung flesh stripped away by a beetle. The agents and Skinner learn that Morley was attempting to genetically create a safer variety of tobacco plant, which accidentally enhanced a ferocious type of tobacco beetle that lays its larvae in people's lungs. Mulder becomes infected with the larvae; Scully and Skinner track down Daniel Weaver - the only test subject to survive Morley's experiments. Scully finds that Weaver's higher-than-average cigarette consumption protected him from the beetles, as nicotine is a powerful insecticide. Scully super-doses Mulder with nicotine, killing his beetle eggs but leaving him with a craving for cigarettes.

Critique This one's a couple of drafts away from being a very good episode. The idea is clever and relevant, that a company's attempts to alter the DNA of a tobacco plant have also affected the composition of the beetles which feed off it. Passive smoking was a particularly topical subject after Oscar nominations were given to The Insider, and it's given a smart X-Files spin here, with scenes generating real tension based upon whether Weaver will light up in front of potential victims. And after the series has spent seven years casting aspersions on government bureaucracy, it's fun to see it take a pot shot at corporate America too - a network of suits who, impervious to FBI interference, seem just as covert and as amoral an organisation as the Syndicate plotting with alien invaders.

It's a great premise, with lots of gore and larvae. But a premise and larvae are all we get, and halfway through, once the episode reveals what its concept is, the story is left with nowhere to go. We get instead puzzling scenes of padding, where test subject Weaver smokes inside a petrol station: we're presumably meant to believe that the cashier upon whom he inflicts his second-hand smoke is doomed, but there's no pay-off. And this is indicative of a final act which offers no real climax either. Weaver delivers a long speech to Skinner, exposing him all the time he does so to his lethal smoke, telling him why he won't dare shoot him - only to have Skinner to shoot him anyway. Mulder is cured of his particularly lurid flesh-eating disease when Scully, as if realising she's in the final few minutes of the show, hits upon the solution as a brainwave. The story never tells us how the passive smoking kills - the early deaths suggest it must be as a result of prolonged exposure. Indeed, the death in the teaser of Scobie, protected as he is by the FBI, could only have taken place sealed away from Weaver and his cigarettes. But later infections take place only on immediate contact with Weaver, and Mulder falls ill after a conversation with him which lasts barely a minute. It's witty to have a cigarette used as a weapon - especially on this series! - but the threat is diluted when it's never made clear in just how much danger any victim is likely to be.

They're all problems you feel could have been ironed out fairly easily - perhaps, as the season finale drew close, everyone just ran out of time. It's a pity: before it runs out of steam, this is entertaining stuff. Tobin Bell gives a terrific performance as Weaver, a man who is happy to live in filth and sees his addiction to nicotine a symbol of America, an inalienable right protected by the Constitution. And it's great to see Mitch Pileggi outside Skinner's office for once, actively aiding Mulder and Scully in their investigation, baulking at an autopsy, and visibly cringing when for once he's on the wrong side of an FBI superior chewing him out and demanding results. (**1/2)

7.19, Hollywood A.D.

Air Date: April 30, 2000
Writer / Director: David Duchovny

Summary As Mulder and Scully look into the bombing of a church crypt, Skinner instructs them to let scriptwriter Wayne Federman - a friend of his from college - tag along and make notes for a motion picture on their investigations. The agents learn that Cardinal O'Fallon, the church priest, was purchasing forged religious documents from a counterculture revolutionary named Micah Hoffman, thinking they were real.

Hoffman's body is found, but he suddenly returns to life, possibly owing to vibrations from a spinning bowl inscribed with the words Christ used to resurrect Lazarus. When Federman's movie comes out, Mulder despairs because it's a bunch of silliness starring Garry Shandling and Tea Leoni. Scully tells Mulder that O'Fallon has murdered the revived Hoffman and then hung himself, even as Mulder spins a cheap replica of the "Lazarus Bowl". Unbeknownst to the agents, this makes a host of the undead come to life and dance about.

Critique Gillian Anderson went for angstful character study and minimalism two weeks ago, and David Duchovny goes for exuberance and comedy and ideas firing off in all different directions. It's just as self-indulgent, and really, just as difficult to sit through. The only saving grace is that it has enough jokes in it that *some* of them are funny.

These funny moments, too, are the ones where Duchovny isn't trying so hard. The way that even the pontiff of the church, the man most likely to be the first American pope, is as much a part of the cell phone lifestyle as a Hollywood writer. The sequence where we see in the far background Scully teaching Tea Leoni how to run, pounding back and forth on the soundstage - and without Scully noticing, Leoni losing interest and taking a call. The ending, too, in which Mulder and Scully get to sit on a fake grassy knoll, and contemplate posterity and the joys of a Bureau credit card, is rather sweet. But - and it's a big "but" - every single time a moment is offered which has the pace or the wit to make you enjoy the gag, Duchovny fetches another item from his kitchen sink and destroys it. So the story ends not on a delicate character moment but with a dance number of zombies, ironically resurrected by cheap plastic merchandise.

It's such a frenetic episode that so appears to be about *everything* - the corrupting influence of modern culture, the irony of a blasphemer believing he is Christ reborn, the sound resonance of every object - that it ultimately ends up being about nothing at all. And the theme that looks the most fun, as pursued in the title and in the teaser, that of a Hollywood studio turning an X-File into bad art, is squandered. The distinction between reality and fantasy is a staple X-Files conceit, but never given such licence for jokes as it is here. Millennium attempted this sort of story last year, and it was awful, partly because the series had never established a style consistent enough to be parodied. The X-Files should have been different; here is a series that really *did* go to movies, which really *did* shift production to California. But what was required was a contrast between a simple and typical X-File, and the way that Hollywood plundered it and distorted it. Instead the X-File itself, something about a bowl that may be able to bring back the dead, is lost within ongoing machinations between forgers and priests. The storyline is so diffuse and offering so little dramatic action, it's a wonder that Hollywood would have wanted to adapt it in the first place.

And that, really, is the problem. This ought to have been something dazzling. But all the discipline Duchovny showed to such great effect in

his debut has been sacrificed; this is a chaotic mess of show-off gags. (The worst of these gags are *nothing* to do with The X-Files, and all to do with in-jokes outside of it. The scenes with Garry Shandling play off the gay attraction Duchovny appeared to demonstrate for him as a guest on Shandling's fictional chat show, The Larry Sanders Show; the sequence where Mulder speculates whether Tea Leoni, Duchovny's real life wife, fancies him or not, is cute and self-referential in the most irritating way.) This is just as pretentious as "all things" - and at least that still seemed to *want* to be about something. In contrast, Hollywood A.D. just feels like a cynical exercise in showing too much cleverness and yet not enough intelligence. (*)

7.20, Fight Club

Air Date: May 7, 2000
Writer: Chris Carter
Director: Paul Shapiro

Summary After two FBI agents beat themselves up, Mulder and Scully investigate a strange case concerning Betty Templeton and Lulu Pfeiffer - two exact duplicates who, wittingly or unwittingly, make people in their vicinity attack one another. Evidence suggests that Betty and Lulu have shadowed each other through seventeen states, triggering personal violence and even shattering physical objects by their mere presence.

Betty and Lulu both vie for the love of wrestler Bert Zupanic, but their rivalry causes an auditorium of people to attack one another. Scully finds that Zupanic also has a double, but bringing the twin to the arena just increases the violence when Zupanic spots his sibling. Afterward, a battered Scully and Mulder theorise that Betty and Lulu, as with Zupanic and his twin, are half-siblings owing to sperm donation. The odds of their meeting was only one in twenty-seven million, but owing to some force that wreaks havoc whenever the siblings meet, such encounters are best avoided.

Critique This is very odd and rather original and almost entirely dreadful.

This might seem like the appropriate time to ask a pertinent question. What on earth has happened to The X-Files in its seventh season?

In the past the series has suffered for two different reasons - always in a state of flux and development, episodes have failed either when they haven't taken into account the fresh direction the series was exploring, or have pushed too hard into those new areas and experimented too wildly. But even the worst of the first six seasons had the sheen of effort to them; the mistakes that were made were, I'd argue, part of the process that produced the successes. Until its somewhat disastrous seventh year, The X-Files was at its least confident in Season One - when, understandably, it drifted around for a while trying to find out what sort of series it was. Episodes like The Jersey Devil or Fire or Gender Bender may not be the most distinguished entries in the canon, but you feel that by dropping the ball with these stories, Chris Carter and company learned from the experience.

Until Season Seven, The X-Files has been typified by a forward momentum. Where the series has ended up - less about scares and more about shocks and quirkiness - may not have been what Chris Carter originally intended, but the process felt natural and unforced. The only stumbling block was when the entire fifth season appeared to be running on the spot to accommodate the first feature film, but the series recovered with a new California-based show which had a new dynamism. The seventh season feels as if it's no longer certain of its own future. At the time Fight Club was made, nobody knew whether it was one of the final episodes ever to be produced. The cast were clearly willing to admit to the press that they'd be relieved should the show be cancelled, there were increasing reports that Duchovny and Anderson had fallen out, and Duchovny was suing the network for lost royalties. The innocence and charm of The X-Files had gone. And with no guaranteed continuation, with the storylines wrapped up, and nothing new to say, Season Seven is a schizophrenic beast. Half the time it doesn't seem to care any more. And the other half it rushes about in a frenzy, like a bull in a china shop, as if keen to play around and have as much fun as possible before the lights go out. Either way it's undisciplined, and either way there's a feeling that there's nothing new to be developed, no new direction that there's the

time to explore. The X-Files, finally, is creatively bankrupt.

Chris Carter's Fight Club is a story so ineptly written and structured, so illogical and haphazard in plot, and so mean-spirited in tone, that it almost feels like a deliberate statement. Kathy Griffin plays two identical doppelgangers, both so biologically and mentally similar that each gives the impression that the one is stalking the other. When they meet, or even think of each other, earthquakes take place, drain covers blow, and everyone in a close vicinity starts fighting. That's pretty much the story. For the length of the episode, the same sequences play out with an increasing sense of déjà vu, until the climax in a wrestling match where the entire audience watching breaks out into fisticuffs too. Including, the final shots reveal, Mulder and Scully themselves, who have clearly beaten each other up with such ferocity that they've both required surgery.

The level of coincidence in the story, which pivots upon the doppelgangers' boyfriend *also* having an unexpected double, is so brazen that it can only be the point: Carter is saying that these stories simply don't make sense any longer. Scully concludes that the only moral from the case she can glean is that it's not worth looking too deeply into the paranormal, which is about a cynical a statement about what The X-Files stands for as Carter could possibly make. Nothing, Carter says, showing us all these doubles (even Mulder and Scully have a pair), is unique, nothing is special. As a series, The X-Files might once have seemed precious, and now it isn't. And to make the point all the clearer, he swaps Mulder and Scully's dialogue about, just to rid them of their characters; he confines them to a few scenes of exposition where they seem to be making reports to a wrestling manager they've only just met, and punching each other's lights out. The final moments of Fight Club are clearly intended to be funny, but it's a particularly jaundiced sense of humour, our heroes scarred and bruised by their own hands.

Fight Club is a marker for a series that seems to want to die now, please. Or if not die, at least *know* whether it has to get back on to the conveyor belt, for another year or two, and find a way to produce something fresh. But for the moment, it doesn't want to make the effort. And ironically, it's tonally one of the most atypical episodes the series ever made, conceived in spite and self-loathing and sheer exhaustion. (*)

7.21, Je Souhaite

Air Date: May 14, 2000
Writer / Director: Vince Gilligan

Summary Anson Stokes, an employee at a self-storage lot in Creve Coeur, Missouri, finds a dark-haired woman, actually a genie, wrapped in a rug. The genie grants Stokes three wishes, but his final wish - invisibility - results in a car hitting him. The invisible corpse puzzles Mulder and Scully, but Stokes' brother Leslie acquires the genie and wishes his brother back to life. This leaves Anson in an undead state, and a mishap causes the brothers' trailer to explode, obliterating both of them.

Mulder takes possession of the genie, whom he names "Jenn". His wish for peace on Earth causes every person save him to vanish, and he uses his second wish to cancel the first. Bested, Mulder uses his third wish to grant Jenn's greatest desire - that she become human and end her servitude.

Critique Thank God for Vince Gilligan, the one member of The X-Files' writing staff who is still coming up with the goods. Je Souhaite is a lovely piece of work, a simple comedy that is sweet and charming, and has to it a quiet unforced profundity. A genie doesn't really fit into the tone of The X-Files - it's a little too silly and fantastical, and it's telling that to explain to the wonderfully stupid Lesley Stokes what one is, Mulder has to sing a sitcom theme tune. But this is the end of an era, the last standalone episode that features Mulder and Scully together, and the device is used as a celebration. Scully at last gets her evidence of the supernatural, giggling like an excitable little girl when she prepares an autopsy of an invisible man. And Mulder tries to beat the system, to be the hero and wish for peace on Earth - only to wipe everyone off the planet in the process. What could easily have been a rather gimmicky little comedy instead becomes an affectionate portrait of our two heroes, just as they're about to be snatched away from us: the last time we'll see them properly

banter, the last time they'll have a chance to sit on a sofa together with beers and watch a Chevy Chase movie.

It's the characters that Gilligan finds worthwhile, the bond between Mulder and Scully which gives The X-Files its heart. And it recognises in the last reel that the series was never really about solving *big* problems and saving the world - as Scully points out, if Mulder could wish all the horrors of the world away, he'd also be ridding it of the very point of human endeavour. The genie - played with a lovely wry touch by Paula Sorge - says that for five hundred years all mankind has had in common is its stupidity, that it always chooses the wrong wish. Gilligan's ultimate point is that wish-fulfilment itself is the stupidity, that nothing worthwhile can be earned by wishing. Anson never notices that his brother is missing his legs, but then, nor does his brother - he'd rather wish for a golden wheelchair than his health. Mulder tries to come up with a foolproof wish that is specific in every last detail and cannot be misinterpreted, believing there's a trick to his being happy; but in the end he needs to do the opposite, to be free and easy and put less effort in. His final act of generosity is to release the genie from a lifetime of overwhelming power - and she is, at last, gratefully able to drink an innocent coffee and watch the world go by. The best things in life, as she says, come from the realisation that you need to live your life moment by moment, not try to change the world around you. In a way one could argue that this is as much against the whole tenor of The X-Files, what this action series stands for, as Fight Club is - it's the exact opposite stance that Amor Fati took at the very start of the season, where Mulder's indolence allows the world to be destroyed - but here instead the moral is warm and winning and full of hope.

If this had been the final standalone episode of the series, as it so easily might have been, it'd have been nevertheless appropriate. After all the seven years of chases and struggles and quests, the tender truth that is out there is that the best thing to seek is the comfort of watching Caddyshack with someone you love. Even as it is, it marks the end of an era: it's a perfect note of bliss which the series will never be able to capture again. (*****)

7.22, Requiem

Air Date: May 21, 2000
Writer: Chris Carter
Director: Kim Manners

Summary Billy Miles, an abductee that Mulder and Scully encountered seven years ago (1.1, Pilot), phones to say that abductions have resumed in Bellefleur, Oregon. Meanwhile, the Cigarette Smoking Man - now confined to a wheelchair and dying - tasks Krycek with recovering a shrouded alien spaceship that collided with a military aircraft in Oregon. The Cigarette Smoking Man believes that this is their best hope of reviving the alien conspiracy.

Krycek betrays the Cigarette Smoking Man and tells Mulder about the spaceship, even as an alien bounty hunter rounds up the Bellefleur abductees. Mulder and Skinner search for the ship while Scully agrees to remain in Washington, D.C., acknowledging concerns that her status as an abductee might make her a target. However, the Lone Gunmen determine that Mulder experienced anomalous brain behaviour similar to that of the abductees, meaning that he's in far greater danger.

A force field keeps Skinner at bay while Mulder finds a group of abductees, Miles included, standing in a circle of light under a spaceship. Mulder joins them, and the bounty hunter steps forward. The light intensifies; Skinner sees the ship departing and finds himself alone. He tells Scully of Mulder's disappearance - even as Scully informs Skinner that while she doesn't know how it's happened, she's pregnant.

Critique Let's suppose, just for a moment, that this really was the end.

There's an air of finality to this episode, of things coming full circle. Mulder and Scully return to the setting of the pilot, are again chasing UFOs. But this time, for all the similarities of the case, so much subtly has changed. Billy Miles is a police officer, and is now old enough not only to have married, but even to be divorced. Teresa Hoese is a wife and mother. Mulder and Scully are remembered by the children who have become adults, and have new responsibilities. Whilst our heroes are still pursuing the same case, whilst their lives appear to have been at standstill for seven years, the world has moved on without them: and yet here they are, still romantically unfulfilled, still denied respect by the FBI they've given their lives to. (As Skinner says to Mulder, after he's been taken apart by an auditor who feels he could conduct his investigations more cheaply on the Internet, "They just don't like you.") They have sacrificed so much - the recurring motif of Scully being barren, Mulder's search for his sister concluded but without firm resolution - and are right back where they started.

There's a wonderful scene which deliberately recalls the pilot, in which Scully comes to Mulder's room at night panicked about her health. At the beginning of the series he can soon allay her fears - telling her that she has mosquito bites, not scars akin to those found on abductees - and the late night conversation between the two of them that ensues allows Mulder to open up about his mission; a friendship is forged. In Requiem, as the sequence is replayed, Mulder calls upon her to abandon her mission, fearing for her, wanting to protect her - he cradles her in bed, reassures her, and makes *her* (and not an alien hunt) the centre of his concern. There's a sense at last of the two of them reaching some sort of maturity, that the world that has grown up without their noticing will claim them too.

And, ultimately, it's not the real world that claims Mulder, but a flying saucer. It's so fitting that he's taken away just as Scully discovers that the real-life responsibilities have won out after all, that she's pregnant. The Cigarette Smoking Man has one last gambit to achieve power, and Krycek's response is to give him an undignified end, tipping his wheelchair down a flight of stairs. So close to death and still smoking, albeit through a hole in his neck, the evil genius of the series is shown to be at last a pathetic cipher. Mitch Pileggi is, in the closing moments, allowed a moment of affirmation to the truth and to the X-Files so sincere, it counts as his most moving performance.

Had this been the ending... the genius of it would have been that it stayed true to the show. That it never tried to come up with some nebulous truth, but right to the very last moment, with Scully's announcement of her pregnancy, kept us guessing. There'd have been a poetic rightness to that.

So what damages this episode? Really, nothing so much as that it wasn't the end. With a future ahead of The X-Files, Scully's pregnancy no longer seems like cruel irony, but a bit of character baggage that will only weigh Scully down over the coming seasons. Mulder's abduction, too, can no longer be the most fitting exit for his character, but just another end of season cliffhanger, of no greater import than burning in a boxcar or faking his own suicide. And the cyclical structure of the story, of closing where it began, now looks nothing more distinctive than a seven-year-old bit of continuity. The boldness of Requiem, really, is all in its willingness to end

so ambiguously. But with two seasons still to go, that ambiguity loses its force, and all the usual mytharc faults come into play; lots of dark mutterings about answers affecting all mankind and regular characters coming to sticky ends. The déjà vu only works if it's the end of the book - if it's just another chapter, it's something we've read too many times before.

After a season that has been lacklustre at best, it does its job at making the audience anticipate the following season and where the show could go from here. That's the problem. Against the odds, after all the disappointments of the year, Requiem is strong enough to leave its audience wanting more. Whether the series should really have gone on to *give* more is another matter altogether. (****)

The X-Files: Season 8

8.1, Within

Air Date: Nov. 5, 2000
Writer: Chris Carter
Director: Kim Manners

Summary Promoted to Deputy Director, Kersh assigns Agent John Doggett to lead a task force and find Mulder. Based upon medical records, Doggett suggests that Mulder's abnormal brain activity (7.2, The Sixth Extinction II: Amor Fati) imperilled his life so much that he faked his abduction rather than let his work be acknowledged as a failure.

The Lone Gunmen trace the spaceship that abducted Mulder to Arizona, and Scully realises that Gibson Praise (6.1, The Beginning) is the next target. Scully, Skinner and Doggett rush there - the latter convinced that Mulder wants to kidnap Gibson. The boy is abducted from the Flemingtown School for the Deaf, and Doggett confronts the kidnapper - who turns around and reveals himself as Mulder - out in the desert. [To be continued.]

Critique And here we are, with The X-Files seven years old, its ratings in decline, its lead actor gone walkabout, with over a hundred and fifty episodes seeming to cover every single aspect of the paranormal there can be. At this stage the most controversial thing the series could do is continue to exist.

The X-Files has long been characterised by an unwillingness to embrace big change; the feature film didn't give the mytharc the jolt it promised, so revelations had to be filtered into the following two seasons to less visible effect. But, in contradiction of that, it's always been very good at subtle reinvention - as the media got more and more frustrated with a show which never appeared to answer the questions they thought were due, it had altered its style towards something more self-mocking and post-modern. By the time Chris Carter had got around to ending the Syndicate conspiracy, or revealing what had happened to Samantha Mulder, it wasn't so much that the viewers had

run out of patience but that the show itself had - the storylines were no longer tonally relevant. By refusing to allow The X-Files to develop its own back story naturally, Carter forced a situation where the show evolved *in spite of* the back story. That was always its greatest strength, that it was more powerful and encompassing a series than the early premise suggested, or that Chris Carter had seeded.

So Within is fascinating, because by removing Mulder as the central focus, a change is *forced* upon the series - and it's adamantly not the change of evolving tone that the show has adapted itself to accept, but something which crashes the gears somewhat. Even the opening title sequence is telling - all those peculiar (and, admittedly, somewhat overfamiliar) images of eyes and shadows are replaced by Duchovny falling into an eye. There's a new mission statement. Whatever it claims, The X-Files is no longer primarily concerned with exploring the paranormal. It's about exploring what happens when your lead actor is absent. And it's going to do that, rather bravely, not by merely soldiering on without him, but by reminding the viewers of his continued absence each week by showcasing it in the titles. Is that a sensible thing to do? Possibly. Only if the pay-off to the Mulder story has due impact, and only - and this is the clincher - if once that pay-off is delivered, the series never again attempts the same stunt. If The X-Files is now about the quest for Mulder, he has to be found - and at that stage, having been found, he can't simply go disappearing once more. The decision puts Chris Carter into a bind. It presupposes that Duchovny's publicised new contract only to commit to half of Season Eight's episodes is a *temporary* respite for the actor, and that if the show lingers on beyond that he'll be back and fully engaged. If not, there's a danger that this entire new storyline will feel like it's a waste of time.

For the moment, though, the changes wrought upon The X-Files give it a new focus that make this the best season opener for many years. It's slow paced - but it's *determinedly* slow, as the series maps out the new path it's taking.

It does this with great skill. The teaser is abrupt and brilliant, leading the viewer to believe that we're being presented simply with a view of Scully's unborn baby, but connecting it with Mulder being an experimental lab rat on board a spaceship - that Mulder is still linked to Scully, even by umbilical cord, is what this story is all about. Scully's grief and anger, coupled with Skinner's newly found compulsion to stand by Mulder and his truth, has a sincerity to it which is very touching; as inconvenient as Duchovny's absence is, it gives a series which had descended largely into self-mockery a renewed urgency. Both Scully and Skinner are reinvigorated by Mulder's disappearance, and Anderson and Pileggi rise to the challenge of redefining characters so long established and making of them something new.

They're helped considerably by Robert Patrick as John Doggett. The introduction of a new lead character was always to be Chris Carter's biggest gamble - and not just for the obvious reasons. To be blunt, The X-Files has had a dreadful track record of introducing recurring characters who have little charm or personality - the last one that made any real impact was Krycek, and that was six years ago. All the others since, your Maritas and Spenders and Fowleys, have failed for one common reason - they've all been so untrustworthy and conspiratorial that they've never had room to breathe. Doggett's introduction is very cleverly handled, as Carter deliberately plays up that very cliché - he's immediately seen as someone in Kersh's pocket, whose first action is to lie to Scully and gather information for the enemy. Carter knows that the audience are immediately going to dislike Mulder's replacement, and so does nothing to hide from it. But it's testament to the honesty that Patrick brings to the performance that little by little you begin to realise that he is nobody's fool and nobody's lackey, but a man of integrity coming at a case not with the flights of fancy the series is used to but with procedural thoroughness and care. Responding to the X-Files with such scepticism could easily have made Doggett look like a reactionary idiot like Spender - when The X-Files has been *this* big a success, you almost feel that the characters too ought to have been watching it. But Robert Patrick is so believable that he manages to make Mulder seem a darker and more ambiguous fig-

ure too, the revelation that he was keeping secrets from Scully suggesting that she (and, by extension, the audience) never knew him as well as we thought. The skill of this is that by the episode's end, and Mulder is seen on the edge of a precipice, he's become something of a threat.

The episode sings when it reinvents the old and introduces the new. It stumbles somewhat when it hearkens back to seasons old storylines. The return of Kersh is contrived but forgivable. Not seen since One Son, he's now a useful character again - if only because with Skinner as a bona fide ally, the series needs someone adversarial once more. That Kersh gets his promotion the day after Mulder's disappearance stretches our credulity a bit - what rotten timing! - but it's just about acceptable. And James Pickens Jr *is* very good in the role.

The return of Gibson Praise almost derails the episode altogether, however. After a creditably clean half-hour in which Mulder's disappearance is analysed from every angle, the story loses focus when it raids the cookie jar of former plot macguffins. Gibson, the key to all the questions in the X-Files, went missing at the start of Season Six; it only takes a few minutes' concerted effort by the FBI to find the lost child two years after they've bothered to remember him. And with all due respect to actor Jeff Gulka, his reappearance isn't as satisfying as Pickens'. As seen in The End, Gibson was a cute kid whose brilliance was offset by youthful vulnerability - but all this time on, after he's had his brain poked at and his head shaved, Gulka is a rather charmless podgy boy with one facial expression. The story honestly doesn't need Gibson Praise, or the associated baggage the character brings - he only manages to make an episode that seemed as if it was giving The X-Files a bold new beginning feel like it's about to offer more of the same old stodge. (****)

8.2, Without

Air Date: Nov. 12, 2000
Writer: Chris Carter
Director: Kim Manners

Summary Gibson escapes, and Mulder vanishes after falling off a cliff. Scully concludes that "Mulder" was actually an alien bounty hunter, sent to abduct Gibson because he's part alien. Scully deduces that the bounty hunter has taken Skinner's form and shoots him in the back of the neck, killing him. The state takes Gibson into protective custody. Doggett is assigned to the X-Files and vows to continue the search for Mulder. Meanwhile, the real Mulder lies strapped to an alien surgical table, surrounded by bounty hunters.

Critique We've seen a lot of this before, of course. Skinner and Scully pointing guns at each other, unsure of their loyalty. The heroes being shapeshifter bounty hunters in disguise. An FBI director conspiring against an agent by tainting his career with the X-Files. Even the sequence where Scully is moved to see a spaceship in the sky - and to realise it's only a helicopter - is familiar.

And yet all the elements have rarely been used so well. This feels like the first time that the paranoia induced by an alien who can steal anyone's identity has been fully exploited - Mulder, Scully and Skinner all get to be villains, and Chris Carter very cleverly keeps us guessing time after time whether anyone is who they claim to be. It's helped enormously by the setting of the Arizona desert being so strangely claustrophobic in spite of itself, echoing (as so many good X-Files do) the isolated community under threat in The Thing. And if we've seen the helicopter shot before, it's different this time because it's John Doggett who gets out.

What makes these replayed elements so successful is that Doggett witnesses them. The sequence where Skinner convinces Doggett that Kersh is trying to discredit him works precisely because Doggett isn't Mulder, isn't a man given over to conspiracy theories; indeed, he's a man who is typically solid and is likely to run the FBI one day. Robert Patrick plays the scene with the

sort of wounded expression of a pet realising that its master wants to hurt him - and it's the way that his mind is gradually opened in the episode that makes the routine so fresh. If he's not ready to accept the paranormal, he's now at least willing to concede the all-too normal, the deceit and the power games that will send him down to the FBI basement.

Of course the story can't resolve. It's typified by a scene in which Scully shouts aimlessly at Mulder in the dark; it's as if the series itself is crying out into the wilderness. But that's also its brilliance, oddly enough. The irony that Scully is right beside the spaceship housing Mulder, that Mulder's one line in the episode is to call despairingly for his partner as she loses trace of him, makes the show dangerous again. Whatever else The X-Files may have been these last two seasons, its experiments in storytelling were symptoms of formula and complacency. That can no longer be the case. Whether The X-Files ought to be continuing is a moot point; it's here anyway, and Chris Carter has met the challenge of that continuation head on. And in a tense episode which returns to the paranoia which summed up The X-Files' early years, it also finds time for a curious beauty. Director Kim Manners makes the desert look stunning by both day and night, the sequence where Scully breaks down realising she may never see her partner again hugely affecting, and the closing scene where a tortured Mulder is approached on all sides by identical bounty hunters marvellously eerie. It's that beauty, emotion and horror which in collision make The X-Files one of the best shows on TV. (*****)

8.3, Patience

Air Date: Nov. 19, 2000
Writer / Director: Chris Carter

Summary Scully and Doggett investigate a double homicide in Burley, Idaho, that possibly involves a large bat-creature. Doggett uncovers a newspaper account of a similar attack in 1956, and Scully believes that the case is connected to Ariel McKesson - a woman who disappeared that year, and whose charred body was discovered just a week ago.

The agents go to Bird Island and find Ariel's husband, Ernie Stefaniuk, who fought the giant bat in 1956. Stefaniuk says that as bats are very close to apes - and apes are close to humans - on the evolutionary ladder, they're dealing with a man who lives and hunts like a bat. The creature wants to kill anyone connected to Stefaniuk's scent, so Stefaniuk has lived in hiding ever since the 1956 incident. The bat-man kills Stefaniuk, then flies away after Scully and Doggett fire several slugs into him. Doggett's performance on the case impresses Scully, and she grants him a desk in Mulder's office.

Critique   Having introduced Doggett to the wonders of the mytharc story, it's time to show him what a monster of the week episode looks like. It's been quite a while since The X-Files has tackled a decent old-fashioned monster show, and there's something refreshing about seeing a teaser in which a doomed couple get offed without irony by a winged predator. Unfortunately, Patience isn't really that decent a monster story at all. It's illogical and silly, and so plodding it doesn't even put in its quota of shocks and scares. It's about a man-bat creature on a revenge spree, having waited forty-four years to pick up the scent of a man responsible for the death of his spouse-bat. Said man is rather stupid, having escaped from the bat only to hide all these years on a little island in utter isolation mere miles away, rather than go and live somewhere - anywhere - a bit safer. That he's managed to get away with this for forty-four years, mind you, only demonstrates that the bat monster is slightly stupider than he is.

But a lot of this works anyway. And that's because the scenes between Doggett and Scully are so good. If the episode was merely about showing how Doggett fitted into a routine X-File, adjusting his traditional cop approach to the paranormal, it would be interesting but obvious. But it's far more about how Scully adjusts to being the expert (in spite of her vociferous denials that she's anything but), how she becomes the one whose theories irritate the local police force, about how she is required to be the investigator who needs to make that imaginative leap into the unknown. It's the very first episode in which Duchovny does not participate, but the spirit of Mulder is in every scene. The episode proper begins with a camera

shot of his nameplate, and ends on the same, with the very words "Fox Mulder" being shut away in a drawer. Scully spends the story trying to compensate for her partner's absence, from the very moment where she brings Doggett up to speed on a new case with a slideshow. She stumbles only when she's trying too hard to be someone she's not - and the best of the episode demonstrates that it's Scully's scientific rationale working in concert with Mulder's lateral thinking that wins through.

The only pity is that this wasn't put to better use in a more exciting episode; this particular case hardly stretched anyone's deductive prowess. As a Mulder and Scully adventure, this would have been bottom of the barrel stuff. Featuring *Doggett* and Scully, there's enough on offer that's new that it gets away with it. Just about. If you're feeling charitable. (**1/2)

8.4, Roadrunners

Air Date: Nov. 26, 2000
Writer: Vince Gilligan
Director: Rod Hardy

Summary   A traveller named Hank Gulatarski boards a bus in Juab County, Utah, then watches as the passengers disembark and stone a man on crutches to death. Moments later, the mob overpowers Gulatarski.

Scully investigates the incident solo and soon finds evidence of cult activity. Some of the locals ask her to give medical aid to the ailing Gulatarski; Scully finds that he's been implanted with a slug-parasite at the base of his spine. She removes part of it, then flees to get help. The parasite within Gulatarski speaks through his voice, telling its disciples that they need to arrange another body swap.

Doggett uncovers records of similar attacks and goes to Utah to find Scully. The cultists capture Scully and implant her with the slug, but Doggett charges to the rescue, yanks out the slug and shoots it. The locals mourn the death of the creature they worshipped, and Scully realises it's in her best interest to keep Doggett better informed.

Critique   Director Rod Hardy's first feature film, Thirst, was about a woman who finds herself unwittingly made the leader of a vampire cult, then discovers that every apparent innocent around her wishes to make her the centre of their unholy obsession. Twenty years later, in his X-Files debut, Hardy tackles a script which almost feels like a homage to that work. Scully is trapped within a desert community whose members do everything in their amiable power to prevent her from leaving - after all, they need her to be the host for the second coming of Jesus. That in true X-Files fashion, "Jesus" in this case is a giant slug which attaches itself to a victim's spine is the source of some rather black humour - there's something truly horrific in watching a group of churchgoers praise the Lord as they stone an unacceptable carrier for Christ to death.

For the first half-hour, this works as a terrific slow burn horror story, in which Scully is wise enough to twig immediately that behind the smiles of a people only too eager to give her free gas and accommodation is something altogether less neighbourly. It's the transition of Gillian Anderson's performance from wry exasperation to outright paranoia, jumping for her gun at the slightest knock at the door, which makes this so effective. Then she becomes a victim, in a scene of grisly horror that recalls Ice but outdoes it - in the first season they'd never have actually put the worm inside the hero. And the story cleverly becomes a gross parody of where the series is taking Scully's character as future mother. She swears at the community, who all but smother her with best wishes and nurturing concern, when she hears them refer to the creature growing inside her as a "him". Vince Gilligan slyly shows the horror of childbirth, of a woman losing control of her body to incubate a new life. And in having that child be something that strangers want to worship, he anticipates the storyarc for the latter part of the season and beyond.

Roadrunners makes the point too that Scully needs a partner to survive; she may not have a Mulder, so she'll have to make do with a Doggett. On the one hand it's intriguing to see Gilligan cut Robert Patrick's role to a minimum, leaving Doggett in the background in the way he'd rightly expect a still-resistant audience would want. On the other, for all the final act scenes where Patrick gets to carry Anderson in

his arms as rescuing hero, it's hardly the best way to develop him as a character. All that The X-Files is doing by treating him this way is turning him into a totem, the symbolic necessary sidekick. It works better than it should, and it helps that the final scene emphasises Scully's mistake in excluding Doggett from her investigation. But for all that, it does make the episode at times feel curiously unbalanced. (****)

8.5, Invocation

Air Date: Dec. 3, 2000
Writer: David Amann
Director: Richard Compton

Summary   Ten years after he disappeared from a school carnival in Dexter, Oklahoma, seven-year-old Billy Underwood resurfaces - looking not a day older than when he vanished. Billy remains mute, but connections surface between him and a five-pointed symbol. One of the locals, Ronnie Purcell, confesses to Doggett that he participated in Billy's kidnapping, murder and burial ten years ago. After Billy's brother Josh is abducted, Purcell names his mother's boyfriend, Cal Jeppy, as his accomplice. Scully and Doggett race to Jeppy's carnival trailer - which features a five-pointed pony ride - and arrest Jeppy, saving the boy. Afterward, Doggett gets a final glimpse of Billy before finding the boy's skeleton.

Critique   Writer David Amann's greatest strength is his ability to elicit real-world reactions out of fantastical situations. His most interesting stories play this to the hilt - so that Terms of Endearment shows the attempts of a devil to produce an ordinary son, and Chimera's depiction of a wife in denial that her marriage is in trouble unleashes a monster within her. Where Invocation excels is in the awkwardness of a family coming to terms with the return of a family member thought lost to them. For ten years, the Underwoods have prayed for their abducted child to be found - and when he is, miraculously having not aged a day, he can't be slotted so easily into a household which has been defined by his absence. The embarrassment of a father realising he has nothing to say to, and nothing to feel for, a little boy who should now be a teenager is very painful - but it's nothing to Kim Greist's excellent turn as a mother who wants to ignore the impossibility of the situation, believing that if she shows enough wide-smiling enthusiasm that she can ignore the crumbling apart of the family she already had.

But where Amann regularly falters is with the bigger picture. There's a great mystery suggested by the reappearance of an unaged boy - and, frankly, of all the many paranormal explanations we could have had, the revelation that he's a ghost seeking justice is the least interesting. There's a clumsiness to much of the plotting, as if Amann is trying so hard to conceal the predictable that he stumbles over himself. That seems to be the reason why we're given very bad scenes, such as the one with the psychic overacting and having a fit. The payoff that she was babbling a children's song backwards is an eerie idea, but the execution is so perfunctory - Scully playing it to Doggett as if rewinding babble backwards is standard FBI procedure - that it's actually very funny. There's so much thrown into the mix here that the emotional subtlety shown in the Underwood scenes is squandered; the white trash stepfather is so vile, it would have been a twist if he *wasn't* a child killer. And sequences where young Billy warns his family about Josh's impending abduction by driving a bloodied knife into the bed walks that fine line between scary and needlessly confusing - and falls off.

The real problem with the episode, though, is that it's clearly designed to give us a further exploration of Doggett. This is the first hint of his own back story, as he engages too personally in a case which has links to his own missing son. But without giving us proper explanation for his feelings, we see a character set up as being solid and reliable now breaking protocol and behaving like a bully. So far, so very Mulder - and when you bear in mind that this is *exactly* the sort of X-File that Mulder too would have linked back to his missing sister, and the angst all feels disappointingly familiar. Coupled with the fact that Doggett is still in denial of the paranormal, he can't help but look a bit foolish. Realistically, of course, you'd expect a novice to the X-Files to be left gaping with incredulity at the suggestion of a ghost - but eight seasons in,

none of the audience are novices any more, and it tests our patience hanging about waiting for Doggett to catch up to this most straightforward of story premises. (**1/2)

8.6, Redrum

Air Date: Dec. 10, 2000
Story: Steven Maeda, Daniel Arkin
Teleplay: Steven Maeda
Director: Peter Markle

Summary On Friday, a lawyer named Martin Wells is confused upon awakening in a prison cell and finding himself transferred by his friend John Doggett and Scully to another location. A mob watches Wells' transfer, and his father-in-law shoots him dead. Time reverses a day, and Wells finds himself on trial for the murder of his wife Vicky. Time reverses to Wednesday, and Wells - who's clearly living the week backwards - gets an increasing number of visions about the murder, glimpsing that his wife's killer has a spider web tattoo on his arm.

As Tuesday dawns, Wells awakens in Doggett's apartment. They learn that the tattoo belongs to Cesar Ocampo, whose brother Hector hung himself after Wells suppressed evidence and got Hector convicted. On Monday - the day of the murder - Wells confesses to Doggett that Hector was convicted of a crime he didn't commit. Wells and Doggett dash to Wells' home, and Doggett shoots the knife-wielding Cesar dead. Time moves forward again, and Wells - having averted a greater tragedy - is incarcerated for tampering with Hector's trial.

Critique As The X-Files moved from scary to quirky, so its influences moved from horror films to the "what if" scenarios posited by shows like The Twilight Zone. Vince Gilligan's stories especially wear their heritage lightly, but the way in which episodes like Monday and Field Trip put a spin upon their origins is by allowing the gimmick to throw up new slants upon the characters of Mulder and Scully. Redrum is another Twilight Zone-like story, this time constructed with great skill by Steven Maeda and Daniel Arkin. But with Doggett in only a minor role, and Scully reduced to cameo status only, it hardly feels like an X-File at all. Indeed, by concentrating upon a guest-star character - however excellently played by Joe Morton - as a man who lives the days following his wife's murder backwards, this feels tonally the least representative episode ever produced under The X-Files banner. Turn the colour down, and you'll be hard pushed not to expect the camera to pan across in those opening cell scenes to Rod Serling, smoking away and narrating. "Portrait of a TV show that's lost its identity..."

The question is whether any of that is really a problem. It's easy to argue that with Duchovny all but gone, and Anderson waiting out her contract, that this is a chance for the series to see just how far it can survive on concept alone. The difficulty only really arises when it becomes clear that The Twilight Zone is hardly a natural template for The X-Files. Chris Carter's baby is all about open-ended ambiguity; Rod Serling's is about neat twists and moral lessons. Martin Wells believes he is living his days backwards for a reason, and what he takes from it, what breaks the spell, is that he needs to be less judgmental of others and must confess to a crime. The more Twilight Zone the feel of X-Files stories, the more we sense that Fate is shaping events - Season Six is full of this sort of stuff. But Fate is ultimately a somewhat unsatisfying protagonist; The Twilight Zone works because it's an anthology of short stories, and each episode plays out in an entirely separate fictive universe. Redrum is a fun story and is cleverly told - it'd have made a great starting point for a movie. But without even trying to find room for its regular cast, it feels more disposable than the simplest standalone monster of the week episode. It exists so that a character we've never seen before and will never see again can learn, without help from anyone else (and only hindrance from Agent Doggett), a few home truths.

With the series in flux, this is an especially unhelpful time to attempt an episode which so abandons the house style; The X-Files urgently needs to assert what it is, not what it isn't. And yet, strangely, it's precisely *because* the series is in flux, and so little of the mainstays of the programme still exist, that The X-Files can just about get away with it. At any point earlier in the show's history this would have been fun but irrelevant. We haven't been told what *is* relevant yet, and while the gap between old mythology

and new is open, episodes like Redrum can creep through. (***1/2)

8.7, Via Negativa

Air Date: Dec. 17, 2000
Writer: Frank Spotnitz
Director: Tony Wharmby

Summary   While Scully seeks treatment for abdominal pain, Skinner and Doggett investigate the deaths of twenty-two cult members and two FBI agents in Pittsburgh. The victims all have axe wounds on their heads, and the FBI agents were found behind locked doors.

Background material suggests the cult leader, Anthony Tipet, believed that a higher realm of being could be reached via the "via negativa", the plane of darkness within oneself. Skinner and Doggett wonder if Tipet's exploration of his inner darkness - combined with his use of an iboga tree bark derivative, a powerful hallucinogenic - have granted him the power to kill people by invading their subconscious thoughts.

Unable to control his abilities, Tipet tries to commit suicide and gravely wounds himself with a saw blade. Soon after, Doggett dreams that he's stalking Scully with an axe. He instead turns the weapon on himself - only to awaken and learn that Tipet has died.

Critique   At last, this is Doggett's true baptism of fire. As in Roadrunners, an episode is given to one agent to cover whilst their partner is indisposed - and with Scully in hospital (and, interestingly, keeping her pregnancy still a secret), this is a case in which Doggett is forced to manage by himself. There's some fun to be had watching his first encounter with the Lone Gunmen, who patronise him and tell him he's way over his head - then grudgingly admit he's not doing badly for a beginner. And it's great to see him partnered with Skinner for a while, acting as sceptive Scully to his more open Mulder. (Seeing that spaceship has clearly turned Walter's life around.)

But elsewhere, fun really isn't the order of the day. This is scary stuff, the tensest episode in many years. And it's that way precisely because this *is* Doggett's case, the control freak losing out to a killer who's invading his dreams. The nightmare imagery is terrific, and Tony Wharmby's direction very skilfully makes even the way people walk down a corridor and turn their heads look unnervingly stylised. If the story were simply about a man who murders people with their dreams it'd be effective enough - it puts an X-File gloss upon a concept made familiar by Freddie Kreuger. But Spotnitz's script goes further than that. It's about achieving a higher consciousness in which you can no longer stop yourself giving into the most bestial and primeval of impulses, in which you lose your identity to becoming an axe-wielding psychopath. In that way it's a blackly witty parody too of the New Age philosophies so prevalent in California. The final act is quite wonderful; Robert Patrick shuffles around the FBI, eyes wide with terror, no longer sure whether he is awake or dreaming, frightened not only of being killed but of turning killer. It's a magnificent performance, and all the more effective because he is the new kid on the block, the man who refuses to admit extreme possibility. When he appears to awake, and sees with baffled horror that he has a third eye in his forehead, it's a metaphor for the way, from now on, he'll have to accept his place amidst the paranormal of The X-Files.

Rarely for a horror, this trades off unease and uncertainty rather than set piece stunts or shocks, and it's all the more powerful for it. At once a thoughtful meditation upon human instinct - in essence are we all really so savage? - and a tale about identity loss which is subtle and Kafkaesque, this is one of the best standalone X-Files in years. (*****)

8.8, Surekill

Air Date: Jan. 7, 2001
Writer: Greg Walker
Director: Terrence O'Hara

Summary   In Worcester, Massachusetts, an assassin shoots a realtor, Carlton Chase, with superhuman accuracy. Chase's business dealings lead Scully and Doggett to AAA-1 Surekill Extermination, where they meet the legally blind Dwight Cooper and his twin brother Randall - who, unbeknownst to them, has the ability to see through walls. The brothers have

been using Randall's advanced eyesight to kill drug dealers and steal their money, with Chase fencing the drugs. However, Randall became infatuated with Chase's girlfriend, Tammi Peyton, and killed him. Dwight realises that Peyton and Chase were embezzling from him, and orders Randall to shoot Peyton - but Randall kills Dwight instead. He's incarcerated, even as Peyton becomes a fugitive.

Critique   My God, this one is dull. So there's this man, right, and he can see through walls... and that's it. No, honestly. With this ability he can shoot people unawares. And he can spy on his brother making out with his girlfriend. The problem is, Randall (he of the X-ray vision) is rather dim. So he doesn't have much imagination to bring to bear on this somewhat ho-hum supernatural ability. His brother (who, ironically, has very *bad* eyesight, tch, what are the odds?) doesn't exactly boast the smartest intellect either. So neither of them can think of anything interesting to do with Randall's gift. There's been something of this done on The X-Files before, where the Stokes brothers in Je Souhaite hadn't the wit to put their new found powers to any use, but that was to comic effect; here there seems to be no such intention. And you watch with open mouthed amazement that writer Greg Walker can spin this premise out for forty-five minutes. Open mouthed but, I'm afraid, with very drooping eyelids. (*)

8.9, Salvage

Air Date: Jan. 14, 2001
Writer: Jeffrey Bell
Director: Rod Hardy

Summary   Following his own funeral, a "deceased" salvage worker named Ray Pearce approaches his friend Curt Delario - and kills him by squeezing his head. Scully and Doggett check out Ray's place of employment, Southside Salvage, but the owner dies in the same fashion. The agents find evidence that researchers at Chambers Technologies were attempting to create an indestructible "smart metal" capable of rebuilding itself, and that exposure to this metal altered Pearce's cellular makeup. Pearce hunts down anyone with a connection to his condition, going after Owen Harris - a Chambers accountant who authorized transfer of the experimental substance through Pearce's employer. Pearce's humanity asserts itself and he refrains from killing Harris, then ends his own existence in a salvage-yard compactor.

Critique   This is a little more interesting than Surekill. But, truth to tell, it's not by much.

Every once in a while, The X-Files would produce a story as generic as this one, and Duchovny and Anderson's best efforts could do little to lift it: with seven seasons of interaction, it was all too easy for the writers to fall into formulaic dialogue for the pair of them. Easy and, I think, forgivable. The eighth season made at first a real effort to find something novel within the most familiar of plotlines, and that was obviously that the series had a new lead character, and that its established co-star had a new relationship to bounce off. The problem with Surekill and Salvage is not simply that they don't give enough for Scully and Doggett to do, it's that what they *do* have is so devoid of personality. You honestly can feel that Scully has been given all of Mulder's old lines, and Doggett all of the old Scully's. The stories expect us to accept a stereotypical position for Doggett and Scully to adopt - and it's unfair, because we don't yet know well enough how they work together for us to have learned what the stereotype is. Patience and Invocation are not the strongest of episodes, but they at least characterised the heroes honestly; Via Negativa went the extra mile to determine that Doggett could *not* simply fall into the routine behaviour of Mulder or Scully.

Salvage is a very silly story. It's about a man who is turning into self-healing metal, making him virtually indestructible. He has the urge to go on a killing spree to exact revenge on the people he feels are responsible for this condition. The clever thing about Jeffrey Bell's script - the *only* clever thing - is that no-one is responsible; there's no conspiracy, no plot. Ray is a victim of circumstance, giving into that modern-day urge to find someone to blame. Just as his wife is wanting to pin his death on Gulf War Syndrome, so Ray too would prefer it if he felt a victim of something insidious rather than an accidental fall guy. It's not a bad theme in itself,

but it's essentially undramatic, and it takes a more skilful storyliner than Bell to build tension out of something which has no antagonist. The characters are achingly dull, Ray's final reach for redemption utterly illogical and unmoving. And without characters to believe in, all we get are a series of increasingly repetitive killings in which a man covered with tin foil murders people.

Salvage would never have made a *great* episode, but if it had only bothered to give a little more depth to Doggett and Scully, it might still have been an entertaining one. As it is, with a plot this mechanical (sorry), neither FBI agent has anything to react to. After seven and a half years on the job, Gillian Anderson has mastered the technique of getting from opening to closing credits without breaking a sweat. But Robert Patrick is still trying hard, and after all the effort he's put in to earlier instalments this year, it's heartbreaking to see him being so wasted. Rather than establish Doggett, this episode seems only to want to make in-jokes about the fact Patrick played a man of living metal in Terminator 2 - the sort of unsubtle nudge nudge wink wink that only undermines the actor's attempts to cast aside the audience's preconceptions about him and build something new. (*)

8.10, Badlaa

Air Date: Jan. 21, 2000
Writer: John Shiban
Director: Tony Wharmby

Summary   An American travelling home from India mysteriously dies in an airport restroom, but flies to Washington, D.C., before emptying all his blood onto a hotel bed. Forensic evidence suggests something stowed away in the man's corpse, even as the perpetrator - a legless beggar - starts menacing two families in suburbia.

Scully and Doggett learn about a type of Siddhi mystic who can alter reality, shrouding themselves from detection. The fakirs' orthodoxy forbids murder, but Scully finds mention of a holy man whose son died in an American chemical plant disaster, and might want revenge. The fakir kills a parent from each of his target families, then goes after their two boys, Trevor and Quinton. Scully intuitively guns down the fakir, even though he appears to her as Trevor. The fakir seems dead, but escapes and returns to begging in an airport in India.

Critique   Badlaa is at its best when it's at its most tasteless. An Indian cripple crawling up the bottom of an obese man on the toilet is *pretty* tasteless. The same stowaway making an impromptu exit from another victim's stomach in the autopsy room isn't for the refined of mind either. Badlaa is The X-Files at its most preposterous - the story of a man who is able to control the limb movements of the corpses he hides in, before letting them drain their blood all over the nice clean sheets of a hotel bedroom.

The problem is that it doesn't have the courage of its convictions. If John Shiban had wanted to write something that pushes the boundaries of the grotesque, he should have gone further. Instead he waters down the horror with too much extraneous detail; this tale of a Sidhi mystic is compromised because a monster which squeezes its way into your insides just isn't enough, and he also can (a) spirit himself through brick walls, (b) turn himself invisible, and (c) alter the perceptions of those about him so he can take on the shape of anyone he chooses. Any of these premises would have been arresting in themselves, but are really all standard X-Files fare - and every time you see an example of them, you wonder why Shiban isn't putting more attention on the bottom invasion concept, which is, at least, *original*. Scully and Doggett spend the episode searching for a motive - why is this chap (played with mesmerising hostility by an unspeaking Deep Roy) making so many random killings against his religious code? And the motive we've given is so depressingly formulaic that its very banality feels tonally askew. In the rush of set pieces, the story never gives us a consistent modus operandi, and framed by revelations that the fakir is just another man seeking revenge for the death of a family member, the weird fantasy elements that might *just* have won us over on their very weirdness get bogged down in the mundane. Lots of the scenes are quite fun to watch - no matter how grisly - but it never really becomes a *story*, just a runaround. (Or more accurately, since Deep Roy spends most of the episode pulling himself about on a wheeled tray, a "rollaround".)

The final act works surprisingly well, considering that it doesn't build to any comprehensible climax. We at last see Scully trying to confront her own lack of confidence - she's required to take on the mantle of Mulder, to become a believer, and it's tearing her apart because she just doesn't feel up to the task. She requires a partner who'll keep her mind open, and Doggett won't do it, actively mocking her theories. She's getting a glimpse of the barrier she gave to Mulder for so many years - except he never let his faith waiver, he kept his determination sharp. At the end of the episode Scully shoots the fakir, even though she still sees a little boy in front of her, and it shakes her to the core. She only does so because she wants to see as Mulder would see. It's this new characterisation of Scully that has been missing from recent humdrum episodes, and turns Badlaa into something a little more interesting. It's still a badly plotted and rather awkward story, but seen as something neither Scully nor Doggett ever come to terms with, that almost feels the point. (**)

8.11, The Gift

Air Date: Feb. 4, 2001
Writer: Frank Spotnitz
Director: Kim Manners

Summary   Doggett finds that Mulder visited Squamash, Pennsylvania, just a week before his abduction, but his files make no mention of the trip. It comes to light that the Hangemuhl family summoned a "soul-eater" that consumes disease, and that Mulder wanted the creature to cure his own illness. However, upon discovering that the soul-eater (who appears as a deformed man) suffered any malady that it cured, Mulder euthanised the creature. The locals buried the soul-eater, but it healed and dug its way free.

The soul-eater cures a woman's kidney disease by eating her whole and then regurgitating her. Doggett takes pity on the soul-eater and tries to make off with it, but the townsfolk insist the soul-eater must continue to cure their illnesses and the sheriff shoots Doggett dead. The soul-eater swallows and regurgitates Doggett, healing him at the expense of its own life.

Critique In a season where even the best episodes have their twists and turns signposted for the audience, this dares to be a bit different. It's structured as a mystery, where for the first half-hour we're given little but unanswered questions. The problem is, however brave the structure, there really isn't the dramatic incidence to keep what's going on very interesting; however thick the atmosphere of the first couple of acts, not an awful lot is really going on. And the puzzle that is most intriguing - why did Mulder keep a case hidden from everyone just before his disappearance, and why did it result in his shooting at someone from point blank range - is ever further elbowed aside to make room for another. Which is why the community of Squamash are running around in the dark getting so excited about an ugly man with long hair.

The Mulder storyline is tantalising, but not very satisfying. When the season opened it suggested there was a Mulder that Scully didn't know, one who was keeping his brain disease a secret. It's a controversial slant on their relationship, but it's justified dramatically if it gives Scully something to react to. But with Gillian Anderson absent for this episode, we see Mulder largely channelled through the dispassionate eyes of Doggett; as in Spotnitz's Via Negativa, Skinner is required to act as Scully in absentia, but his protective horror that Mulder could be a liar or a murderer feels as if it's coming from the wrong character. Too much of the episode is sold to us as being about Mulder - the promo ads firmly place Duchovny's fleeting cameo in the story at the centre of its publicity, and the teaser is naturally all about his return to the show. But the story really isn't an exploration of Mulder whatsoever; his totemic appearance to Doggett at the end of the story confirms that he's reduced to a symbol here, a symbol of what Doggett must become. And whilst this is a very good episode for Doggett's development - as all Spotnitz's episodes seem to be - and Robert Patrick rises to the challenge admirably, it's not the character study we were promised on the tin.

The final act is very powerful, as Doggett is obliged to take on Mulder's role, and show compassion to a monster that everyone else seeks to exploit. The monster's shot dead for his pains, but the soul-eater, a creature that can take the sickness from a man, absorbs Doggett's death. It's a great notion, but I wonder at the wisdom of it here, when in only a few weeks' time Mulder's own resurrection from the dead will become the pivot point for the season. And the final sequence, though well performed by Patrick and Pileggi, is rather problematic. Skinner urges Doggett to suppress the truth of the case; it's odd that the series this year has become a show which actively urges cover-ups. The X-Files' central mission seems to have been turned on its head. (**)

8.12, Medusa

Air Date: Feb. 11, 2001
Writer: Frank Spotnitz
Director: Richard Compton

Summary In Boston, a police officer is found dead on a subway car with much of his flesh stripped away. Scully advises via radio as Doggett leads a team - including Lieutenant Bianco, another police officer - into the subway tunnel to investigate. They discover three more bodies and a strange patch of seawater. A marine biologist at Boston University studies a sample of the seawater puddle and finds it contains a medusa - small creatures, possibly from the sea, that rely on calcium to move and provide bioluminescence. Human sweat seems to trigger a fatal reaction from the medusa, and before long Doggett is infected with the creatures. With a train approaching - and the likelihood that the medusa will infect everyone aboard - Doggett generates a spark that electrifies the medusa-laden puddles, killing the creatures and curing himself.

Critique On paper at least, this is the right episode at the right time. It's a simple thriller with a beginning, a middle and an end, it moves at a reasonable pace, and it holds the attention. It should have been more tense - Frank Spotnitz's story is basically sound, but it could do with a few more moments of jeopardy amid the brooding claustrophobia. And given the potential of the setting, with a posse exploring the dark tunnels of the underground train system for face-burning killers, Richard Compton's direction is disappointingly bland. Whenever we catch a glimpse of what's going on through Doggett's head camera, all fuzzy shots and ambiguity, it looks horrifying. But once the scenes cut back to Doggett directly, the atmosphere dissipates.

But although it's not a story which tries as hard as it might, it's so recognisably generic that it's entertaining to watch anyway. It plays like a disaster movie, with the routine set of stereotypes: there's the man in charge of getting the trains running back on time, no matter the risk to human life (or his intelligence); and there's the grunt with a gun and an authority problem, who's going to panic and run out on the hero. It ought to matter, if only because Spotnitz's storyline doesn't have enough fun with the clichés - both these characters should at least to have fulfilled the dramatic expectations and died horribly. But it doesn't, because the thinness of the supporting cast only emphasises the growing depth of trust between Scully and Doggett.

The eighth season has treated its two leads very curiously; the best character studies have seen Scully and Doggett working in isolation. Whenever a story requires them to be together as a unit, they seem to flounder. Rather cleverly, Spotnitz's story separates them once more, but puts the pair into constant contact, so that both of them vitally need to stay in communication. It does wonders for the way their relationship is portrayed. Scully is still unwilling to tell her partner about her pregnancy (although, according to the timeline of the series, she really ought to be dropping sprog by now), and so elects to guide Doggett from the control room. The guilt she feels for leading the expedition from safety is palpable, and her growing concern for Doggett's health as he's infected feels much more personal. He goes into the tunnel her partner in name only, of no greater importance than anyone else on the team - but she feels such responsibility for him that, by the time he emerges, they're closer than before. Doggett is required to examine his faith in Scully too, when Lieutenant Bianco keeps putting it to the test. Showing disapproval of the way she won't accompany him, referring to her in ironic terms as "the boss", Doggett is the one character underground who keeps a clear head - and it's through his dialogue

with Scully that he is able to survive.

It's by no means a good episode; the teaser never really makes sense in light of the revelations offered, the appearance of the mute boy is a messy contrivance, and the ending is too abrupt. But it does its job, it sharpens our understanding of our heroes, and brings them closer together just as they seemed to be drifting apart for good. (**1/2)

8.13, Per Manum

Air Date: Feb. 18, 2001
Writers: Chris Carter, Frank Spotnitz
Director: Kim Manners

Summary   A man named Duffy Haskell approaches Scully and Doggett, claiming that his girlfriend - Kath McCready, an alien abductee - was killed by her doctors after giving birth to an alien child. The case makes Scully recall events from the previous year: having been rendered infertile as a result of her abduction, Scully learned that artificial insemination might be possible using ova of hers that Mulder recovered (4.14, Memento Mori) from a government lab. Mulder agreed to serve as Scully's sperm-donor, but the insemination failed.

Back in the present day, Haskell advises a pregnant abductee named Mary Hendershot to seek Scully's help. Scully and Hendershot visit the Walden-Freedman Army Research Hospital so doctors there can induce Hendershot's labour, but Doggett discovers that the *real* Duffy Haskell died in 1970. The attending physicians take Hendershot's offspring; Scully is drugged unconscious after glimpsing that the baby is an alien. Scully awakens and is unconvincingly told that Hendershot birthed a boy. She realises that from the very start, Haskell was part of an operation designed to acquire Hendershot's alien baby.

Critique   After a few weeks of the season losing itself in vague fumbling, this is something of a relief. It's a story which seems to offer a direction for The X-Files. Whether that direction is the wisest one is open to question, perhaps; of all the ways that Chris Carter and his team could have dealt with Scully's pregnancy, to go down the conspiracy retread and suggest alien foetuses is one of the most obvious. But it has to be said that after half a season in which the pregnancy has only been *alluded* to in clever but throwaway visual references - the slug in Roadrunners, the hand peeping out from the stomach in Badlaa - it's about time that it was addressed directly. And for all the fears that the teaser may give us of its alien baby storyline horribly blatant (it looks a bit like the opening gag to Small Potatoes, but with fewer chuckles), Per Manum is impressive as a remarkably assured piece of work that is all *about* preserving its ambiguity.

Structurally, the flips between the present with Doggett and the past with Mulder are handled with great skill. What raises it above the mere series of flashback comparisons that made The Gift so frustrating is the subtlety of the writing and the acting. We're invited to care about the pregnancy at last, because we can see how much it means to Scully not through her denials and her melancholic self-regard, but through the reactions of her best friend. The scene where she and Mulder discuss whether he will donate sperm for her final chance at motherhood is just beautiful - she already accepts that he will refuse, and he's awkward and scared but so very very proud. And it's bookended brilliantly by the comfort Scully can take from Mulder at the end of the episode when it appears the pregnancy hasn't taken. Seeing Mulder and Doggett compared at last not as agents but as people who share Scully's life makes sense at last of her caution with Doggett, why she still resists trusting him with her personal life. And it shows more clearly than we've seen all year her absolute *need* for Mulder to be found, and her fear that being a mother will have her removed from that quest. Anderson gives her best work of the year, someone who had to resort to half-truths and cover-ups to protect her miracle child and the man she loves. And Robert Patrick is great too, downplaying the hurt he feels to be so cut out from her life, and still behind the scenes doing his best to look after her. The scene where he swears his support to her in the hospital at the end feels at last like a real apotheosis in their relationship.

The brilliance of Per Manum is that the emotions are all written with such sensitivity and direct clarity, it allows the plot of obfuscation

and lies to work well in contrast. All this running around hospitals and looking angstful was exactly the sort of thing which felt so tiring in Season Four. But with a plot that is both shocking in its implications, and constantly keeps you guessing, the conspiracy tale here does something it's not done for ages - it actually intrigues. This is a terrific return to form, an episode which is thrilling and dark and yet emotionally sincere. I was losing hope. (*****)

8.14, This Is Not Happening

Air Date: Feb. 25, 2001
Writers: Chris Carter, Frank Spotnitz
Director: Kim Manners

Summary Teresa Hoese - one of the abductees who vanished alongside Mulder - is found moments after a UFO is spotted in Helena, Montana. As Hoese's injuries correspond to incidents involving cults, Doggett recruits Agent Monica Reyes - a ritual crimes expert, and also someone who's "sensitive" to certain energies in the universe - for help. Reyes discovers the corpse of Gary Cory, who was also taken with Mulder.

Hoese is kidnapped by a doomsday cult leader named Absalom and taken to a farm where Jeremiah Smith (4.1, Herrenvolk) heals her wounds. The agents storm the farm and discover that Absalom and Smith are attempting to find and heal all such abductees.

Skinner gives Scully the tragic news that Mulder's dead body has been found in a field. Scully races to collect Smith so he can heal Mulder, but a UFO appears and blazes light down into the farm. The UFO disappears, and Scully is horrified to find Smith gone. [To be continued.]

Critique The odd thing about The X-Files, in retrospect, is that it's rarely had the occasion to do big "sweeps" episodes that become events in their own right. If you look at the promo trailers (all lovingly preserved on the DVD boxsets) you can sometimes sense the frustration of the publicity department as they try to stress the shocking importance of every other upcoming adventure! The consequences of which will mean nothing's ever the same again! All with the audience knowing full well that the programme stubbornly resists series-changing stunts. When in Season Six it was decided at last to wrap up the conspiracy storyline, and the ads went wild promising "Full Disclosure!", it was as if the series was at last making good on its promise to produce a full alien invasion and a detailed explanation of all we'd been watching for the last few years. And what we were given, really, was a bunch of men standing about waiting to be fried in a warehouse.

Ironically, it's not until Season Eight, with its popularity on the wane, that The X-Files has at last the opportunity to deliver an episode that genuinely feels long-awaited. Mulder may have disappeared from the action, but he's there in the title sequence every week - and even if the search for him isn't integral to that many episodes, his absence still feels of importance in even the most desultory of instalments. Now, "The Search for Mulder is Over!" scream the promos. And Chris Carter teases the audience with his return brilliantly. The publicity leads you to expect something triumphant. But from the start there's a funereal air to the episode, as Scully and Skinner face up to the fact that although they *may* find Mulder, the probability is that he'll be dead. It'd almost be better not to find him at all. One of the best moments in the episode concerns UFO-hunter Richie, and his attempts to find his abducted boyfriend Gary ever since the events of Requiem. After all his efforts, he only succeeds in seeing him one last time on an autopsy table - and then he's gently dismissed, the body's been identified, the job's been done. The comparison is clear. Scully too begins to realise that if she finds the object of her quest, he may simply be face down dead in the woods somewhere.

And the central tragedy of This Is Not Happening is that this is *exactly* what comes to pass. And that it was of her own doing. Ever since Mulder's abduction, Scully has tried to fill his shoes - and it's been a struggle for her. At the last hurdle she falters; by treating Jeremiah Smith and Absalom with FBI procedure in a strictly scientific way, rather than making that leap of faith, she prevents them from finding Mulder and bringing him back to life. It's a despairing end - in spite of her best endeavours, she's failed to open her mind as completely as

she needed to. Gillian Anderson does great work here, showing both the excitement of new hope when she begins to understand what Smith is doing, and the dawning horror that she has compromised him.

The best aspects of these latter-day mytharc episodes is that with so much of the plot baggage out of the way, the writers have more opportunity to focus on the characters and the emotional crises that they are facing. Whilst a lot of the plotting in Season Eight has been rather perfunctory, gone too is the purple prose and the ponderous voiceovers. The scene between Scully and Skinner, as they contemplate starlight, could so easily have been forced and pretentious, but instead has a tenderness to it which feels wholly natural. Cleverest of all is the way that we finally learn something of Doggett's back story - the three days he spent looking for his son - and the context is perfect. It doesn't feel like shoehorned exposition at all, but something which comes out to illustrate the dread fear of finding Mulder dead.

There are moments which feel a bit awkward and self-conscious; the ad break which reveals Jeremiah Smith wears Nike shoes is laughably overdramatic. The phrase "this is not happening" might have best been used only once - or even not at all. And the introduction of Agent Monica Reyes is rather forced; Annabeth Gish does her best to charm, but she's required to be so happy and quirky and brilliant that with this particular episode's atmosphere, she comes across as someone trying to start a conga at a funeral. But overall this is great stuff. On the one hand, it's a wonderful tease of an episode, announcing the return of Duchovny only to deny him a single line of dialogue and make him a disfigured corpse. On the other, it's far more than a tease, being a sincere exploration of hope beyond hope - and the disillusionment it can bring. (*******)

8.15, DeadAlive

Air Date: April 1, 2001
Writers: Chris Carter, Frank Spotnitz
Director: Tony Wharmby

Summary Mulder's funeral is held, and three months pass until fishermen working off Cape Fear in North Carolina find the body of Billy Miles (7.22, Requiem). When Miles' lips start moving, Skinner and Doggett realise that perhaps Mulder isn't dead after all and dig him up. Mulder is clinically alive, but his body is in an advanced state of decay.

Miles sheds his calcified skin, an act that restores him to health. Absalom tells Doggett that he and Smith were "healing" the abductees so they wouldn't be resurrected as aliens, part of an alien takeover scheme. Mulder is similarly afflicted, and Krycek offers to give Skinner the vaccine that will save him - but only if Skinner prevents Scully's child from coming to term. Skinner refuses to trust Krycek and tries to terminate Mulder's life support - an act that fortuitously drops Mulder's temperature and kills the virus. Scully gives Mulder a course of antivirals, facilitating his recovery.

Critique DeadAlive is somewhat compromised by its scheduling. It opens with Mulder's funeral, then leads into a title sequence from which Duchovny's name has been removed, as if suggesting he won't be back, that this whole announcement he'd be returning for the latter half of the season has been a cruel joke; the episode proper begins with the caption "three months later". Scully is now visibly pregnant, and Doggett is being offered reassignment. And Mulder has spent a quarter of a year underground in a coffin. Broadcast nearly a month after This Is Not Happening, you can get some measure of the importance of stressing that time has passed - but had other episodes been scheduled in the interim, had some of the standalone episodes been given a little extra weight by being set after Mulder's fatal return, then his revival here would surely have had more impact. Just imagine how it might have felt had Mulder's death not been presented as a cliffhanger, but a real story conclusion - and

then the series carried on regardless. (It's a complaint I'd level at the season as a whole; This Is Not Happening was compromised by Per Manum, which gave its audience just too much Duchovny action to make his return quite as spectacular as it should have been. And earlier episodes, in which Scully is trying hard to *be* Mulder whilst not lifting a finger to find him in the meantime, may have acquired an extra pathos had the cases been pursued in the light of his death.)

It still works very well, and that's because DeadAlive is tonally very different from the episode before it. This Is Not Happening was atmospheric and doom-laden - DeadAlive is a slice of sci-fi hokum, with action scenes, bits of grisly horror (the sequence where Billy Miles sheds his skin in the shower is especially nasty), and, above all, a re-examination of the show's mythology. Krycek is back, along with his nanobyte machine that gave Skinner so much trouble in Season Six. And there's further exploration of an alien invasion, this time reversing the idea of having aliens gestate inside humans by instead returning abducted humans who'll become aliens after they die. It could easily be something of a muddle, but what holds it together is Agent Doggett. This is Robert Patrick's episode, approaching the convoluted mytharc in front of him with a determination to cut through it and find the heart of it. He doesn't understand or respect the insanity of the stories he's told, but it's by pursuing them anyway that Mulder is saved - and his own career is shattered. The final scene is very powerful: Mulder and Scully are back together again, and Doggett is no longer required to be a placeholder character awaiting Duchovny's return from sabbatical. Robert Patrick watches them embrace, then creeps away unobserved.

Only The X-Files could spend so much time anticipating the return of a lead character, and then come up with a story suggesting it'd be an act of mercy to kill him before he's transformed into an alien monster. Carter and Spotnitz take an episode which could so easily have been an exercise in running on the spot - its job, after all, is to revive Mulder, which it only does in its closing minutes - and instead mines it for every moral dilemma it can get. Doggett's decision to reject his promotion is done to prevent the closure of the X-Files, but by saving Mulder he'll become the unwanted third wheel. Skinner is given the choice between the life of Mulder and the life of Scully's child - and having spent a season trying to find Mulder nevertheless decides the only way he can protect the baby is to kill his friend. And Scully is pitch perfect, the desperate hope on her face that Mulder is alive after months of burial weighing against her medical certainty that he can never recover. That the script juggles these themes with such clarity and so little apparent effort is something it would have struggled with badly a few seasons ago - that it can also revive Mulder in a scene that is touching for its humour and simplicity is the icing on the cake. (*****)

8.16, Three Words

Air Date: April 8, 2001
Writers: Chris Carter, Frank Spotnitz
Director: Tony Wharmby

Summary   Kersh denies Mulder's reinstatement to the X-Files, saying that he's satisfied with Doggett's success rate. Meanwhile, a census worker named Howard Salt - one of Absalom's colleagues - dies while trying to forcibly obtain an audience with the President, claiming that aliens are taking over the United States. Upon learing of Salt's death, Absalom captures Doggett and first confirms that his neck doesn't contain telltale signs of an alien vertebrae, then takes him to the Federal Statistics Center. Absalom hopes to find hard evidence of Salt's claims - and also intends that Doggett will spread the truth afterward - but guards at the facility kill Absalom.

The Lone Gunmen find protected Statistics Center files on Salt's hard drive. Knowle Rohrer - whom Doggett served with in the Marines, and who works for the Department of Defense - provides the password to the files ("fight the future"), which can only be accessed at the Center. Mulder breaks into the building, but Doggett realises that Mulder has been lured into a trap and helps him escape. Rohrer continues to insist that he's helping Doggett in his quest for answers - but unbeknownst to Doggett, Rohrer has an alien vertebrae.

Critique   This follows a very familiar premise - during an investigation, the X-Files agents are set up in a sting operation. It's remarkably similar in concept to Per Manum, even down to the identity of Doggett's dubious Deep Throat, Knowle Rohrer. Indeed, there's a sense of déjà vu about the episode - quite deliberately, I feel: there's conspiracy and doublecrossing and vital information stored on discs that can't be downloaded in time. And the point of all this is only to emphasise how different The X-Files universe now feels, the familiarity of the ingredients only making us more aware that the mix is never going to be the same again. Mulder is back, but he's not the same Mulder. He says right from the beginning that he doesn't know how to fit in, and that his world has changed in the six months he's been absent. Scully is expecting, and has a new partner who has won her respect. And no matter how many wisecracks he may throw her way, Mulder never looks comfortable sitting in an office that is no longer his. He throws himself into a new mission to expose the truth in a frenzy, as if wanting to make up for lost time. So he denies what he has suffered, and in his arrogance believes he can discern the real motives behind everything within minutes of his being back on the job. Doggett is a traitor; the Lone Gunmen are weak and spineless; Scully has gone over to the other side.

It's painful to watch. This isn't what we wanted from Mulder's return. But it's brilliantly well handled, and emotionally true. Duchovny is excellent here, in no way seeking to be likeable or comforting. With the series having spent so long anticipating his return, it's an act of wonderful cruelty that as soon as he's back it gives us a lead who is so cold and selfish. The scene where he first encounters Doggett is terrific; Doggett rises from his chair with a smile and a handshake, but Mulder is so certain of a conspiracy that he pushes him down violently. And in doing so the series draws a clear line between the approaches of Mulder and Doggett; whilst the past fifteen episodes have demonstrated how a career cop like Doggett needs the imaginative zeal of a Mulder, it's telling that Doggett is so stung by the accusations brought against him that he suspects he's been set up by his confidants. We are given a story in which Doggett struggles to save Mulder from a trap, risking both his own life and his own credibility by doing so. For all Mulder's galvanism and vigour, it's hard to imagine how he could have had the patience or emotional intelligence to stand back and reach the same conclusions.

Three Words is a thriller in which the main plot is something of a macguffin. And some of the details of the action are very perfunctory; Absalom's jail break is as convenient as Mulder and Doggett's from the census bureau. But it returns to one of The X-Files' greatest strengths, making everyone and everything a source of distrust and suspicion. Scully acts like any regular X-Files fan, desperately grateful that Mulder has returned, and hurt and rejected that he's not as warm or as fun as he used to be. From the triumphant conclusion to DeadAlive, Three Words in contrast provides a slow and difficult tale of disillusionment. It's brave and it's heartfelt, and it's extremely well performed by all concerned. Mulder is wrong - you really can't go home again. (*****)

8.17, Empedocles

Air Date: April 15, 2001
Writer: Greg Walker
Director: Barry K Thomas

Summary   In New Orleans, a recently unemployed office worker named Jeb Dukes observes a fiery car accident - followed by a man, bathed in flames, merging with Dukes' body. Afterward, Dukes murders the employers who just fired him.

At the crime scene, Monica Reyes gets a vision of a charred body, which is very similar to the vision she experienced while investigating the death of Doggett's son Luke. Reyes asks Mulder for help, telling him that Doggett shared her vision but refuses to acknowledge it. Mulder postulates that "evil" can transmit from person to person like a disease. Dukes takes his niece hostage, but Doggett and Reyes save the girl - before Dukes spasms and dies, the "evil" within him passing into his sister Katha. Doggett apprehends Katha when she becomes violent, and hopes that by keeping her restrained, the "evil" within her will stay trapped.

Critique   The awkward relationships at the heart

of the new X-Files are given further exploration this week. This time it's Doggett's turn to push Mulder about, as he suspects that his private life is being turned into a case for his predecessor to investigate. The irony is, of course, that Mulder has no interest in Doggett at all, and it's with supreme indifference that he is drawn into this study of evil as a disease. Doggett's back story has been handled with considerable subtlety so far; whereas Mulder's tale of his sister's abduction was being presented as series credo right from the pilot, Doggett has treated the death of his son as something very painful and secretive. At first glance the set-up seems strikingly familiar, as if Chris Carter wants to lend his new lead actor added depth by giving him baggage concerning a missing relative. But what's fascinating is the difference; Mulder's life becomes all about an acceptance of the paranormal in his rationalisation of his sister's loss, whilst for Doggett consideration of extreme possibilities belittles the tragedy. It suggests, too, that there was some other avenue he should have explored to have saved his son. So for Doggett denial of unexplained phenomena becomes a safety net, a means by which he can feel he never betrayed his son's future. Empedocles cleverly puts this denial at the very heart of the story. Scully tells Doggett how she resisted belief for so long out of fear, and even Mulder reminds him that his way into FBI work was through the harsh reality of the violent crimes unit, that his flirtation with unseen forces was a way of understanding the bizarre inhumanity he witnessed.

At the other extreme we have Monica Reyes, a woman who keeps an open mind to *everything*, who so outMulders Mulder that Annabeth Gish's breezy performance literally leaves David Duchovny's jaw drooping. This is a far better episode for Gish than her introductory one, where her character was somewhat swamped in the unfolding mythology of the series as a whole. With Reyes due to return in Season Nine, we're left with the interesting notion of a character who needs to believe *less*, whose journey may just have to be to toughen up and become more cynical. Potentially, this is very clever. The Mulder and Scully development always seemed one-sided; whatever the mission statements to the contrary - how Scully's scien-

---

tific approach curbed Mulder's undisciplined theorising to find a common truth - the reality was that over the years, the lesson learned was that Scully frankly needed to shut up and open her eyes a bit.

The X-File in itself is an interesting concept, but left frustratingly vague. But it's commendable that, as Mulder points out, there is no easy comfort for Doggett to find as he opens himself up to accept the paranormal. Empedocles isn't about solving the murder of Doggett's son, or curing Doggett of his oh-so grumpy scepticism. At its best it's a character study which gives its new leads some background depth and, better yet, somewhere new to develop. It does less well, interestingly enough, with Mulder and Scully - their banter about pizza delivery men feels very forced, and after the truthful awkwardness of Three Words, Duchovny and Anderson only manage another sort of awkwardness altogether. But that's not necessarily a bad thing. Empedocles is a workmanlike storyline that stands out because it so firmly looks to the future. (***1/2)

8.18, Vienen

Air Date: April 22, 2001
Writer: Steven Maeda
Director: Rod Hardy

Summary When an Galpex Petroleum worker is mysteriously fried by radiation, Doggett travels to an oil rig in the Gulf of Mexico - only to find Mulder already there, believing the worker's death is tied to aliens. Scully's autopsy reveals that the dead man had a latent immunity to the alien black oil, and that he was murdered because his oil-infected co-workers couldn't control him. The oil-tainted crewmen besiege Mulder and Doggett, who wreck the rig's radio to prevent the crewmen from contacting an alien mothership. The two of them escape in a helicopter moments before the crewmen blow up the rig. Mulder tells Doggett that Galpex must be stopped from drilling further, and concedes that Doggett is the only bit of credibility the X-Files has left.

Critique So, for all the stories featuring the black oil, there'd somehow never been one set on an oil rig! Until Vienen. The odd thing,

though, is that the black oil hasn't been part of The X-Files storyline since the feature film, and so this sudden return to it seems curiously out of date. It's not even as if writer Steven Maeda could find any new twists to give the idea - you get your sequences of eye clouding, and one act ends when a man is infected as oil pours into his screaming mouth - but there's nothing to link this slice of old mythology to the new. Because we're now in a story which deals with invasion through alien possession, the black oil can only remind us that this particular theme has been well explored already - and there are indeed moments here which echo scenes in Three Words, such as the one where Doggett (again) is threatened by a man who needs to check whether he's still human or not.

This is a ponderous episode which only breaks into the sprint it needs in the final few minutes, and offers little of the shocks or tension it promises. The story's purpose, quite openly, is to team Mulder and Doggett together on a case, so that in the closing scene Mulder can hand over the baton of the X-Files to his successor. Though that finale is well played, it's not been earned by an episode which so obviously *should* be exploring the relationship between the two agents but in practice does little more than have them lazily snipe at each other. You can see how this *might* have worked, a tale in which Mulder and Doggett put aside their differences and learn to respect one another. But the only teamwork they really manage is in jumping off an exploding rig together - their greatest contribution to the story is that they're good at running away, which doesn't give either of them much dignity. (**)

8.19, Alone

Air Date: May 6, 2001
Writer / Director: Frank Spotnitz

Summary Agent Leyla Harrison is temporarily assigned to take Scully's place when she goes onto maternity leave. Doggett and Harrison venture to Ellicot, New York, after two men - Gary Sacks and his father Arlen - are sprayed with some sort of reptile venom. Mulder is drawn into the investigation, and checks out a mansion owned by Herman Stites.

Unable to set work aside, Scully determines

that the reptile venom hardens a person's skin, enabling the internal organs to liquefy. Mulder determines that Stites was labouring to develop a new species of reptile, and Harrison deduces that Stites *is* the reptile, able to assume human form. Blinded by Stites' venom, Doggett follows Mulder's instructions and fires his weapon, killing Stites. Harrison opts to not return to the X-Files, leaving Doggett the only agent on duty in the department.

Critique   Frank Spotnitz has written a huge number of X-Files episodes over the years, and quite a few Millennium's and Lone Gunmen's to boot. But I've never had much cause to be impressed by his meat-and-potatoes writing style until Season Eight. He's been the real brains behind this year of The X-Files, the hardest working writer, the most consistent at examining old characters like Mulder and Scully and exploring new ones like Doggett. And if the season went through a lull in its middle episodes, Spotnitz's achievements this year have been considerable. He's taken a show that has outlived its usefulness and become complacent, and given it a renewed urgency.

So if anyone is qualified to write a story which is so unashamedly an exercise in nostalgia, it's Spotnitz. And if there's any time for it to happen, it's now. And this is largely rather sweet; Mulder and Scully are out of the FBI, but neither can resist getting back into their old grooves when Doggett is in danger. For the last time, Mulder is on a stakeout eating sunflower seeds, and Scully is in scrubs yet again doing an autopsy, only this time over the bulk of her pregnant stomach. (And it's amusing that after so much effort was spent in Season Two concealing Gillian Anderson's *real* pregnancy, that here Spotnitz the director emphasises it.) There are old props to look at. And Doggett is partnered with a veritable X-Files fan who can point out references to past episodes from classic series. Jolie Jenkins gives a lovely performance as Agent Harrison, the Mulder / Scully wannabe, on her first case acting out her fantasies and coming to realise that crawling through underground tunnels and being blinded by monsters isn't as much fun as it's cracked up to be.

If there's a problem with all this, it's the way in which it's emphasised that this week's X-File is a rather low-key humdrum affair. There's even a certain wit to this familiarity, but it inevitably wears thin. It's telling, though, that in the end it's the fan who realises the true nature of Stites, with Doggett blinded by inexperience and Mulder blinded by complacency. And the final scenes are smashing, with Mulder risking Doggett's bullet to kill the creature, and Duchovny finally accepting Patrick as the show's new lead actor. The sequence in the hospital, too, as Agent Harrison gets to ask Mulder and Scully the beleaguered question of how they got home from the Antarctic in the feature film - a plothole in a script that Spotnitz himself wrote, and a familiar fan nitpick - is very funny, and touchingly feels like it's marking the end of the Mulder / Scully era of the series. As a story, Alone may not be much to write home about. But as an affectionate celebration it's a winner, and the one episode of comedy in a very dark season. (***1/2)

8.20, Essence

Air Date: May 13, 2001
Writer: Chris Carter
Director: Kim Manners

Summary   Billy Miles, reborn as an alien-human hybrid (8.15, DeadAlive), begins to systematically kill anyone connected to the conspiracy to harvest alien offspring (8.13, Per Manum). As Mulder, Doggett and Skinner find Scully's prenatal records at a cloning facility, Scully realises that her baby nurse - Lizzy Gill - is more than she seems. Gill concedes that she's part of a team that had some success in combining alien DNA from the Roswell incident with human ova to produce alien offspring. The children didn't live long, but they yielded tissue and stem cells. Gill says that Scully's child isn't an alien, but is a "perfect" child with no human frailties.

Krycek helps Scully elude Miles, insisting that the aliens fear her child because it's superior to them. Scully goes into hiding with Monica Reyes, even as a rooftop struggle ends with Mulder pushing Miles into a garbage compactor, pulverizing him. [To be continued.]

8.21, Existence

Air Date: May 20, 2001
Writer: Chris Carter
Director: Kim Manners

Summary While a piece of Billy Miles' metallic spine replicates and grows him a new body, Krycek tells Mulder that Miles represents a type of "replacement human" to aid in the repopulation of Earth. Scully's baby represents a threat to Miles and those like him. Knowle Rohrer tells Doggett that Scully's child stems from a military experiment to generate a supersoldier, and that Miles is a program prototype.

Mulder realises that Krycek is working with Rohrer, and has misdirected them to leave Scully's child undefended. Krycek moves to kill Mulder, but Skinner shoots him dead. Rohrer goes missing in a car explosion. Scully and Reyes take refuge at a location suggested by Doggett: the abandoned town in Georgia where he was born. Several human-replicants find them and mutely watch as Scully goes into labor. The replicants depart, evidently because the child isn't what they expected, just as Mulder arrives.

Doggett assigns Reyes to the X-Files, and the two of them tell Kersh that he's under investigation for possible ties to Rohrer. Meanwhile, Mulder learns that Scully has named their son "William" after Mulder's father.

Critique It's one of the hallmarks of this peculiar long-running series that decisions taken eight years ago come back to haunt the show. So a young actor cast to be in the opening minutes of the pilot episode is now, by a quirk of plot, required to act as an unstoppable Terminator figure. It's not a part you would automatically cast Zachary Ansley in, but the incongruity of his slight build is actually surprisingly effective. The last ten minutes of the episode are wonderfully tense, as this thin and unassuming young man credibly manages to get all the cast racing around the FBI in panic. So good, in fact, is this final act of the story that it almost makes up for an episode which sadly returns to the style of the traditional mytharc instalment. So there's a lot of heated exposition, none of which is ever *quite* clear enough to be actually helpful. And in these scenes there's usually one FBI agent so angry that he interrupts the information, only to be stopped by a calmer counterpart. Early on in the episode, Mulder gets so furious with Frances Fisher's nanny that Doggett has to intervene; later on Doggett is the one so angered by Krycek that he needs to be stopped by Mulder. And so on - it's like a strange dance of shouting men. And it's too familiar a dance, this, where a little (but never enough) explanation is offered to increase the jeopardy but reduce understanding.

It's not that there aren't pleasures to be had: it's worth watching the episode just to see Mulder and Doggett on a case together, finally as frustrated but respectful equals. But after a mythology this year that has done so well in making the emotions count and keeping the pretension and the red herrings at bay, it's disheartening to return to a style that feels this outdated, this *cluttered*, as it piles earnest plot point onto plot point. Right from the opening narration, which describes the miracle of childbirth with so many adjectives it seems like they're on special offer this week, you can sense you're in trouble. And though there's great opportunity for suspense and intrigue - the nanny tampering with Scully's medicine, for example - there isn't the attention given them to make them work. It's an old complaint I level at these storyarc episodes, which date right back to when the words "To be continued" first flashed up on the screen: frenetic, airless plotting does not necessarily make good drama. (**)

Critique There's some great stuff in here. The entire death scene of Krycek, for example, is superb. Krycek has never been a comprehensible character, his loyalties shifting as the mythology dictates, and yet Nicholas Lea here is so passionate and regretful as he prepares to kill Mulder, you can almost believe he'd always been reluctantly cheering his enemy on. His shooting by Skinner is unusually brutal, Lea's face contorted in its moment of death with a shock that the last of his nine lives is over. I love the image of Krycek's prosthetic hand reaching uselessly for the gun as well. And Mulder's silence afterwards, and the way he refuses to discuss what Skinner has done, speaks volumes.

There are some terrific set pieces too. Car chases where supersoldiers are clinging impossibly to the side of speeding vehicles. Skinner being knocked out by a fist punching through the door of a moving lift. A metal vertebra creepily rebuilding itself on the autopsy table. There's lots of action and running about - but, ultimately, it's all just making time until the moment Scully can give birth. The episode focuses upon our heroes' attempts to keep Scully safely in hiding so she can drop her sprog in peace - and therefore there's no hiding the anticlimax. Once she's been found by the aliens who watch so impassively as she pushes out her newborn, they just get back in their cars and drive away. Chris Carter so overloads the Christ symbolism here, with the Star of Bethlehem, the manger, even the Lone Gunmen appearing as three kings bearing gifts, that almost anything other than Scully producing a fountain of light from her cervix to an angelic choir would have seemed disappointing. So the way that the birth is merely shrugged off is especially frustrating.

In a way I can see noble intent behind this. There's something dramatically ironic to this, that after all the expectation of Scully giving a virgin birth to the saviour of mankind, what we get instead is "just" an ordinary miracle. There's a human life here, against all the odds - what *should* be more remarkable than that? And I would buy that, on condition that the series stuck with it. If Season Nine could refrain from giving Baby William strange powers, or putting him at the centre of more conspiracy, then this would at least be a dignified ending. But that is not to be. And it leaves the series in an awkward position. Certainly the last scene is intended to be a touching resolution to the Mulder / Scully story, but the events of the episode have gone so far from making them simple or ordinary people that the intimacy of a shared kiss over their child seems contrived.

This, though, is still where the Mulder and Scully story should have ended. They've both left the FBI. They have a child. The conspiracy is over. The scene where Doggett tells Mulder in the car that it's time for him to stop, that he's given away so many years of his life, feels like the production team at last accepting Duchovny's own protestations that he's spent eight years in the same role on the same TV show. The worst thing they could do now, in Duchovny's absence, is to continue the series with a focus upon Scully. It effectively makes the eighth season development redundant. There's no need to bring Scully back. The scene where Doggett and Reyes stand up to Kersh and begin an investigation on him is very promising. (Even if it would have been more effective still had we seen Kersh guilty of what he's being accused of.) Robert Patrick has done a sterling job on this season of The X-Files, giving it a new purpose and commitment, and the writers have matched his efforts by turning Doggett into so much more than a mere replacement. But it's worrying that they haven't bothered to do the same with his new partner. Annabeth Gish is fine, but Reyes has been given only half-hearted attention, and has been too often a series of comic tics and eccentricities. (The prime one in this episode being her imitation of whale song.) The reason Ten Thirteen have held back is abundantly clear: Gillian Anderson is still under contract. To them, The X-Files without Mulder *or* Scully still seems unthinkable, and that's the problem - because the story has now been put into a position where one continuing without the other does a disservice to their emotional journey. If the show is to survive, it needs to cut loose now. Invest in a new beginning, build upon the fine work of Robert Patrick and ensure that it doesn't go to waste. Season Eight has made many mistakes, but overall it's been a triumph against the odds, and at the very least much better than the audience had any right to expect.

Onwards to the final season. But first - a little light relief... (**1/2)

The Lone Gunmen: Season 1

1.1, Pilot

Air Date: March 4, 2001
Writers: Chris Carter, Vince Gilligan,
John Shiban, Frank Spotnitz
Director: Rob Bowman

Summary   A hacker / thief named Yves Adele Harlow out-foxes the Lone Gunmen at the E-Com-Con Corporation in Virginia, stealing a powerful Octium IV chip. Meanwhile, Byers is told that his estranged father Bertram has died in a car crash - then discovers that Bertram faked his death when an assassin tried to silence him.

Bertram - who has access to Department of Defense files - explains that a shadow faction of the government is attempting to use a war games simulation, "Scenario 12D", to bring down a flight over Manhattan, rocking world stability and boosting arms sales. Byers and his father discover that the targeted flight is being flown by remote and aimed at the World Trade Center. Frohike convinces Yves to lend them the Octium chip, enabling him and Langly to sever the remote control. The pilots steer the plane to safety, and Frohike swipes the chip from Yves - enabling the Gunmen to publish its secrets.

Critique   Of course, it's impossible to watch this episode any more with innocence. The irony is that it's the pilot for a comedic action adventure show, something to amuse, something to make us laugh. And its first wacky plotline is a terrorist plot to fly a passenger plane into the World Trade Centre. Screened a mere six months before the horrors of 9/11, it's acquired a rather dubious reputation and you can see why: it's not even that it seems to predict the atrocity, it's that it reveals that the terrorists are just a smokescreen for the *American government* who want to create a national disaster so great it'll reinvigorate the arms trade. Bloody hell.

On its own terms, actually, that's quite a witty idea. But if it's hard now to watch scenes of the plane flying over the Manhattan skyline, it's harder still to watch the naivety of the resolution. Once the Lone Gunmen override the flight computer with a snazzy microchip, the crisis is averted. We see Byers and his dad get off the plane, easily able to chat, not a passenger in tears, not a photographer to be seen. And the global terror that would have been produced had a plane crashed into the World Trade Centre somehow never comes to pass, by a lucky escape that at the last moment the pilot was able to fly over the very top of it.

Right from the start, Ten Thirteen demonstrate that they can concoct bits of action adventure thrills, but cannot imagine the real-life consequences of even a near miss. The world would have changed anyway. And that might be quite right that they can't - really, why should they? It's a bit of escapism, for God's sake. But it's still typical of an approach we've seen time and time again on The X-Files, in which potentially world changing threats are foiled and discoveries are made each week, but because there's some near miss is built into the plot it's always enough to ensure that the series format never has to change. Every season they'll find a spacecraft on a shoreline, or a boy who can read minds, or a microchip that will prove alien life - and next week we'll go right back to where we started, Mulder chasing around after monsters with his always sceptical partner. The X-Files can't deal with consequences. And what 9/11 showed the world is that there really had to be consequences, that the world literally could alter completely overnight.

Now, I'm not going so far as to say that this single pilot for another series altogether killed off The X-Files. But it did suddenly make it look very superficial. I pity the poor writers - after over two hundred episodes of imaginative hokum, one of their most unlikely plots comes true. And worse, it took place in a series so tonally unassured that it can't but help leave you cringing. If Duchovny and Anderson had been left to ponder the implications in their brooding earnestness, it'd have been bad enough. Instead we've got the Three Stooges. It feels like a Keystone Kops movie anticipating the Holocaust.

That The Lone Gunmen went to series at all seems peculiar enough. In 1997, Ten Thirteen's Millennium emphasised all that they were proud of in The X-Files, and in consequence out came something that was even darker and more violent and more disturbing. Come 2001, it's telling of The X-Files' lighter self-parodic tone that the perfect spin-off is a comedy series. It really doesn't do the actors any favours at all. Tom Braidwood and Dean Haglund have always been perfectly serviceable as comic relief bit parts, but stretching their shtick to forty-five minutes removes their charm. Bruce Harwood has improved massively on his early awkward performances, but he's not a leading man; the attempts to give him depth here involve him standing around a lot looking angstful and removing all the inflection from his dialogue. They're given a new adversary, Yves Harlow, played without warmth or chemistry by Zuleikha Robinson; her only real achievement here is that she makes the Lone Gunmen look like better actors. The best comedy performance is from Jim Fyfe as hacker "Kimmy the Geek", effectively resurrected after his "brother" Jimmy the Geek's death in Three of a Kind.

As action adventure, it never breaks a sweat - the greatest tension evoked in the first half is watching everyone stand around a computer trying to download something. And as a comedy it's mannered and false. There are a few good lines, and it all looks expensive - but as you watch all these computer hacks squabble over software whilst playing violent virtual reality games, it strikes you that they're all just silly children. And if someone ever flies a plane into the World Trade Centre, I'd want someone just a little more grown-up fighting for us all. (*1/2)

1.2, Bond, Jimmy Bond

Air Date: March 11, 2001
Writers: Vince Gilligan, John Shiban, Frank Spotnitz
Director: Bryan Spicer

Summary   Intelligence operatives slay a hacker named Alex Goldsmith, who was in the employ of Philanthropic Outreach Enterprises (POE). The Gunmen look into the company, discovering that its charity minded CEO - Jimmy Bond - is trying to develop a variant of football that blind people can play.

It's revealed that the ruling party of Belasmirsk, a breakaway Soviet republic, is using POE as a shell company to acquire a large stockpile of nerve gas. Langly is captured and taken to the Belasmirsk Embassy, then ordered to hack into e-stock accounts and steal $50 million - that the ruling party will spend on nerve gas weapons. Yves blocks Langly's transaction, using his access to drain the ruling party's bank account of millions, bankrupting them. Langly escapes and the Gunmen return home - to find that Jimmy, needing a cause to support, has become their new benefactor.

Critique   This is a lot more consistent, with a much more confident tone, and if anything serves as a far better pilot than the first episode. The plotline itself is very pedestrian, involving arms dealers and hacking, and fizzles out into a stream of technobabble rather listlessly by the end. But when the episode is allowed to deliver solely upon comic sequences, it mostly works well. The teaser, in which Frohike poses as a martial arts expert, is pretty amusing and parodies the fight stunts of Asian cinema very well. The sequence where the Lone Gunmen all have to work together in a frenzy to fake autographs on a golf caddy is lovely. And the highlight is the blind football team, one of those jokes which really shouldn't work on paper but in practice is laugh out loud funny, in part thanks to the amiable gusto of Jimmy Bond, played by Stephen Snedden.

Indeed, as an introduction for Snedden, this works a treat. His performance is loud and hardly subtle, but he brings a likeable charm to a series composed of characters who, by nature of their roles in The X-Files, are paranoid and bickering. Zuleika Robinson continues to underwhelm as Yves, however; if she tried to be any more arch, she'd turn into a bridge.

This is light, forgettable entertainment. It doesn't have the pace or the wit to work as well as it might - for every clever gag there's a scene in which someone vomits or falls over. But it passes the time very amiably, which is exactly what it set out to do. (***1/2)

1.3, Eine Kleine Frohike

Air Date: March 16, 2001
Writer: John Shiban
Director: David Jackson

Summary A man named Michael Wilhelm asks the Gunmen to help determine if a pastry baker named Anna Haag is "Madame Dauvos", a World War II poisoner who eliminated several French resistance members, Wilhelm's father included. Since Haag has placed ads trying to find her lost son, and as Dauvos had a tryst with a man who looked like Frohike, Frohike agrees to learn the truth by posing as Haag's offspring.

Yves learns that Wilhelm *himself* is Dauvos' son, that he's a former member of the East German secret police, and that he's using Frohike as a decoy to see if Haag poisons him. Madame Dauvos is revealed as Haag's neighbor, Louella Everidge, who became friends with Haag because she had a similar background as a means of anonymously looking for her own son. Everidge is arrested, and Yves claims the bounty on Wilhelm.

Critique Okay. So this is the one where Frohike poses as the son to an old German lady who used to poison members of the French Resistance during the war. He goes to her house, and although he's pushing fifty, she scrubs him in the bath and dresses him in lederhosen. But what's priceless is, because she's a German, and a member of the master race, she's a humourless old bat who makes him do pushups and go jogging! Poor old Frohike, in his fake blue eyes and blonde wig! But he's no time to complain, he's got a mission. You see, the way he can positively identify the woman as a Nazi is by the distinctive birthmark of Germany she'll have on her bottom - so cue lots of great set pieces as women pull down their skirts to reveal their identities, and Frohike stalks his putative mum with a camera in the shower!

Ten Thirteeen are never at their best when playing with cultural stereotypes, be it Russians, Native Americans, or the British. But an entire race has never been held up for ridicule the way it is so witlessly here. This is the first episode of The Lone Gunmen which doesn't even pretend the plot makes sense - by the time the last act stutters into play, in which Stephen Snedden

manages an entirely perfect impersonation of Alan Dale with a face mask, and the neighbour reveals her secret plan to track down her criminal son by befriending *another* German woman from the exact same village who was *also* tracking down her child, you realise that John Shiban must think that in comedy anything goes. And that's not the case. Comedy is rather hard to pull off; flinging lots of sight gags at the screen with no logical storyline to bind them isn't funny. There's something to be said when the sneering xenophobia leaves such a bad taste in the mouth that you almost feel relieved as the series gets back to its trademark vomiting and falling over.

Almost worst of all, the episode occasionally wants to reach out to us through the wave of stereotypes to tell us we should be *feeling* something. The sequence where Frohike and "mother" bond over the removal of toupees achieves a sentimentality so forced and unearned, it borders on actual genius. (*)

1.4, Like Water for Octane

Air Date: March 18, 2001
Writer: Collin Friesen
Director: Richard Compton

Summary In flashbacks from the Gunmen's youth, Byers in 1974 declares that he wants to become a bureaucrat and spread democracy; Langly in 1982 argues with his father, a farmer, about how computers are the future; and Frohike in 1967 has an altercation with a football team captain.

In the present, Yves tricks the Gunmen into searching for the Studebaker Lark, a water-powered car created in 1962 by the late Stan Mizer, thinking she can seize it herself. Evidence suggests that the car is hidden in a military silo - that the government demolishes. The Gunmen learn that the car is actually located on the farm of JT Guthrie, whose father was friends with Mizer. Mr Vast - Yves' current employer - tries to kill everyone involved and seize the car on behalf of the oil companies, who know the world's oil is running out. Jimmy overpowers Vast, and the Gunmen agree that the car must be destroyed, as it would actually increase consumption and devastate the environment.

Critique The comedy's much more restrained here, which is all to the good. Even though there's a scene where Dean Haglund gets to roll his eyes and squirm as he puts his arm up a bull's backside, it *does* have a payoff in the final act when a villain needs to be despatched. The premise is interesting, too; the best bit of the episode being the explanation of how a water powered car, at first glance so environmentally friendly, would only succeed in making the planet even more ecologically unsound because of the boom it would cause in the manufacture of cars.

But, for all the intelligence behind it, it's dramatically rather dull. Events don't flow naturally in the story - incidents lead coincidentally to incidents. As soon as we hear that the car may be buried within a silo, we also learn that the silo is to be destroyed *that day*. As soon as we learn that Langly's father had a friend with the initials JT, we stumble across his son, who just happens to have named a bull after his dead dad. They're all coincidences that could have been smoothed out with a bit of effort - but there is no effort to the plotting, there's a sense of "it'll do" because the series is only a comedy.

The last scene is touching, its paean to inaction and anticlimax actually making an ending which is *all* anticlimax feel emotionally satisfying. And Stephen Snedden's Jimmy is still the best thing in the series, his amicable enthusiasm honestly infectious - the look of joy on his face when he realises the Lone Gunmen are still alive is lovely. But it's telling that we still don't know or care for the leads, who only respond to the adventure in a series of predictably snide ways. The opening sequence, in which we see them all reaching moments of apotheosis as children, is a very funny idea. But it would only really work if we had a better idea of who these people were as adults. (**)

1.5, Three Men and a Smoking Diaper

Air Date: March 23, 2001
Writer: Chris Carter
Director: Bryan Spicer

Summary The Gunmen attempt to prove that Senator Richard Jefferson is corrupt, and was possibly involved in the death of Barbara Bonabo, a campaign staffer. They find a baby boy - possibly the Senator and Bonabo's love child - alone in an apartment, and do their best to care for him. Jock, a member of Jefferson's staff, comes clean that he's been covering for his boss' drunkenness and infidelities for years. Bonabo was given tranquilizers to try and keep her docile, but unwisely went for a drive and perished in a car accident. The Senator takes custody of his son and makes a clean accounting of his bad behavior to the press, but none of the revelations damn his re-election bid.

Critique This is the first episode since the pilot in which Langly doesn't vomit. He does get pissed on, though, for an unfeasibly long time, and just stands there taking it with the patented Dean Haglund look of grumpiness. (He could perhaps have just moved out of the way.) And there's a lot of farting too, and even more simulated farting, as Frohike poses as a man who has gas problems. In the overcrowded genre of men-coping-with-babies, this may well be the only one where the baby seems more grown up than the storyline.

But still, we don't watch The Lone Gunmen for subtlety. This week, to go with the baby plot, our intrepid heroes try to bring down a senatorial candidate. He's a philanderer, plays the saxophone, and just happens to sound like Bill Clinton. Again, it's a mark of the show's innocence that it makes a Democrat adulterer its target of disdain, and cannot conceive of the Bush administration around the corner. The story is ponderous and illogical, and ends with an extraordinary final scene in which all the Lone Gunmen make friends with Clinton-lite, and cheer him on as they watch the polling results. So what was the point of the story then? There wasn't one. Moving on... (*)

1.6, Madam, I'm Adam

Air Date: March 30, 2001
Writer: Thomas Schnauz
Director: Bryan Spicer

Summary A man named Adam Burgess finds strangers living in his house and that all record of his identity has disappeared. He asks for help from the Gunmen, who find wiring running from Burgess' neck to his cerebral cortex. They determine that Burgess is really Charlie Muckle - a drunk and general ne'er-do-well who submitted himself to one Dr DiVico for treatment. Using electrical devices and virtual reality simulations, DiVico transformed Muckle into the more agreeable Burgess. The Gunmen convince Charlie to reclaim his original identity, become a better person and reunite with his wife Lois.

Critique Of the rash of paranoid thrillers that were released in the wake of The X-Files, one of the most interesting was the series Nowhere Man. This episode feels like a comic version of that, as a man goes to his home only to find another couple live there, the neighbours have never heard of him, and his entire identity has been wiped. The concept is good - so good, in fact, that Nowhere Man was able to milk it for twenty-five episodes. And Stephen Tobolowsky gives a strong and likeable performance as the nowhere man we're concerned with here. For the first time, The Lone Gunmen has a story which is an intriguing mystery, and is able to showcase a performance of great skill.

It's such a relief to be carried along by a story that it takes a while to realise that in the second half the plot has badly gone off the rails. It's the need to be a *comedy* above all else that does Madam, I'm Adam in - and so what is essentially a rather poignant tale of a man realising his entire remembered life is a virtual reality fantasy is lost somewhat in scenes of strident humour. To discover you're wiping your original personality because you're a lowlife who doesn't treat your wife well is dramatic and human and very sad - to reveal that said wife is a wrestling dwarf is clearly only done to add some hilarious spice. And in a story which is all about the comparison of a perfect (if synthetic) existence compared to a harder but more honest reality, we really need that reality to be some-

thing grounded and identifiable. Thomas Schnauz's script is gentle and amiable at all the key moments, but grinds gears when it's trying to be colourful and wacky. Tobolowsky is increasingly required to throw temper tantrums whenever he sees short people, and it's an indication of how good his performance is that this tedious one joke repetition doesn't undermine his character too badly.

Madam, I'm Adam is promising, though, and shows evidence of the series wanting to engage with ideas rather than prat falls. Certainly the final act, in which the Gunmen try to persuade Adam back into the real world, is the best and wittiest use of virtual reality than Ten Thirteen have attempted in any of their series. The episode as a whole doesn't really work, but scenes as good as this one show there's a quality just wanting to break through. Here's hoping.

(Oh, and rather oddly, Frohike at one point says that he doesn't think they need call Mulder to the case yet. Which is just as well, as at this point during the broadcast, he's dead and buried in a coffin.) (***)

1.7, Planet of the Frohikes (or A Short History of My Demeaning Captivity)

Air Date: April 6, 2001
Writer: Vince Gilligan
Director: John T Kretchmer

Summary Someone claiming to be held captive by the Department of Defense sends the Gunmen a plea for help, but they soon discover that the note originated from a super-smart chimp named Peanuts. Yves repeats a rumor that the government wants to create hyper-intelligent animals to work as undercover agents, and the Gunmen's involvement enables Peanuts to escape. The authorities capture Byers, Langly and Jimmy, but agree to trade them for Peanuts. A chimp named Bobo is surrendered in Peanuts' place, tricking those involved into releasing the Gunmen. Peanuts is then free to live in a zoo, caged up with his beloved: a chimp named Lady Bonkers.

Critique Monkeys are funny. You can't go wrong with monkeys. In this episode the Lone Gunmen team up with an intelligent chimp called Peanuts - or, since he wants to reject his "slave" name, called Simon White-Thatch Potentloins. And although it feels very much like a backhanded compliment, the series finally finds its level. It's terribly silly, nonsensical stuff, but it's also (at last!) actually very funny. Vince Gilligan's script is full of great jokes, and despite the obvious visual gag of having a monkey behave like a human, these jokes are for once based on verbal wit rather than slapstick. The collision between these two styles of comedy is best exemplified in the wonderful teaser, where a room of monkeys bashing away gibberish on computer keyboards cuts to one secretly writing his memoirs: "A Short History of My Demeaning Captivity". The sight joke is funny; that Peanuts' autobiography has such a pompous title is funnier still.

Using the synthesised voice of Edward Woodward (Peanuts likes the British accent), the monkey runs rings around the Lone Gunmen. After a stalled attempt in the pilot episode to give them a little dignity, they've never been put in so humiliating a position as here, bested by an animal. It's done with such good nature that it's honestly charming, but in an ironic way the very effectiveness of this approach surely rings the death knell for the series. How can The Lone Gunmen sustain itself when the best episode of its run reveals them all to be sub-simian? Once again, Jimmy Bond is the stand out of the group, and he gets the funniest of Gilligan's lines. The sequence where he affects surprise that a monkey has sent him an email - because he doesn't have an Internet account - raises comic stupidity to hilarious new heights. And it's great that at the end of the episode Jimmy is the one most on Peanuts' wavelength and saves the day. It's about time that one of the cruellest aspects of the show - that Jimmy is regularly bullied by the characters we're supposed to care about - is addressed as pointedly as it is here.

It's not perfect. The plotting is rather haphazard. You almost don't care because the jokes are so good, but somewhere in the final act the story becomes such a convoluted mess, it can

no longer be ignored. And Zuleikha Robinson has far too much to do. Here we are, halfway through the series' run, and she has barely found a second emotional register. But besides that, this episode is lovely, a skilful bit of comedy with a terrific premise, made with a confidence the programme has so far lacked. (****)

1.8, Maximum Byers

Air Date: April 13, 2001
Writers: Vince Gilligan, Frank Spotnitz
Director: Vincent Misiano

Summary A reader of *The Lone Gunmen* asks Byers and company to help free her son, Douglas Pfieffer, a death row inmate convicted of murdering the owner of the Wally Burger chain. Byers and Jimmy infiltrate Pfieffer's prison disguised as inmates, even as Langly and Frohike learn that Jeremy Walsh - Pfieffer's lawyer - contracted him to commit the killing as part of a crooked land deal. Walsh also framed another convict, Wallace Krendel Atherton, for a second murder.

The Gunmen convince Pfieffer to admit Walsh's involvement, and also to claim responsibility for the death that Atherton allegedly caused. Walsh is jailed, Pfieffer is executed as scheduled, and Atherton is freed - vowing to devote his life to aiding an oppressed species: cockroaches.

Critique This one opens with the team on board a cruise liner trying to track down Elvis Presley... masquerading as one of his own impersonators. And it ends with Byers getting his face slapped by a grieving mother whose son has been executed for murder, and a curious reflection on the meaning of death. Tonally this one is all over the place, moving from scenes of light comedy to ugly prison drama, and it can only be deliberate. It's a pity, then, that its boldness really doesn't work that well at all. Maximum Byers gives every indication of an attempt at something a little more sophisticated than usual, but the series simply hasn't yet got the maturity to pull it off. It quite openly sets up a comparison between prison as a comic setting as seen in TV genre shows (Langly even comments that the plot, in which our heroes pose as inmates to rescue an innocent man, is a cliché used by tired series in their fourth seasons), and the harsh reality of incarceration. And it invites the audience to accept the episode on both levels at once - as an A-Team parody, and as a drama about crime and punishment.

Playing with an audience's expectations is certainly very ambitious and laudable. But it falls apart, because the contrast isn't made clearly enough. And, crucially, for all Jimmy's horrified mutterings that jail isn't at all like it's seen on telly, the realism just isn't there - the cells look like cheap studio sets, so indeed it looks *exactly* the way it is on telly. Ultimately the most brutal thing we see in the story is a cockroach being fried with a cigarette, and that just isn't strong enough. It's a tale which wants to have its cake and eat it too; it tries to be a feel-good comedy about a man who when freed can devote his life to the betterment of insects, and it also tries to be something more dour in which a mother's tears for her convict son may ultimately turn out to be undeserved. The direction doesn't make much sense of it: when does it allow the jaunty Presley music of Jailhouse Rock, and when does it play on the heartstrings? And the story spends so much time juggling its themes it doesn't spend enough time on the plot - sequences where Byers earnestly tries to talk to Pfieffer in the infirmary, or where Yves plays a southern belle temptress, grow wearisome with repetition. Stephen Sneddon, the most consistent actor on the series, looks utterly floored by the hoops he's being asked to jump through, and eventually elects for an awkward and subdued performance which doesn't tip the tonal balance to either side. That sums it all up, really; for the episode to have worked, as parodic laughfest or redemptive drama, let alone both, it would require a lot of confidence. What we have here is a script and production which nervously walk a tightrope. (**)

1.9, Diagnosis: Jimmy

Air Date: April 20, 2001
Writer: John Shiban
Director: Bryan Spicer

Summary   The Gunmen go to Washington state and attempt to record a poacher meeting with

his buyers, but Jimmy smacks into a tree while skiing. He's hospitalised, and becomes convinced that one of the physicians there - Dr Bromberg - is actually Richard Milliken, the murderous "Doctor of Death" from Denver. Yves realises that the *real* "Doctor of Death" is Greg Ballucci, an anesthesiologist, and saves Jimmy before he becomes Ballucci's next victim. She also alerts the authorities to shut down the poacher's operation.

Critique   This may not be the worst episode of The Lone Gunmen, but it's the blandest. John Shiban offers two storylines here, and neither are very funny nor very dramatic. In one the Lone Gunmen track down someone who sells pelts of grizzly bears. Cue sequences of our hapless heroes being caught in animal traps and disguising themselves as wild beasts - and a bizarrely bad monologue from Byers in which he links his support of animal rights to a childhood fascination with Gentle Ben. In the second story, Jimmy is in hospital with a broken leg, and becomes convinced that one of his doctors is a murderer. We get scenes of a lustful nurse jabbing him in the bottom with a syringe, and a dreadful squib of sentiment in which Jimmy attempts to reunite his grouch of a roommate with his estranged son. The worst crime of the episode is that it takes the ironic charm of Stephen Snedden and slowly dribbles it away until his idiot savant shtick is spent. Zuleika Robinson sleepwalks her way, as ever, through the hour - but for once she looks as if she's got the right idea. (*)

1.10, Tango de los Pistoleros

Air Date: April 27, 2001
Writer: Thomas Schnauz
Director: Bryan Spicer

Summary   The Gunmen venture to Miami, intent on revenging themselves upon Yves by spoiling one of her crooked deals. They learn that Leonardo Santavos - an Argentinean businessman / smuggler and competitive tango dancer - has taken possession of some missile defense secrets, and will likely pass the information along at the dance competition. Yves worms her way into Santavos' life, becoming his new dance partner.

Frohike gets the Gunmen into the contest by renewing his former dance career as "El Lobo". Santavos asks Yves to eliminate the pesky Langly, who fakes his own demise. Santavos' enforcer, Cuccino, realises the deception, deems Yves as treacherous and moves to kill her. Santavos - who's fallen for Yves - takes a knife intended for her and dies, but the authorities round up all the other criminals and recover the stolen information. Yves shares a last dance with Jimmy.

Critique   This is a welcome change of pace. Thomas Schnauz's plot may be rather illogical, but the story has a certain fire to it; his tale of Latin American passions around a dance of love and death has real style. And Bryan Spicer's direction is terrific - his handling of the teaser gives the episode from the start a cool beauty it never loses.

But for all the skill involved, it's a story which centres around the series' femme fatale, and that's where it comes unstuck. Now, it'll be obvious to any reader that I'm not the greatest fan of Zuleika Robinson. It's nothing personal. I'm sure she's a charming woman, and very kind to animals. I've no doubts even that she's a decent actress (most recently she's doing a fine job guesting in the fifth season of Lost). But her interpretation of Yves is fundamentally unappealing. She needs to be a woman of mystery and danger, as Signy Coleman provided as Susanne Modeski. And it may be because the series is making too much of her each week to maintain that mystery, or that since she's a regular her character needs a bit more grounding - but Zuleika Robinson seems caught between too stools: too omnipresent to be as distant as the stories try to make her, too vague to be interesting enough to justify her constant reappearances each week. She's required to smoulder, but sashaying as she walks all the time just doesn't cut it, her inflection pitched at the emotionless or the wooden. In this episode it's not Robinson's fault; this story calls for a passion that's entirely outside what we understand about Yves. We're asked to believe that not only a dangerous smuggler whose billions have been acquired through merciless paranoia will, at the climax, take an assassin's knife for Yves' sake;

we're also invited to believe that there is such a dangerous ambiguity to Yves that she really might murder Langly in cold blood. She needs to inspire faith in those who'd never easily trust her, whilst still pushing the audience away. It's just too much of a leap, and it typifies one of the major problems with the series as a whole.

And this is an episode that emphasises, as other episodes before have only suggested, that the heroes of the show are only ever to be beaten and humiliated by a cleverer hacker than they are. Working on her own, with better technology, Yves is always streets ahead of the titular main cast. And she's a terrible character - hiding under constant anagrams of Lee Harvey Oswald doesn't give her mystery, it gives her OCD. With Jimmy Bond always there to provide the voice of conscience, it's clear that the Lone Gunmen are being squeezed out of their own spin-off. The closing moments say it all, as Jimmy and Yves dance the tango on their own. The Lone Gunmen may have been the comic relief in The X-Files, but they were rarely bunglers, and there was a touch of brilliance to their eccentricities. Now if they want to hack into a computer they even have to call in Kimmy, who's able to breach state security by pressing a single button.

Tom Braidwood has the most fun this week, and the revelation that Frohike is a tango legend called El Lobo, with broken hearts behind him, is lovely. His own turn on the dance floor isn't necessarily convincing, but it's great fun nonetheless and a highlight of the story. But otherwise this is an episode which underlines, even when you remove some of the more childish excesses of the comedy, how The Lone Gunmen has a void at its very centre. All television shows take a little while to settle down and find their groove - The X-Files and Millennium were certainly no exception, and it was in their constant shifting about trying to find out whether the groove they'd opted for suited them that both series produced their best work. But as The Lone Gunmen cools down and starts showing a bit of style, it's hard to see what on earth it has to develop. (**1/2)

1.11, The Lying Game

Air Date: May 4, 2001
Writer: Nandi Bowe
Director: Richard Compton

Summary Jeff Strode, Byers' former roommate, is seemingly killed while undertaking a blackmail scheme - and video evidence suggests that the murderer is FBI Assistant Director Walter Skinner. FBI agents detain the Gunmen, and Skinner explains that he faked Jeff's death - all part of a scheme to stop Russian mobsters from selling plutonium on the black market. The Gunmen discover that Byers was actually roommates with Jeff's "sister" Carol - who was once a man named Carl. Events converge at a night club, where Skinner and his operatives arrest the criminals and seize the plutonium.

Critique One could justifiably argue that an episode in which The X-Files directly collides with The Lone Gunmen does the spin-off series no good at all. By investigating Skinner for murder, our heroes only manage to jeopardise an FBI sting operation run by more credible characters than they are; in fact, throughout the episode, the Lone Gunmen do *nothing* to bring about a successful conclusion to the case. (That's a first, even for them.) And by bringing Skinner in, a series which is having difficulty establishing a workable identity for its stars suffers still further, feeling even more like a satellite to a better show than it did when the references weren't so blatant.

And yet, The Lying Game is good fun. There's a coherent plot to be enjoyed, there's a wit to the dialogue, and there's even an attempt at something rather touching in the way that Byers tries to protect the privacy of an old friend who's had a sex change operation. It's amusing to see Jimmy and Yves, who alone of the regulars have never had any dealings with The X-Files, become ever more convinced that Walter Skinner is committed to evil and in the pay of Russian mobsters. And the final act is genuinely very funny, as Mitch Pileggi - playing Jimmy-disguised-as-Skinner - at last gets a chance to let his hair down (in a manner of speaking), and delights in playing a widely grinning corrupt parody of his regular role. It may be telling that the most comic performance in the episode comes from an X-Files regular rather than from the series proper, but that's partly because we're seeing Skinner played against type. It seems pointless to go against the flow anyway; Lone Gunmen is on borrowed time now, and is clearly resorting to the parent series to prop it up. It might as well have the fun it can have whilst it lasts. Who can they bring in next week? Oh, look, Mulder and Morris Fletcher! (***1/2)

1.12, All About Yves

Air Date: May 11, 2001
Writers: Vince Gilligan, John Shiban, Frank Spotnitz
Director: Bryan Spicer

Summary An e-mail from a military server entitled "Romeo 61" causes the Gunmen to encounter a Man in Black, Morris Fletcher (X-Files 6.4, Dreamland). He tells the heroes that "Romeo 61" is a group of unidentified individuals who commit seemingly motiveless crimes - and who were possibly behind every notable bombing, disaster and assassination since at least 1952. Fletcher also says that Yves has stolen information pertaining to something called "the Maharon Project", that he'll be killed if this is discovered, and that he needs the Gunmen's help to retrieve it.

Clues lead the Gunmen to the Fenix Atlantic Corporation, which purportedly has a massive data storage vault holding a treasure trove of secrets. The Gunmen break into the vault, while Yves tries to pass the "Maharon" information - actually a list of "alien abductees" who were brainwashed by the likes of Fletcher, along with details concerning governmental cover stories and procedures - to her contact, Fox Mulder.

Yves fails to meet up with Mulder, realising that "Romeo 61" is nothing more than a trap set for her - which the Gunmen have walked into - to retrieve the information. Fletcher and his goons capture Yves when she goes to Fenix to help the Gunmen, then surround Byers, Frohike and Langly. [To be continued (in name only; this cliffhanger is never resolved).]

Critique Now that The Lone Gunmen has thrown in its all with The X-Files, it seems apt that this opens with a wicked parody of its current season - with Michael McKean, playing

Fletcher, apparently abducted by aliens. It even seems that he's on the same set as the one we keep seeing David Duchovny experimented on every now and again - and that something which was taken so earnestly on the parent show only weeks ago is being played for laughs here. Yes, McKean being tortured by a fat alien in an unconvincing costume is rather sly. Later on Mulder appears in a somewhat forced cameo, but the way that Jimmy gushes to him as a fan asking about the supposed abduction ("I *was* abducted by aliens!") raises a smile.

And it's odd that by tying itself closer to the themes of The X-Files, The Lone Gunmen actually finds its own voice. Looking back at the series, one can applaud Ten Thirteen's attempts to make it a show that didn't trade upon the alien or the paranormal - but combined with an highly overt comic tone, all that succeeded in doing was making a homegrown menace seem rather ineffectual and spoken in a variety of bad European accents. All About Yves is often very funny, principally because it brings back Morris Fletcher - his lazy womanising Man in Black is the perfect foil for the rather pompous Lone Gunmen. (Their scenes together seem to be a replay of their encounter in Dreamland II - which, of course, none of them would remember.) But there's also the return of elements that have been largely missing since the pilot: intrigue and tension. Yves is at her best here as a genuinely ambiguous figure who may be something darker than our heroes had believed - Zuleikha Robinson does a much better job now she's required to play something other than smug boredom. And the scenes where the Lone Gunmen make their way into the Atlantic Corporation are actually *suspenseful*, in a series which has always sold out such stuff in favour of easy laughs.

It'd perhaps be an exaggeration to say that The Lone Gunmen was finding its feet just as it was cancelled. The reason why All About Yves works as well as it does is that it feeds off exactly the elements that make The X-Files such a success. But this is likeable and confident, and it does seem therefore a real missed opportunity that it all ends on an unfulfilled "To Be Continued" announcement. It's an indication of how enjoyable the episode is on its own terms

that even though this is merely the opening chapter to an unfinished novel it's still so satisfying, when so many of the completed stories feel like damp squibs. (****)

1.13, The Cap'n Toby Show

Air Date: June 1, 2001
Writers: Vince Gilligan, John Shiban,
Frank Spotnitz
Director: Carol Banker

Summary Two stage hands from a children's programme - the Cap'n Toby Show - are found murdered. The Gunmen visit the studio where the show - a childhood favourite of Langly's - is filmed, and discover that the dead men were actually FBI agents. Moreover, it seems that a spy ring intent on relaying information to China has usurped the show's format. To Langly's horror, Cap'n Toby himself is implicated in the scheme and charged with espionage. The killer is revealed as Agent Blythe of the CIA, a turncoat who has modified the show's "Magic Portal" to display messages that can be seen by use of special glasses. Yves incapacitates Blythe, and Cap'n Toby is exonerated.

Critique This is the "missing" episode, a story presumably held over for screening during the second season, and only broadcast some weeks after the series finale and the cancellation of the show. It's a light throwaway story, and you can see why the network seemed almost apologetic in the way they scheduled it after the main run of episodes was over. But although there's nothing climactic about this, there's a breezy charm to it which is very endearing. It doesn't attempt to go for big laughs or stunts, and so this tale of lost innocence has an almost effortless feel to it, in marked contrast to the hysterical comedy of the series proper. It's Dean Haglund's finest hour too, as he sweetly portrays a Langly who can only feel disillusioned when his childhood TV favourite show gets a hip-hop theme tune and loses its simplicity to Hollywood soullessness. It'd be tempting to draw parallels here - that the Cap'n Toby Show is a light piece of fun that's about to make its final episode, unable to sustain itself in the smear of twenty-first century cynicism - but that's clearly not the intention. The story's appeal is that it isn't trying to be too smart or bitter, that instead it's presenting a feel-good tale about the enduring power of escapism.

It's not an especially well-told story; it feels oddly like a first draft, the plotting rather clunky, the ending lacking a true punch. Maybe that's why it was held over from original broadcast: to give it a bit more work in the editing room. But it has a subtlety to it which is missing from most of The Lone Gunmen episodes, and a relaxed tone which isn't trying to be strident. It's tempting to think of this as something of a workmanlike template for that cancelled second season, a basic average of what a more thoughtful and restrained Lone Gunmen series could produce. It's forgettable stuff, but sincere and amiable. There are worse ways for series to bow out. (***1/2)

The X-Files: Season 9

9.1, Nothing Important Happened Today

Air Date: Nov. 11, 2001
Writers: Chris Carter, Frank Spotnitz
Director: Kim Manners

Summary   A dark-haired woman who can breathe underwater drowns Carl Wormus, a deputy administrator for the EPA, and then eliminates Roland McFarland, a worker at a water reclamation facility. Back in Washington, D.C., Doggett and Reyes' case against Kersh begins dying for lack of evidence. Reyes' former lover, Assistant Director Brad Follmer, stonewalls their investigation on Kersh's behalf.

Doggett tries to consult with Mulder - but finds that he's vanished, and that Scully refuses to talk about his absence. Skinner and Doggett look into Wormus and McFarland's deaths, investigating McFarland's water plant. Just as they find a number of files pertaining to "chloramines", Follmer and his men apprehend Skinner. Doggett hides in a water tank - and is pulled under water by the dark-haired woman. [To be continued.]

Critique   This isn't quite the dullest season opener to The X-Files - that dubious distinction must be taken by Redux. But at least Redux was merely the dreadful sandwich filler of a story which felt urgent and emotional and did something major to its main characters. Nothing Important Happened Today is about an internal investigation at the FBI of a character who was never that central in the first place; Kersh is an effective obstruction to any number of X-Files cases, but he can hardly be considered a lead villain, and we've yet to see him in any position that could honestly be thought compromising. As a result, Doggett and Reyes going after Kersh has nothing of the verve that we had in previous seasons when Mulder faced up to the Cigarette Smoking Man, and instead seems something rather petty and vengeful. It's appropriately small-fare stuff in an episode which feels like a celebration of inaction - with Scully, Skinner et al lining up to tell Doggett to stop doing anything which might be halfway interesting. Mulder going into hiding is just the beginning of a story in which everyone seems to be acting out of character; Scully's defeatism, coupled with her new lack of principles, not only gives her feet of clay but also makes her wearying to watch - within the course of one episode, it's as if she's stopped being an FBI agent and become nothing more than a harassed mother. The wrongness of it all is typified by the way everyone keeps calling each other by their first names; it's a small point, but it just makes the characterization feel slightly off. And with the greatest discovery made this week being that Reyes has an on / off relationship with yet-another spoke in the wheel of the FBI, you struggle to find anything useful this episode achieves. Cary Elwes does Gish no favours here; had he played Follmer as the reluctant bureaucrat suggested by the script, Reyes' affection for him wouldn't have seemed so contrived. As it is, with Elwes intent upon dripping insincerity in every scene, Reyes can only look cheap. For all Existence's problems, the ending felt big and triumphant; this episode, set only two days later, has all the passion of a wet Monday morning.

Director Kim Manners gets the meat out of the few action sequences there are; the teaser is particularly effective. But since these sudden jolts of adrenalin are all variations on the same theme - Lucy Lawless dragging her victims into water to drown - they soon lose their impact. We're left with rivetting scenes of Baby William making a mobile spin, or Reyes breaking her pencil, for any nerve-wrenching drama. I appreciate what the title means, and its historical irony - they're the words George III put in his diary the day that American independence was declared - but with the explanation not forthcoming until next week, and headlining an episode as arthritically paced as this one, a rethink might have been in order. (*)

9.2, Nothing Important Happened Today II

Air Date: Nov. 18, 2001
Writers: Chris Carter, Frank Spotnitz
Director: Tony Wharmby

Summary   The dark-haired woman, Shannon McMahon, breathes air into Doggett's lungs and keeps him underwater as a means of avoiding detection. McMahon tells Doggett that she and the late Knowle Rohrer are bioengineered combat units - the products of a "supersoldier" program going back fifty years. McMahon claims to hate what she's become, and wants to expose persons involved in lacing the water supply with chloramine - a molecularly-tailored substance that will alter the unborn and create a whole generation of supersoldiers.

Reyes finds that McMahon works for the Justice Department and killed Wormus and McFarland because they were whistle-blowers - and has been hoodwinking the agents to find the dead men's accomplice. The third whistle-blower is revealed as the captain of a Navy ship that's carrying a secret laboratory. Rohrer turns up alive and kills the captain, then attacks Doggett. McMahon decapitates Rohrer, but his headless body shoves an arm through her torso and they both fall into the ocean. Scully, Doggett and Reyes find that the secret lab is designed to manipulate ova for transplant, fleeing just prior to a bomb destroying the ship.

Critique   There is at least the semblance of drama here, but this second episode isn't significantly better than the first. The supersoldier idea is fine in essence, and worked last year quite well when it had something more personal to play off, be it either the means of Mulder's return from the dead or the fears surrounding Scully's pregnancy. But with the baby born and Mulder gone, this storyline has been moved to prime position - and, frankly, it isn't interesting enough. It might work as a monster of the week notion (as in Eve, or Sleepless), but as the centre of The X-Files' mythology it seems very uninspired - after the conspiracy of alien invasion, this doesn't feel like the climax to the ongoing story but a coda. This time water is being used as the means to infect the world with alien matter, and we're supposed to treat this as

a revelation - but it's no different to the oil or the bees; it's little wonder that Scully looks as exasperated as she does. The episode feels laboured. New actors like Cary Elwes and Annabeth Gish are going through the routines of being allies one moment and enemies the next, as if this isn't a dance we've seen played out over the last few seasons from every conceivable angle. And old lags like Gillian Anderson and Mitch Pileggi seem barely able to stifle their yawns at the proceedings.

After Season Eight succeeded in giving The X-Files a whole new lease of life, it's dispiriting to see it here as something so flaccid and listless. The clichés just keep coming, so that by the end it'd be a shock if Shannon McMahon *wasn't* some ambiguous double agent, or *didn't* open her eyes after death. Never before has the series seemed so tired and so irrelevant. I find it significant, perhaps, that the episode ends on a dedication to a man who died in the attack on the World Trade Center. As shown with the pilot for The Lone Gunmen, the world of escapist terrorism and espionage that is the substance for this show has changed and become much darker - and, whether consciously or not, this tepid and cautious season opener seems to reflect that. (*)

9.3, Daemonicus

Air Date: Dec. 2, 2001
Writer / Director: Frank Spotnitz

Summary   After two men with demon faces murder Darren and Evelyn Mountjoy, a married couple in Weston, West Virginia, the victims are found around their kitchen table with the word "Daemonicus" (a word meaning "Satan" or "demon possession") spelled out on a Scrabble board. Doggett and Reyes follow a lead concerning Kenneth Richman, a serial killer who escaped from a nearby mental institution, questioning Josef Kobold, one of Richman's fellow inmates. Kobold helps the agents find Richman's accomplice dead in the woods.

Richman strikes again and kills Dr Monique Sampson. Kobold prompts the agents to accompany him to a marina - where Richman briefly captures Scully before shooting himself. Kobold then escapes, causing Doggett to realise that Kobold played everyone from the start to facilitate his getaway. Worse, Kobold arranged events so that pieces of the victims' names spell out the word "daemonicus".

Critique There's some very attention-seeking direction here, with strange cross fades and exaggerated camera points of view. But it's really not enough to distract from what is a very clumsy script that doesn't so much leap from set piece to set piece as lurch. The focus of the episode is all over the place. It begins as a story which seems designed to give emphasis to Reyes, and that's all to the good because Annabeth Gish desperately needs a stronger character to be working with; after Spotnitz did such sterling work last season developing Doggett, it's a natural hope that he can do the same for Monica here. But although there's an interesting attempt at first to shake her out of her complacency, to allow her to see evil as a reality rather than just a New Age concept, Spotnitz too quickly loses interest in her. Instead he gives his attention once more to Doggett, who again reacts angrily to suggestions of the paranormal, and is goaded by Kobold as being a man who has specific reasons for denying supernatural forces. We *know* all this; it's just a rehash of what was explored more subtly and with greater power in Empedocles. By the time Kobold is mocking Doggett for not being as good as the "long gone" Mulder, it feels as if the series is mocking itself too, putting focus on a vulnerability it really can't afford.

But that's really just one aspect of a story which feels, in spite of itself, hell-bent on emphasising its flaws. The three FBI agents do little but bicker amongst themselves, and then at the end lose their game with the Devil. Scully has become a teacher at the FBI academy, and that rather prompts the unfortunate sensation that all this chasing around after demons is something she fits in after work as some sort of hobby. She stands in front of her class, talks about the X-Files - and we cut to a roomful of teenagers who all look bored to death, and can't wait to race out at the end of the lecture hall as soon as the bell rings. Is this *really* the signal The X-Files should be sending out in its ninth year, that it's something now so establishment that all the kids want nothing to do with it?

Daemonicus needed to be something that would have made the kids sit up. It needed to be scary. In the season opener, Scully gets emotional when something happens that science can't explain - namely, that the mobile above her baby's head moved without being touched. This week Reyes detects the presence of evil, and does so by alluding to something she can't explain... and it's that the fan above her head has stopped working. Not the two corpses sitting at the Scrabble board, not the snakes that worm out of a victim's stomach. The fan. Stopped. Working. Apart from this season's fixation with things designed to rotate being a source of mystery and wonder, it's another illustration that this new season needs to try a little harder. (*1/2)

9.4, 4-D

Air Date: Dec. 9, 2001
Writer: Steven Maeda
Director: Tony Wharmby

Summary Reyes, Doggett and Follmer attempt to apprehend Erwin Lukesh - a serial killer who cuts out women's tongues - but Lukesh kills Reyes by slitting her throat. Doggett confronts Lukesh in an alley, but Lukesh disappears, then reappears behind Doggett and shoots him with Reyes' gun.

Oblivious to these events, Reyes is unpacking boxes in her apartment when Skinner phones to say that Doggett is comatose. Ballistics match his wound to Reyes' gun, and an eyewitness, Lukesh, has identified her as the assailant. Doggett wakes up paralyzed, unable to speak, but taps out Lukesh's name in Morse Code.

Reyes determines that Lukesh can flit between parallel Earths, that he *did* kill her in another reality and that this alternate version of Doggett somehow followed him through. Lukesh goes to kill Reyes, but Follmer shoots him dead. Doggett communicates that Reyes should end his life and enable the other Doggett to return, as two versions of them can't exist in the same reality. Reyes pulls Doggett's life support - and finds herself back in her apartment, with "her" Doggett offering her a housewarming gift of Polish sausages.

Critique   Last year Steven Maeda wrote in Redrum a smart little thriller that owed a lot to The Twilight Zone, but in sidelining its lead characters didn't give it much to do with The X-Files. Here he's in Rod Serling mode again, and this time the premise doesn't seem as well thought through. The parallel universe set up is a terrific idea, and the suggestion that Lukesh uses an alternate reality as merely the place where he can safely act out his sick serial killer fantasies is very effective. The X-Files always plays its banality of evil card very well, and what is more disturbing than a character who uses a unique gift of exploring an entire new world as nothing more than a rubbish bin for all his emotional garbage? But it's such a high concept idea that Meada finds it hard to manoeuvre any of his characters credibly to posit it; the sequence where Reyes puts to Doggett her outlandish understanding of the story, and asks him whether he can find any other scenario that better fits the facts, is such a leap into fantasy that it's almost funny. The story first requires that the FBI suspect Reyes of Doggett's shooting, and then once the sci-fi premise is raised it's dramatically essential that this subplot is abandoned so that the story can move on. The logic behind these parallel universes is never explained, neither how Lukesh is able to manipulate them, nor why Doggett believes that dying in one would save his life in another. Maeda's spinning a lot of plates here, and he asks us and his characters to take an awful lot on trust.

But, you know, it's worth it. Because if Redrum suffered by being emotionally distant, 4-D earns its stripes by at last restoring to the series a pulse. Maeda very skilfully mines each scene for its maximum emotional impact. Lukesh may be a vicious psychopath, but the agonised grief he feels when he realises he's going to have to kill his own mother is fantastic; it may not humanise the brute, but it's very real, and is played by Dylan Haggerty with great conviction. Better yet are the scenes featuring Annabeth Gish, who is finally given a showcase that makes Reyes so much more than a New Age fanatic or someone who's sleeping with the boss. Her revelation to Lukesh that she knows his world-crossing secret is a stand out, brimming over with utter disgust; the fear and courage she shows as Doggett asks her to test the limits of her beliefs and turn off his life support machine is Gish's best performance yet. At the end of the day, this is the story in which Doggett and Reyes at last seem to assume the mantle of Mulder and Scully. (Indeed, for her few appearances in the story, Gillian Anderson looks somewhat irrelevant, like a ghost from series past.) High in concept but very down to earth in the way it explores its implications, this is just the sort of story The X-Files needs to reinvent itself. (****)

9.5, Lord of the Flies

Air Date: Dec. 16, 2001
Writer: Thomas Schnauz
Director: Kim Manners

Summary   A teen named Bill seemingly dies while performing a daredevil stunt, but an autopsy reveals that he actually perished because a swarm of flies ate out the contents of his head. Doggett and Reyes question Bill's classmates, and see the lice carve the words "Dumb Ass" into the back of David Winkle, another teen. The culprit is revealed as Dylan Lokensgard, a teen secretes pheromones that make insects obey him, and has been exacting punishment against anyone who makes trouble for the object of his affections: Winkle's girlfriend Natalie. The agents find that both Lokensgard and his mother are a biological anomaly somewhere between human and insect, and that Mrs Lokensagard killed Dylan's father because he was merely human. Exposed, Mrs Lokensgard takes her son and goes into hiding.

Critique   The final scene gives you an indication of what this is trying to be, as the fireflies spell out the words "I Love You" outside a girl's window. It wants to be a Rain King, or a Terms of Endearment, and would like to recapture the sweet and charming feel of those early Season Six experiments. But the reason those episodes worked as very strange comedies is because at that stage The X-Files was brimming over with a certain type of confidence, and because Duchovny and Anderson were breezily comfortable testing the limits of their characters. Here in Season Nine an attempt at the same style falls flat on its face; there is no confidence any more, so no-one knows what tone they should be pitching for in script or direction or performance. And you end up with something which looks rather embarrassing and - even worse - rather embarrassed. Dr Rocky Bronzino is an overacted and overwritten character who screams "comedy" at the screen, and Mark Snow goes overboard trying to suggest that each scene has the hilarity and the heart this sort of love story would need to work. But it's just not convincing.

The X-Files is draining the trough of teenage angst again, and the results are rarely pretty. Here at least there's some bite to Thomas Schnauz's depiction of a generation so pampered and so superficial that they deliberately make cable programmes for TV in which they hurt themselves. And there is a sly wit to the scenes in which teenagers get nostalgic about what it was like when they were kids - here is an episode, if nothing else, which takes all the devastations of new adulthood and hormonal change with its tongue firmly in its cheek. At times this approach almost dignifies a script in which the plot mechanics are mundane in the extreme and the characterisations vague and uninteresting - you feel that this may just be the point. Gillian Anderson is allowed to relax a bit and give a wry Scully who's all too aware that what's going on around her is ridiculous; if she's not exactly enjoying herself, at least she doesn't look as awkward as she has so far this season. The same can't be said for Robert Patrick or Annabeth Gish, who walk through the story with the sense that there's something very bad smelling right under their noses. (*1/2)

9.6, Trust No 1

Air Date: Jan. 6, 2002
Writers: Chris Carter, Frank Spotnitz
Director: Tony Wharmby

Summary Scully finds herself entangled with a woman named Patti and her unnamed husband (henceforth called "the Man on the Street"), who claim that their daughter, like William, is a product of the supersoldier program. The Man on the Street, who works for the National Security Agency, hopes that Mulder can learn more about the offspring's condition.

A Shadow Man running a clandestine surveillance operation on Scully contacts her, claiming to have information vital to Mulder's survival. Mulder is slated to return on a train at a pre-arranged time, but the Shadow Man kills the Man on the Street at the rendezvous - and Scully realises that the latter was trying to protect her from the former, his employer.

The Shadow Man jumps on the train to confront Mulder, but Mulder leaps off the train near a quarry. The Shadow Man follows, but - as Mulder suspected - the quarry's iron compound exerts a magnetic pull on the enormous amount of iron in the Shadow Man's blood, pulling him into a fine mist. Mulder goes back into hiding.

Critique Gillian Anderson is back in the limelight again, and gives her most assured performance so far this season. Some of the discussion about surveillance is very interesting, especially the idea that there's no such thing as "the middle of nowhere" any more; the series began in 1993 when mobile phones were state of the art and the Internet was used mostly by people in offices, and now The X-Files is made in a world of CCTV. And the growing use of camera images, and the piano score, manage to make this episode have a different feel to any we've seen before - quite an accomplishment this late in the show's run.

But.

At its best, Trust No 1 is still an exercise in futility. It's a story about a plot to lure Mulder out of hiding. The thing is, we can't watch this series in innocence any more. We don't sit on the edge of our seats wondering if David Duchovny might make an appearance. He isn't going to. He's gone. He's not coming back. (Well, I suppose he might do, you may tempt him back for a final guest appearance if you cancelled the whole show, but that'd be a bit self-defeating, wouldn't it, Chris? Chris?) At this stage of The X-Files' run, you can get the impression that the behind-the-scenes cast disputes are better followed by the public than the storylines on the series themselves. Last year Duchovny's absence could be credibly built around a story which was all about his inevitable return; an episode like Trust No 1 could have worked at such a time, because

Mulder's reappearance had been made a vital part of the season. Now it's not only an irrelevant consideration, it's damaging. It takes the focus from all the actors who are still there on the show, and diverts it uselessly. It feels like a reprise of all we went through on Season Eight, of the way viewers' patiences were tested. Except this time there isn't going to be a pay-off. The final act seems to consist of little more than characters in a darkened quarry shouting desperately for Mulder - but Mulder isn't going to reply, guys, and if that isn't a metaphor for what we've seen on Season Nine so far, I don't know what is.

As I said, this is an exercise in futility *at best*. At worst is the implication not only for Mulder's character but Scully's too. We've been sold the premise of the ninth season on some fairly vague bases, and they're now exposed in horrible glory. Mulder cannot return because his life is under such threat - and we now finally see what that threat is, and it's guest-star Terry O'Quinn standing at a railway station with a gun. Mulder's faced worse in *comedy* episodes. The script can heighten the danger of the supersoldiers as much as it likes, but it honestly needs to *show* them doing something bad to make that real. O'Quinn's great presence in the story amounts to nothing more than sending Scully off on a laborious wild goose chase, and shaking a lot around iron. That's the threat; that's what's kept Mulder away from his child and the woman he loves all *season*. The supersoldiers have one real power, their sensational ability to survive things; it's a useful skill, no doubt, but on its own terms makes them about as menacing as a pack of rechargeable batteries. And it gets worse! O'Quinn tells Scully that either Mulder or the baby must die. *Either* Mulder *or* the baby. So, what they're saying is, by running away as fast as his legs can carry him, Mulder is choosing to let the baby be the fall guy. Is that it? Is that what Mulder's heroism has been reduced to?

The worrying suggestion is that The X-Files' credo has changed. In Season Eight our heroes were on the side of cover-up and subterfuge, and the truth was something best concealed. In Season Nine it's gone further - the best thing the central character can do (and, unfortunately, this episode demonstrates that the series still sees Mulder as central) is to hide. Hiding may be the most sensible line of defence, but it's not the dramatic choice for an adventure series. When we finally glimpse Mulder - in long shot, obviously, and played by an extra - his only course of action is to run away. Run away as fast as you can, Mulder! Run for the hills! Last week they broadcast Lord of the Flies! God knows what Season Nine has lined up for us next!

We can't recognise Mulder any more. His absence changes who he is. Who's this peculiar man who writes poetic email that's headed "Dearest Dana"? Who's Scully, who writes back that she's "physically shaking" to read his words, who was once the protagonist but now becomes a gullible patsy at her first chance to see her lover again? Who investigates cases now based upon how relevant they are to her baby, and will put fellow agents in danger to get that information? Is this really what the series is going to have to be now, something which warps both Mulder and Scully because it can't find a way of letting either of them go? (*)

9.7, John Doe

Air Date: Jan. 13, 2002
Writer: Vince Gilligan
Director: Michelle MacLaren

Summary   Doggett awakens in Sangradura, Mexico, with no ID and no memory of his past, and accepts a job from two men - Domingo and Nestor - repairing vehicles to help smuggle immigrants across the American border. Scully, Reyes and Skinner intensify efforts to find Doggett, who was last seen in Texas trailing Hollis Rice, the vice president of a bank.

The cause of Doggett's amnesia - a caballero who erases people's memories by extending talons into their heads, and who was ordered by a cartel to make Doggett disappear - independently decides that Doggett is too dangerous to let live. Matters degenerate until Skinner and Mexican federal officials round up the caballero and his associates. Doggett's recollections of his dead son help to crumble the caballero's memory block, restoring him to normal.

Critique   If Trust No 1 taught us anything, it's that characters can be redefined by their absence. John Doggett was the highlight of Season Eight. As sceptic newbie to Scully, it was his development which humanised the series once more and gave renewed focus to mysteries which would otherwise have seemed clichéd or overfamiliar. In Season Nine, though, Doggett is sceptic to both Scully *and* Reyes, and he looks as a result little more than a curmudgeonly killjoy. Vince Gilligan's script starts afresh with Doggett by wiping his memory and dumping him in a small town in Mexico. He has to learn at heart who he is, and it's his journey of self-discovery which can re-establish him to our eyes as a man of integrity, of strength, and of great suffering. It's not an easy process either; it's interesting, as Domingo says, that the first thing Doggett learns about himself is that he doesn't keep his word. During his period of amnesia he's led to believe that he's a murderer, and almost as a fait accompli turns killer. When he meets Reyes again, he's learned in typical X-Files style to trust no-one, and his first instinct is to attack her.

Robert Patrick gives an extraordinary performance, probably his best take on Doggett we've yet seen. When Nestor complains that there's something "different" about the nameless American, he's absolutely right; Doggett stands out not just because we know he's a lead character, but amidst the corruption of a town owned by an organised crime cartel is someone who's seeking a *truth*. What gives him a mission is the vague memory of a son whose name he can't recall; what gives him back his full identity is the realisation that that son is dead. That Doggett has to learn afresh that his child was murdered, and to live the raw grief of that once more, is the crux of the episode. This is the pain that has been removed from him, and the pain that he's fought so hard to win back.

Gilligan is a playful writer, but creditably writes this script with a directness that gives it real power. There's a brooding languor to the plot which is unusual - the first ten minutes feature no regular cast member but Doggett - but it has such a confidence that it's gripping. The direction, by newcomer Michelle Maclaren, is earthy and brutal, the oversaturated lighting making the town hot and oppressive. There's such dirty realism to this that its late dip into the paranormal feels honestly surprising. John Doe shows that there's still a fresh take to be had on The X-Files after all; the contrast to the tepid episodes before it is so great that it actually gives you a jolt. (*****)

9.8, Hellbound

Air Date: Jan. 27, 2002
Writer: David Amann
Director: Kim Manners

Summary Three ex-convicts are murdered in Novi, Virginia, their bodies skinned after one of them predicted that he'd die in such a fashion. Scully uncovers files pertaining to a quartet of similar murders dating back to 1960; the dates of death match when the current victims were born, suggesting that their souls are being reincarnated. Moreover, Reyes finds newspaper clippings from an incident in 1868, in which four men skinned a prospector over a mining dispute but went unpunished.

Reyes pieces together that Detective Van Allen is the reincarnated prospector, and that he's been skinning his former assailants in each of their reincarnated lives, then committing suicide to restart the cycle. Van Allen assaults his fourth target, Dr Lisa Holland, but Doggett and Reyes shoot and kill him. Reyes speculates that she witnessed the killings in her own past lives, but was unable to stop them. Meanwhile, a child is born elsewhere with Van Allen's eyes.

Critique For its first half this plays out like a particularly grisly version of Squeeze, with a series of murders echoing cases that took place in 1960. But writer David Amann is only too aware of The X-Files cliché, and uses it to misdirect our expectations of what the episode is really about... although the victims, all skinned alive, perhaps represent the high point of the series' trading in gore, the dialogue and the plotting in contrast are delightfully subtle. There's a genuine suspense to the story, as Amann cleverly leads us down several blind alleys, throwing suspicion at first on hothead Ed as the killer when he's just a frightened victim waiting in the wings. And there's a real sense of horror to the murders, as time is taken to show how these ex-cons - who are being killed in the most inhumane manner imaginable - are struggling hard to reinvent their lives and put their criminal pasts behind them. It's that air of thwarted redemption which gives so much heart to what could simply have been another gorefest, and throws the standard X-Files vengeance yarn into sharp relief.

For the weight of the past is exactly what this story is about. And in the end the episode owes less to Squeeze and more to The Field Where I Died, as generation after generation of reincarnated souls are butchered in revenge for an unpunished murder of the nineteenth century. The high concept idea works better here than in the Morgan and Wong story too, precisely because it's used as a hook to tell an exciting horror story, and sensibly allows the premise some ambiguity. That Reyes is in some way connected to this cycle of killings is very clever; that, for all her desperate need to understand, we never find out the specifics of that connection is cleverer still. The Field Where I Died suffered because once Mulder found his past lives he could barely be shut up giving full accounts of them all, and it became more of an acting exercise than a demonstration of storytelling. Amann has tapped into something missing from The X-Files for a while, knowing just when to *stop* painting the picture, knowing that what's left unexplained is far more scary.

It's not a flawless episode. Reyes feels a bond to the case from the moment she sees a photograph of the first skinned victim; the script (understandably) wants Reyes' conviction that there's something paranormal going on to be part of the suspense. Right from her first episode, though, she's been responding to her feelings with no logical reason. In 4-D, just a few weeks ago, she seized upon the high concept as the story dictated, just as she does here. What's meant to stand out as a plot twist here has been exhausted already, and now looks like standard Reyes behaviour - Amann has been compromised by lazy treatments of Reyes in previous stories, and it means his own depiction of her here can't have the impact it should, nor does it allow the explanation of Reyes' unease and legacy to be revelatory. But this is nevertheless a standout episode, revelling in a horror and a tension that the show hasn't even dabbled in for quite a while.

This too is the first episode transmitted since Chris Carter announced that the show was facing certain cancellation. From this point on, all episodes are advertised as being part of an "end game". How that subtly affects audience's expectations of the stories, and whether that makes them have greater or lesser power, remains to be seen. But from now on there's a shift in the way that any X-Files episode can be perceived. Doggett and Reyes are on their way out - for better or for worse, there's no longer time to develop the characters, just to start plotting their departures. (****)

9.9, Provenance

Air Date: March 3, 2002
Writers: Chris Carter, Frank Spotnitz
Director: Kim Manners

Summary Border police in North Dakota stop a motorcyclist carrying some rubbings with markings akin to the spaceship that Scully examined in Africa (7.1, The Sixth Extinction). Doggett learns that the border-runner was Robert Comer, an FBI agent assigned to infiltrate UFO cultists in Canada, but who seems to have thrown in with the group. Comer's rubbings seem to originated from a second spaceship in Canada.

Scully shoots Comer when he tries to kill William. She finds a metallic fragment from the spaceship in Comer's jacket; the object flies across the room and comes to rest, spinning in mid-air, above William.

Kersh tells Scully that the UFO group made threats against Mulder, and that before going rogue, Comer sent word that Mulder was dead. Reyes and Scully worry that the cultists want to kill Mulder's son, so Scully gives William to the Lone Gunmen for safekeeping. However, one of the cultists - a woman in an overcoat - intercepts the Gunmen and abducts the boy. [To be continued.]

Critique Pity poor Scully. There she is, abducted by her own government, who strap her down and whip out her ovaries. She can't have children. Then, a few years later, she finds out she has a daughter. It's a miracle!... except the daughter has an unfortunate habit of bleeding green acid and - well - dying. She's right back where she started; she mourns a bit, but seems to have forgotten about her daughter in time for the feature film. And a few years later she gets pregnant. It's a miracle!... except the son has a telekinetic ability, and a strange cult wants to kidnap him, and some other group altogether want to kill him. And if you scratch him, who knows, he's probably *so* alien he'll bleed green acid too. It's tough being a mum.

Pity poor Gillian Anderson. The X-Files once gave her the opportunity to play a strong, capable FBI agent who could solve cases of the paranormal, conduct impossible autopsies, and still hold her own in the odd comedy episode. Now she's in a series that both she and her character' have outgrown, popping up for cameo appearances in the standalone stories and having to portray a mother who's always crying, shouting or looking miserable in the mythology outings. Anderson is always a reliable hand at the occasional bout of angst, but it was rationed out in previous seasons, and was usually something to do with the fate of Mulder. That was good; we cared for Mulder too. The angst we see now is for a baby, and as an audience we are expected to share that angst just *because* it's a baby. To have the same emotional connection to it that a mother would, by making it a super-infant that can rotate bits of metal above its head and may well be a Christ-like figure who can ensure mankind's survival, the writers are doing their level best to make this the least empathetic child in television history. Anderson has so much more range than can be shown here, and yet she's reduced to being selfish and obsessed, to withholding medical help from dying men, to seeing the arrival of a spaceship as a message intended only for her as a mother. Back in The Jersey Devil, Scully thought she wouldn't make a very good mum. She was right.

And pity poor us. Because a series which was once about extreme possibility and about opening the door to alternate perception has become this inward looking and tedious. The characters no longer make sense, they've been so required to dance through the little conspiracy hoops that there's no consistency any more. Skinner has somehow forgotten the development he underwent since Requiem, and seems genuinely offended by suggestions of corruption within the FBI. Doggett is so angry because he's been excluded from an X-File that he raids the Assistant Director's office - for the sake of the plot, he's actually become Mulder. The Lone Gunmen are such idiots that less than two minutes after taking care of Super Baby, they've had it stolen. (Of course, as their own series showed, they have such a winning way with babies; at least this time Chris Carter resisted the urge of having them pissed all over.) And Mulder's dead. Perhaps. It's funny; the last time Mulder "appeared", the story failed because we knew full well that Duchovny wasn't returning. In the meantime Carter has announced that with the series concluding Duchovny will be making an appearance in the finale. It's really not the time to play as a possible truth that Mulder's dead; ironically, it's a premise which might have worked only a few weeks ago. (*)

9.10, Providence

Air Date: March 10, 2002
Writers: Chris Carter, Frank Spotnitz
Director: Chris Carter

Summary Scully questions Comer after close proximity with the alien fragment heals him. He tells Scully that the UFO cult, led by Zeke Josepho, believes that aliens have proper dominion over Earth, and that the spaceship in Canada houses the physical manifestation of God. William is foretold as a saviour who will thwart the aliens if his father is alive, or rule the aliens if Mulder is dead. Thinking that Mulder has been slain, Josepho now wants to protect William, but Cromer attacked the boy to stop the alien plan. Scully leaves as one of her superiors, actually a super-solider, takes the fragment.

Josepho tells Scully of his belief that the supersoldiers are the future of mankind. He offers to let Scully see William, but only if she brings him proof that Mulder is dead. Scully and Reyes track the cultists to Alberta, and find them excavating the spaceship.

William starts crying as the ship emits a bright light, then takes off and flies away. Scully and Reyes approach the tattered, enflamed remains of the work tent and find the cultists charred to death - but William is miraculously unharmed.

Critique   Chris Carter directs the teaser very well, which at last shows the supersoldiers doing something interesting - they're in the Iraq war, they're soldiers, and they're frankly super! And the sequences in which Josepho's cult try to open the spacecraft have an eeriness to them which recalls the conclusion of Raiders of the Lost Ark.

Otherwise, though, this is horrible. More Scully tears and snot. More hospital bedside scenes (it's a mythology episode, so it's de rigueur that *someone* should be in a coma), and this time Doggett wakes up because he's somehow had a woman in his head giving him plot spoilers. With the clumsy emphasis upon religion in all its forms this week, with Reyes genuflecting before crosses, and Josepho thinking he's got the house of God beneath his feet, Doggett may well have been taking instruction from Mary Magdalene. There's some hilariously bad dialogue - bring me the head of Fox Mulder, indeed! - but most of it is just tediously clunky. There's a scene at the beginning which seems little more than a chance for Scully and Skinner to play potato / potahto. (You call it a task force, I call it a whitewash! You call it protection, I call it the FBI trying to eliminate us! You call it dialogue, I call it playing with words.) Skinner has a speech in which he tells Reyes of his depressing experiences in Vietnam - it's so inappropriate to her concern for Doggett, it's surprising she doesn't pull the plug on her partner there and then.

This is shallow and pretentious, and internally inconsistent. We've got these supersoldiers who can survive almost anything. Then there's Agent Comer, who can survive anything as long as he's holding onto a bit of metal scripture. Then there's Baby William, who can survive being reduced to ashes by a spaceship ascent because... I don't know, isn't he Jesus, or something? Ten Thirteen now have at the centre of their mythology a situation dependent on Mulder and a baby. One of them is absent, and one of them can't talk. Who in their right minds makes the climax to a nine-year storyline revolve around two characters who can't contribute to the action? (*)

9.11, Audrey Pauley

Air Date: March 17, 2002
Writer: Steven Maeda
Director: Kim Manners

Summary   Reyes falls comatose due to a car accident, then awakens in an empty doppelganger of a hospital that's floating in a dark void. She meets two fellow patients, Stephen Murdo and Mr Barreiro, who think they're either dead or in transit to Heaven, and also keeps glimpsing a woman named Audrey Pauley. Murdo and Barreiro both vanish from the hospital as Dr Jack Preijers terminates their life-support systems back in the real world.

Doggett befriends Pauley, a nurse's aide who has a small model of the hospital that she can "visit" by "going inside her head". He determines that Preijers has been unduly murdering his patients, but Preijers - sensing the game is up - gives Pauley a lethal injection. Pauley enters the duplicate hospital and tells Reyes to jump into the void - she does so, returning to her body as the hospital vanishes with Pauley inside. Doggett discovers Pauley's body and apprehends Preijers.

Critique   Steven Maeda fulfils the promise he showed in episodes like 4-D and Redrum by producing a Twilight Zone-like script which is clever, thoughtful, and ultimately very moving. It boasts some of the oddest visual imagery ever seen in an X-Files episode: Monica leaving a hospital only to find it suspended in a cloudy void, the monochrome souls of the dead trapped inside a doll's house. But it works principally because this is a very simple tale of faith and love that is told with strict economy and no frills. Basically it's a story in which Doggett fights against all hope to keep a comatose Reyes alive - but because he's too afraid to tell her he loves her, this gives both Patrick and Gish at last a sense of true partnership. The irony being, of course, that they're separated for most of the episode. Had this been a story of Scully or Mulder, it'd almost seem too pat and obvious. It's *because* this features agents we're still only getting to know, and who are still only getting to feel for each other, that it has its power.

It's written and directed with so much restraint, which makes sequences of Doggett crying all the more affecting, and scenes in which trapped souls expire all the more chilling. Tracey Ellis gives a lovely performance as Audrey, autistic and believing herself of no use to anyone; the scene where she awkwardly reaches out for the distraught Doggett's hair, not knowing how to react to his display of emotion, is beautiful. This is what The X-Files should be doing now; you can see its influences in Rod Serling, even down to the black and white of the hospital, but it has an intelligence and an imagination and an emotional truth that is pure X-Files. Stories like this make it a pity the show is to end soon - this would have been the template on which to have built a series starring Doggett and Reyes. (*****)

9.12, Underneath

Air Date: March 31, 2002
Writer / Director: John Shiban

Summary   As a police officer in 1989, John Doggett helped to catch Bob Fassl - "the screwdriver killer" who murdered seven people. But in the modern day, DNA evidence clears Fassl and mandates his release.

Doggett, Reyes and Scully investigate the murder of Fassl's cellmate, who was killed by an unidentified bearded man. Forensic evidence determines that the bearded man and Fassl are close relatives, although Fassl doesn't have any family. Reyes theorises that Fassl, a devout Catholic, is so terrified to recognize his sinful nature that it manifests as a different person, both mentally and physically. Doggett and Reyes pursue the bearded man into the sewers, where they find several people that he's killed. Reyes shoots the bearded man to save Doggett; in death, the bearded man reverts to being Fassl.

Critique   His writing partners have all turned director over the past two seasons, and at last John Shiban joins the club. Shiban has been on The X-Files since Season Three, and over his stint has acquired the reputation of being the donkey of the writing staff. It's more than a little unfair, but his episodes largely do seem to lack some of the spark of his fellows' efforts, and he comes across as being something of a "meat and potatoes" writer. Underneath is a case in point. At first glance there's little here we haven't seen before; the story of a Jekyll and Hyde character who metamorphoses into an evil self whenever he wants to kill is very familiar, and was last seen in Chimera only two years ago. And a lot of the visuals are trademark X-File moments too, whether it be the surprise appearance of a face in the bathroom cabinet mirror, or the climactic fight in a sewer.

But as a director, Shiban makes Underneath shine. He hits upon a wonderful device early on, watching the murders through Fassl's eyes, as he looks on in horror as his victims instantaneously jump from being alive to dying before him. And he elicits great performances from his guest stars - W Earl Brown gives an excellent portrait of a freed convict wholly unequipped to deal with the real world and only wanting to escape back to the safety of confinement. Mary-Margaret Lewis also gives a stand out performance as his attorney, whose concern and admiration for Fassl borders almost upon the flirtatious, and who reacts with starchy primness when a man who has been incarcerated for thirteen years fails to live up to all her humanitarian ideals.

But it's especially in his depiction of the series regulars that Shiban succeeds. It's Doggett's episode, really; a man who, like Shiban, has built his career at the "meat and potatoes" end of the job, finds to his growing horror that a case from his beat-cop past is yet another X-File in disguise. Over the course of two days, in which he obsessively *needs* to prove to himself that his former police success was as solid as he thought, he discovers that his partner feloniously framed evidence, and that his promotion to detective was based upon a mistake. His journey echoes that of Scully in Shiban's Badlaa last year, fearing at the story's end that he's inadequately experienced to pursue an X-File, but it's handled with far greater subtlety here. For the first time this year Gillian Anderson and Annabeth Gish are both allowed enough screen time and character that they are able to give Robert Patrick proper support.

The plot crumbles away a bit in the final act - just why did Fassl hide all his victims underneath the house of an attorney he hadn't even met yet? But this is an episode which is solid and efficient and boasts characters who have real dimensions to them; it's an essential addition to a series which needs a bit more of that meat and potatoes in its diet. (***1/2)

9.13, Improbable

Air Date: April 7, 2002
Writer / Director: Chris Carter

Summary Reyes takes an interest in the "Triple Zero" killer - a man who's murdering women and leaving the same triple zero mark on their bodies. Meanwhile, the killer, "Mad Wayne", is shadowed by a lover of games named Mr Burt - who feels confident that Wayne won't harm him because it doesn't fit "the pattern".

Scully determines that the body marks are actually 666, the sign of the devil. She and Reyes encounter Burt, who makes them play checkers until they realise that Mad Wayne kills trios of women based upon their hair colour. Reyes speculates that numbers drive the universal order and might also influence human behaviour, as if people were checkers on a board. Mad Wayne tries to make Scully and Reyes - a redhead and a brunette - his next victims, but Doggett arrives and shoots him. Burt disappears, leaving the agents uncertain as to his identity. An aerial view, however, reveals Burt's face as being woven into the city's infrastructure - suggesting that he was actually God.

Critique The X-Files first properly started debating free will and determinism back in Season Three with Clyde Bruckman's Final Repose, and it's a subject to which it has returned several times. It's a serious theme, and suggests a universe which allows no sense of achievement or point, in which events may be fated (as in The Goldberg Variation) or repeat over and over again until they can be put back on track (as in Monday). It's so serious a theme, in fact, that it can really only be treated playfully - and Improbable is The X-Files' last word on the subject. What better character to provide the answers, it says, than God himself?

Burt Reynolds gives a teasing and charming performance as Mr Burt, the mysterious figure who dances and sings and jokes his way through this serial killer episode. The joy of his God is that he *wants* to be surprised - that the girl who wastes all her money in a one-armed bandit might one day hit a lucky streak, that the psychopath next to him at the bar will rebel against his instincts and not murder her in the restroom. This is Clyde Bruckman writ large - a character that can see the future, and knows the ugliness of the world it reflects. Unlike Clyde, though - and simply by dint of being God - he can see the multiple threads and connections and coincidences that give the world sense anyway. There's much talk in the episode by Reyes and Scully about the theory that everything can be reduced to a mathematical equation; Scully resists the idea, not only because it takes all the impossible complexity of the universe and makes it simple, but because also it reduces *her* to the level of a checker piece on a board. God, though, can see the equation before him, and can exult in it. In all the events around him he can make out a shape - so that the roadworks and the scraping of a pram and the fanning of a newspaper become an orchestrated song and dance number to a tune only he can hear.

He can hear it - and, for forty-five glorious minutes, so can we. The brilliance of Chris Carter's direction is that we see Improbable from God's point of view. It plays out as an exaggerated comedy to a backdrop of perky music. The Goldberg Variation was a story about how multiple coincidences always tipped themselves in favour of one lucky man - it was amusing, but by definition very contrived. Improbable does a similar thing, but this time we're not looking at the contrivance from an outsider perspective - and the result is giddy, silly, charming and bizarre. Carter's direction is clever because, unlike Goldberg, he insists on punctuating the choreography of head tilting and corridor walking with a story that is brutal and gruesome. God cannot be appalled by the murderer - he knows he's a character in his own fiction - and tells him he loves him with a smile, suggesting that he "choose better" whilst believing that he won't. And we become complicit in this; we're the audience looking on, seeing within these strange X-Files episodes of killing and horror the same routines that keep us entertained week after week. It's wonderful that as the series enters its final episodes, we are invited to look upon it as a safe and predictable piece of light entertainment - and to judge it accordingly. We've seen so many murders on this programme now that a few committed to the background of French pop music can only lend them a little extra flavour.

It doesn't entirely work. Carter is aiming for the sunny charm of a movie like Amelie - hence the profusion of Europop songs. But the set pieces of lip synching and coordinated movement need to be executed that little bit *better* to have the effect he's after. A very witty script, which takes in causal effect and numerology and Einstein theories for starters, gets a bit buried by a style so self-indulgent that it often obscures its own dark cleverness. You rather suspect that self-indulgence is the very point, that this is overripe and overdirected and overconscious, but that means that it tests the viewers' patience. (My wife *hates* this episode with a rare passion.) And the final sequence of lip synching is especially awkward and goes on for far too long. But this is such a breathlessly mad bit of television that even as you resist its dizziness, you may well find yourself bowled over by its chutzpah. It's not as smart as it thinks it is. But it's still pretty smart. (****)

9.14, Scary Monsters

Air Date: April 14, 2002
Writer: Thomas Schnauz
Director: Dwight Little

Summary   Agent Harrison (8.19, Alone) approaches Scully about Tommy Conlon, an eight year old who believes that a monster killed his mother. Doggett and Reyes visit Tommy and his father Jeffrey in Fairhope, Pennsylvania. In rapid succession, Doggett finds monsters in Tommy's room and briefly falls into a void, and the local sheriff is revealed as a zombie.

The agents deduce that when Tommy is afraid, his imagination conjures forth monsters that kill anyone who believes in them. Armed with his scepticism, Doggett pretends to burn down the house with Tommy inside, rendering the lad unconscious. Afterward, state psychiatrists numb Tommy's imagination by having him watch an endless stream of television.

Critique   "I made this!" says the little boy, handing Reyes his cartooned picture of her being eaten from the inside. He echoes the chirpy voice of the child at the end of each and every Ten Thirteen episode - whether that be Grotesque or Home or the Season Two finale of Millennium, that little kid would be there, proudly declaring his ownership in all apparent innocence. This episode is really rather wonderful, a sly little story about the imagination and how it can be let loose to create scary monsters, from a production team that has had fun creating a fair few of them and is about to shut up shop.

Where the self-references are about horror and the creation of it, this story excels. The teaser which shows a little boy scared by the childhood cliché of something nasty hiding under the bed; the way that Doggett and Reyes are trapped in an isolated house by the elements with no means of reaching the outside world. Like Alone last year, which this episode echoes not only with the presence of Agent Harrison, it's a story which wallows in the stereotypes to make a point about the genre of scares and laughs that The X-Files has helped to shape. It only suffers when the self-reference is less about the creativity, and more about fan criticisms of later seasons. "If Agent Mulder were here, he'd carry on," sulks Harrison early in the story, and too much of the episode plays out as a frustrated attack upon the viewers who've switched channels since the heydays of Mulder and Scully. If this were a story which was attempting to showcase the efficacy of their successors that would be more acceptable - but with only a handful of episodes to go before the plug is pulled, it looks more like sniping at the audience who are still left to complain. (And when the next story is called Jump the Shark, you do wonder quite how bitter The X-Files writers have become now they're consigning their show to history.) The constant references to past adventures that Harrison made in Alone were sweet and celebratory - here they feel more like carping. Even when Harrison admits that Doggett was better suited to the case than Mulder, it's because of his "lack of imagination".

It's a shame, because these more obvious examples of self-analysis detract from the cleverer ones that serve as the main theme to the story. And Thomas Schnauz writes with pace and wit; the scenes where Scully resignedly conducts an autopsy on a dead cat on her kitchen table in the middle of the night - her apron sporting the motto "Something smells goooood!" - are the funniest of the season. Only a few weeks after Audrey Pauley, Scary Monsters loses some impact once it becomes clear that this adventure is a flight into one person's fantasies - but it's great fun to watch, it's clever and intriguing, and it has a climax which is both satisfying (Doggett's trick with the gas can, turning the boy's imagination back on himself, is lovely) and knowing (the scene where Tommy's imagination is stuffed by multi-channel TV ought to feel nothing more than a punchline, but is strangely eerie as well). All the remaining episodes are lined up to offer different sorts of farewells to The X-Files; as a valediction to the series, and the writing process behind it, this comic thriller works better than most. (****)

9.15, Jump the Shark

Air Date: April 21, 2002
Writers: Vince Gilligan, John Shiban,
Frank Spotnitz
Director: Cliff Bole

Summary   Morris Fletcher (The Lone Gunmen 1.12, All About Yves), now formerly of Area 51, approaches Doggett and Reyes with information about a supersoldier, Yves Adele Harlow. The Lone Gunmen track Harlow as she murders Professor Houghton, a marine biologist. The Gunmen determine that Yves isn't a supersoldier after all, and that Fletcher set them up to find Yves on behalf of her father, an international arms dealer and terrorist.

Yves has been eliminating scientists who developed a deadly virus with her father's backing, claiming that a man is equipped with a virus-containing vessel that will decay at precisely eight o'clock. The Gunmen intercept the man in question, John Gillnitz, as he attends a bioethics forum. With Gillnitz's virus set to kill thousands, the Gunmen seal him - and themselves - in an airtight section of the building. Gillnitz dies, and Yves and Jimmy Bond say goodbye before the Gunmen meet the same fate. Afterward, Skinner gets special dispensa-tion for the Gunmen to be buried at Arlington National Cemetery.

Critique   I think the decision that The X-Files host an episode of Millennium after its cancellation was misguided, but I can see the reasoning behind it. Millennium had been an intriguing show which may not have enjoyed the mass popular success of The X-Files, but at its best certainly enjoyed its critical success. There was obvious dramatic value in having the two series cross over when they'd been kept apart so carefully during Millennium's run. And, of course, it *was* New Year 2000 - it was the right time to give that series closure.

The Lone Gunmen is another matter altogether. No-one was crying out to see what would happen if Frohike, Byers and Langly popped into the world of The X-Files - they'd been there half the ninth season already, and making barbed comments about their spin-off show's cancellation in a way that was presumably meant as a wink to the audience, but came across more as a grumpy two-fingered salute. The Millennium crossover never forgot that it was an X-File first and foremost, with Mulder and Scully taking the lead and Frank Black relegated to supporting character only. With only a few episodes of The X-Files left to run, you have to question the wisdom of handing one of those precious slots over to be *dominated* by a series which had barely staggered to a half season. Because Jump the Shark doesn't really try to be an X-Files story at all: its cinematography and its music are all Lone Gunmen through and through, and The X-Files regulars are minor players. (Though they appear in the opening credits, Scully and Skinner only appear in one scene.)

I'm not a fan of The Lone Gunmen, but my objections here are not simply that The X-Files has been hijacked for a week by a series I don't like very much. Indeed, a little of the breezy lowbrow comedy that had been its house style might have been a refreshing change in a season which has only featured these characters so far in the most turgid of mythology stories. But there's nothing celebratory about this final outing for the three unlikely heroes; right from the teaser we are assured that they aren't going to win, and so it transpires. They're mocked for their computer skills (so need Kimmy the Geek to do the difficult hacking), they're ridiculed for their incompetence (ruining yet another of Yves' schemes with disastrous consequences). They talk about how old they are, and how they should give up their newspaper - we realise they haven't put out a single issue since their own series folded. What this story needed to do, surely, was to provide these losers with a moment of glory. But rather than sending them off at the end of the series with renewed faith in their work, the episode instead decides... to gas them all to death.

The pity of all this is that you can tell from the po-faced (and ghastly) funeral orations that the writers thought that burying them at Arlington National Cemetery with war veterans could *be* that moment of glory. But it's tonally so wrong for them that it just feels like a weird anticlimax. At their end, these most anti-establishment of characters join the establishment. There's nothing tragic about their deaths; there's nothing in the manner of how they die that reveals anything about who they were or what skills they had. They merely elect to die behind a glass window door because The X-Files universe is wrapping up. It's not even as if it's tonally right for the episode itself. Jump the Shark lacks all the comic energy that made all the better instalments of The Lone Gunmen a guilty pleasure, and instead drags itself along by having long scenes of characters typing at keyboards. Eine Kleine Frohike had a greater build-up to a tragic climax than this. When Frohike pulls the alarm that sentences himself and his friends to death, it's not with courage or determination but weariness. It's such a *bland* way of dying that for a moment you feel you must have missed the point, that something more dramatic is going to kick in. And so it's merely the most disappointing moment in an episode which so steadfastly refuses to catch fire. The Lone Gunmen deserved better. No, worse than that - *we* deserved better. (*)

9.16, William

Air Date: April 28, 2002
Story: David Duchovny, Frank Spotnitz, Chris Carter
Teleplay: Chris Carter
Director: David Duchovny

Summary Doggett apprehends a disfigured man who gains access to the X-Files office using Mulder's access card. The man identifies himself as Daniel Miller, who says that he's seeking information about a government experiment that was designed to turn him into an alien, but which failed and left him scarred. Doggett comes to suspect, and an initial DNA test confirms, that the man is actually Mulder.

The disfigured man injects William with a metallic liquid, then comes clean that he's actually Jeffrey Spender - Mulder's half-brother, who was shot and left for dead (6.12, One Son). Spender says that the injection deactivated William's alien abilities and made him human, thereby stopping the Cigarette Smoking Man's masterplan. He claims that William will always be in danger from the aliens, whereupon Scully makes the grave decision to erase all trace of William's identity and put him up for adoption. A farm family takes in the child, who's safe in his new home.

Critique There's a similar game being played here to the one in Trust No 1, as a story teasingly suggests that we might be about to see Mulder again. But at least this time the game seems a fair one. If Mulder isn't back, then there is still David Duchovny, this time behind the camera rather than in front of it. And rather than be a runaround that gets nowhere pointlessly, William uses the question of whether or not Mulder has returned to ask questions about Scully and her baby, and about where the series can go from here. It does this, in part at least, by having a Mulder figure - albeit one that's hideously scarred. Trust No 1 placed Mulder at the centre of the episode, and his one contribution was to appear in long distance played by an extra. Here Scully and Doggett get to play off and converse with a man who might be Mulder, to react to him and feel pity for him, and even put to him all the questions that a frustrated audience has been wanting to ask. It's fascinating to see how angry Scully is behind her desperate need to see her lover again - her outburst to the faux Mulder, demanding to know why the hell he can't be with her as father and as partner, is terrific, giving Gillian Anderson some real emotional fire after a season of ineffective weeping. And the way that Doggett awkwardly tries to sympathise with his predecessor, offering him almost patronising support before threatening "Mulder" when he suspects he may have harmed his own child, is very telling.

One of the reasons this works so well is that, by making the faux Mulder so deformed, the audience and Scully are left in a quandary, hoping for some resolution, hoping that this figure really is an old friend - and yet wanting any other resolution but this. We can see this actor in heavy make-up isn't Duchovny, but that doesn't matter; you can still believe this *might* be Ten Thirteen's compromise, the way they can bring Mulder back without having to hire a reluctant actor. And the solution to the mystery is satisfying, even as it is contrived - a rare example of The X-Files reaching back into its convoluted past and pulling out an old character whose return is genuinely confounding. Some of the plotting is plain wrong: two half-brothers would *not* share the same DNA. But the emotional journey of Scully is so sincerely written and performed that it doesn't matter as much as it perhaps should.

And the story never lies; Chris Owens' mutilated Jeffrey Spender never once pretends that he actually *is* Mulder either to the FBI or to the audience, instead taking advantage of circumstances which allow his truths to be seen as prevarications. Owens does a great job too of making Spender both sympathetic and yet utterly amoral. The scene in the interrogation room, where he sadly accepts the brunt of Scully's anger, and calmly explains how he's only lived in pain these years to destroy the plans of his hated father, is ironically the most powerful he's ever been.

But all of this is a clever smokescreen, designed to distract us from the episode's true purpose. It's rather a pity that the title gives it away, because had the importance of William to Spender's mission been revealed as a surprise twist, it may well have been more convincing.

But even in the teaser we're invited to ask the question: what could happen that would persuade Scully to give up her adored and long-sought miracle child for adoption? And the answer is... nothing very believable, sadly. Scully's character development for years has subtly been about the denial of her right to a child; if she wasn't going to give it away for the sake of its own protection after a UFO cult abducted it, then why should she because Jeffrey Spender of all people comes along and informs her that it's under threat?

The business with William then all feels too pat. Having spent so much time in this season and the last discussing the importance of William's special powers, to have him cured of them all with one simple injection feels laughably bathetic. Even a flu shot needs a booster now and then, but saviour-of-mankind syndrome requires just the one jab. Now that he's no longer superhuman, it seems odd that *this* should be the moment when Scully gives him up. The story even tries to address the inadequacy of his protection - if Scully, an FBI agent who *knows* how much danger her son is in can't take care of him, why should two random strangers do any better? Gillian Anderson does her best with the lines she is given, but her performance can't square this particular circle.

It feels like the production team are trying to close a chapter. Making the baby normal is a sensible thing to do; the "alien baby" storyline has always been something of a non-starter, partly because it puts a character who can't contribute in any way to the drama at the centre of the action, and partly because it was always the most banal of all the possible explanations for Scully's pregnancy. (It was sent up, years before The X-Files was a glint in Chris Carter's eye, as a particularly outrageous storyline in the comedy series Soap - and you know there's something wrong with a premise if it's handled more credibly in a spoof.)

The adoption just feels tacked on. With only three episodes to go, do they really *need* to have Scully lose the baby? It's already done its damage to the show, preventing Scully from taking an active lead - what good does it do anybody now to jettison it from the programme altogether when there's no time to put that right? It indicates two things. Firstly, a desire on behalf of Ten Thirteen to get rid of any taint of a failed storyline. And secondly, to give a series in its dying weeks another bit of angst to mine. Last week it killed off the Lone Gunmen, this week they have Scully reject her infant son. It's the belief that this more melodramatic style has greater depth than something more considered and more hopeful that is the shame of it. Had this story ended with Scully knowing that she has a baby that's no more special than any other in the world - and seen that as something to celebrate - it'd have had a little profundity to it, and removed some of the contrivance of how he lost his powers in the first place. As it is, it's all just a bit too much to bear. (***)

9.17, Release

Air Date: May 5, 2002
Story: John Shiban, David Amann
Teleplay: David Amann
Director: Kim Manners

Summary One of Scully's students, Rudolph Hayes, displays amazing insight and suggests that the same killer murdered two seemingly unconnected women. Hayes also demonstrates an interest in the case of Doggett's murdered son, insisting that a mobster named Nicholas Regali killed the boy after a man named Robert Harvey - who died in 1978 - abducted him.

Agent Follmer tells the agents that Hayes is actually a mental patient named Stuart Mimms, and might have killed Luke Doggett himself. Mimms is arrested, but claims he read about the case in the newspaper and gained insight from studying photographs of Luke's death. Agent Follmer is revealed as having accepted bribes for years to keep Regali out of prison. Over-confident, Regali all but admits to Doggett that Harvey, a paedophile, abducted Luke and took him to Regali's home - but that the boy saw Regali's face, and was killed to silence him. Doggett moves to kill Regali, but Follmer, finding some vestige of conscience, shoots the mobster first.

Critique In the rush to tie up all the loose threads of The X-Files, it'd have been all too easy to have given the story of Doggett and his son's murder rather short shrift. Indeed, with

the minimal emphasis that the case has been given in the series, one might argue it didn't even require such closure, that The X-Files had bigger issues to worry about. But it's *because* of the very low-key way in which Doggett's background has been explored that Release packs the punch that it does. The last two seasons of the series have made many mistakes, but one of its successes has been the subtlety with which Doggett's tragedy has been handled. It has never been allowed to dominate, the details of the story so drip-fed that we only fully understand the manner of Luke Doggett's abduction within this episode. And that's absolutely right for Doggett, a man who is so self-composed that he hasn't allowed the pivotal moment of his life to be worn like a character badge. For years Mulder was always identified by his quest for his sister - Doggett, more effectively, has carried the loss of his son as a private grief. The skill of Release is not only that it's so emotionally powerful, but that it retroactively makes Doggett's memories in John Doe so much more moving; we only learn here that his recall of Luke - who wakes his Dad to proudly show how he can ride a bike - is the moment of his kidnap. And it's a testament to the unforced realism here in Release that a week after *another* episode which determined the fate of a small child, that this one, in which the little boy never even appears, is so much more involving. Baby William's story was nothing if not rather laboured - Luke Doggett's was so gently handled that it sang.

By the time the mystery of Samantha was resolved in Season Seven, it had been used for years as an easy source of emotion whenever a storyline needed to become grand and iconic. Whatever else the ending for Samantha is, it's certainly contrived; any simple explanation of what had happened to Mulder's sister would have been an anticlimax. On the contrary, Release works because the reason for Luke's death is so simple - insultingly, terribly so. In the wrong place at the wrong time, he is in a position to identify a man working for the mob - so he's erased without a second thought. It's the bluntness of the act, that something so casual could have destroyed a marriage and taken a life, that's so hard hitting. And it works wonders that Release is a story which is free of paranormal influences. There's no inherited evil to be faced (as suggested in Empedocles), there's no alien conspiracy, there's no starlight. Doggett is given more dignity than that. Robert Patrick's performance is given more dignity than that.

It's the very realism of David Amann's script that makes watching Release so cathartic. The eager hope that Doggett shows when he approaches the bright young cadet with a genius for profiling; the awkward pain Doggett's wife feels when he asks her to confront the details of their son's death once more. Amann has always been the *truest* writer of emotion on the series, the one who'll find the sincerity within the most ludicrous of storylines. It's here, in a story of real grief and real distress, when Doggett's feelings are so exposed that he'll leap for the slightest chance for closure, that Amann does his best work on The X-Files.

Robert Patrick and David Amann are given sterling support. Jared Poe takes the schizophrenic profiler and gives him a quiet passion for his gift which makes him very credible. Barbara Patrick, playing Doggett's wife, brings an honesty to her performance that could only have felt more real being opposite her real-life husband. And Cary Elwes is at his best here. Follmer never matured into an interesting character in his own right, but as the corrupt cop whose sensibilities are shaken when he realises he's been taking bribes all these years from a child killer, he becomes believable. (*****)

9.18, Sunshine Days

Air Date: May 12, 2002
Writer / Director: Vince Gilligan

Summary Two young men, Blake McCormick and Michael Daley, break into what they believe is the house where *The Brady Bunch* was filmed - but the escapade ends with McCormick being flung through the air and killed. A curious Daley later returns to the house and sees the "Brady" family sitting down for dinner, then is likewise flung to his death.

Doggett, Reyes and Scully realise that the house owner, Oliver Martin, possesses a formidable psychokinesis that enables his thoughts to become reality. Dr John Rietz, a parapsychologist who examined Martin back in 1970, says the boy's talent faded with age but has now returned. Martin's health deteriorates, and Doggett realises that he'll die if he keeps using his power. As Martin's power diminishes when he's happy, and he was most happy when he had Rietz as a surrogate father, Rietz agrees to stay in Martin's life and keep him company - on the condition that Martin never uses his power again.

Critique Vince Gilligan has been The X-Files' most consistent writer, and this episode acts as his fond farewell. Like many of his comedies, it works as a comment upon the series itself: it knows that there's only one story to go, that the show has had its day, and that everything that *can* be investigated has now *been* investigated. "With this, the X-Files can go on forever!" enthuses a delighted Skinner, turned by a genius psychokinetic into an acrobat doing cartwheels in midair. It's a tale of a man fixated on a popular TV show, so lonely that he derives comfort from its literal presence around him. He's taken on the identity of a forgotten late addition to the cast from the days when it was nearing cancellation. And the dilemma he faces is whether he can find a way of living without it, because constant exposure to the fantasy, however reassuring, is slowly killing him.

For all of Gilligan's skill with black comedy - and there are some fine examples of it here - he's basically an optimistic writer, who sees that the important things to care about in life aren't nebulous truths wrapped in conspiracies, but people. In this regard he's always somewhat stood at odds with the very tone of The X-Files; in just one week's time, Chris Carter will bring back a Mulder who'll be prepared to sacrifice his happiness with Scully in order to uncover the same mysteries he's always pursued. Gilligan is too much of a humanist not to think that this sort of heroism is utter bunk. He *gives* Scully the proof of the paranormal she's been needing all these years, the display of psychokinesis that the amazed scientists declare will rewrite the physics books. Gilligan has shown this sort of scenario before: Scully's thrill in having an invisible man to show the world in Je Souhaite, or Mulder's growing dissatisfaction with being able to demonstrate alien existence in Field Trip. For Gilligan the truth isn't necessarily with the discovery, it's the journey along the way that matters, and the influence that has upon the characters. He takes great pleasure in showing an Agent Doggett who's really starting to *enjoy* the way he's adapting to his work solving bizarre cases, for example. And at the end of the episode, as Reyes takes his hand, Scully reminds us that the victory of The X-Files is not in the big revelations but in the intimate character moments.

Typically too Gilligan appears to be taking a pot shot at recent developments in the series' mythology. As a kid, Oliver Martin was able to make objects float, he's proclaimed to be the one who can change the world. Who does that remind you of? At the end of the story he has to be rid of his ability. To effect this, Oliver is shown the love of a surrogate father, and a chance to connect back into the real world. William, in contrast, is injected with a bit of metal. For all the angst and the tears that have characterised the alien baby episodes, the solution to them was depressingly mechanical. It's Gilligan, with his comic take on the same themes, who provides the *emotional* solution that Chris Carter should have taken.

Truth to tell, this is not one of Gilligan's very best stories. It's tonally all over the place; it sets up Oliver Martin as a man who kills his intruders, but then drops that darker side of the plot when it decides instead to make Oliver more sympathetic. Michael Emerson does his best in the part, but seems rather confused as to which side of Oliver is more important - the loner with a dangerous power, or the performing seal who is looking for love. Though there's much to enjoy here, it means that the fable isn't as touching as it wants to be: two years ago when Gilligan wrote Je Souhaite, which also acted as a goodbye to the series and echoed many of the themes here, he much more successfully got the balance right between the sweet and the macabre. But there's an eeriness to the Brady Bunch house which is terrific - I love the way that the anodyne kids of a sitcom end up looking for all the world like the dead girls in The Shining - and the sequence where Oliver turns his living room into a peaceful green hill is magical. And, let's face it, there's something wonderful too about The X-Files offering as its penultimate case a story as profoundly bizarre as this one - it's not its funniest comedy, nor its most

assured, but it's one of its most imaginative. (***1/2)

9.19-20, The Truth

Air Date: May 19, 2002
Writer: Chris Carter
Director: Kim Manners

Summary   Mulder breaks into the Mount Weather complex in Bluemont, Virginia, and finds computer information pertaining to a mobilization of alien forces on December 22, 2012. Knowle Rohrer intercepts Mulder, and in the ensuing scuffle - in which the late Krycek appears to help Mulder - Rohrer is electrocuted. Mulder is arrested and charged with Rohrer's death, and an FBI hearing is held to determine his fate within the bounds of a military court. Skinner acts as Mulder's defence attorney.

From the witness chair, Scully details the core government conspiracy to hide the existence of aliens. In her account, a meteor came to Earth millions of years ago from Mars, carrying the biological material needed to create the human race. The meteor also had a virus that turned some prehistoric men into an alien life form; those aliens died in the last ice age, and the virus went dormant underground.

Thriving in oil deposits, the virus later surfaced and communicated with the UFO involved in the Roswell incident. From the Roswell crash, the government learned of the alien plot to recolonise Earth. A private alliance was forged with the aliens, as a means of stalling for time to develop a vaccine against the virus. Test subjects were identified through tags in their smallpox vaccination scars. Scully's abduction, and that of many other women, owed to government experiments to create a race of alien-human hybrids for the aliens to use as slaves. The undertaking ended when faceless alien rebels killed the conspirators (6.12, One Son).

The late X appears in Mulder's cell, helping him to locate Marita Covarrubias. She testifies that the conspiracy still exists, just with new players. Gibson Praise also testifies, and says that one of Mulder's judges isn't human. Finally, Doggett talks about a military project to create invulnerable supersoldiers.

Mulder is sentenced to death, but Skinner and Doggett help him escape. The government cracks down on the X-Files and empties the office. Mulder and Scully head for the Texas-New Mexico border and find Pueblo ruins housing the person who led Mulder to the Mount Weather complex: the Cigarette Smoking Man. He explains that aliens avoid the site because of its high levels of magnetite, the same material that brought down the Roswell UFO. Moreover, the Cigarette Smoking Man confirms that the alien invasion is set for December 22, 2012 - the date that marks the end of the Mayan calendars.

Doggett and Reyes arrive at the site and encounter the very-much-alive Knowle Rohrer - who is pulled apart by the magnetite deposits. Mulder and Scully flee in Rohrer's van, and Doggett and Reyes make their own escape, as military helicopters arrive and blast the Cigarette Smoking Man's home with missiles, killing him.

Afterward, in a Roswell motel, Mulder suggests to Scully that the dead - as part of some greater force - can speak to the living. Scully concurs, and the two of them remain on the run from the law.

Critique   It all begins promisingly enough. There are helicopters, and secret bases carved inside mountains, and Mulder running down gantries from soldiers, and high falling stunts! It looks a bit James Bond, and suggests that The X-Files is going to go out with something rather dynamic.

But not a chance. Courtroom drama can be extraordinarily gripping; it focuses upon characters justifying themselves under pressure, eliminating the excess flab of action and cutting to motives and beliefs. What it should never be used for, though, is a simple expository tool. You have to feel sorry for Mitch Pileggi, who tries his hardest here with lots of long but irrelevant speeches. Skinner makes the worst defence lawyer imaginable. Mulder is on trial for murder - and Skinner chooses to address these charges by treating the powers that be to a clip show. "Tell me, Jeffrey Spender, not seen as a recurring character since Season Six, how does the mythology arc relate to you?" "Explain to us all, Agent Scully, not your commitment to

your partner, but the function of the black oil virus, with particular reference both to the feature film and Season Three." Once in a while, as these legal dramas demand, the prosecution will object, but realistically every single person in that courtroom should have been on their feet and shouting at Skinner to stick to the point.

And it gets worse! The courtroom set-up is a means by which Chris Carter can bring back all the living characters for a panto walk-down. As for the dead ones... well, Mulder can now see ghosts. No-one else can see them, so we might think they're in his imagination. Fair enough. But X is able to hand Mulder a piece of paper with an address on it, which suggests he's got some sort of tangible presence. Steven Williams did a sterling job on the early years of the series as Mulder's ambiguous informer - now he comes back from the grave to act like a ghoulish Yellow Pages. And after having gone to all that trouble of squeezing himself back into existence, just so we can see the clips through the eyes of Marita Covarrubias, Mulder interrupts the proceedings when she begins to say something which might actually be *helpful*. Poor old X. He must wonder why he bothered, poor dead soul.

He's not the only corpse who's useless. There's Krycek, whose great contribution to the episode is holding open a door. Then there are the Lone Gunmen, materialising just as Mulder takes a piss. In an otherwise terrible episode a few weeks ago, the Gunmen died refusing to give up on their desire to expose the truth; their final moments in the series are spent urging Mulder to give up. Classy.

The dead achieve nothing. The living simply provide a running commentary to X-Files episodes more interesting than this one. And the terrible thing is, that as we hear The X-Files mythology laid out before us at breakneck speed - all the oil and the supersoldiers and the smallpox vaccinations and the magic babies - you realise that the whole thing is pants. Chris Carter intends this not only to be an explanation of the way the backstory has worked, but a celebration of it. And instead, it reminds you you've spent nine years, *nine sodding years*, watching something that's very very silly indeed. We've had a promise of "the truth". And the fact of the matter is, the series long ago outgrew it. We're not learning anything new from the long monologues here, we're simply hearing story synopses with all the wit and the action taken out of them. For years The X-Files has sold itself as being a show with secrets, that in its final year Chris Carter seems to have forgotten that he's already revealed them. There's nothing new to be learned. Except one thing, that is. Something the Cigarette Smoking Man thinks will scare Scully. Something Mulder knows, but won't dare reveal to his partner for fear it may break her. The piece of information that Smoking Man has kept Mulder alive for all these years, just for the joy of destroying him with.

... it's a date. The alien invasion will commence on December 22nd, 2012. (Just in time to ruin Christmas.)

Smoking Man says that it's a piece of knowledge that has terrified all US presidents since Truman. Oh, really? We live in a world where people shrug if they're told that global warming might destroy the planet by the next *generation*. Is this really what the series was about? Those cryptic comments in early seasons that the "date is set" - they're referring to an event that won't take place until The X-Files is in its *nineteenth season*? The X-Files has a reputation for delaying its story climaxes, to the detriment of the first feature film, but this is ridiculous. It makes it hard to accept any of the feverish urgency that the Syndicate showed every other month when a mytharc two-parter popped up in the schedules. In the very second episode of the series, Mulder asks Deep Throat on the running track, "They're here, aren't they?" I guarantee that the show would not have reached its ninth season had Deep Throat winked benignly and said, "Mulder, they're coming in 2012. Don't worry - you'll have retired by then." Dear God. How can

you take an alien invasion seriously when they've already set a precise date this many years in advance? Who are they, a bunch of intergalactic obsessive compulsives? What did they have to do, schedule it around work like a vacation? Did they get a cheaper travel deal booking this far in advance?

It matters little that the mythology revelations turn out to be a damp squib. The mytharc has been running on the spot for so long that had something new and exciting been revealed here, it'd have only felt as if Chris Carter had been holding out on the good stuff. The problem is more that this is how a series which has been brilliant - frequently, truly *brilliant* - chooses to define itself in the summing up. This is Chris Carter's truth. And it's that Mulder and Scully are ultimately swamped by a storyline that barely gives a damn about their characters or their journey. David Duchovny is brought back so he can sit silently in a courtroom for three quarters of an hour. He tells Scully that he's prepared to sacrifice their life together for something greater than they are - and the one thing that the series has demonstrated, time and time again, is that these two characters are *far* greater than any series mythology could hope to be. The final scene reaches out for character resolution, but the moment's been squandered - what Mulder and Scully have been has been dwarfed by all the exposition and the turgid solemnity and the blandness of the plot. They've been made to look foolish, these heroes of ours. Because they've taken a foolish story more seriously than the relationship they've been forging with the audience for nearly a decade. That, ultimately, is the truth that's offered here. And it leaves a bad taste in the mouth. (*)

The X-Files: I Want to Believe

Release Date (US): July 25, 2008
Release Date (UK): August 1, 2008
Writers: Frank Spotnitz, Chris Carter
Director: Chris Carter

Summary Six years after leaving the FBI, Scully is now employed as a doctor at a Catholic hospital, while the fugitive Mulder leads a solitary existence in a secluded house. Elsewhere, FBI Agent Monica Bannan is kidnapped, and Joseph Crissman - a defrocked priest convicted of paedophilia - claims to have psychic visions of the crime. Joe's "visions" enable him to lead FBI agents to unearth a severed arm buried in the snow.

The paranormal aspect of the case convinces Agent Dakota Whitney to recruit Mulder, who - with Scully's encouragement - accepts the FBI's offer of amnesty in exchange for his help. Scully assists Mulder up to a point, but also struggles, against opposition from her fellow doctors, to advocate a risky course of treatment for a dying young boy named Christian.

When a second woman is kidnapped, Joe's visions lead the agents to find an entire cache of buried corpses and body parts. The agents determine that the kidnapped women had the same blood type, and suspicion falls upon Janke Dacyshyn, a courier shuttling organs intended for transplant. Dacyshyn's boyfriend, Franz Tomczeszyn, was among the youths abused by Father Joe, but an attempt to corner Dacyshyn results in his pushing Whitney to her death.

Scully visits Father Joe, repulsed by his crimes but wanting to know why he told her "Don't give up" in the course of finding the bodies. Joe expresses bafflement as to what made him say such a thing, then suffers a seizure and is hospitalized, in the advanced stages of lung cancer.

Mulder finds Dacyshyn and shadows him along a snowy road, but Dacyshyn pushes Mulder's car off a cliff with a snowplow. Pulling himself free, Mulder finds a small compound where Russian physicians have been taking body parts from compatible donors and grafting them to Tomczeszyn, who's dying of cancer. Able to sever a person's head and keep it alive, the physicians put the second kidnap victim -

Cheryl Cunningham - on ice, intending to transplant Tomczeszyn's head onto her body.

Mulder's prolonged absence prompts Scully to contact Walter Skinner, who uses the FBI's resources to triangulate the position of Mulder's car. Dacyshyn overpowers Mulder and prepares to kill him with an axe, but a clue given by Joe helps Scully to find the compound. She incapacitates Dacyshyn, enabling Skinner to round up Dacyshyn's associates while Scully revives Cunningham. Tomczeszyn's severed head perishes, and Joe dies in the same instant. Mulder remains convinced that the men's fates were linked, even as Scully - motivated by Joe's words of encouragement - performs the surgery needed to save Christian's life. Afterward, and apparently on Mulder's suggestion that he and Scully should leave behind their lives spent in darkness, the agents are seen in a rowboat headed toward a tropical island.

Critique British film critic Mark Kermode was understandably bemused by the second X-Files movie. He approached it with a remembered fondness for the TV series, which had hinged he felt upon the sexual tension between Mulder and Scully, their will-they won't-they dalliances as much the cement of the series as the hunting of aliens. He discovered that the dalliance was long over - the sexual tension had been consummated, and produced a kid. And with that gone, so too had the chemistry between Duchovny and Anderson. In producing a belated sequel six years after the series finished, Chris Carter was clearly trading off nostalgia and affection for a television show that had felt a centrepiece of the 1990s. But he'd cornered himself. In being true to where the series had left the story, and in respect of the fans who had watched it 'til the end, he had to acknowledge all the latter year twists and turns. Mulder and Scully, quite rightly, had developed since the first movie teased its audiences with unspoken romance and a near kiss. But that development isn't big screen friendly, and the point at which it left our heroes puzzled rather more viewers than Kermode.

It's to Chris Carter's credit, then, that he doesn't try to paper over the cracks. He could so easily have tried to misdirect the audience, to put Mulder and Scully back in the midst of a generic sci-fi movie, to have them leap around performing stunts as if they were still in their twenties, and lazily repeat all the clichés that might have sated the most primal X-Files fix. He refuses. The two leads no longer work for the FBI - and, against expectations, remain stubbornly outside the FBI at the movie's conclusion, Scully's victory isn't a triumph over a monster, but the hope of performing an operation on a sick child. And they're not fighting aliens. Indeed, they're only touching base with the paranormal in the most determinedly low key way. Anyone watching the second X-Files movie straight after the first is in for a shock, because tonally they couldn't be more dissimilar. Fight the Future tried to be epic and grandstanding, full of explosions and alien goo and guest appearances from all the supporting cast of the show. I Want to Believe is a sombre story about faith and redemption, in which a paedophile priest hopes with his psychic visions of abducted women to atone for past crimes. There are *no* explosions. There are *no* gunshots, even. It's a thriller only insofar that it features characters we recognise from a thriller series, who spend at least the first half of the running time deciding whether or not even to take part in the proceedings. (Mulder first, then Scully; it feels a little like a dance.)

On the one hand it's hard not to admire a summer movie which resists so hard the lure of being a brainless box-office blockbuster. And Chris Carter's direction is bold and cinematic - I love the way that he regularly makes jump cuts between two contrasting pieces of action. The opening sequences of Father Joe leading the FBI across the ice, punctuated by flashes of the abduction they're investigating, are electric. So too is the dread of Agent Drummy opening the organ container to find a severed head, cut with Mulder and Agent Whitney's pursuit of the perpetrator. It all looks beautiful - the scenes of snow falling on the desolate icescapes sets the mood perfectly for this chilly tale of a modern-day Frankenstein kidnapping women to use for body parts.

It desires to confound the audience's expectations of what The X-Files can be, to remind us

that the series wasn't all sci-fi hokum and was often focused upon detection and crime. But it's in danger too often of not giving that audience much else in return. Since The X-Files ended, its target viewer has moved on to shows like CSI, which tell these sorts of stories with greater flair, greater pace, and - it must be said - greater authority. The first movie was criticised for seeming to be two TV episodes stuck together; the second movie feels more like *one* episode stretched out. And what is really lacking at the heart of I Want to Believe are any characters. It's not simply that Mulder and Scully aren't the stock stereotypes that your average cinemagoer might expect - it's that they're not much of *anything*, really. There's a coldness to both of them which is very distancing. On paper the idea is sound - Scully finds Mulder once again, and tempts him out of retirement onto a case which will reinvest him both with a faith in the world and in himself. But on the screen Mulder is denied any passion whatsoever; he's not the genius maverick of yesteryear, but a rather earnest adviser to the FBI who seems merely more gullible than the others. Carter attempts to give Scully more of an emotional storyline, placing her in a dilemma whether she should be putting a dying child through surgery. But it takes up far too much screen time, and crucially takes Scully away from the story proper, and from Mulder. We paid our money to see Mulder and Scully together again, but to all intents and purposes Scully would rather hang around with a child with brain disease, and Mulder with Billy Connolly's Father Joe. There are some very well played scenes between Duchovny and Anderson as they reaffirm their complex feelings for each other - but they're given little foundation. Tellingly, the movie never makes it clear whether they begin the drama estranged or not. The opening scenes play both ways, that they've long broken off a relationship, or are still sleeping together and able to enter each other's houses without causing surprise. Carter had a chance for a great reunion scene between the two of them, whichever way he'd intended to play the relationship - but it's thrown away to coyness.

The first half feels rather laboured. The second half is mostly very good, with the serial killer storyline downplaying any attempts to charm or be spectacular, instead offering haunting images of a frightened woman in a human battery farm. There are no characters to be found amongst the villains, but that's part of what's impressive - it's the utter anonymity of the crimes which make them so uncompromising. That's the real bravery of what Carter and Spotnitz have done, to have offered up a movie which promises to be a crowd-pleaser sequel to a hit TV show, and given instead something as odd and as dark as a European horror movie. But in doing so, it still pulls a trick on its audience that it doesn't really justify elsewhere. It's a reunion movie in which the most impressive performance is from guest star Billy Connolly, not the stars reunited. It's a TV tie-in which seems tonally closer to Millennium than the show it's reviving. It's not a bland movie, or a cynical one, and that's to be applauded. But it's a film to be admired rather than liked, and

admired more for its intent than what it actually pulls off.

And what of the future? I can't believe there'll be a third movie. Not because of the poor box office: the movie opened the week after The Dark Knight broke records, and will doubtless make up its small budget on DVD sales. Not because The X-Files has run out of stories to tell - after two hundred episodes, the second movie still managed to feel fresh and original - but because of its reluctance to engage with the audience. At its peak The X-Files *was* the zeitgeist; it managed to tap into a sense of pre-millennial paranoia and summed up the mood of a decade. Now it stubbornly refuses to give that same audience the post-millennial comfort it craves, the wallow in nostalgia we were waiting for. It's the most foolish thing about this movie. It's also the most wonderful.

A future for The X-Files. I can't believe it. I can't. But I want to believe. (**1/2)

ABOUT TIME

1970-1974

SEASONS 7 TO 11 (SECOND EDITION)

THE UNAUTHORIZED GUIDE TO
DOCTOR WHO

1970-1974
SEASONS 7 TO 11
(SECOND EDITION)

TAT WOOD

Out Now... In the *About Time 3* second edition, Tat Wood vastly expands upon the Jon Pertwee Era, bringing this installment of the *About Time* series up to the size and elaborate depth of its fellows.

New essays in this second edition will include "The Daemons - What the Hell are They Doing?", "Where Were Torchwood When All This Was Happening?" and "Is This Any Way to Run a Galactic Empire?"

Many existing essays and entries have been greatly retooled, and evidence from the new *Doctor Who* series (unbroadcast when this book first published) has been taken into account. In every regard, this book displays the eye-popping complexity readers expect from the *About Time* range.

(At present, Mad Norwegian has no plans to do second editions of the other *About Time* volumes.)

ISBN: 978-0-9759446-7-7
MSRP: $29.95

www.madnorwegian.com

*1150 46th St
Des Moines, IA
madnorwegian@gmail.com*

**mad
norwegian
press**

MORE DIGRESSIONS
PETER DAVID

A new collection of 'But I Digress' columns

FOREWORD BY HARLAN ELLISON

Out Now... The first compilation of its kind in 15 years, *More Digressions* collects about 100 essays from Peter David's long-running *But I Digress* column (as published in the pages of *Comics Buyer's Guide*). For this entirely new collection, David has personally selected *But I Digress* pieces written from 2001 to the present day, and also included many personal reflections and historical notes.

Topics covered in this collection include Peter's thoughts on comic book movies, his pleasing and sometimes less-than pleasing interactions with fandom, his take on the business aspects of the comic-book industry, his anecdotes about getting married and having children, his advocacy of free speech and much more.

More Digressions features a new foreword by the legendary Harlan Ellison, and sports a cover by J.K. Woodward (*Fallen Angel*) that highlights some of David's comic-book creations.

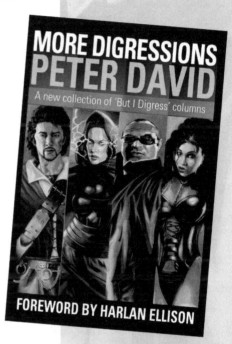

ISBN: 978-1935234005
Retail Price: $24.95

www.madnorwegian.com

1150 46th St
Des Moines, IA 50311
madnorwegian@gmail.com

Robert Shearman

... is probably best known as a writer for Doctor Who, where he reintroduced the Daleks in the show's BAFTA winning first series, in an episode nominated for a Hugo Award. But he has long worked as a writer for radio, television and the stage. He has received several international awards for his theatre work, including the Sunday Times Playwriting Award, the World Drama Trust Award, and the Guinness Award for Ingenuity in association with the Royal National Theatre. His plays have been regularly produced by Alan Ayckbourn, and on BBC Radio by Martin Jarvis. His first book, Tiny Deaths, was nominated for the Edge Hill Story Prize and the Frank O'Connor International Short Story Award, and won the World Fantasy Award. His second collection, Love Songs for the Shy and Cynical, is forthcoming in November.

Publisher / Editor-in-Chief
Lars Pearson

**Senior Editor /
Design Manager**
Christa Dickson

Associate Editor
Joshua Wilson

Technical Support
Marc Eby

The publisher wishes to thank...
Robert Smith?, Michael and Lynne Thomas, Jim Boyd, George Krstic, Kelli and Brandon Griffis, Dave and Tracy Gartner, and that nice lady who sends me newspaper articles.

1150 46th Street
Des Moines, Iowa 50311
info@madnorwegian.com
www.madnorwegian.com